KEN LAMUG

MISCHIEF AND MAYHEM

THE CURSED BUNNY

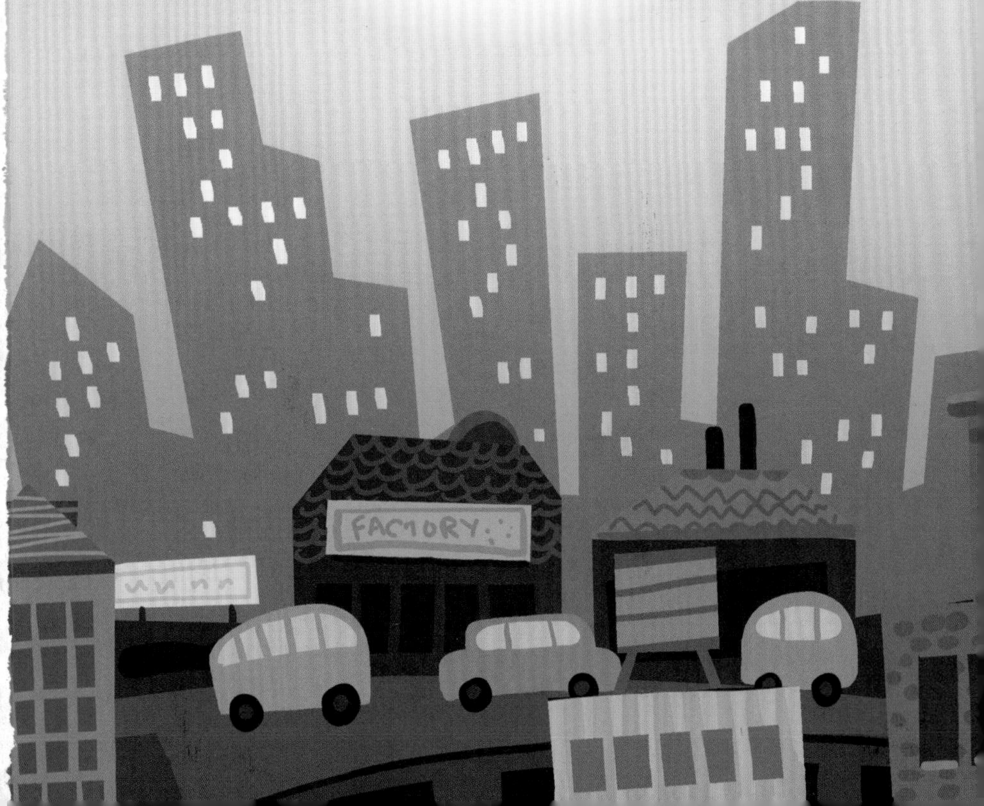
FACTORY

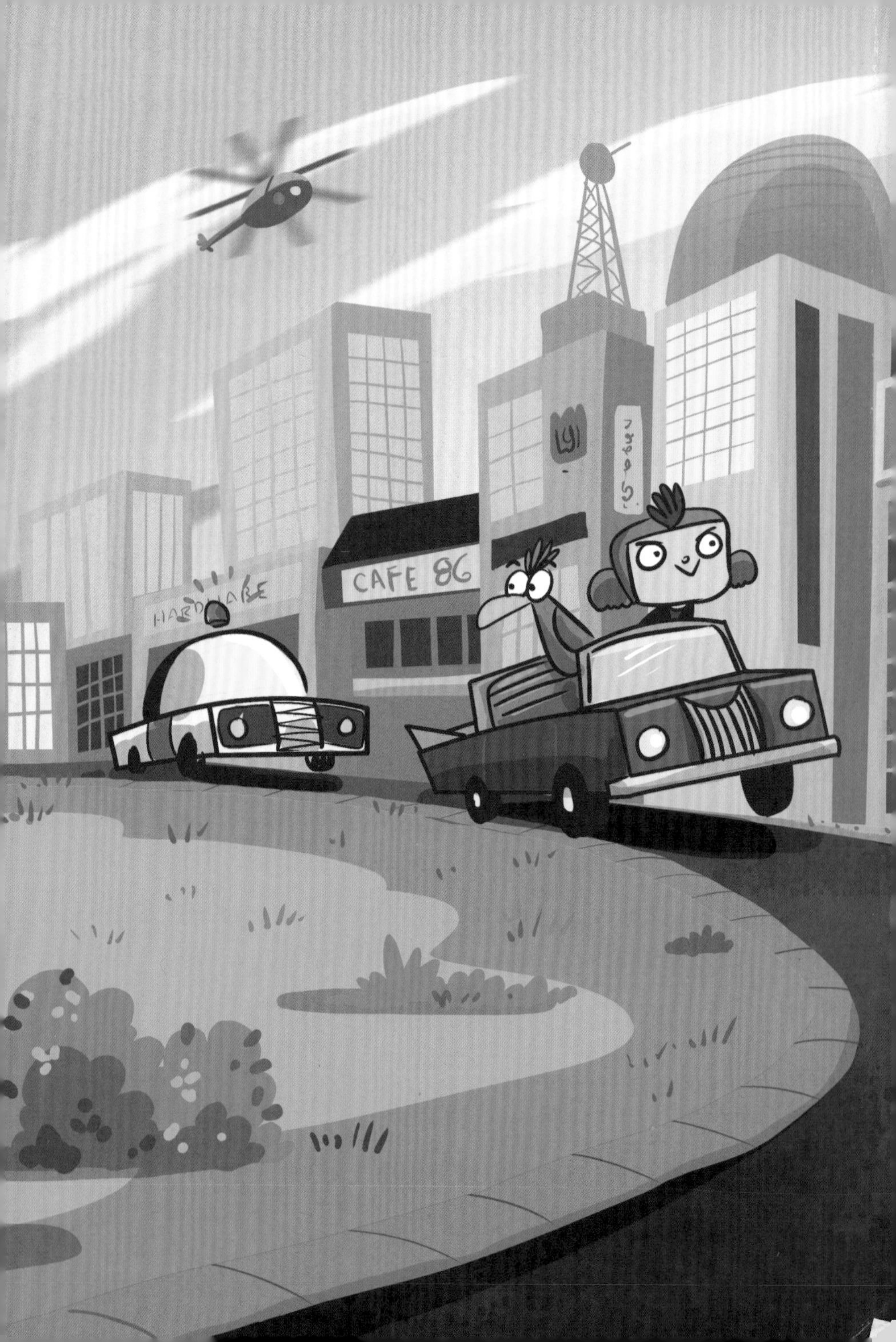
CAFE 86

KEN LAMUG

MISCHIEF AND MAYHEM

THE CURSED BUNNY

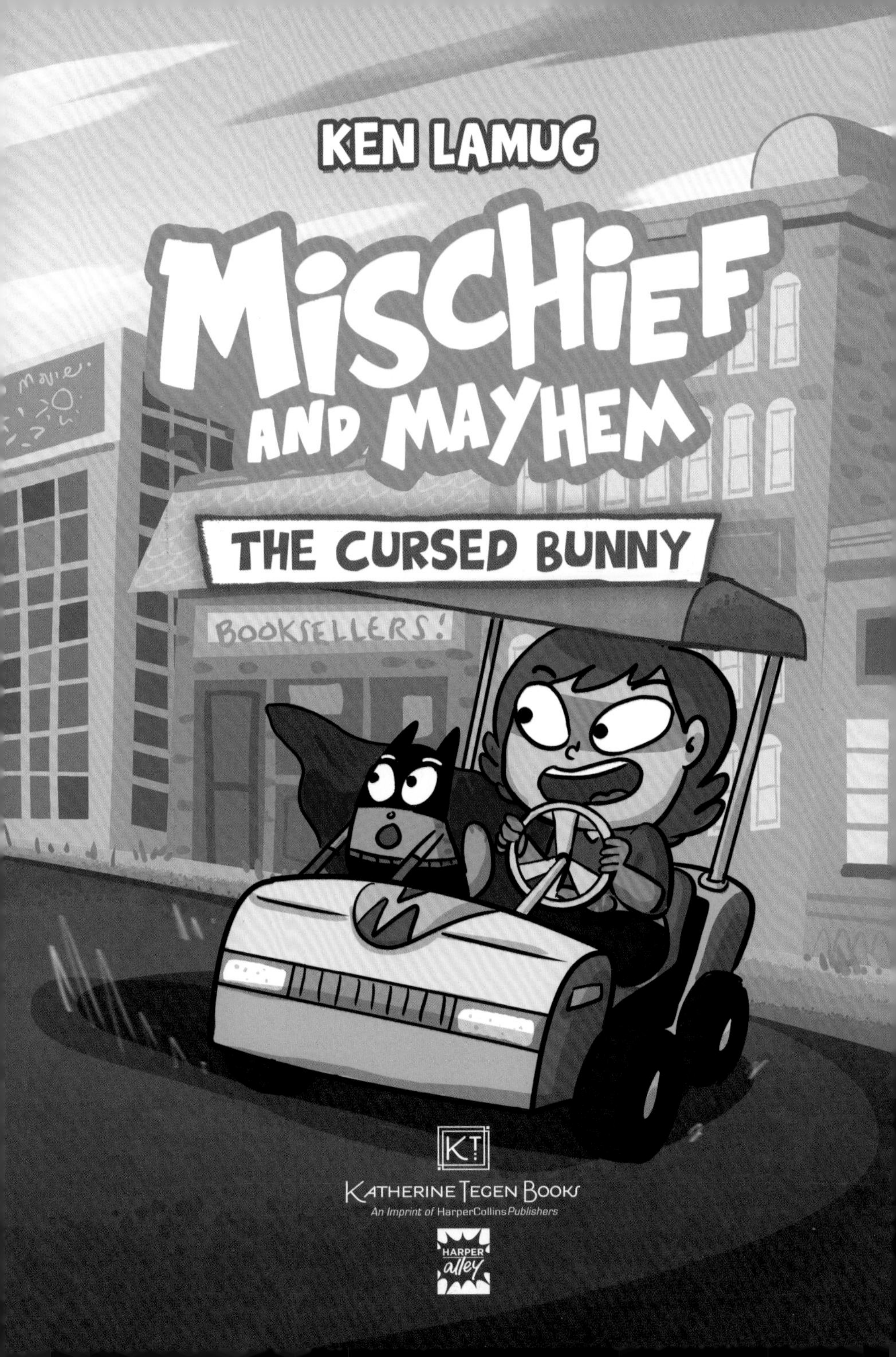
BOOKSELLERS!

KT
KATHERINE TEGEN BOOKS
An Imprint of HarperCollinsPublishers
HARPER alley

HarperAlley is an imprint of HarperCollins Publishers.
Katherine Tegen Books is an imprint of HarperCollins Publishers.

Mischief and Mayhem #2: The Cursed Bunny
Copyright © 2022 by Ken Lamug
All rights reserved. Manufactured in Italy.

No part of this book may be used or reproduced in any manner whatsoever without written
permission except in the case of brief quotations embodied in critical articles and reviews. For
information address HarperCollins Children's Books, a division of HarperCollins Publishers,
195 Broadway, New York, NY 10007.
www.harpercollinschildrens.com

Library of Congress Control Number: 2021950864
ISBN 978-0-06-297079-4 (hardcover) — ISBN 978-0-06-297078-7 (pbk.)

The artist used Clip Studio Paint to create the digital illustrations for this book.
22 23 24 25 26 RTLO 10 9 8 7 6 5 4 3 2 1
❖
First Edition

FOR TOM.
THANKS FOR SHOWING ME THE WILD SIDE.

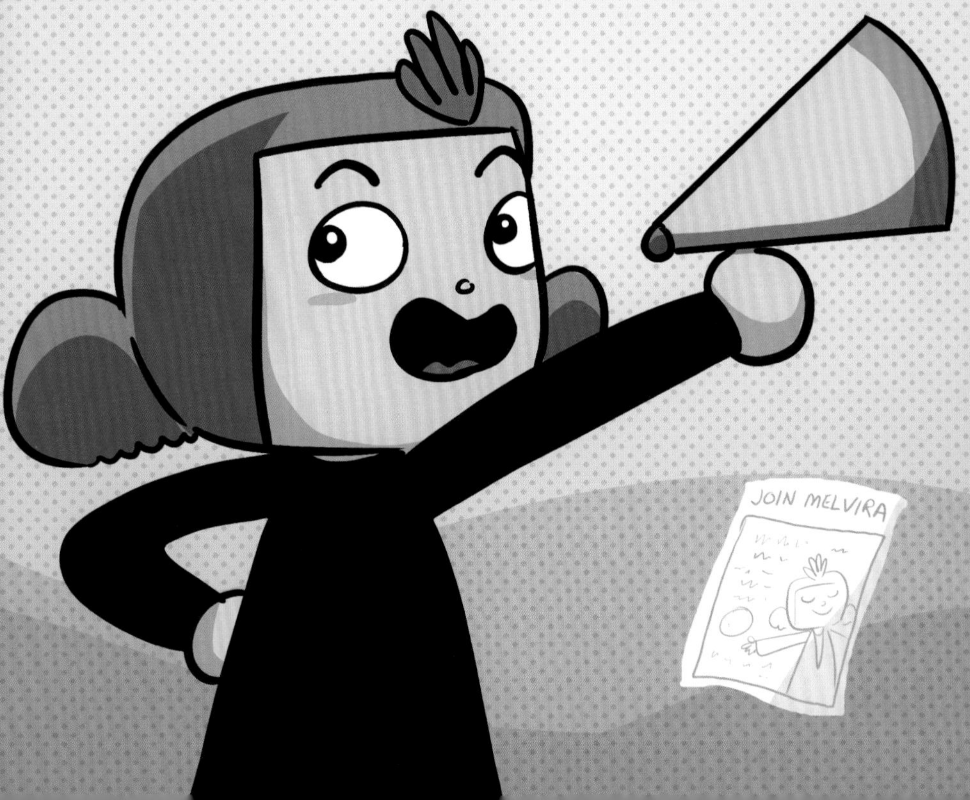
JOIN MELVIRA

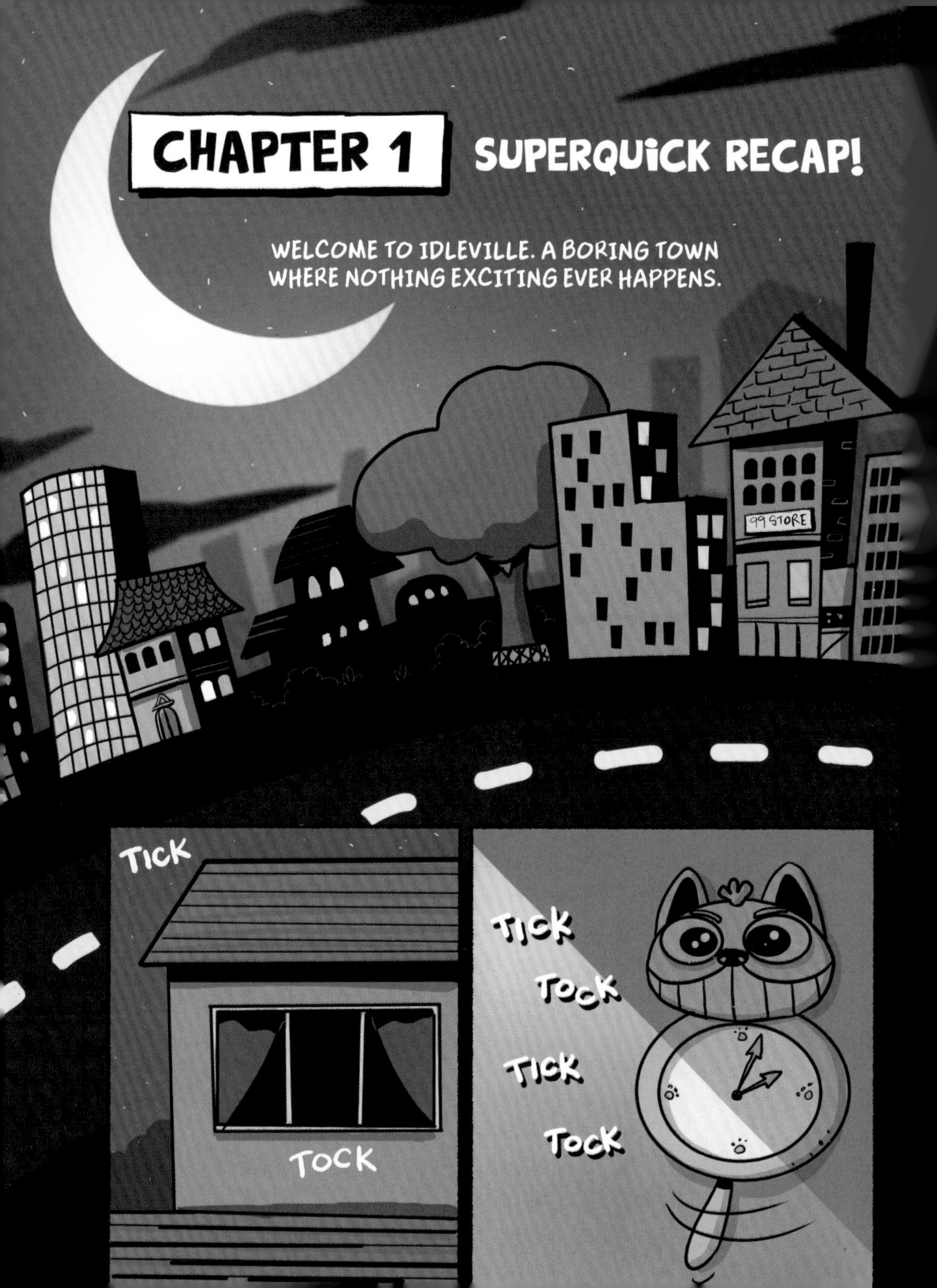
CHAPTER 1
SUPERQUICK RECAP!
WELCOME TO IDLEVILLE. A BORING TOWN WHERE NOTHING EXCITING EVER HAPPENS.
99 STORE
TICK
TOCK
TICK
TOCK
TICK
TOCK

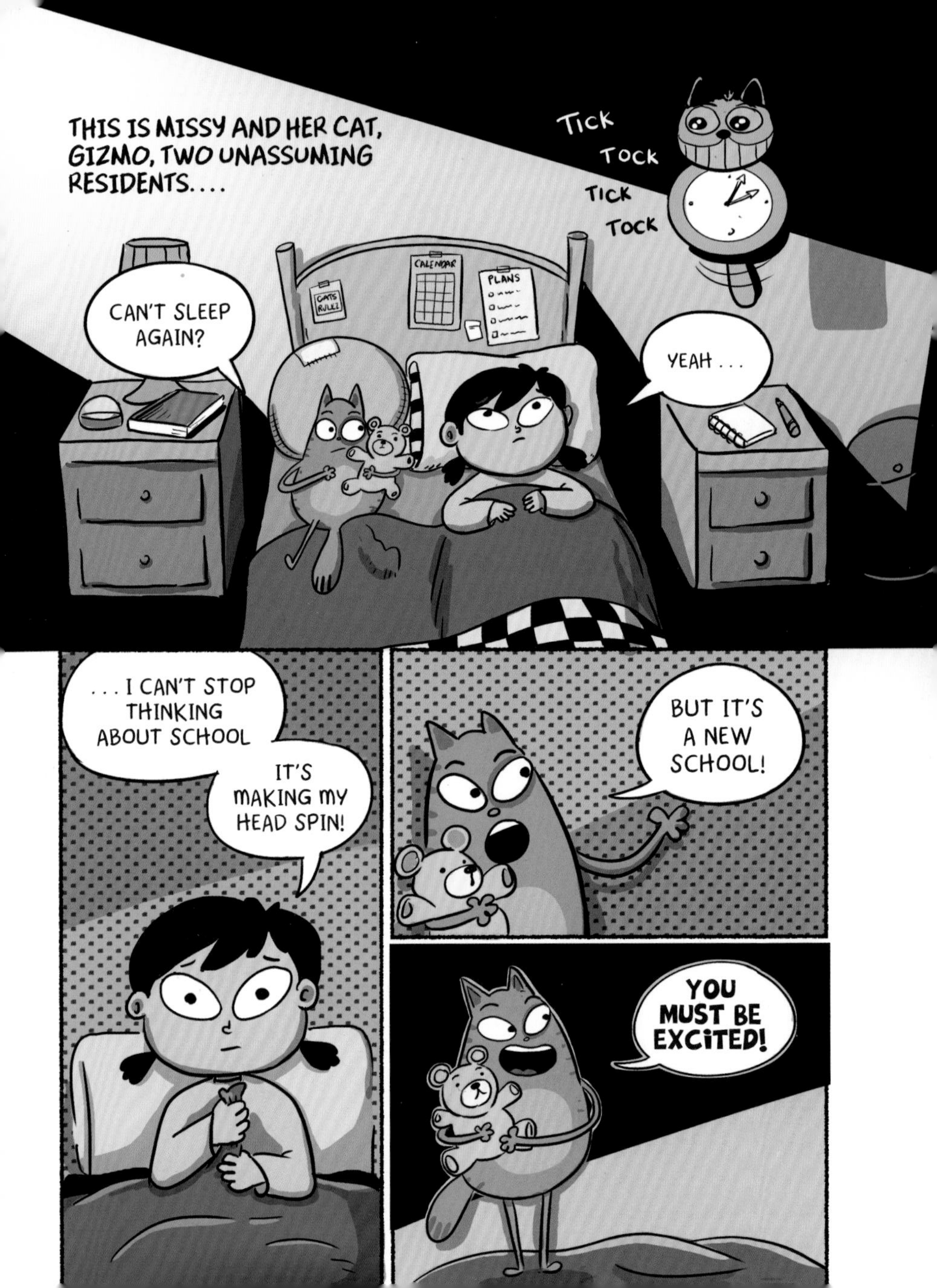
THIS IS MISSY AND HER CAT, GIZMO, TWO UNASSUMING RESIDENTS....
TICK
TOCK
TICK
TOCK
CALENDAR
PLANS
CATS RULEZ
CAN'T SLEEP AGAIN?
YEAH...
...I CAN'T STOP THINKING ABOUT SCHOOL
IT'S MAKING MY HEAD SPIN!
BUT IT'S A NEW SCHOOL!
YOU MUST BE EXCITED!

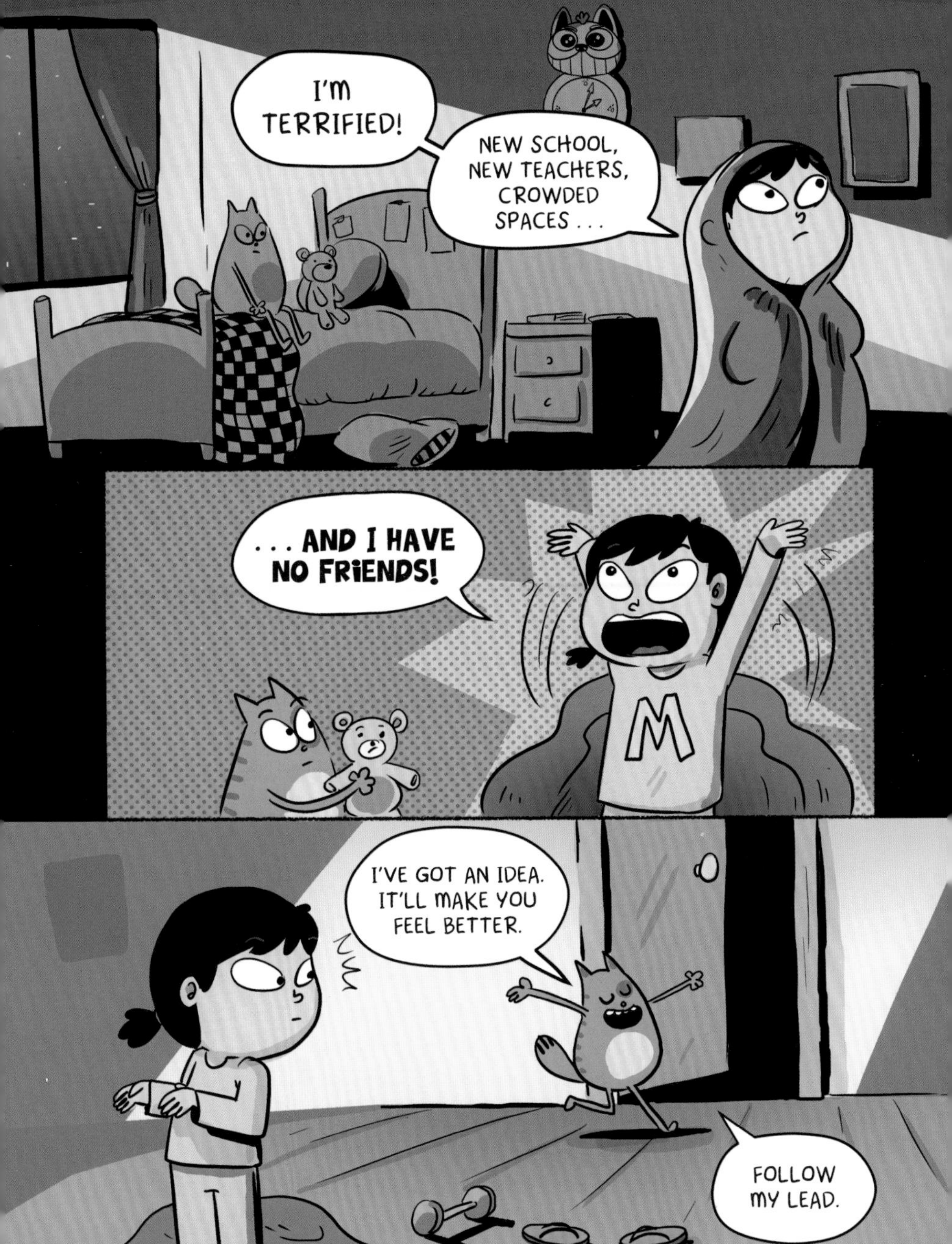
I'M TERRIFIED!
NEW SCHOOL, NEW TEACHERS, CROWDED SPACES . . .
. . . AND I HAVE NO FRIENDS!
I'VE GOT AN IDEA. IT'LL MAKE YOU FEEL BETTER.
FOLLOW MY LEAD.

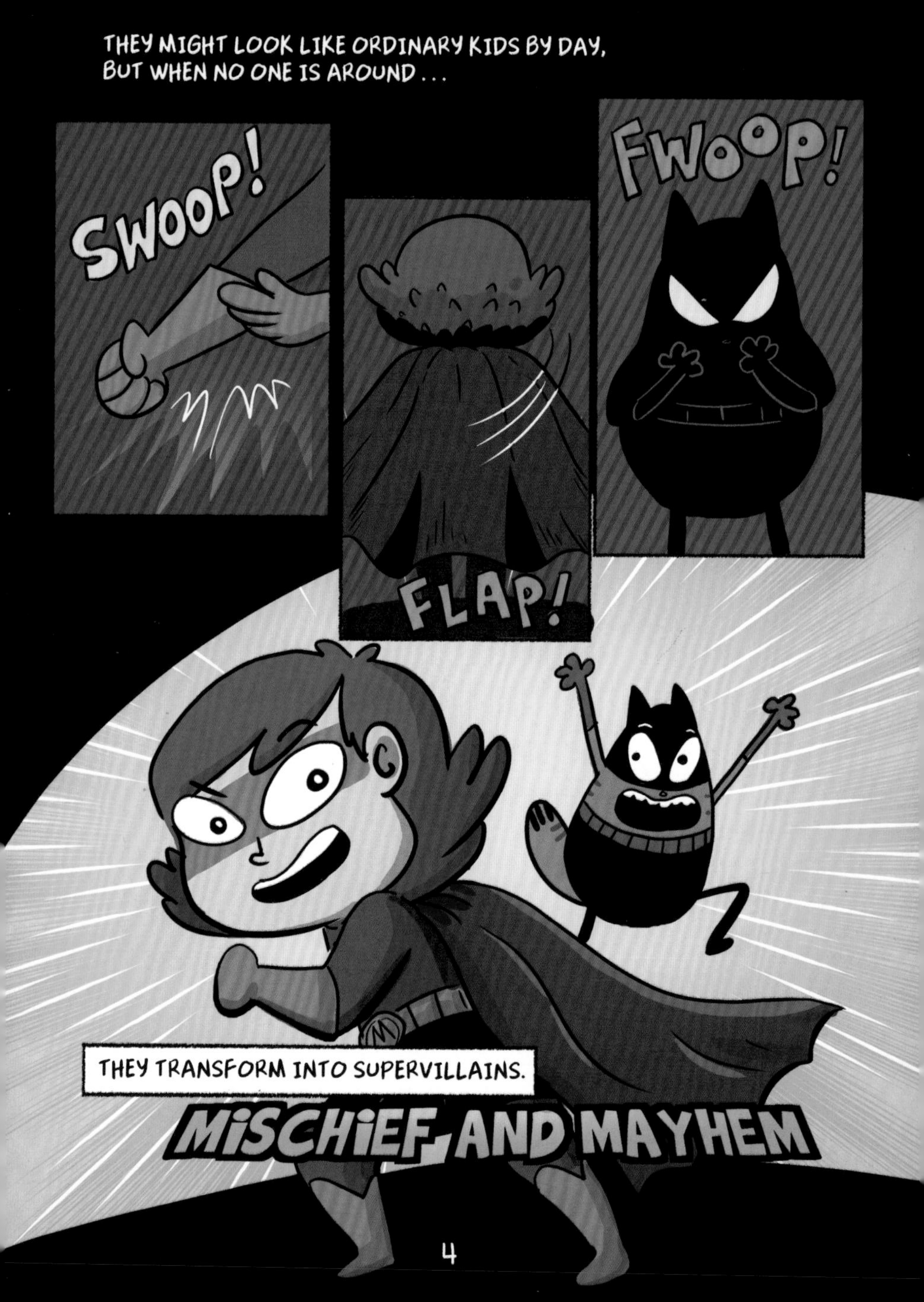
THEY MIGHT LOOK LIKE ORDINARY KIDS BY DAY,
BUT WHEN NO ONE IS AROUND . . .
SWOOP!
FLAP!
FWOOP!
THEY TRANSFORM INTO SUPERVILLAINS.
MISCHIEF AND MAYHEM

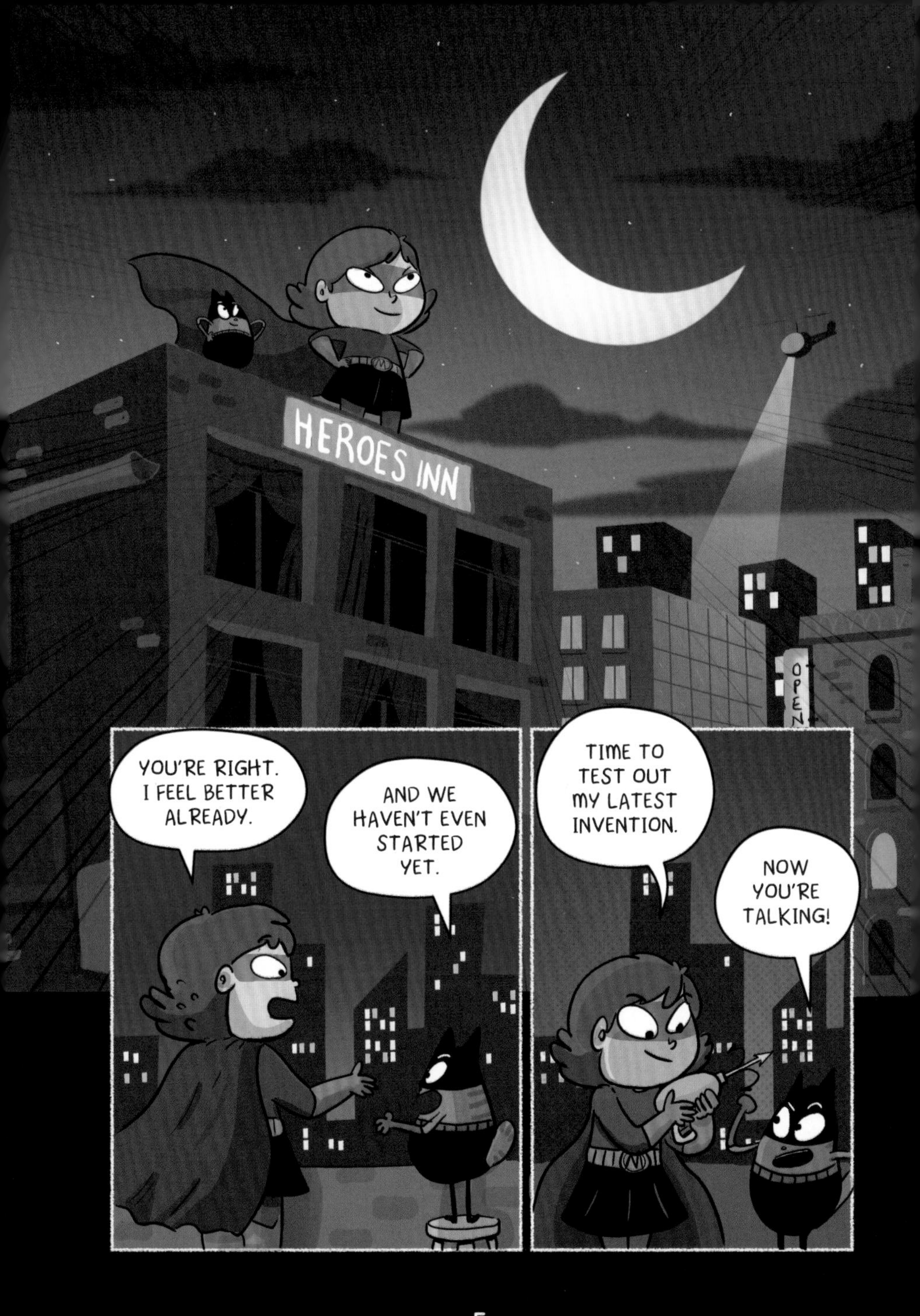
HEROES INN
OPEN
YOU'RE RIGHT. I FEEL BETTER ALREADY.
AND WE HAVEN'T EVEN STARTED YET.
TIME TO TEST OUT MY LATEST INVENTION.
NOW YOU'RE TALKING!

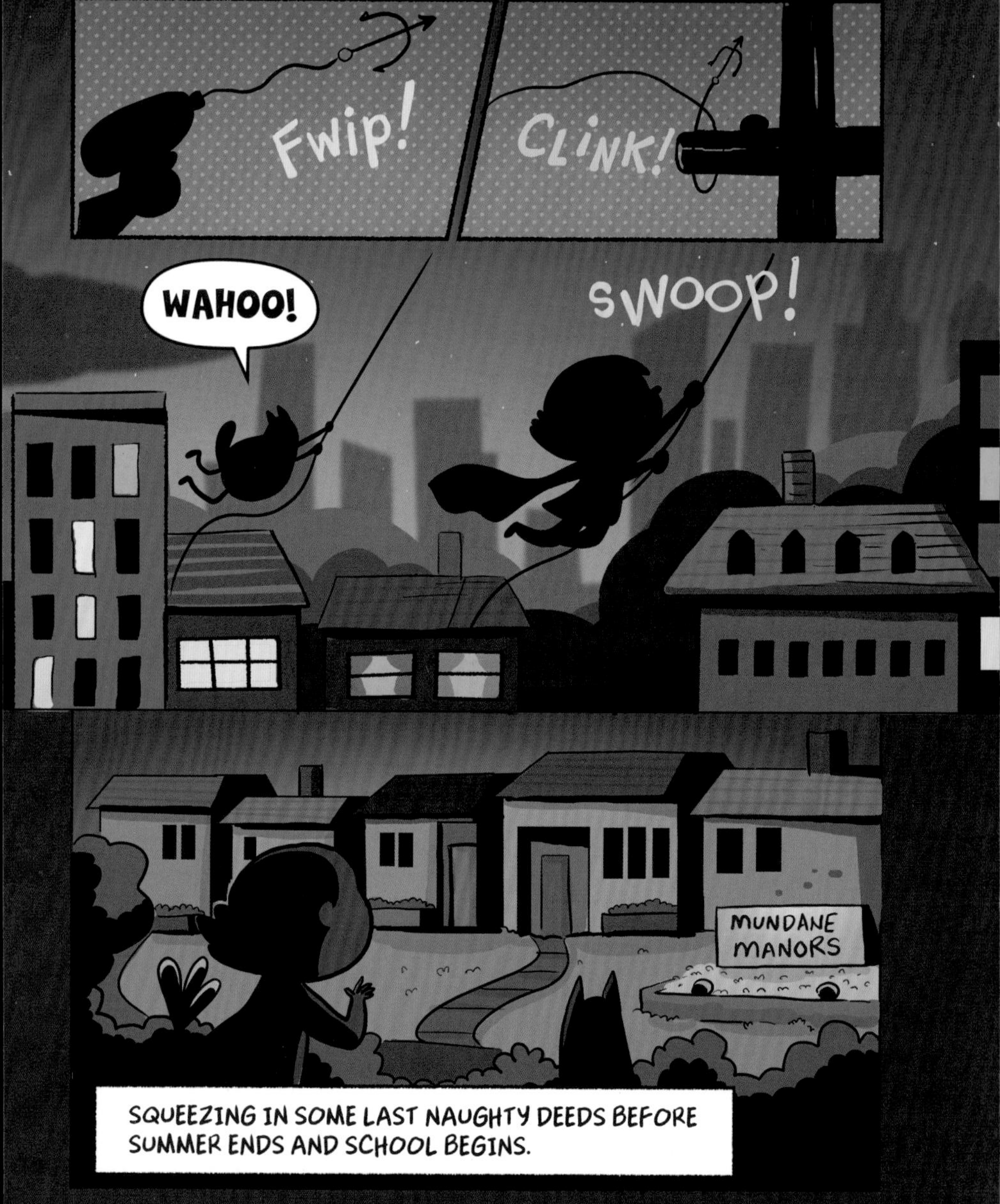
FWIP!
CLINK!
WAHOO!
SWOOP!
MUNDANE MANORS
SQUEEZING IN SOME LAST NAUGHTY DEEDS BEFORE SUMMER ENDS AND SCHOOL BEGINS.

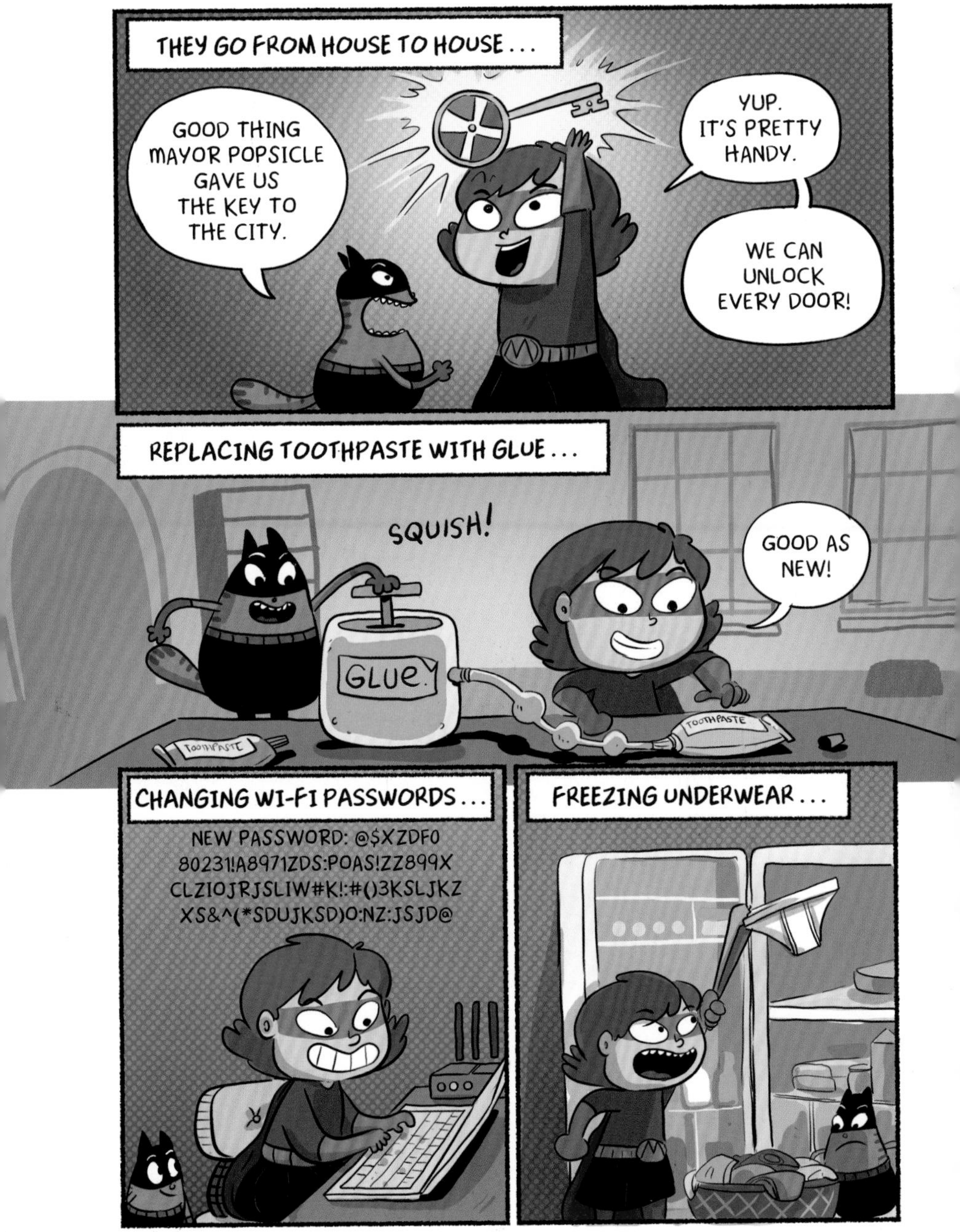
THEY GO FROM HOUSE TO HOUSE . . .
GOOD THING MAYOR POPSICLE GAVE US THE KEY TO THE CITY.
YUP. IT'S PRETTY HANDY.
WE CAN UNLOCK EVERY DOOR!
REPLACING TOOTHPASTE WITH GLUE . . .
SQUISH!
GLUE
GOOD AS NEW!
TOOTHPASTE
TOOTHPASTE
CHANGING WI-FI PASSWORDS . . .
NEW PASSWORD: @$XZDF0
80231!A8971ZDS:POAS!ZZ899X
CLZIOJRJSLIW#K!:#()3KSLJKZ
XS&^(*SDUJKSD)O:NZ:JSJD@
FREEZING UNDERWEAR . . .

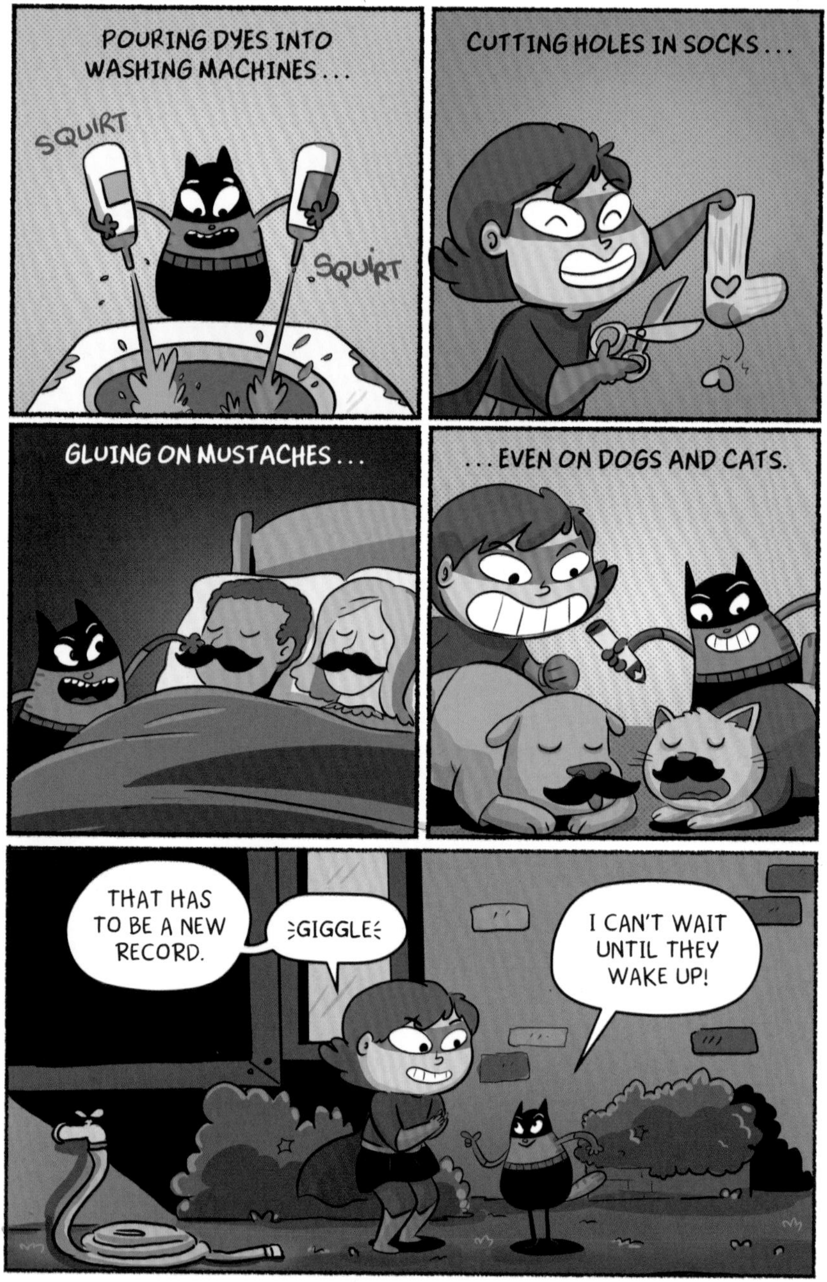
POURING DYES INTO WASHING MACHINES . . .
SQUIRT
SQUIRT
CUTTING HOLES IN SOCKS . . .
GLUING ON MUSTACHES . . .
. . . EVEN ON DOGS AND CATS.
THAT HAS TO BE A NEW RECORD.
GIGGLE
I CAN'T WAIT UNTIL THEY WAKE UP!

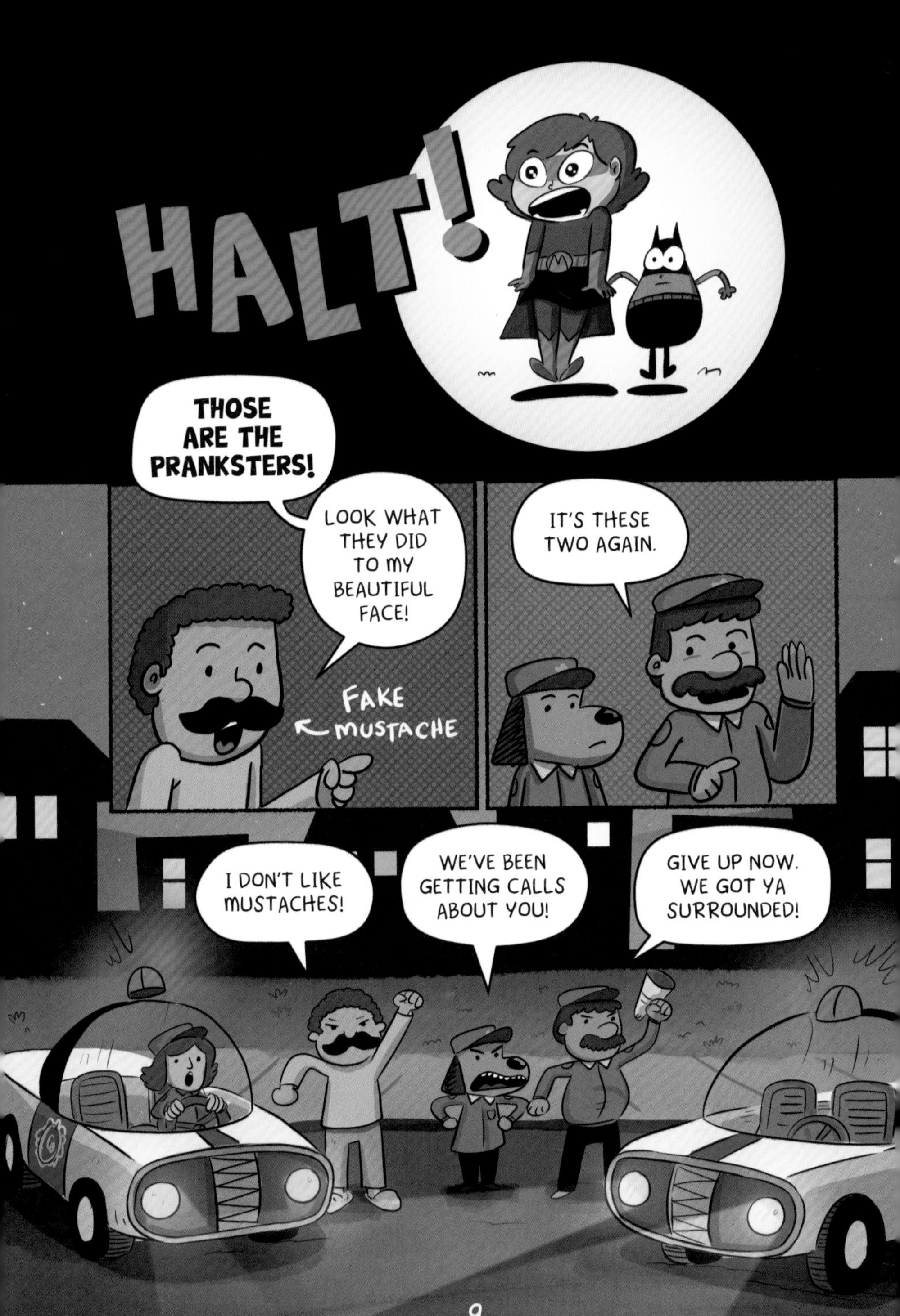
HALT!
THOSE ARE THE PRANKSTERS!
LOOK WHAT THEY DID TO MY BEAUTIFUL FACE!
FAKE MUSTACHE
IT'S THESE TWO AGAIN.
I DON'T LIKE MUSTACHES!
WE'VE BEEN GETTING CALLS ABOUT YOU!
GIVE UP NOW. WE GOT YA SURROUNDED!

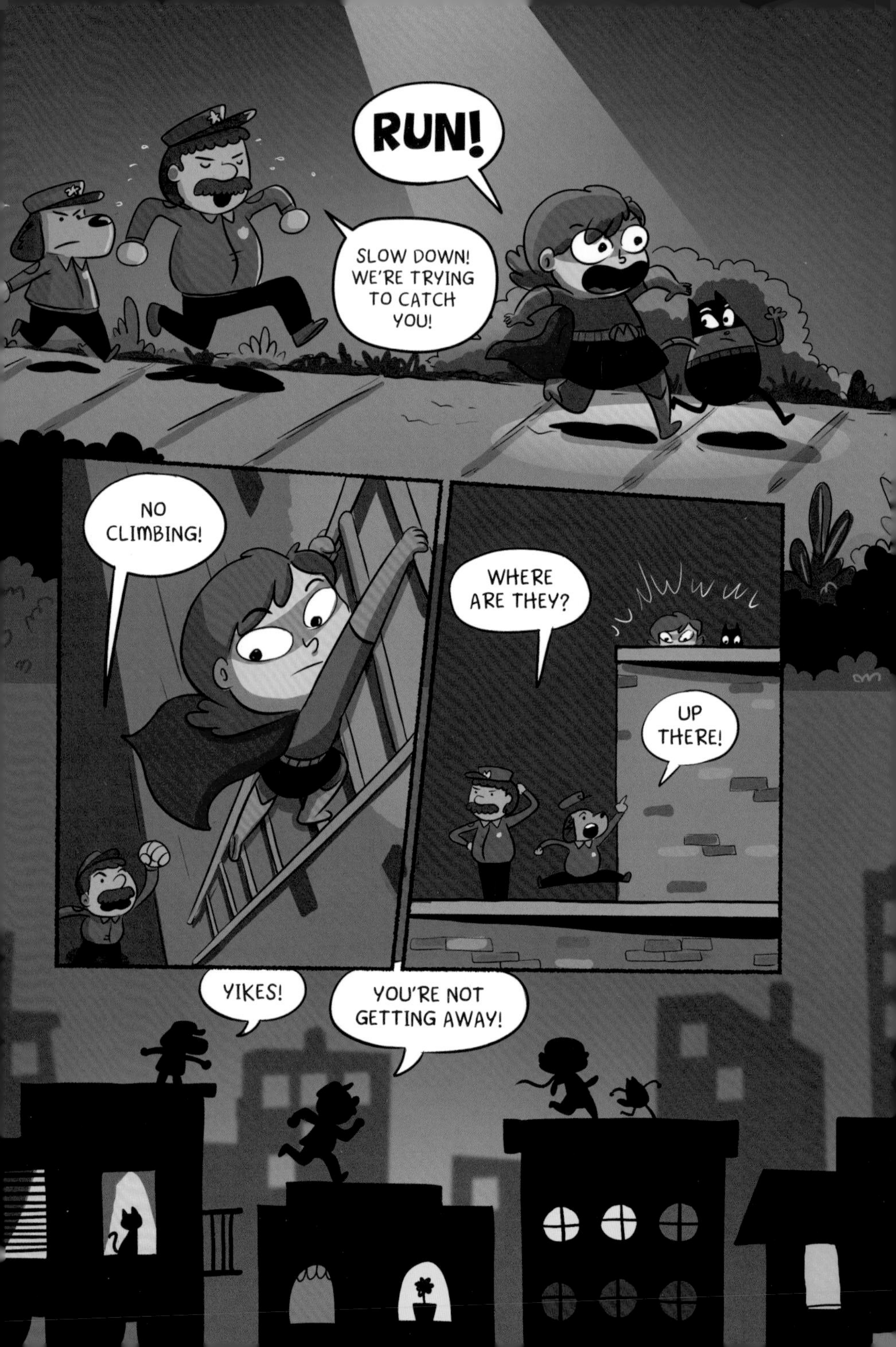
RUN!
SLOW DOWN! WE'RE TRYING TO CATCH YOU!
NO CLIMBING!
WHERE ARE THEY?
UP THERE!
YIKES!
YOU'RE NOT GETTING AWAY!

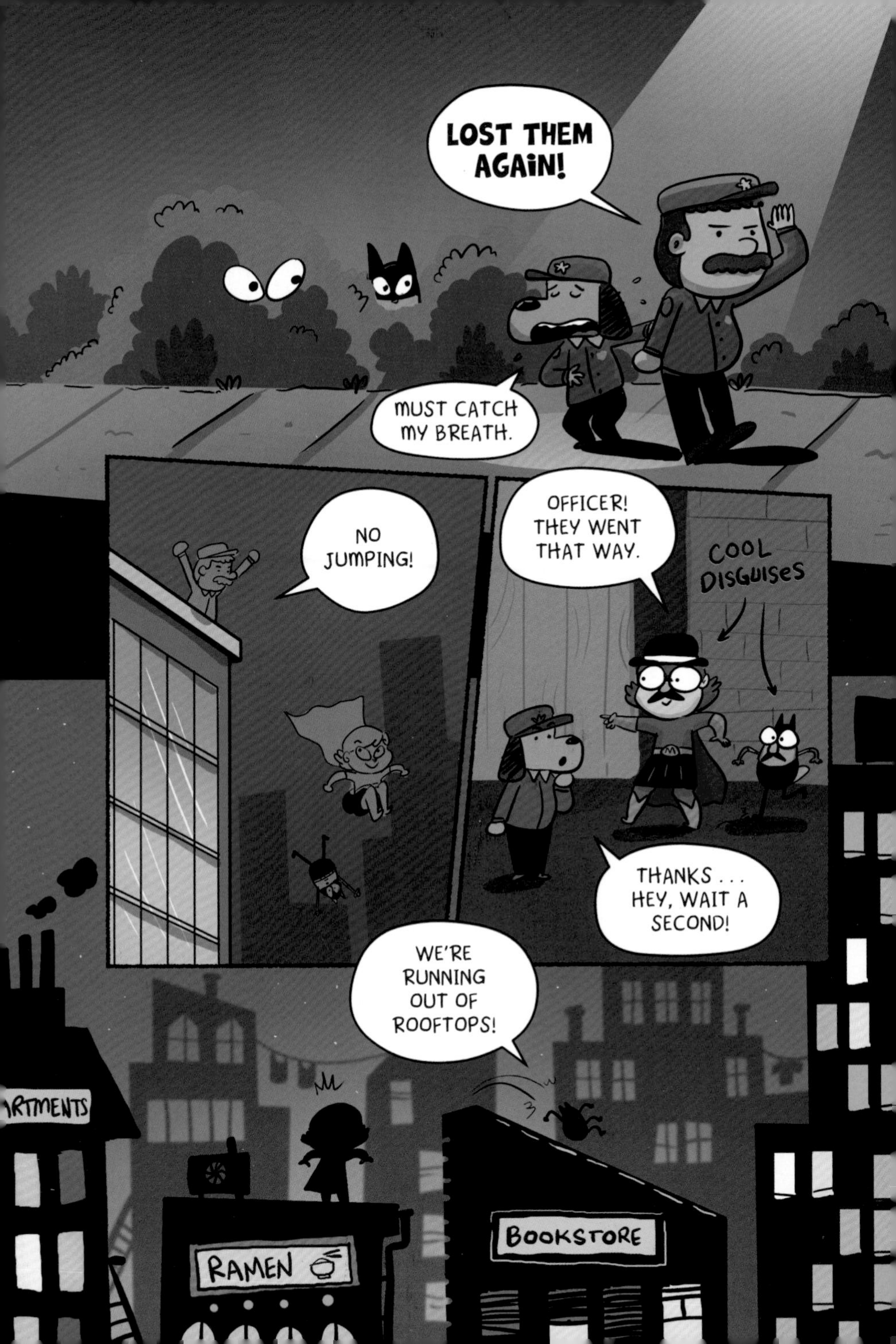
LOST THEM AGAIN!
MUST CATCH MY BREATH.
NO JUMPING!
OFFICER! THEY WENT THAT WAY.
COOL DISGUISES
THANKS . . . HEY, WAIT A SECOND!
WE'RE RUNNING OUT OF ROOFTOPS!
RTMENTS
RAMEN
BOOKSTORE

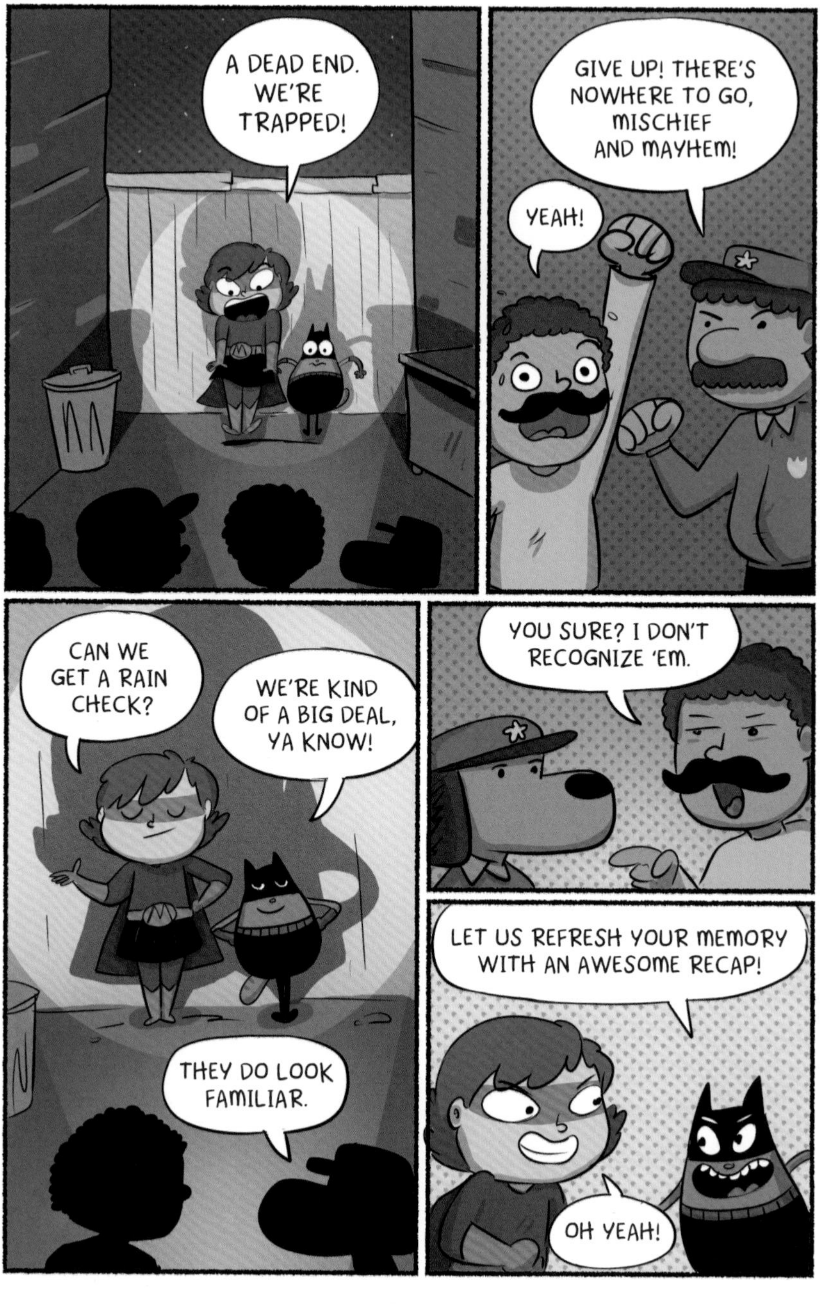
A DEAD END. WE'RE TRAPPED!
GIVE UP! THERE'S NOWHERE TO GO, MISCHIEF AND MAYHEM!
YEAH!
CAN WE GET A RAIN CHECK?
WE'RE KIND OF A BIG DEAL, YA KNOW!
THEY DO LOOK FAMILIAR.
YOU SURE? I DON'T RECOGNIZE 'EM.
LET US REFRESH YOUR MEMORY WITH AN AWESOME RECAP!
OH YEAH!

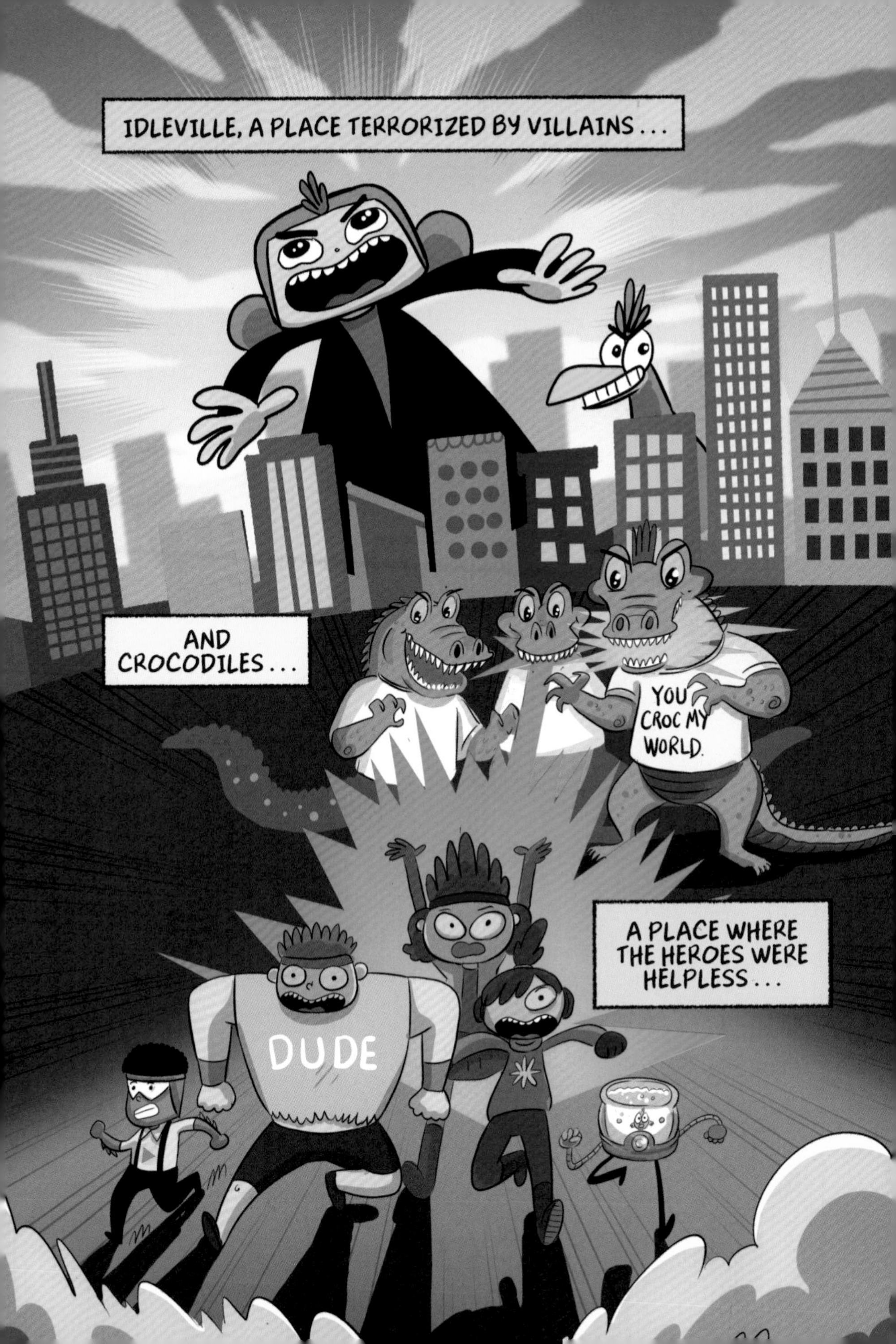

IDLEVILLE, A PLACE TERRORIZED BY VILLAINS . . .
AND CROCODILES . . .
YOU CROC MY WORLD.
A PLACE WHERE THE HEROES WERE HELPLESS . . .
DUDE

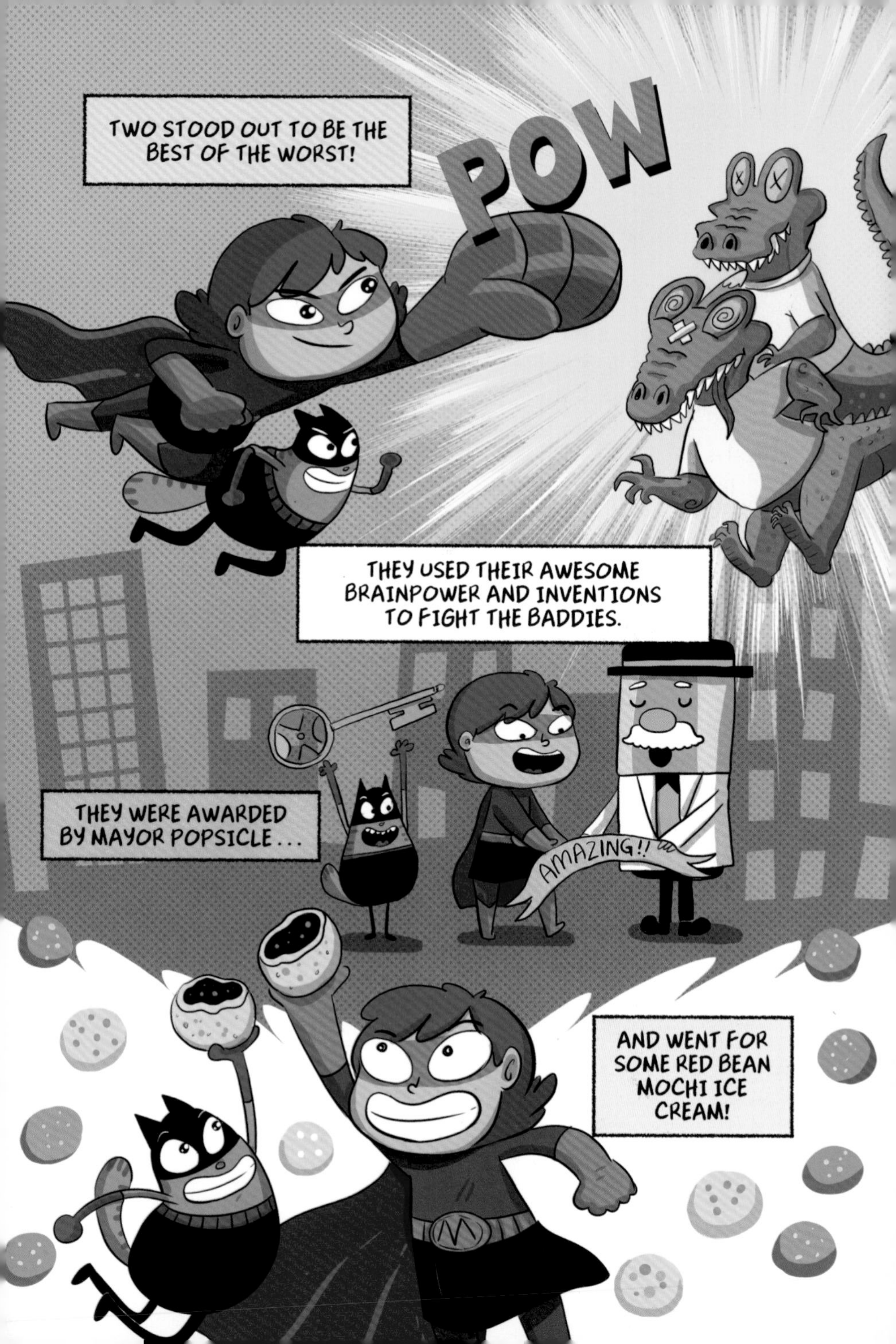
TWO STOOD OUT TO BE THE BEST OF THE WORST!
POW
THEY USED THEIR AWESOME BRAINPOWER AND INVENTIONS TO FIGHT THE BADDIES.
THEY WERE AWARDED BY MAYOR POPSICLE . . .
AMAZING!!
AND WENT FOR SOME RED BEAN MOCHI ICE CREAM!

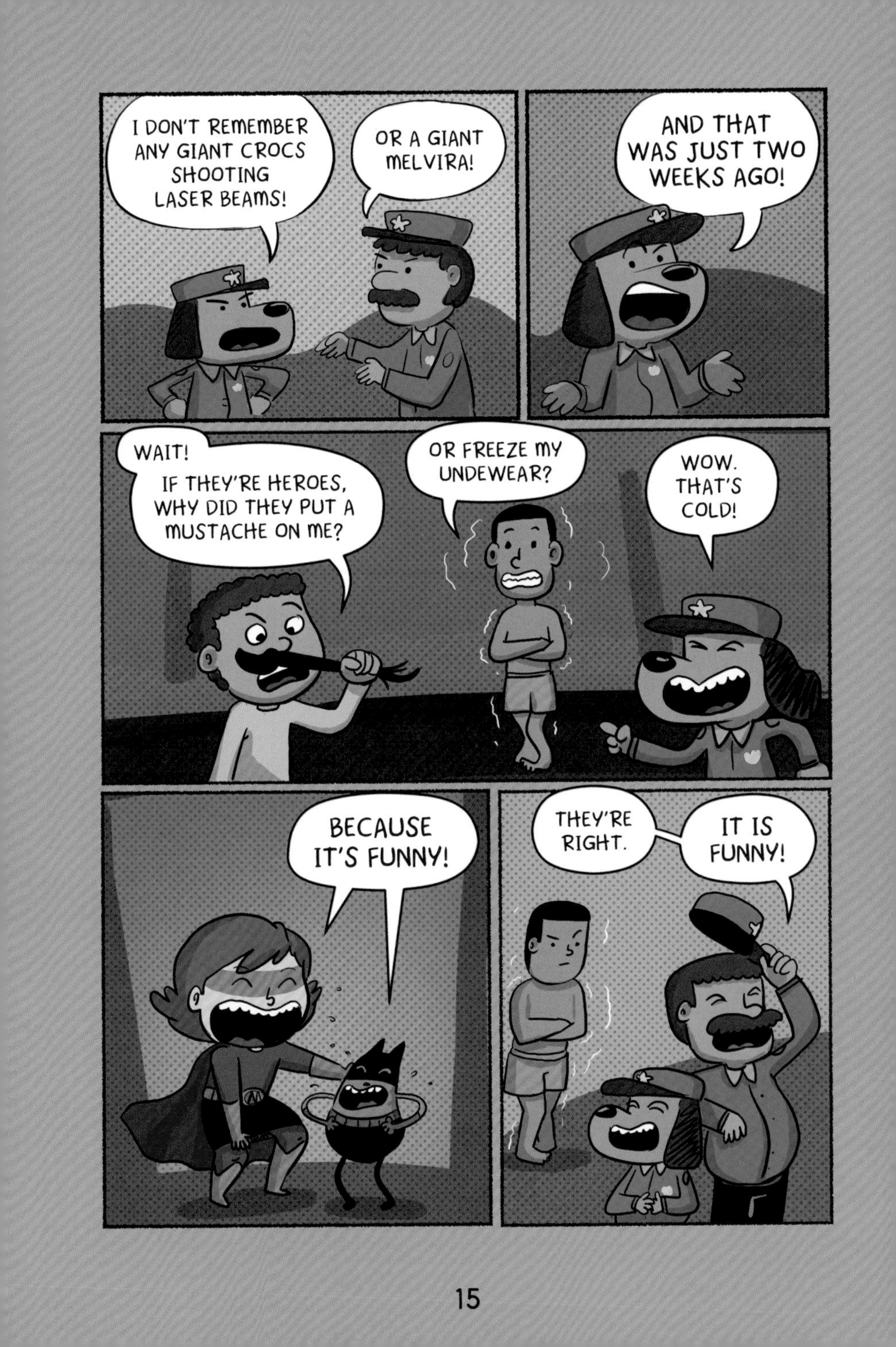
I DON'T REMEMBER ANY GIANT CROCS SHOOTING LASER BEAMS!
OR A GIANT MELVIRA!
AND THAT WAS JUST TWO WEEKS AGO!
WAIT!
IF THEY'RE HEROES, WHY DID THEY PUT A MUSTACHE ON ME?
OR FREEZE MY UNDEWEAR?
WOW. THAT'S COLD!
BECAUSE IT'S FUNNY!
THEY'RE RIGHT.
IT IS FUNNY!

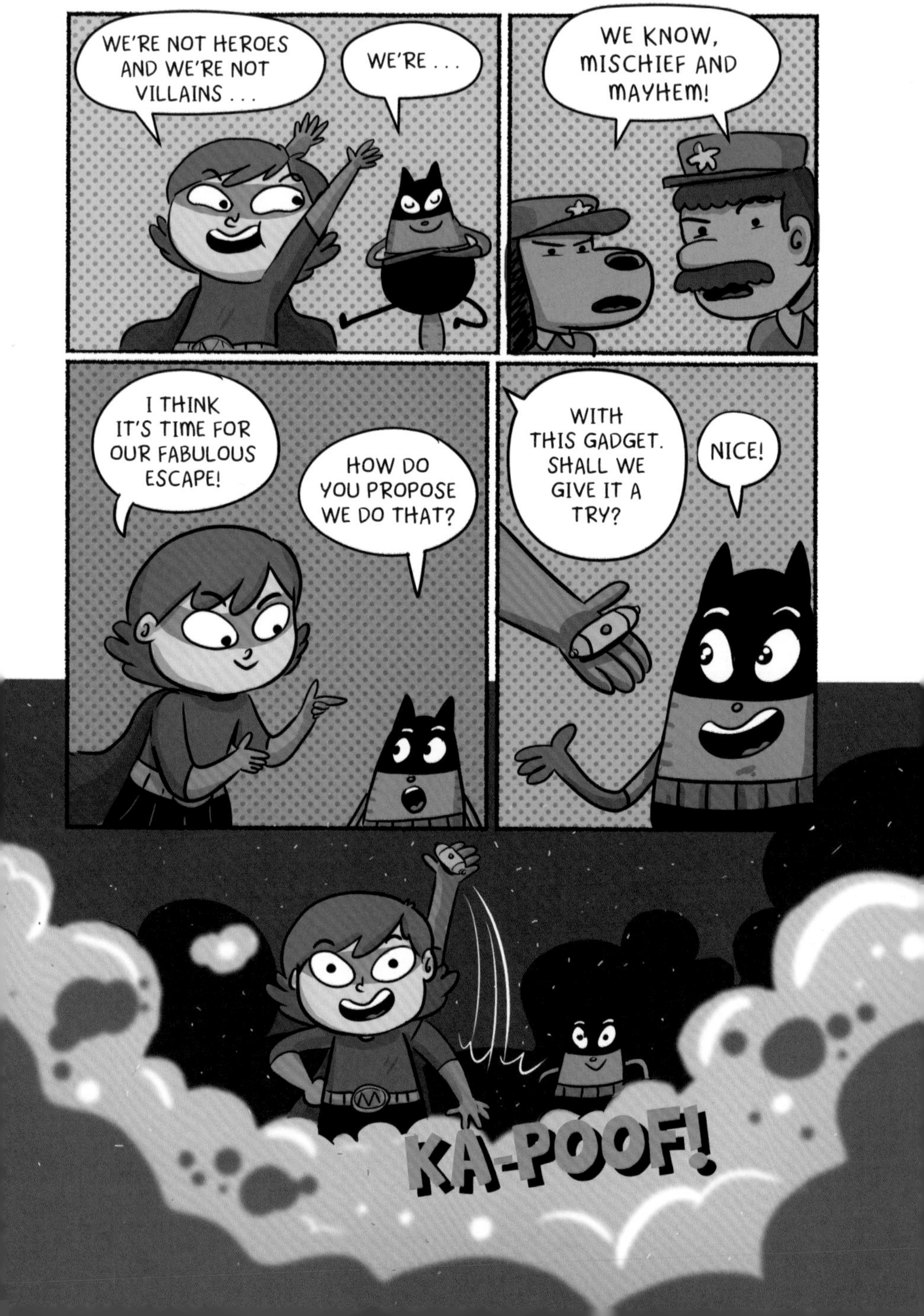
WE'RE NOT HEROES AND WE'RE NOT VILLAINS . . .
WE'RE . . .
WE KNOW, MISCHIEF AND MAYHEM!
I THINK IT'S TIME FOR OUR FABULOUS ESCAPE!
HOW DO YOU PROPOSE WE DO THAT?
WITH THIS GADGET. SHALL WE GIVE IT A TRY?
NICE!
KA-POOF!

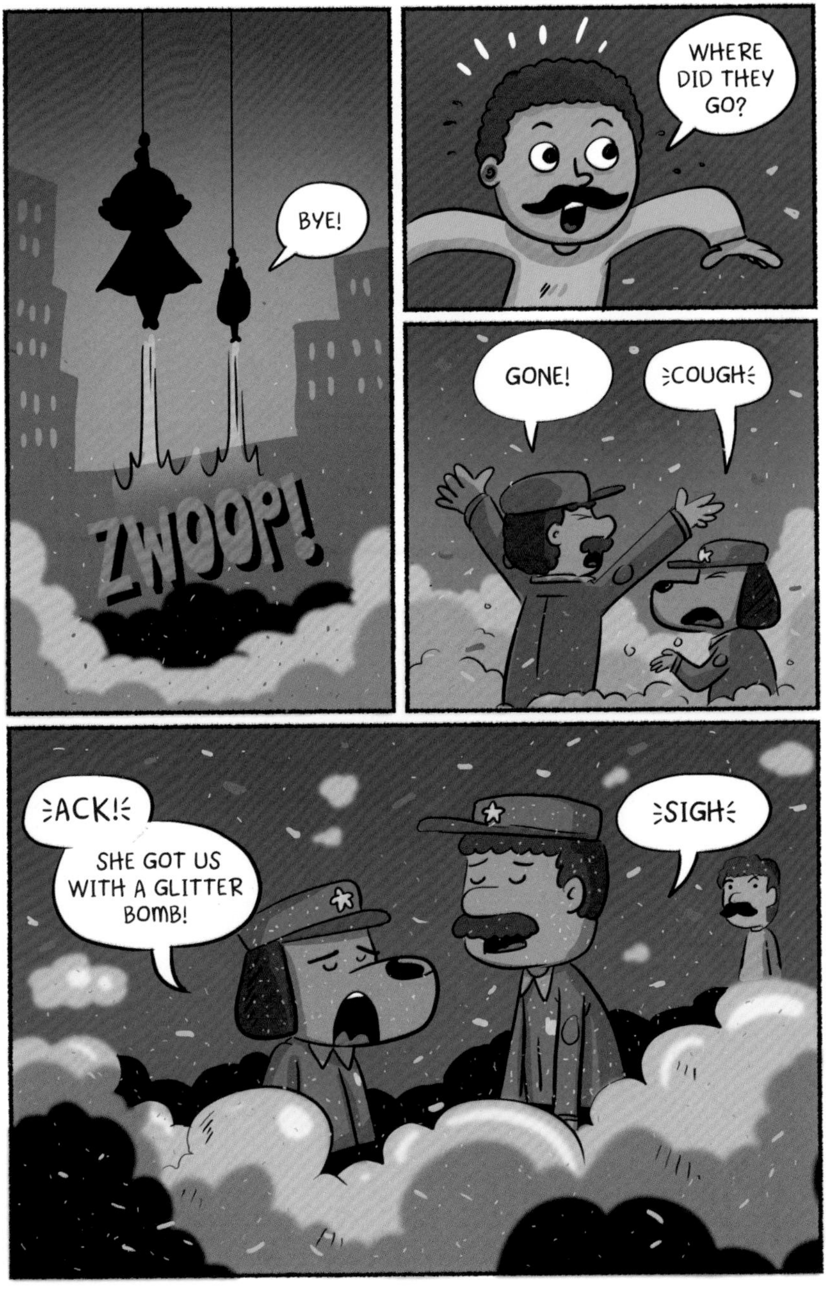
BYE!
ZWOOP!
WHERE DID THEY GO?
GONE!
COUGH
ACK!
SHE GOT US WITH A GLITTER BOMB!
SIGH

CHAPTER 2

MEET THE LEAGUE OF VILLAINS

IN A REMOTE VOLCANO ISLAND SOMEWHERE...

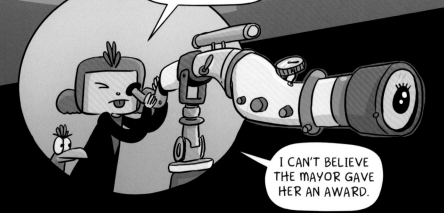

LOOK AT MISCHIEF AND MAYHEM HAVING ALL THAT FUN!

I CAN'T BELIEVE THE MAYOR GAVE HER AN AWARD.

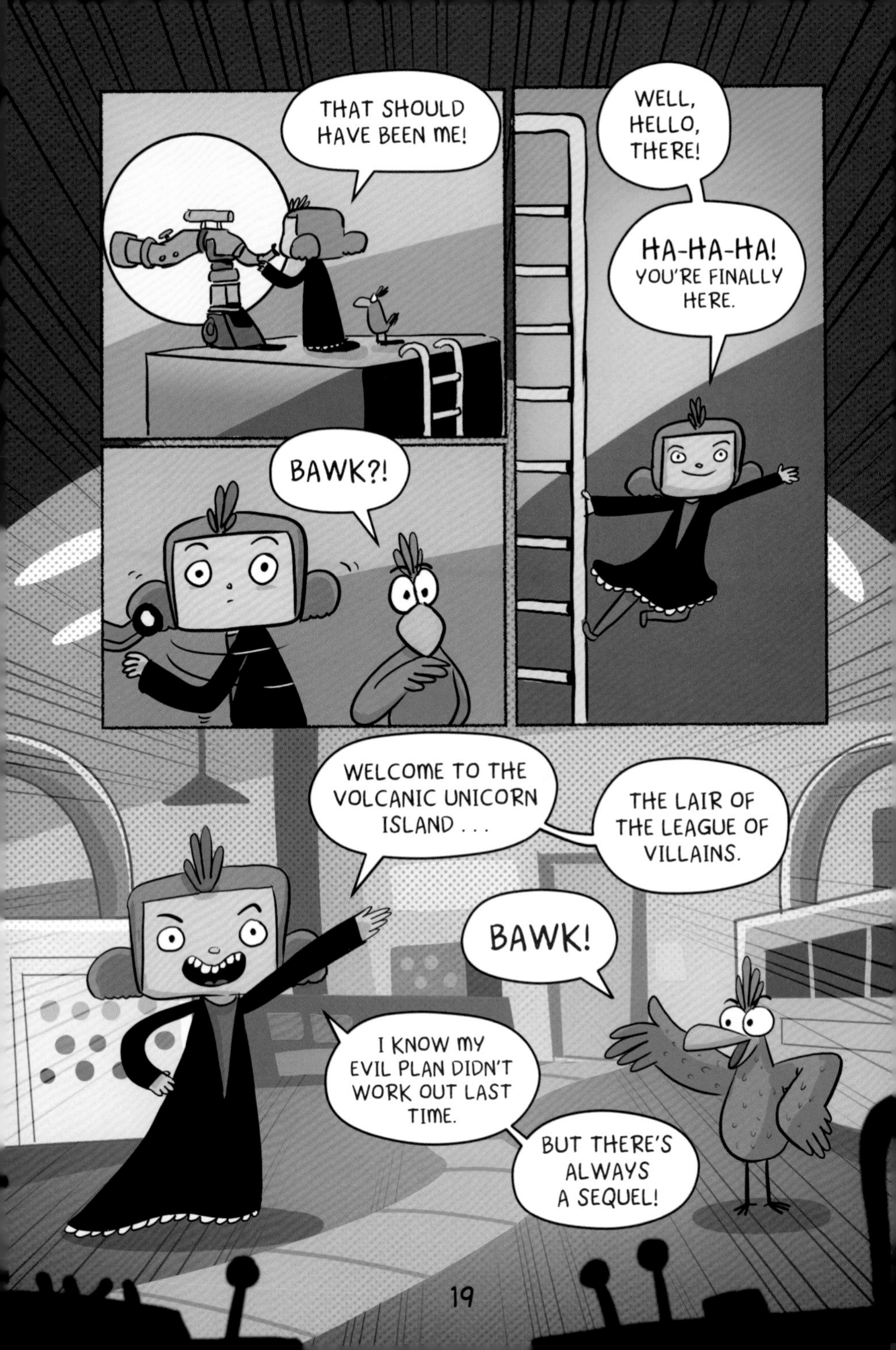
THAT SHOULD HAVE BEEN ME!
WELL, HELLO, THERE!
HA-HA-HA! YOU'RE FINALLY HERE.
BAWK?!
WELCOME TO THE VOLCANIC UNICORN ISLAND . . .
THE LAIR OF THE LEAGUE OF VILLAINS.
BAWK!
I KNOW MY EVIL PLAN DIDN'T WORK OUT LAST TIME.
BUT THERE'S ALWAYS A SEQUEL!

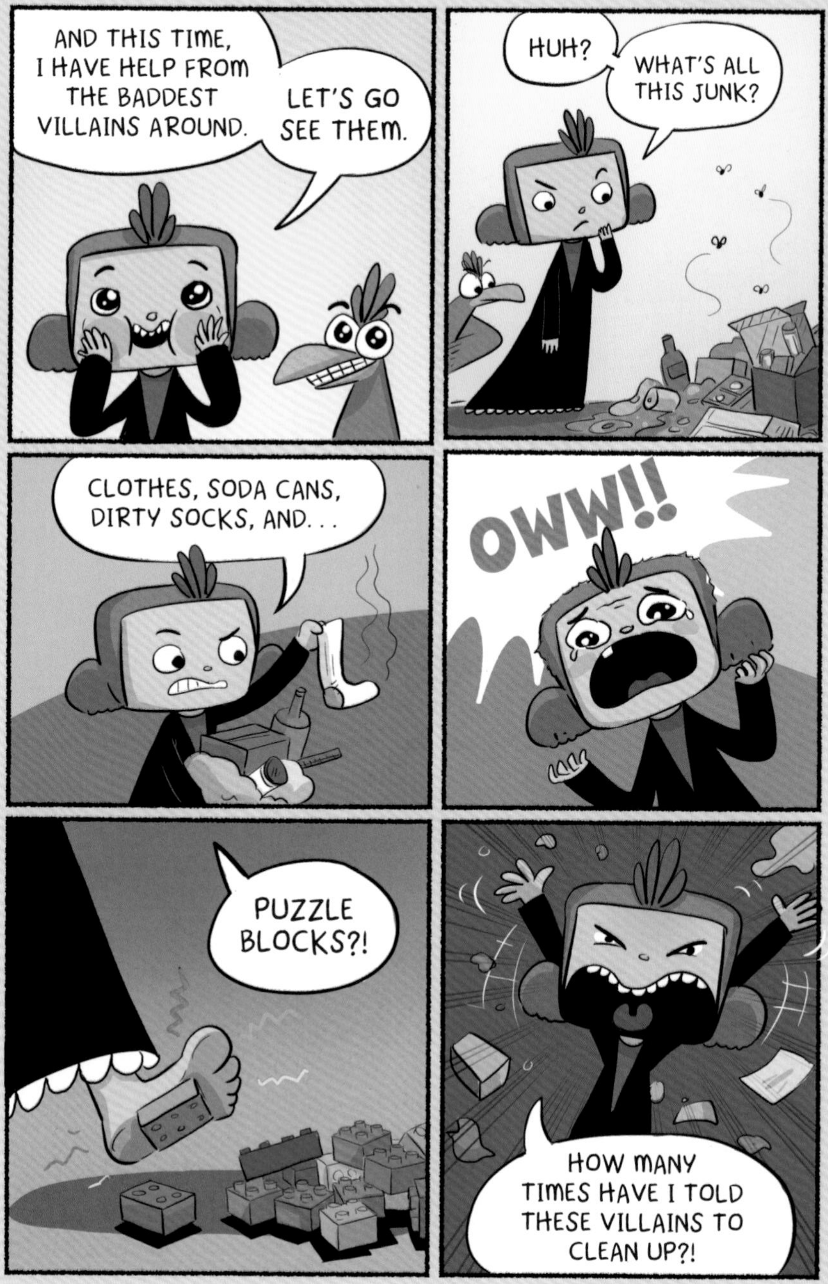
AND THIS TIME, I HAVE HELP FROM THE BADDEST VILLAINS AROUND.
LET'S GO SEE THEM.
HUH?
WHAT'S ALL THIS JUNK?
CLOTHES, SODA CANS, DIRTY SOCKS, AND. . .
OWW!!
PUZZLE BLOCKS?!
HOW MANY TIMES HAVE I TOLD THESE VILLAINS TO CLEAN UP?!

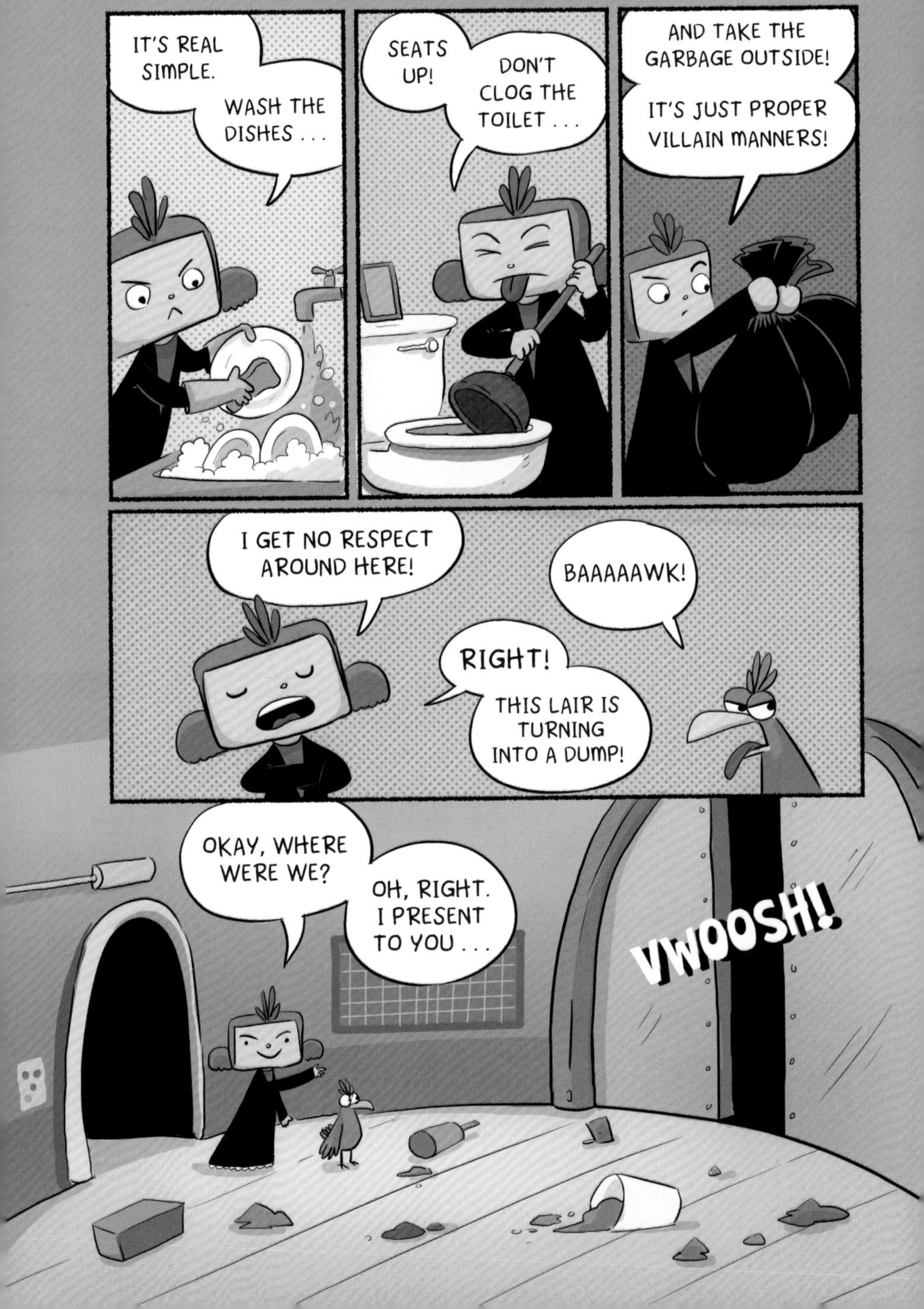
IT'S REAL SIMPLE.
WASH THE DISHES . . .
SEATS UP!
DON'T CLOG THE TOILET . . .
AND TAKE THE GARBAGE OUTSIDE!
IT'S JUST PROPER VILLAIN MANNERS!
I GET NO RESPECT AROUND HERE!
BAAAAAWK!
RIGHT!
THIS LAIR IS TURNING INTO A DUMP!
OKAY, WHERE WERE WE?
OH, RIGHT. I PRESENT TO YOU . . .
VWOOSH!

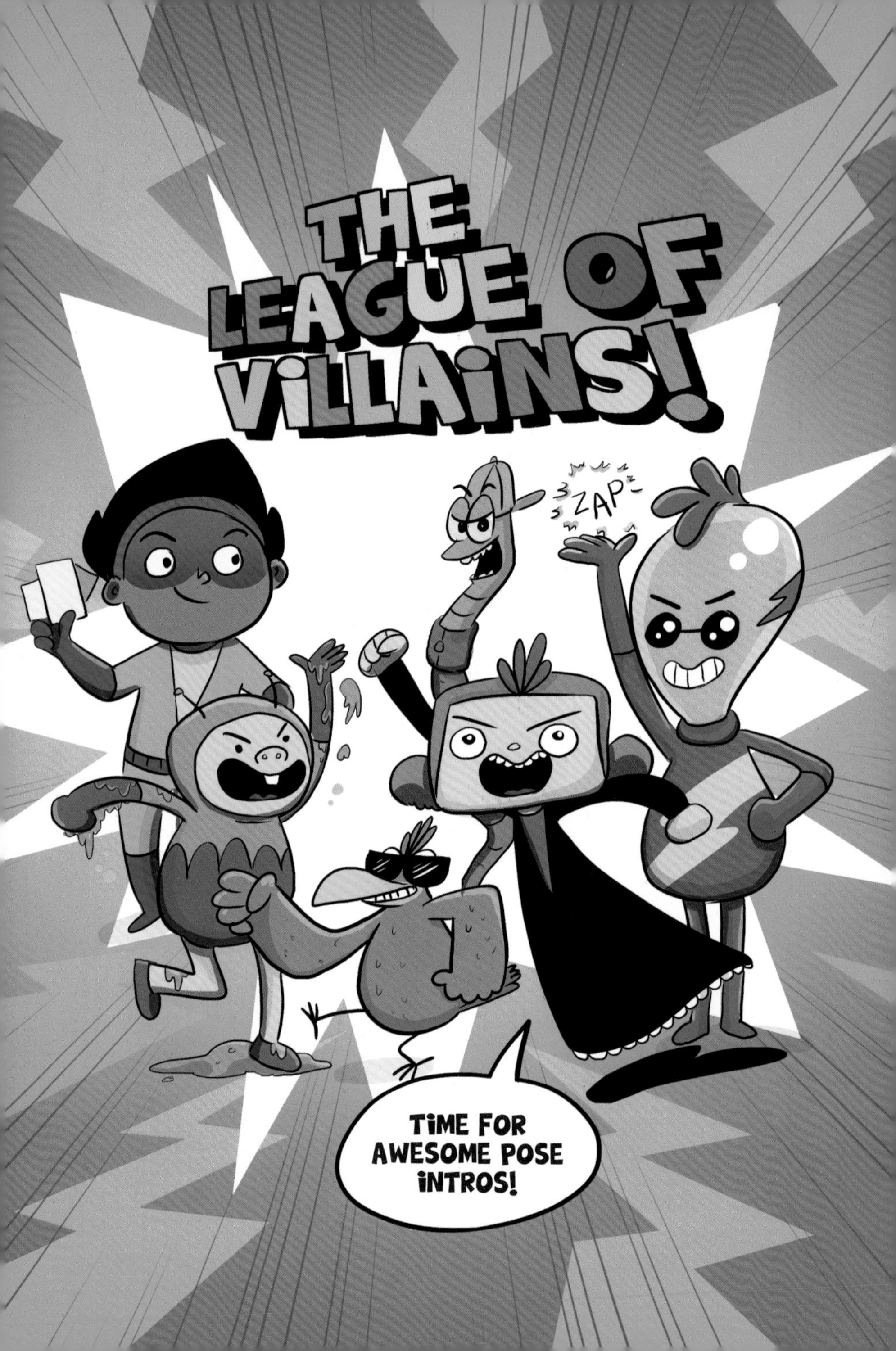
THE LEAGUE OF VILLAINS!
ZAP
TIME FOR AWESOME POSE INTROS!

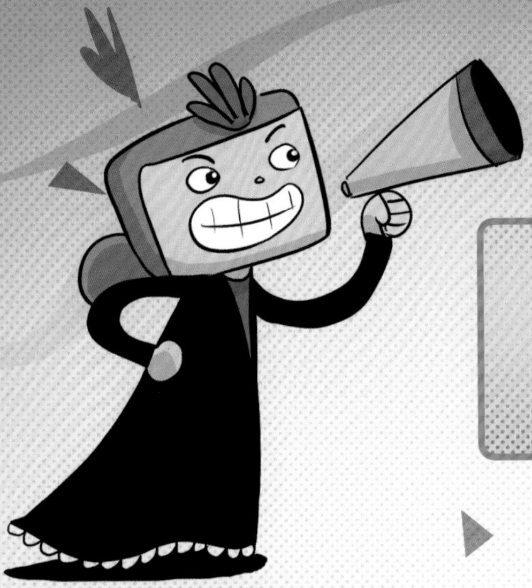

MELVIRA!

She's super evil, super smart, and has the power to transform!

CLAW

Melvira's trusted sidekick!

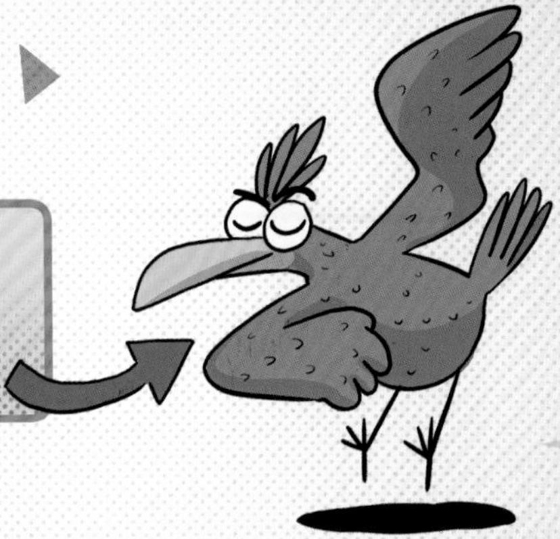

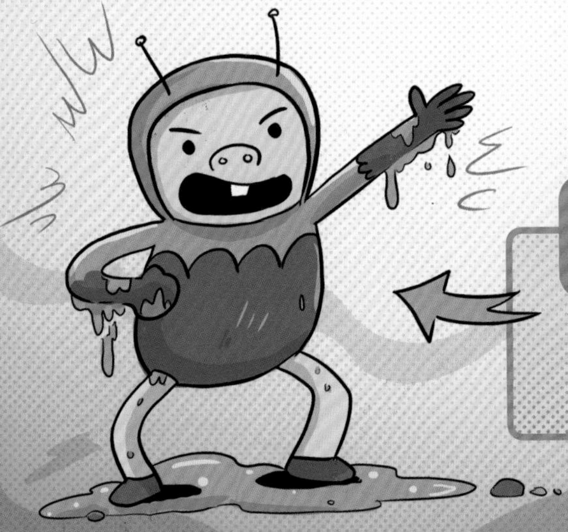

STICKY FINGERS

He has an endless supply of ooze!

PAPER CUT

She slices and dices using paper! Her weapon of choice? Sticky notes!

Light bulb head!

ZAP

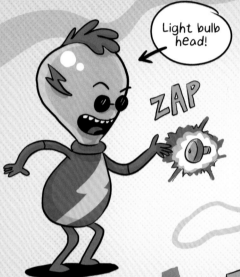

STATICO

He'll zap you with his unlimited power of static electricity!

EARWORM

He may be tiny, but you'll never get his catchy tunes out of your head!

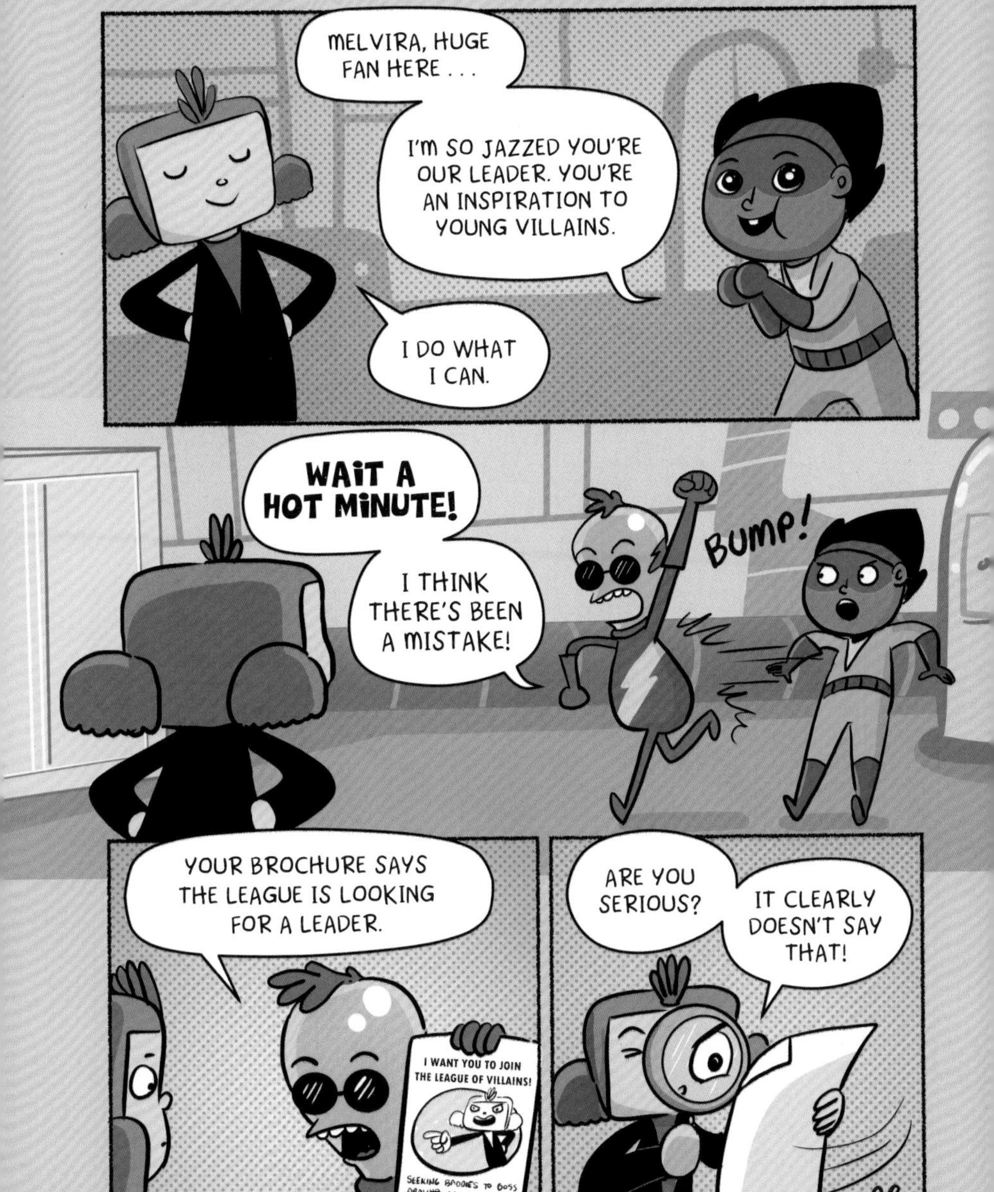
MELVIRA, HUGE FAN HERE . . .
I'M SO JAZZED YOU'RE OUR LEADER. YOU'RE AN INSPIRATION TO YOUNG VILLAINS.
I DO WHAT I CAN.
WAIT A HOT MINUTE!
I THINK THERE'S BEEN A MISTAKE!
BUMP!
YOUR BROCHURE SAYS THE LEAGUE IS LOOKING FOR A LEADER.
I WANT YOU TO JOIN THE LEAGUE OF VILLAINS!
ARE YOU SERIOUS?
IT CLEARLY DOESN'T SAY THAT!
SWIPE.

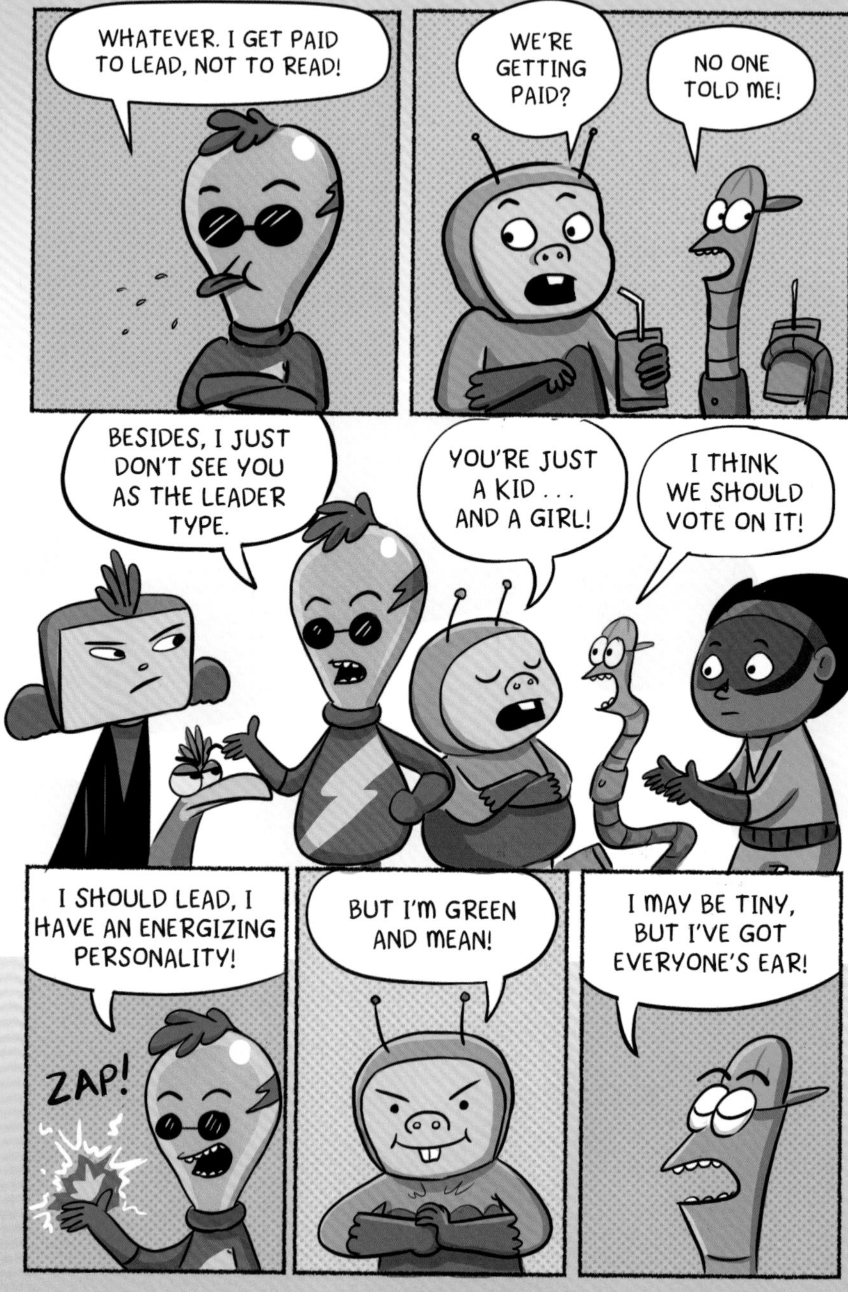
WHATEVER. I GET PAID TO LEAD, NOT TO READ!
WE'RE GETTING PAID?
NO ONE TOLD ME!
BESIDES, I JUST DON'T SEE YOU AS THE LEADER TYPE.
YOU'RE JUST A KID . . . AND A GIRL!
I THINK WE SHOULD VOTE ON IT!
I SHOULD LEAD, I HAVE AN ENERGIZING PERSONALITY!
ZAP!
BUT I'M GREEN AND MEAN!
I MAY BE TINY, BUT I'VE GOT EVERYONE'S EAR!

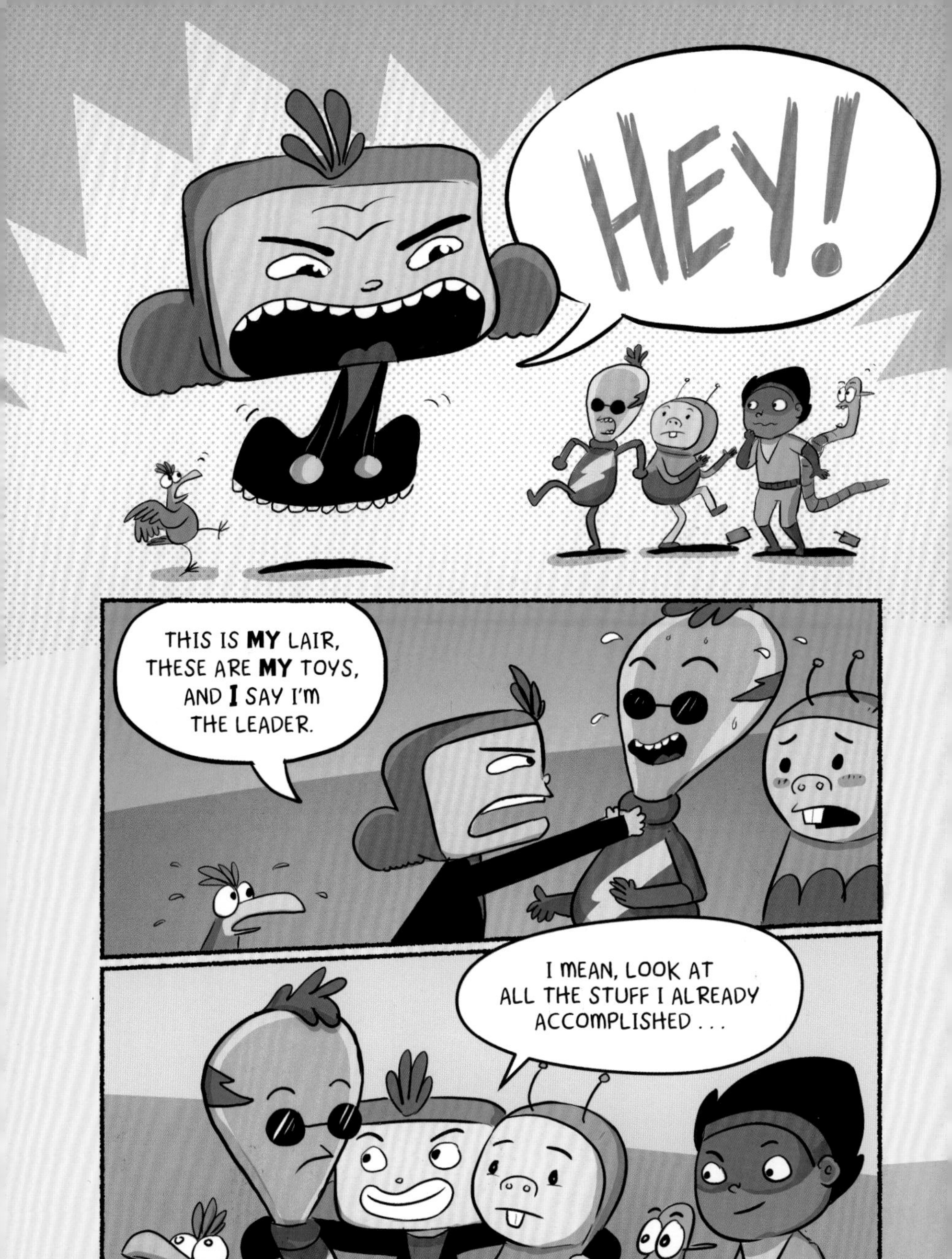
HEY!
THIS IS MY LAIR, THESE ARE MY TOYS, AND I SAY I'M THE LEADER.
I MEAN, LOOK AT ALL THE STUFF I ALREADY ACCOMPLISHED . . .

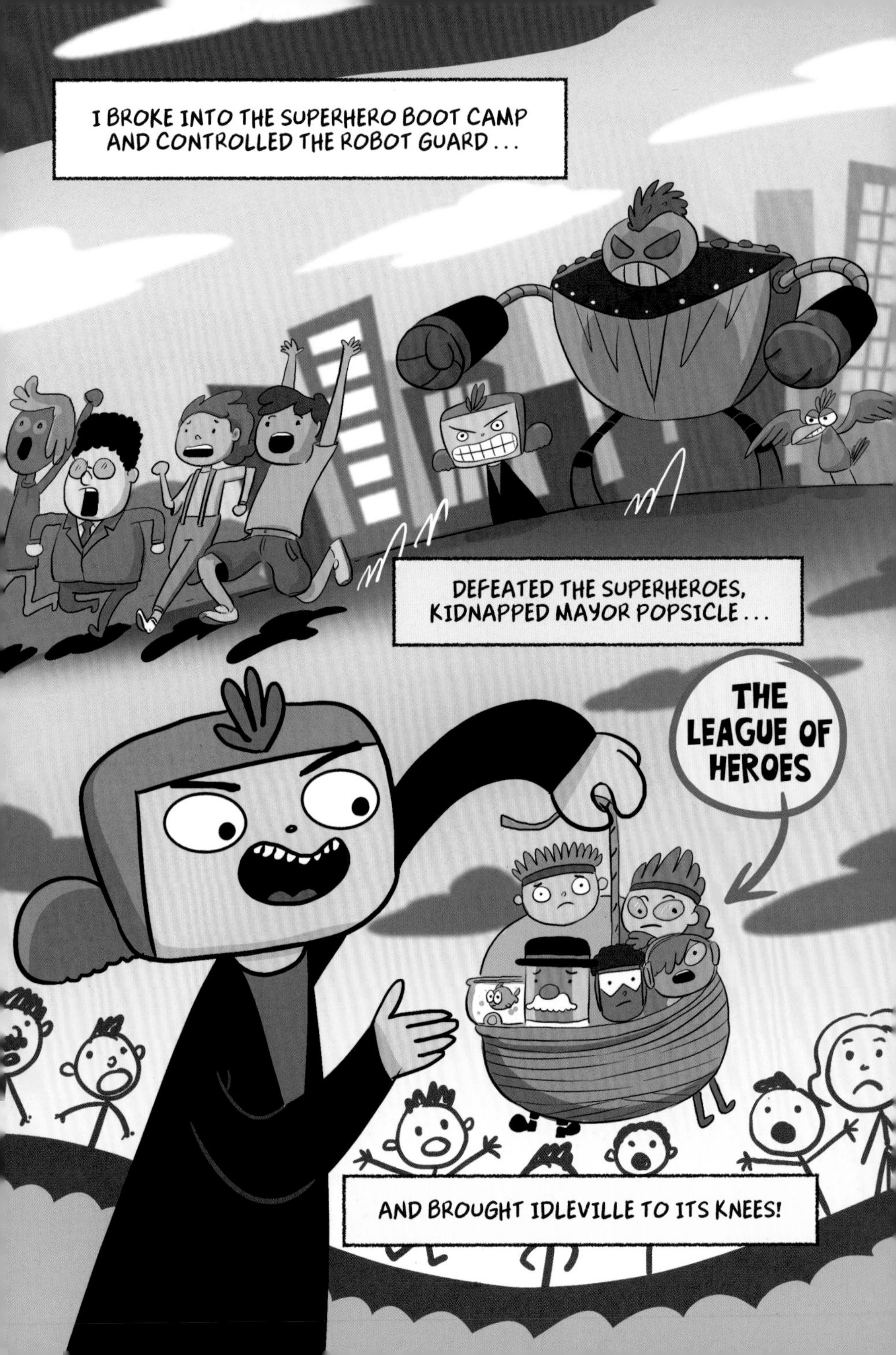
I BROKE INTO THE SUPERHERO BOOT CAMP AND CONTROLLED THE ROBOT GUARD . . .
DEFEATED THE SUPERHEROES, KIDNAPPED MAYOR POPSICLE . . .
THE LEAGUE OF HEROES
AND BROUGHT IDLEVILLE TO ITS KNEES!

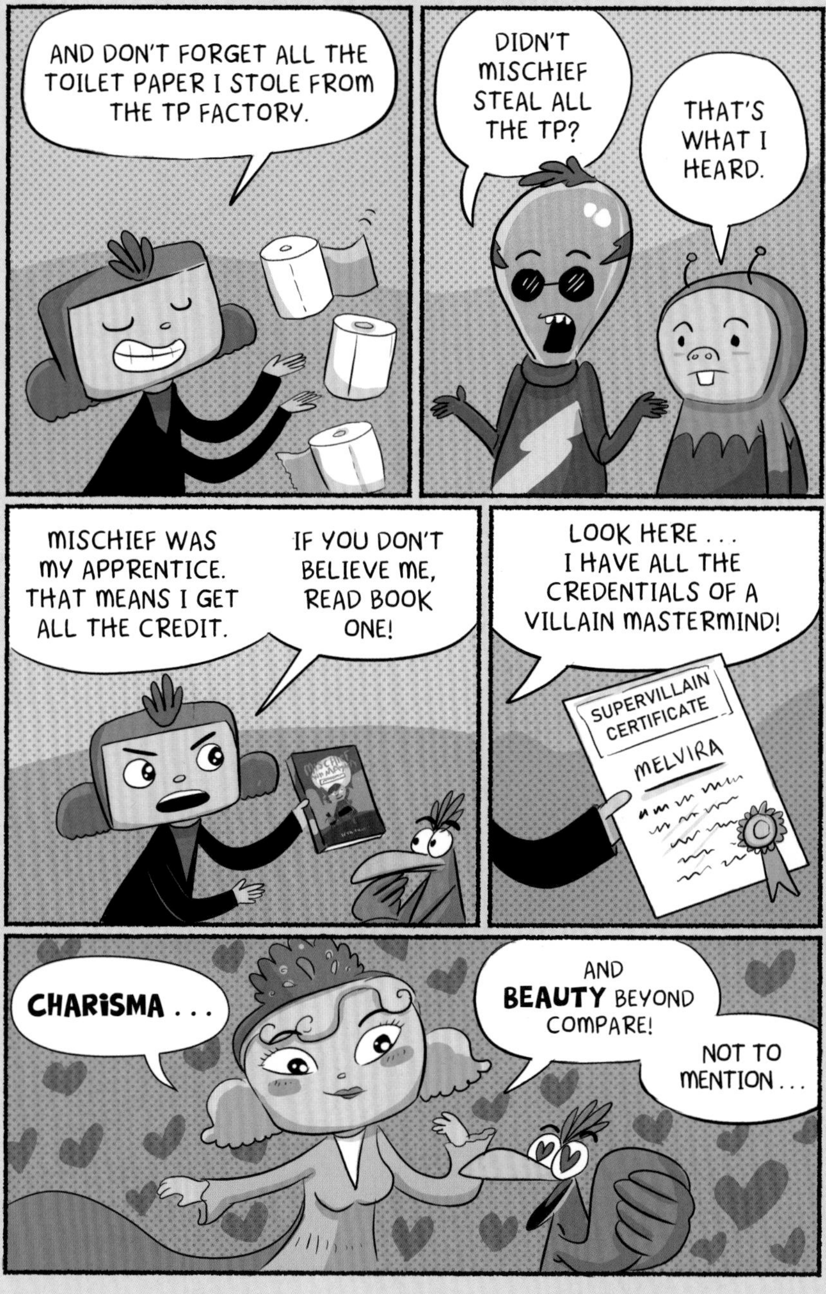
AND DON'T FORGET ALL THE TOILET PAPER I STOLE FROM THE TP FACTORY.
DIDN'T MISCHIEF STEAL ALL THE TP?
THAT'S WHAT I HEARD.
MISCHIEF WAS MY APPRENTICE. THAT MEANS I GET ALL THE CREDIT.
IF YOU DON'T BELIEVE ME, READ BOOK ONE!
LOOK HERE . . . I HAVE ALL THE CREDENTIALS OF A VILLAIN MASTERMIND!
SUPERVILLAIN CERTIFICATE
MELVIRA
CHARISMA . . .
AND BEAUTY BEYOND COMPARE!
NOT TO MENTION . . .

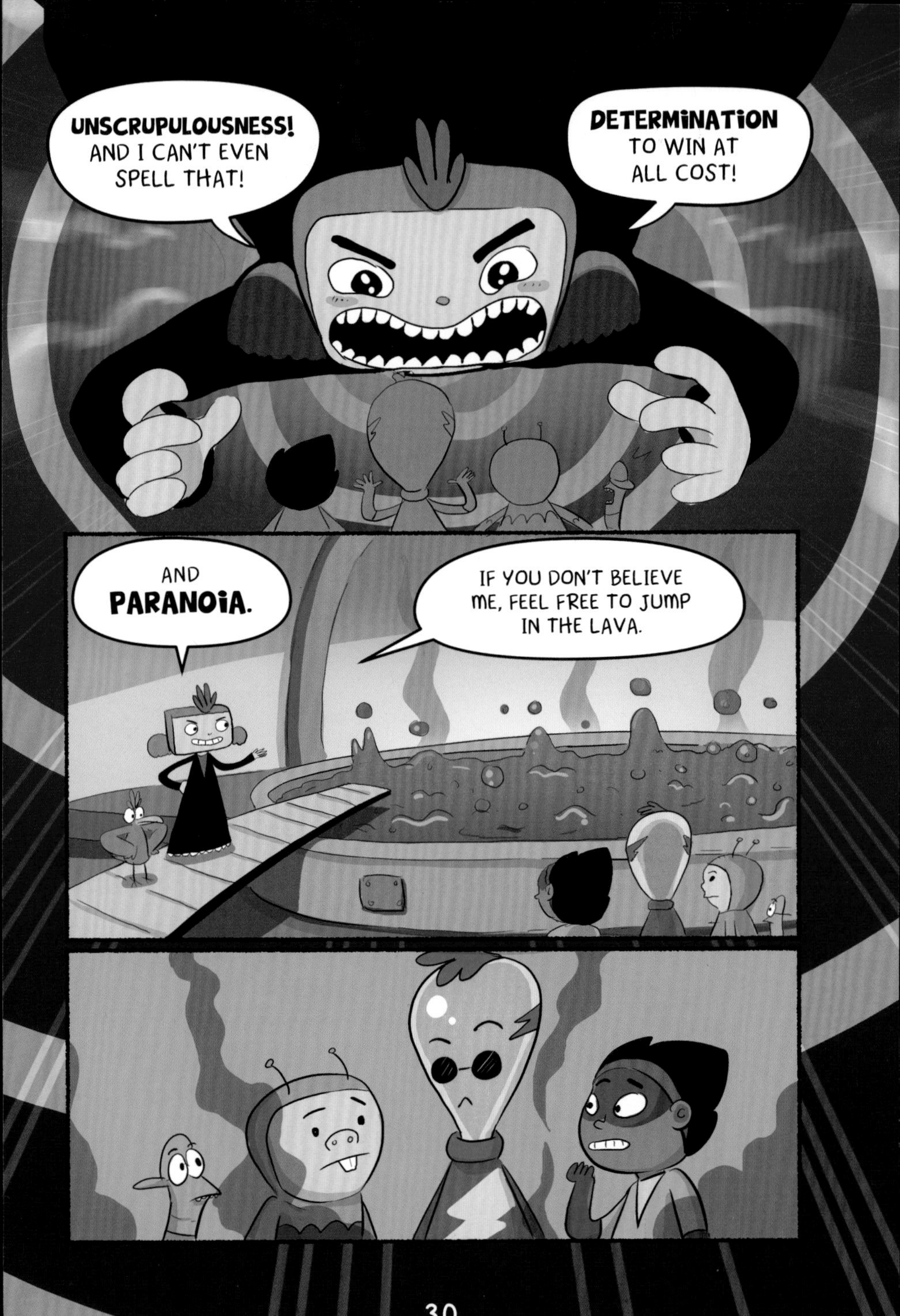
UNSCRUPULOUSNESS! AND I CAN'T EVEN SPELL THAT!
DETERMINATION TO WIN AT ALL COST!
AND PARANOIA.
IF YOU DON'T BELIEVE ME, FEEL FREE TO JUMP IN THE LAVA.

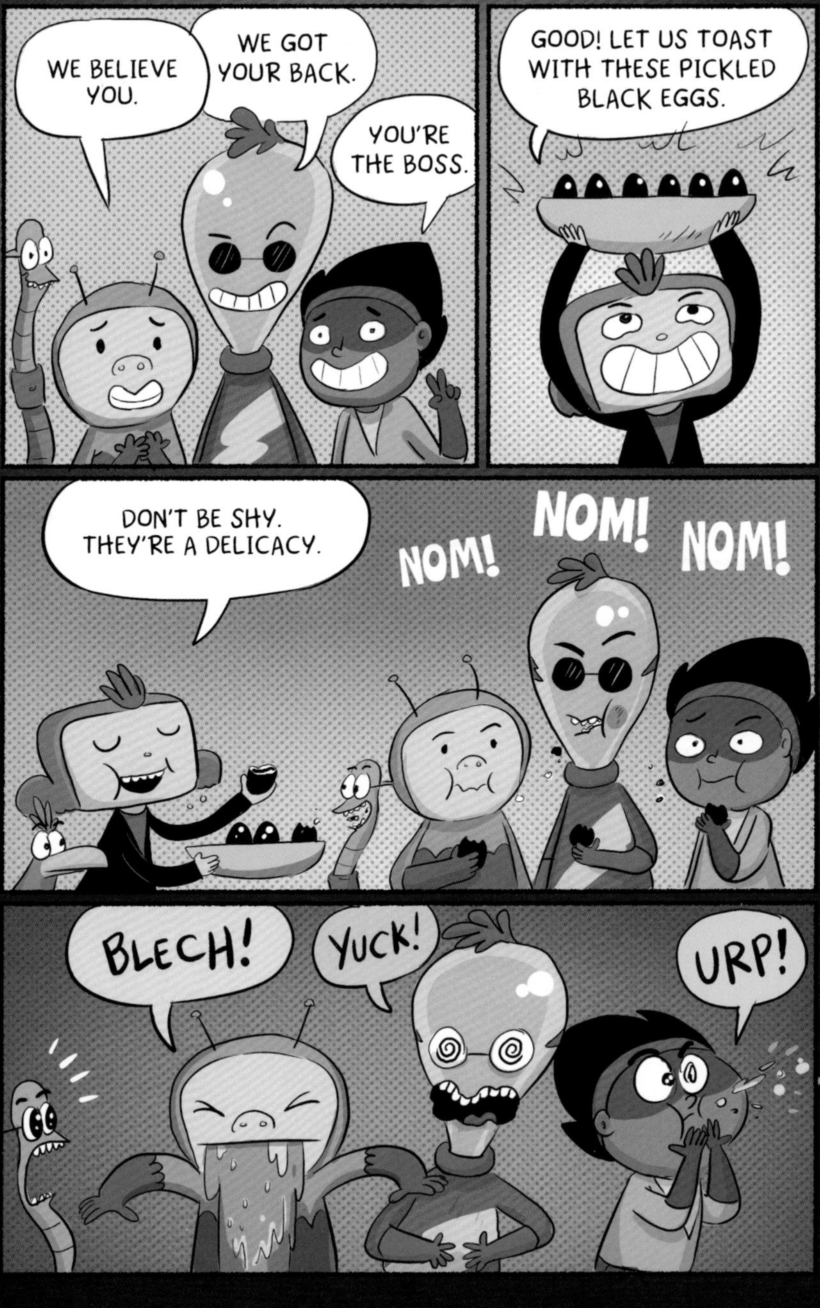
WE BELIEVE YOU.
WE GOT YOUR BACK.
YOU'RE THE BOSS.
GOOD! LET US TOAST WITH THESE PICKLED BLACK EGGS.
DON'T BE SHY. THEY'RE A DELICACY.
NOM!
NOM!
NOM!
BLECH!
YUCK!
URP!

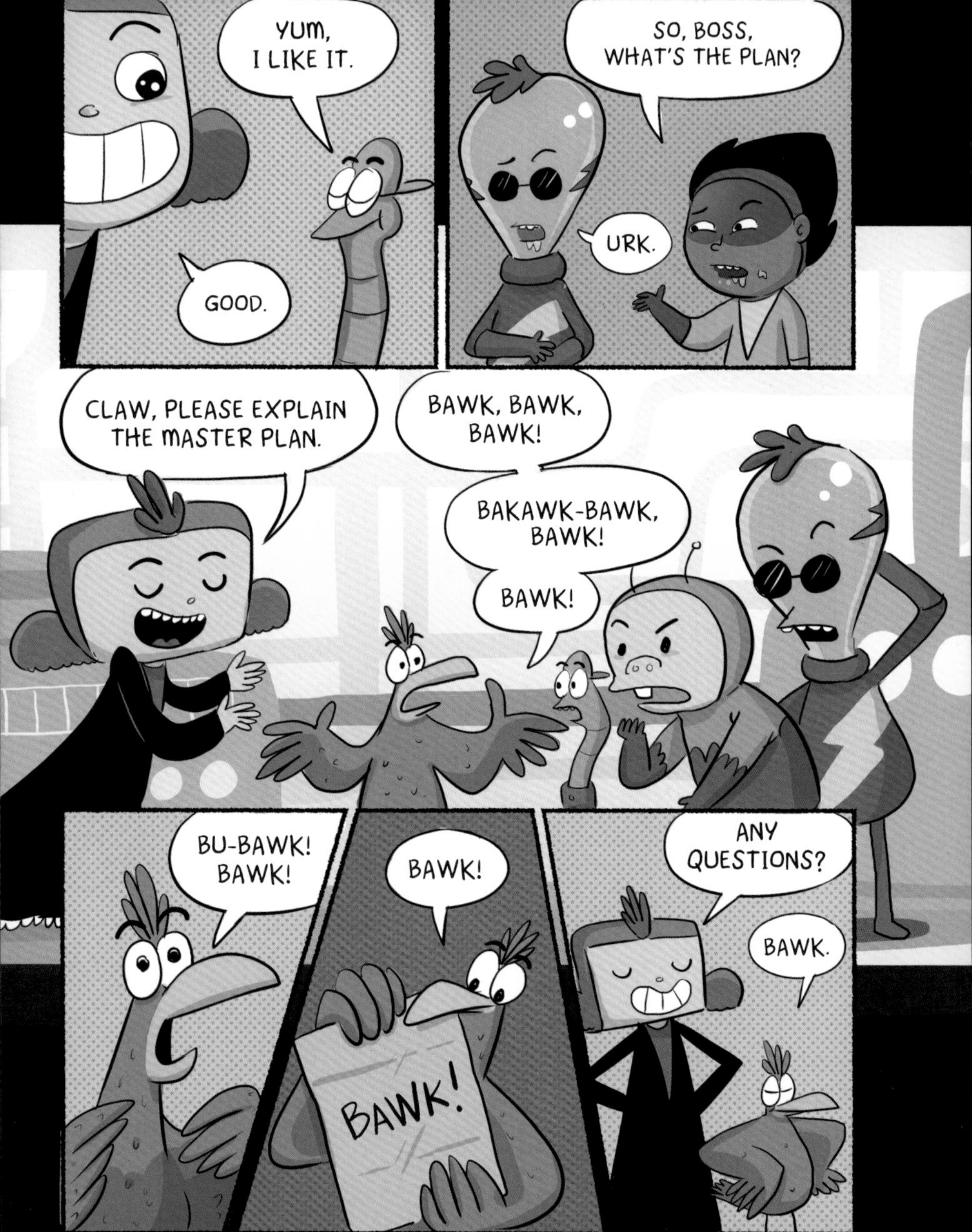
YUM, I LIKE IT.
GOOD.
SO, BOSS, WHAT'S THE PLAN?
URK.
CLAW, PLEASE EXPLAIN THE MASTER PLAN.
BAWK, BAWK, BAWK!
BAKAWK-BAWK, BAWK!
BAWK!
BU-BAWK! BAWK!
BAWK!
BAWK!
ANY QUESTIONS?
BAWK.

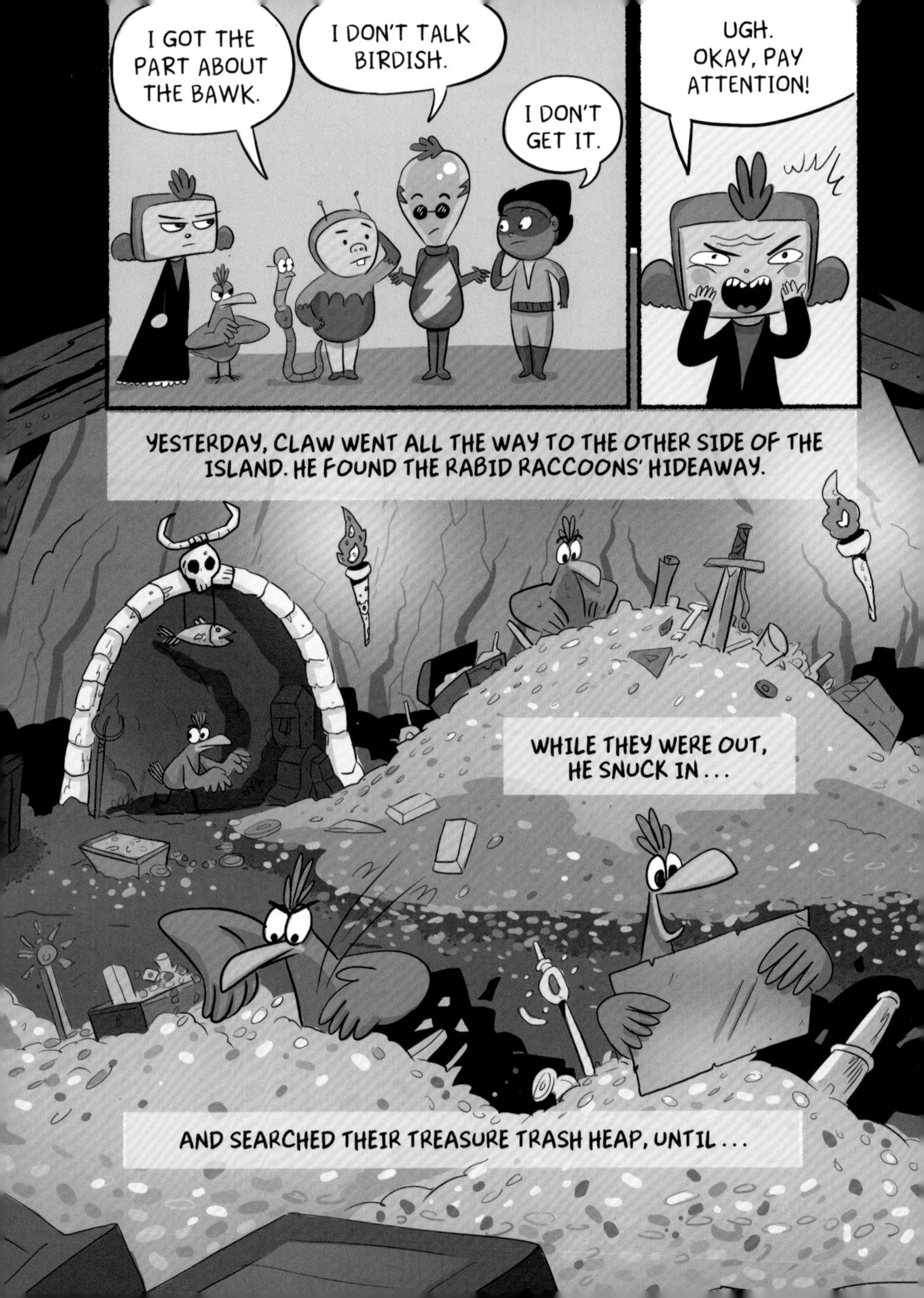
I GOT THE PART ABOUT THE BAWK.
I DON'T TALK BIRDISH.
I DON'T GET IT.
UGH. OKAY, PAY ATTENTION!
YESTERDAY, CLAW WENT ALL THE WAY TO THE OTHER SIDE OF THE ISLAND. HE FOUND THE RABID RACCOONS' HIDEAWAY.
WHILE THEY WERE OUT, HE SNUCK IN . . .
AND SEARCHED THEIR TREASURE TRASH HEAP, UNTIL . . .

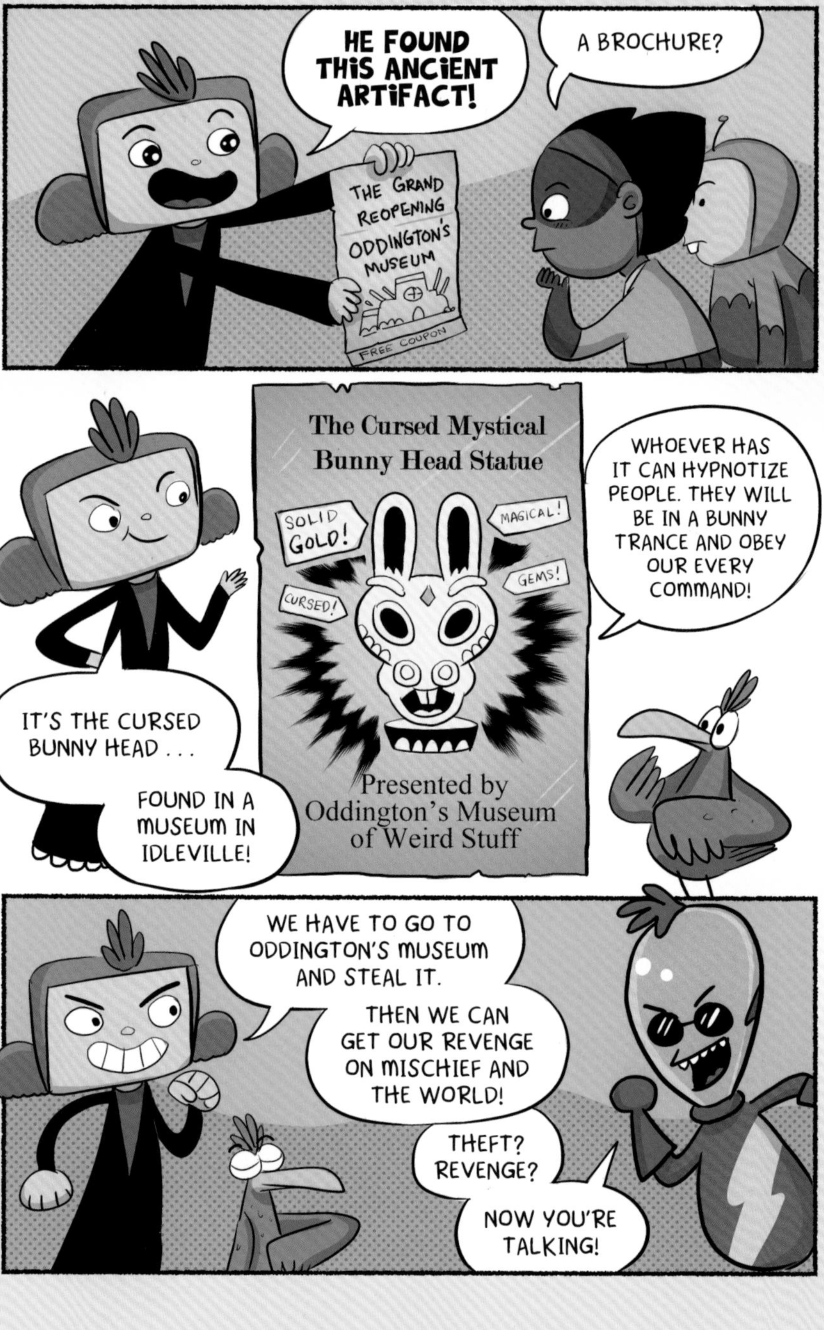
HE FOUND THIS ANCIENT ARTIFACT!
A BROCHURE?
THE GRAND REOPENING
ODDINGTON'S MUSEUM
FREE COUPON
The Cursed Mystical Bunny Head Statue
SOLID GOLD!
MAGICAL!
GEMS!
CURSED!
Presented by Oddington's Museum of Weird Stuff
WHOEVER HAS IT CAN HYPNOTIZE PEOPLE. THEY WILL BE IN A BUNNY TRANCE AND OBEY OUR EVERY COMMAND!
IT'S THE CURSED BUNNY HEAD . . .
FOUND IN A MUSEUM IN IDLEVILLE!
WE HAVE TO GO TO ODDINGTON'S MUSEUM AND STEAL IT.
THEN WE CAN GET OUR REVENGE ON MISCHIEF AND THE WORLD!
THEFT? REVENGE?
NOW YOU'RE TALKING!

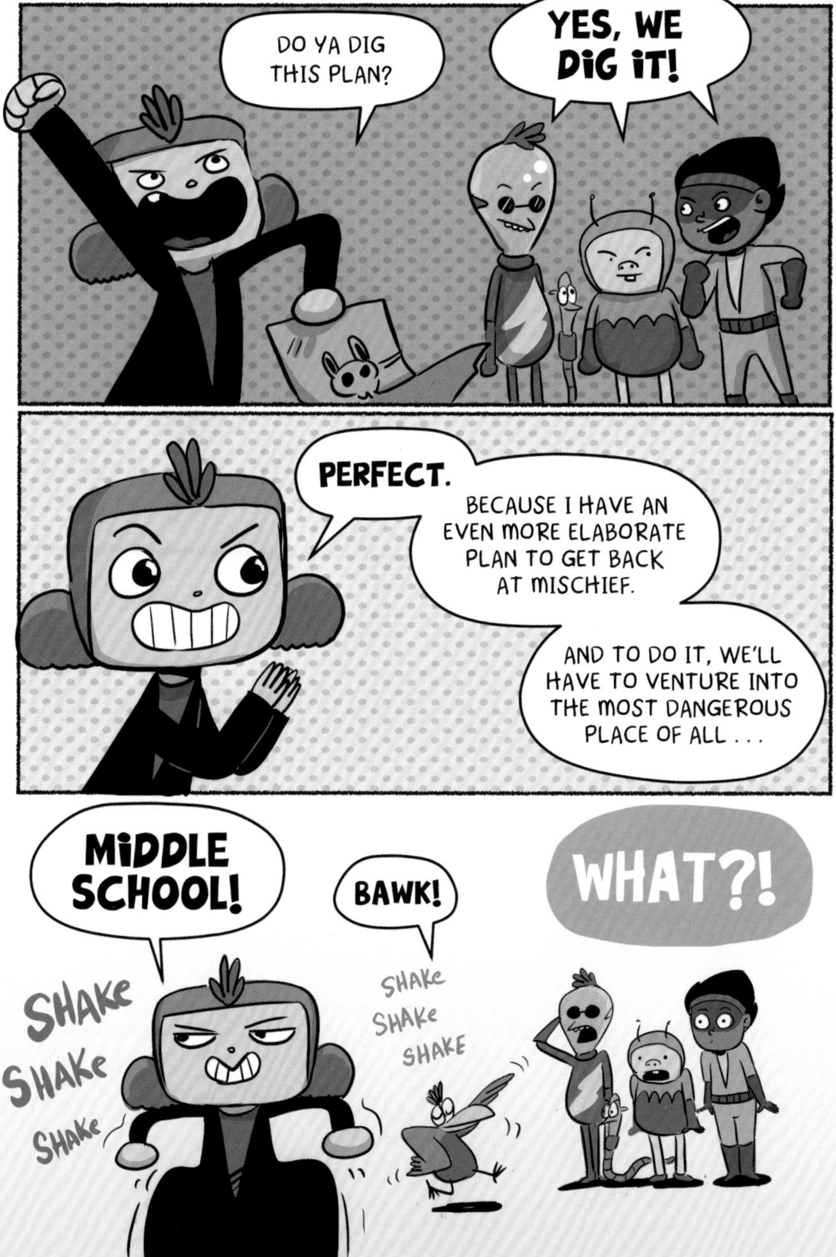
DO YA DIG THIS PLAN?
YES, WE DIG IT!
PERFECT.
BECAUSE I HAVE AN EVEN MORE ELABORATE PLAN TO GET BACK AT MISCHIEF.
AND TO DO IT, WE'LL HAVE TO VENTURE INTO THE MOST DANGEROUS PLACE OF ALL . . .
MIDDLE SCHOOL!
BAWK!
WHAT?!
SHAKE
SHAKE
SHAKE
SHAKE
SHAKE
SHAKE

CHAPTER 3

THE NEW KID ON THE BLOCK

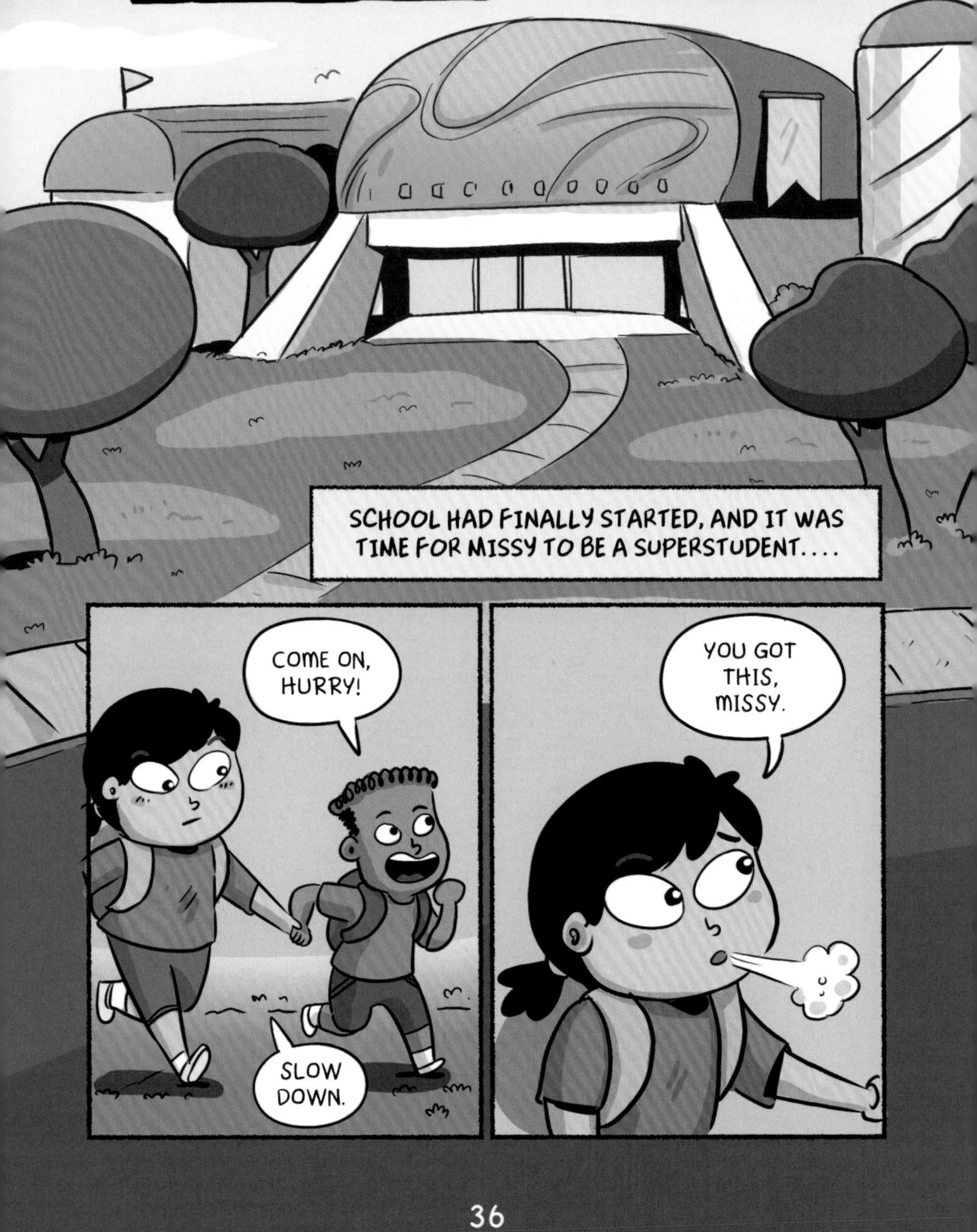

SCHOOL HAD FINALLY STARTED, AND IT WAS TIME FOR MISSY TO BE A SUPERSTUDENT....
COME ON, HURRY!
SLOW DOWN.
YOU GOT THIS, MISSY.

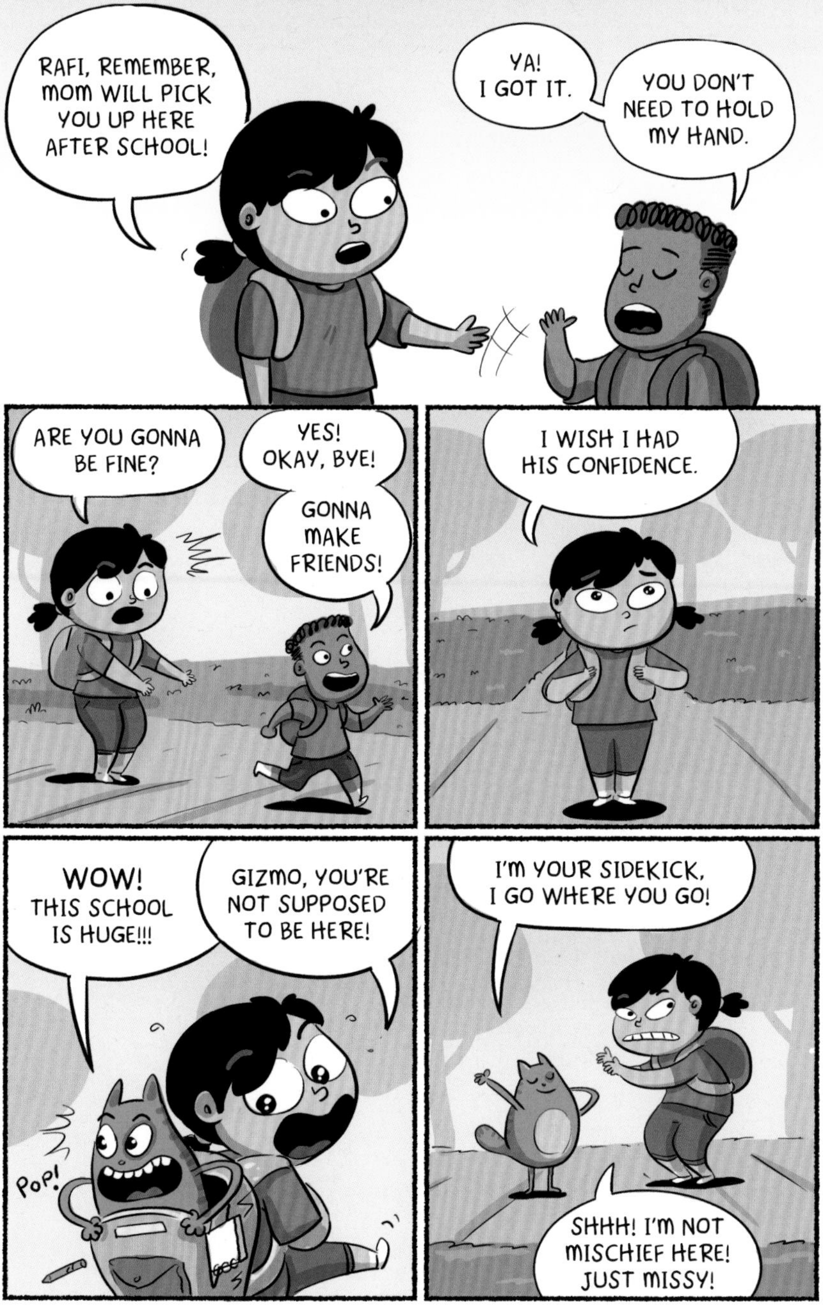
RAFI, REMEMBER, MOM WILL PICK YOU UP HERE AFTER SCHOOL!
YA! I GOT IT.
YOU DON'T NEED TO HOLD MY HAND.
ARE YOU GONNA BE FINE?
YES! OKAY, BYE!
GONNA MAKE FRIENDS!
I WISH I HAD HIS CONFIDENCE.
WOW! THIS SCHOOL IS HUGE!!!
POP!
GIZMO, YOU'RE NOT SUPPOSED TO BE HERE!
I'M YOUR SIDEKICK, I GO WHERE YOU GO!
SHHH! I'M NOT MISCHIEF HERE! JUST MISSY!

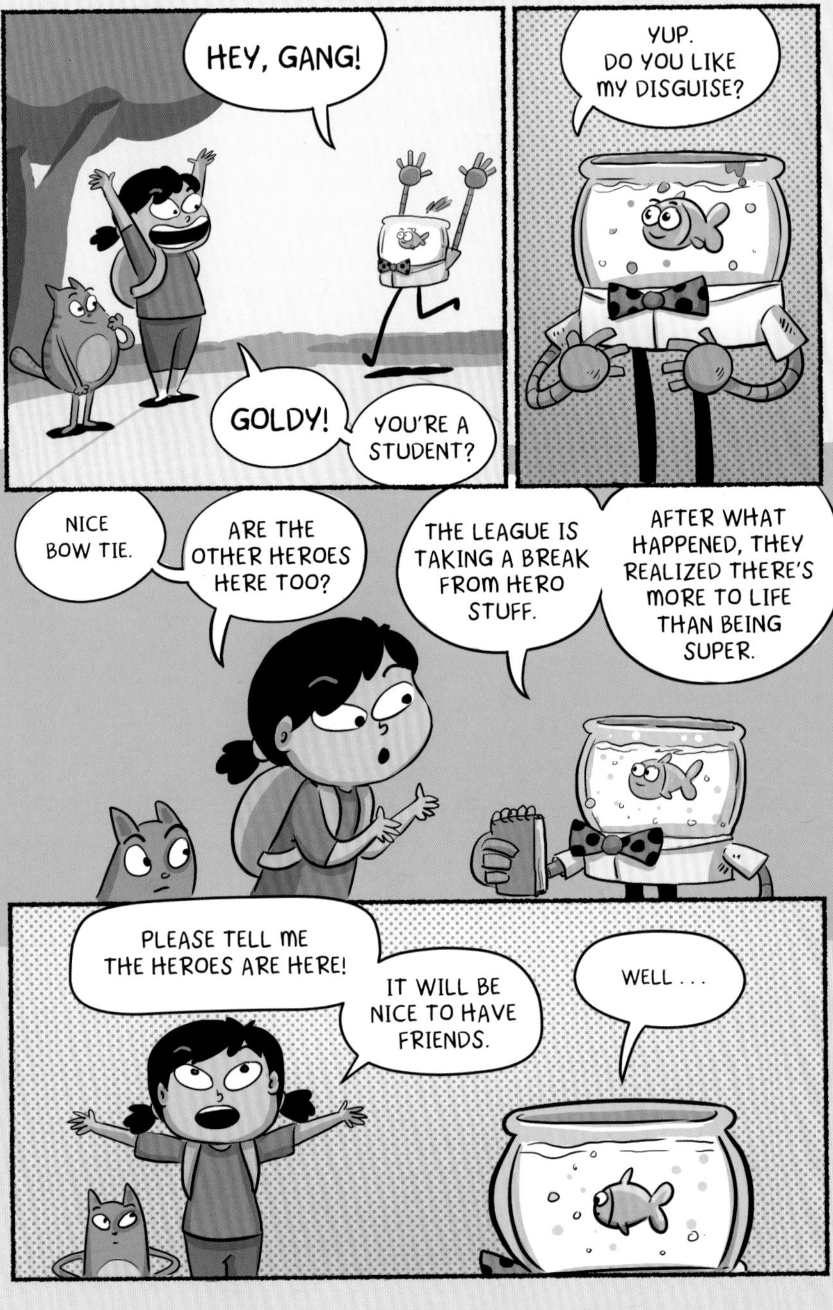
HEY, GANG!
GOLDY!
YOU'RE A STUDENT?
YUP. DO YOU LIKE MY DISGUISE?
NICE BOW TIE.
ARE THE OTHER HEROES HERE TOO?
THE LEAGUE IS TAKING A BREAK FROM HERO STUFF.
AFTER WHAT HAPPENED, THEY REALIZED THERE'S MORE TO LIFE THAN BEING SUPER.
PLEASE TELL ME THE HEROES ARE HERE!
IT WILL BE NICE TO HAVE FRIENDS.
WELL . . .

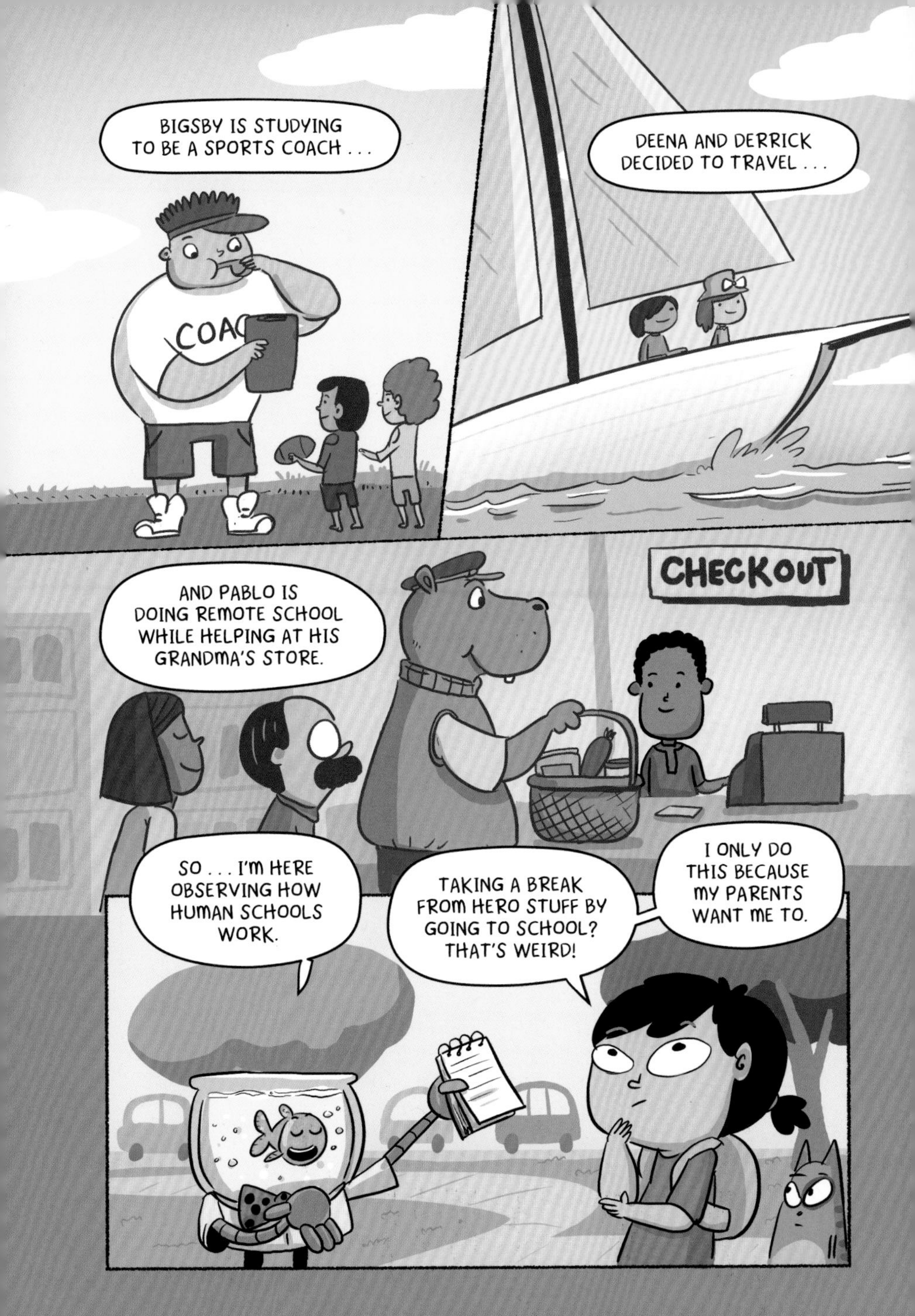
BIGSBY IS STUDYING TO BE A SPORTS COACH . . .
COAC
DEENA AND DERRICK DECIDED TO TRAVEL . . .
CHECKOUT
AND PABLO IS DOING REMOTE SCHOOL WHILE HELPING AT HIS GRANDMA'S STORE.
SO . . . I'M HERE OBSERVING HOW HUMAN SCHOOLS WORK.
TAKING A BREAK FROM HERO STUFF BY GOING TO SCHOOL? THAT'S WEIRD!
I ONLY DO THIS BECAUSE MY PARENTS WANT ME TO.

THE PRESSURES OF GOING TO SCHOOL

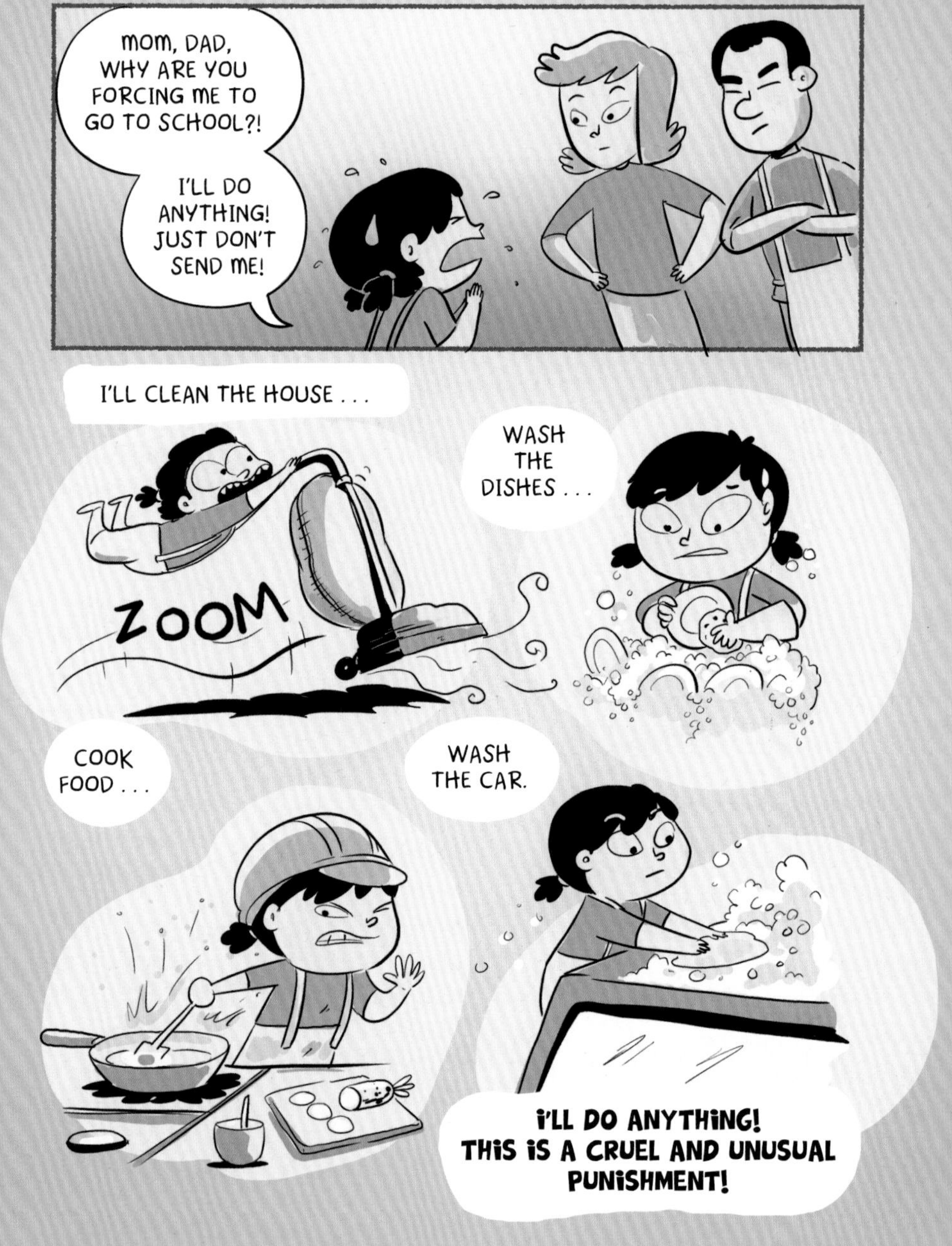
MOM, DAD, WHY ARE YOU FORCING ME TO GO TO SCHOOL?!
I'LL DO ANYTHING! JUST DON'T SEND ME!
I'LL CLEAN THE HOUSE . . .
ZOOM
WASH THE DISHES . . .
COOK FOOD . . .
WASH THE CAR.
I'LL DO ANYTHING! THIS IS A CRUEL AND UNUSUAL PUNISHMENT!

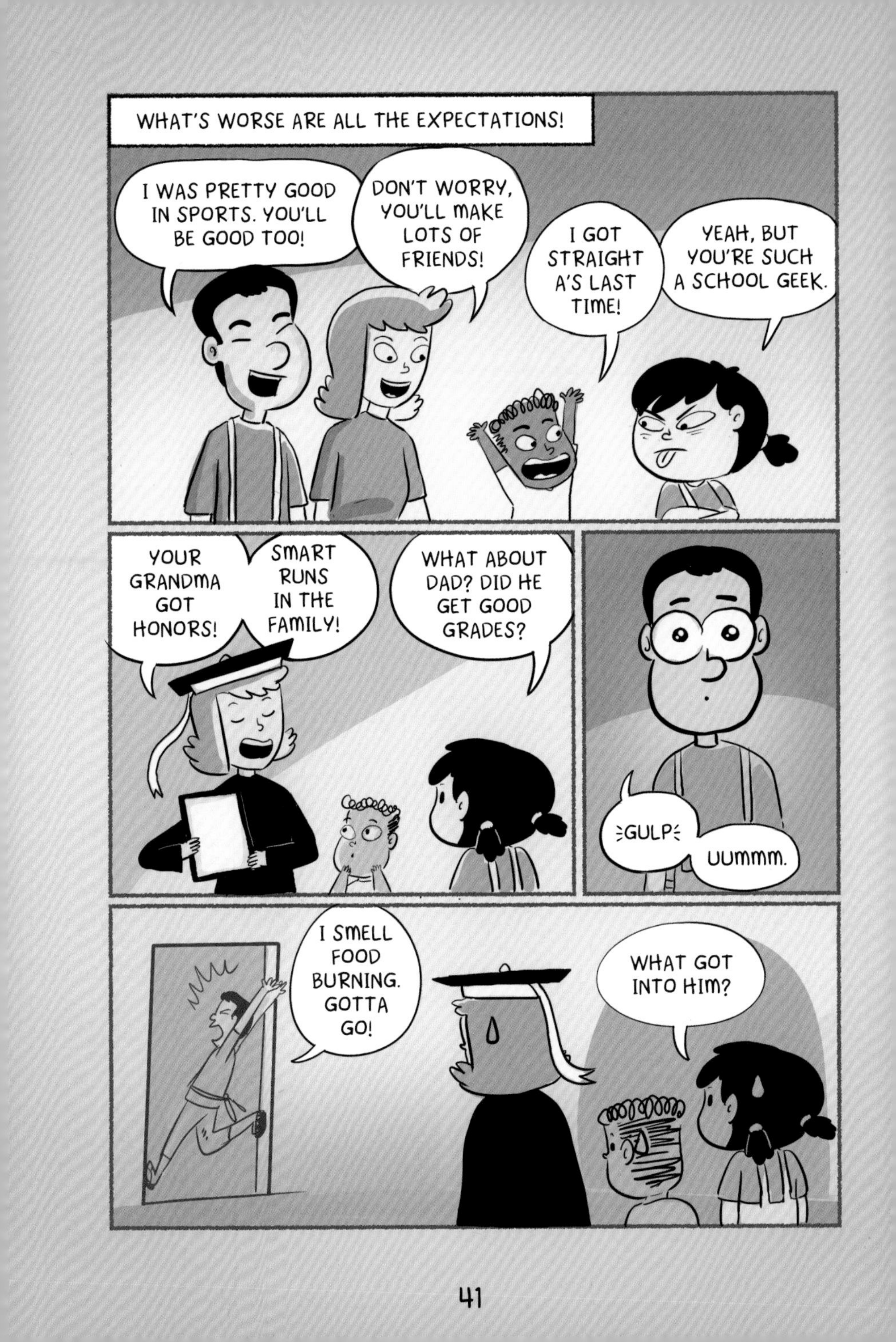
WHAT'S WORSE ARE ALL THE EXPECTATIONS!
I WAS PRETTY GOOD IN SPORTS. YOU'LL BE GOOD TOO!
DON'T WORRY, YOU'LL MAKE LOTS OF FRIENDS!
I GOT STRAIGHT A'S LAST TIME!
YEAH, BUT YOU'RE SUCH A SCHOOL GEEK.
YOUR GRANDMA GOT HONORS!
SMART RUNS IN THE FAMILY!
WHAT ABOUT DAD? DID HE GET GOOD GRADES?
GULP
UUMMM.
I SMELL FOOD BURNING. GOTTA GO!
WHAT GOT INTO HIM?

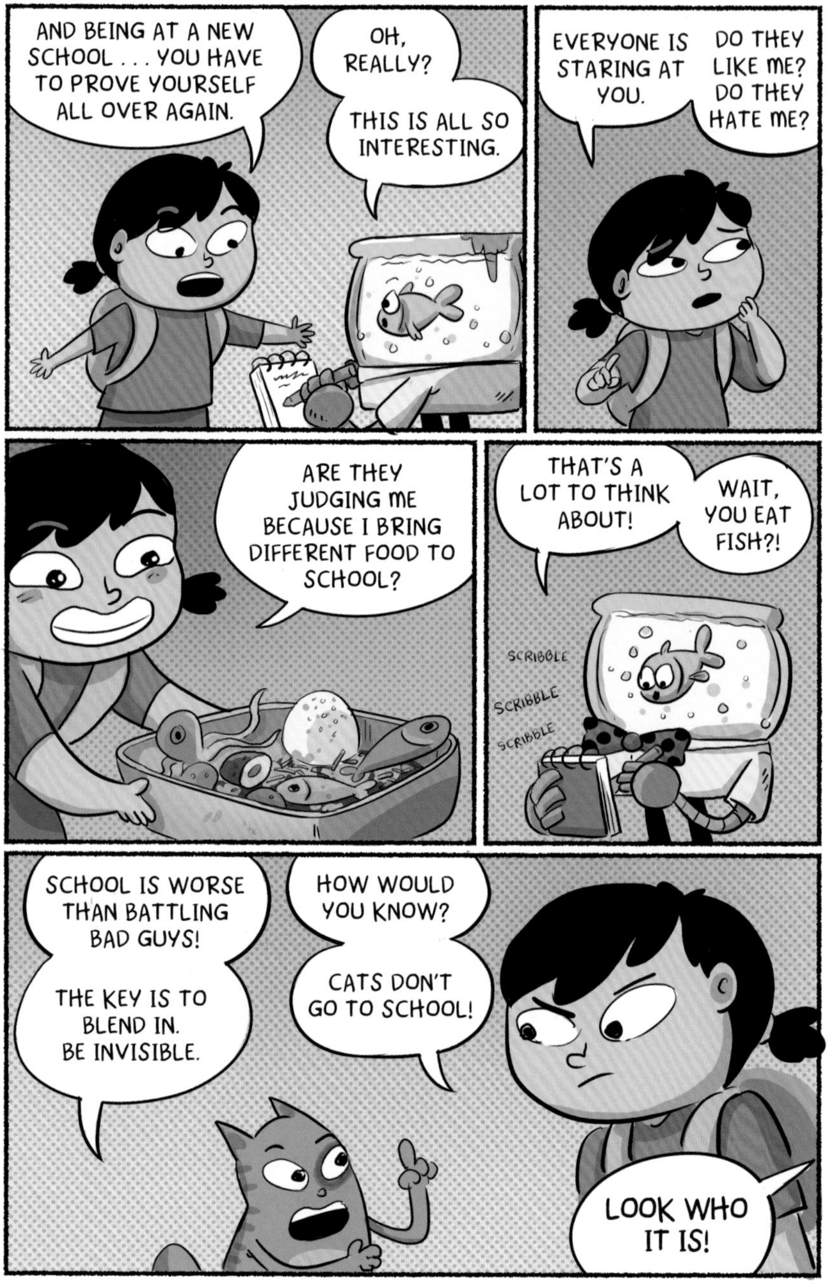
AND BEING AT A NEW SCHOOL . . . YOU HAVE TO PROVE YOURSELF ALL OVER AGAIN.
OH, REALLY?
THIS IS ALL SO INTERESTING.
EVERYONE IS STARING AT YOU.
DO THEY LIKE ME? DO THEY HATE ME?
ARE THEY JUDGING ME BECAUSE I BRING DIFFERENT FOOD TO SCHOOL?
THAT'S A LOT TO THINK ABOUT!
WAIT, YOU EAT FISH?!
SCRIBBLE
SCRIBBLE
SCRIBBLE
SCHOOL IS WORSE THAN BATTLING BAD GUYS!
THE KEY IS TO BLEND IN. BE INVISIBLE.
HOW WOULD YOU KNOW?
CATS DON'T GO TO SCHOOL!
LOOK WHO IT IS!

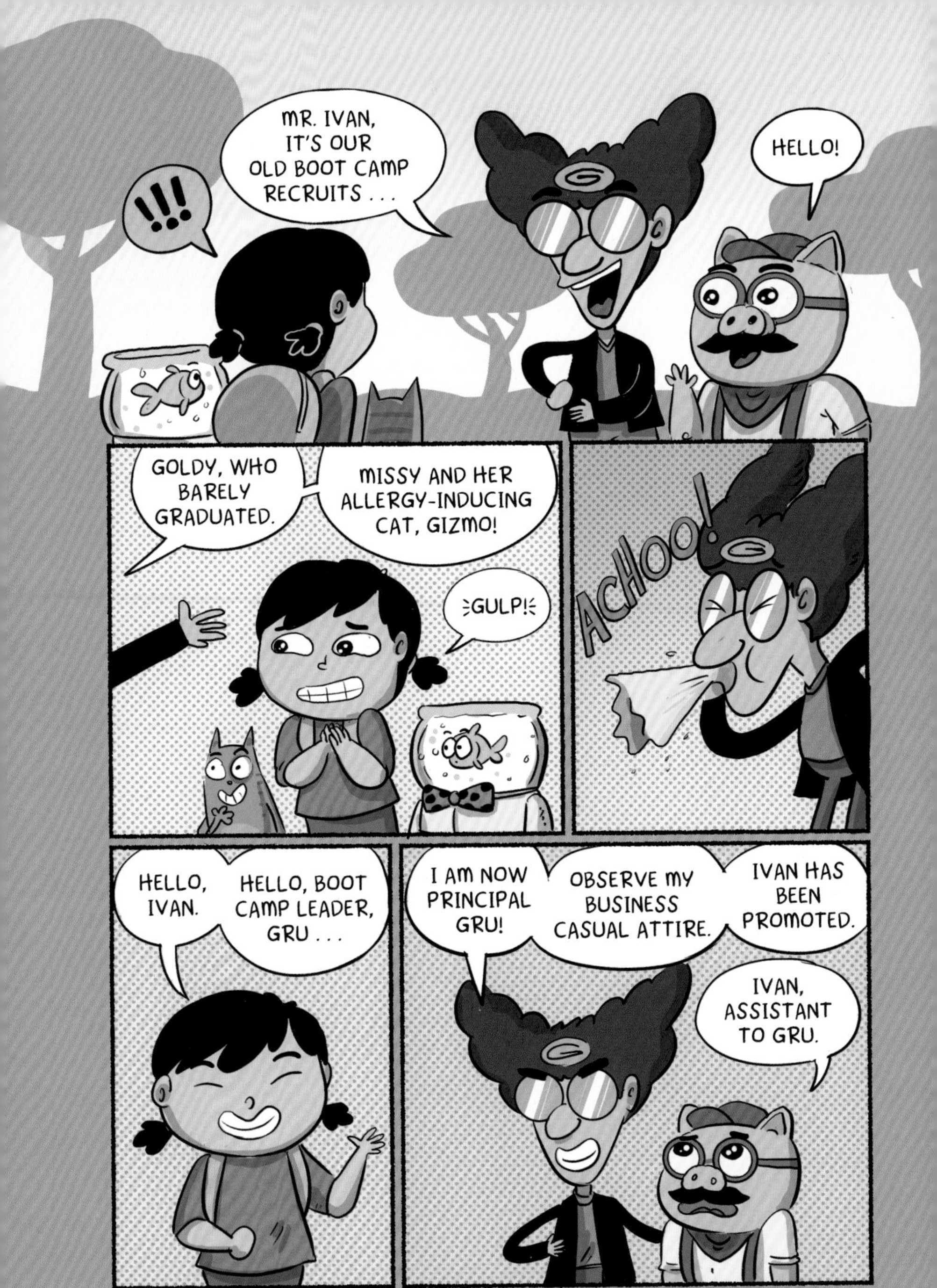
!!!
MR. IVAN, IT'S OUR OLD BOOT CAMP RECRUITS . . .
HELLO!
GOLDY, WHO BARELY GRADUATED.
MISSY AND HER ALLERGY-INDUCING CAT, GIZMO!
GULP!
ACHOO!
HELLO, IVAN.
HELLO, BOOT CAMP LEADER, GRU . . .
I AM NOW PRINCIPAL GRU!
OBSERVE MY BUSINESS CASUAL ATTIRE.
IVAN HAS BEEN PROMOTED.
IVAN, ASSISTANT TO GRU.

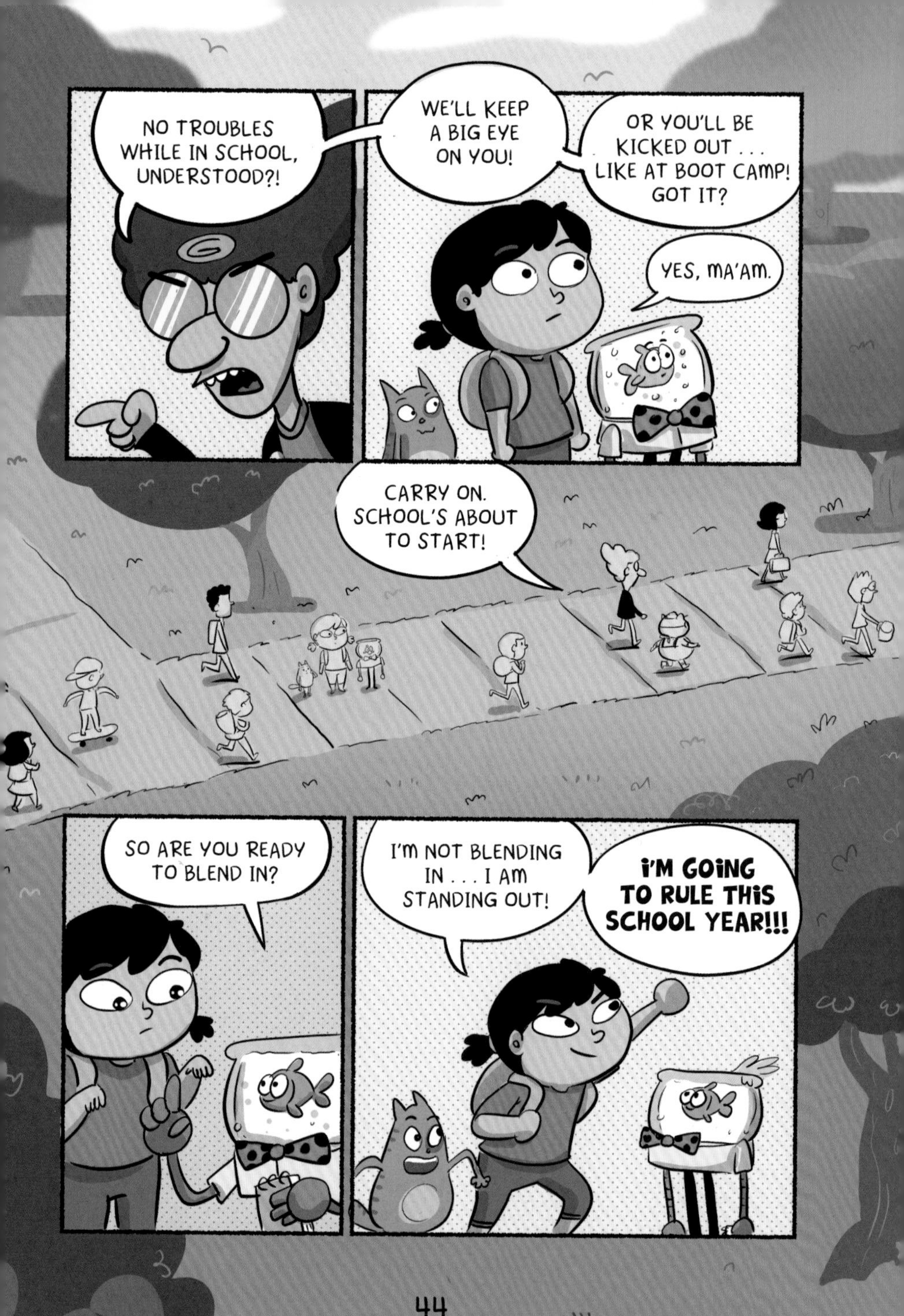
NO TROUBLES WHILE IN SCHOOL, UNDERSTOOD?!
WE'LL KEEP A BIG EYE ON YOU!
OR YOU'LL BE KICKED OUT . . . LIKE AT BOOT CAMP! GOT IT?
YES, MA'AM.
CARRY ON. SCHOOL'S ABOUT TO START!
SO ARE YOU READY TO BLEND IN?
I'M NOT BLENDING IN . . . I AM STANDING OUT!
I'M GOING TO RULE THIS SCHOOL YEAR!!!

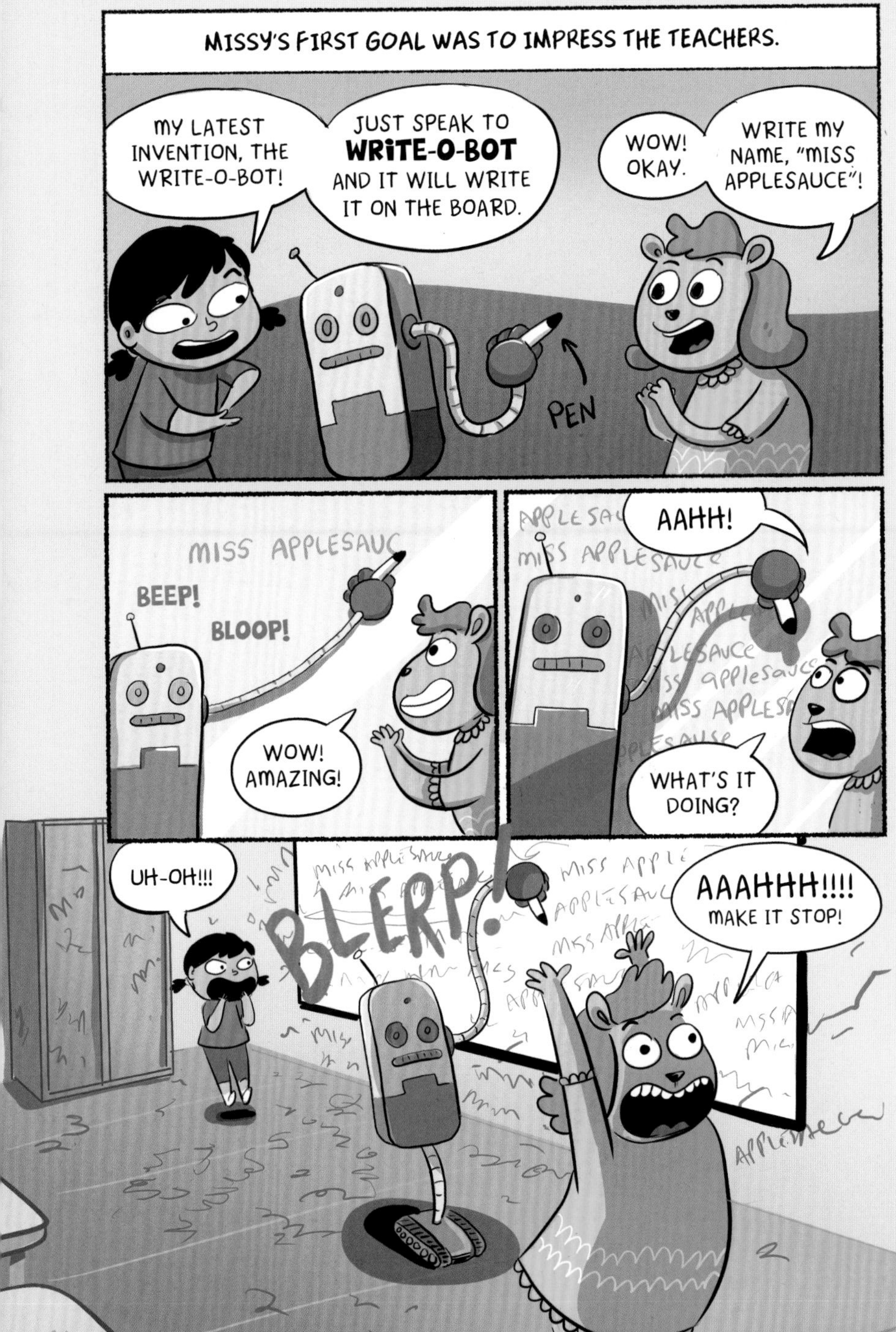
MISSY'S FIRST GOAL WAS TO IMPRESS THE TEACHERS.
MY LATEST INVENTION, THE WRITE-O-BOT!
JUST SPEAK TO WRITE-O-BOT AND IT WILL WRITE IT ON THE BOARD.
WOW! OKAY.
WRITE MY NAME, "MISS APPLESAUCE"!
PEN
MISS APPLESAUC
BEEP!
BLOOP!
WOW! AMAZING!
AAHH!
WHAT'S IT DOING?
UH-OH!!!
BLERP!
AAAHHH!!!! MAKE IT STOP!

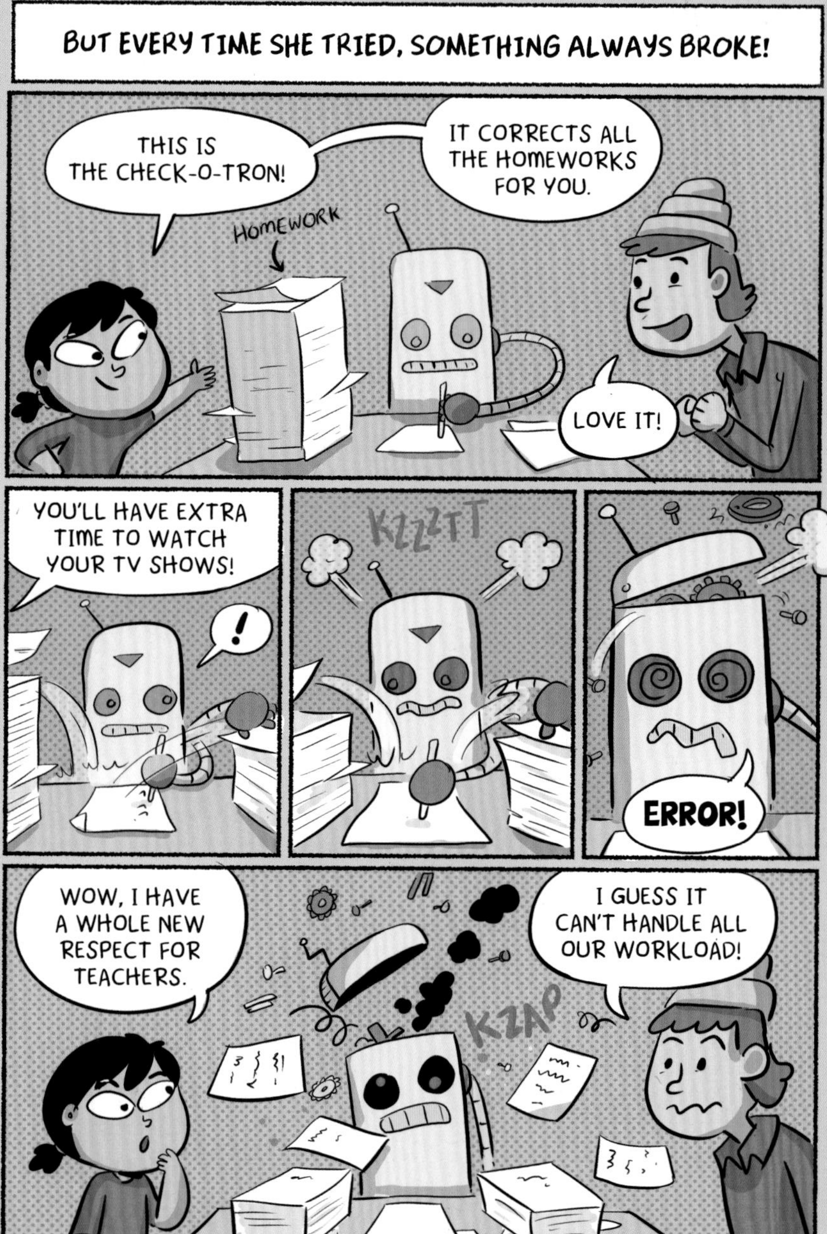
BUT EVERY TIME SHE TRIED, SOMETHING ALWAYS BROKE!
THIS IS THE CHECK-O-TRON!
IT CORRECTS ALL THE HOMEWORKS FOR YOU.
HOMEWORK
LOVE IT!
YOU'LL HAVE EXTRA TIME TO WATCH YOUR TV SHOWS!
!
KZZZTT
ERROR!
WOW, I HAVE A WHOLE NEW RESPECT FOR TEACHERS.
I GUESS IT CAN'T HANDLE ALL OUR WORKLOAD!
KZAP

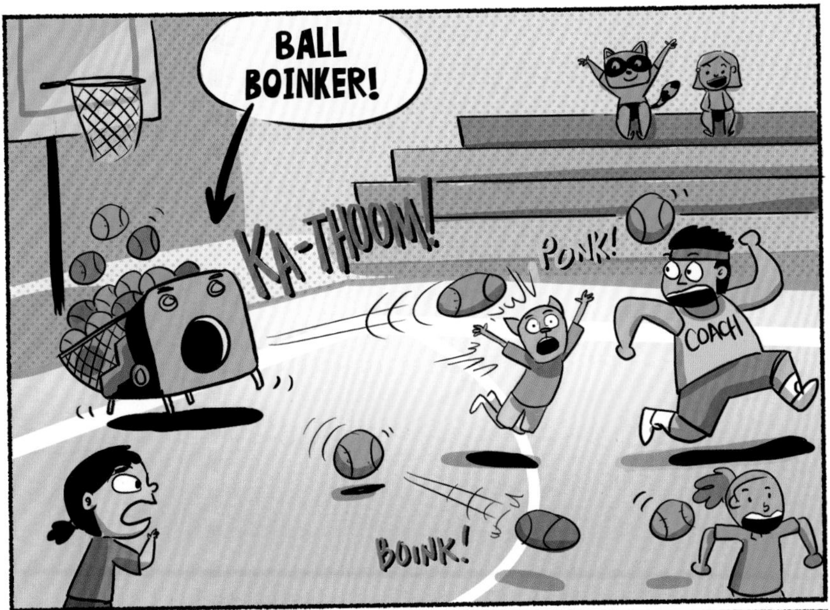
BALL BOINKER!
KA-THOOM!
PONK!
COACH
BOINK!

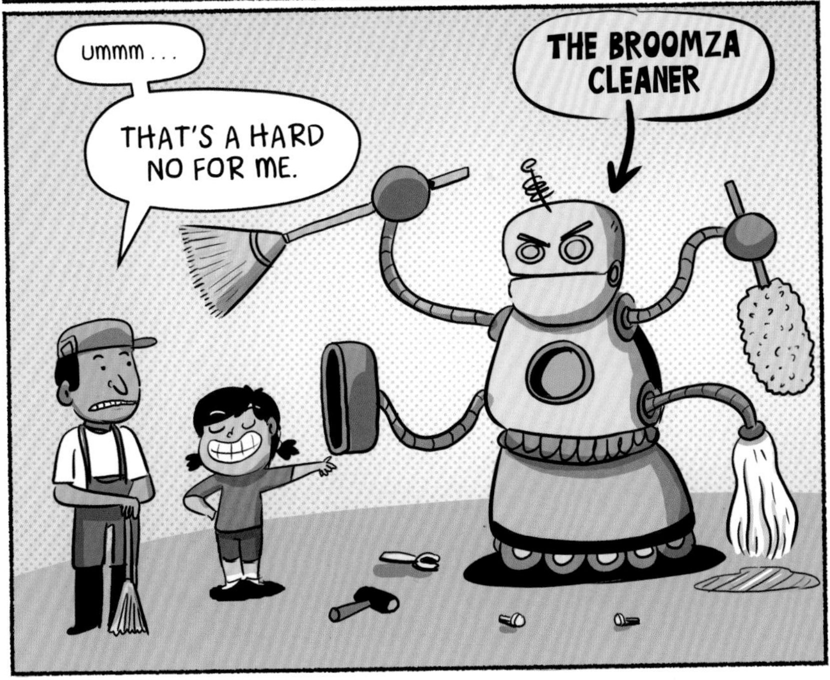
Ummm . . .
THAT'S A HARD NO FOR ME.
THE BROOMZA CLEANER

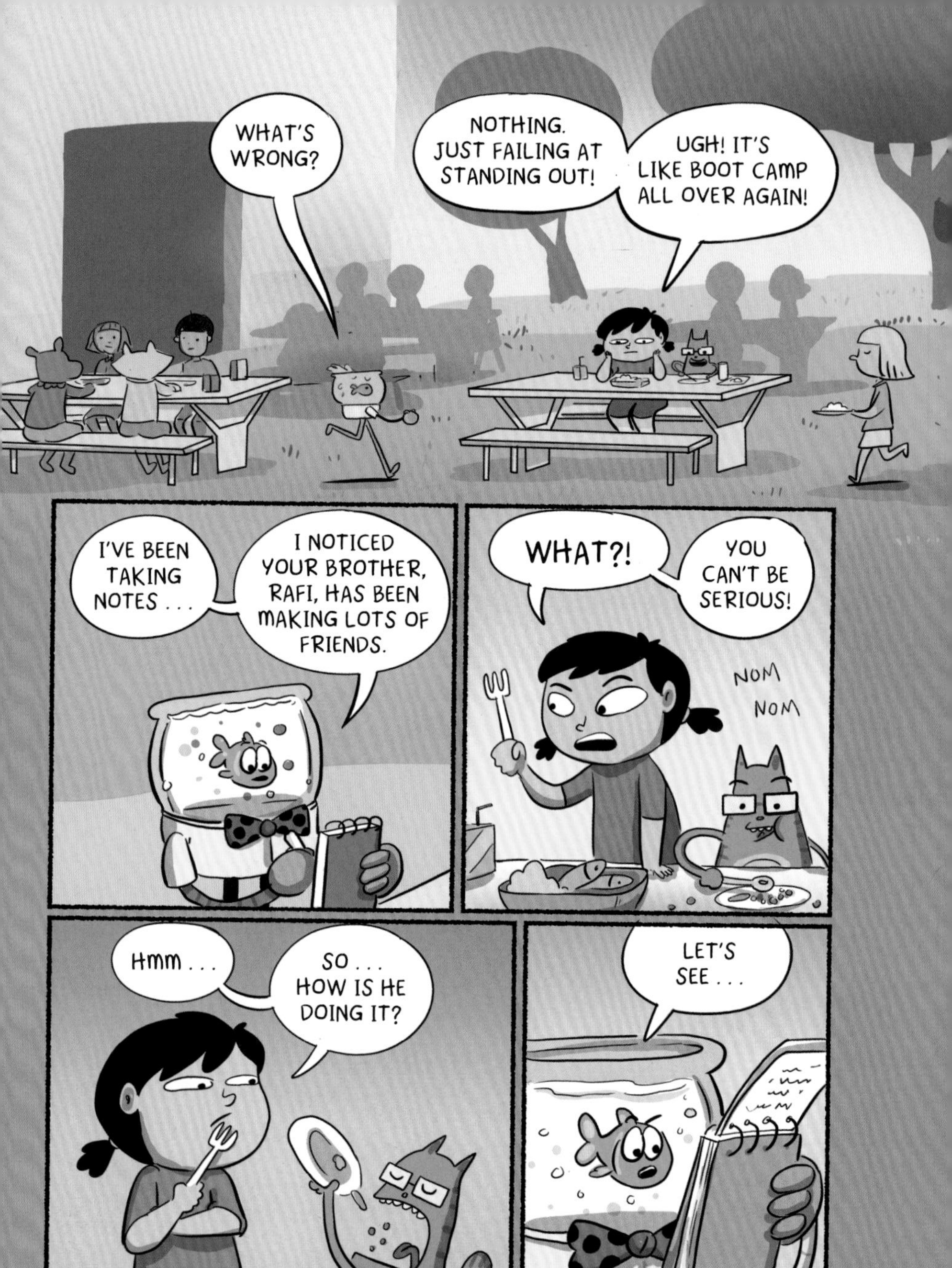
WHAT'S WRONG?
NOTHING. JUST FAILING AT STANDING OUT!
UGH! IT'S LIKE BOOT CAMP ALL OVER AGAIN!
I'VE BEEN TAKING NOTES . . .
I NOTICED YOUR BROTHER, RAFI, HAS BEEN MAKING LOTS OF FRIENDS.
WHAT?!
YOU CAN'T BE SERIOUS!
NOM
NOM
Hmm . . .
SO . . . HOW IS HE DOING IT?
LET'S SEE . . .

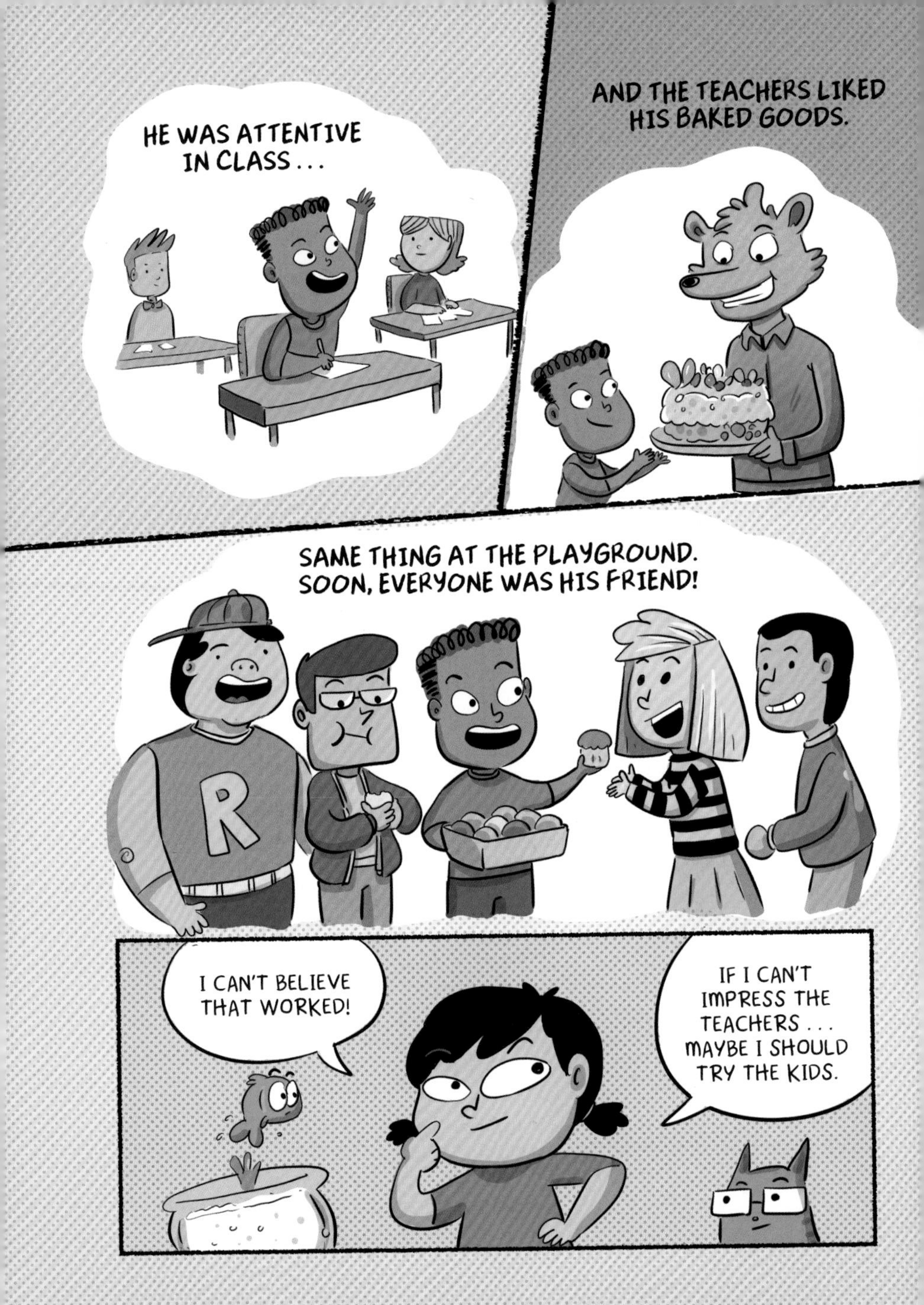
HE WAS ATTENTIVE IN CLASS . . .
AND THE TEACHERS LIKED HIS BAKED GOODS.
SAME THING AT THE PLAYGROUND. SOON, EVERYONE WAS HIS FRIEND!
R
I CAN'T BELIEVE THAT WORKED!
IF I CAN'T IMPRESS THE TEACHERS . . . MAYBE I SHOULD TRY THE KIDS.

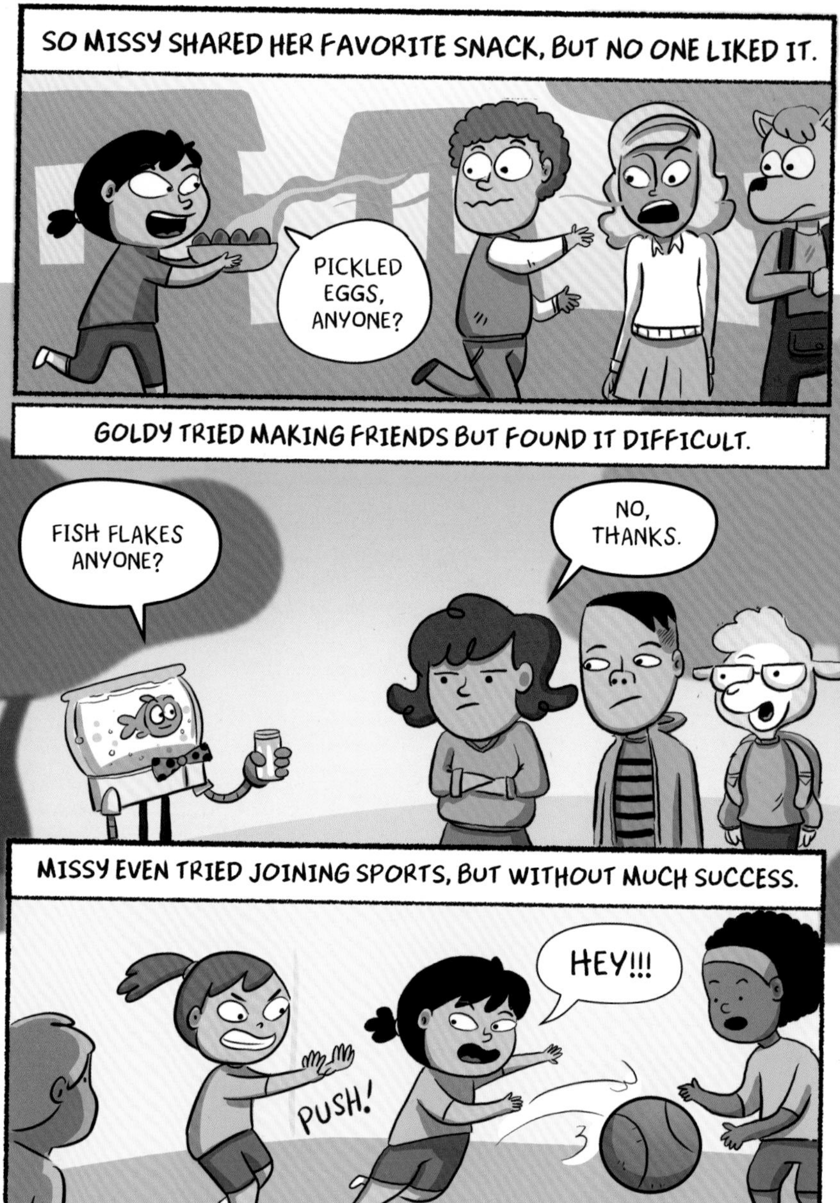
SO MISSY SHARED HER FAVORITE SNACK, BUT NO ONE LIKED IT.
PICKLED EGGS, ANYONE?
GOLDY TRIED MAKING FRIENDS BUT FOUND IT DIFFICULT.
FISH FLAKES ANYONE?
NO, THANKS.
MISSY EVEN TRIED JOINING SPORTS, BUT WITHOUT MUCH SUCCESS.
PUSH!
HEY!!!

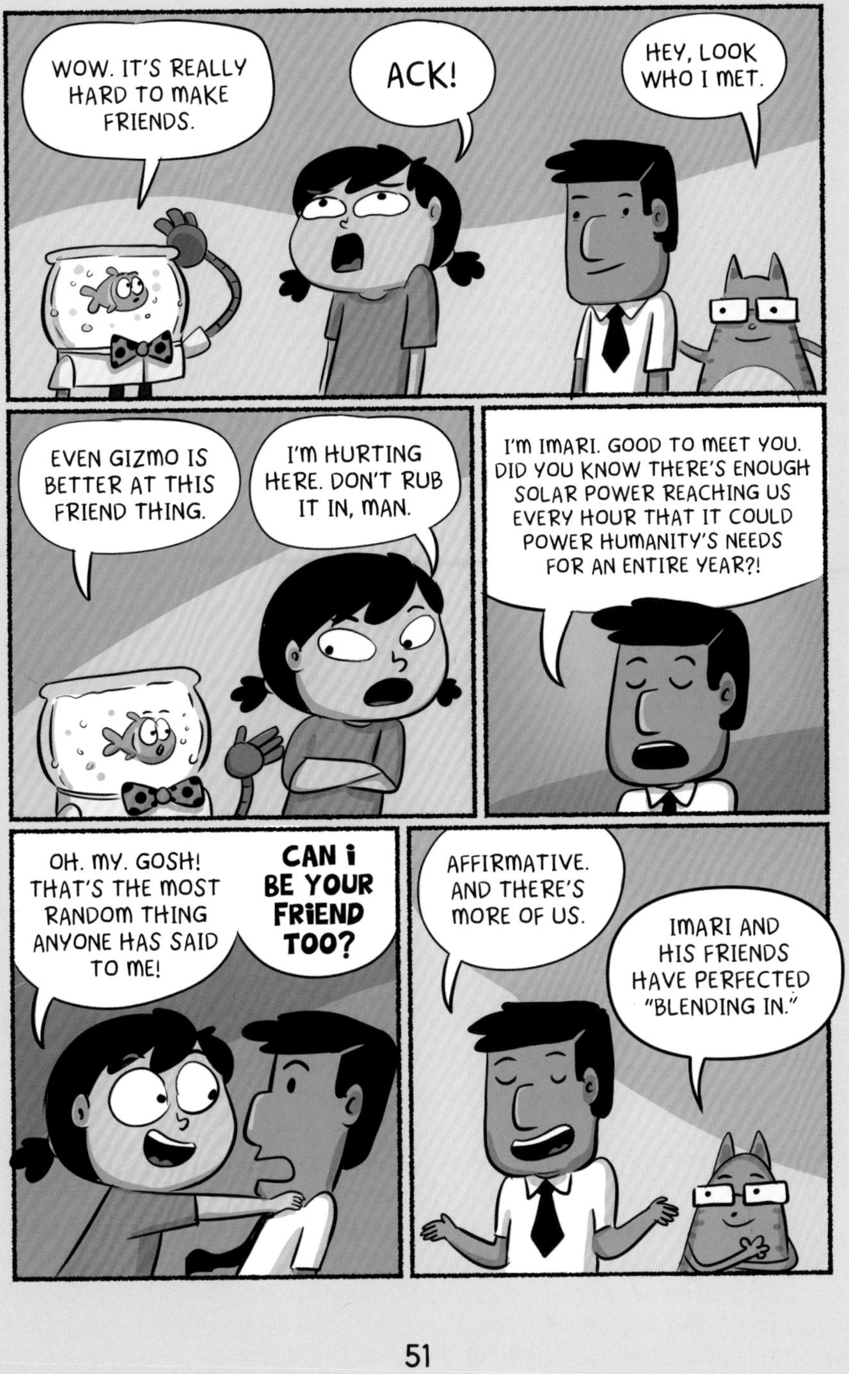
WOW. IT'S REALLY HARD TO MAKE FRIENDS.
ACK!
HEY, LOOK WHO I MET.
EVEN GIZMO IS BETTER AT THIS FRIEND THING.
I'M HURTING HERE. DON'T RUB IT IN, MAN.
I'M IMARI. GOOD TO MEET YOU. DID YOU KNOW THERE'S ENOUGH SOLAR POWER REACHING US EVERY HOUR THAT IT COULD POWER HUMANITY'S NEEDS FOR AN ENTIRE YEAR?!
OH. MY. GOSH! THAT'S THE MOST RANDOM THING ANYONE HAS SAID TO ME!
CAN I BE YOUR FRIEND TOO?
AFFIRMATIVE. AND THERE'S MORE OF US.
IMARI AND HIS FRIENDS HAVE PERFECTED "BLENDING IN."

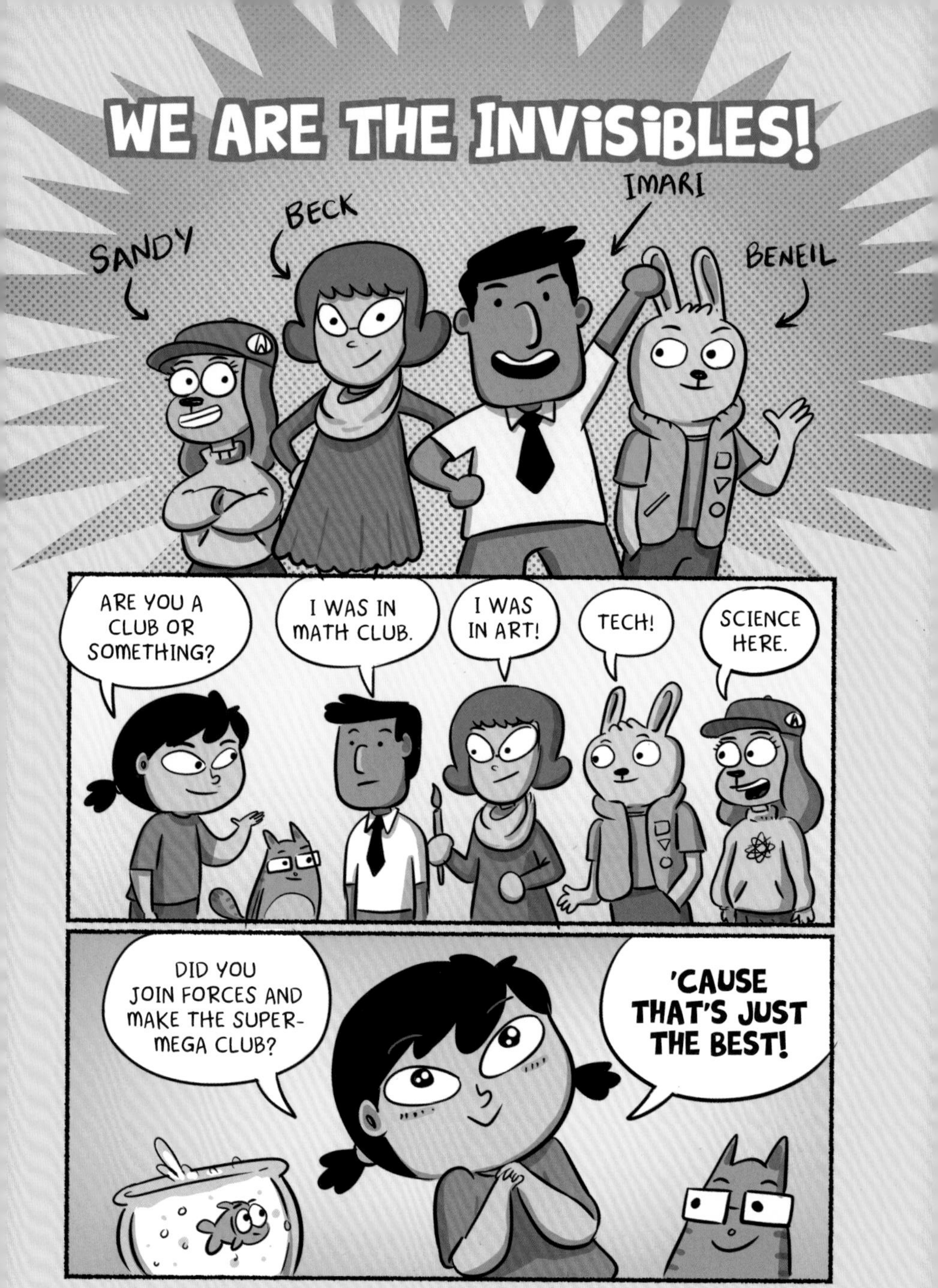

WE ARE THE INVISIBLES!
SANDY
BECK
IMARI
BENEIL
ARE YOU A CLUB OR SOMETHING?
I WAS IN MATH CLUB.
I WAS IN ART!
TECH!
SCIENCE HERE.
DID YOU JOIN FORCES AND MAKE THE SUPER-MEGA CLUB?
'CAUSE THAT'S JUST THE BEST!

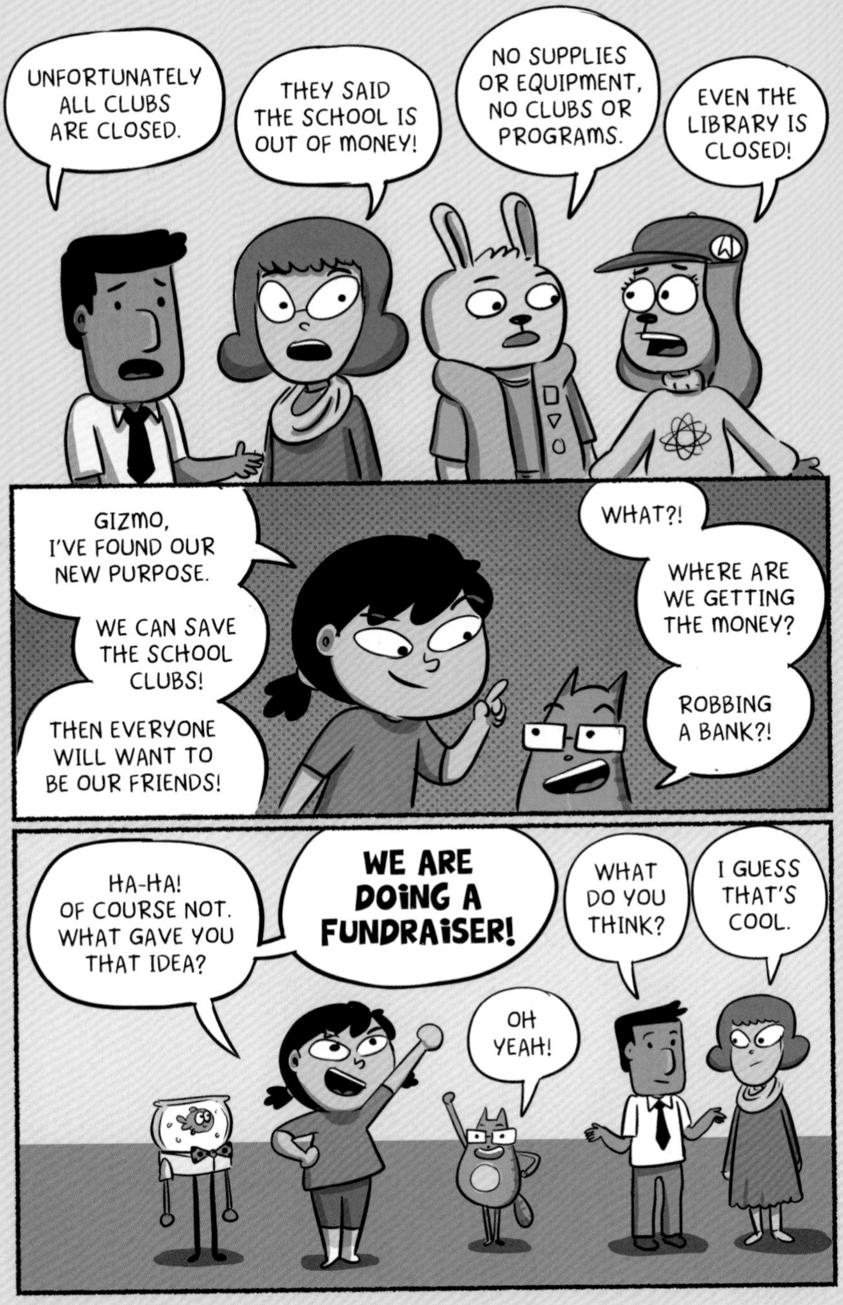
UNFORTUNATELY ALL CLUBS ARE CLOSED.
THEY SAID THE SCHOOL IS OUT OF MONEY!
NO SUPPLIES OR EQUIPMENT, NO CLUBS OR PROGRAMS.
EVEN THE LIBRARY IS CLOSED!
GIZMO, I'VE FOUND OUR NEW PURPOSE.
WE CAN SAVE THE SCHOOL CLUBS!
THEN EVERYONE WILL WANT TO BE OUR FRIENDS!
WHAT?!
WHERE ARE WE GETTING THE MONEY?
ROBBING A BANK?!
HA-HA! OF COURSE NOT. WHAT GAVE YOU THAT IDEA?
WE ARE DOING A FUNDRAISER!
OH YEAH!
WHAT DO YOU THINK?
I GUESS THAT'S COOL.

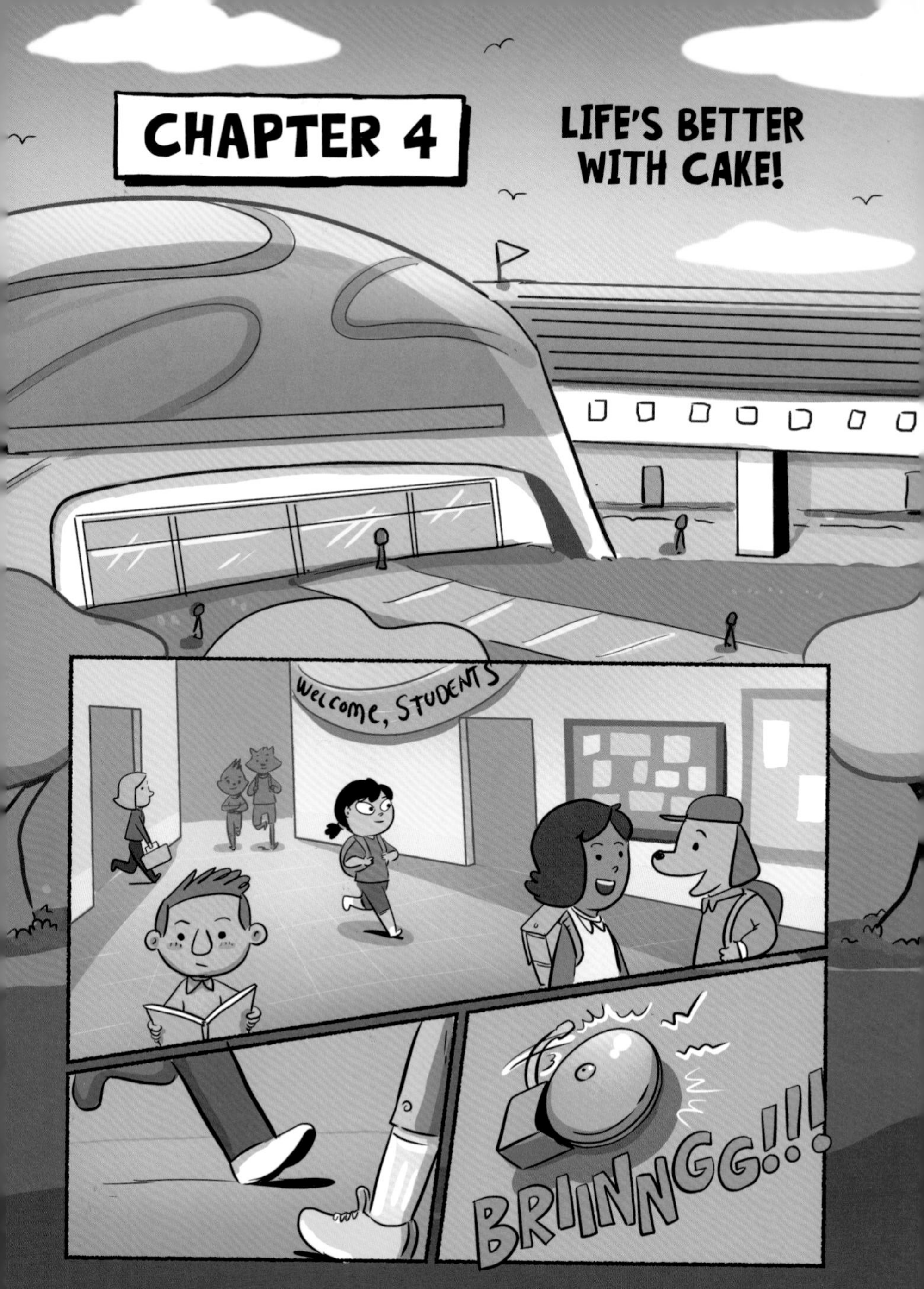
CHAPTER 4
LIFE'S BETTER WITH CAKE!
Welcome, STUDENTS
BRIINNGG!!!

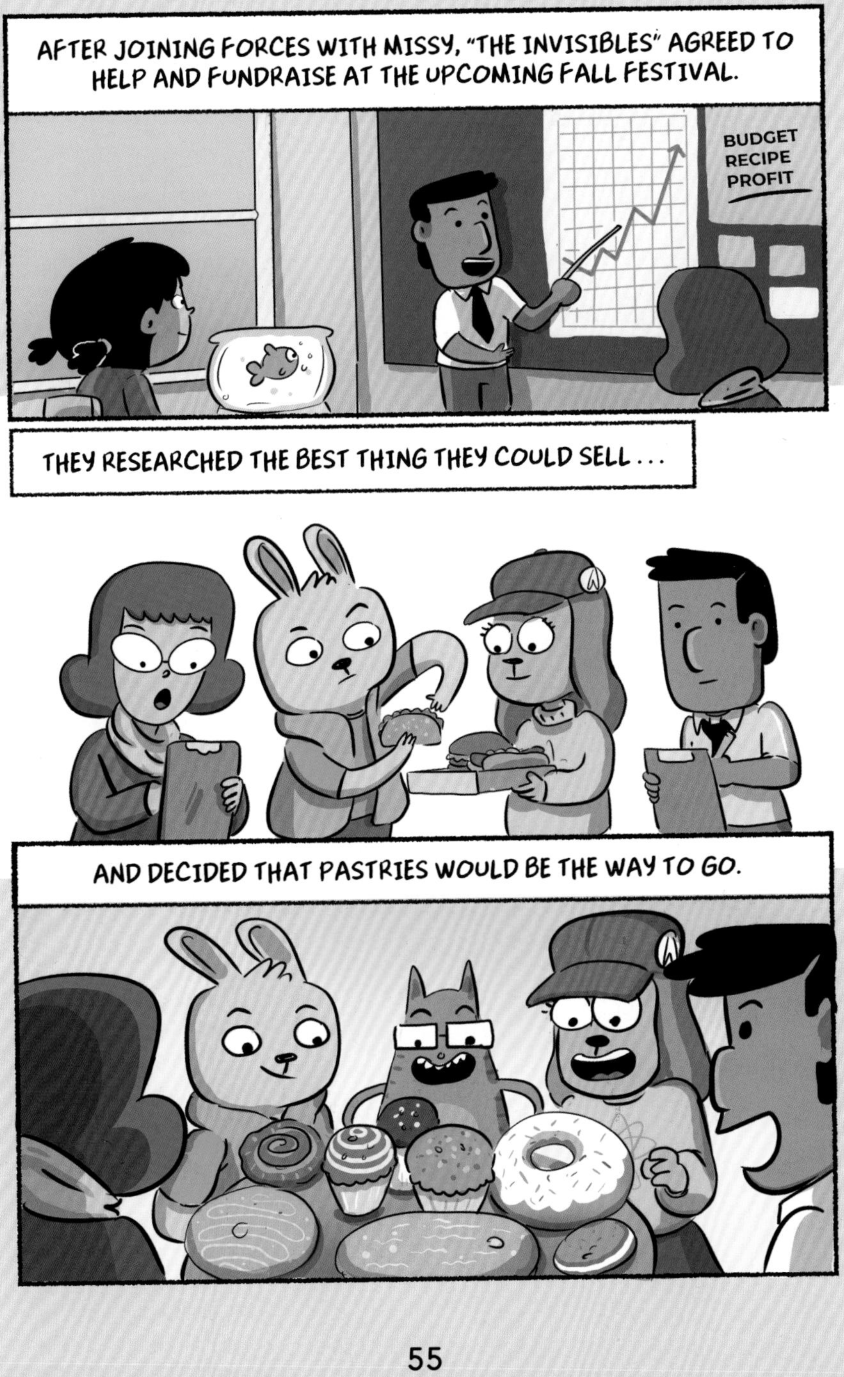
AFTER JOINING FORCES WITH MISSY, "THE INVISIBLES" AGREED TO HELP AND FUNDRAISE AT THE UPCOMING FALL FESTIVAL.
BUDGET
RECIPE
PROFIT
THEY RESEARCHED THE BEST THING THEY COULD SELL . . .
AND DECIDED THAT PASTRIES WOULD BE THE WAY TO GO.

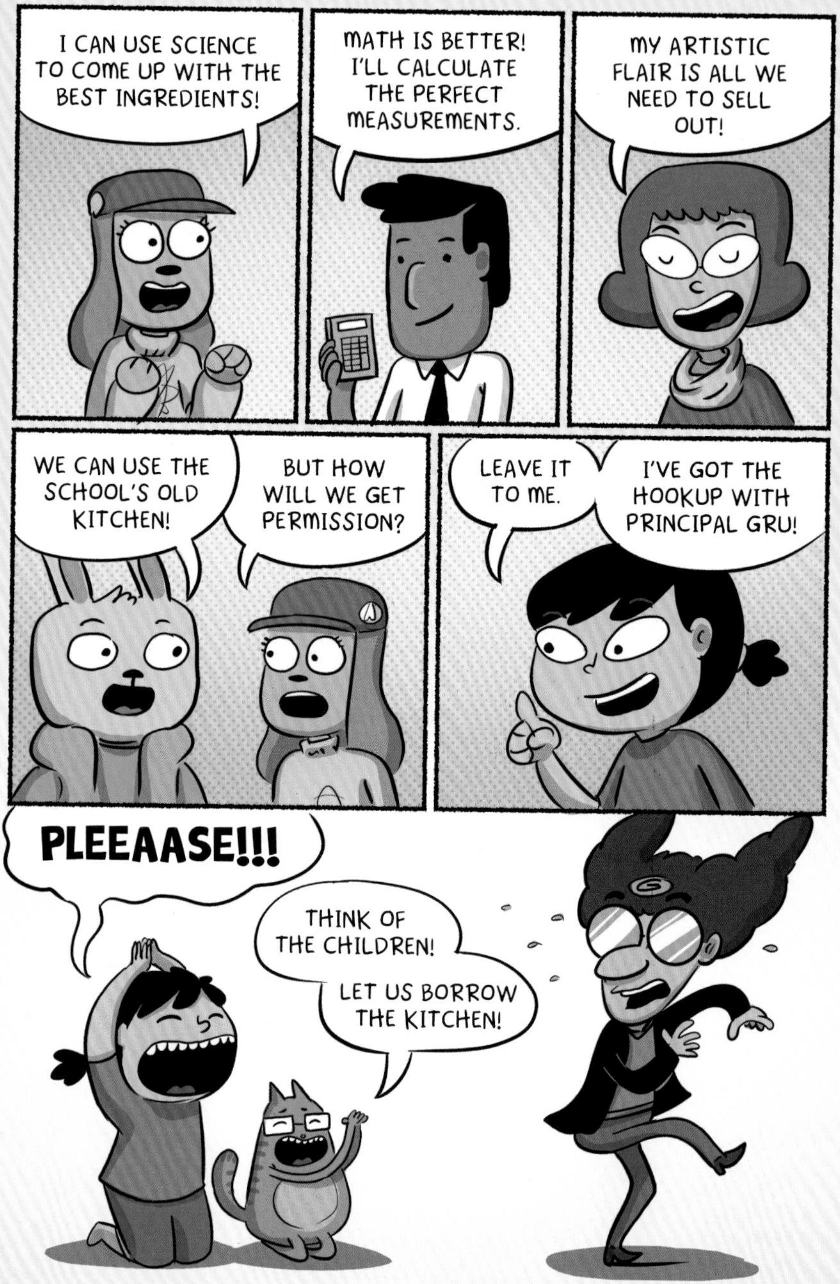
I CAN USE SCIENCE TO COME UP WITH THE BEST INGREDIENTS!
MATH IS BETTER! I'LL CALCULATE THE PERFECT MEASUREMENTS.
MY ARTISTIC FLAIR IS ALL WE NEED TO SELL OUT!
WE CAN USE THE SCHOOL'S OLD KITCHEN!
BUT HOW WILL WE GET PERMISSION?
LEAVE IT TO ME.
I'VE GOT THE HOOKUP WITH PRINCIPAL GRU!
PLEEAASE!!!
THINK OF THE CHILDREN!
LET US BORROW THE KITCHEN!

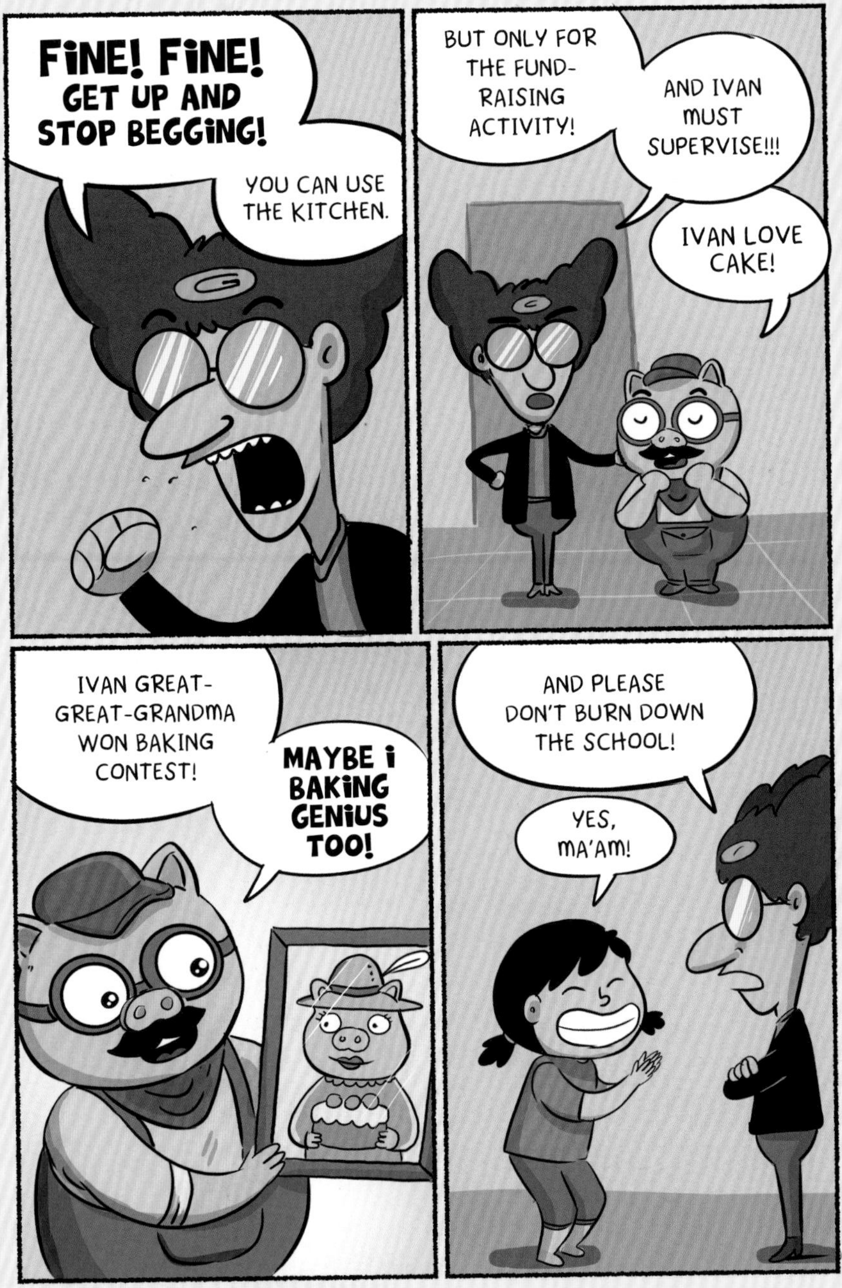
FINE! FINE!
GET UP AND STOP BEGGING!
YOU CAN USE THE KITCHEN.
BUT ONLY FOR THE FUND-RAISING ACTIVITY!
AND IVAN MUST SUPERVISE!!!
IVAN LOVE CAKE!
IVAN GREAT-GREAT-GRANDMA WON BAKING CONTEST!
MAYBE I BAKING GENIUS TOO!
AND PLEASE DON'T BURN DOWN THE SCHOOL!
YES, MA'AM!

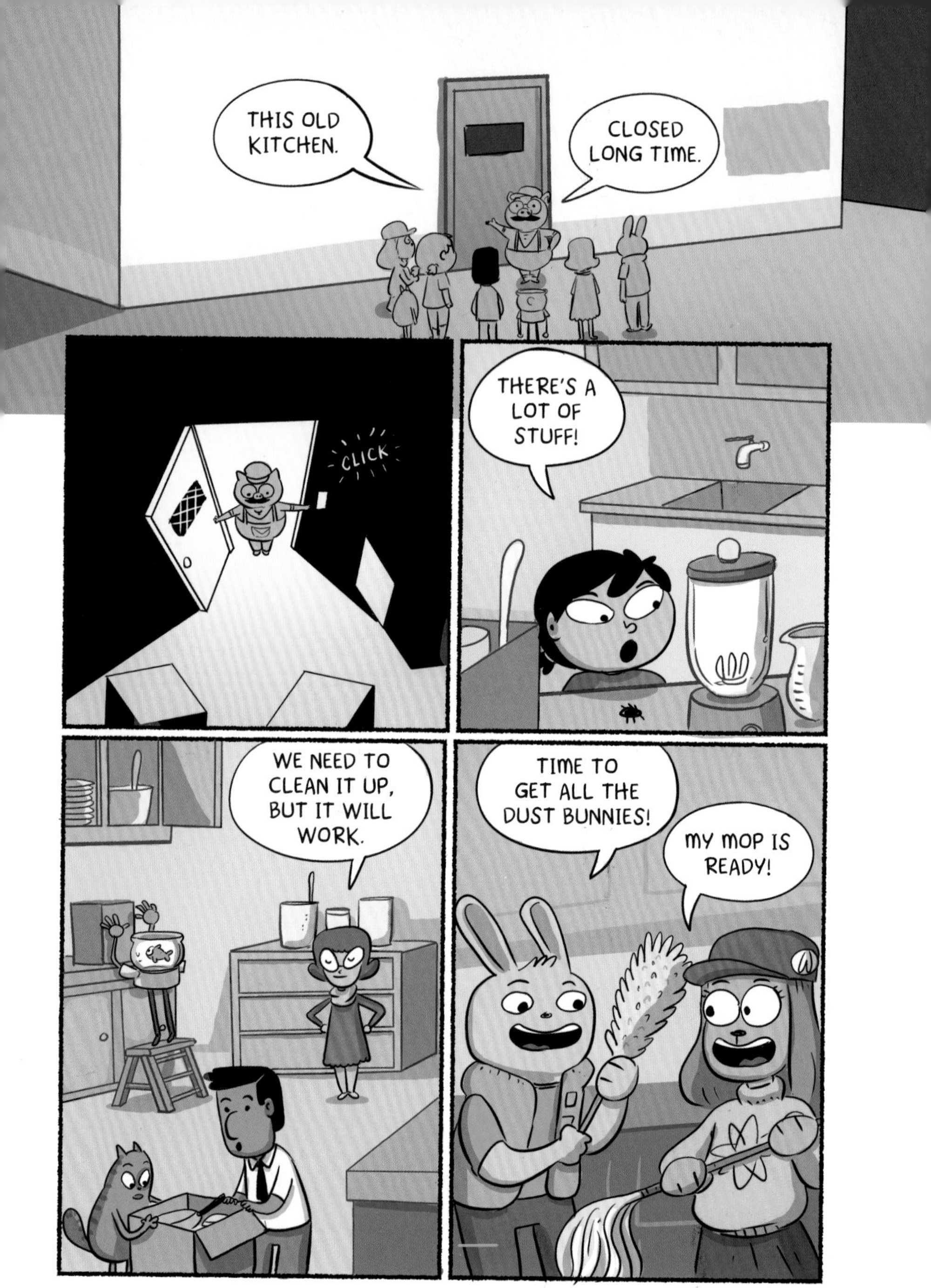
THIS OLD KITCHEN.
CLOSED LONG TIME.
CLICK
THERE'S A LOT OF STUFF!
WE NEED TO CLEAN IT UP, BUT IT WILL WORK.
TIME TO GET ALL THE DUST BUNNIES!
MY MOP IS READY!

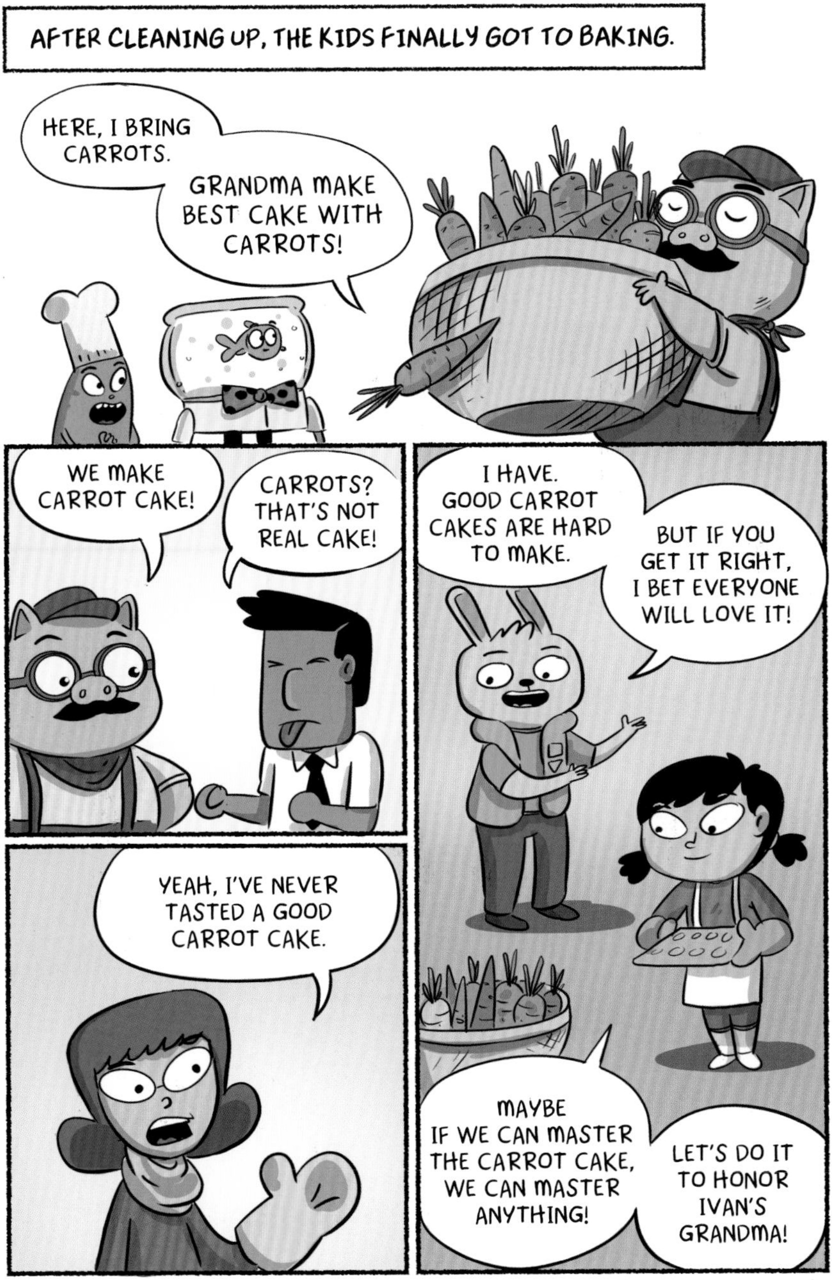
AFTER CLEANING UP, THE KIDS FINALLY GOT TO BAKING.
HERE, I BRING CARROTS.
GRANDMA MAKE BEST CAKE WITH CARROTS!
WE MAKE CARROT CAKE!
CARROTS? THAT'S NOT REAL CAKE!
YEAH, I'VE NEVER TASTED A GOOD CARROT CAKE.
I HAVE. GOOD CARROT CAKES ARE HARD TO MAKE.
BUT IF YOU GET IT RIGHT, I BET EVERYONE WILL LOVE IT!
MAYBE IF WE CAN MASTER THE CARROT CAKE, WE CAN MASTER ANYTHING!
LET'S DO IT TO HONOR IVAN'S GRANDMA!

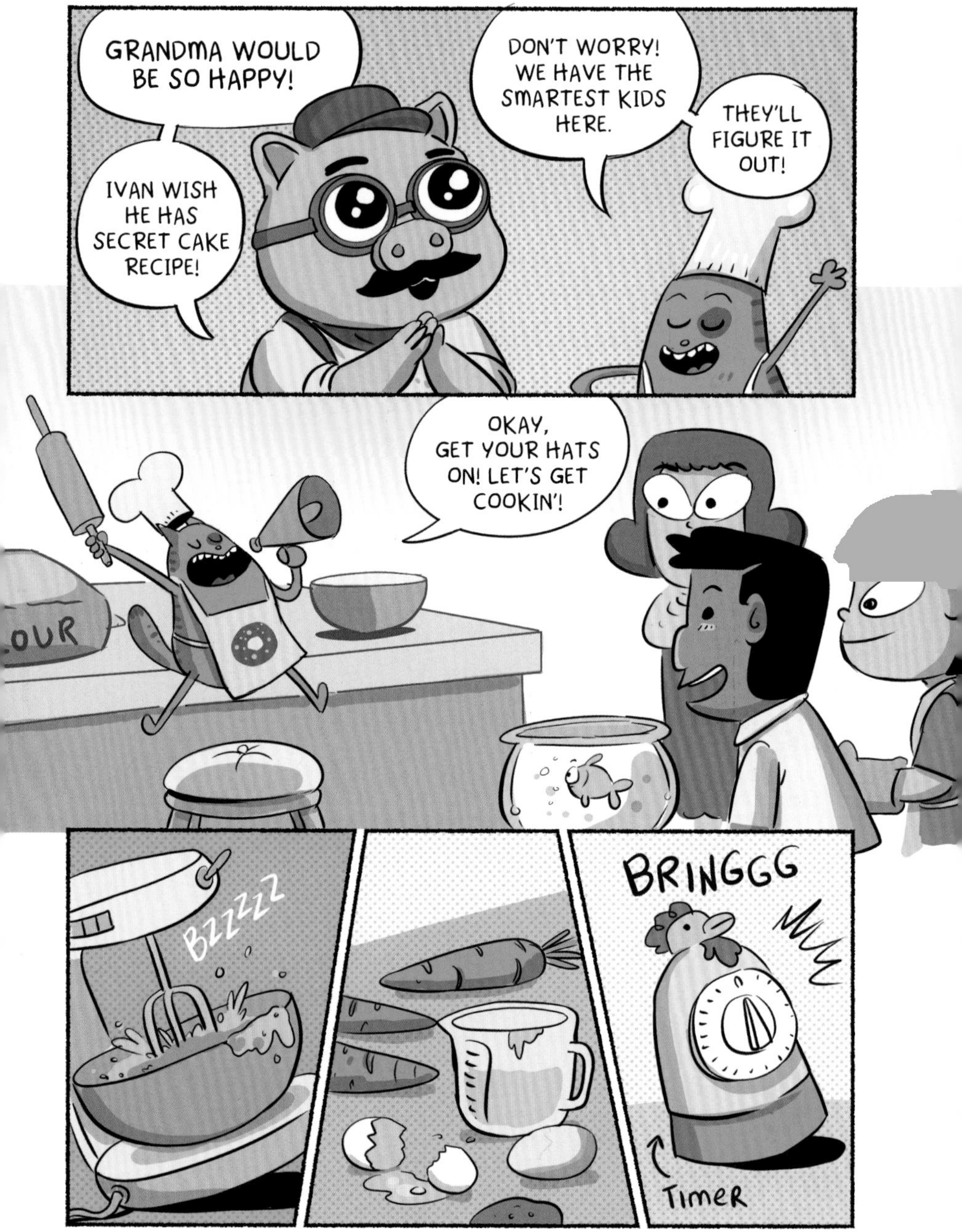
GRANDMA WOULD BE SO HAPPY!
IVAN WISH HE HAS SECRET CAKE RECIPE!
DON'T WORRY! WE HAVE THE SMARTEST KIDS HERE.
THEY'LL FIGURE IT OUT!
OKAY, GET YOUR HATS ON! LET'S GET COOKIN'!
OUR
BZZZZZ
BRINGGG
Timer

LET'S MAKE CARROT CAKE!

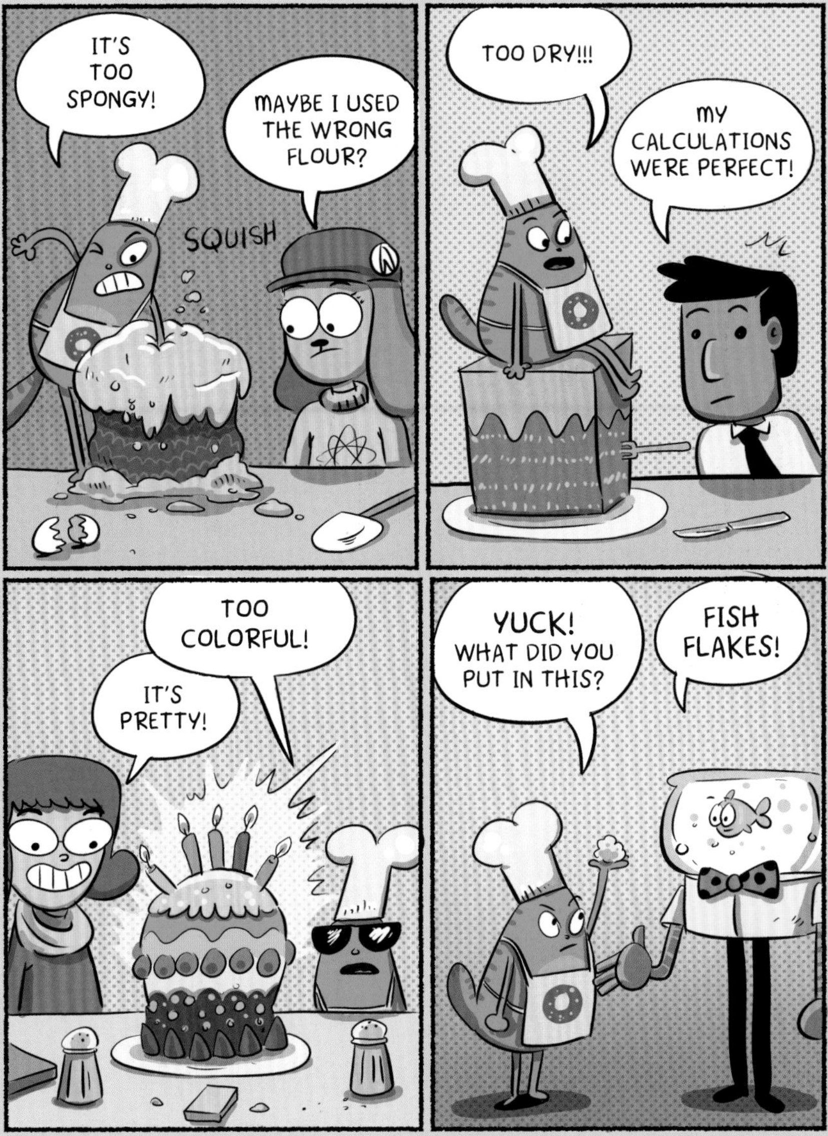
IT'S TOO SPONGY!
MAYBE I USED THE WRONG FLOUR?
SQUISH
TOO DRY!!!
MY CALCULATIONS WERE PERFECT!
TOO COLORFUL!
IT'S PRETTY!
YUCK! WHAT DID YOU PUT IN THIS?
FISH FLAKES!

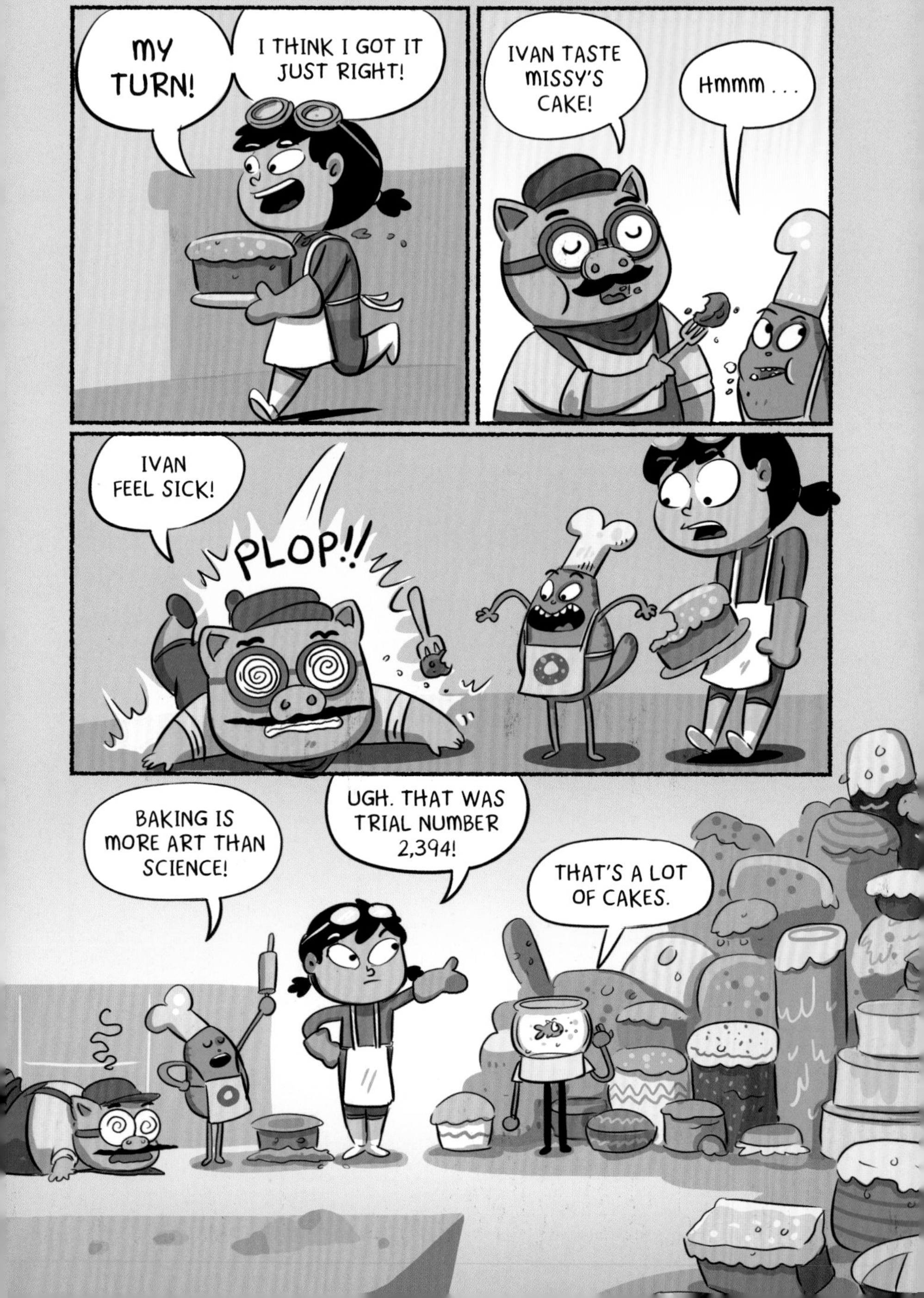

MY TURN!
I THINK I GOT IT JUST RIGHT!
IVAN TASTE MISSY'S CAKE!
Hmmm . . .
IVAN FEEL SICK!
PLOP!!
BAKING IS MORE ART THAN SCIENCE!
UGH. THAT WAS TRIAL NUMBER 2,394!
THAT'S A LOT OF CAKES.

THERE WERE SO MANY BAD BATCHES OF CARROT CAKE, THE KIDS STORED THEM IN THE MEGA-SIZED FRIDGE.

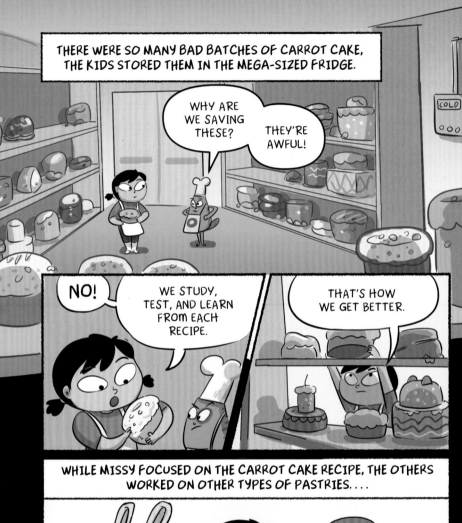

WHY ARE WE SAVING THESE?

THEY'RE AWFUL!

NO!

WE STUDY, TEST, AND LEARN FROM EACH RECIPE.

THAT'S HOW WE GET BETTER.

WHILE MISSY FOCUSED ON THE CARROT CAKE RECIPE, THE OTHERS WORKED ON OTHER TYPES OF PASTRIES. . . .

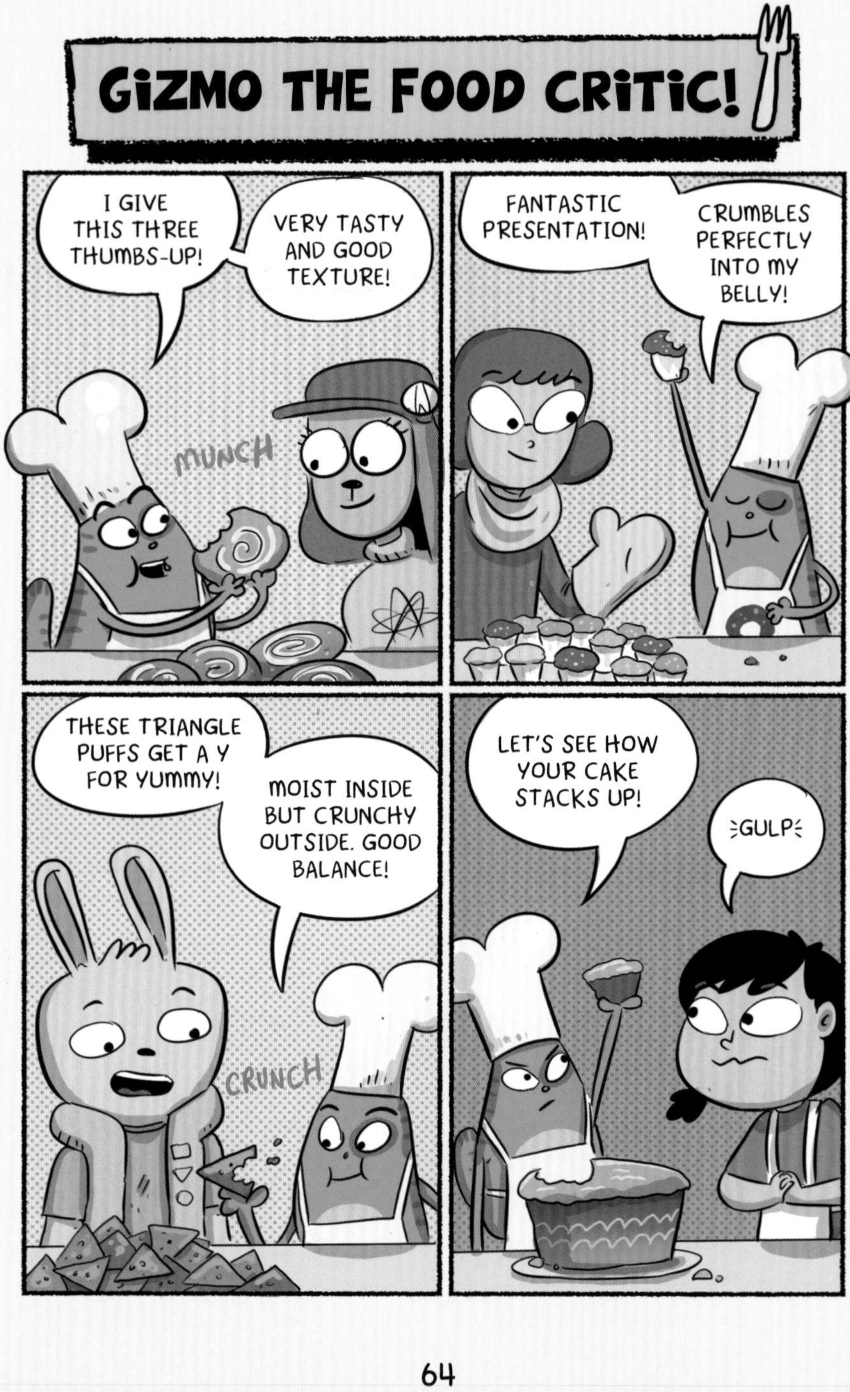
GIZMO THE FOOD CRITIC!
I GIVE THIS THREE THUMBS-UP!
MUNCH
VERY TASTY AND GOOD TEXTURE!
FANTASTIC PRESENTATION!
CRUMBLES PERFECTLY INTO MY BELLY!
THESE TRIANGLE PUFFS GET A Y FOR YUMMY!
MOIST INSIDE BUT CRUNCHY OUTSIDE. GOOD BALANCE!
CRUNCH
LET'S SEE HOW YOUR CAKE STACKS UP!
GULP

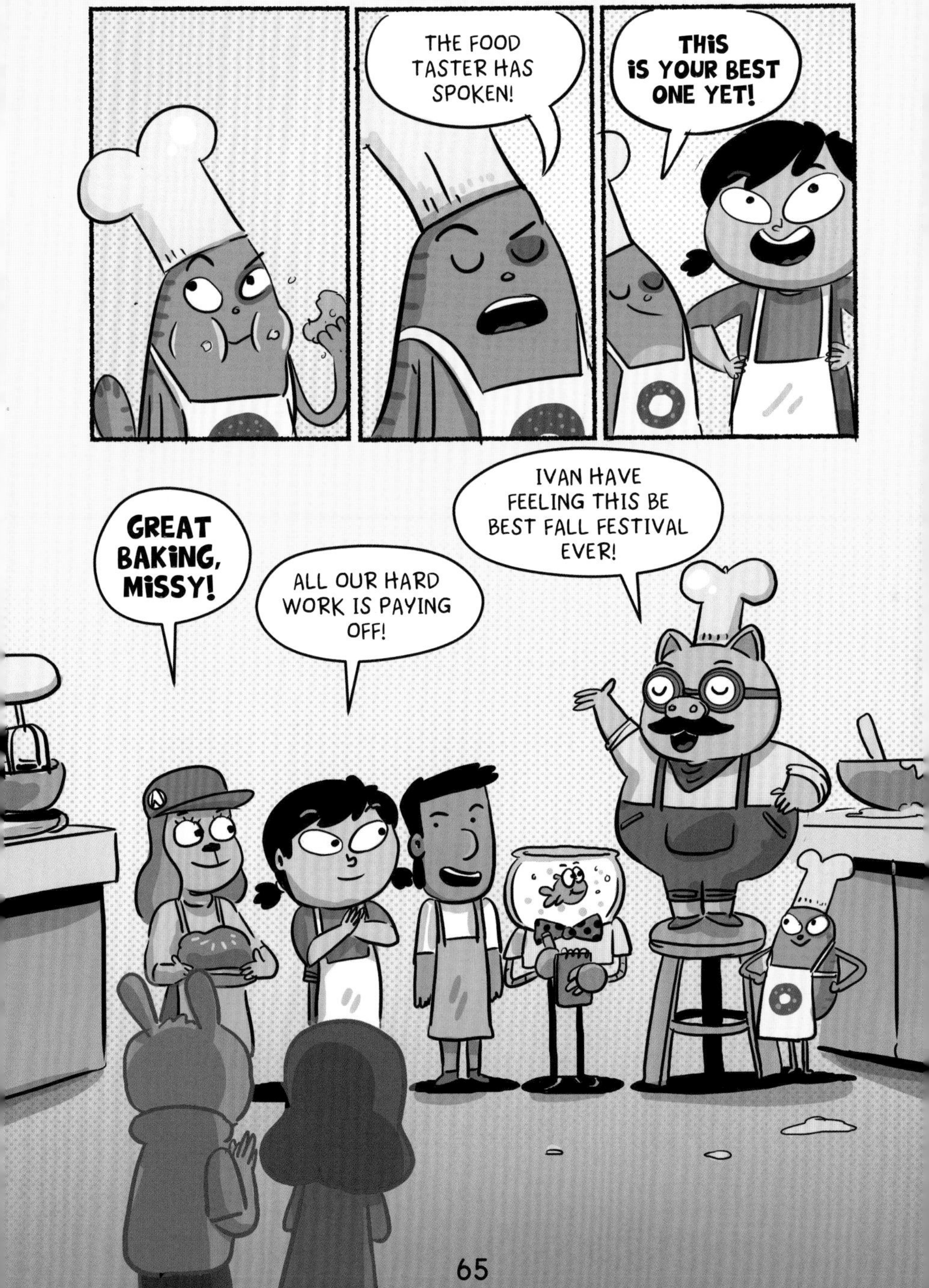
THE FOOD TASTER HAS SPOKEN!
THIS IS YOUR BEST ONE YET!
GREAT BAKING, MISSY!
ALL OUR HARD WORK IS PAYING OFF!
IVAN HAVE FEELING THIS BE BEST FALL FESTIVAL EVER!

CHAPTER 5 SCHOOL TIME FOR VILLAINS

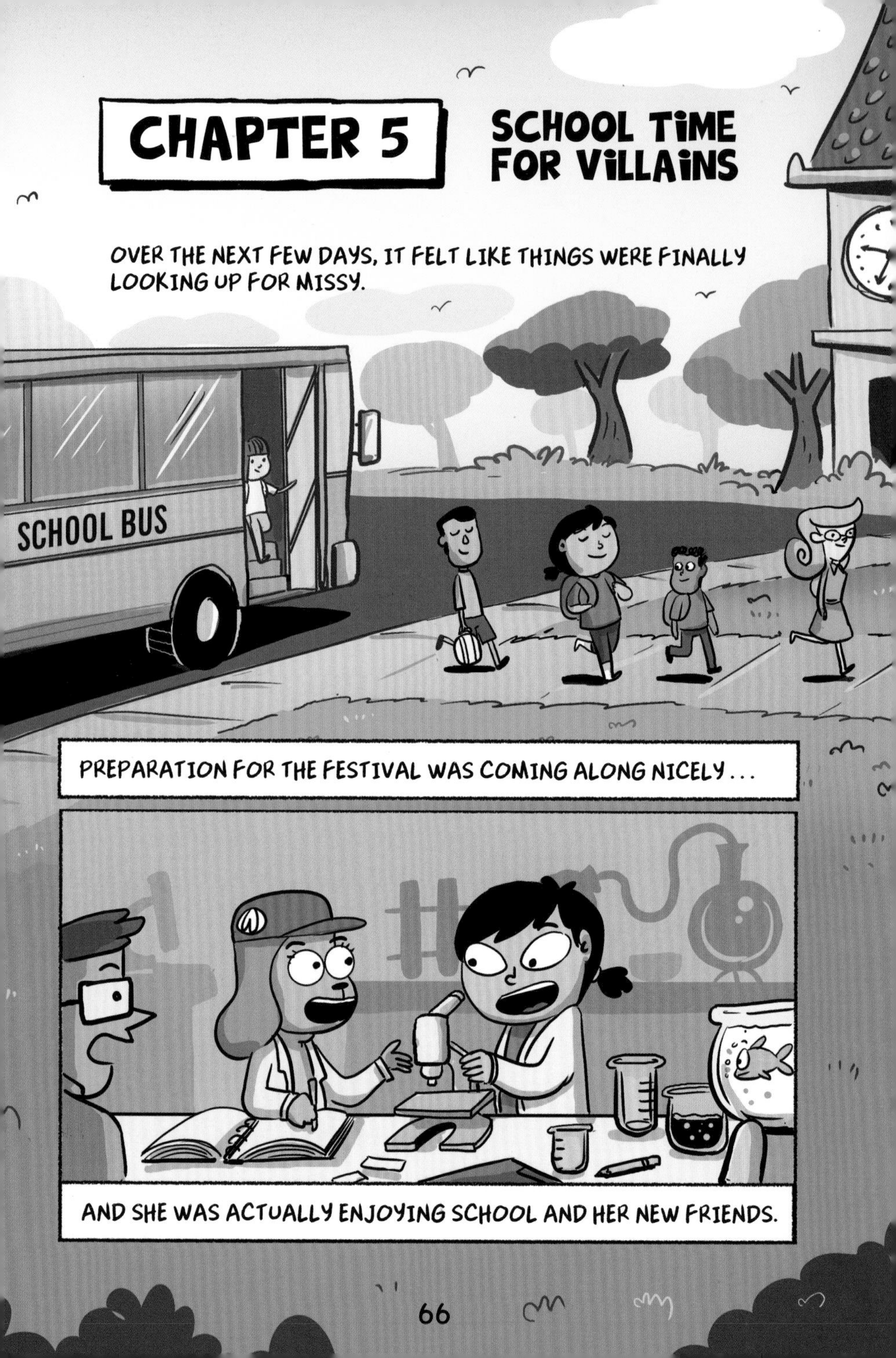
OVER THE NEXT FEW DAYS, IT FELT LIKE THINGS WERE FINALLY LOOKING UP FOR MISSY.
SCHOOL BUS
PREPARATION FOR THE FESTIVAL WAS COMING ALONG NICELY . . .
AND SHE WAS ACTUALLY ENJOYING SCHOOL AND HER NEW FRIENDS.

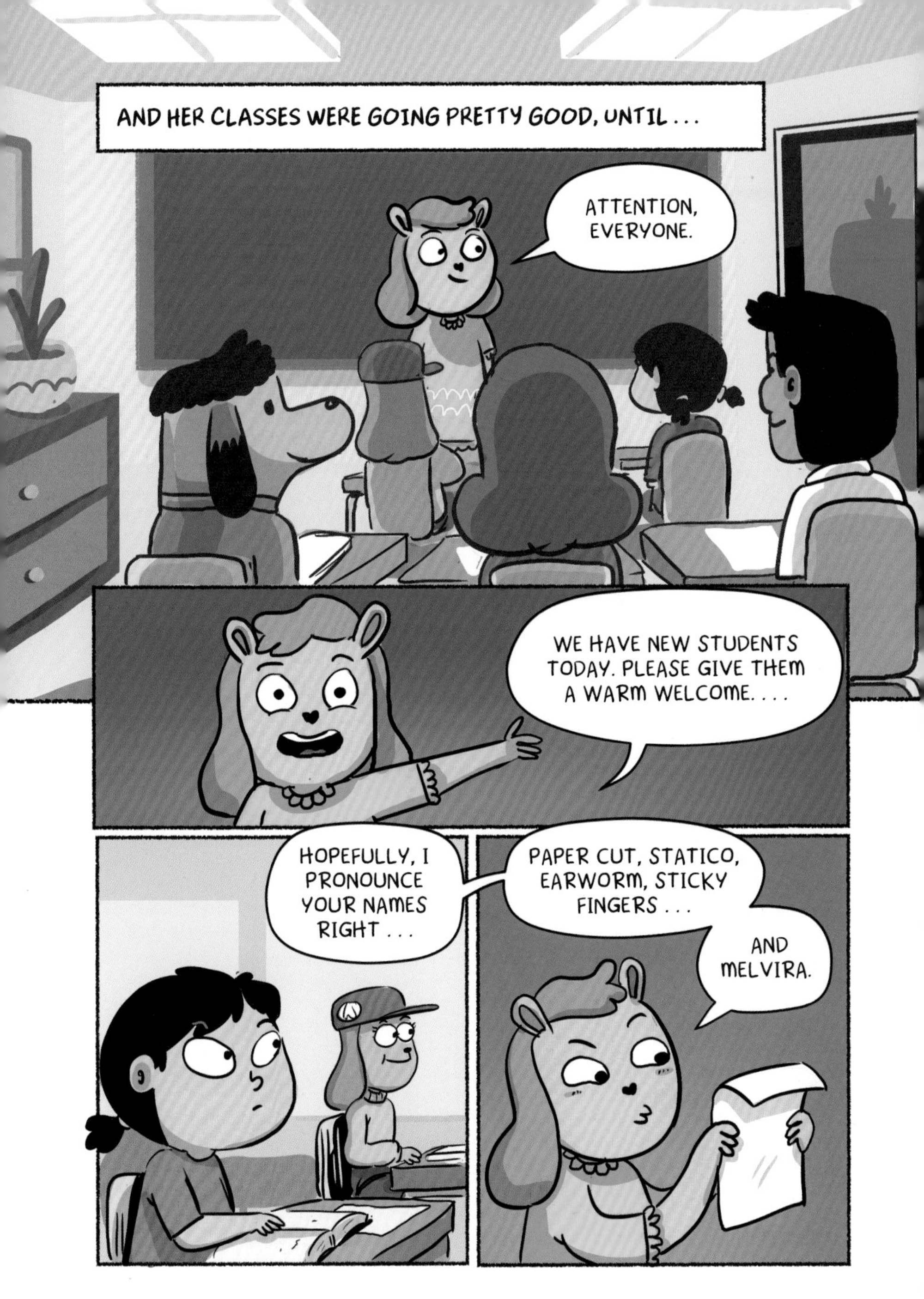
AND HER CLASSES WERE GOING PRETTY GOOD, UNTIL . . .
ATTENTION, EVERYONE.
WE HAVE NEW STUDENTS TODAY. PLEASE GIVE THEM A WARM WELCOME. . . .
HOPEFULLY, I PRONOUNCE YOUR NAMES RIGHT . . .
PAPER CUT, STATICO, EARWORM, STICKY FINGERS . . .
AND MELVIRA.

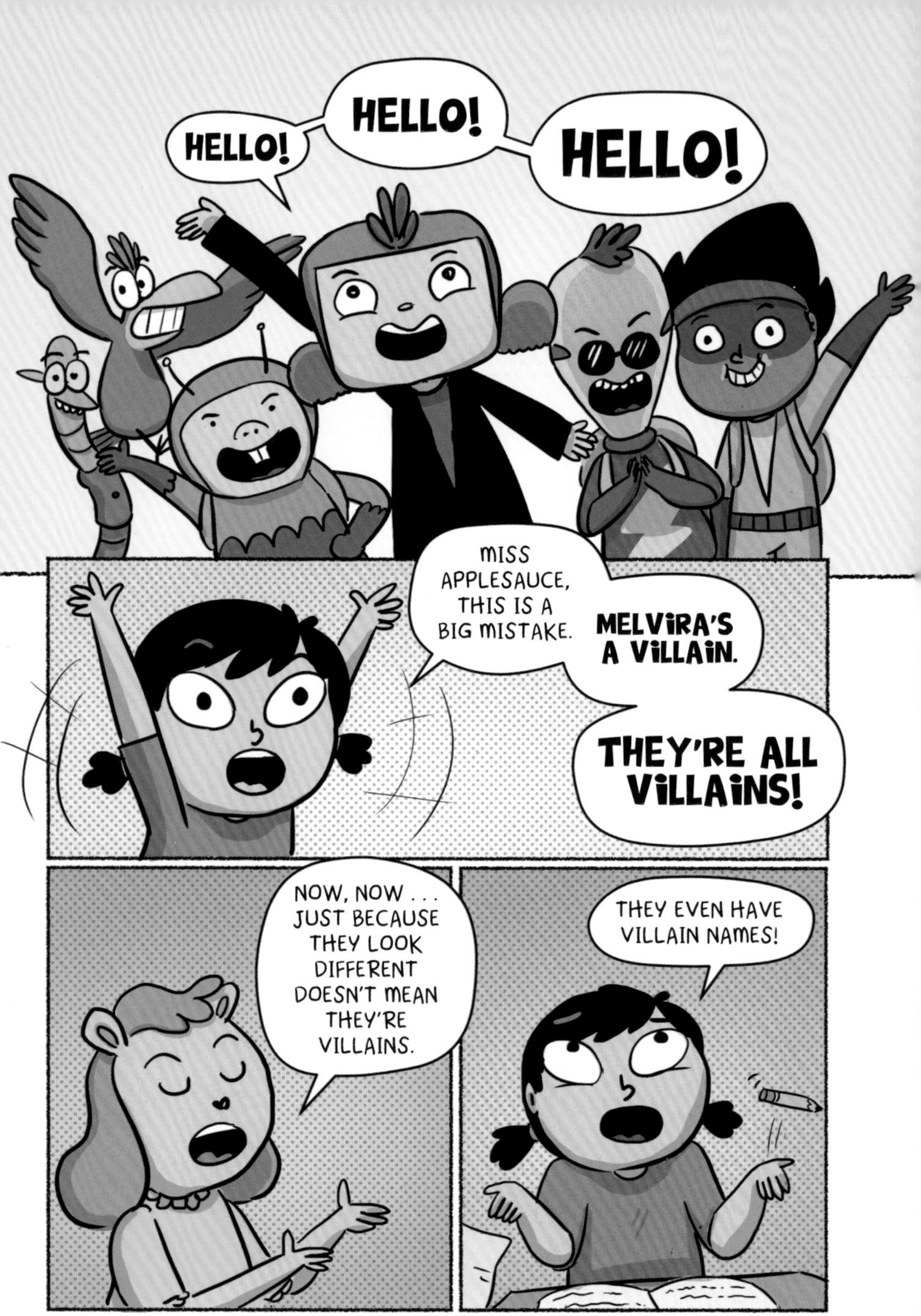
HELLO!
HELLO!
HELLO!
MISS APPLESAUCE, THIS IS A BIG MISTAKE.
MELVIRA'S A VILLAIN.
THEY'RE ALL VILLAINS!
NOW, NOW . . . JUST BECAUSE THEY LOOK DIFFERENT DOESN'T MEAN THEY'RE VILLAINS.
THEY EVEN HAVE VILLAIN NAMES!

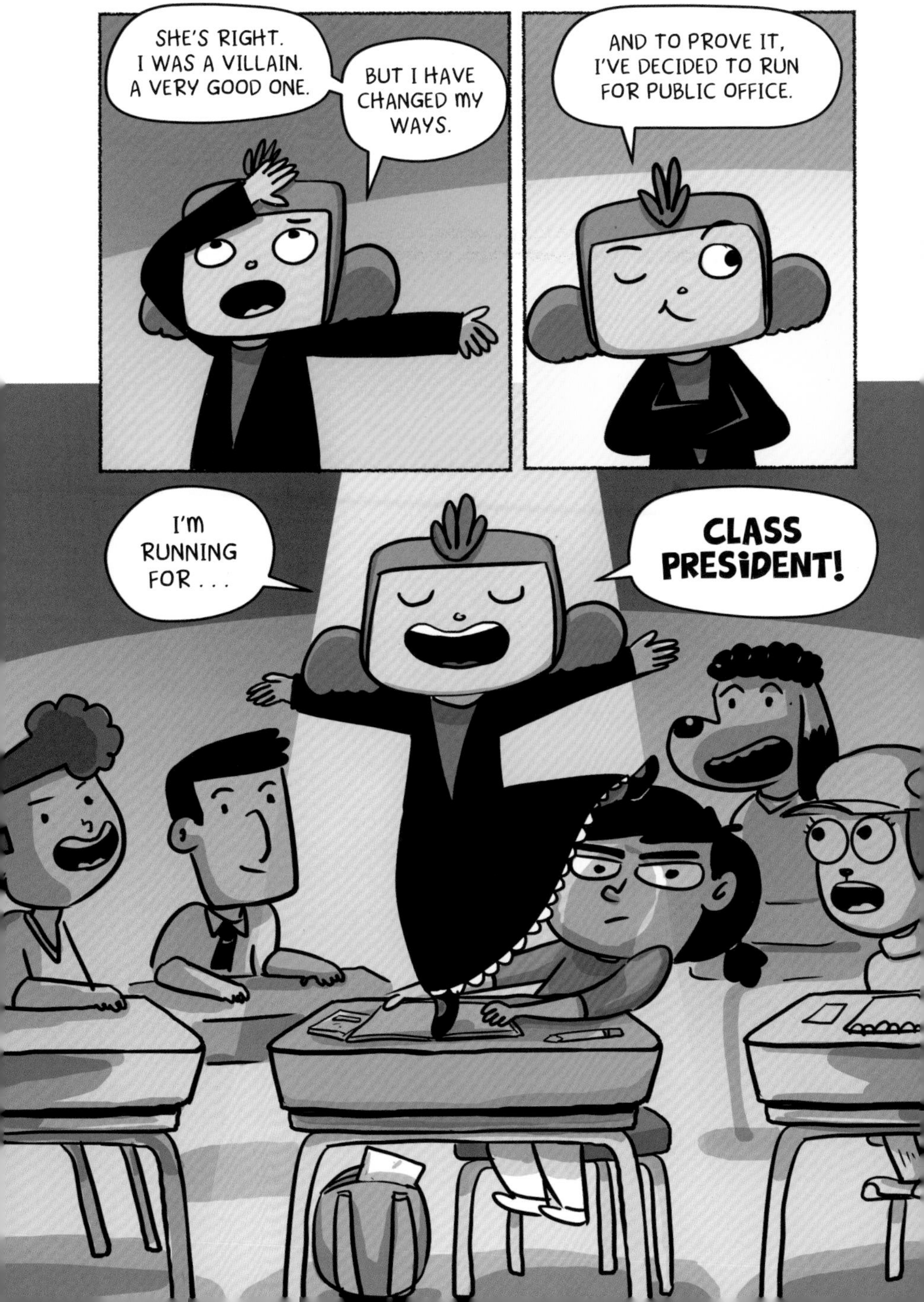
SHE'S RIGHT. I WAS A VILLAIN. A VERY GOOD ONE.
BUT I HAVE CHANGED MY WAYS.
AND TO PROVE IT, I'VE DECIDED TO RUN FOR PUBLIC OFFICE.
I'M RUNNING FOR . . .
CLASS PRESIDENT!

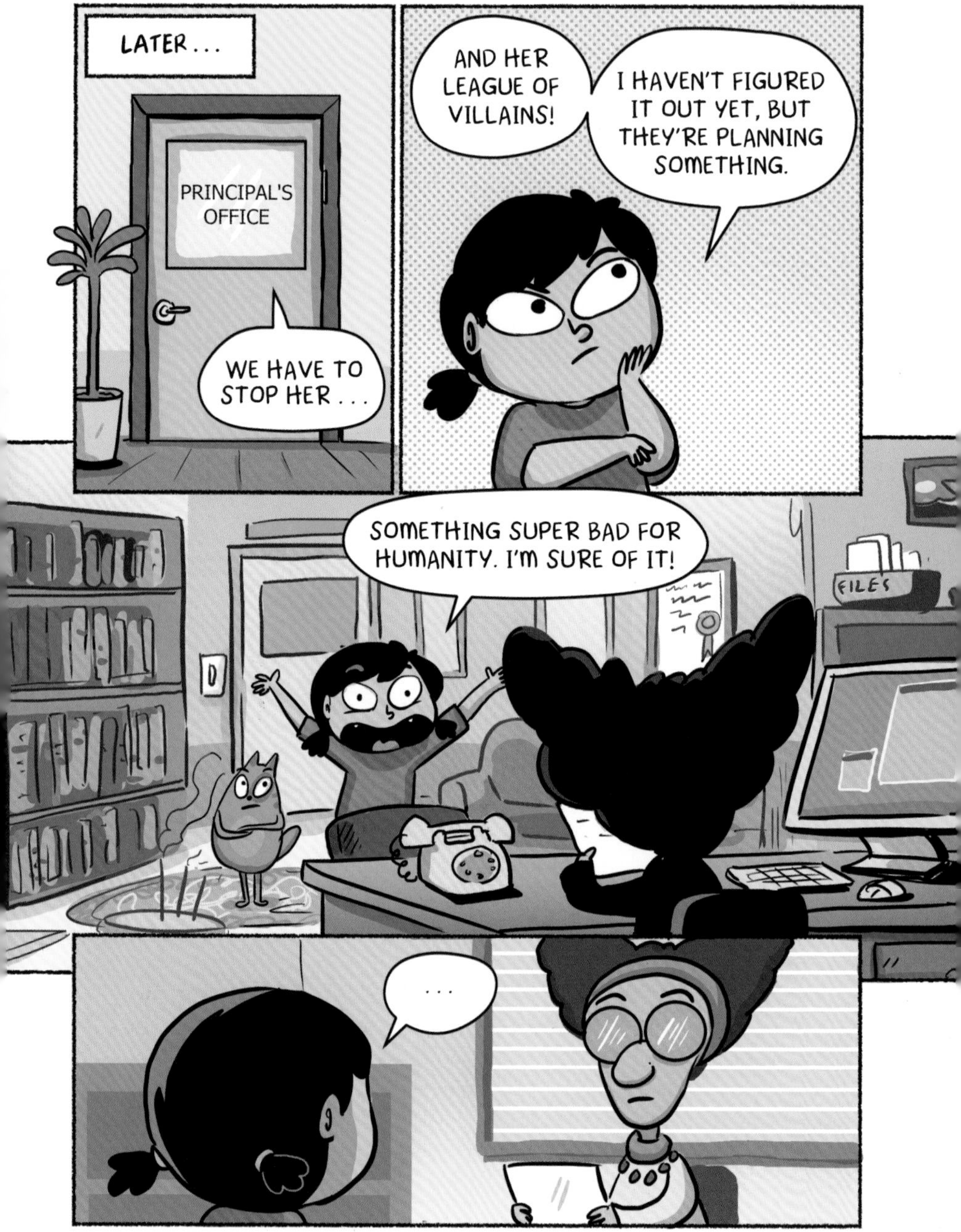
LATER . . .
PRINCIPAL'S OFFICE
WE HAVE TO STOP HER . . .
AND HER LEAGUE OF VILLAINS!
I HAVEN'T FIGURED IT OUT YET, BUT THEY'RE PLANNING SOMETHING.
SOMETHING SUPER BAD FOR HUMANITY. I'M SURE OF IT!
FILES
. . .

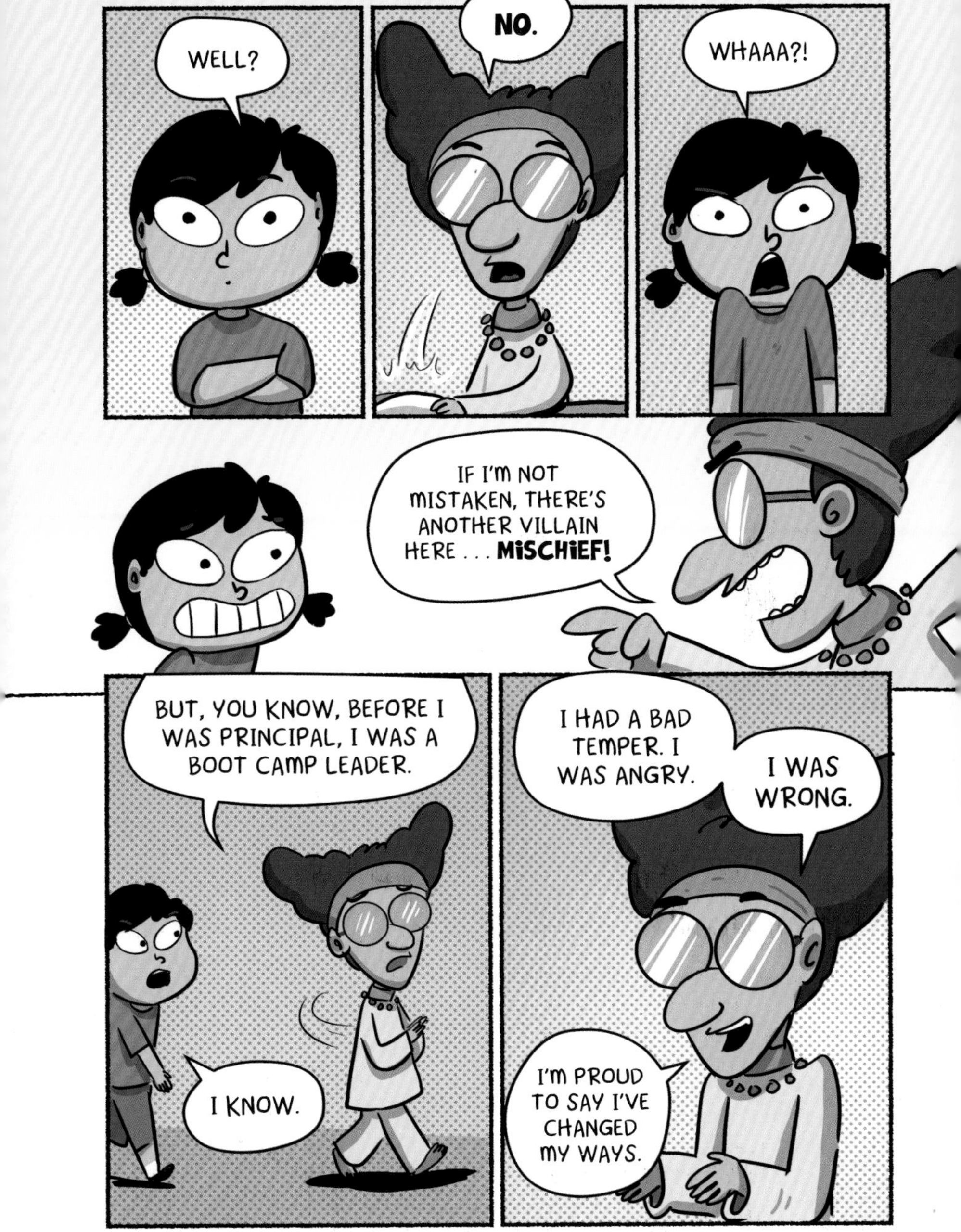
WELL?
NO.
WHAAA?!
IF I'M NOT MISTAKEN, THERE'S ANOTHER VILLAIN HERE . . . MISCHIEF!
BUT, YOU KNOW, BEFORE I WAS PRINCIPAL, I WAS A BOOT CAMP LEADER.
I KNOW.
I HAD A BAD TEMPER. I WAS ANGRY.
I WAS WRONG.
I'M PROUD TO SAY I'VE CHANGED MY WAYS.

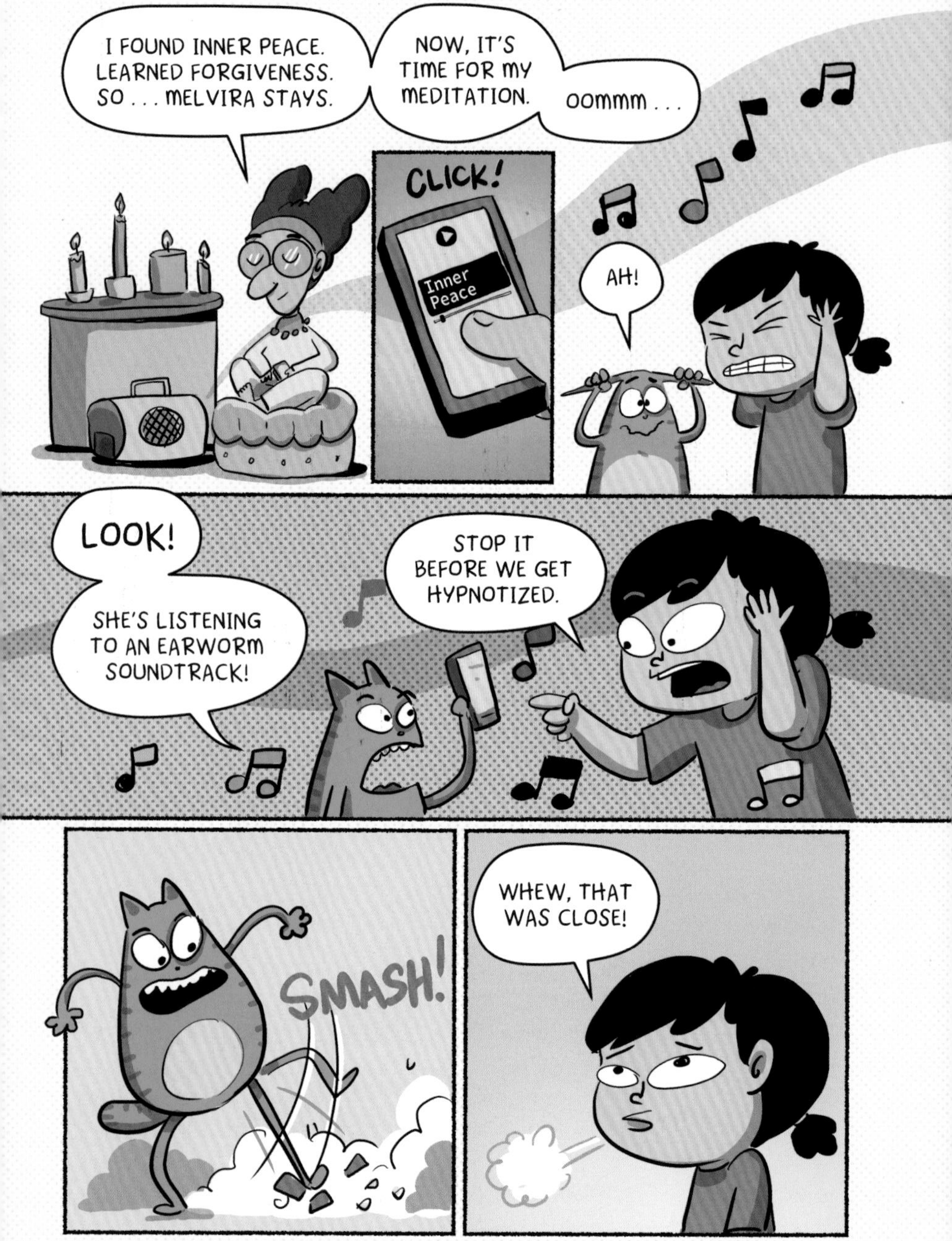
I FOUND INNER PEACE. LEARNED FORGIVENESS. SO . . . MELVIRA STAYS.
NOW, IT'S TIME FOR MY MEDITATION.
OOMMM . . .
CLICK!
Inner Peace
AH!
LOOK!
SHE'S LISTENING TO AN EARWORM SOUNDTRACK!
STOP IT BEFORE WE GET HYPNOTIZED.
SMASH!
WHEW, THAT WAS CLOSE!

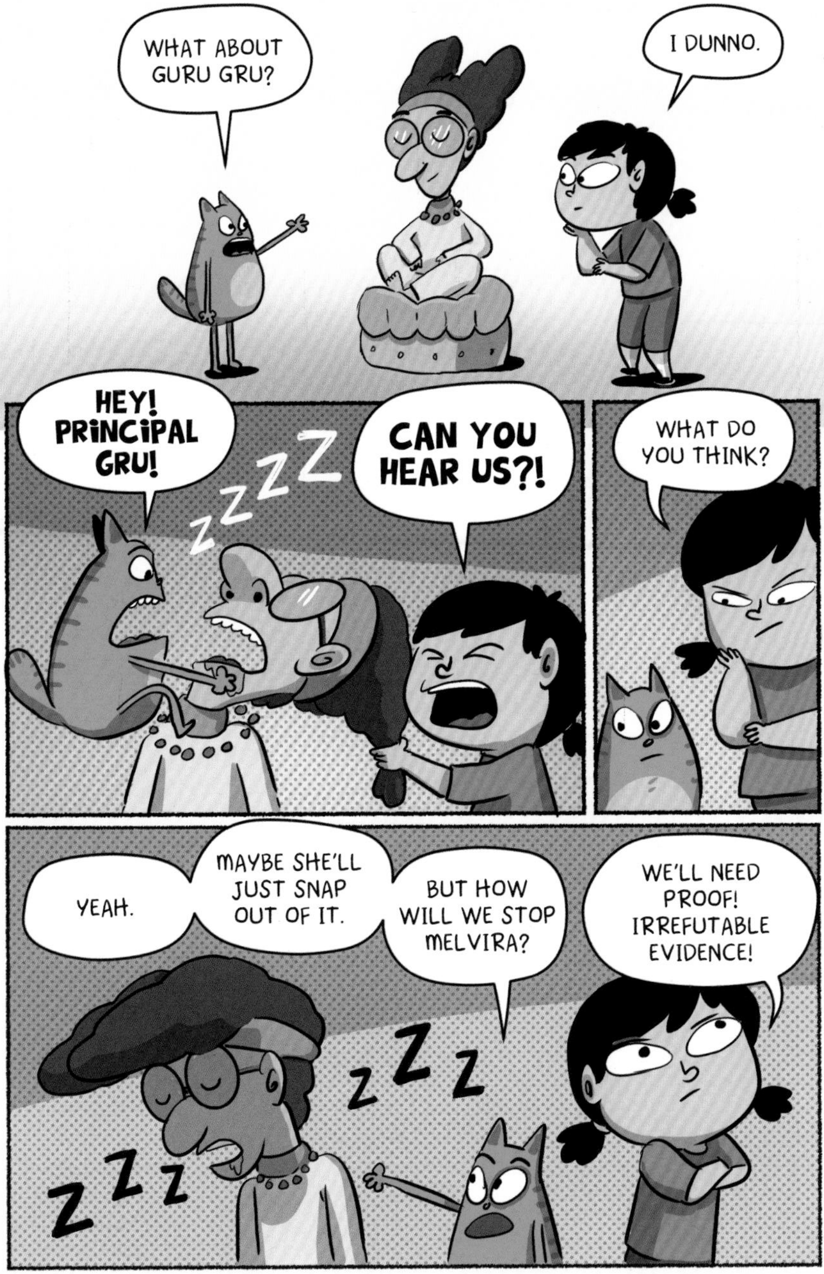
WHAT ABOUT GURU GRU?
I DUNNO.
HEY! PRINCIPAL GRU!
ZZZZZ
CAN YOU HEAR US?!
WHAT DO YOU THINK?
YEAH.
MAYBE SHE'LL JUST SNAP OUT OF IT.
BUT HOW WILL WE STOP MELVIRA?
WE'LL NEED PROOF! IRREFUTABLE EVIDENCE!
ZZZ
ZZZ

VILLAINS IN SCHOOL

SCHOOL WASN'T EASY FOR THE VILLAINS EITHER. IN FACT, THEY HATED EVERYTHING ABOUT IT.

WE'RE LATE FOR SCHOOL!

FIVE MORE MINUTES.

≶SNORT≶

THEY WERE CAUGHT CHEATING ON TESTS...

AGAIN?!

YOU'RE NOT EVEN HIDING IT!

HOW ELSE ARE WE SUPPOSED TO GET THE RIGHT ANSWERS?

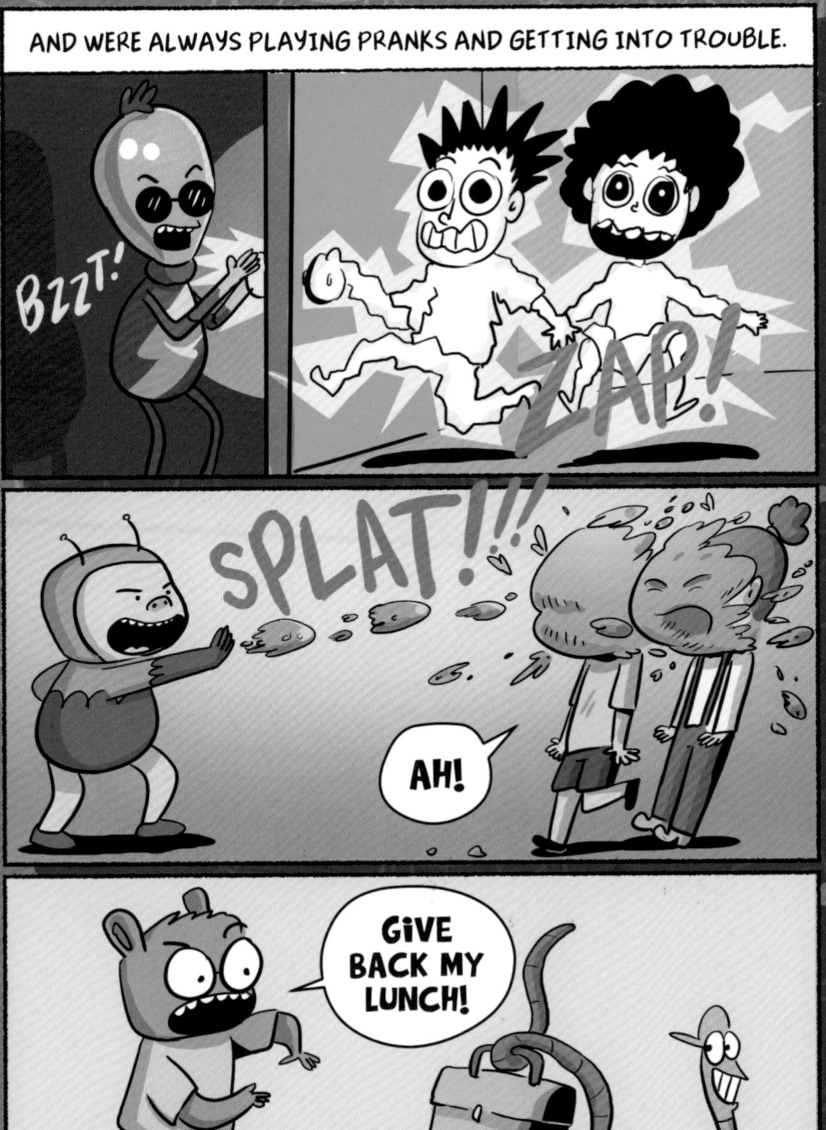
AND WERE ALWAYS PLAYING PRANKS AND GETTING INTO TROUBLE.
BZZT!
ZAP!
SPLAT!!!
AH!
GIVE BACK MY LUNCH!
YOINK!

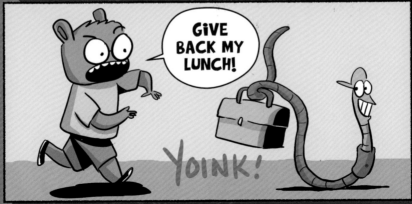

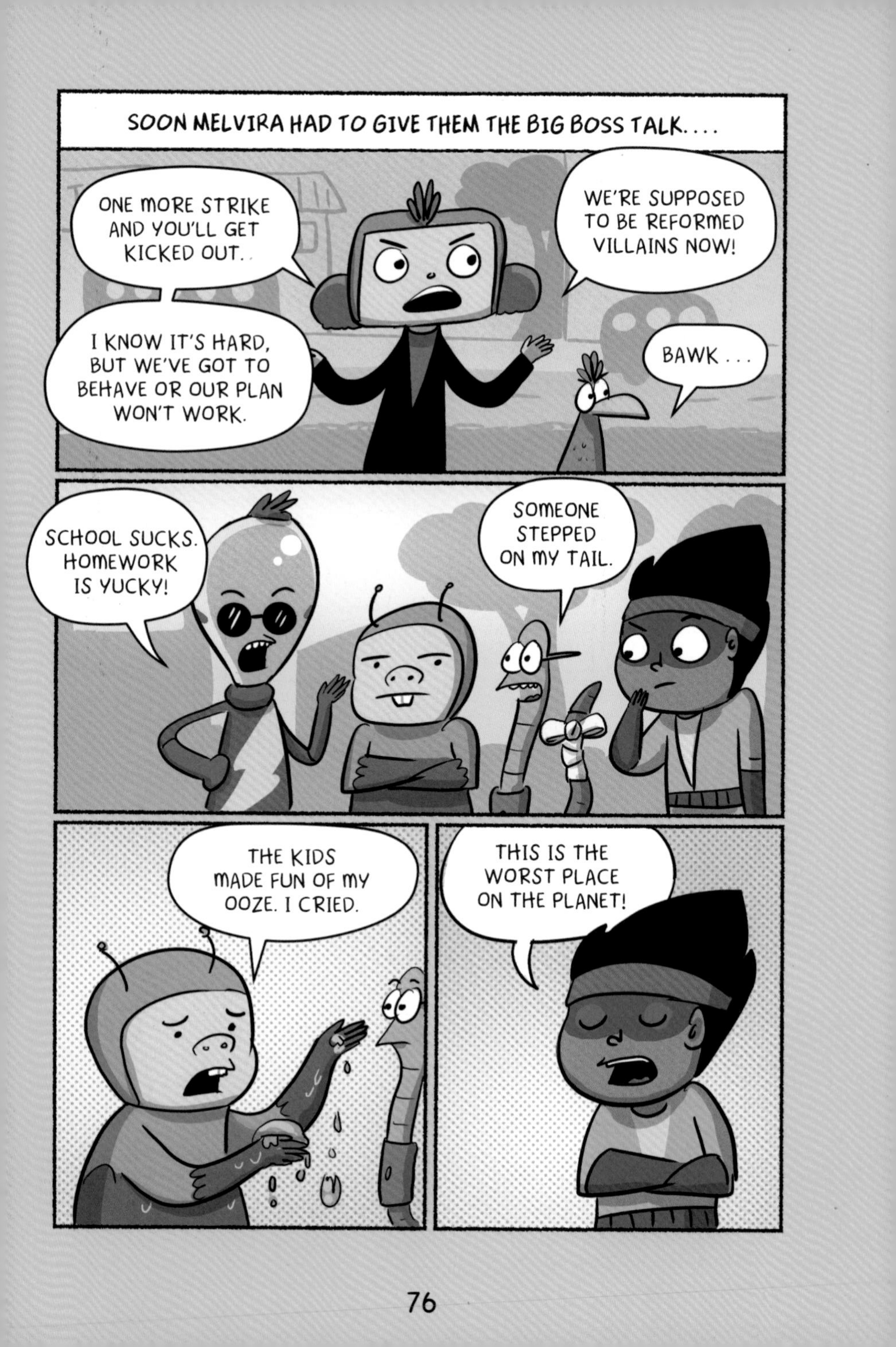
SOON MELVIRA HAD TO GIVE THEM THE BIG BOSS TALK. . . .
ONE MORE STRIKE AND YOU'LL GET KICKED OUT. . .
I KNOW IT'S HARD, BUT WE'VE GOT TO BEHAVE OR OUR PLAN WON'T WORK.
WE'RE SUPPOSED TO BE REFORMED VILLAINS NOW!
BAWK . . .
SCHOOL SUCKS. HOMEWORK IS YUCKY!
SOMEONE STEPPED ON MY TAIL.
THE KIDS MADE FUN OF MY OOZE. I CRIED.
THIS IS THE WORST PLACE ON THE PLANET!

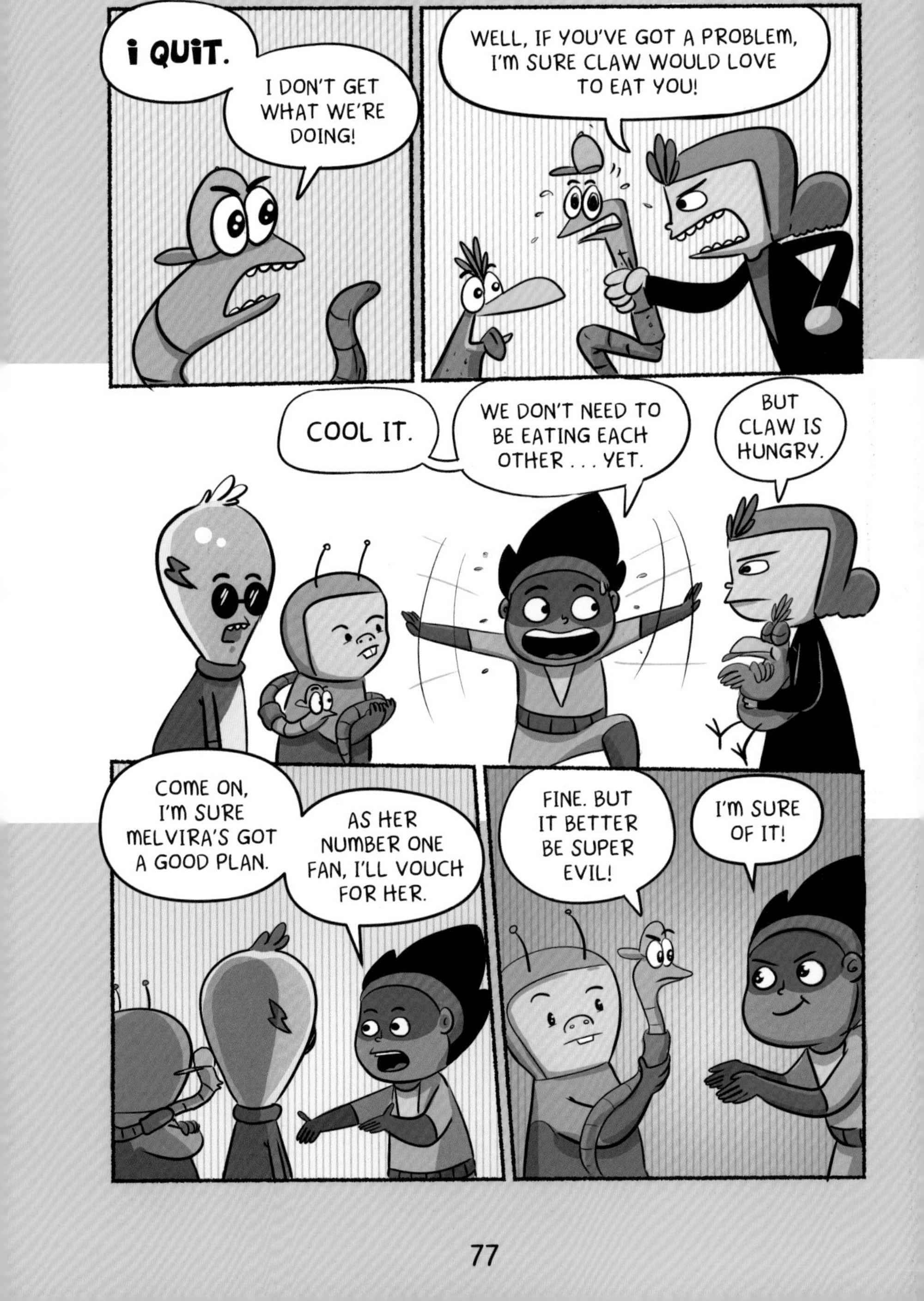
I QUIT.
I DON'T GET WHAT WE'RE DOING!
WELL, IF YOU'VE GOT A PROBLEM, I'M SURE CLAW WOULD LOVE TO EAT YOU!
COOL IT.
WE DON'T NEED TO BE EATING EACH OTHER . . . YET.
BUT CLAW IS HUNGRY.
COME ON, I'M SURE MELVIRA'S GOT A GOOD PLAN.
AS HER NUMBER ONE FAN, I'LL VOUCH FOR HER.
FINE. BUT IT BETTER BE SUPER EVIL!
I'M SURE OF IT!

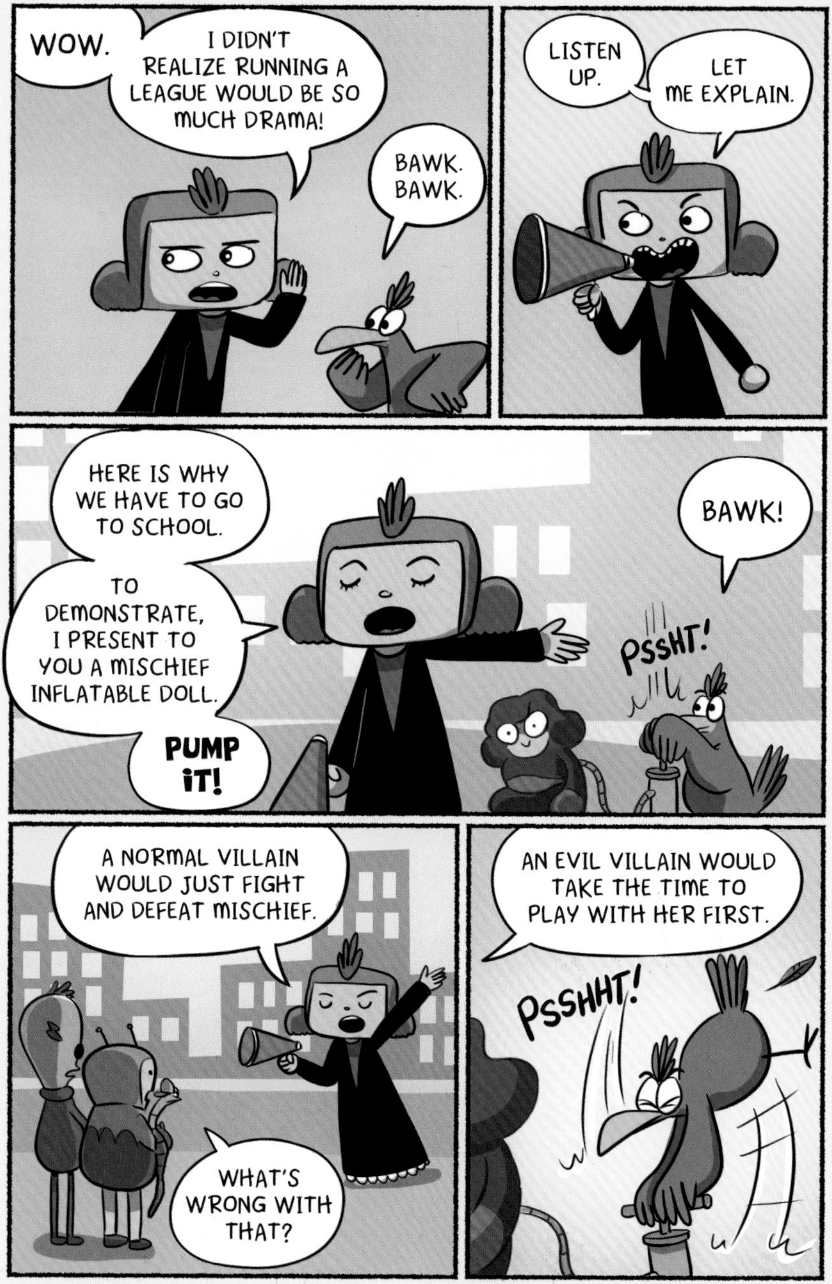
WOW.
I DIDN'T REALIZE RUNNING A LEAGUE WOULD BE SO MUCH DRAMA!
BAWK. BAWK.
LISTEN UP.
LET ME EXPLAIN.
HERE IS WHY WE HAVE TO GO TO SCHOOL.
TO DEMONSTRATE, I PRESENT TO YOU A MISCHIEF INFLATABLE DOLL.
PUMP IT!
BAWK!
PSSHT!
A NORMAL VILLAIN WOULD JUST FIGHT AND DEFEAT MISCHIEF.
WHAT'S WRONG WITH THAT?
AN EVIL VILLAIN WOULD TAKE THE TIME TO PLAY WITH HER FIRST.
PSSHHT!

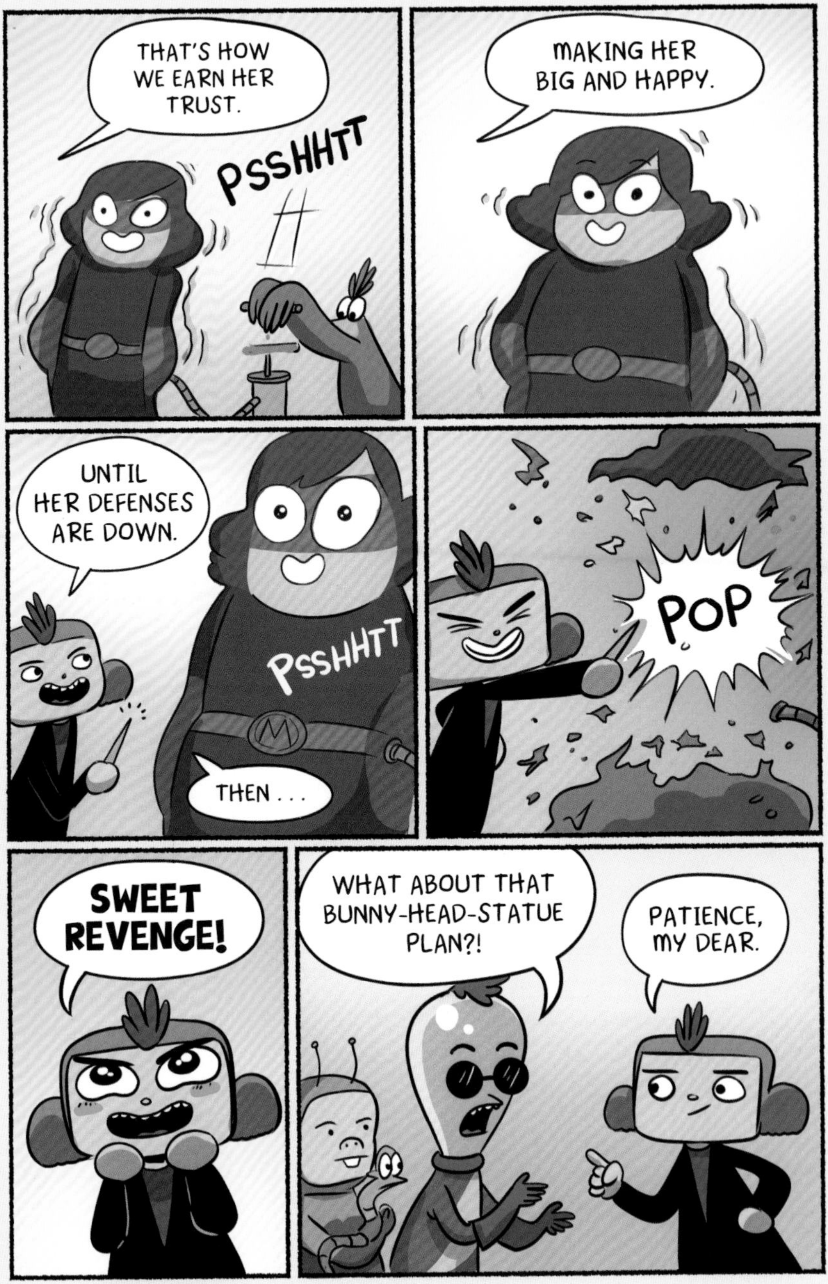
THAT'S HOW WE EARN HER TRUST.
PSSHHTT
MAKING HER BIG AND HAPPY.
UNTIL HER DEFENSES ARE DOWN.
PSSHHTT
THEN . . .
POP
SWEET REVENGE!
WHAT ABOUT THAT BUNNY-HEAD-STATUE PLAN?!
PATIENCE, MY DEAR.

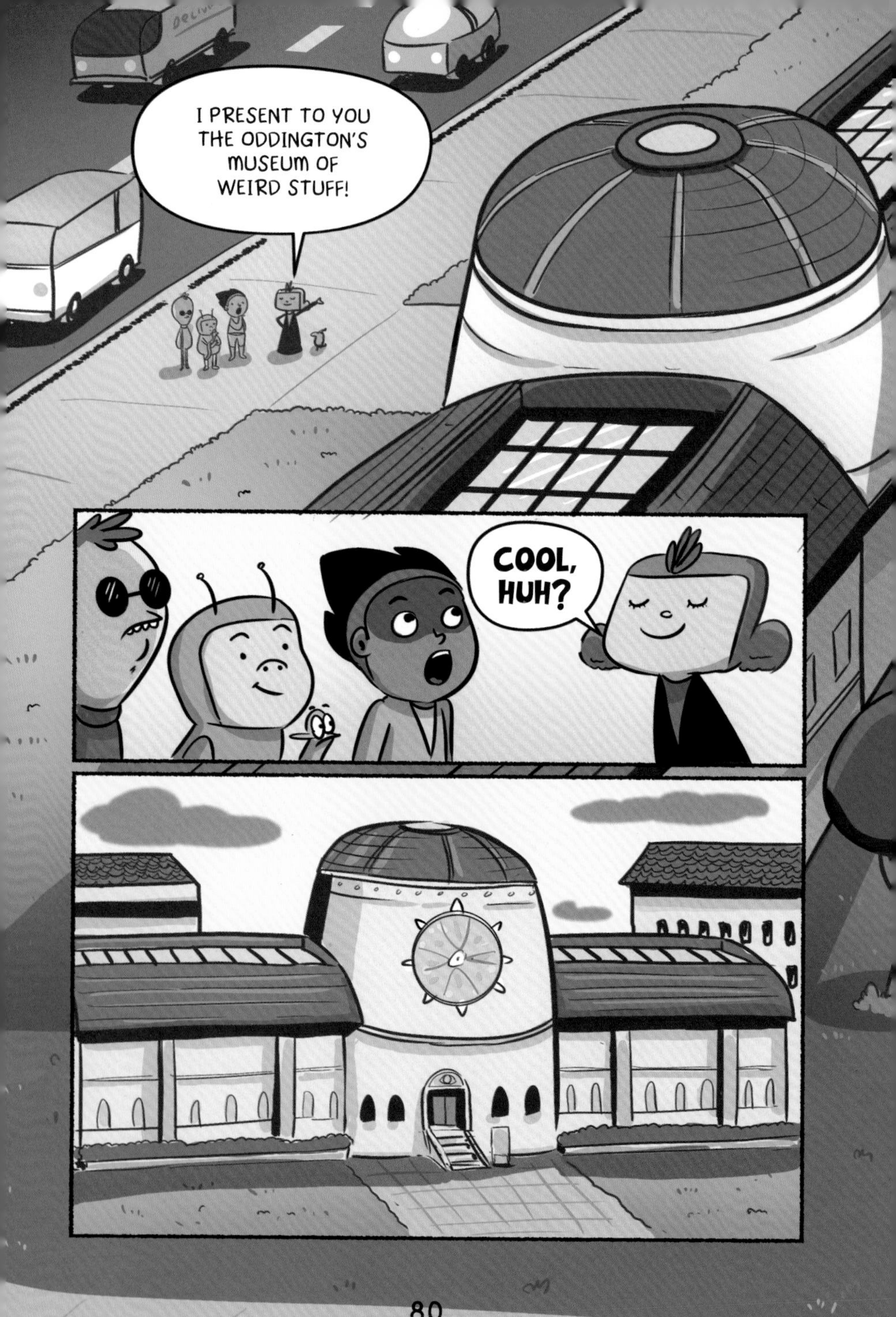
I PRESENT TO YOU THE ODDINGTON'S MUSEUM OF WEIRD STUFF!
COOL, HUH?

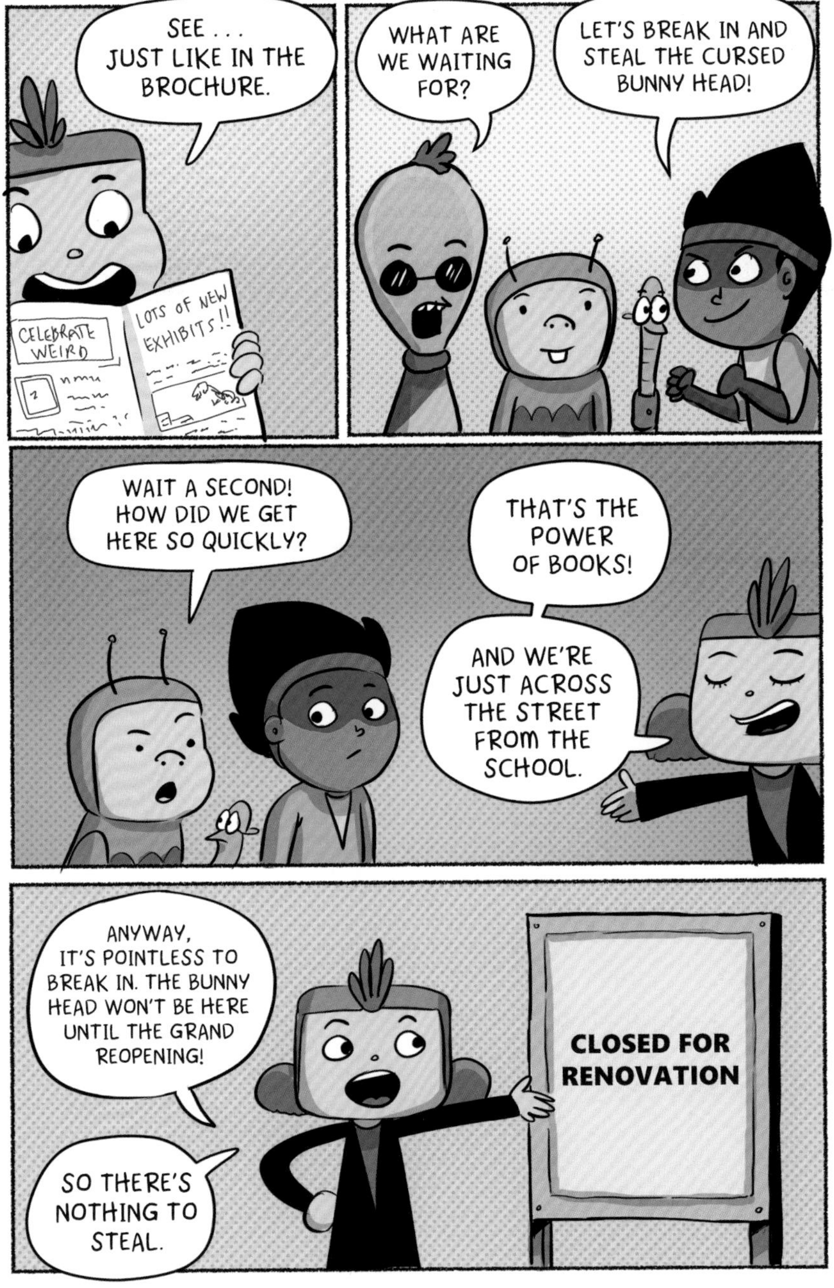
SEE . . . JUST LIKE IN THE BROCHURE.
CELEBRATE WEIRD
LOTS OF NEW EXHIBITS!!
WHAT ARE WE WAITING FOR?
LET'S BREAK IN AND STEAL THE CURSED BUNNY HEAD!
WAIT A SECOND! HOW DID WE GET HERE SO QUICKLY?
THAT'S THE POWER OF BOOKS!
AND WE'RE JUST ACROSS THE STREET FROM THE SCHOOL.
ANYWAY, IT'S POINTLESS TO BREAK IN. THE BUNNY HEAD WON'T BE HERE UNTIL THE GRAND REOPENING!
SO THERE'S NOTHING TO STEAL.
CLOSED FOR RENOVATION

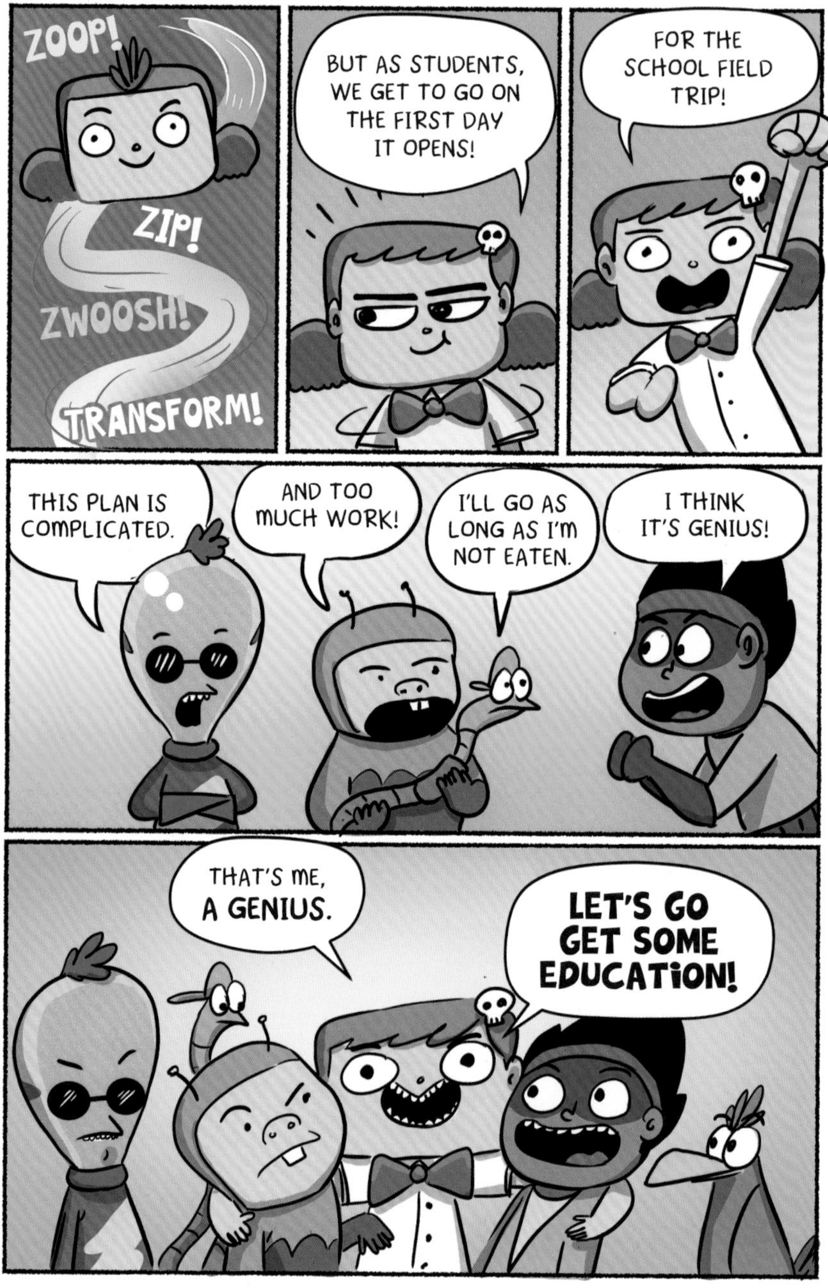
ZOOP!
ZIP!
ZWOOSH!
TRANSFORM!
BUT AS STUDENTS, WE GET TO GO ON THE FIRST DAY IT OPENS!
FOR THE SCHOOL FIELD TRIP!
THIS PLAN IS COMPLICATED.
AND TOO MUCH WORK!
I'LL GO AS LONG AS I'M NOT EATEN.
I THINK IT'S GENIUS!
THAT'S ME, A GENIUS.
LET'S GO GET SOME EDUCATION!

CHAPTER 6

DETECTIVE MISSY ON A MISSION

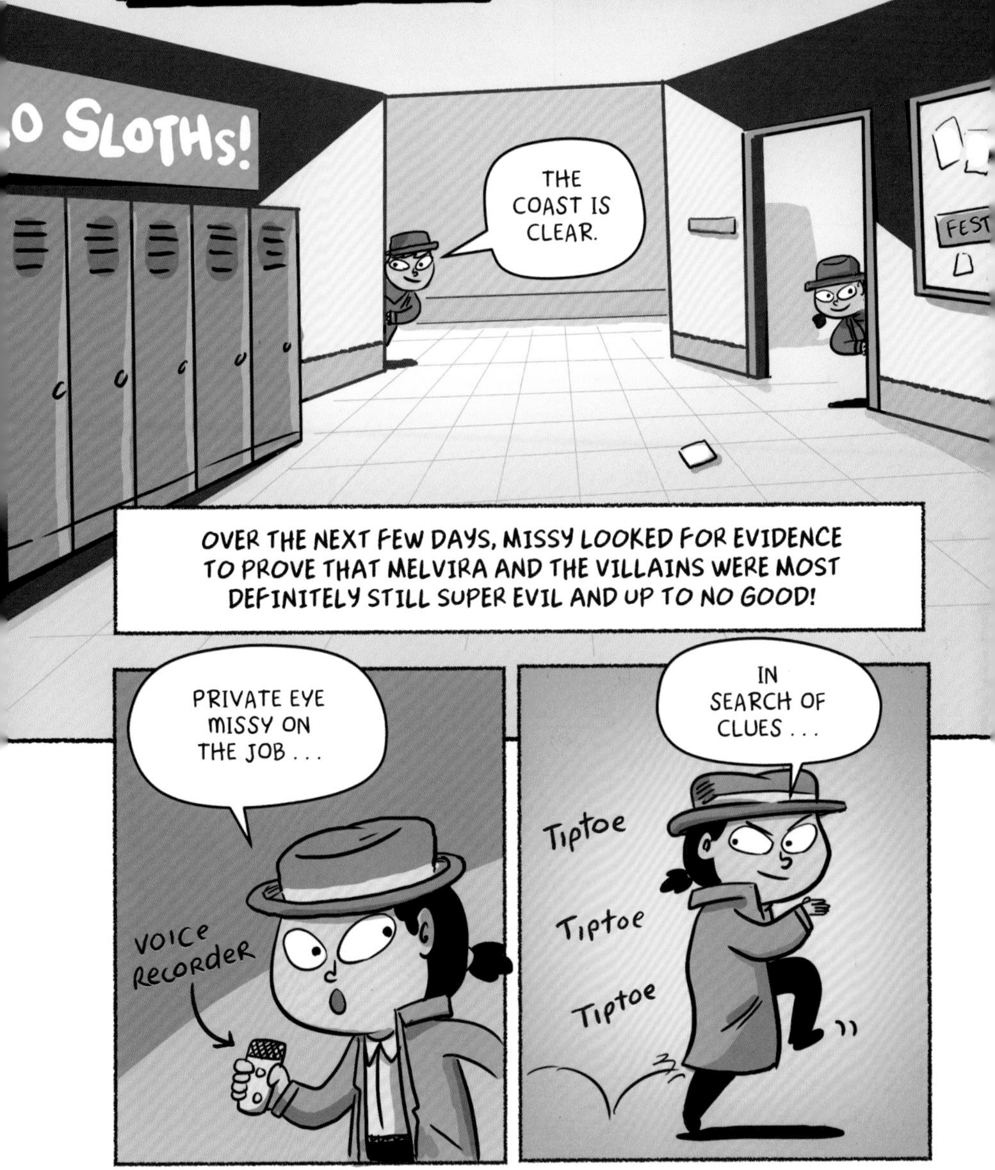
O SLOTHS!
THE COAST IS CLEAR.
FEST
OVER THE NEXT FEW DAYS, MISSY LOOKED FOR EVIDENCE TO PROVE THAT MELVIRA AND THE VILLAINS WERE MOST DEFINITELY STILL SUPER EVIL AND UP TO NO GOOD!
PRIVATE EYE MISSY ON THE JOB . . .
VOICE RECORDER
IN SEARCH OF CLUES . . .
Tiptoe
Tiptoe
Tiptoe

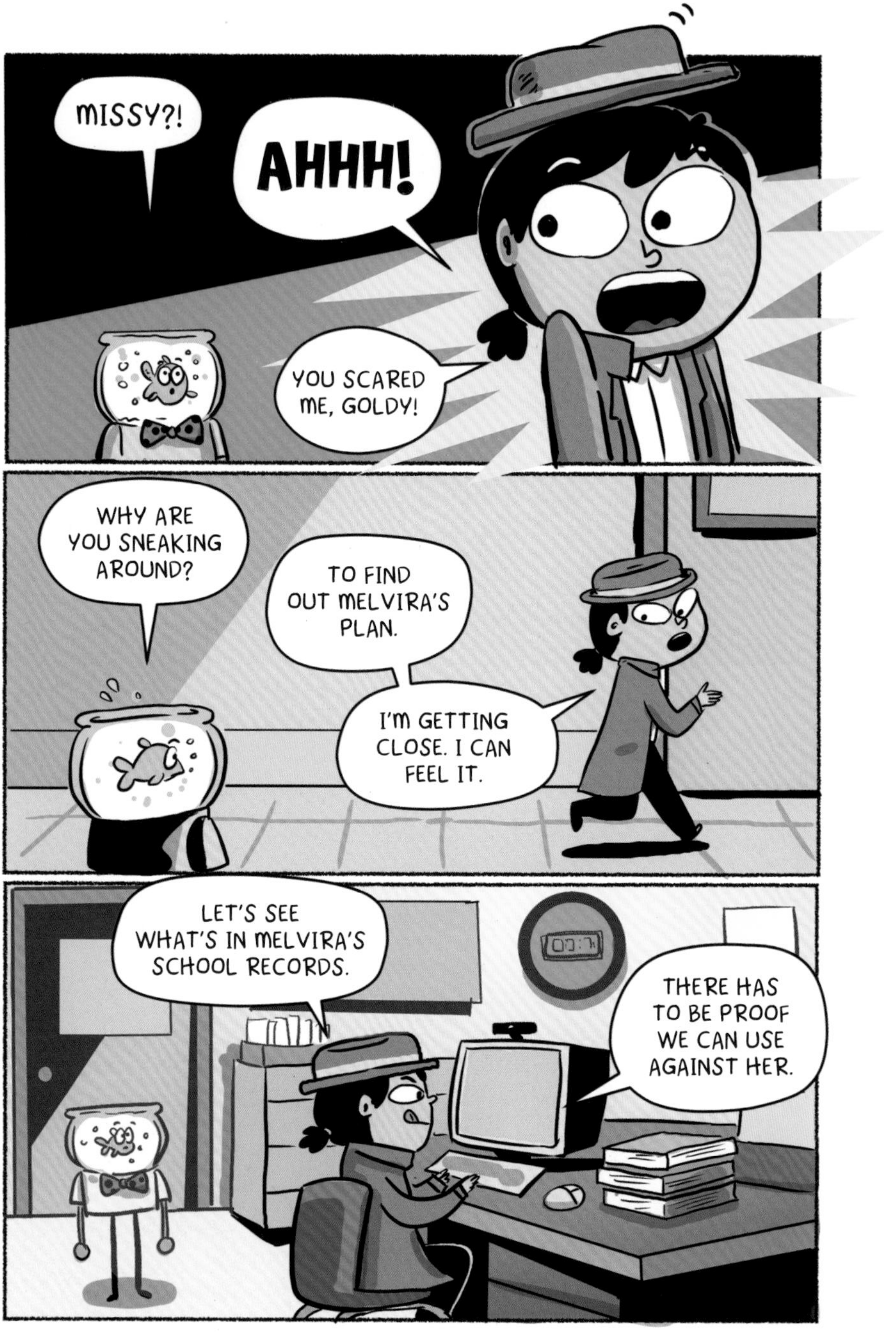
MISSY?!
AHHH!
YOU SCARED ME, GOLDY!
WHY ARE YOU SNEAKING AROUND?
TO FIND OUT MELVIRA'S PLAN.
I'M GETTING CLOSE. I CAN FEEL IT.
LET'S SEE WHAT'S IN MELVIRA'S SCHOOL RECORDS.
THERE HAS TO BE PROOF WE CAN USE AGAINST HER.

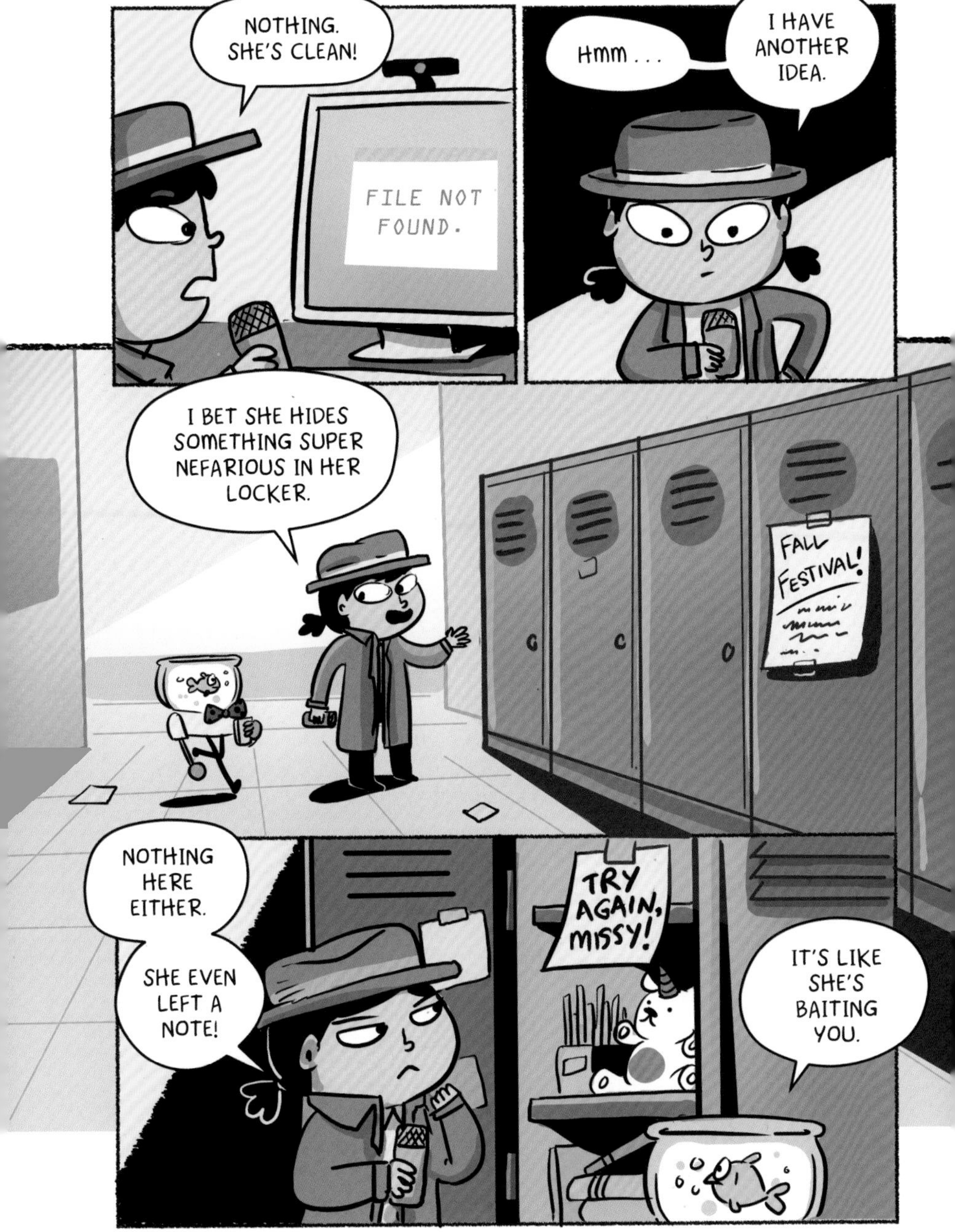
NOTHING. SHE'S CLEAN!
FILE NOT FOUND.
Hmm . . .
I HAVE ANOTHER IDEA.
I BET SHE HIDES SOMETHING SUPER NEFARIOUS IN HER LOCKER.
FALL FESTIVAL!
NOTHING HERE EITHER.
SHE EVEN LEFT A NOTE!
TRY AGAIN, MISSY!
IT'S LIKE SHE'S BAITING YOU.

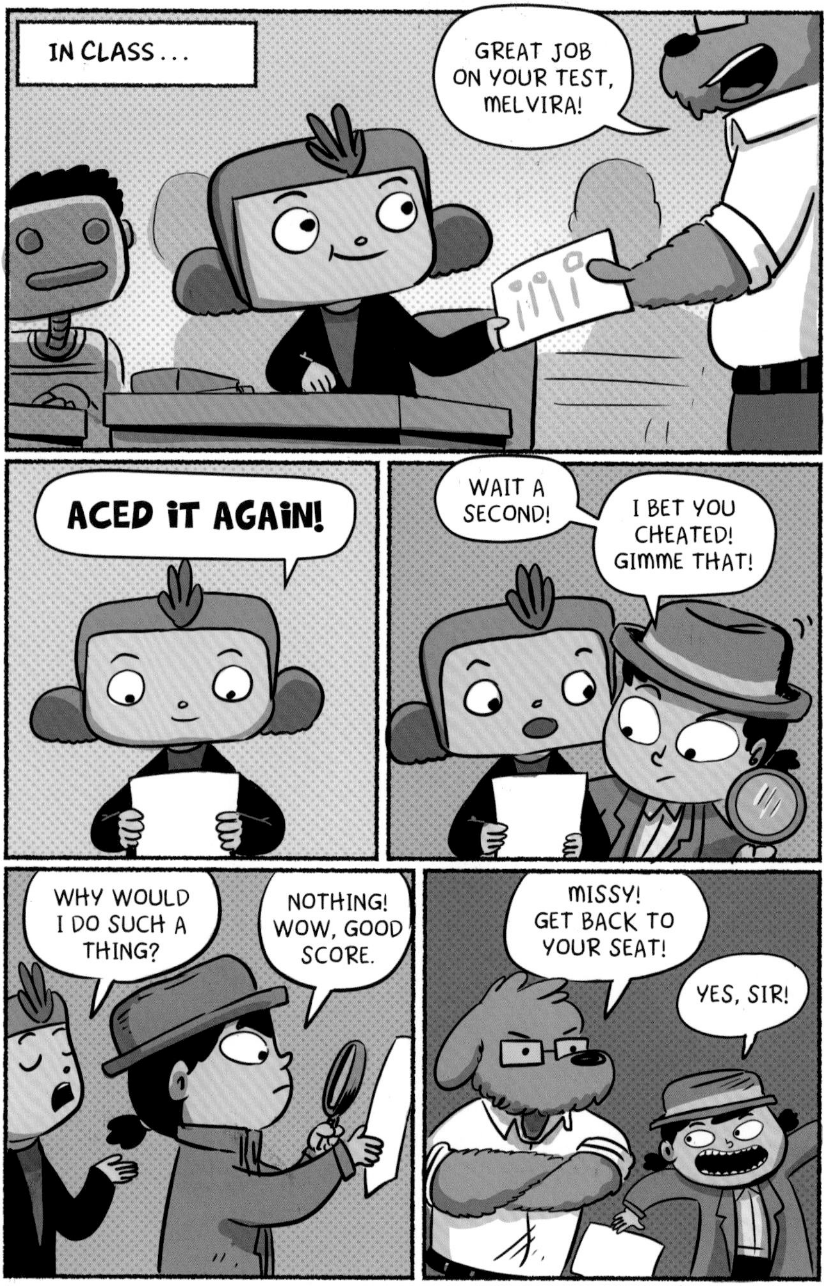
IN CLASS...
GREAT JOB ON YOUR TEST, MELVIRA!
ACED IT AGAIN!
WAIT A SECOND!
I BET YOU CHEATED! GIMME THAT!
WHY WOULD I DO SUCH A THING?
NOTHING! WOW, GOOD SCORE.
MISSY! GET BACK TO YOUR SEAT!
YES, SIR!

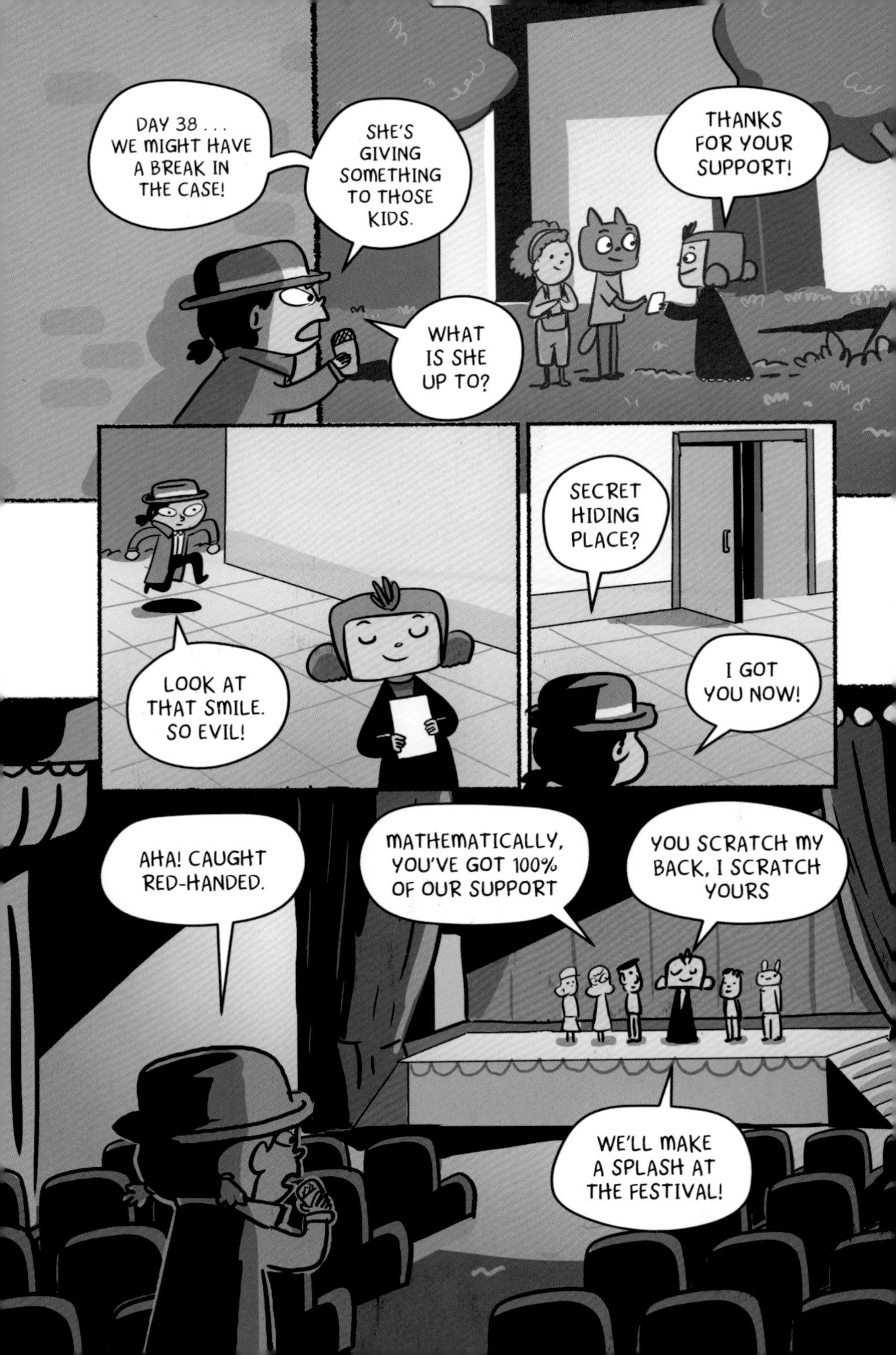
DAY 38 . . . WE MIGHT HAVE A BREAK IN THE CASE!
SHE'S GIVING SOMETHING TO THOSE KIDS.
WHAT IS SHE UP TO?
THANKS FOR YOUR SUPPORT!
LOOK AT THAT SMILE. SO EVIL!
SECRET HIDING PLACE?
I GOT YOU NOW!
AHA! CAUGHT RED-HANDED.
MATHEMATICALLY, YOU'VE GOT 100% OF OUR SUPPORT
YOU SCRATCH MY BACK, I SCRATCH YOURS
WE'LL MAKE A SPLASH AT THE FESTIVAL!

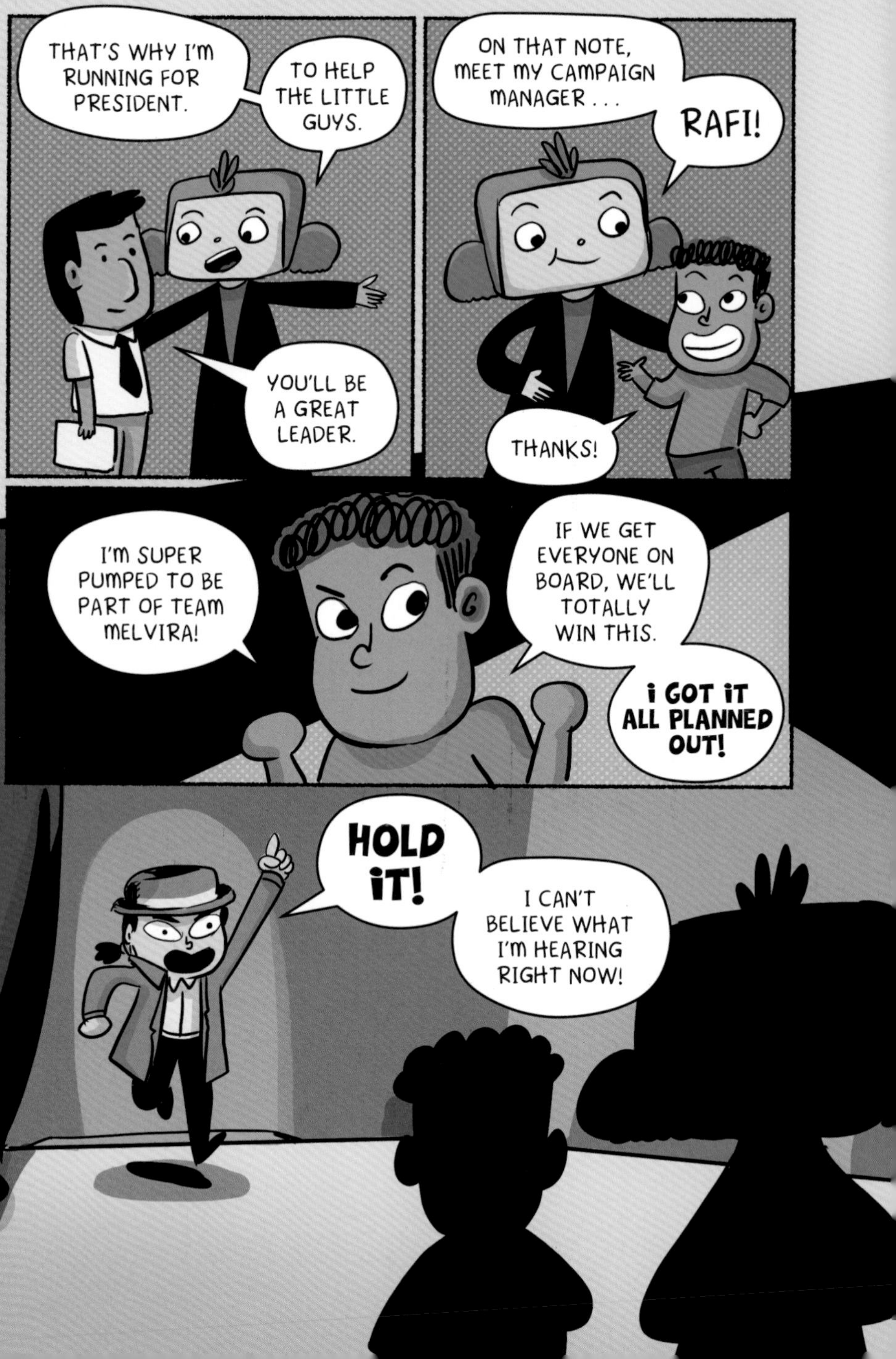
THAT'S WHY I'M RUNNING FOR PRESIDENT.
TO HELP THE LITTLE GUYS.
YOU'LL BE A GREAT LEADER.
ON THAT NOTE, MEET MY CAMPAIGN MANAGER . . .
RAFI!
THANKS!
I'M SUPER PUMPED TO BE PART OF TEAM MELVIRA!
IF WE GET EVERYONE ON BOARD, WE'LL TOTALLY WIN THIS.
I GOT IT ALL PLANNED OUT!
HOLD IT!
I CAN'T BELIEVE WHAT I'M HEARING RIGHT NOW!

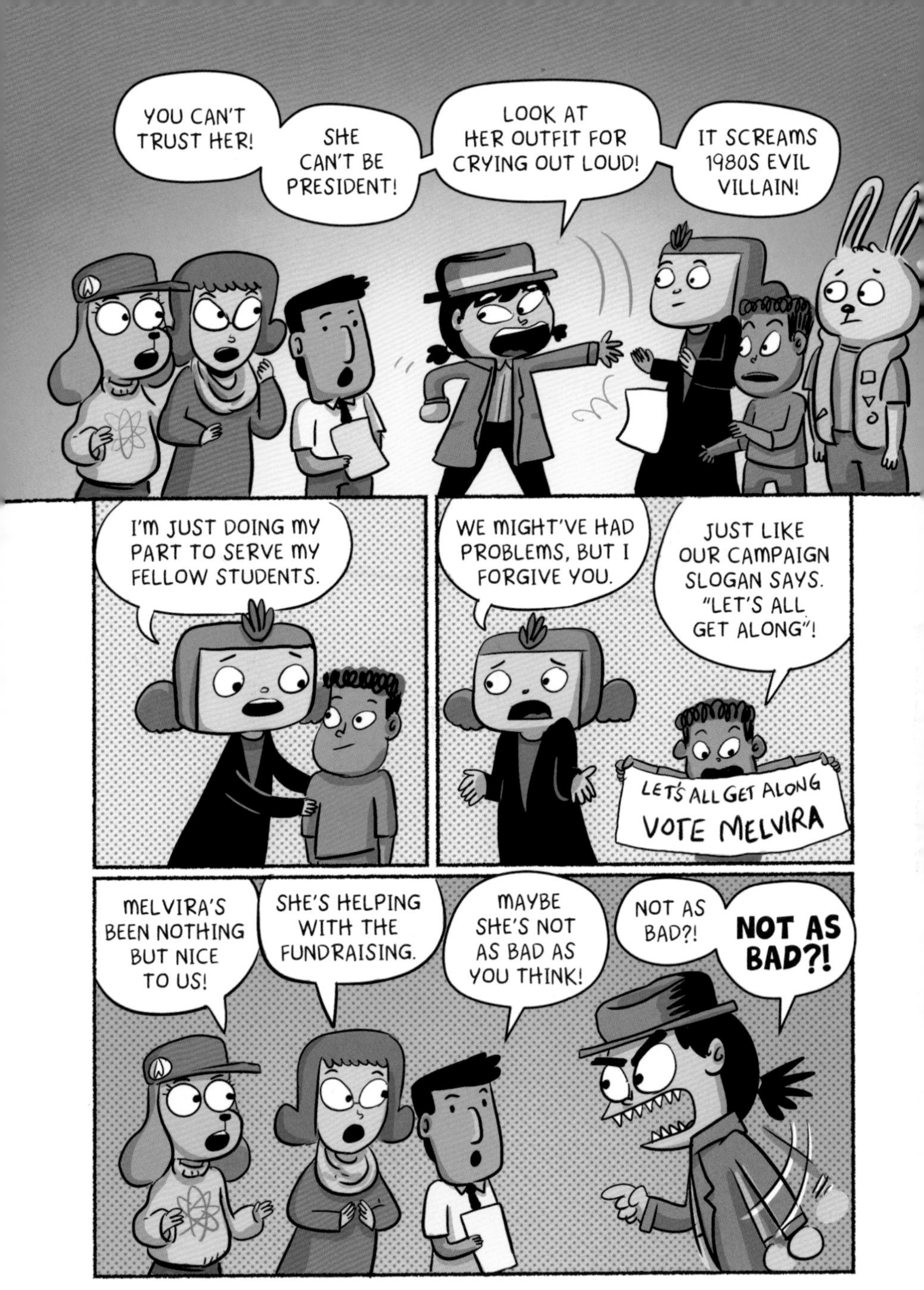
YOU CAN'T TRUST HER!
SHE CAN'T BE PRESIDENT!
LOOK AT HER OUTFIT FOR CRYING OUT LOUD!
IT SCREAMS 1980S EVIL VILLAIN!
I'M JUST DOING MY PART TO SERVE MY FELLOW STUDENTS.
WE MIGHT'VE HAD PROBLEMS, BUT I FORGIVE YOU.
JUST LIKE OUR CAMPAIGN SLOGAN SAYS. "LET'S ALL GET ALONG"!
LET'S ALL GET ALONG
VOTE MELVIRA
MELVIRA'S BEEN NOTHING BUT NICE TO US!
SHE'S HELPING WITH THE FUNDRAISING.
MAYBE SHE'S NOT AS BAD AS YOU THINK!
NOT AS BAD?!
NOT AS BAD?!

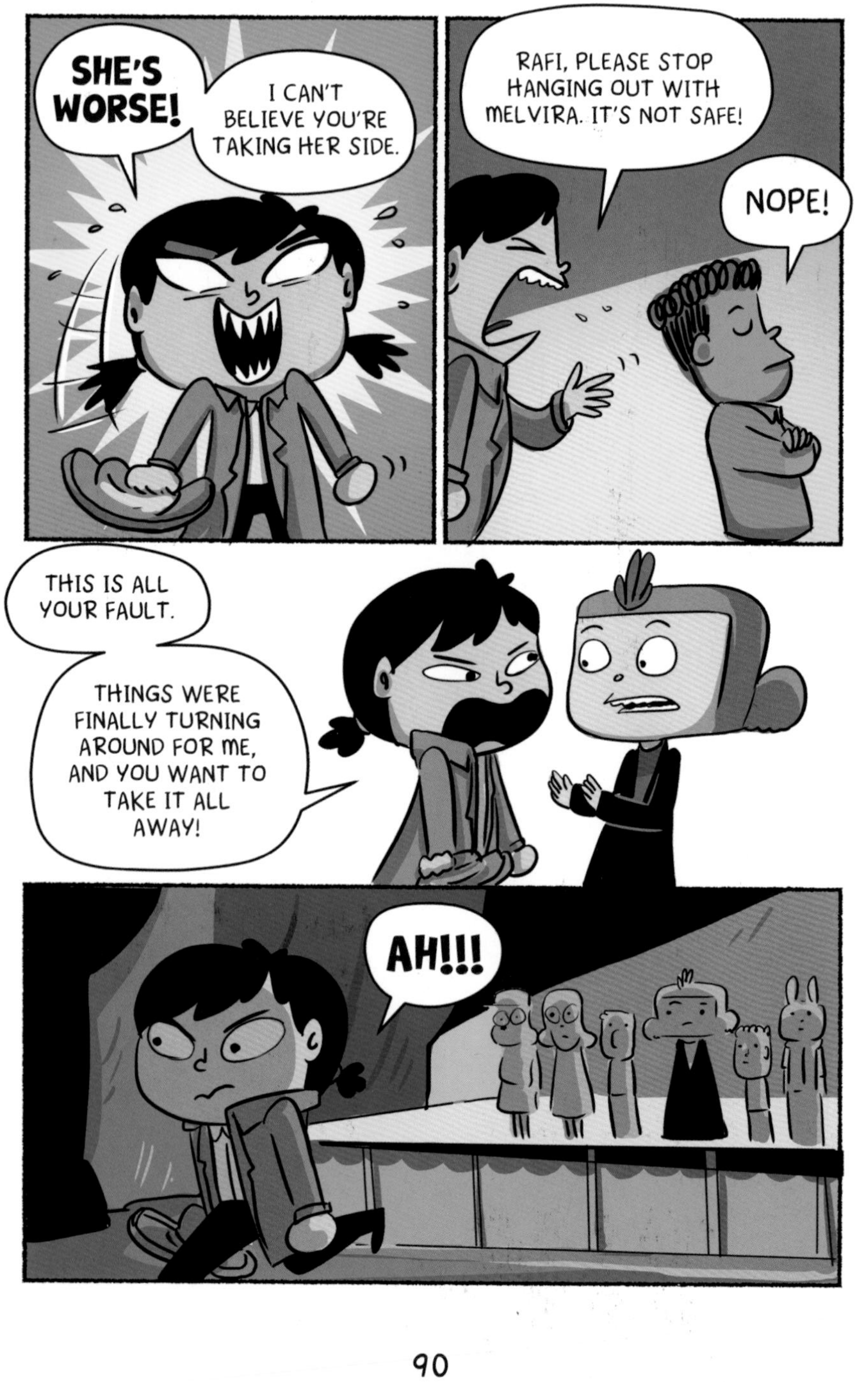
SHE'S WORSE!
I CAN'T BELIEVE YOU'RE TAKING HER SIDE.
RAFI, PLEASE STOP HANGING OUT WITH MELVIRA. IT'S NOT SAFE!
NOPE!
THIS IS ALL YOUR FAULT.
THINGS WERE FINALLY TURNING AROUND FOR ME, AND YOU WANT TO TAKE IT ALL AWAY!
AH!!!

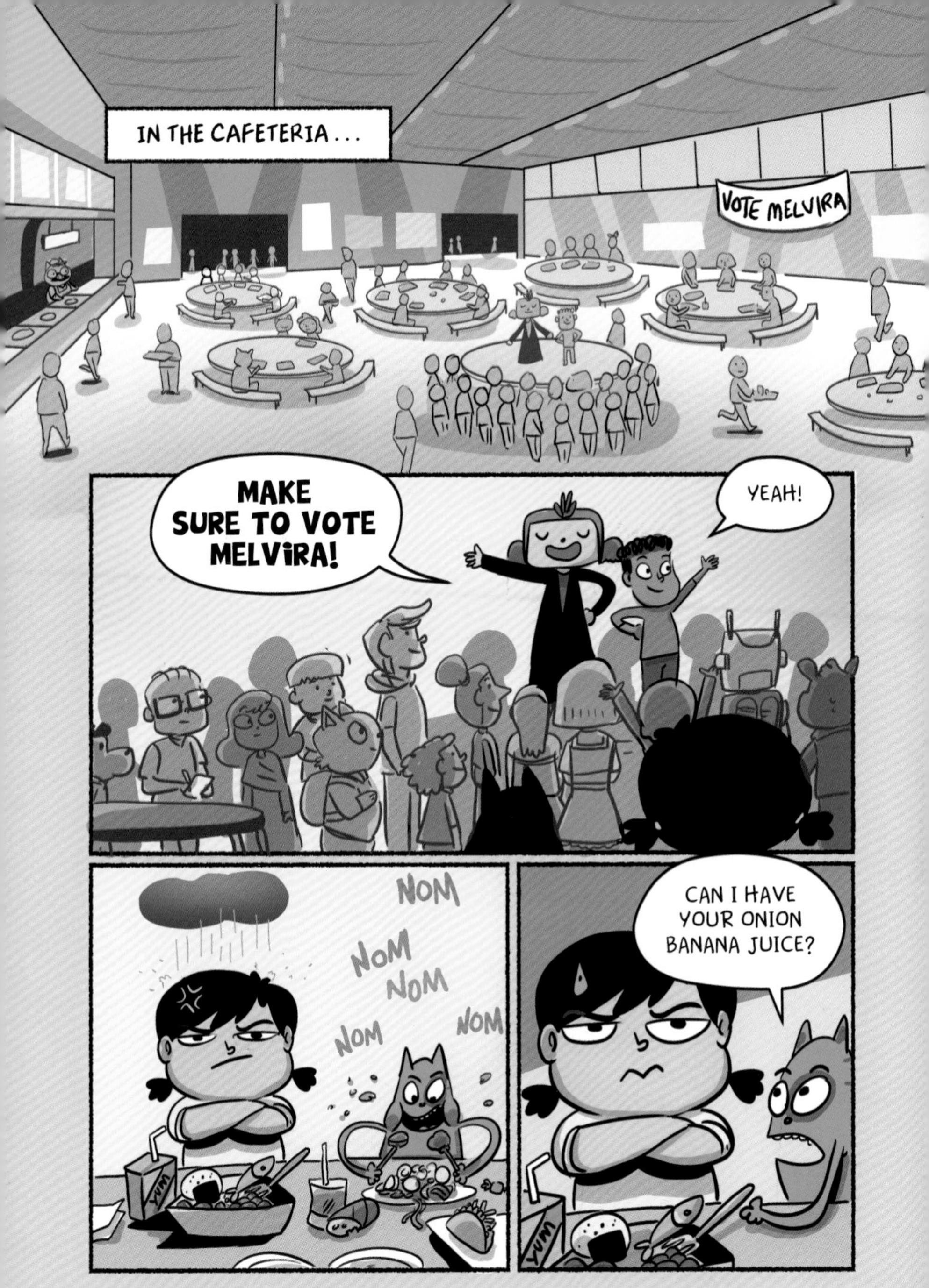
IN THE CAFETERIA . . .
VOTE MELVIRA
MAKE SURE TO VOTE MELVIRA!
YEAH!
NOM
NOM
NOM
NOM
NOM
YUM
CAN I HAVE YOUR ONION BANANA JUICE?
YUM

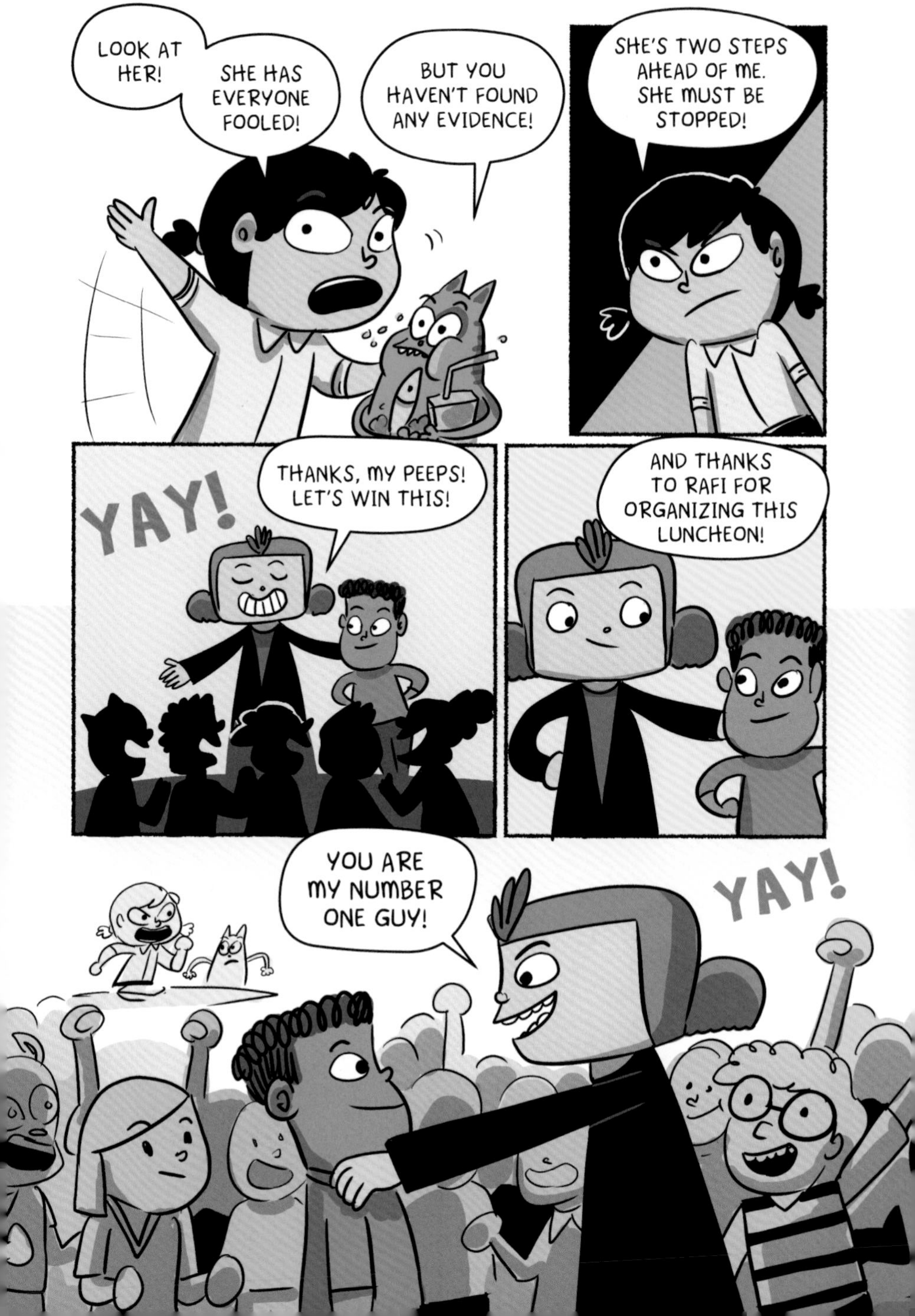
LOOK AT HER!
SHE HAS EVERYONE FOOLED!
BUT YOU HAVEN'T FOUND ANY EVIDENCE!
SHE'S TWO STEPS AHEAD OF ME. SHE MUST BE STOPPED!
YAY!
THANKS, MY PEEPS! LET'S WIN THIS!
AND THANKS TO RAFI FOR ORGANIZING THIS LUNCHEON!
YOU ARE MY NUMBER ONE GUY!
YAY!

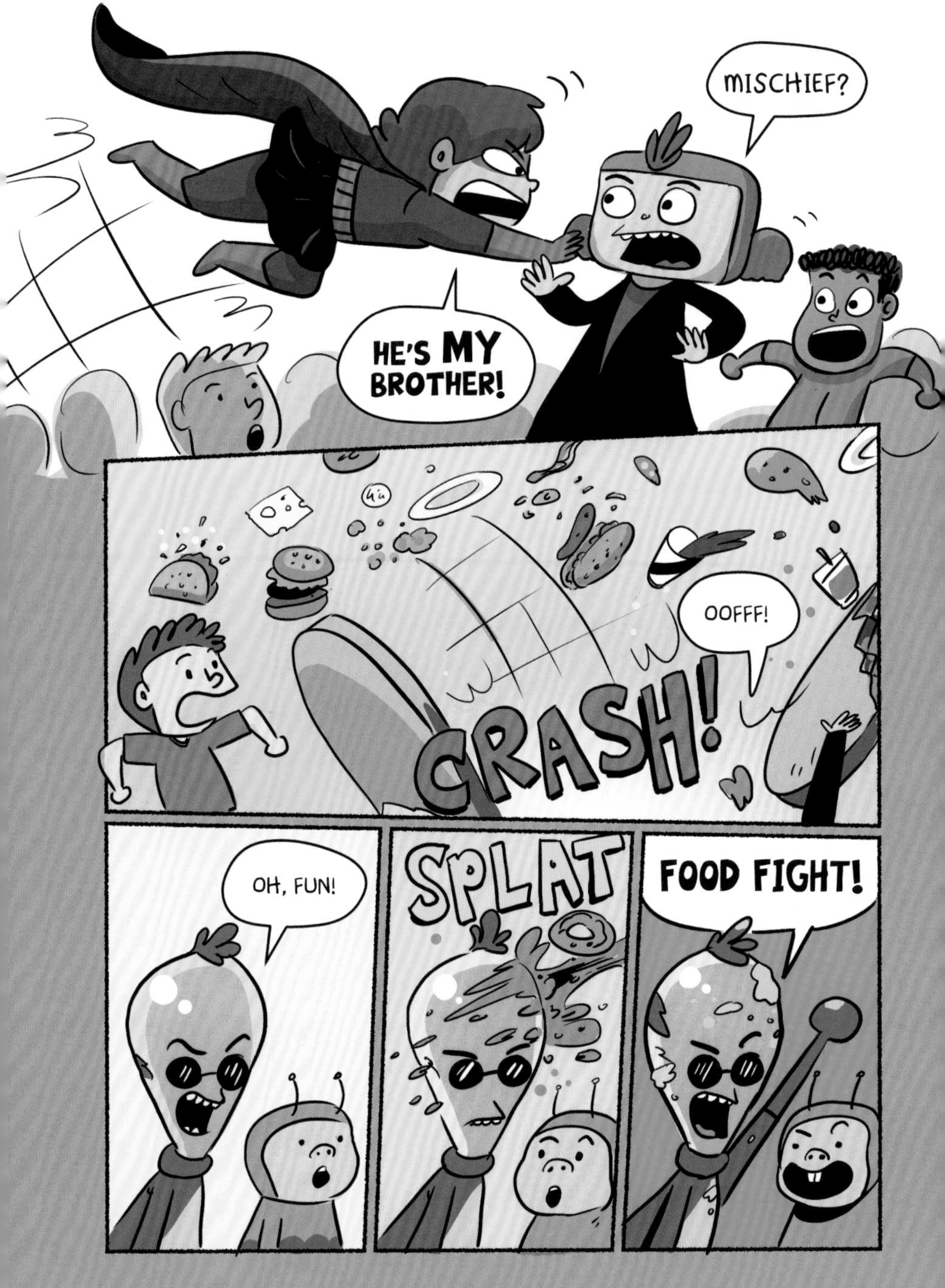
MISCHIEF?
HE'S MY BROTHER!
OOFFF!
CRASH!
OH, FUN!
SPLAT
FOOD FIGHT!

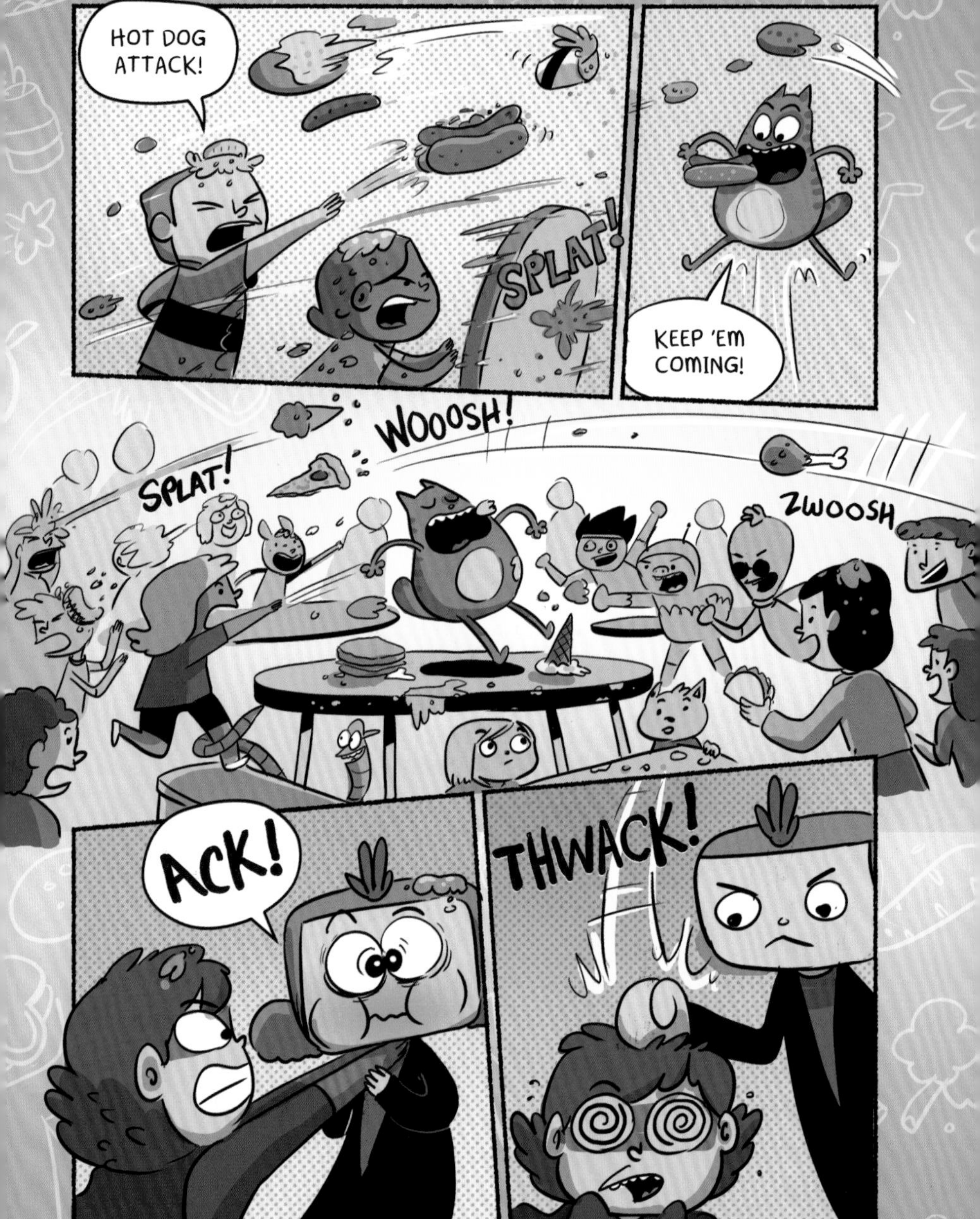
HOT DOG ATTACK!
SPLAT!
KEEP 'EM COMING!
WOOOSH!
SPLAT!
ZWOOSH
ACK!
THWACK!

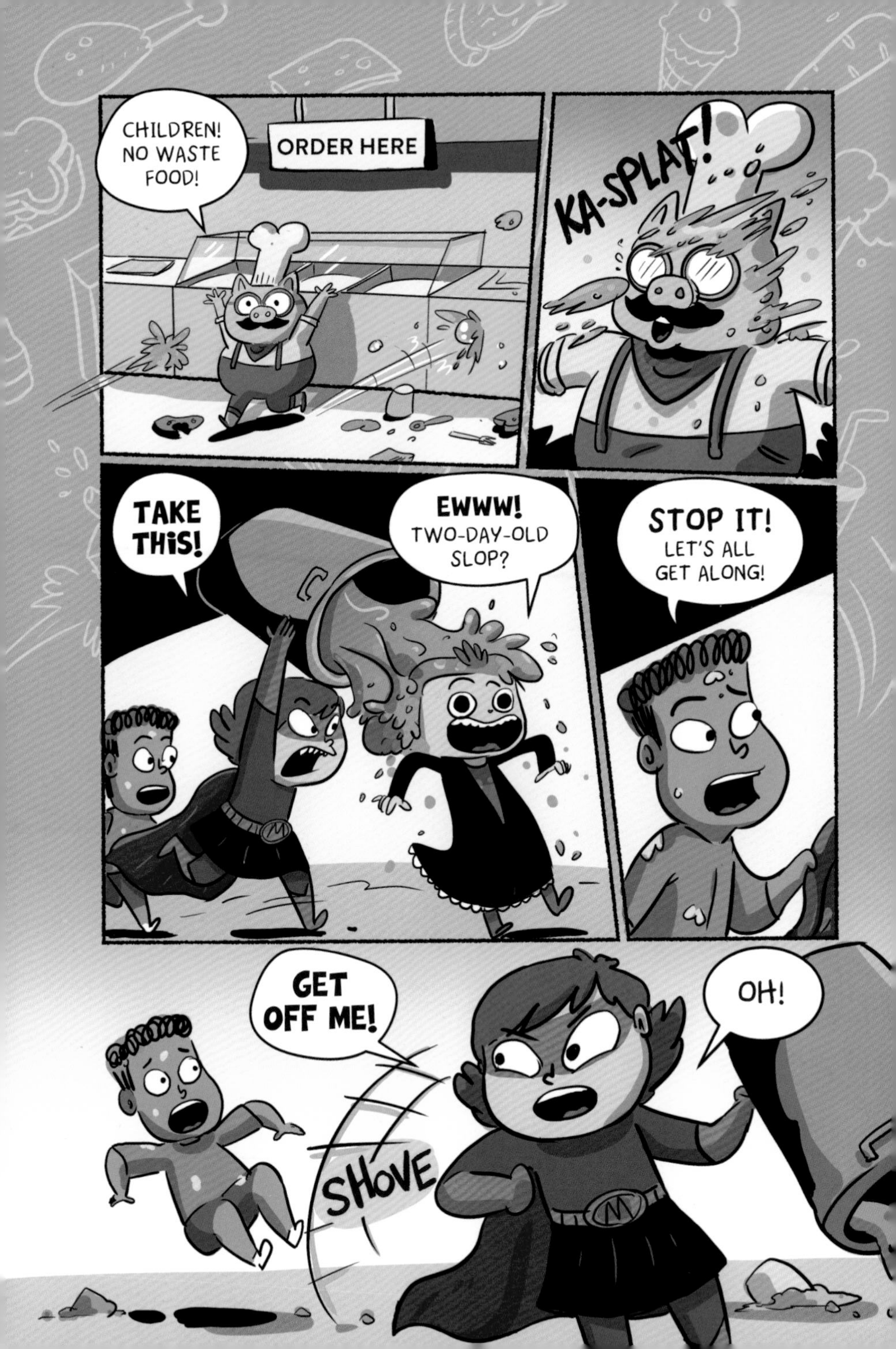
ORDER HERE
CHILDREN! NO WASTE FOOD!
KA-SPLAT!
TAKE THIS!
EWWW! TWO-DAY-OLD SLOP?
STOP IT! LET'S ALL GET ALONG!
GET OFF ME!
SHOVE
OH!

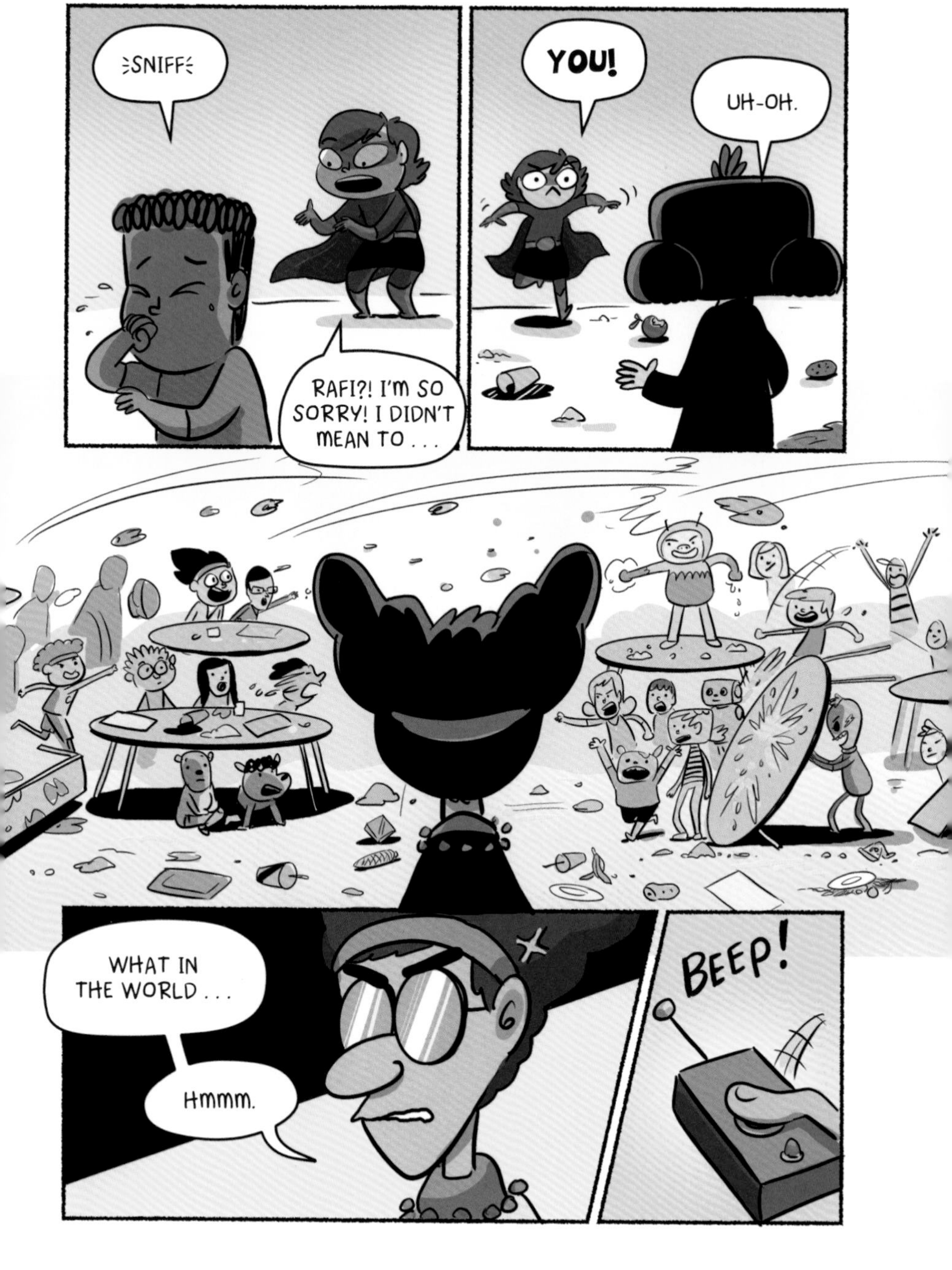
SNIFF
RAFI?! I'M SO SORRY! I DIDN'T MEAN TO . . .
YOU!
UH-OH.
WHAT IN THE WORLD . . .
Hmmm.
BEEP!

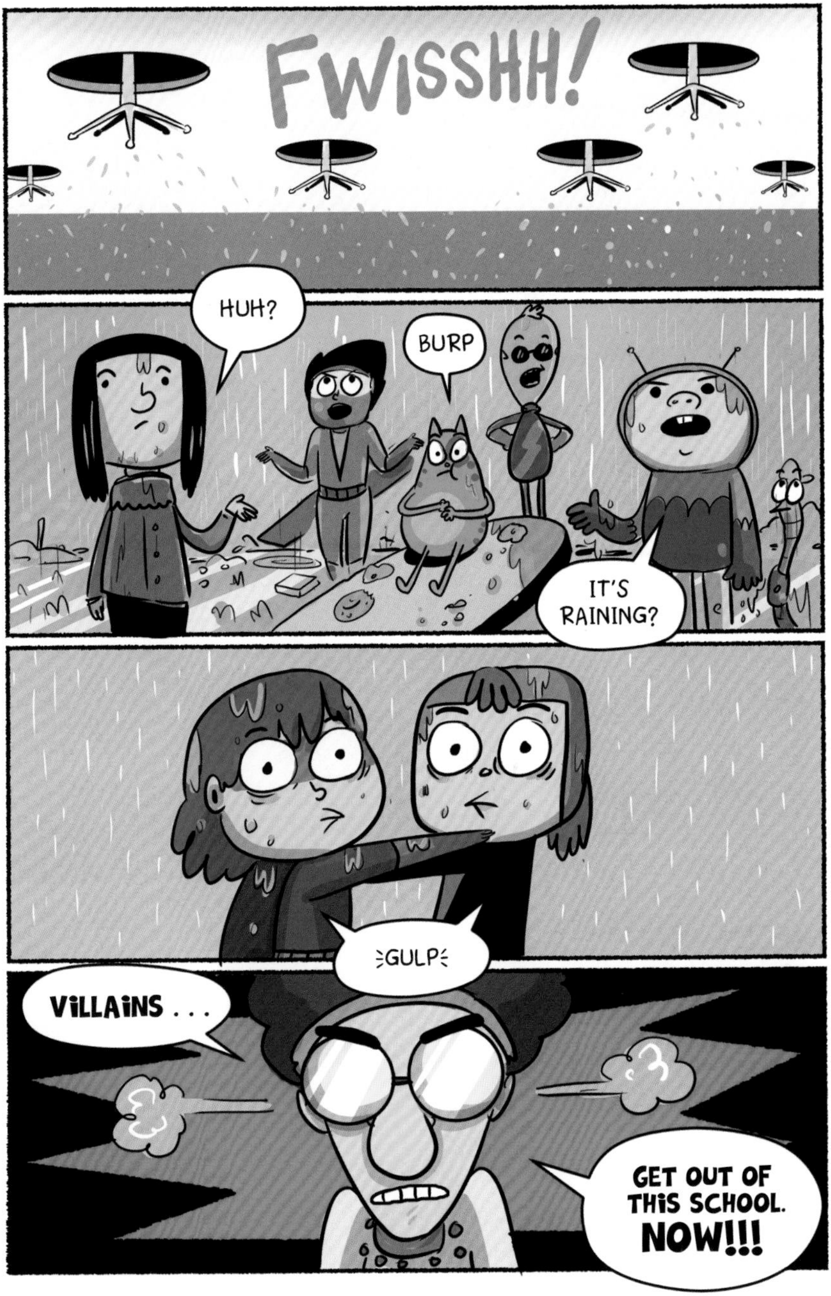
FWISSHH!
HUH?
BURP
IT'S RAINING?
GULP
VILLAINS . . .
GET OUT OF THIS SCHOOL. NOW!!!

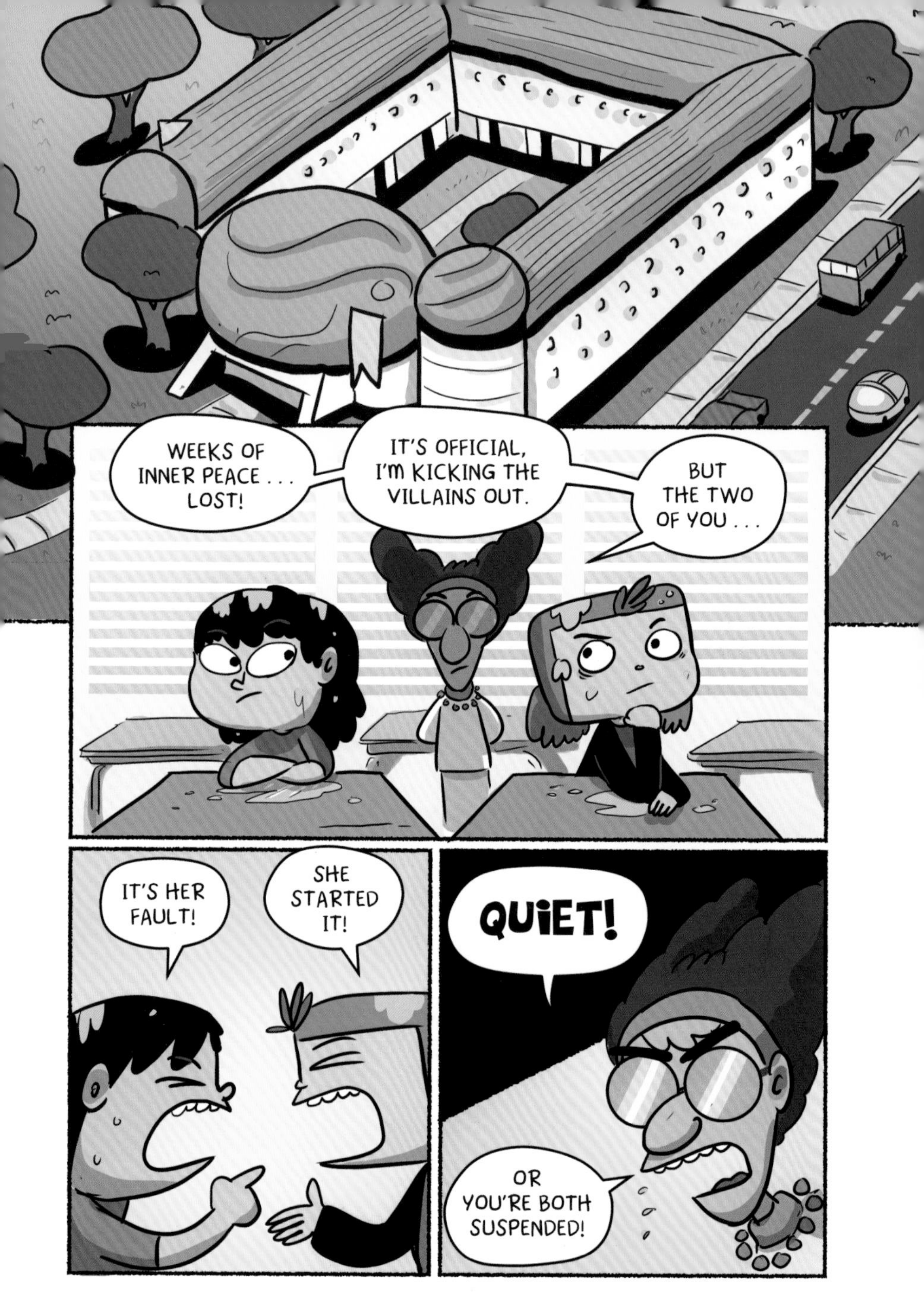
WEEKS OF INNER PEACE . . . LOST!
IT'S OFFICIAL, I'M KICKING THE VILLAINS OUT.
BUT THE TWO OF YOU . . .
IT'S HER FAULT!
SHE STARTED IT!
QUIET!
OR YOU'RE BOTH SUSPENDED!

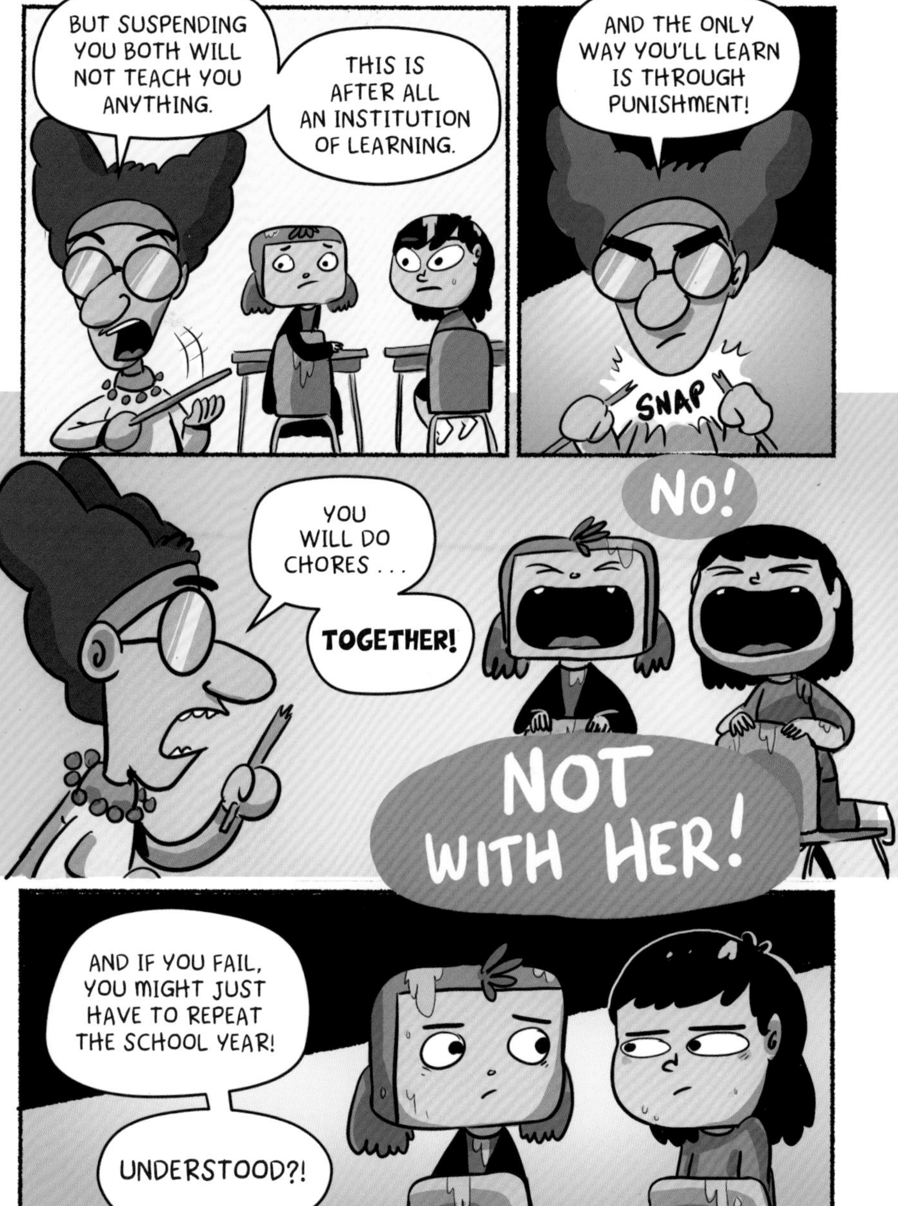
BUT SUSPENDING YOU BOTH WILL NOT TEACH YOU ANYTHING.
THIS IS AFTER ALL AN INSTITUTION OF LEARNING.
AND THE ONLY WAY YOU'LL LEARN IS THROUGH PUNISHMENT!
SNAP
YOU WILL DO CHORES . . .
TOGETHER!
NO!
NOT WITH HER!
AND IF YOU FAIL, YOU MIGHT JUST HAVE TO REPEAT THE SCHOOL YEAR!
UNDERSTOOD?!

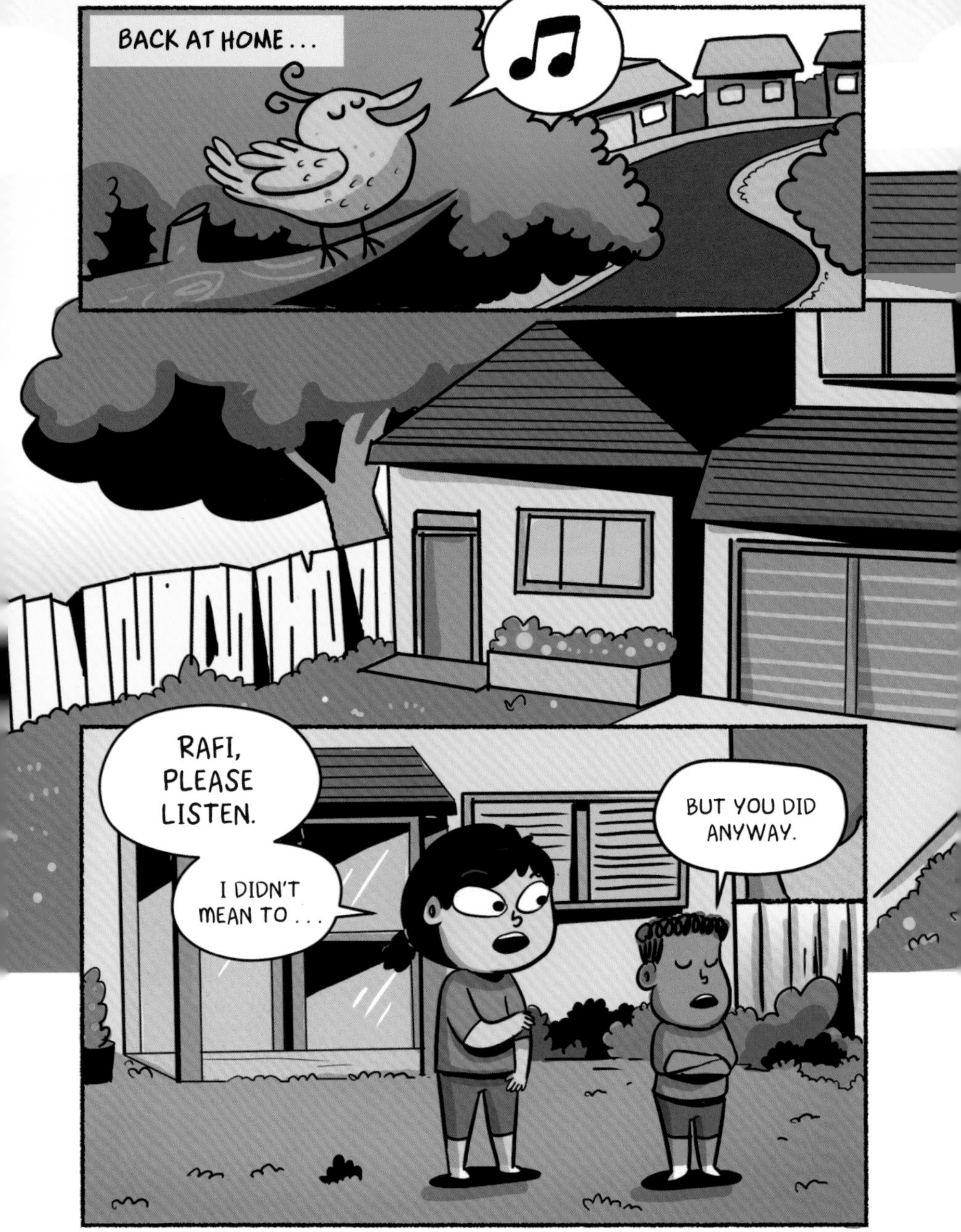
BACK AT HOME . . .
♫
RAFI, PLEASE LISTEN.
I DIDN'T MEAN TO . . .
BUT YOU DID ANYWAY.

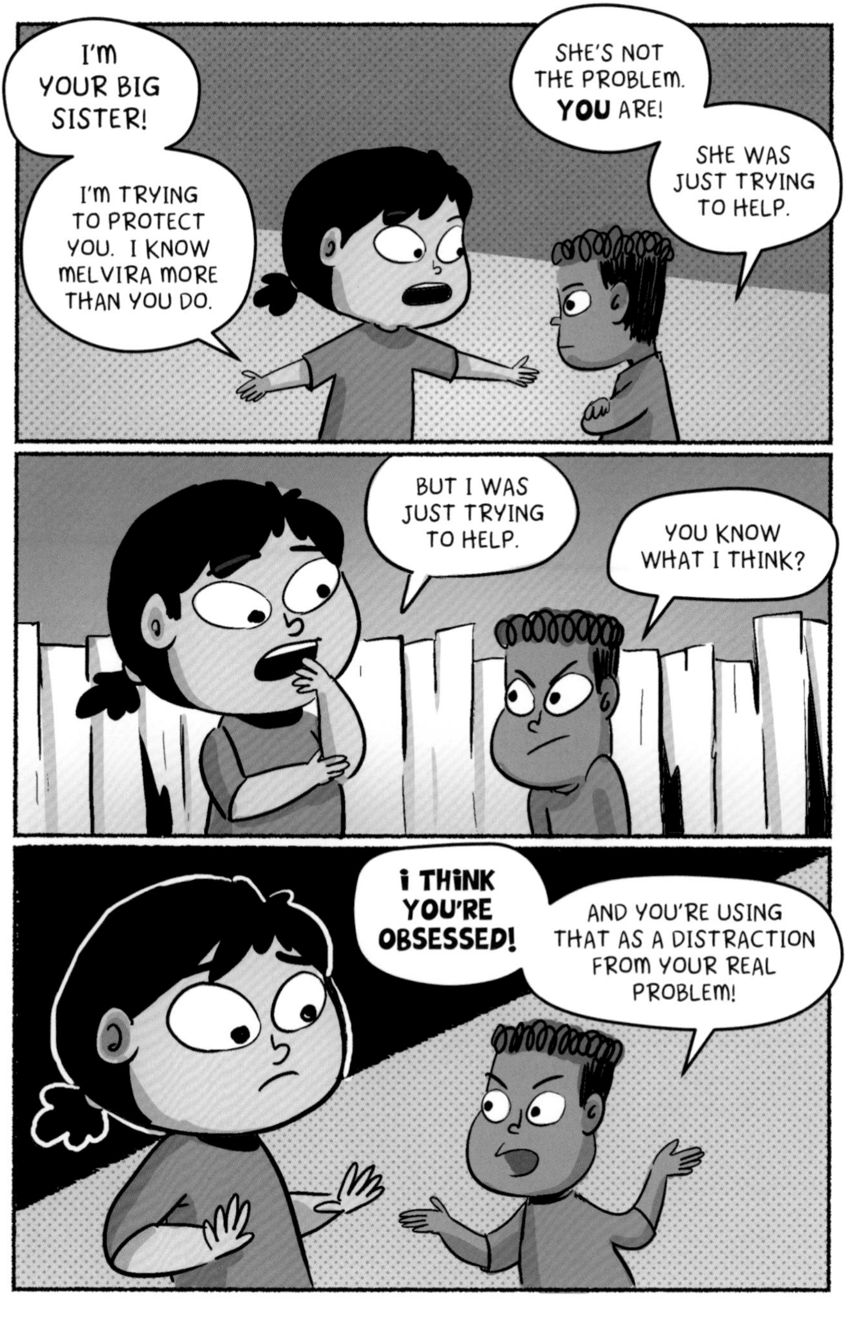
I'M YOUR BIG SISTER!
I'M TRYING TO PROTECT YOU. I KNOW MELVIRA MORE THAN YOU DO.
SHE'S NOT THE PROBLEM. **YOU** ARE!
SHE WAS JUST TRYING TO HELP.
BUT I WAS JUST TRYING TO HELP.
YOU KNOW WHAT I THINK?
I THINK YOU'RE OBSESSED!
AND YOU'RE USING THAT AS A DISTRACTION FROM YOUR REAL PROBLEM!

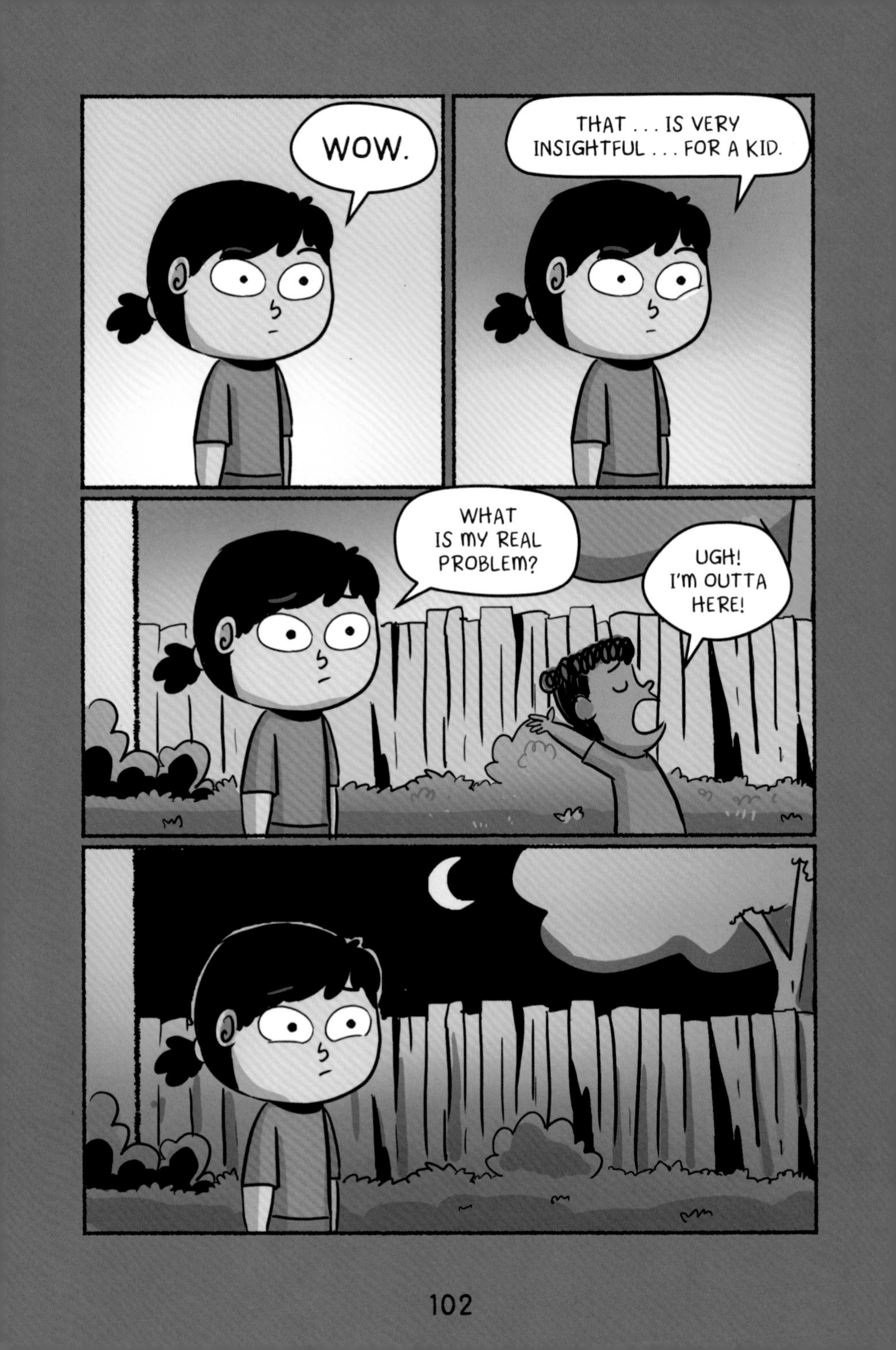
WOW.
THAT . . . IS VERY INSIGHTFUL . . . FOR A KID.
WHAT IS MY REAL PROBLEM?
UGH! I'M OUTTA HERE!

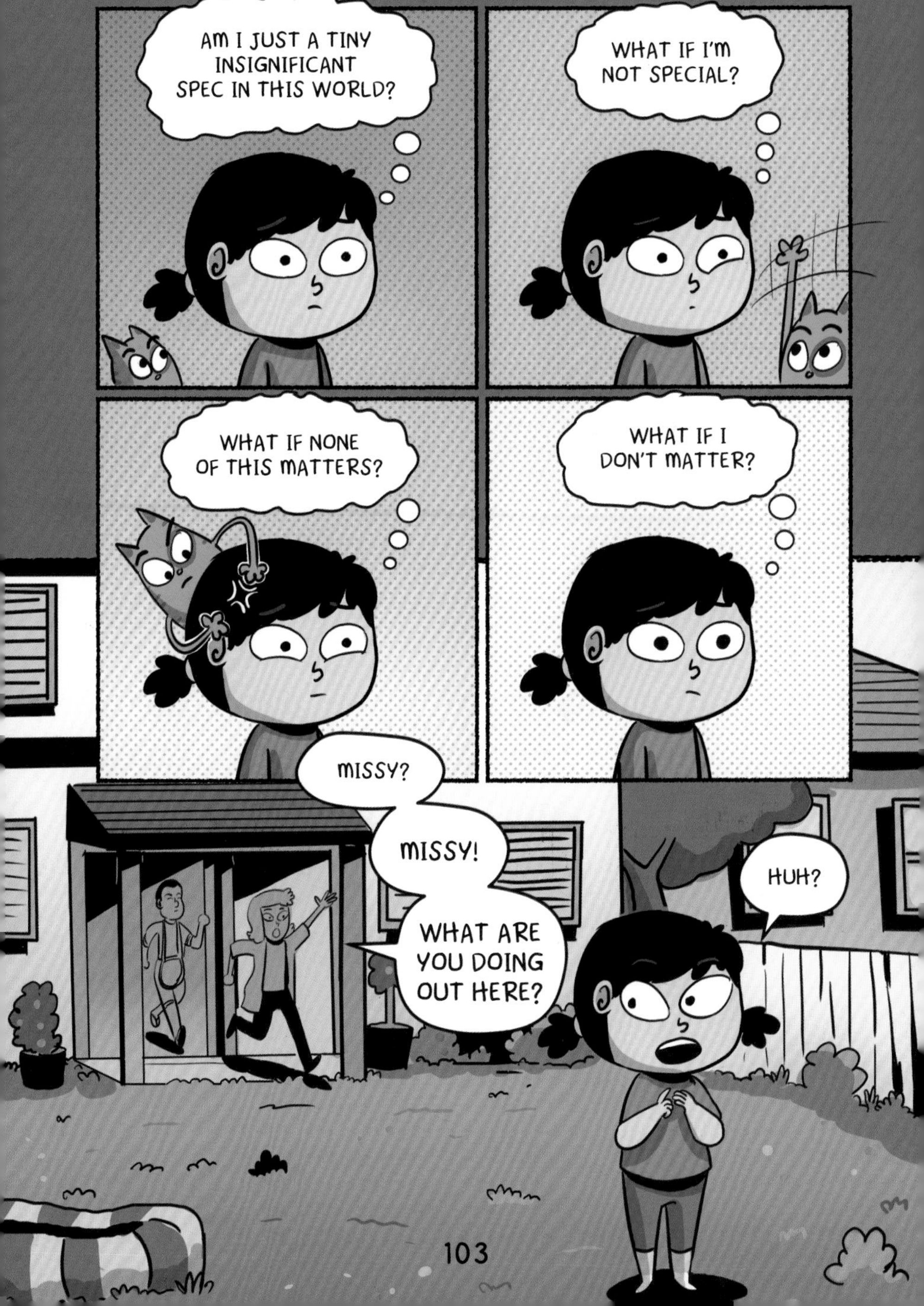
AM I JUST A TINY INSIGNIFICANT SPEC IN THIS WORLD?
WHAT IF I'M NOT SPECIAL?
WHAT IF NONE OF THIS MATTERS?
WHAT IF I DON'T MATTER?
MISSY?
MISSY!
WHAT ARE YOU DOING OUT HERE?
HUH?

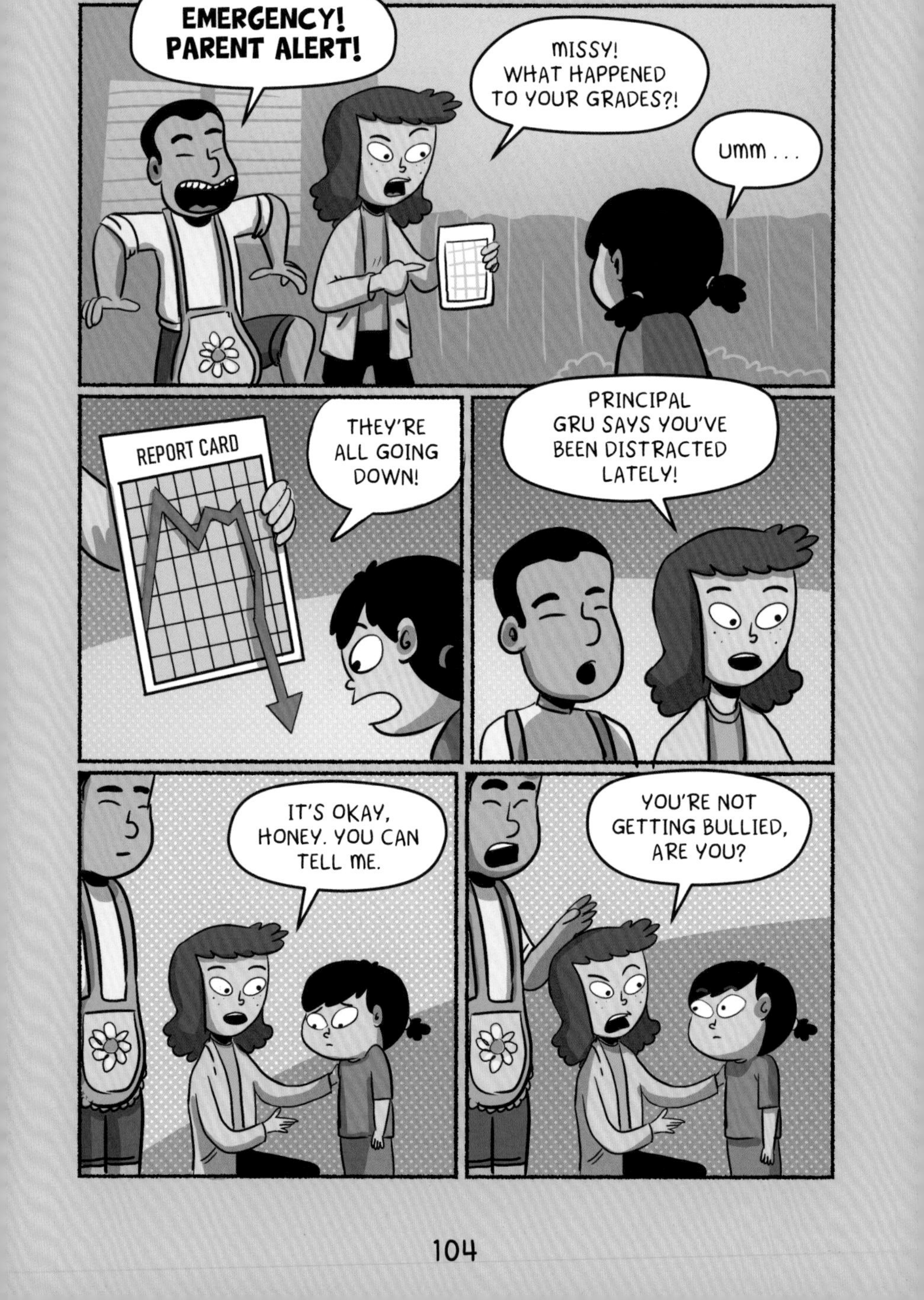
EMERGENCY! PARENT ALERT!
MISSY! WHAT HAPPENED TO YOUR GRADES?!
UMM . . .
REPORT CARD
THEY'RE ALL GOING DOWN!
PRINCIPAL GRU SAYS YOU'VE BEEN DISTRACTED LATELY!
IT'S OKAY, HONEY. YOU CAN TELL ME.
YOU'RE NOT GETTING BULLIED, ARE YOU?

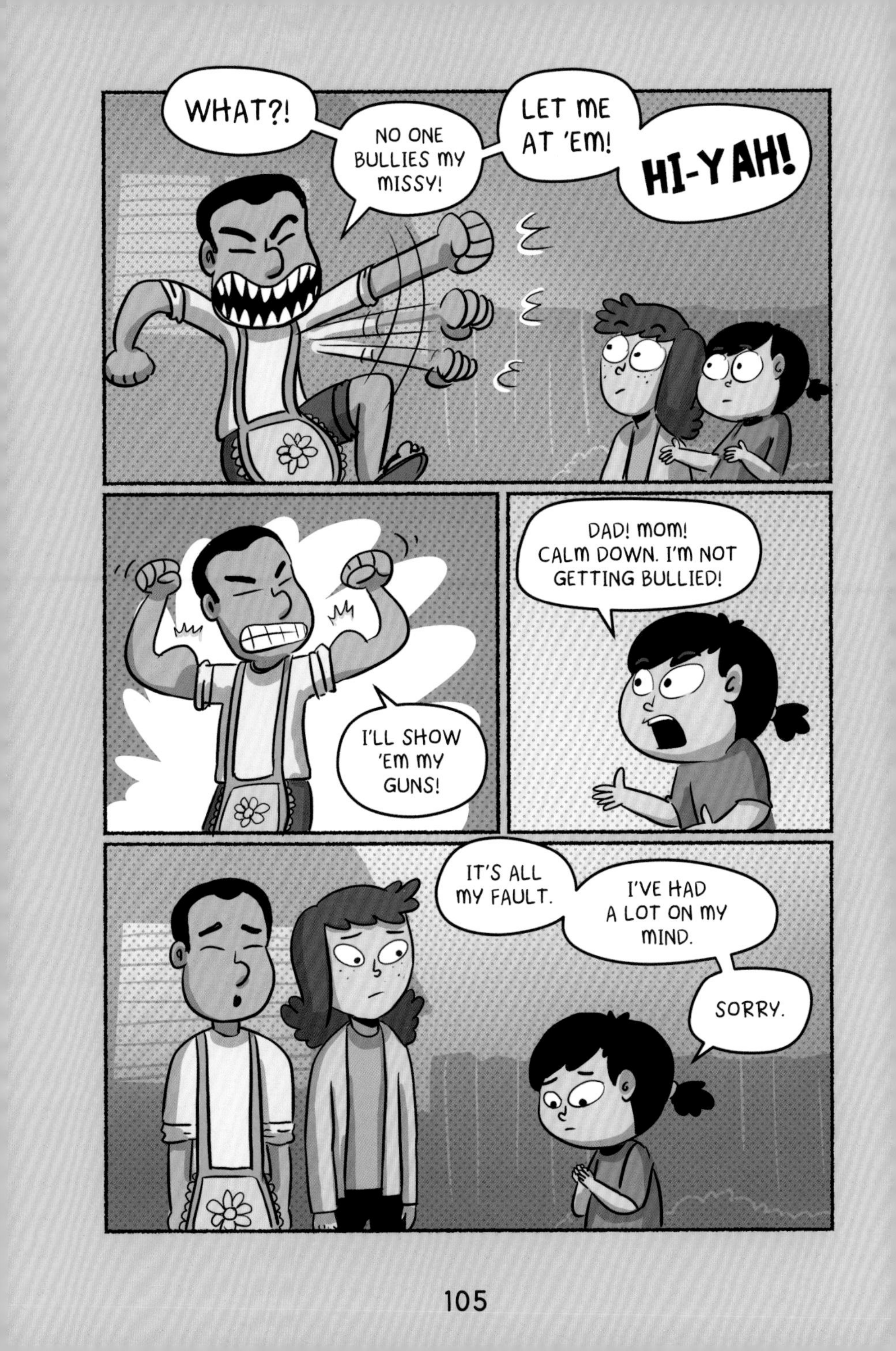
WHAT?!
NO ONE BULLIES MY MISSY!
LET ME AT 'EM!
HI-YAH!
DAD! MOM! CALM DOWN. I'M NOT GETTING BULLIED!
I'LL SHOW 'EM MY GUNS!
IT'S ALL MY FAULT.
I'VE HAD A LOT ON MY MIND.
SORRY.

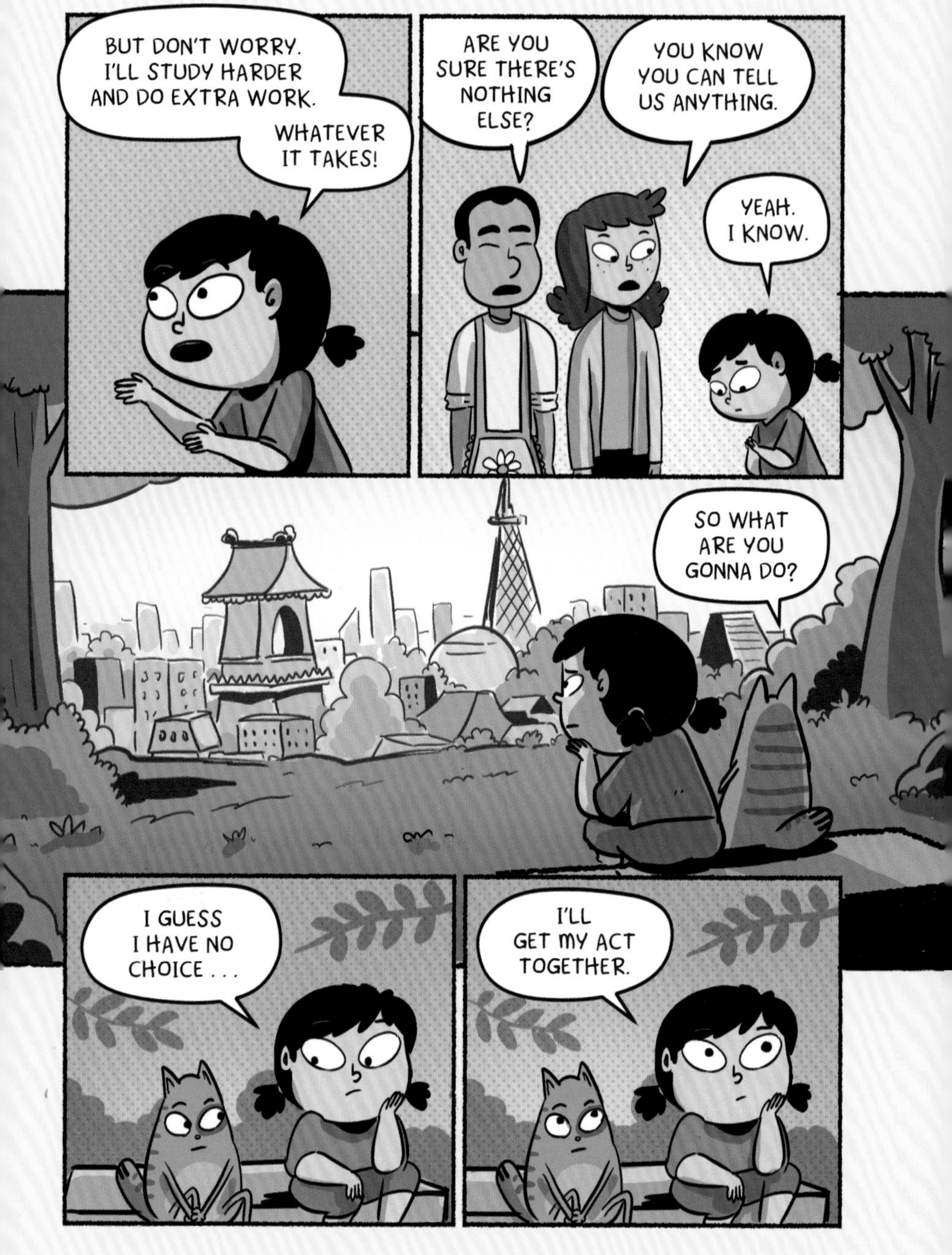
BUT DON'T WORRY. I'LL STUDY HARDER AND DO EXTRA WORK.
WHATEVER IT TAKES!
ARE YOU SURE THERE'S NOTHING ELSE?
YOU KNOW YOU CAN TELL US ANYTHING.
YEAH. I KNOW.
SO WHAT ARE YOU GONNA DO?
I GUESS I HAVE NO CHOICE . . .
I'LL GET MY ACT TOGETHER.

CHAPTER 7

TURNING A NEW FEATHER

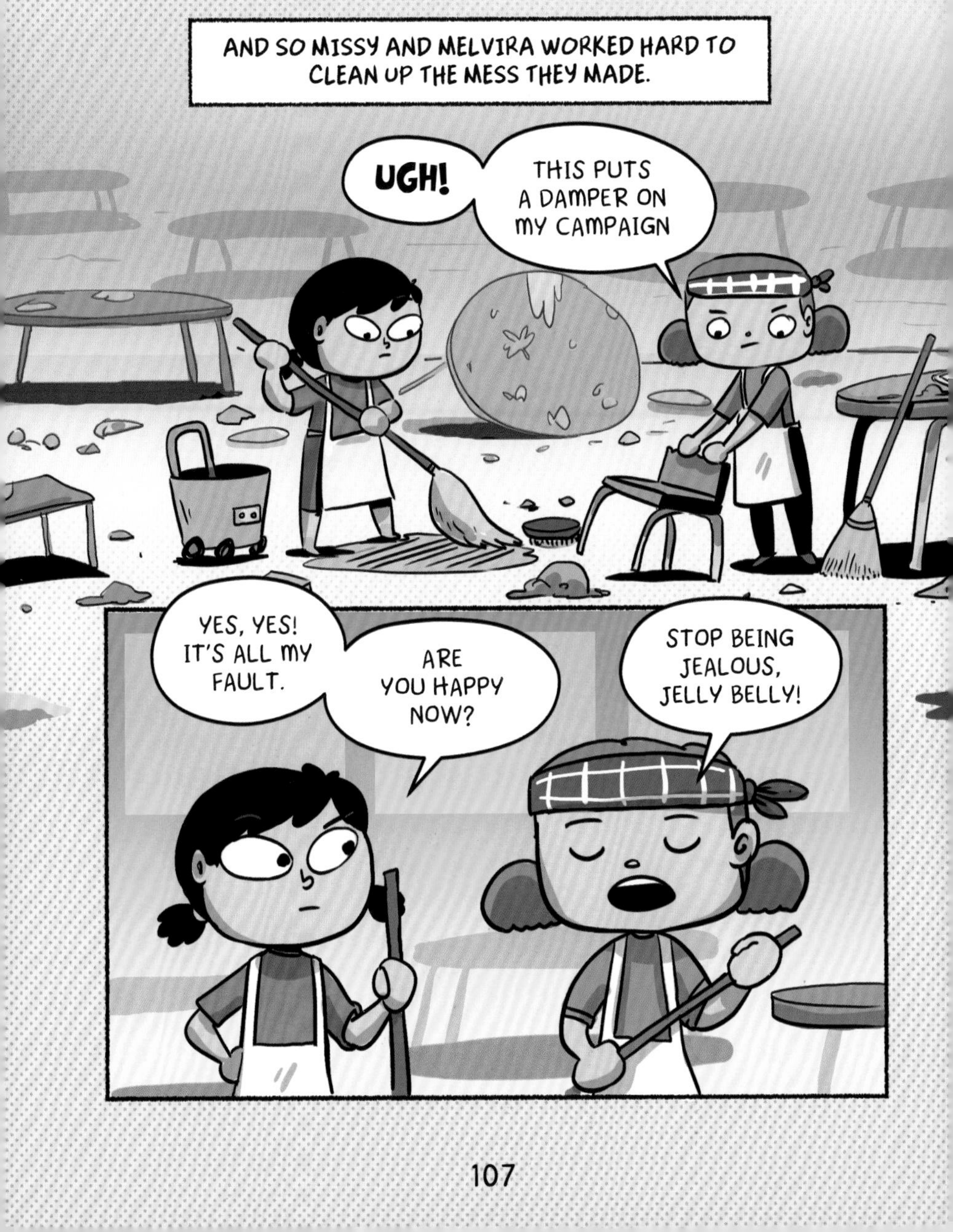
AND SO MISSY AND MELVIRA WORKED HARD TO CLEAN UP THE MESS THEY MADE.
UGH!
THIS PUTS A DAMPER ON MY CAMPAIGN
YES, YES! IT'S ALL MY FAULT.
ARE YOU HAPPY NOW?
STOP BEING JEALOUS, JELLY BELLY!

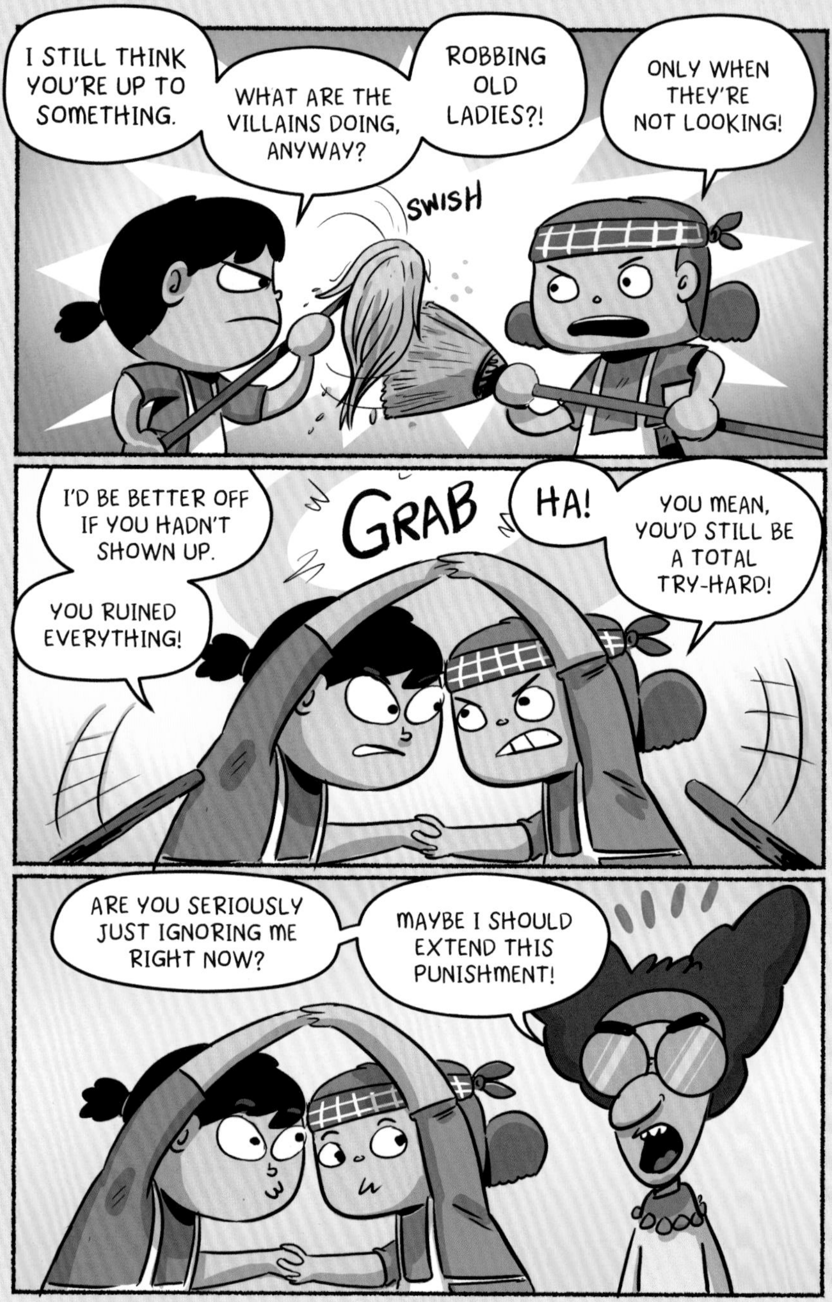
I STILL THINK YOU'RE UP TO SOMETHING.
WHAT ARE THE VILLAINS DOING, ANYWAY?
ROBBING OLD LADIES?!
ONLY WHEN THEY'RE NOT LOOKING!
SWISH
GRAB
I'D BE BETTER OFF IF YOU HADN'T SHOWN UP.
YOU RUINED EVERYTHING!
HA!
YOU MEAN, YOU'D STILL BE A TOTAL TRY-HARD!
ARE YOU SERIOUSLY JUST IGNORING ME RIGHT NOW?
MAYBE I SHOULD EXTEND THIS PUNISHMENT!

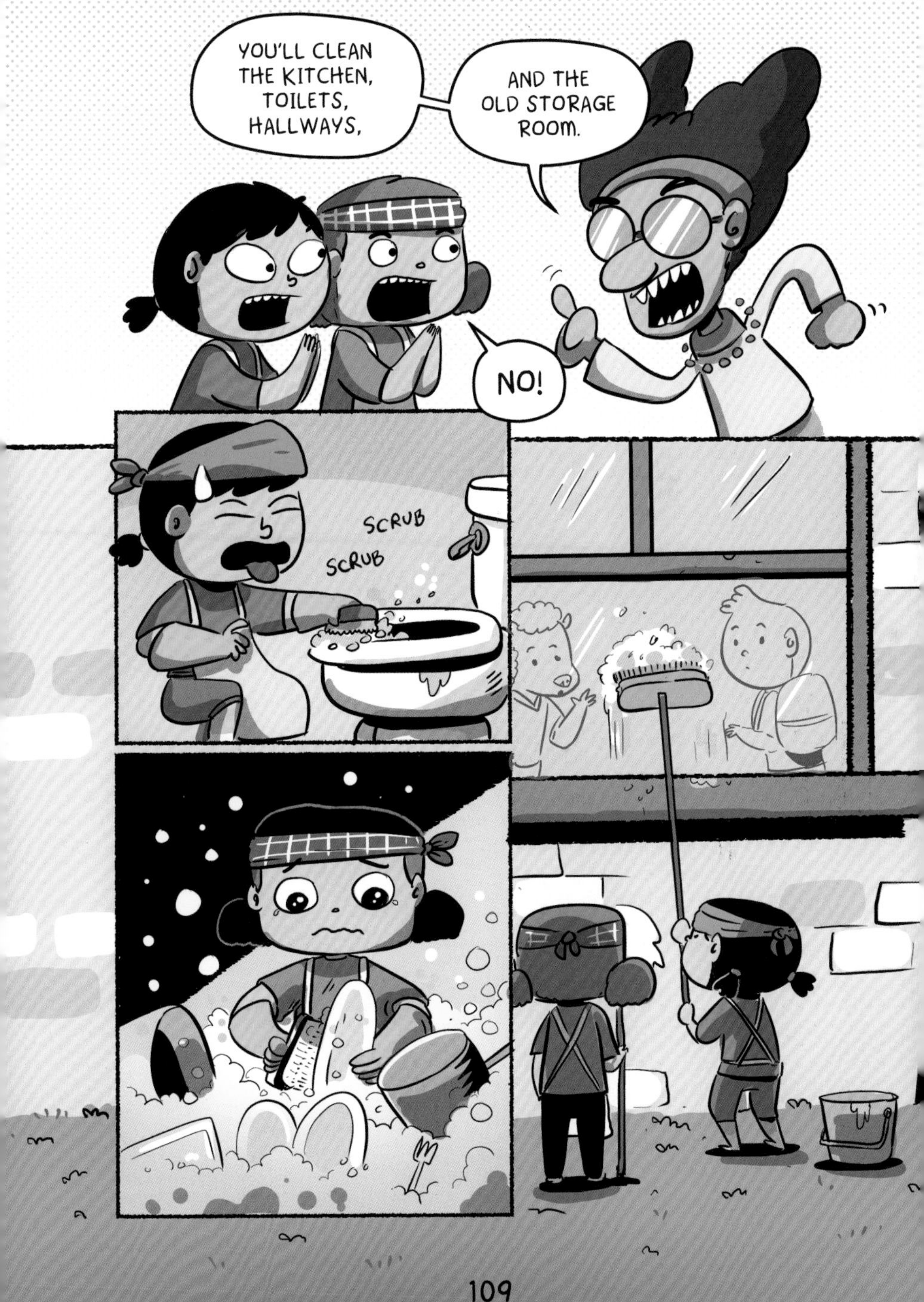
YOU'LL CLEAN THE KITCHEN, TOILETS, HALLWAYS,
AND THE OLD STORAGE ROOM.
NO!
SCRUB
SCRUB

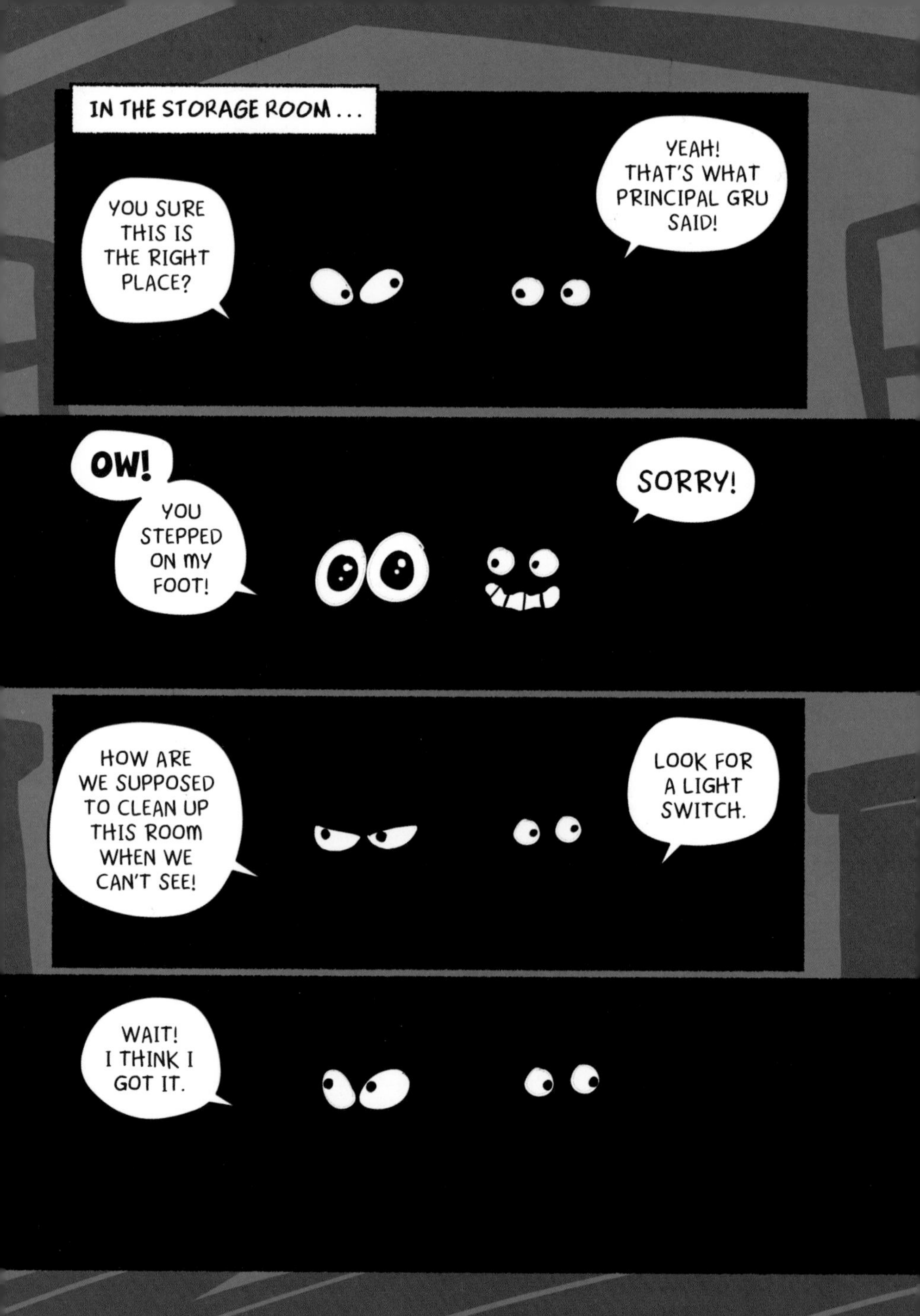
IN THE STORAGE ROOM . . .
YOU SURE THIS IS THE RIGHT PLACE?
YEAH! THAT'S WHAT PRINCIPAL GRU SAID!
OW!
YOU STEPPED ON MY FOOT!
SORRY!
HOW ARE WE SUPPOSED TO CLEAN UP THIS ROOM WHEN WE CAN'T SEE!
LOOK FOR A LIGHT SWITCH.
WAIT! I THINK I GOT IT.

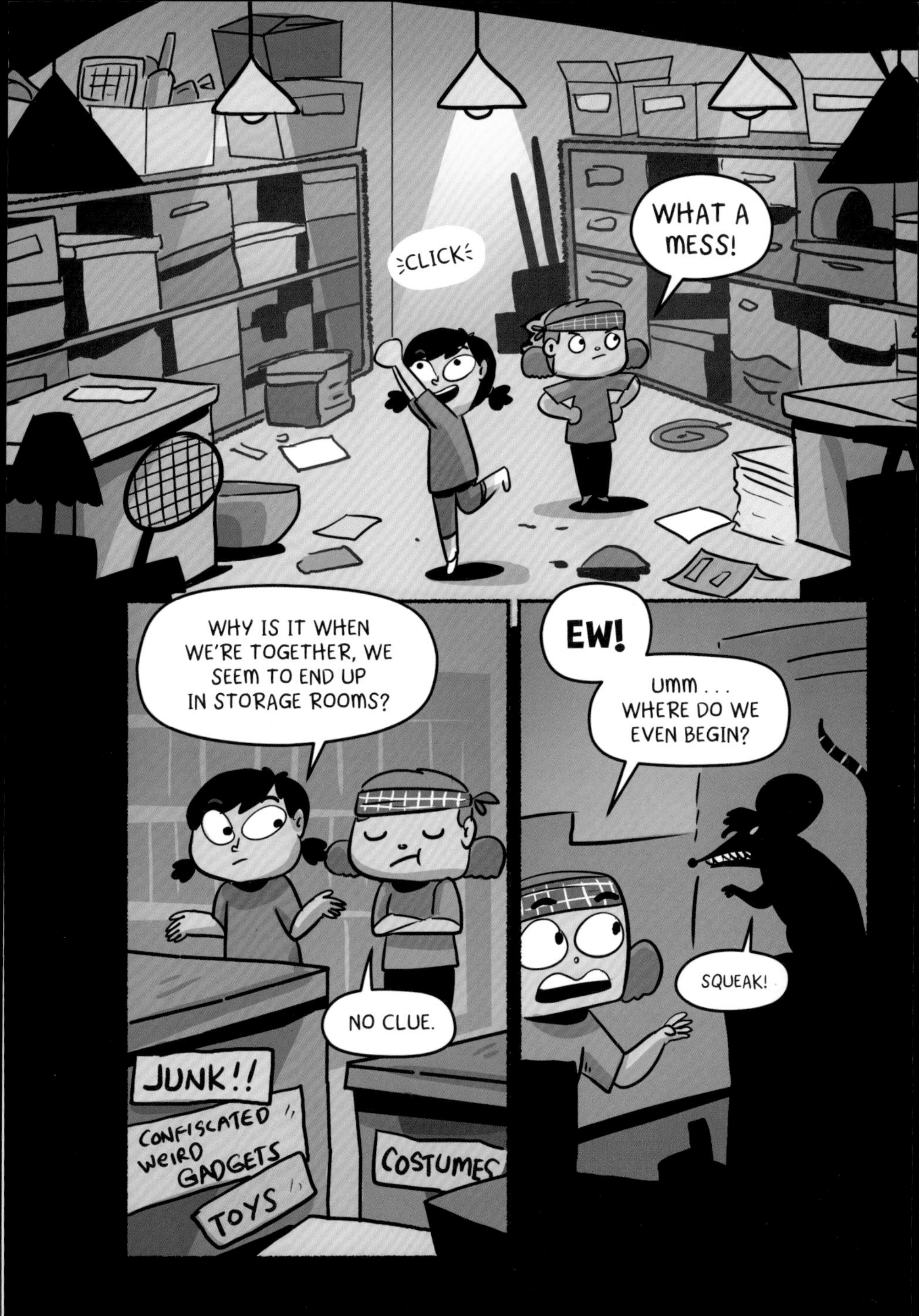
CLICK
WHAT A MESS!
WHY IS IT WHEN WE'RE TOGETHER, WE SEEM TO END UP IN STORAGE ROOMS?
NO CLUE.
JUNK!!
CONFISCATED WEIRD GADGETS
TOYS
COSTUMES
EW!
Umm . . . WHERE DO WE EVEN BEGIN?
SQUEAK!

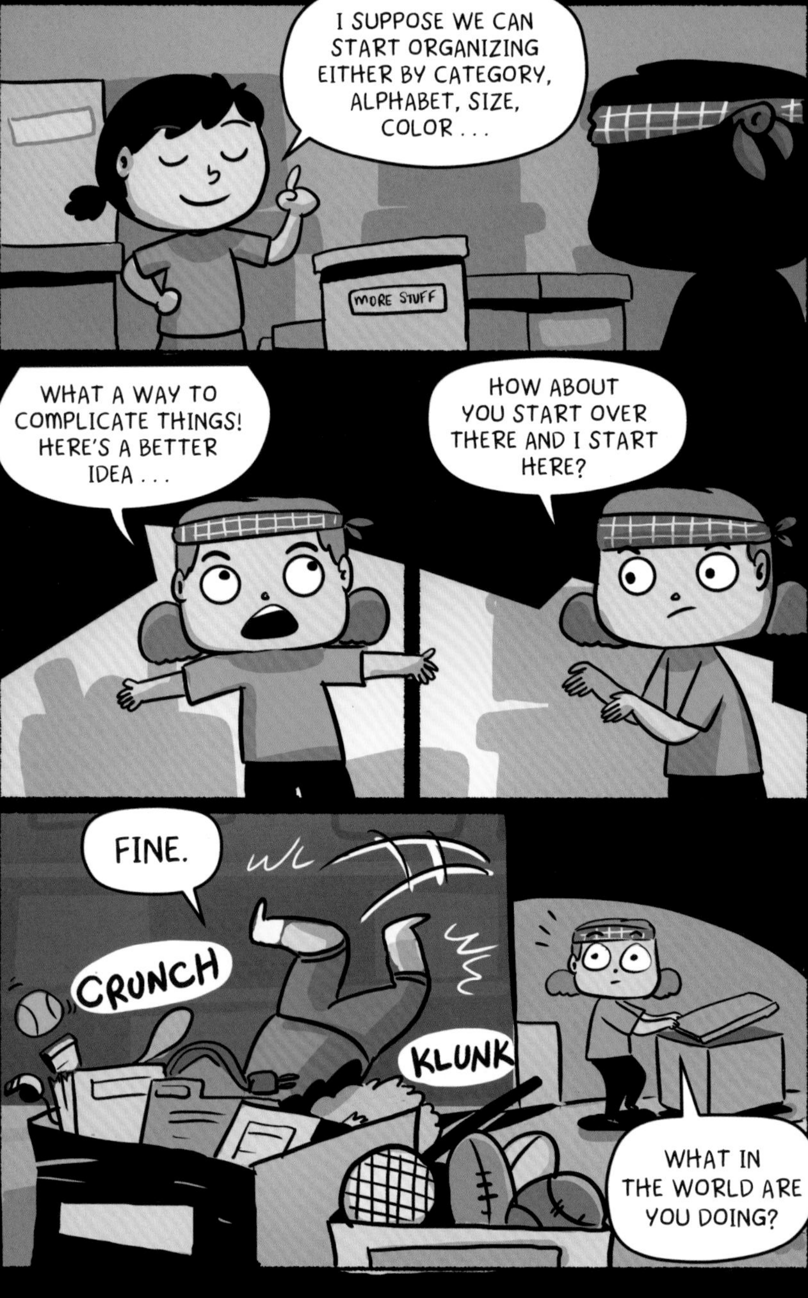

I SUPPOSE WE CAN START ORGANIZING EITHER BY CATEGORY, ALPHABET, SIZE, COLOR . . .
MORE STUFF
WHAT A WAY TO COMPLICATE THINGS! HERE'S A BETTER IDEA . . .
HOW ABOUT YOU START OVER THERE AND I START HERE?
FINE.
CRUNCH
KLUNK
WHAT IN THE WORLD ARE YOU DOING?

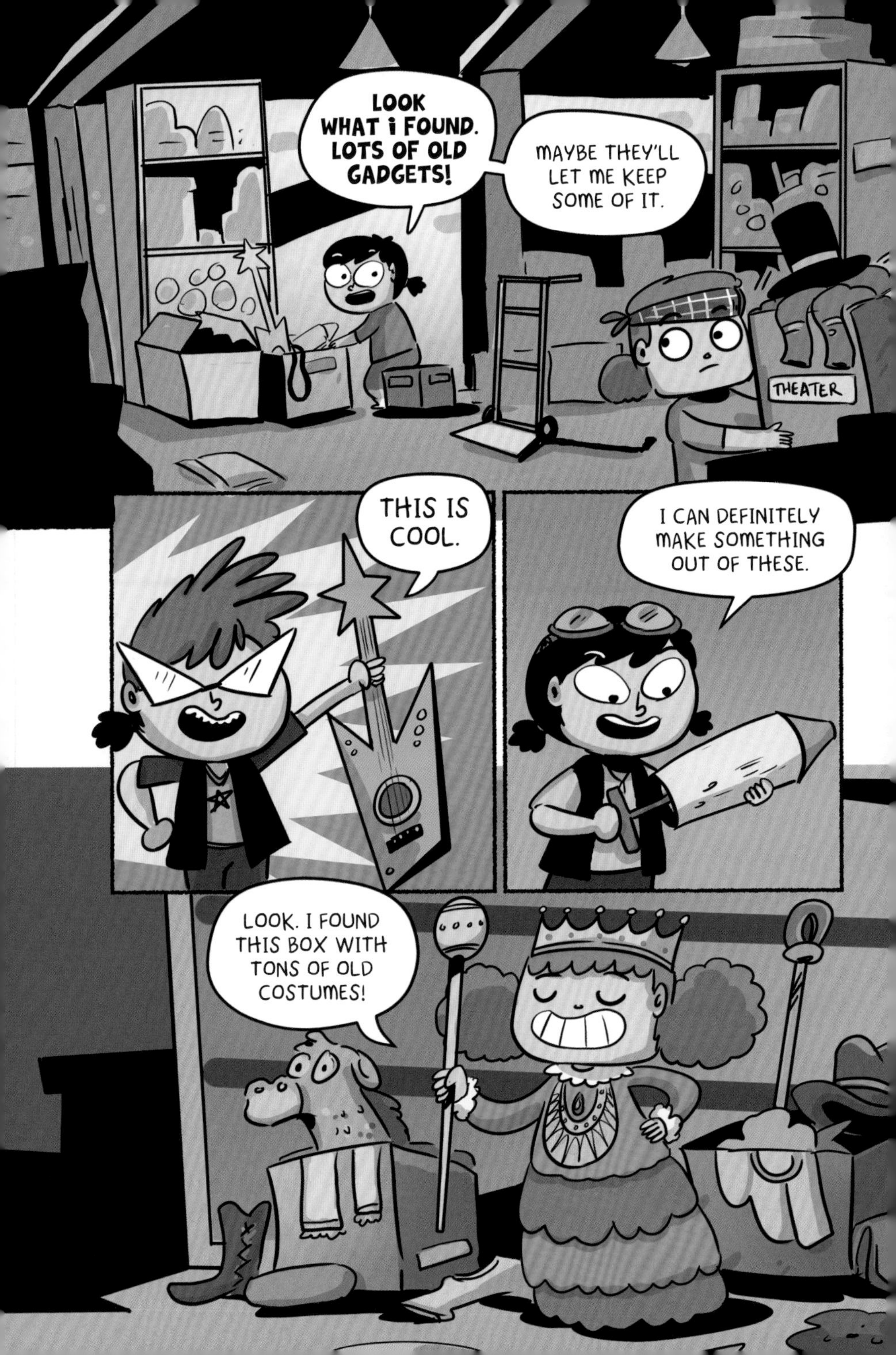
LOOK WHAT I FOUND. LOTS OF OLD GADGETS!
MAYBE THEY'LL LET ME KEEP SOME OF IT.
THEATER
THIS IS COOL.
I CAN DEFINITELY MAKE SOMETHING OUT OF THESE.
LOOK. I FOUND THIS BOX WITH TONS OF OLD COSTUMES!

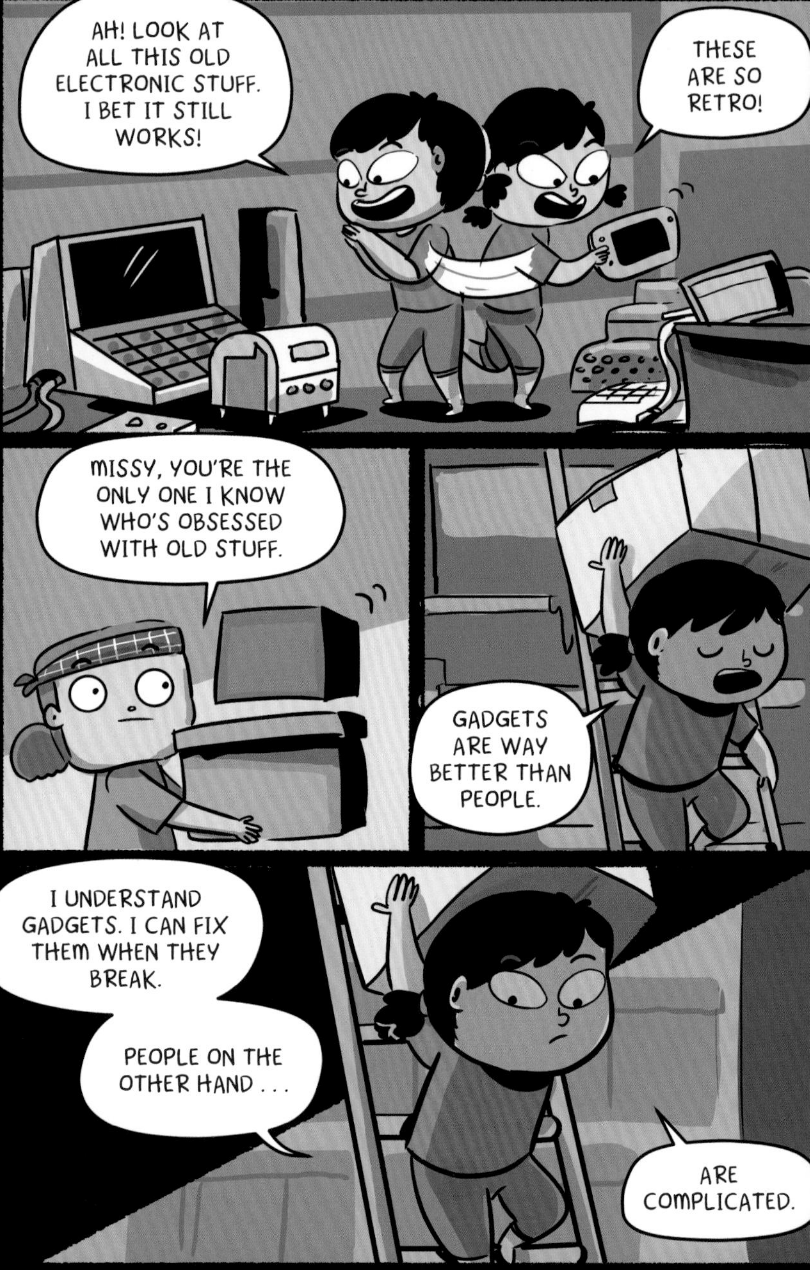
AH! LOOK AT ALL THIS OLD ELECTRONIC STUFF. I BET IT STILL WORKS!
THESE ARE SO RETRO!
MISSY, YOU'RE THE ONLY ONE I KNOW WHO'S OBSESSED WITH OLD STUFF.
GADGETS ARE WAY BETTER THAN PEOPLE.
I UNDERSTAND GADGETS. I CAN FIX THEM WHEN THEY BREAK.
PEOPLE ON THE OTHER HAND . . .
ARE COMPLICATED.

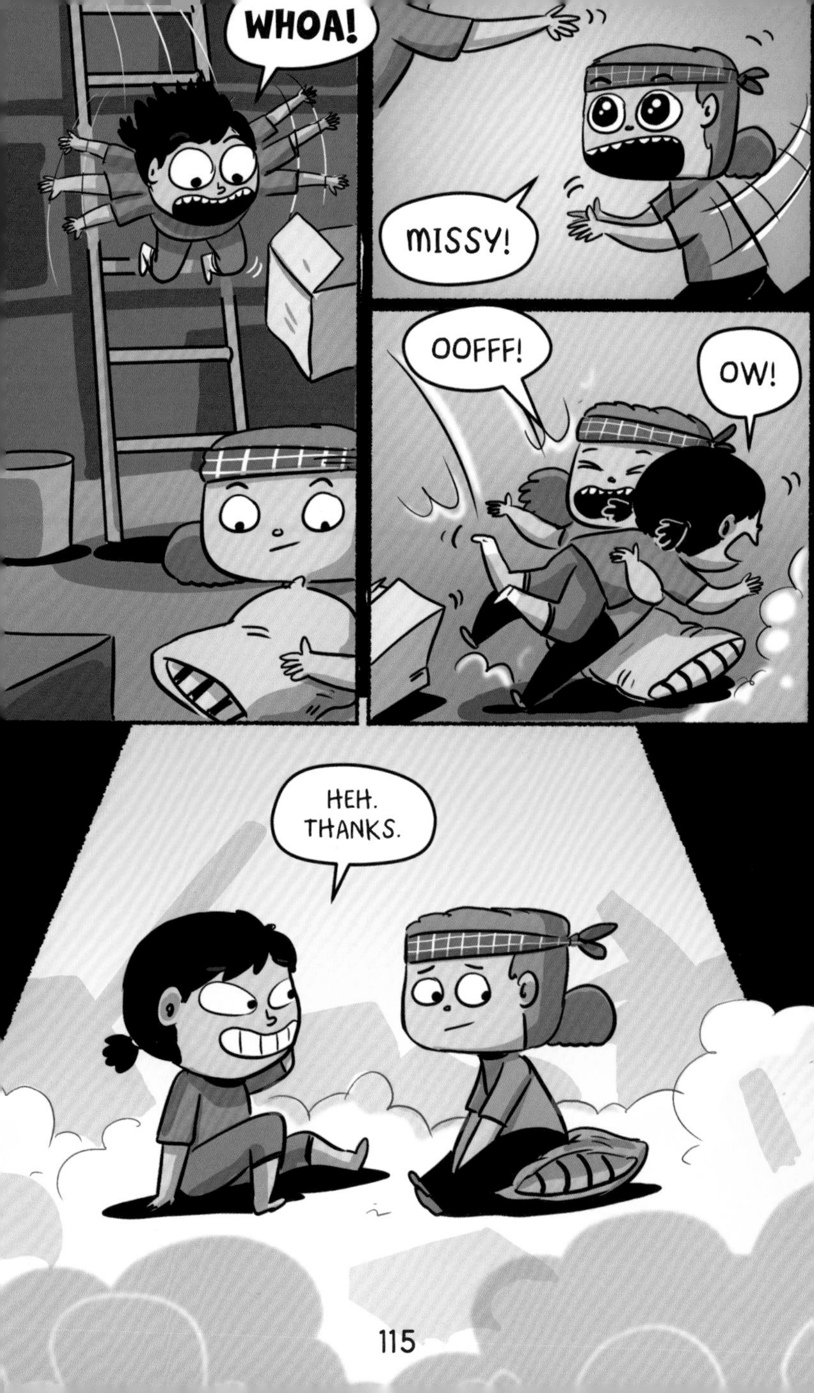
WHOA!
MISSY!
OOFFF!
OW!
HEH. THANKS.

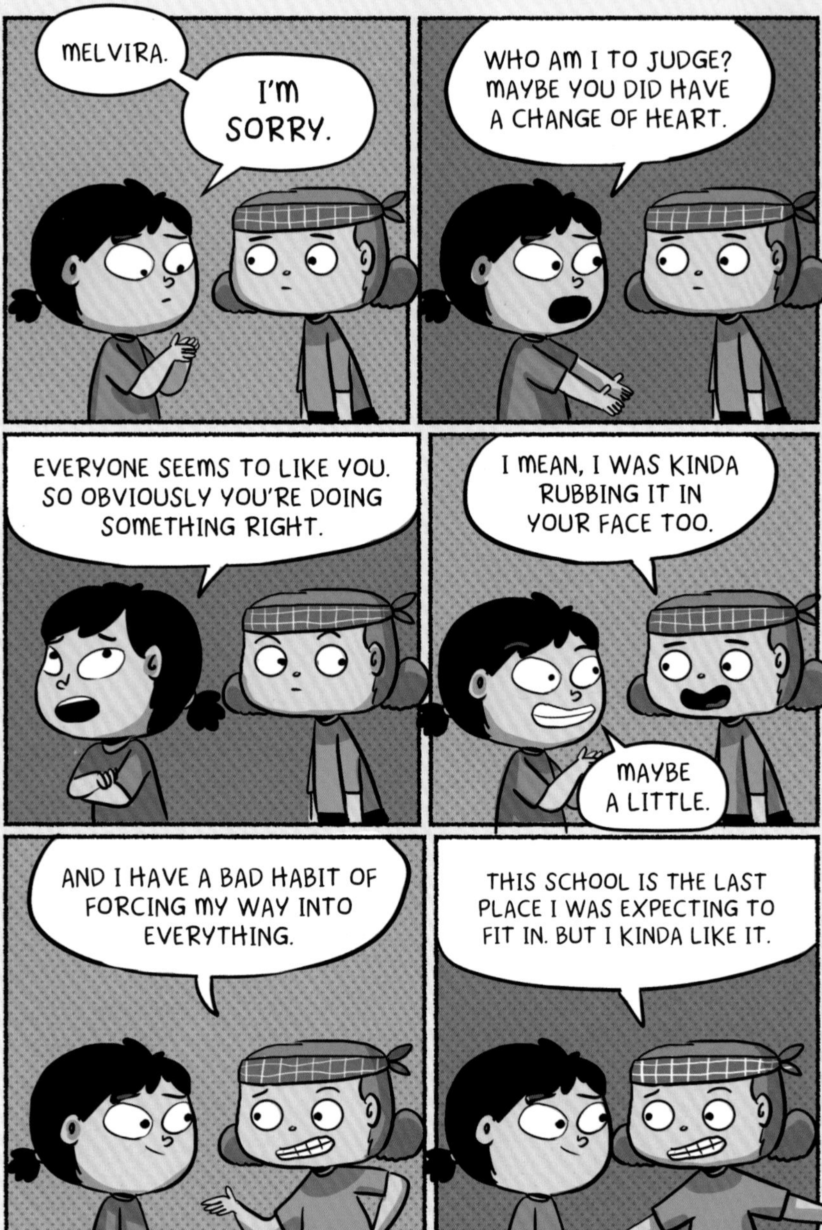
MELVIRA.
I'M SORRY.
WHO AM I TO JUDGE? MAYBE YOU DID HAVE A CHANGE OF HEART.
EVERYONE SEEMS TO LIKE YOU. SO OBVIOUSLY YOU'RE DOING SOMETHING RIGHT.
I MEAN, I WAS KINDA RUBBING IT IN YOUR FACE TOO.
MAYBE A LITTLE.
AND I HAVE A BAD HABIT OF FORCING MY WAY INTO EVERYTHING.
THIS SCHOOL IS THE LAST PLACE I WAS EXPECTING TO FIT IN. BUT I KINDA LIKE IT.

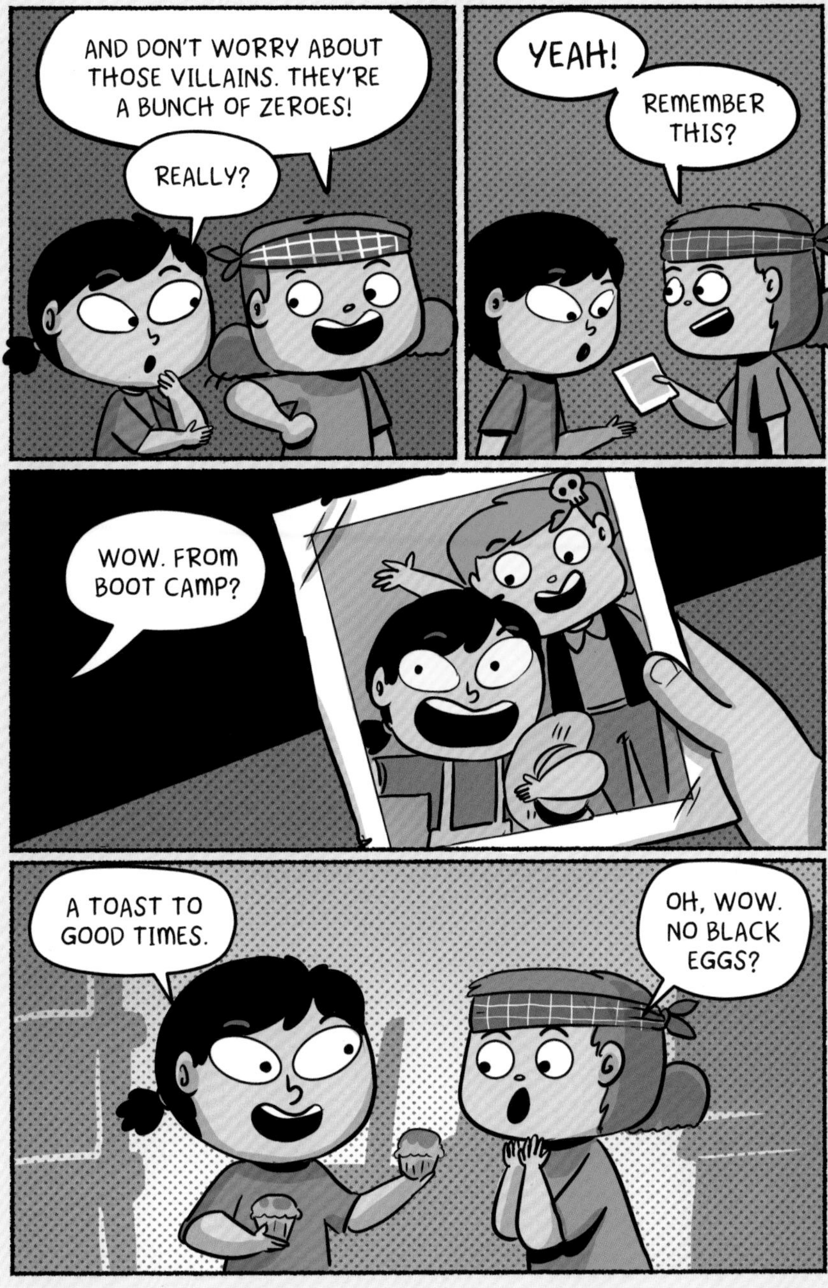
AND DON'T WORRY ABOUT THOSE VILLAINS. THEY'RE A BUNCH OF ZEROES!
REALLY?
YEAH!
REMEMBER THIS?
WOW. FROM BOOT CAMP?
A TOAST TO GOOD TIMES.
OH, WOW. NO BLACK EGGS?

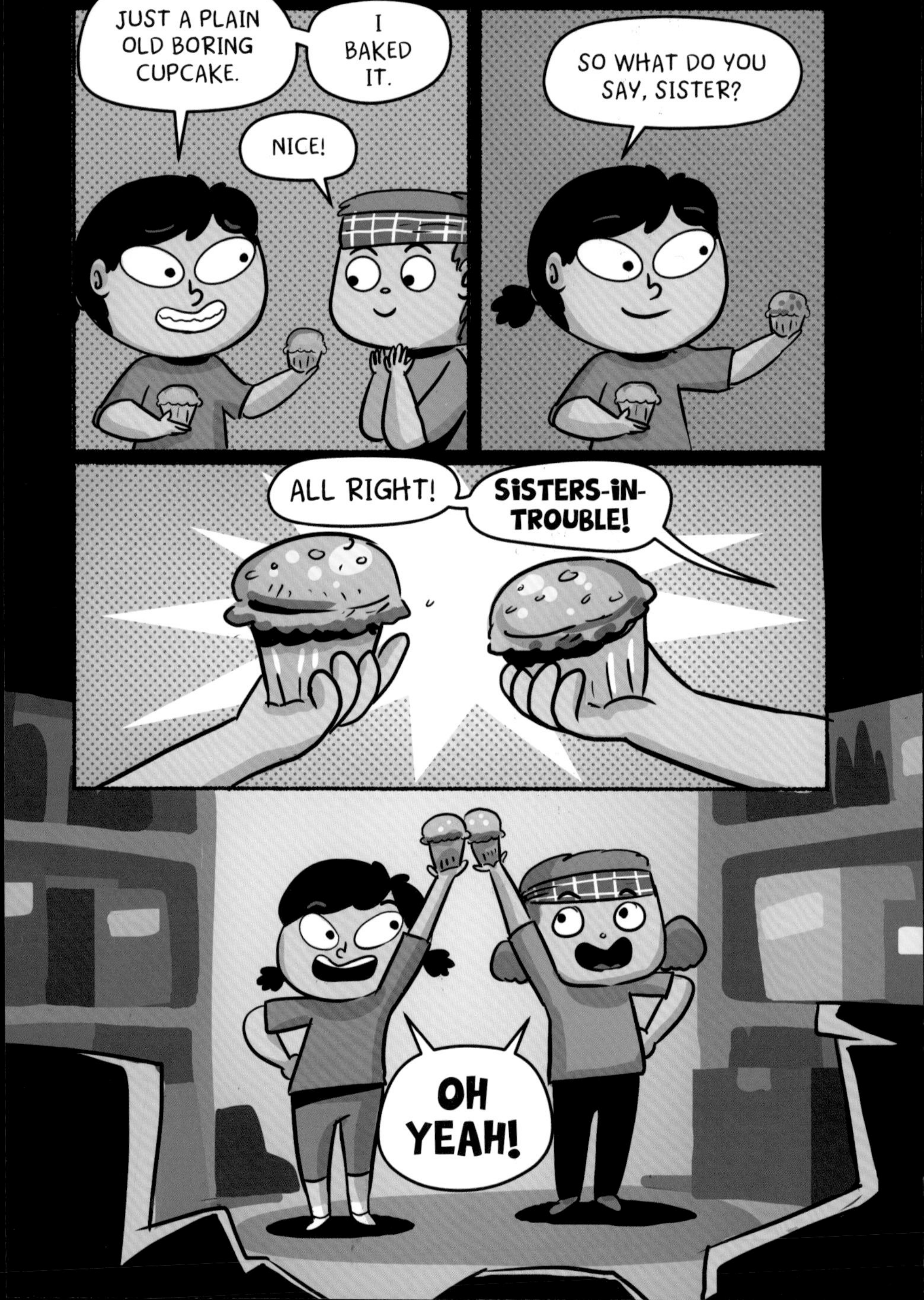
JUST A PLAIN OLD BORING CUPCAKE.
I BAKED IT.
NICE!
SO WHAT DO YOU SAY, SISTER?
ALL RIGHT!
SISTERS-IN-TROUBLE!
OH YEAH!

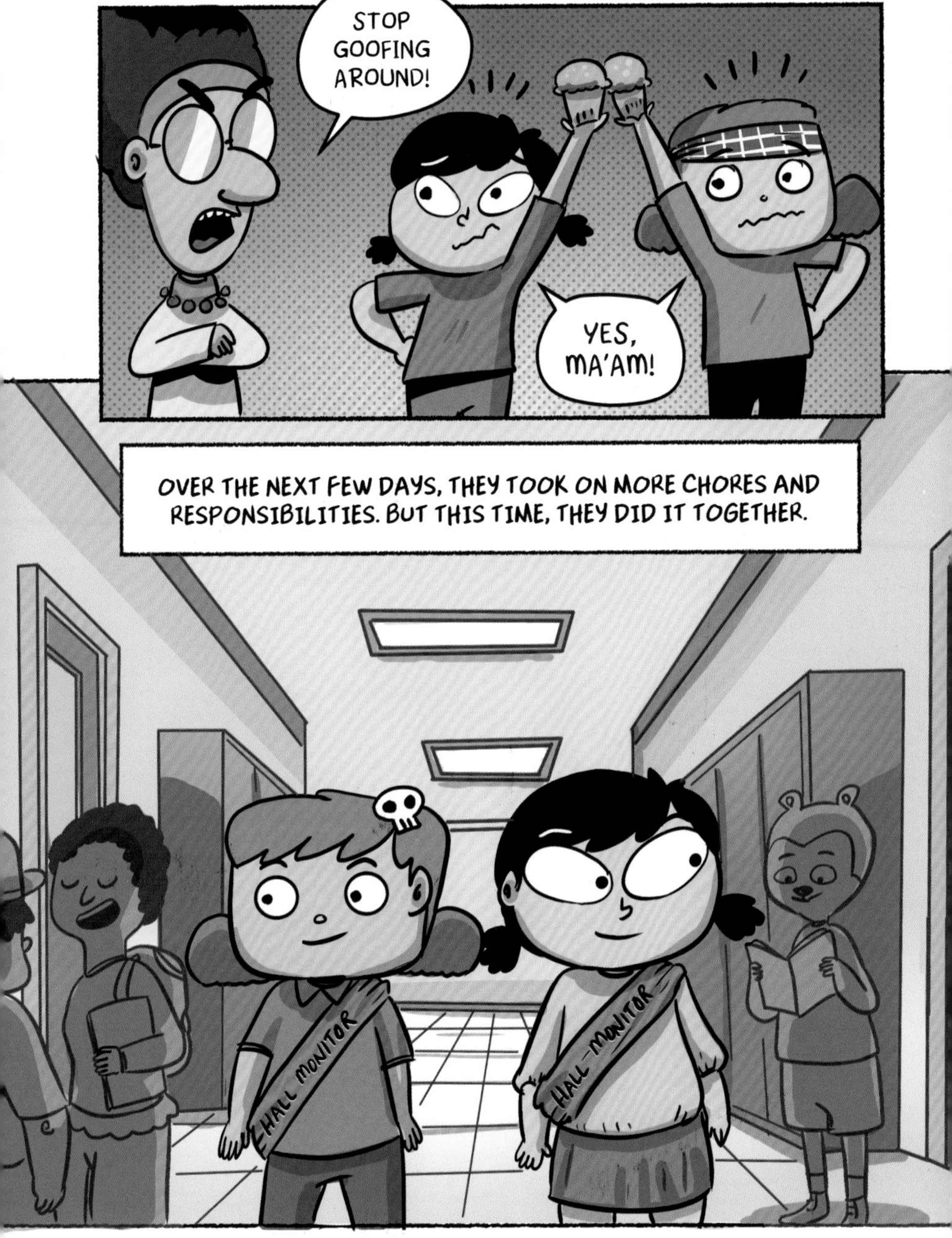
STOP GOOFING AROUND!
YES, MA'AM!
OVER THE NEXT FEW DAYS, THEY TOOK ON MORE CHORES AND RESPONSIBILITIES. BUT THIS TIME, THEY DID IT TOGETHER.
HALL MONITOR
HALL-MONITOR

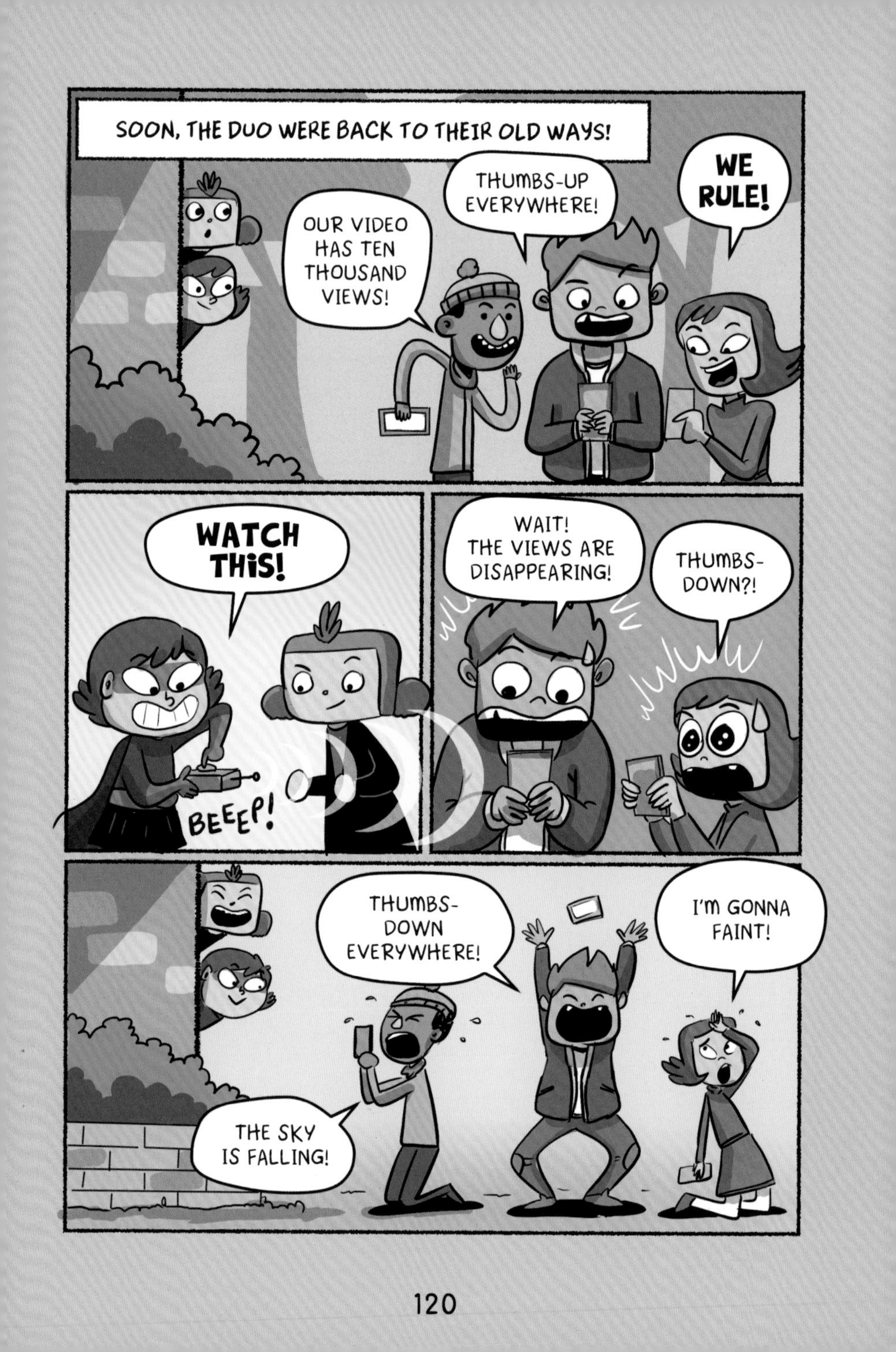
SOON, THE DUO WERE BACK TO THEIR OLD WAYS!
OUR VIDEO HAS TEN THOUSAND VIEWS!
THUMBS-UP EVERYWHERE!
WE RULE!
WATCH THIS!
BEEEP!
WAIT! THE VIEWS ARE DISAPPEARING!
THUMBS-DOWN?!
THUMBS-DOWN EVERYWHERE!
I'M GONNA FAINT!
THE SKY IS FALLING!

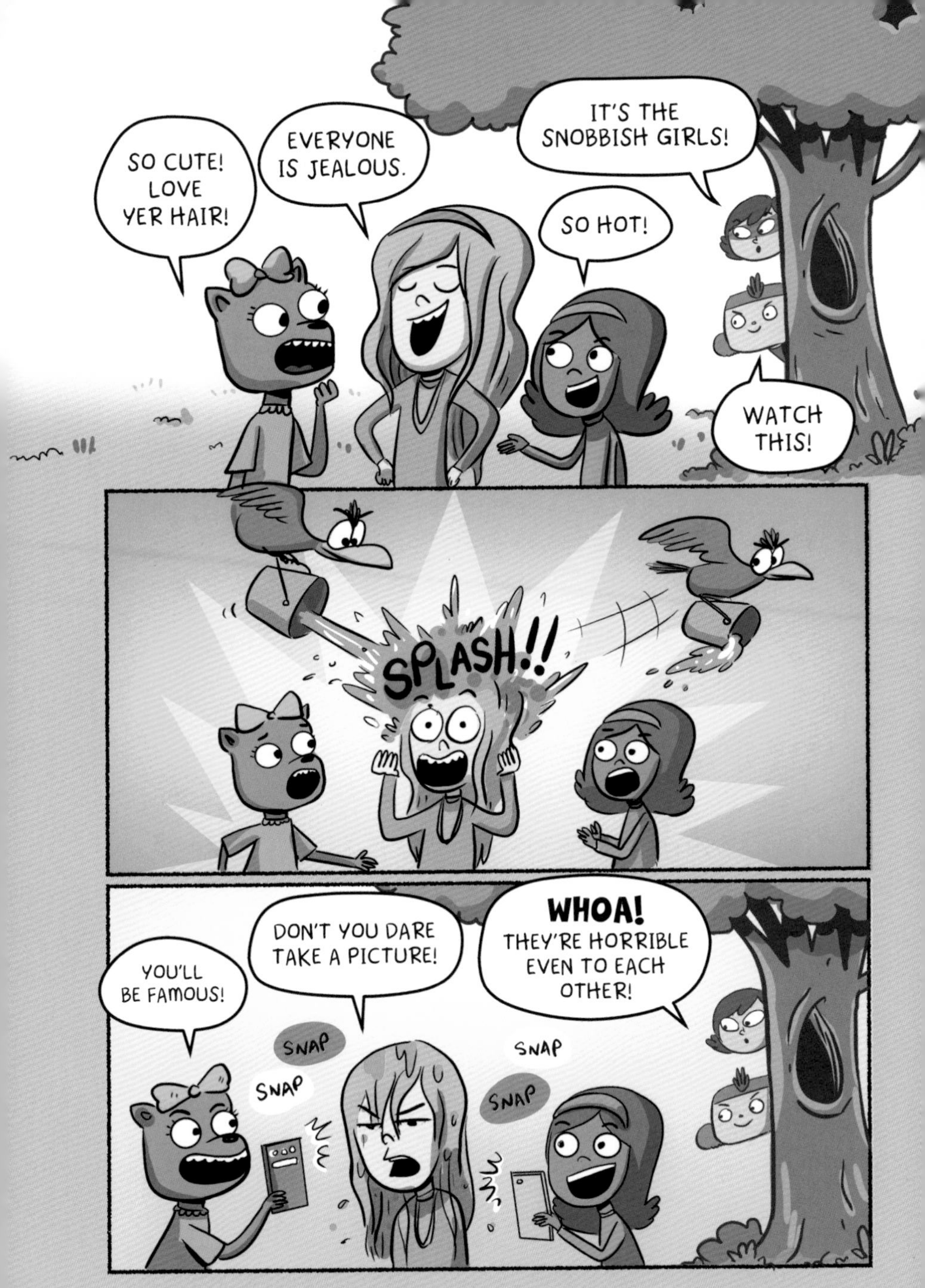
SO CUTE! LOVE YER HAIR!
EVERYONE IS JEALOUS.
SO HOT!
IT'S THE SNOBBISH GIRLS!
WATCH THIS!
SPLASH!!
YOU'LL BE FAMOUS!
DON'T YOU DARE TAKE A PICTURE!
WHOA! THEY'RE HORRIBLE EVEN TO EACH OTHER!
SNAP
SNAP
SNAP
SNAP

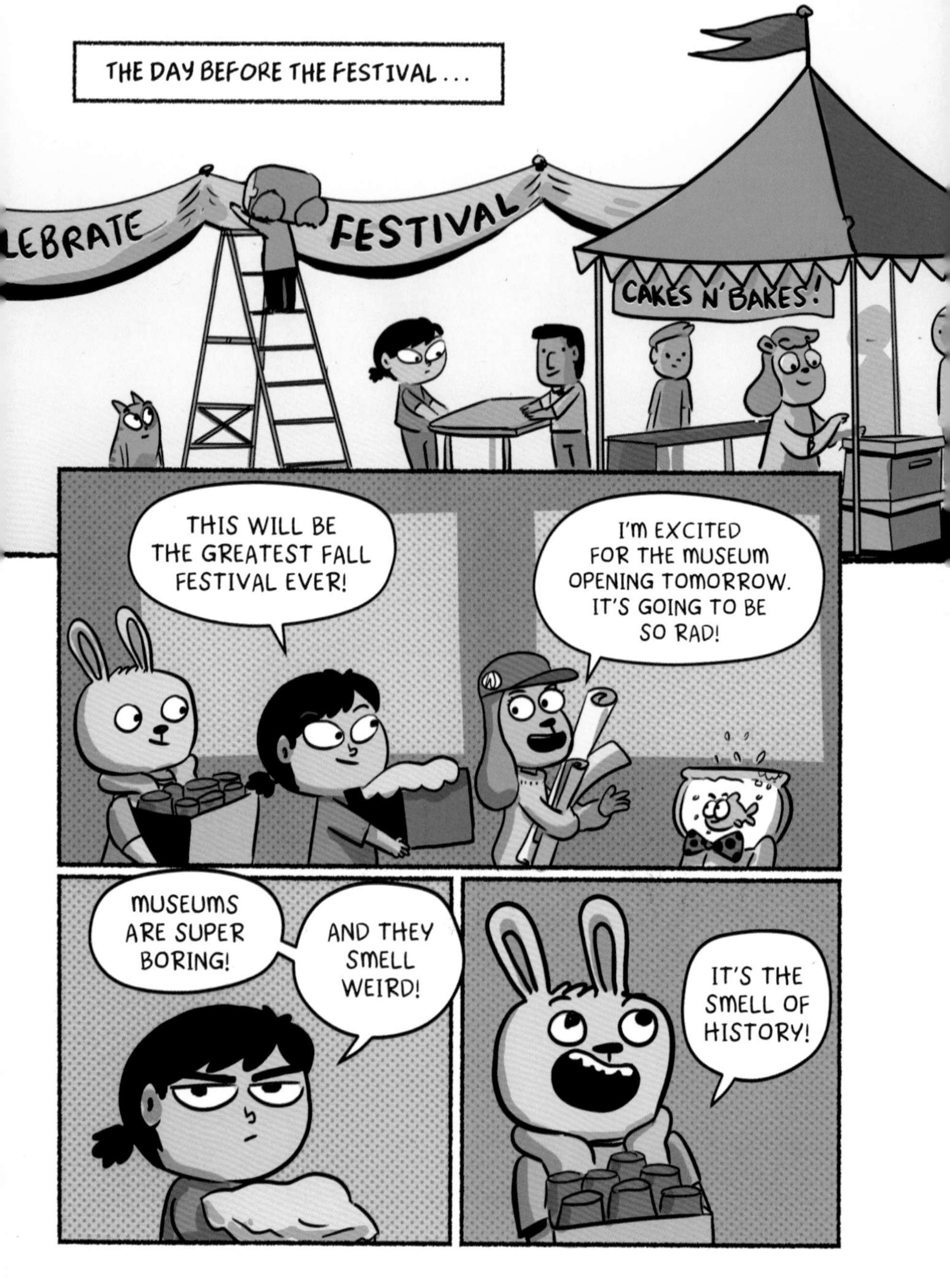
THE DAY BEFORE THE FESTIVAL . . .
LEBRATE
FESTIVAL
CAKES N' BAKES!
THIS WILL BE THE GREATEST FALL FESTIVAL EVER!
I'M EXCITED FOR THE MUSEUM OPENING TOMORROW. IT'S GOING TO BE SO RAD!
MUSEUMS ARE SUPER BORING!
AND THEY SMELL WEIRD!
IT'S THE SMELL OF HISTORY!

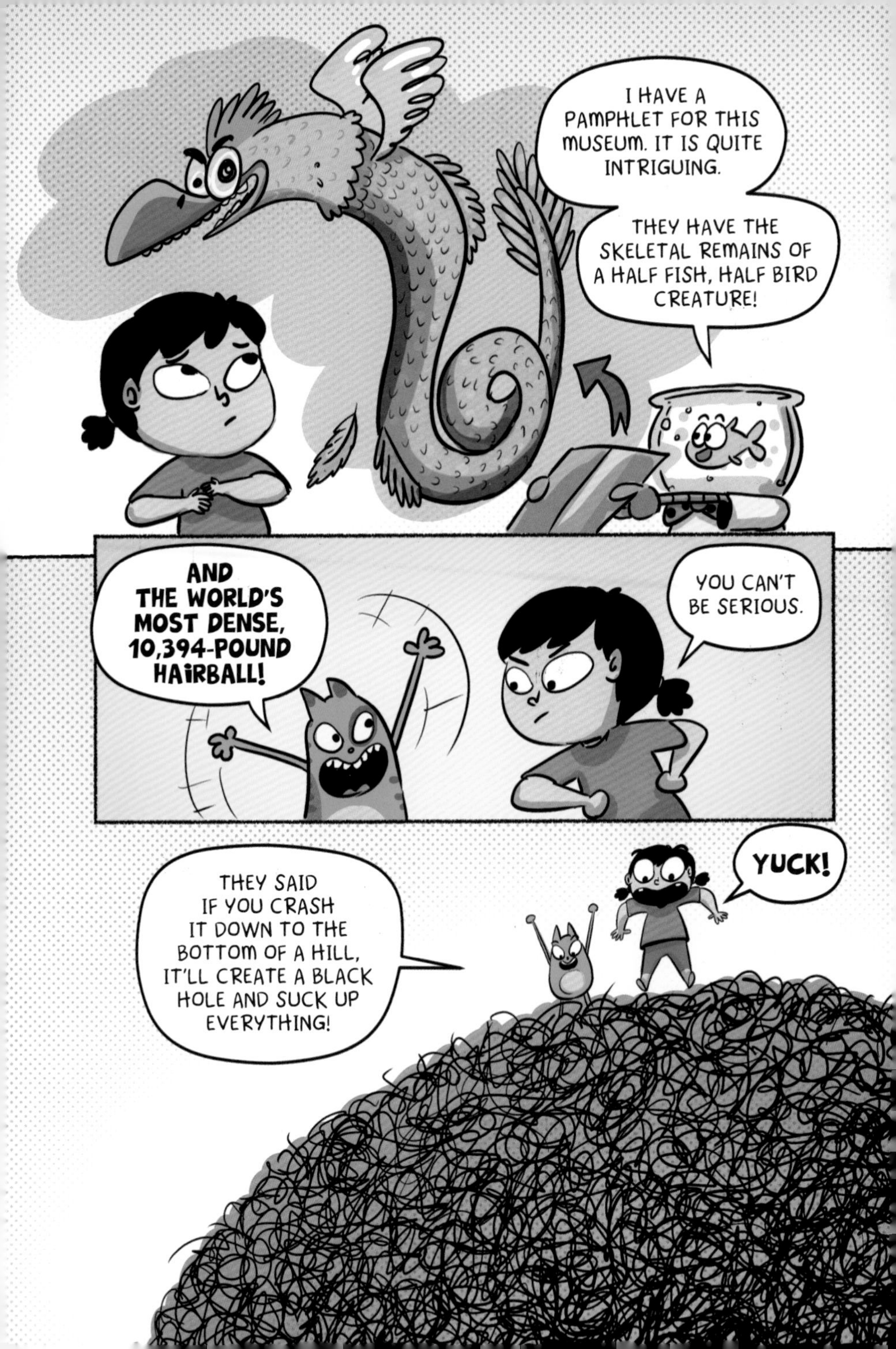
I HAVE A PAMPHLET FOR THIS MUSEUM. IT IS QUITE INTRIGUING.
THEY HAVE THE SKELETAL REMAINS OF A HALF FISH, HALF BIRD CREATURE!
AND THE WORLD'S MOST DENSE, 10,394-POUND HAIRBALL!
YOU CAN'T BE SERIOUS.
THEY SAID IF YOU CRASH IT DOWN TO THE BOTTOM OF A HILL, IT'LL CREATE A BLACK HOLE AND SUCK UP EVERYTHING!
YUCK!

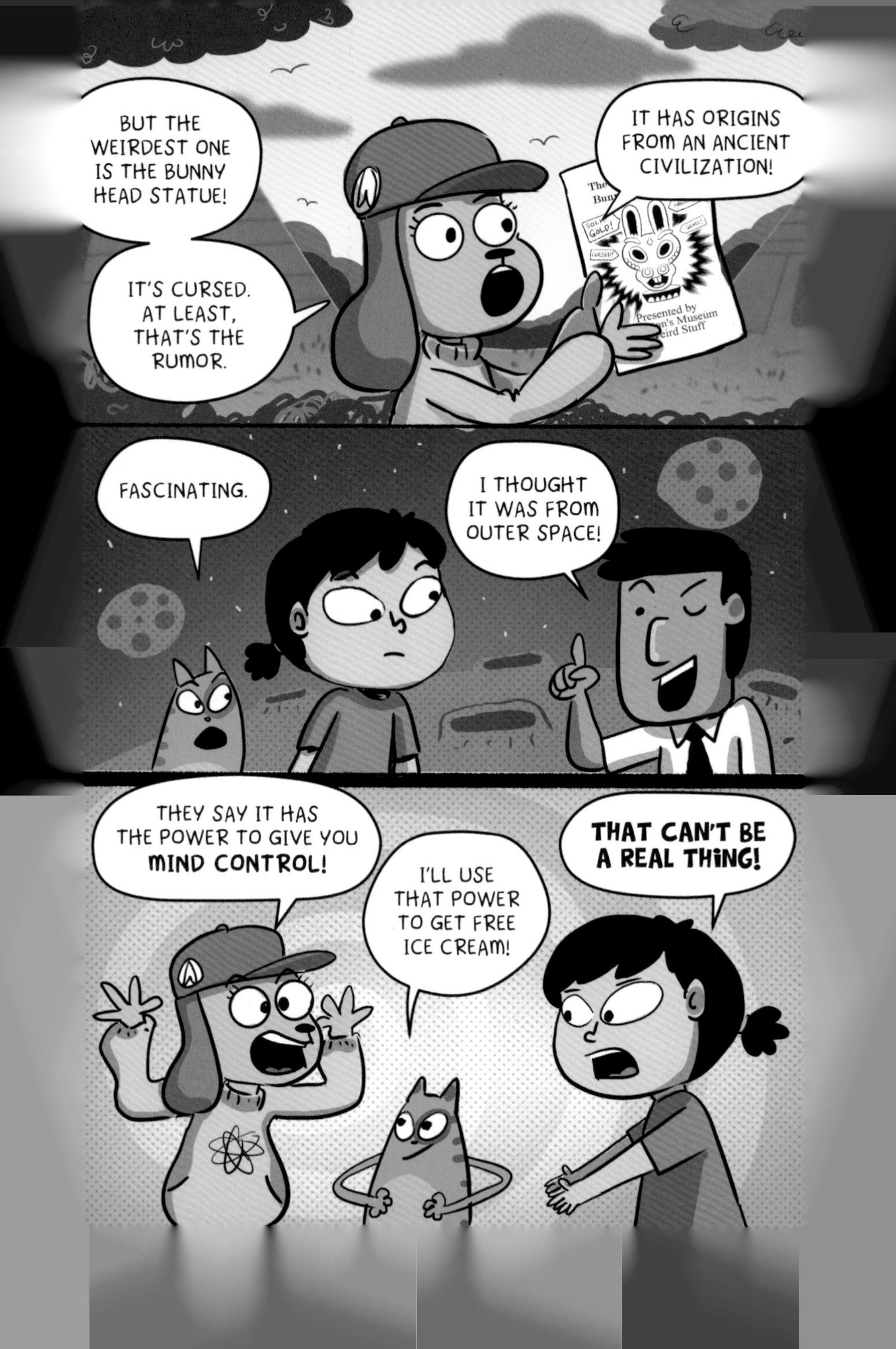
BUT THE WEIRDEST ONE IS THE BUNNY HEAD STATUE!
IT'S CURSED. AT LEAST, THAT'S THE RUMOR.
IT HAS ORIGINS FROM AN ANCIENT CIVILIZATION!
Presented by
FASCINATING.
I THOUGHT IT WAS FROM OUTER SPACE!
THEY SAY IT HAS THE POWER TO GIVE YOU **MIND CONTROL!**
I'LL USE THAT POWER TO GET FREE ICE CREAM!
THAT CAN'T BE A REAL THING!

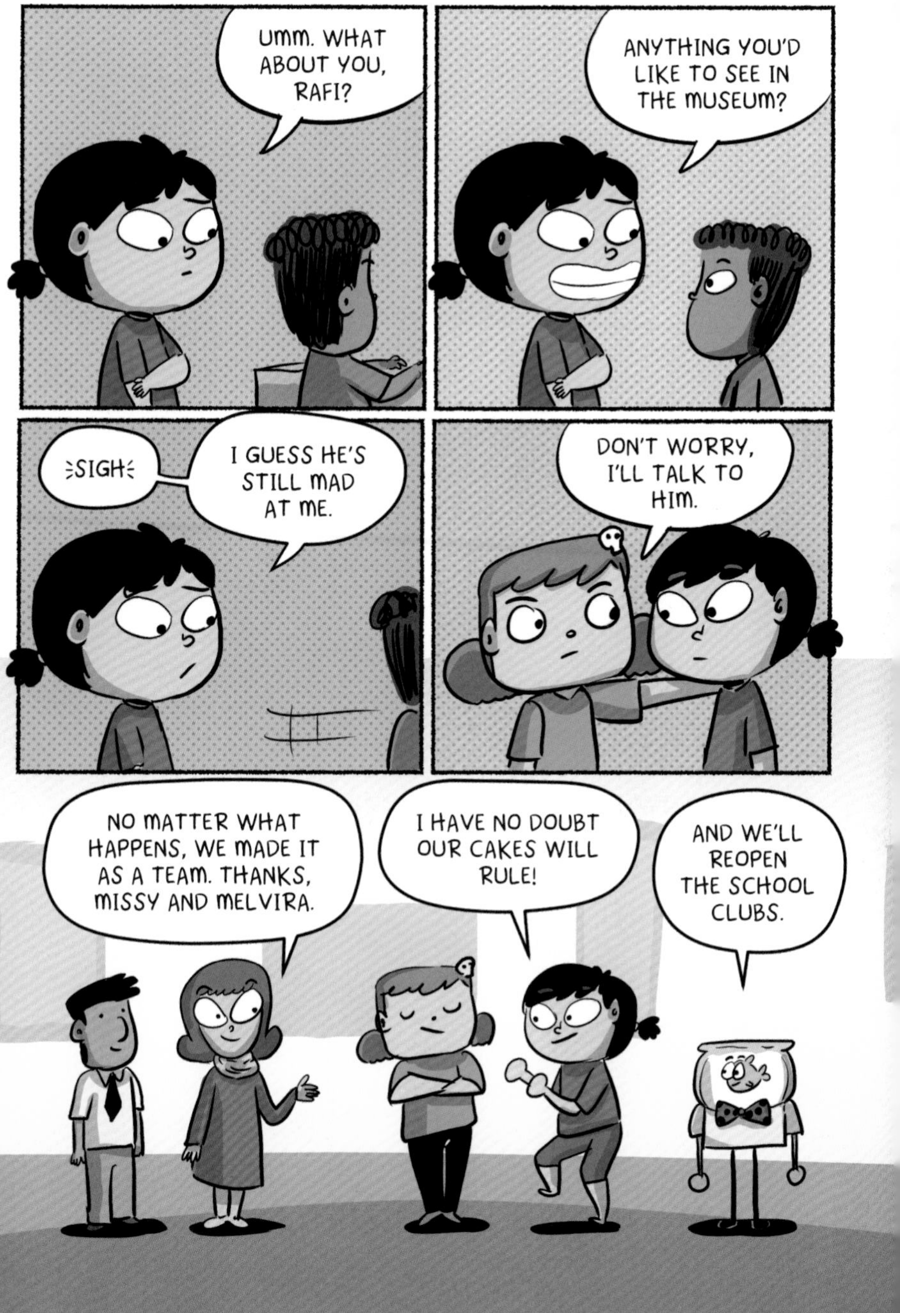
UMM. WHAT ABOUT YOU, RAFI?
ANYTHING YOU'D LIKE TO SEE IN THE MUSEUM?
SIGH
I GUESS HE'S STILL MAD AT ME.
DON'T WORRY, I'LL TALK TO HIM.
NO MATTER WHAT HAPPENS, WE MADE IT AS A TEAM. THANKS, MISSY AND MELVIRA.
I HAVE NO DOUBT OUR CAKES WILL RULE!
AND WE'LL REOPEN THE SCHOOL CLUBS.

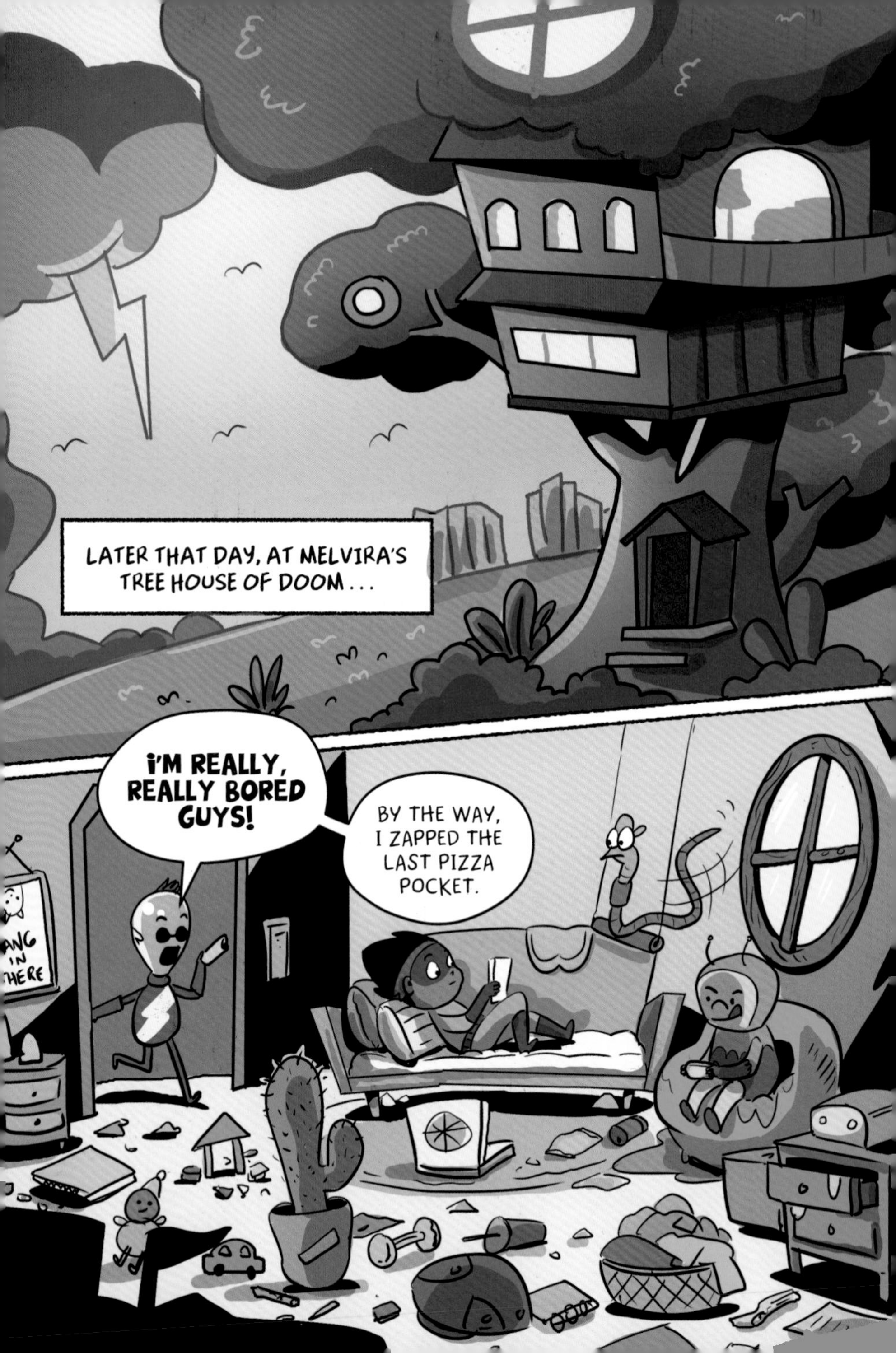
LATER THAT DAY, AT MELVIRA'S TREE HOUSE OF DOOM . . .
I'M REALLY, REALLY BORED GUYS!
BY THE WAY, I ZAPPED THE LAST PIZZA POCKET.
ANG IN THERE

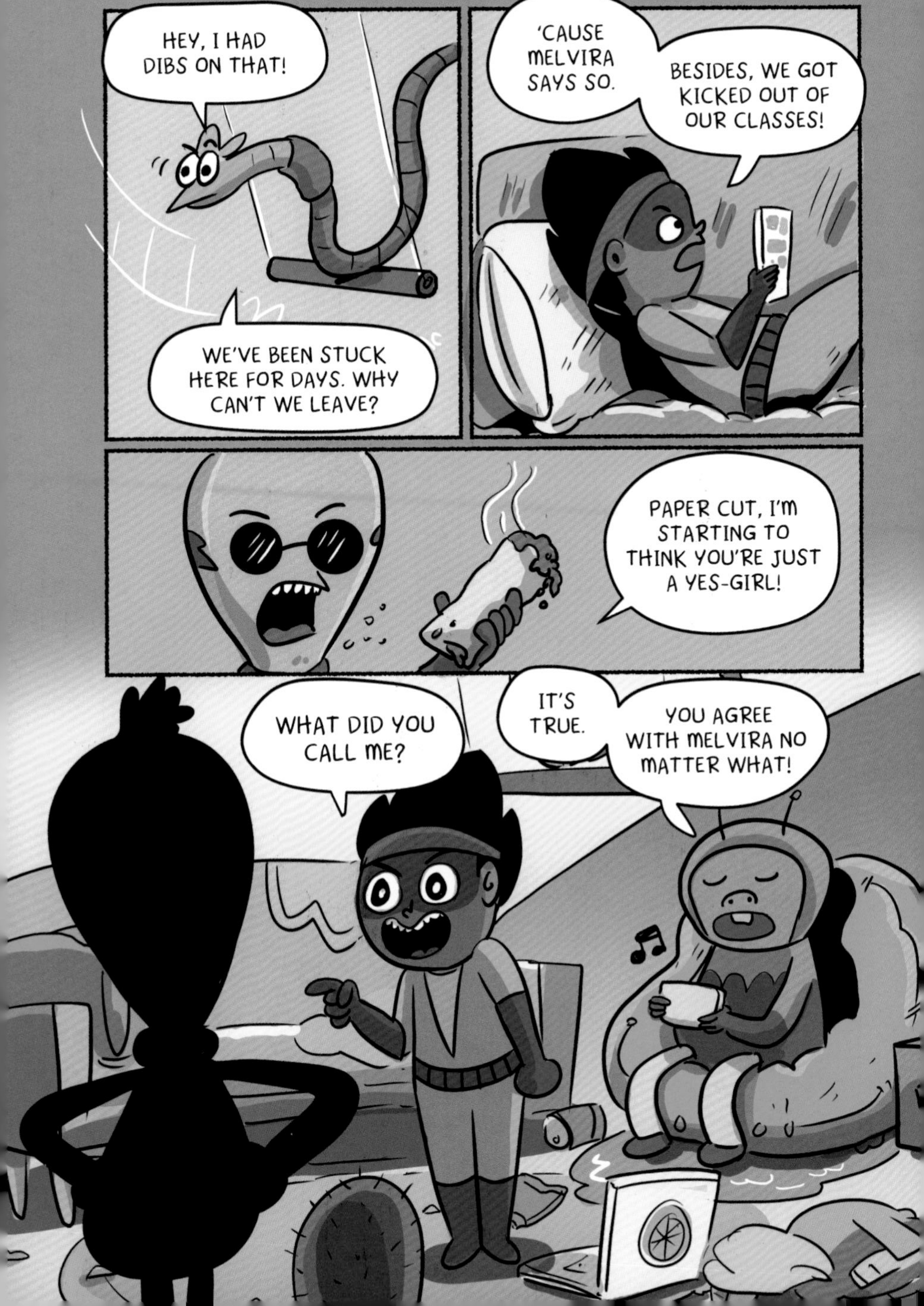
HEY, I HAD DIBS ON THAT!
WE'VE BEEN STUCK HERE FOR DAYS. WHY CAN'T WE LEAVE?
'CAUSE MELVIRA SAYS SO.
BESIDES, WE GOT KICKED OUT OF OUR CLASSES!
PAPER CUT, I'M STARTING TO THINK YOU'RE JUST A YES-GIRL!
WHAT DID YOU CALL ME?
IT'S TRUE.
YOU AGREE WITH MELVIRA NO MATTER WHAT!

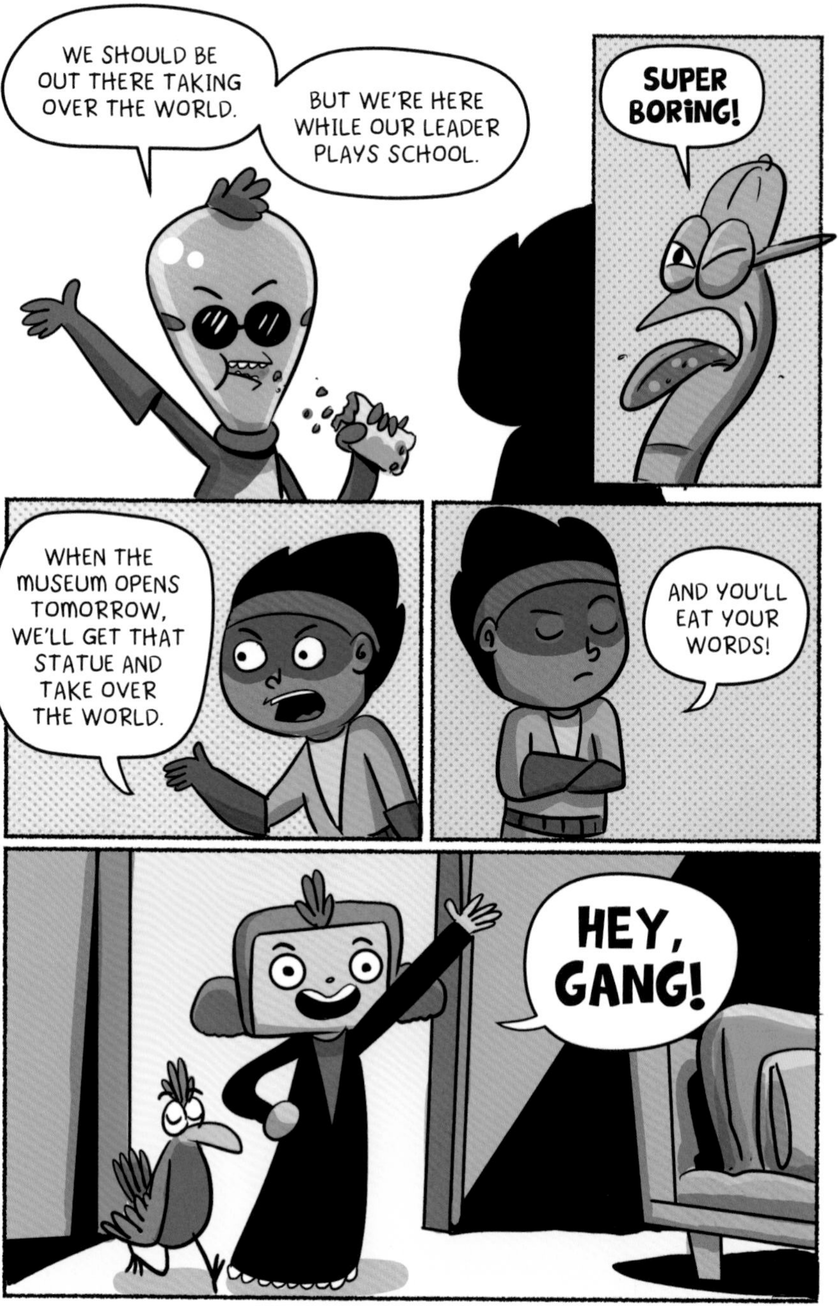
WE SHOULD BE OUT THERE TAKING OVER THE WORLD.
BUT WE'RE HERE WHILE OUR LEADER PLAYS SCHOOL.
SUPER BORING!
WHEN THE MUSEUM OPENS TOMORROW, WE'LL GET THAT STATUE AND TAKE OVER THE WORLD.
AND YOU'LL EAT YOUR WORDS!
HEY, GANG!

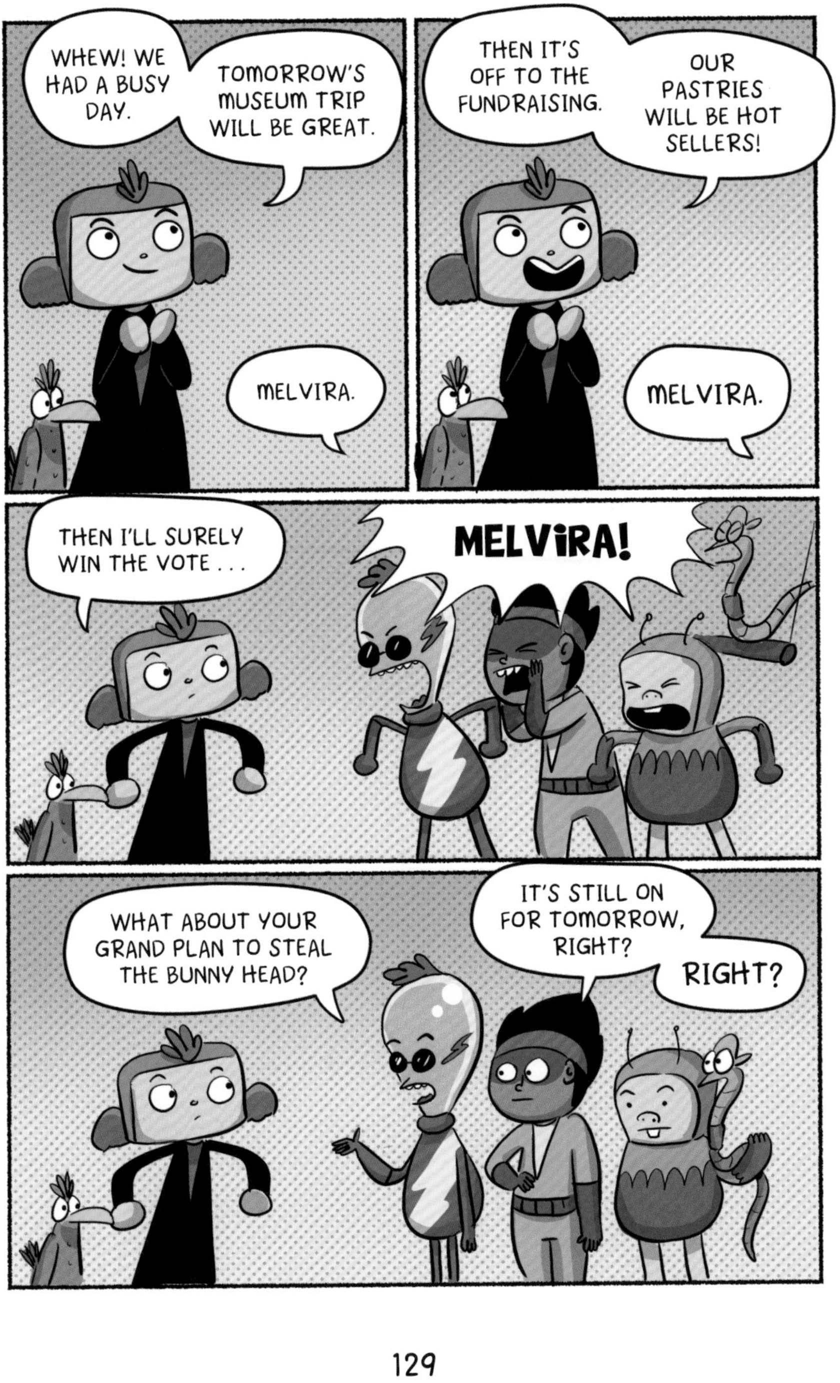
WHEW! WE HAD A BUSY DAY.
TOMORROW'S MUSEUM TRIP WILL BE GREAT.
MELVIRA.
THEN IT'S OFF TO THE FUNDRAISING.
OUR PASTRIES WILL BE HOT SELLERS!
MELVIRA.
THEN I'LL SURELY WIN THE VOTE . . .
MELVIRA!
WHAT ABOUT YOUR GRAND PLAN TO STEAL THE BUNNY HEAD?
IT'S STILL ON FOR TOMORROW, RIGHT?
RIGHT?

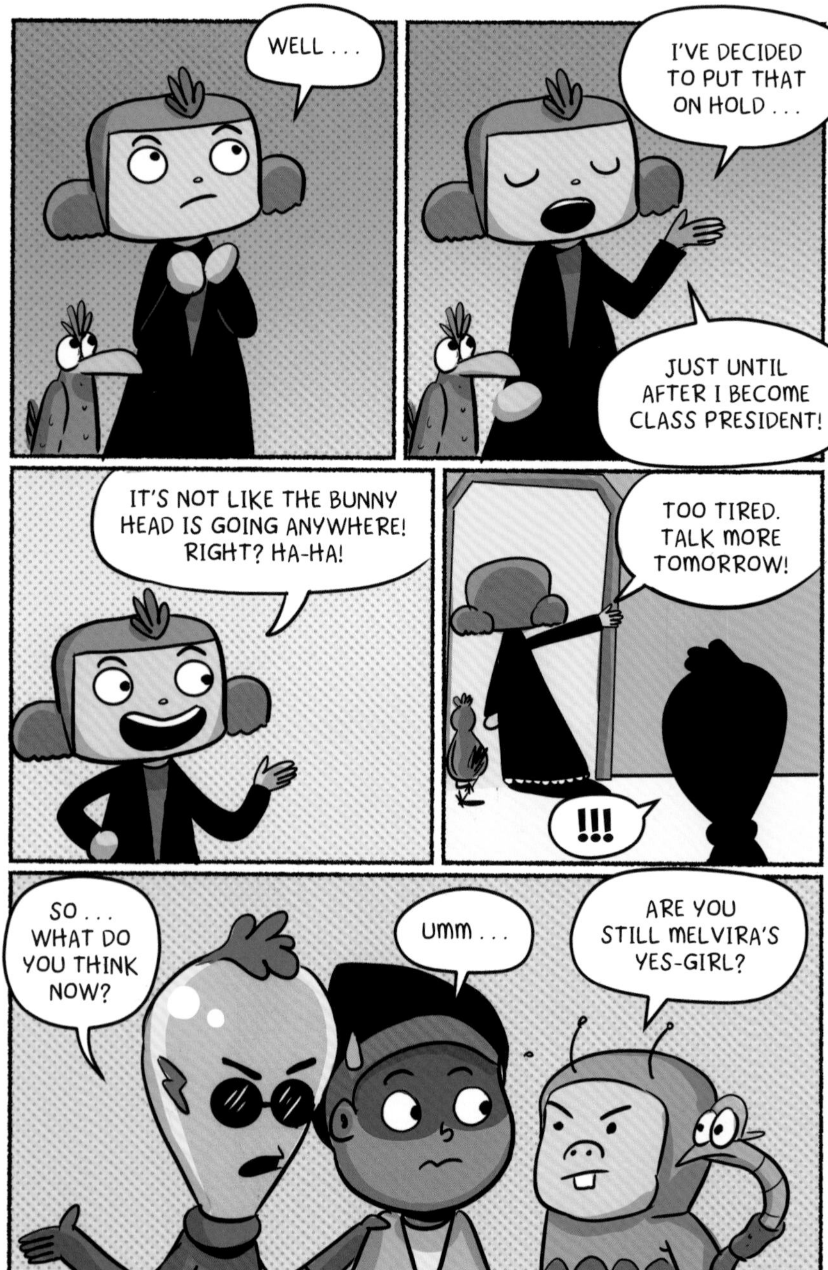
WELL . . .
I'VE DECIDED TO PUT THAT ON HOLD . . .
JUST UNTIL AFTER I BECOME CLASS PRESIDENT!
IT'S NOT LIKE THE BUNNY HEAD IS GOING ANYWHERE! RIGHT? HA-HA!
TOO TIRED. TALK MORE TOMORROW!
!!!
SO . . . WHAT DO YOU THINK NOW?
UMM . . .
ARE YOU STILL MELVIRA'S YES-GIRL?

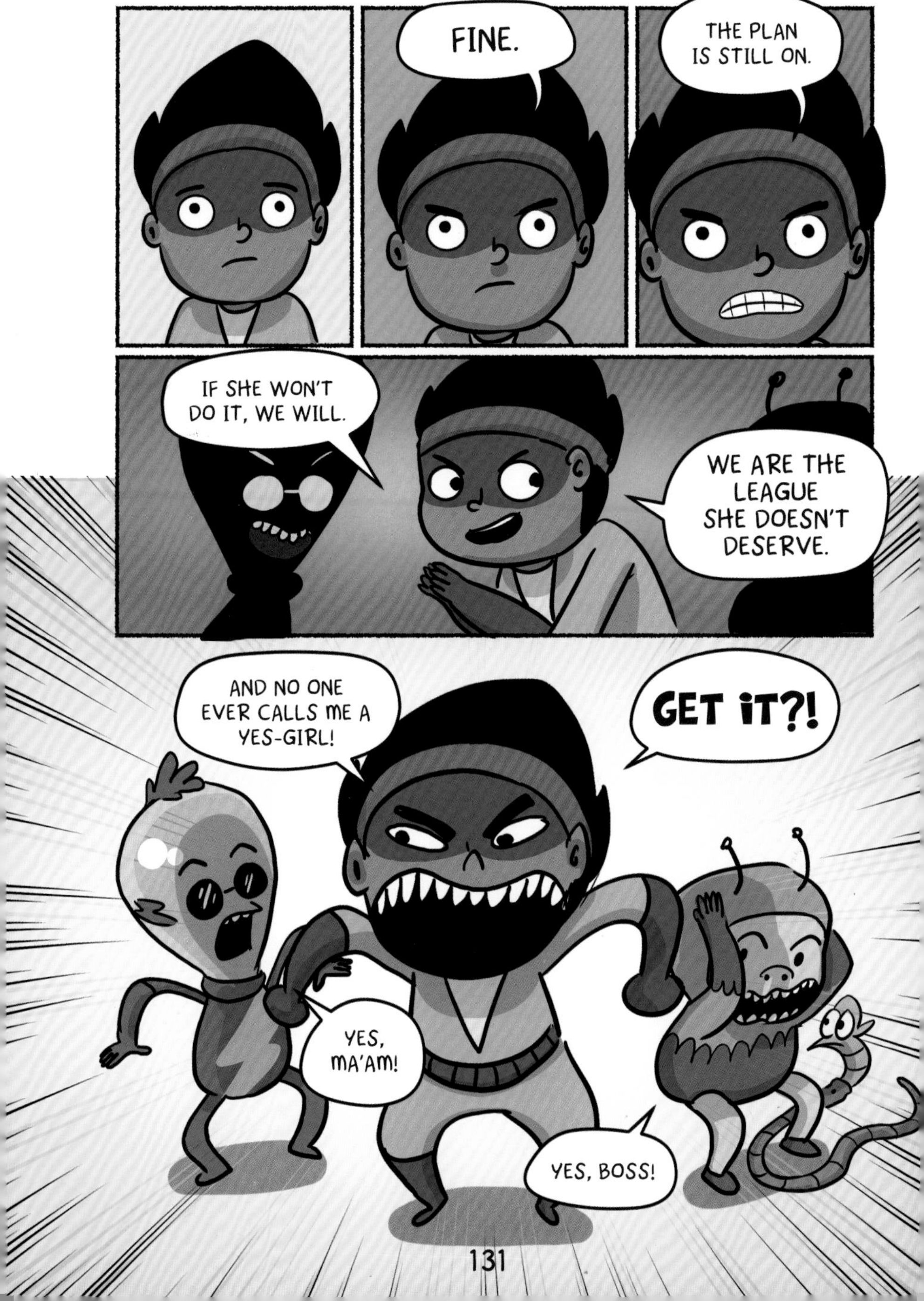
FINE.
THE PLAN IS STILL ON.
IF SHE WON'T DO IT, WE WILL.
WE ARE THE LEAGUE SHE DOESN'T DESERVE.
AND NO ONE EVER CALLS ME A YES-GIRL!
GET IT?!
YES, MA'AM!
YES, BOSS!

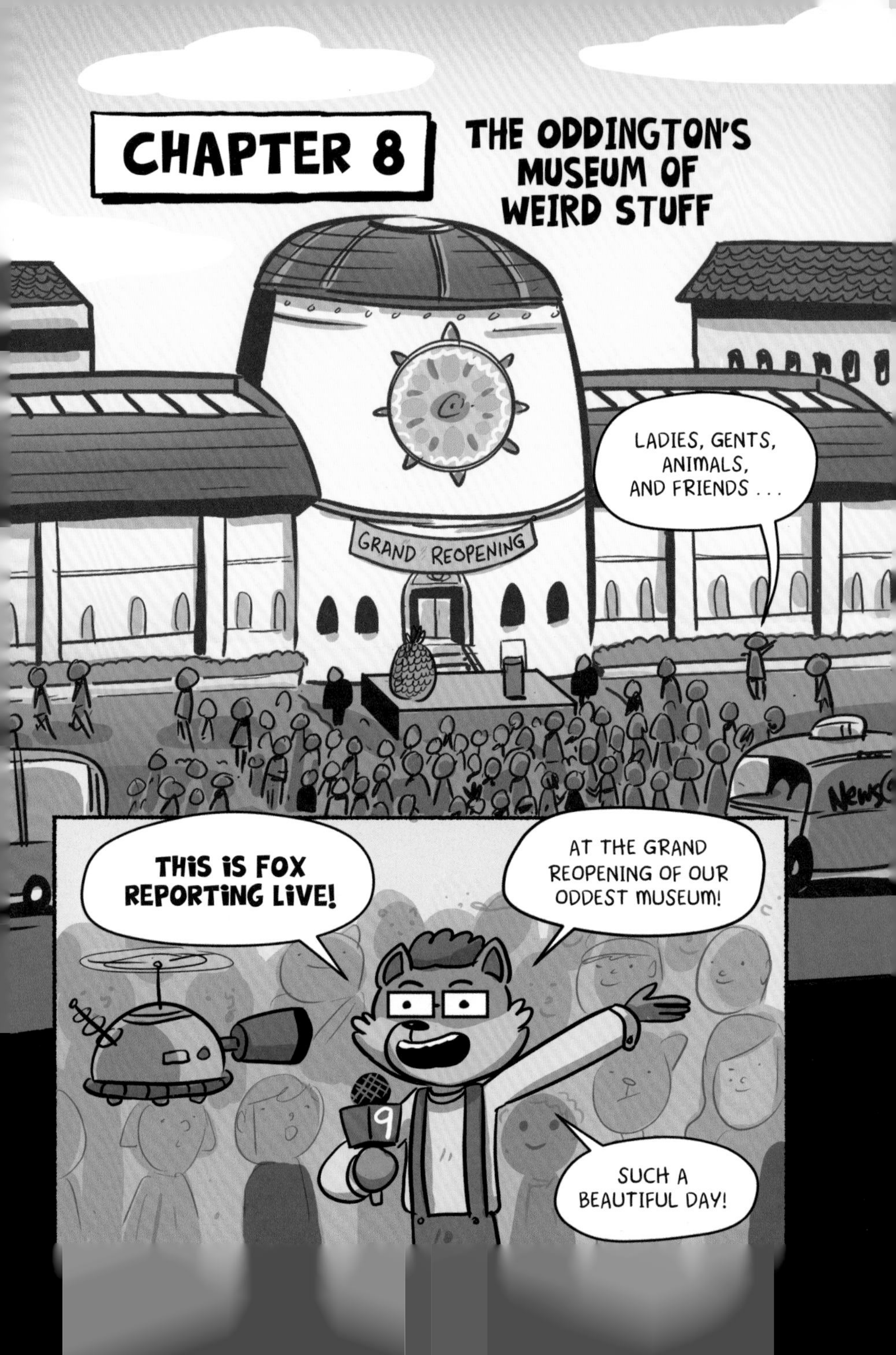
CHAPTER 8
THE ODDINGTON'S MUSEUM OF WEIRD STUFF
GRAND REOPENING
LADIES, GENTS, ANIMALS, AND FRIENDS . . .
THIS IS FOX REPORTING LIVE!
AT THE GRAND REOPENING OF OUR ODDEST MUSEUM!
SUCH A BEAUTIFUL DAY!

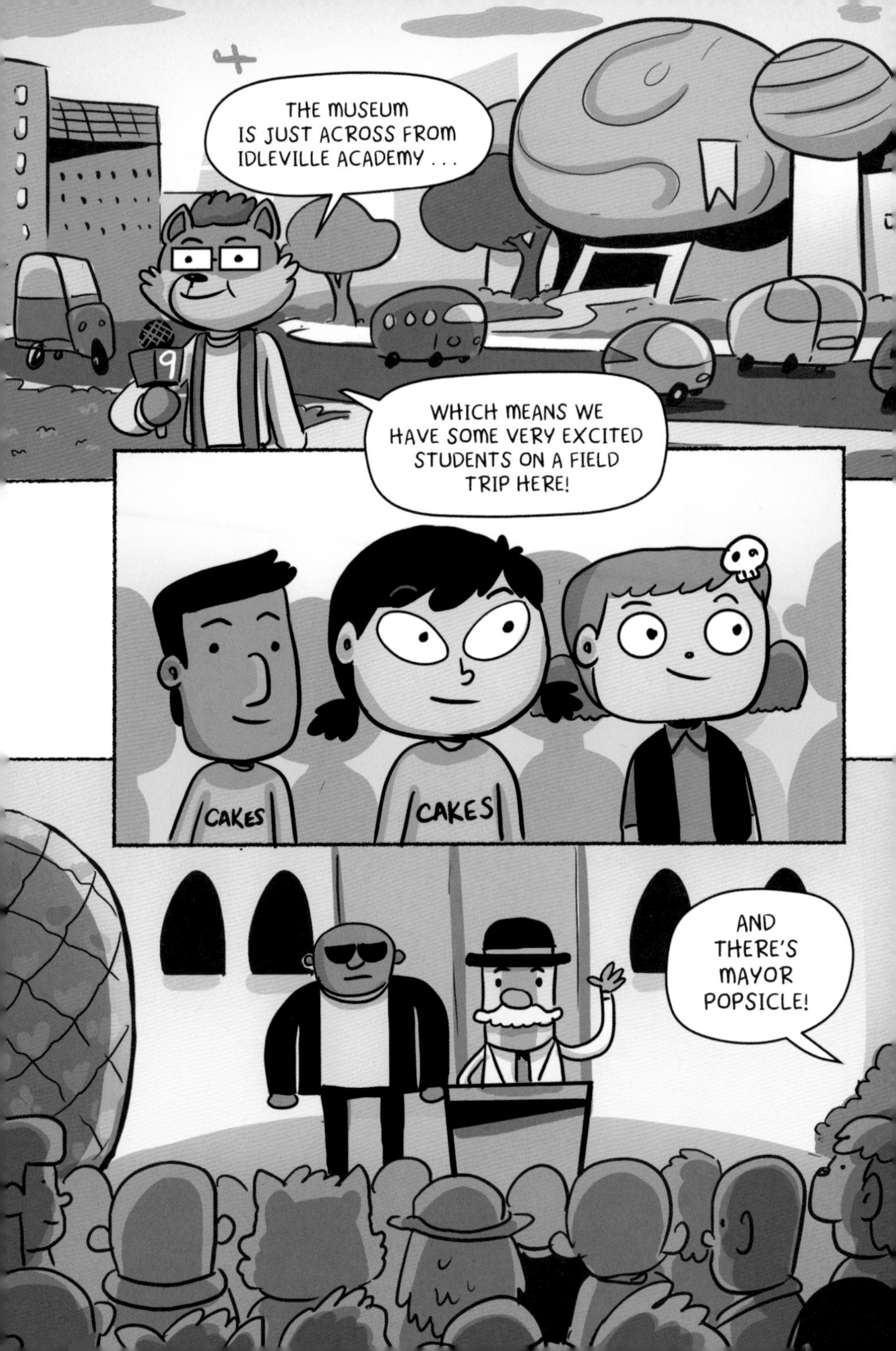

THE MUSEUM IS JUST ACROSS FROM IDLEVILLE ACADEMY . . .
9
WHICH MEANS WE HAVE SOME VERY EXCITED STUDENTS ON A FIELD TRIP HERE!
CAKES
CAKES
AND THERE'S MAYOR POPSICLE!

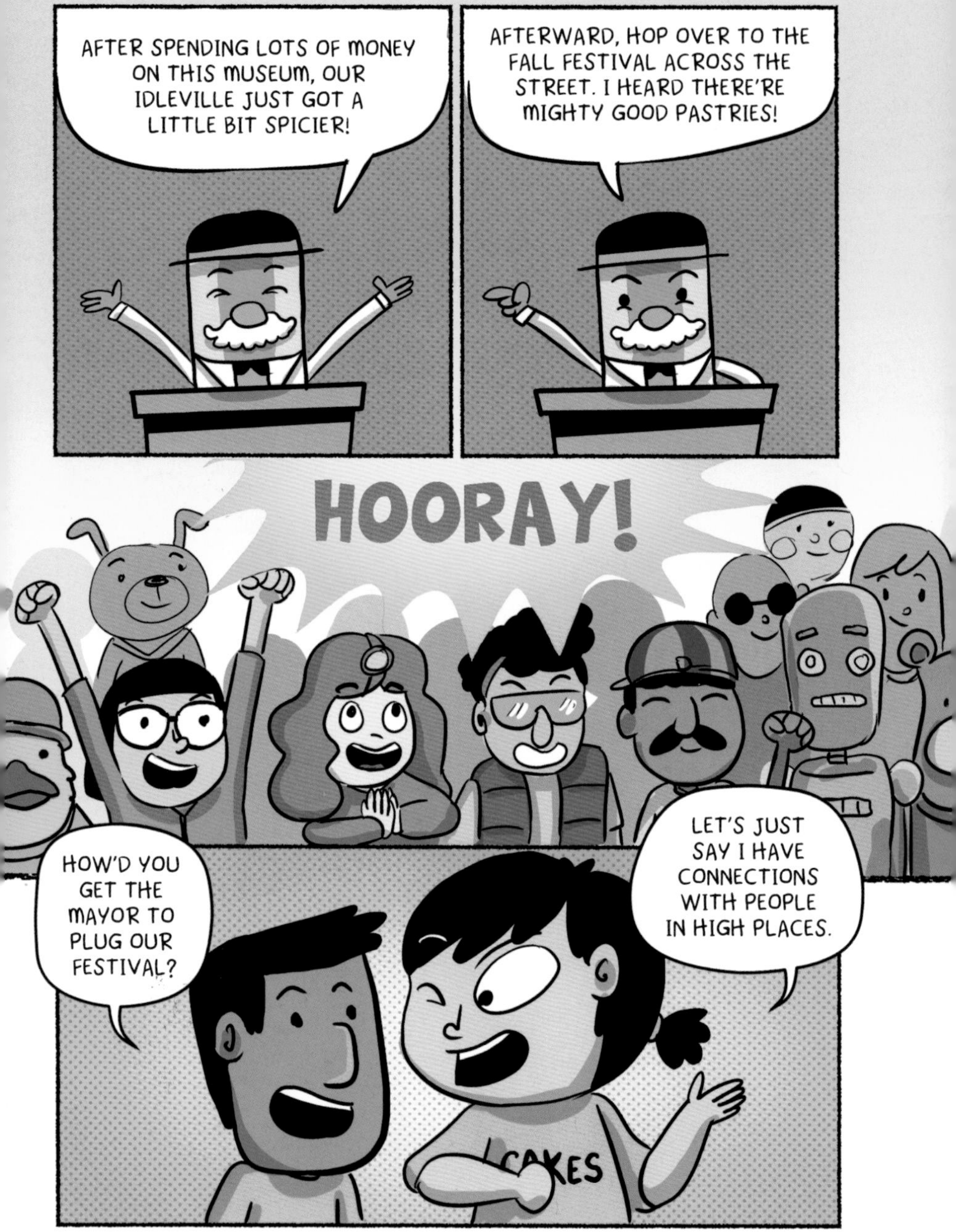
AFTER SPENDING LOTS OF MONEY ON THIS MUSEUM, OUR IDLEVILLE JUST GOT A LITTLE BIT SPICIER!
AFTERWARD, HOP OVER TO THE FALL FESTIVAL ACROSS THE STREET. I HEARD THERE'RE MIGHTY GOOD PASTRIES!
HOORAY!
HOW'D YOU GET THE MAYOR TO PLUG OUR FESTIVAL?
LET'S JUST SAY I HAVE CONNECTIONS WITH PEOPLE IN HIGH PLACES.
CAKES

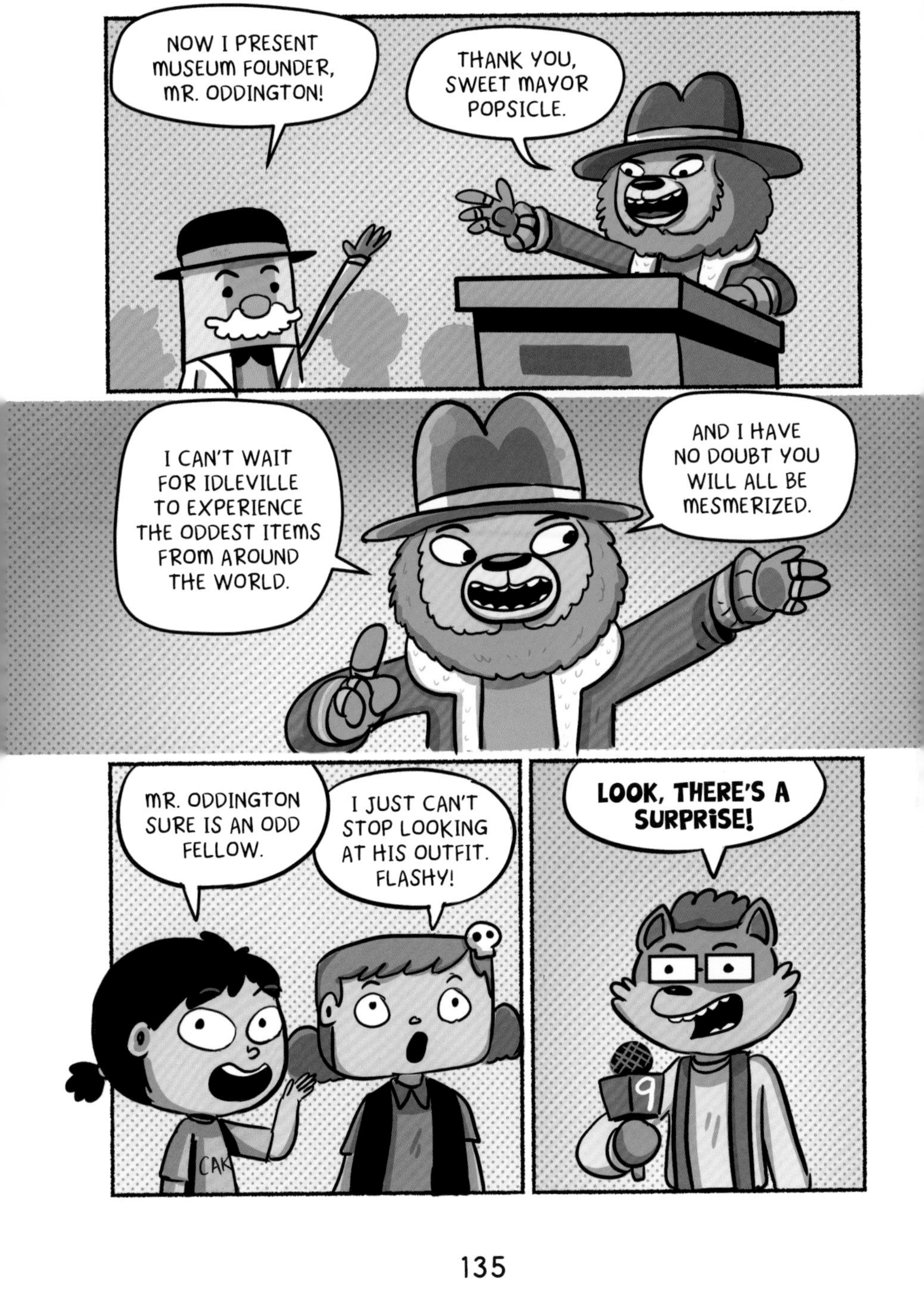
NOW I PRESENT MUSEUM FOUNDER, MR. ODDINGTON!
THANK YOU, SWEET MAYOR POPSICLE.
I CAN'T WAIT FOR IDLEVILLE TO EXPERIENCE THE ODDEST ITEMS FROM AROUND THE WORLD.
AND I HAVE NO DOUBT YOU WILL ALL BE MESMERIZED.
MR. ODDINGTON SURE IS AN ODD FELLOW.
I JUST CAN'T STOP LOOKING AT HIS OUTFIT. FLASHY!
LOOK, THERE'S A SURPRISE!

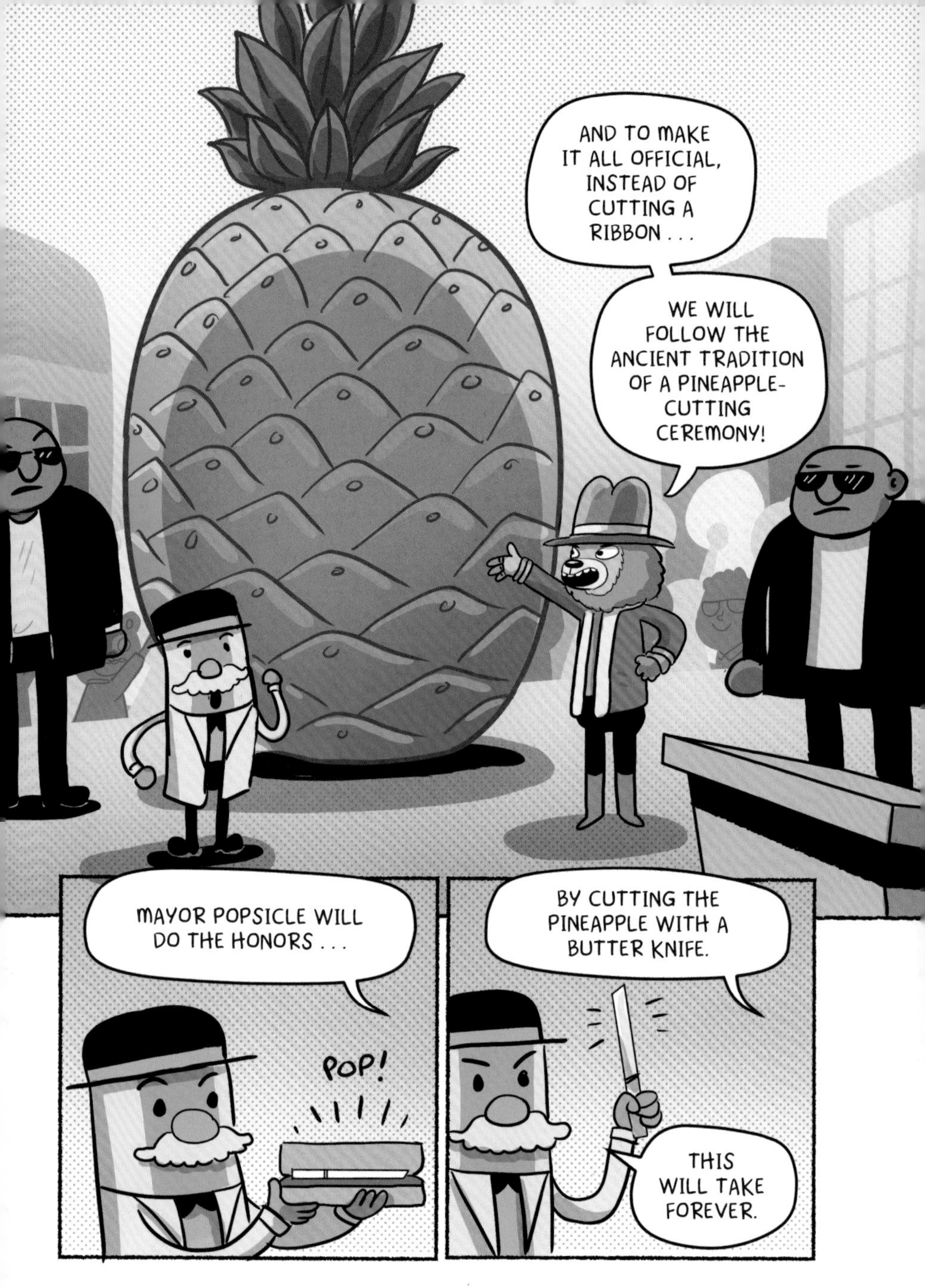
AND TO MAKE IT ALL OFFICIAL, INSTEAD OF CUTTING A RIBBON . . .
WE WILL FOLLOW THE ANCIENT TRADITION OF A PINEAPPLE-CUTTING CEREMONY!
MAYOR POPSICLE WILL DO THE HONORS . . .
POP!
BY CUTTING THE PINEAPPLE WITH A BUTTER KNIFE.
THIS WILL TAKE FOREVER.

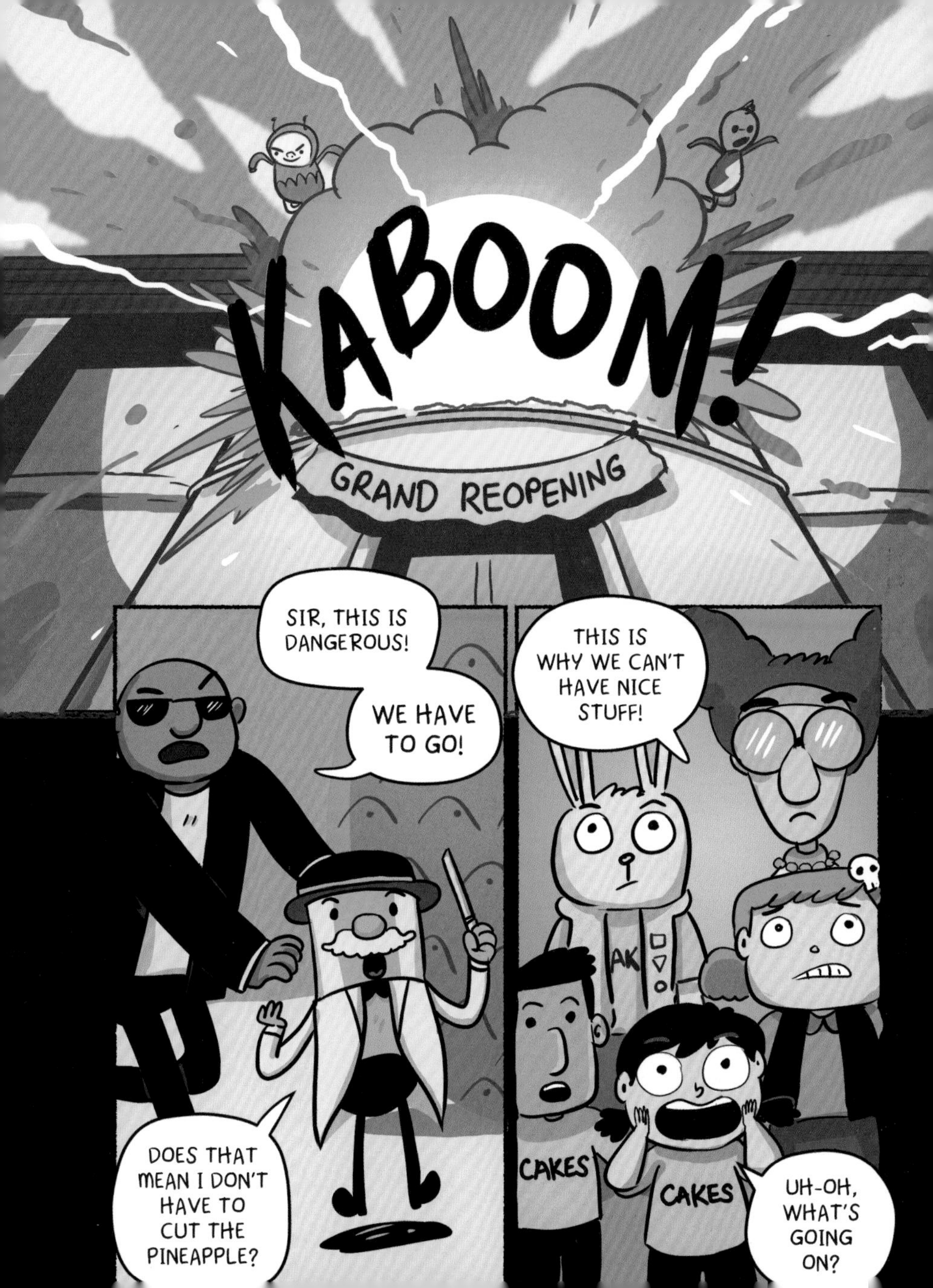
KABOOM!
GRAND REOPENING
SIR, THIS IS DANGEROUS!
WE HAVE TO GO!
DOES THAT MEAN I DON'T HAVE TO CUT THE PINEAPPLE?
THIS IS WHY WE CAN'T HAVE NICE STUFF!
CAKES
CAKES
UH-OH, WHAT'S GOING ON?

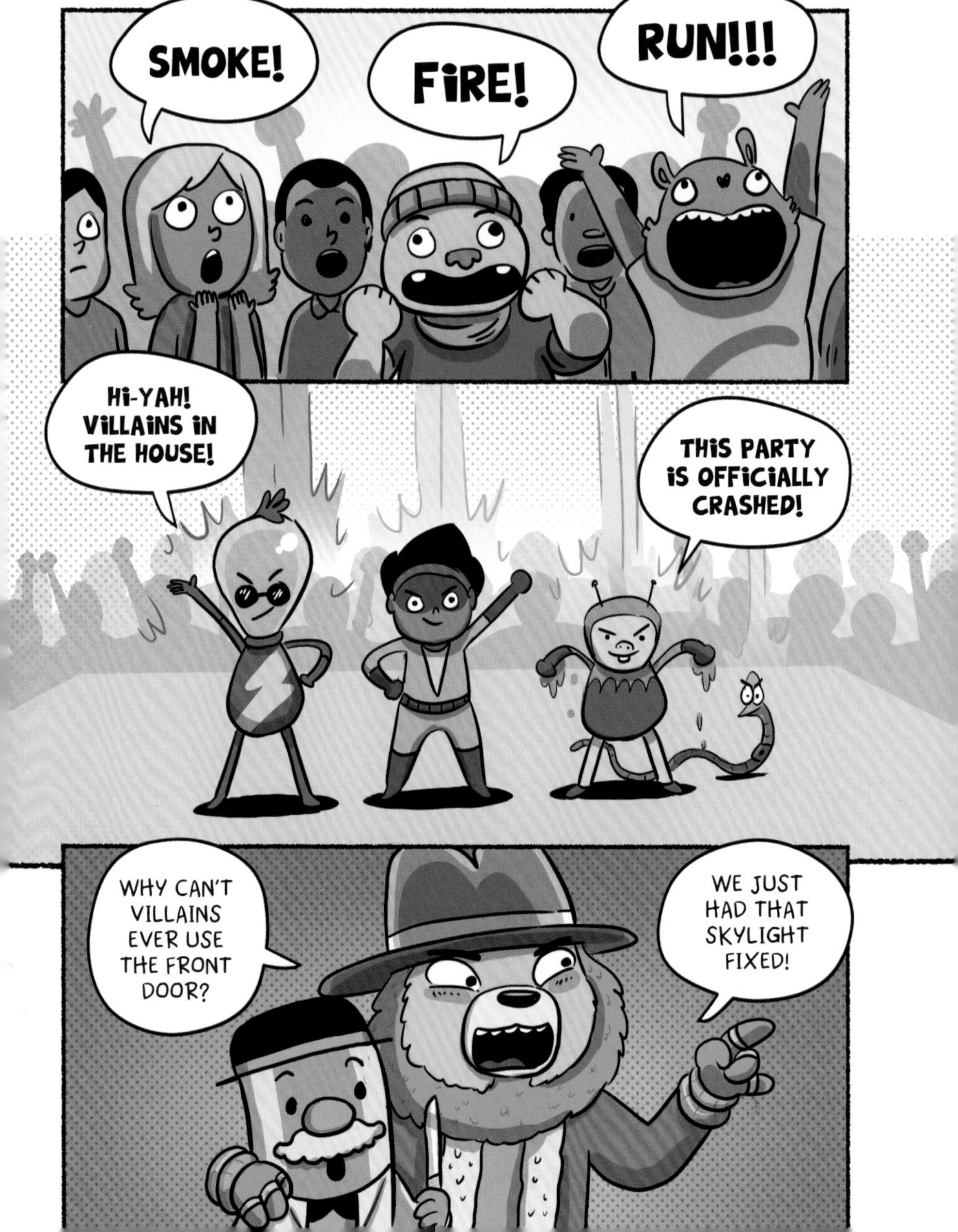
SMOKE!
FIRE!
RUN!!!
HI-YAH! VILLAINS IN THE HOUSE!
THIS PARTY IS OFFICIALLY CRASHED!
WHY CAN'T VILLAINS EVER USE THE FRONT DOOR?
WE JUST HAD THAT SKYLIGHT FIXED!

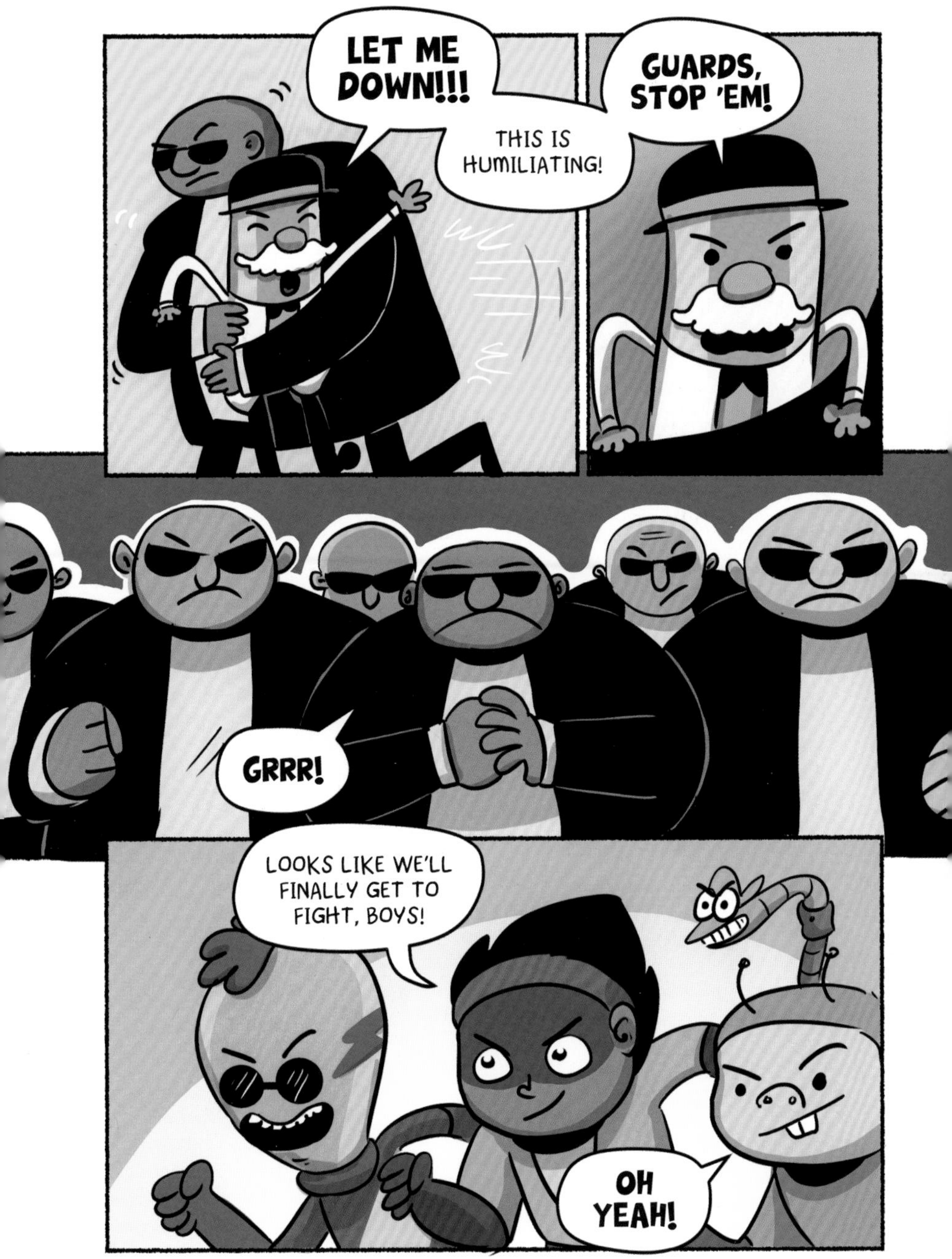
LET ME DOWN!!!
THIS IS HUMILIATING!
GUARDS, STOP 'EM!
GRRR!
LOOKS LIKE WE'LL FINALLY GET TO FIGHT, BOYS!
OH YEAH!

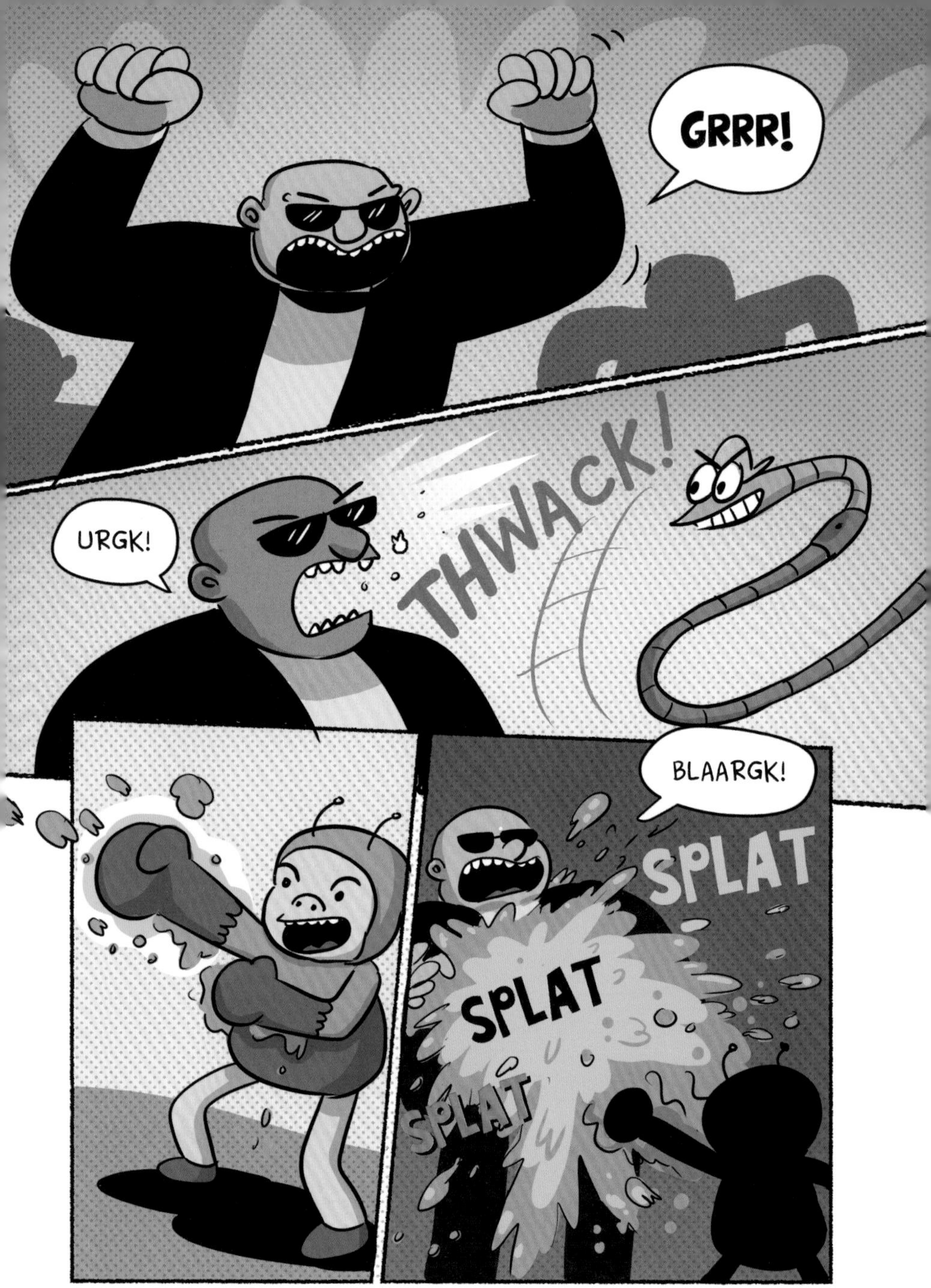
GRRR!
URGK!
THWACK!
BLAARGK!
SPLAT
SPLAT
SPLAT

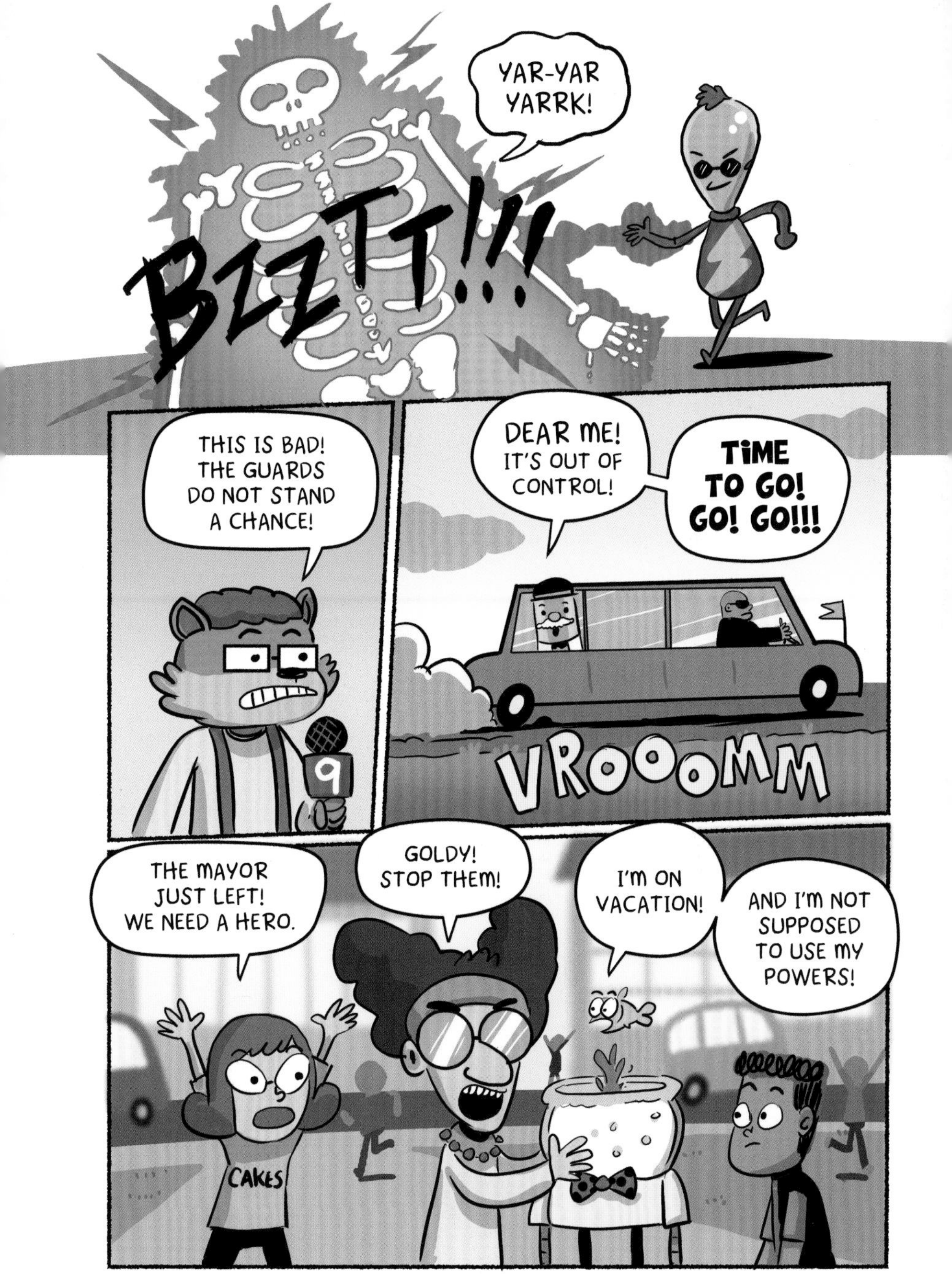
YAR-YAR YARRK!
BZZTT!!!
THIS IS BAD! THE GUARDS DO NOT STAND A CHANCE!
9
DEAR ME! IT'S OUT OF CONTROL!
TIME TO GO! GO! GO!!!
VROOOMM
THE MAYOR JUST LEFT! WE NEED A HERO.
GOLDY! STOP THEM!
I'M ON VACATION!
AND I'M NOT SUPPOSED TO USE MY POWERS!
CAKES

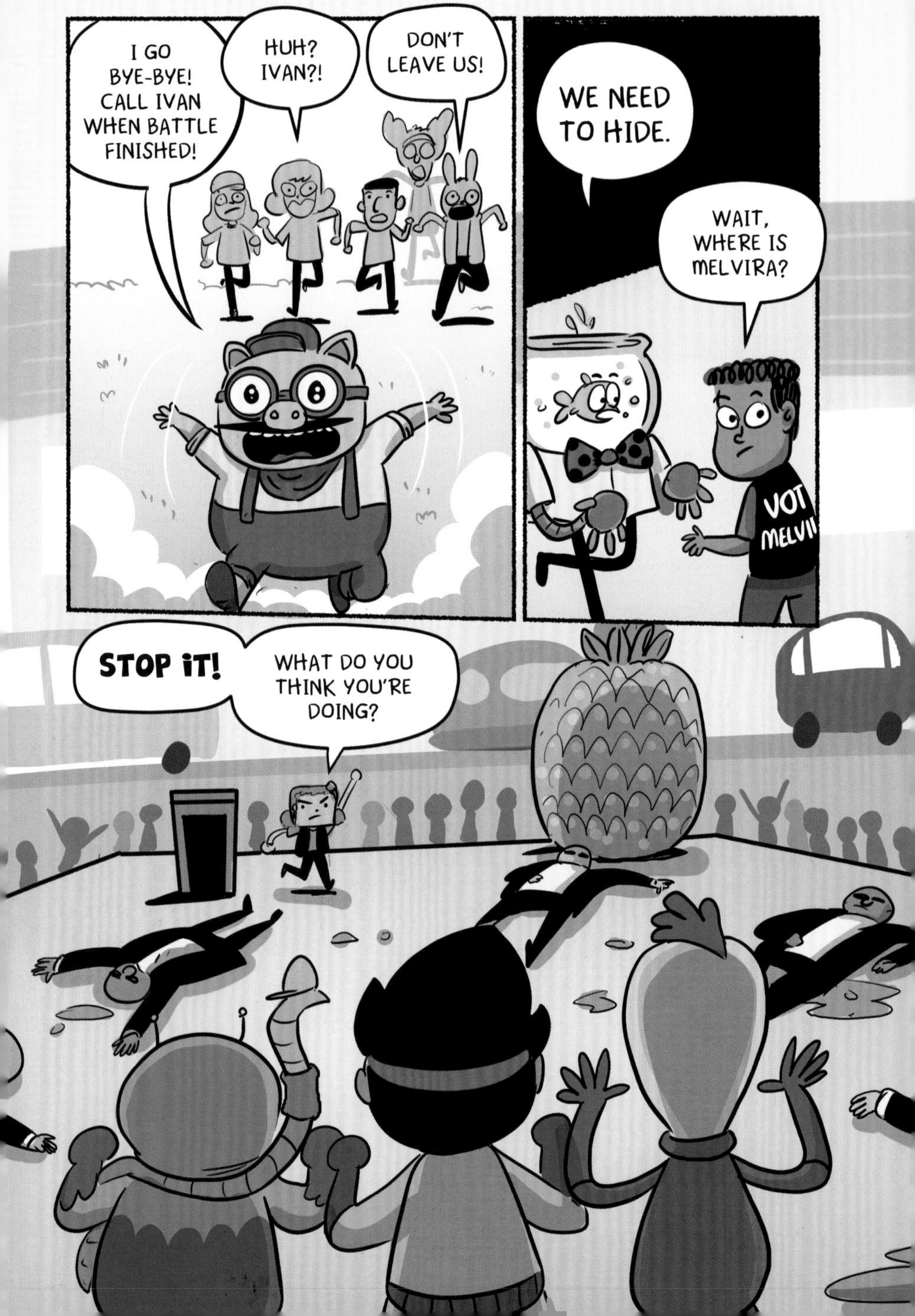
I GO BYE-BYE! CALL IVAN WHEN BATTLE FINISHED!
HUH? IVAN?!
DON'T LEAVE US!
WE NEED TO HIDE.
WAIT, WHERE IS MELVIRA?
VOT MELVI
STOP IT!
WHAT DO YOU THINK YOU'RE DOING?

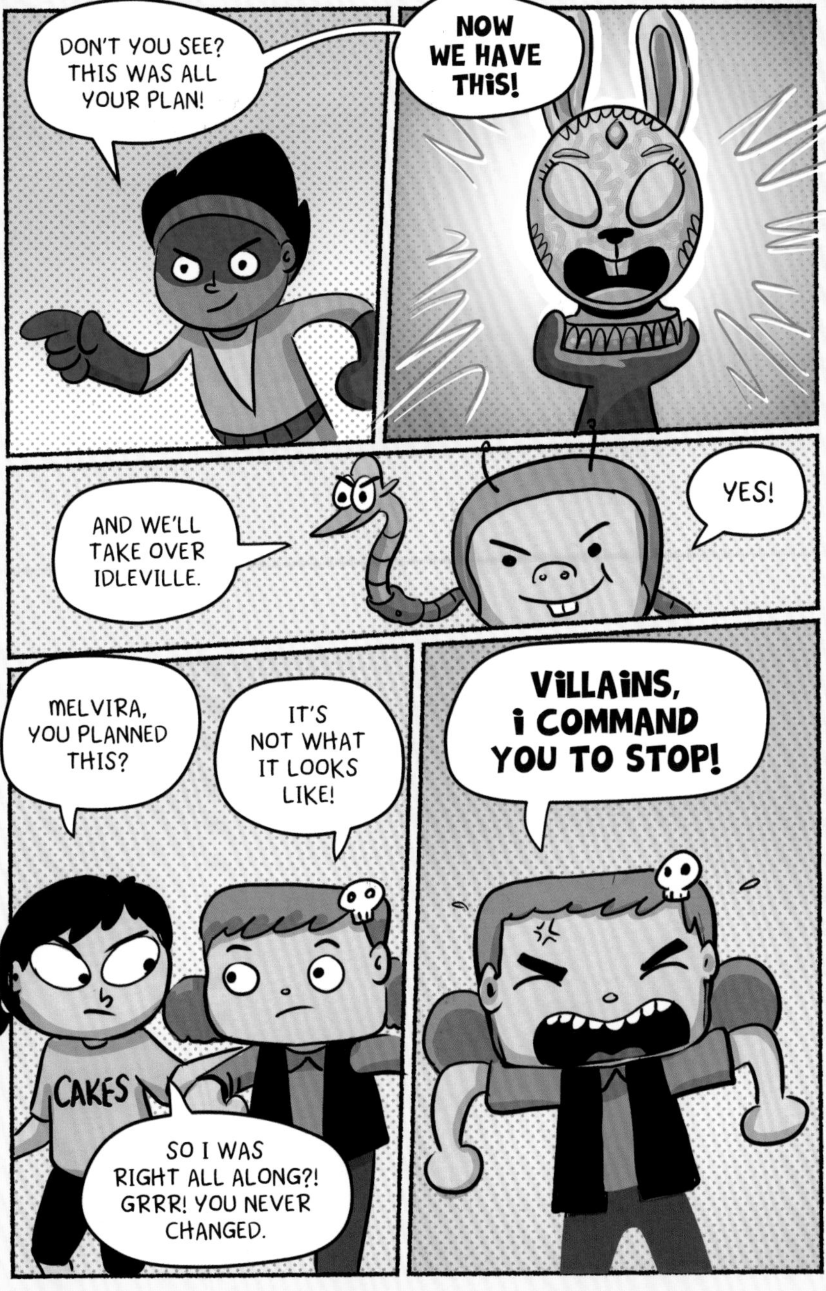
DON'T YOU SEE? THIS WAS ALL YOUR PLAN!
NOW WE HAVE THIS!
AND WE'LL TAKE OVER IDLEVILLE.
YES!
MELVIRA, YOU PLANNED THIS?
IT'S NOT WHAT IT LOOKS LIKE!
CAKES
SO I WAS RIGHT ALL ALONG?! GRRR! YOU NEVER CHANGED.
VILLAINS, I COMMAND YOU TO STOP!

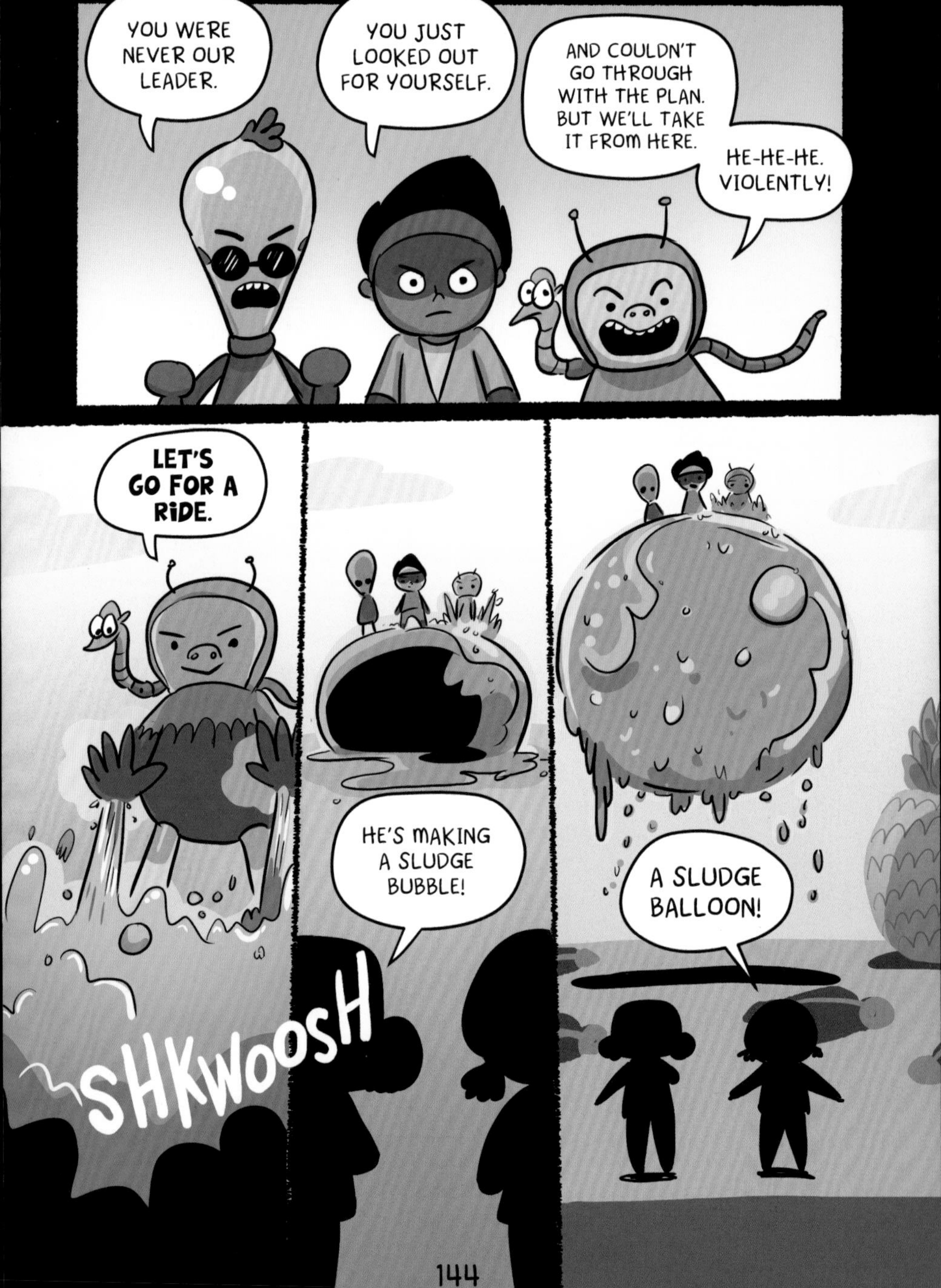
YOU WERE NEVER OUR LEADER.
YOU JUST LOOKED OUT FOR YOURSELF.
AND COULDN'T GO THROUGH WITH THE PLAN. BUT WE'LL TAKE IT FROM HERE.
HE-HE-HE. VIOLENTLY!
LET'S GO FOR A RIDE.
SHKWOOSH
HE'S MAKING A SLUDGE BUBBLE!
A SLUDGE BALLOON!

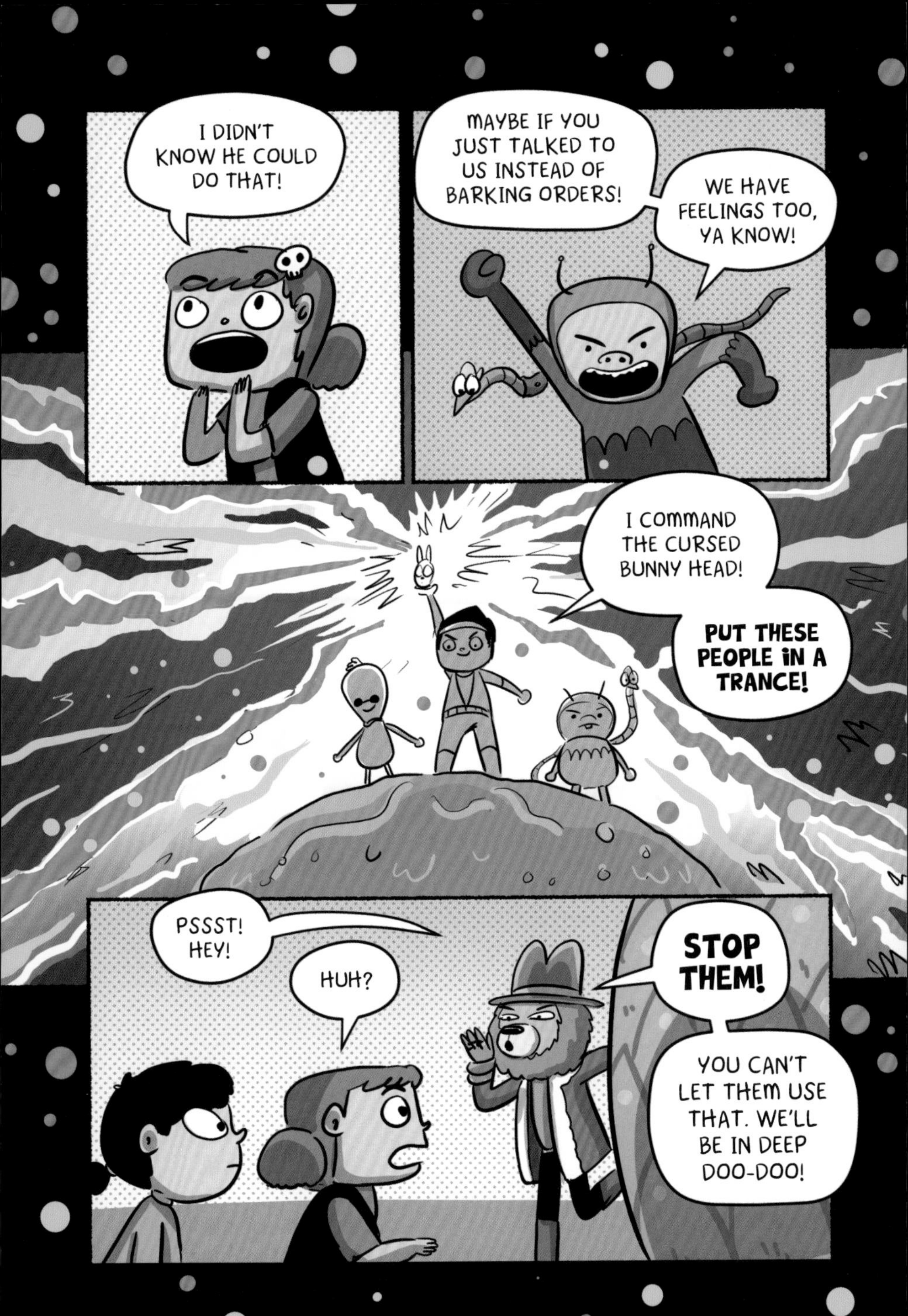
I DIDN'T KNOW HE COULD DO THAT!
MAYBE IF YOU JUST TALKED TO US INSTEAD OF BARKING ORDERS!
WE HAVE FEELINGS TOO, YA KNOW!
I COMMAND THE CURSED BUNNY HEAD!
PUT THESE PEOPLE IN A TRANCE!
PSSST! HEY!
HUH?
STOP THEM!
YOU CAN'T LET THEM USE THAT. WE'LL BE IN DEEP DOO-DOO!

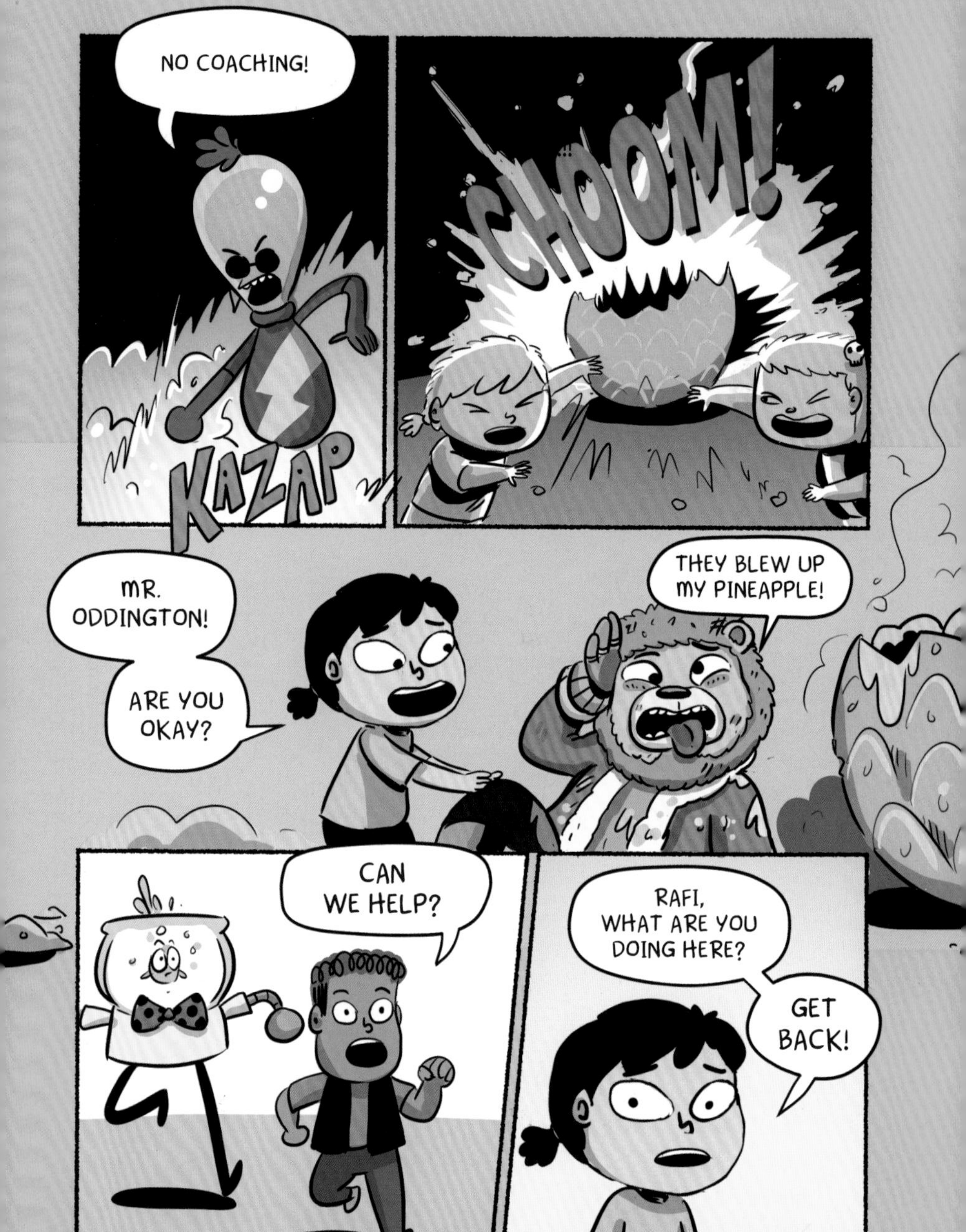
NO COACHING!
KAZAP
CHOOM!
MR. ODDINGTON!
ARE YOU OKAY?
THEY BLEW UP MY PINEAPPLE!
CAN WE HELP?
RAFI, WHAT ARE YOU DOING HERE?
GET BACK!
CAKES

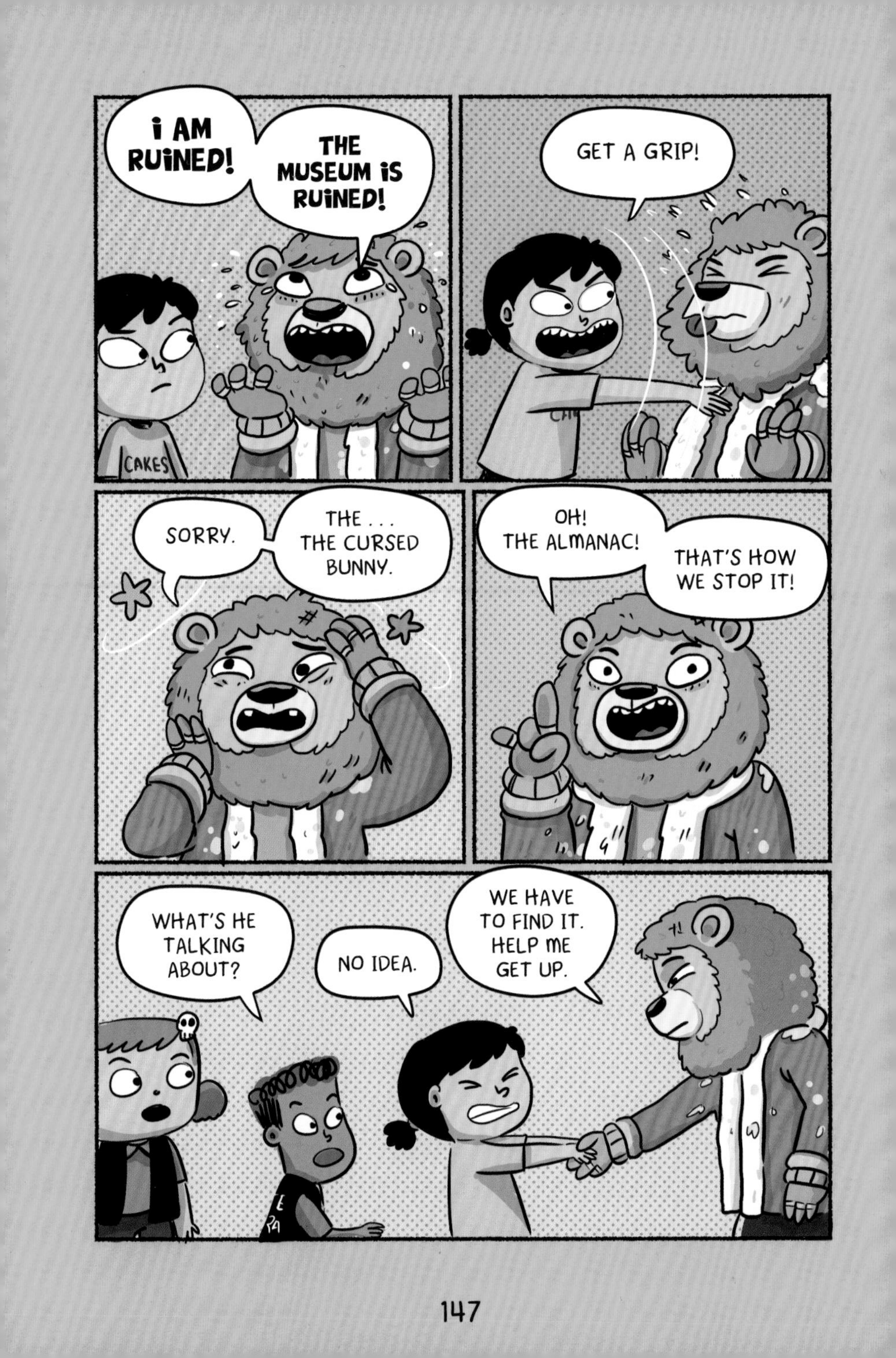
I AM RUINED!
THE MUSEUM IS RUINED!
GET A GRIP!
CAKES
SORRY.
THE . . . THE CURSED BUNNY.
OH! THE ALMANAC!
THAT'S HOW WE STOP IT!
WHAT'S HE TALKING ABOUT?
NO IDEA.
WE HAVE TO FIND IT. HELP ME GET UP.

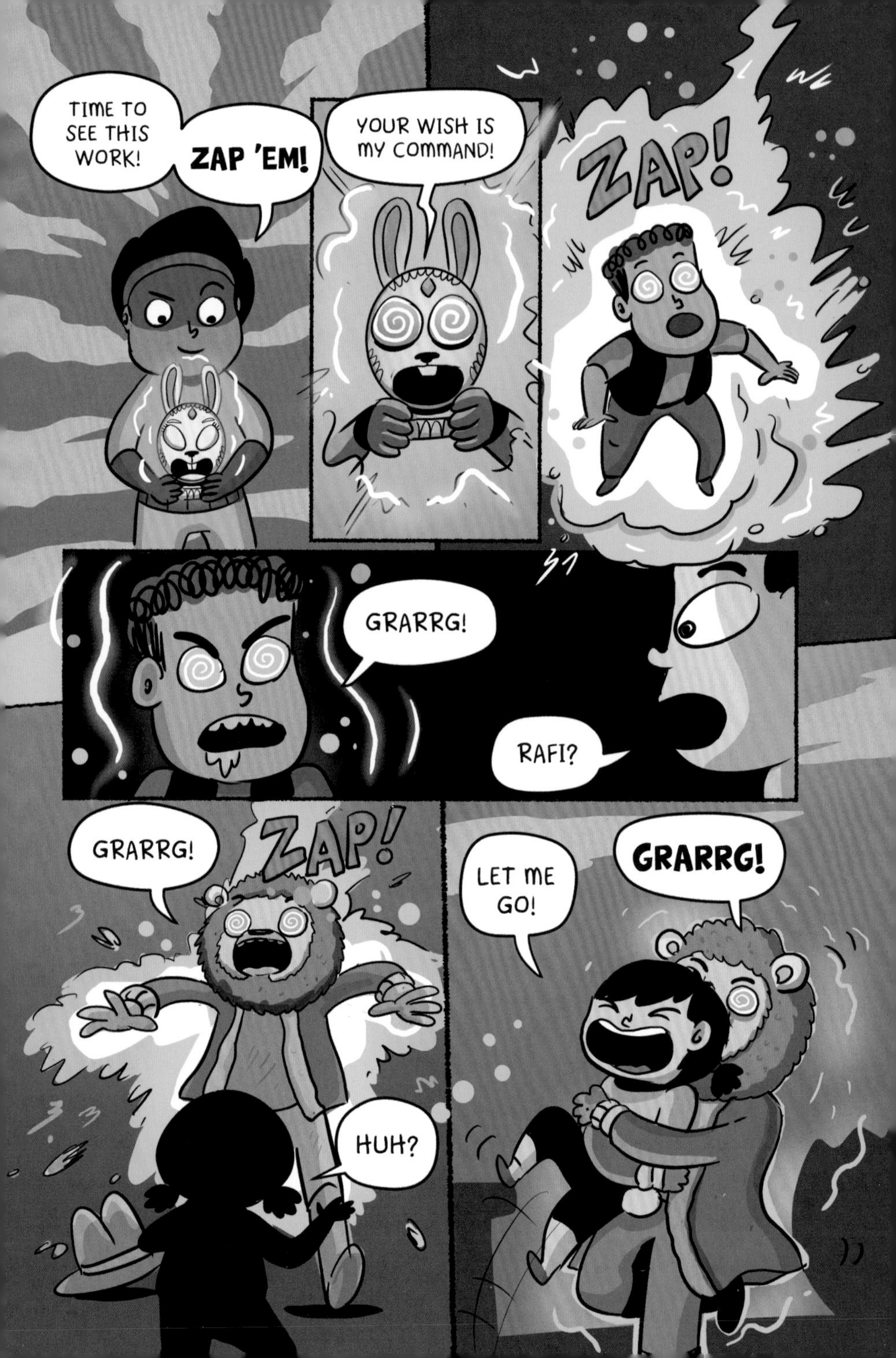
TIME TO SEE THIS WORK!
ZAP 'EM!
YOUR WISH IS MY COMMAND!
ZAP!
GRARRG!
RAFI?
GRARRG!
ZAP!
HUH?
LET ME GO!
GRARRG!

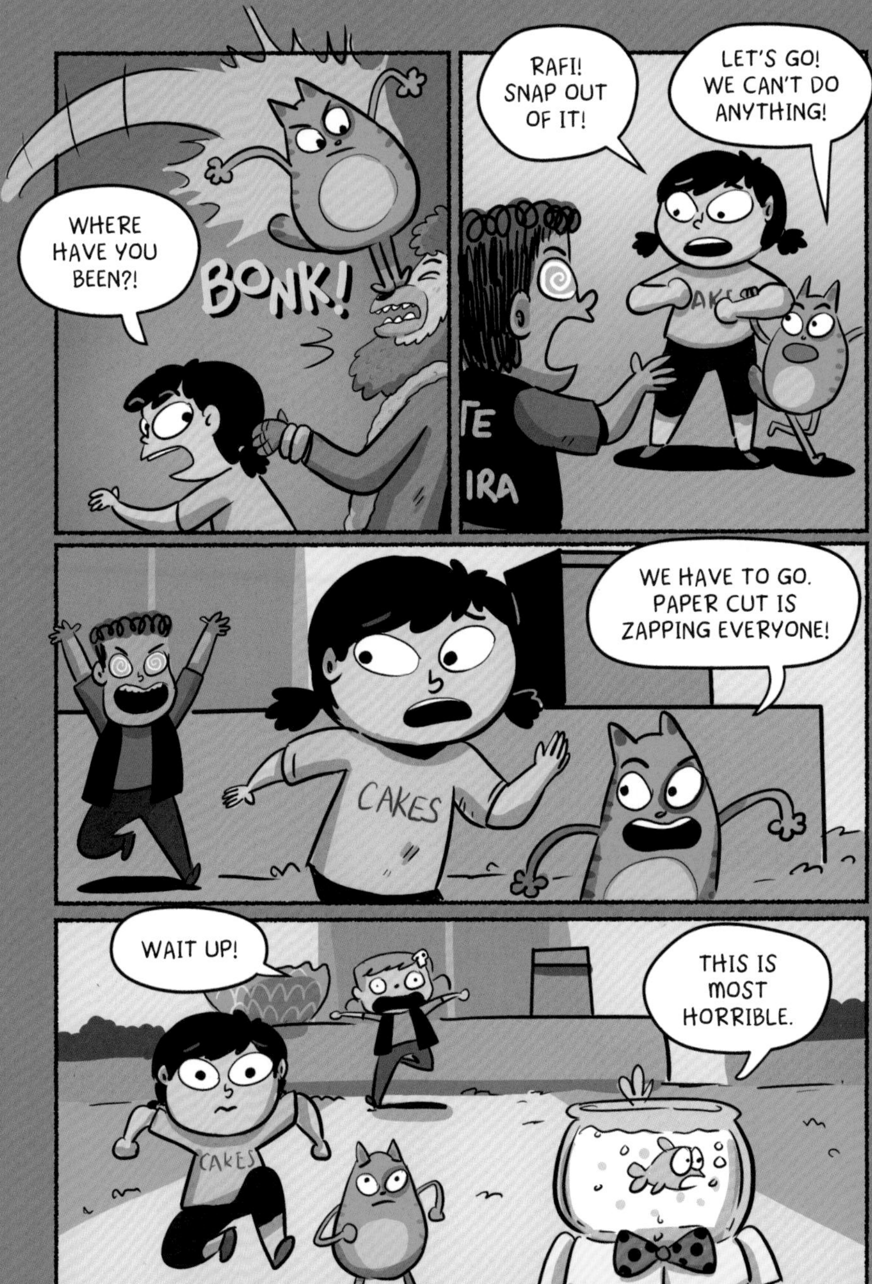
WHERE HAVE YOU BEEN?!
BONK!
RAFI! SNAP OUT OF IT!
LET'S GO! WE CAN'T DO ANYTHING!
WE HAVE TO GO. PAPER CUT IS ZAPPING EVERYONE!
CAKES
WAIT UP!
THIS IS MOST HORRIBLE.
CAKES

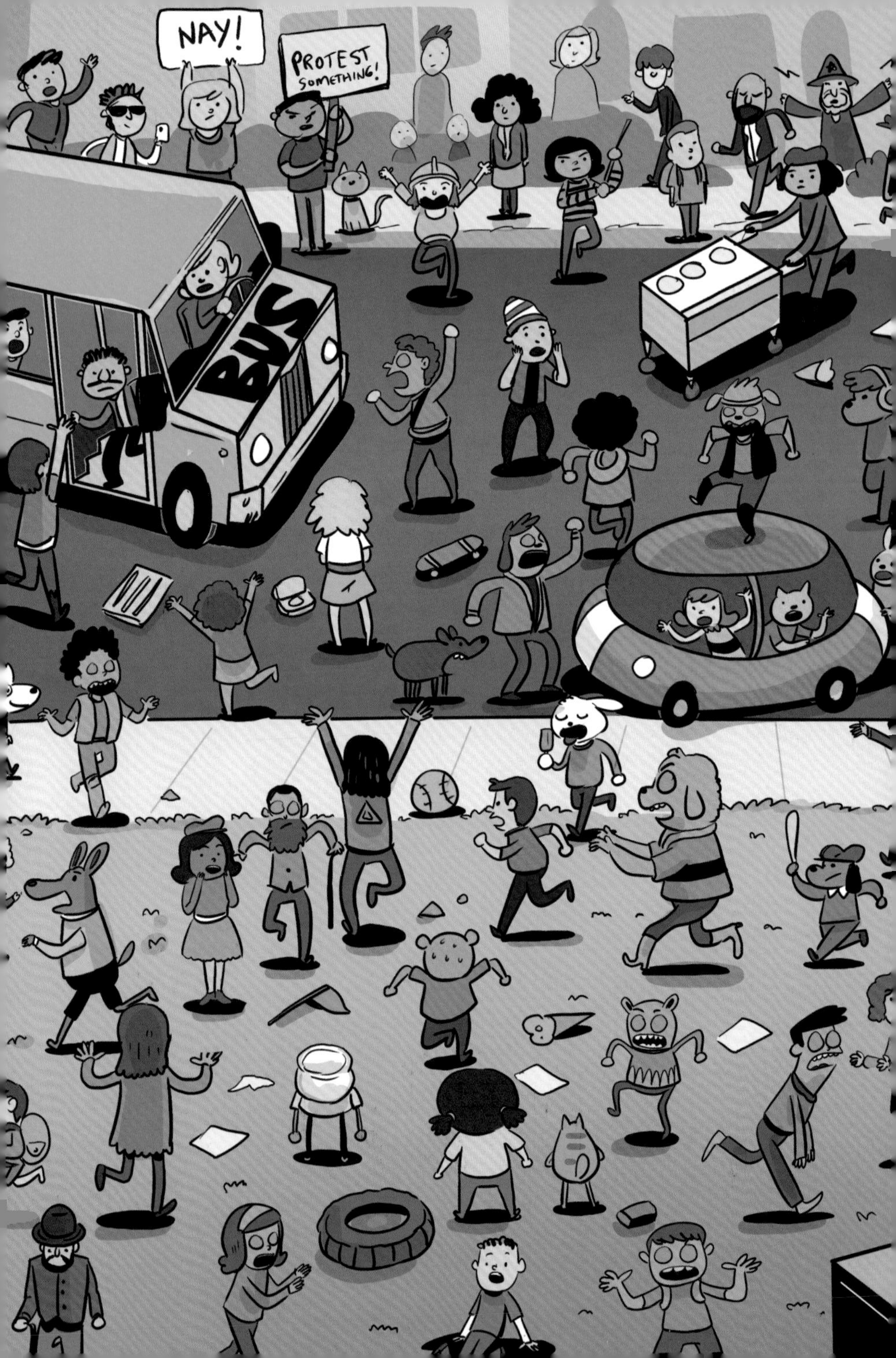
NAY!
PROTEST SOMETHING!
BUS

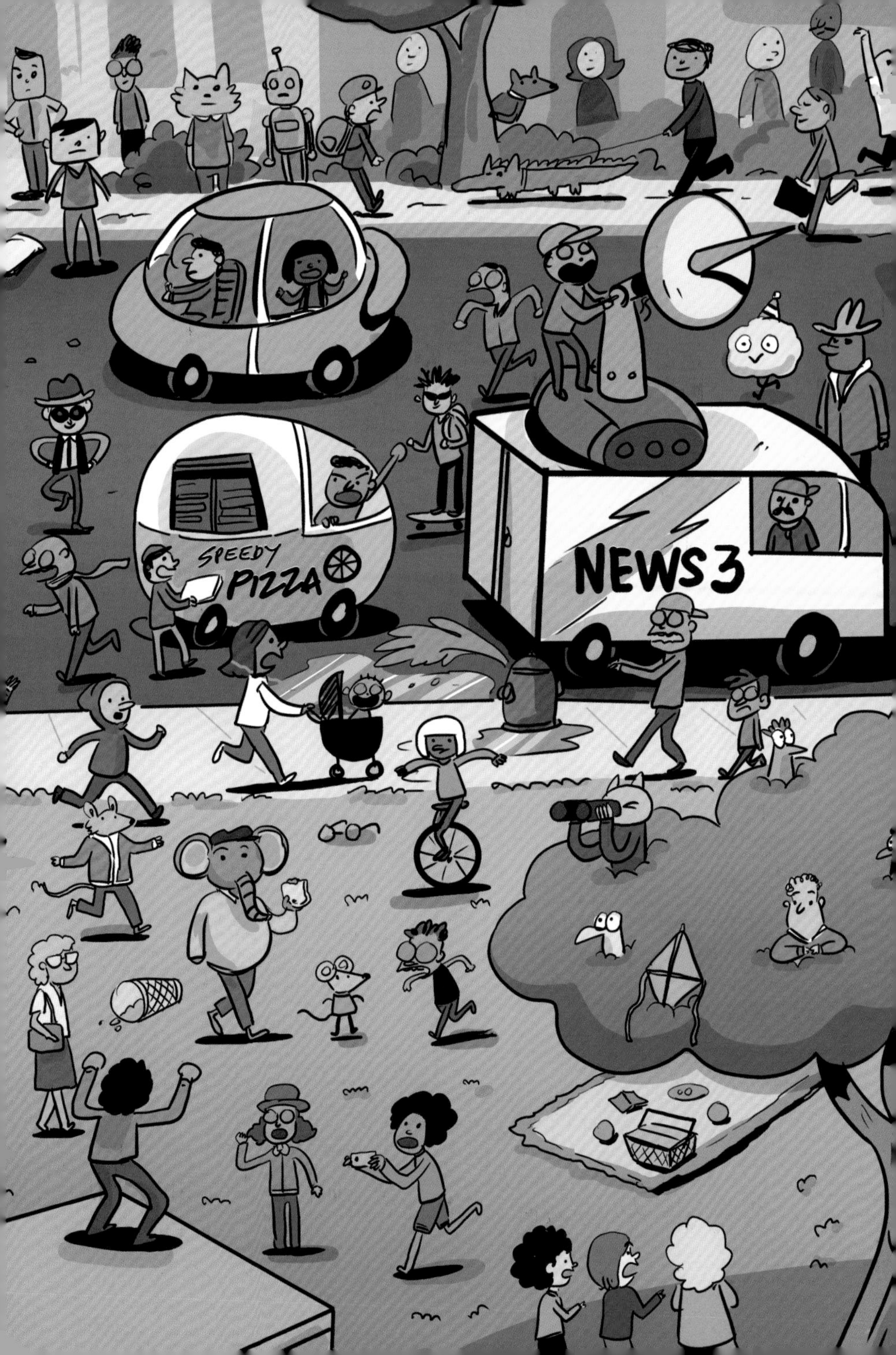
SPEEDY
PIZZA
NEWS 3

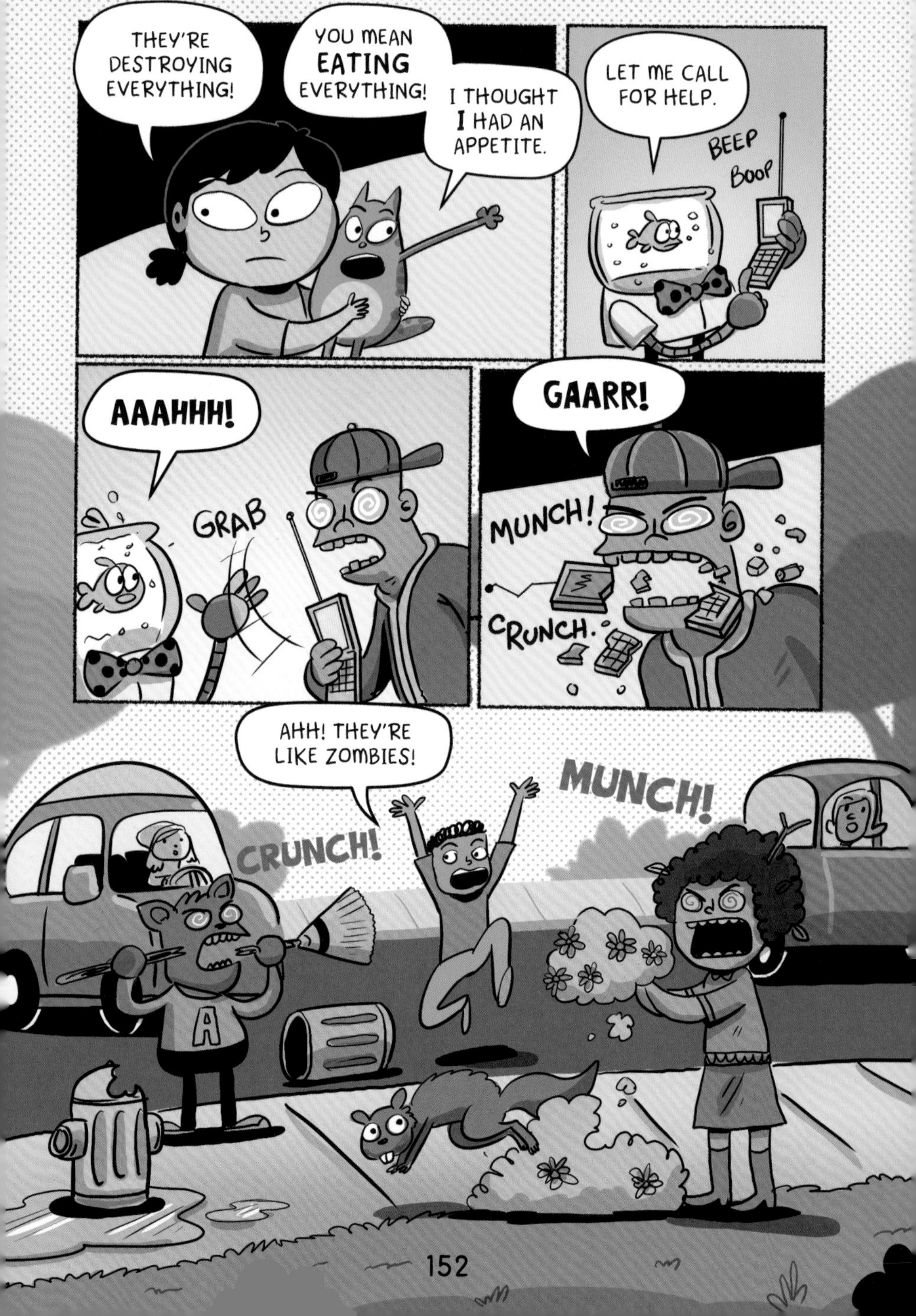
THEY'RE DESTROYING EVERYTHING!
YOU MEAN **EATING** EVERYTHING!
I THOUGHT **I** HAD AN APPETITE.
LET ME CALL FOR HELP.
BEEP
BOOP
AAAHHH!
GRAB
GAARR!
MUNCH!
CRUNCH.
AHH! THEY'RE LIKE ZOMBIES!
MUNCH!
CRUNCH!
A

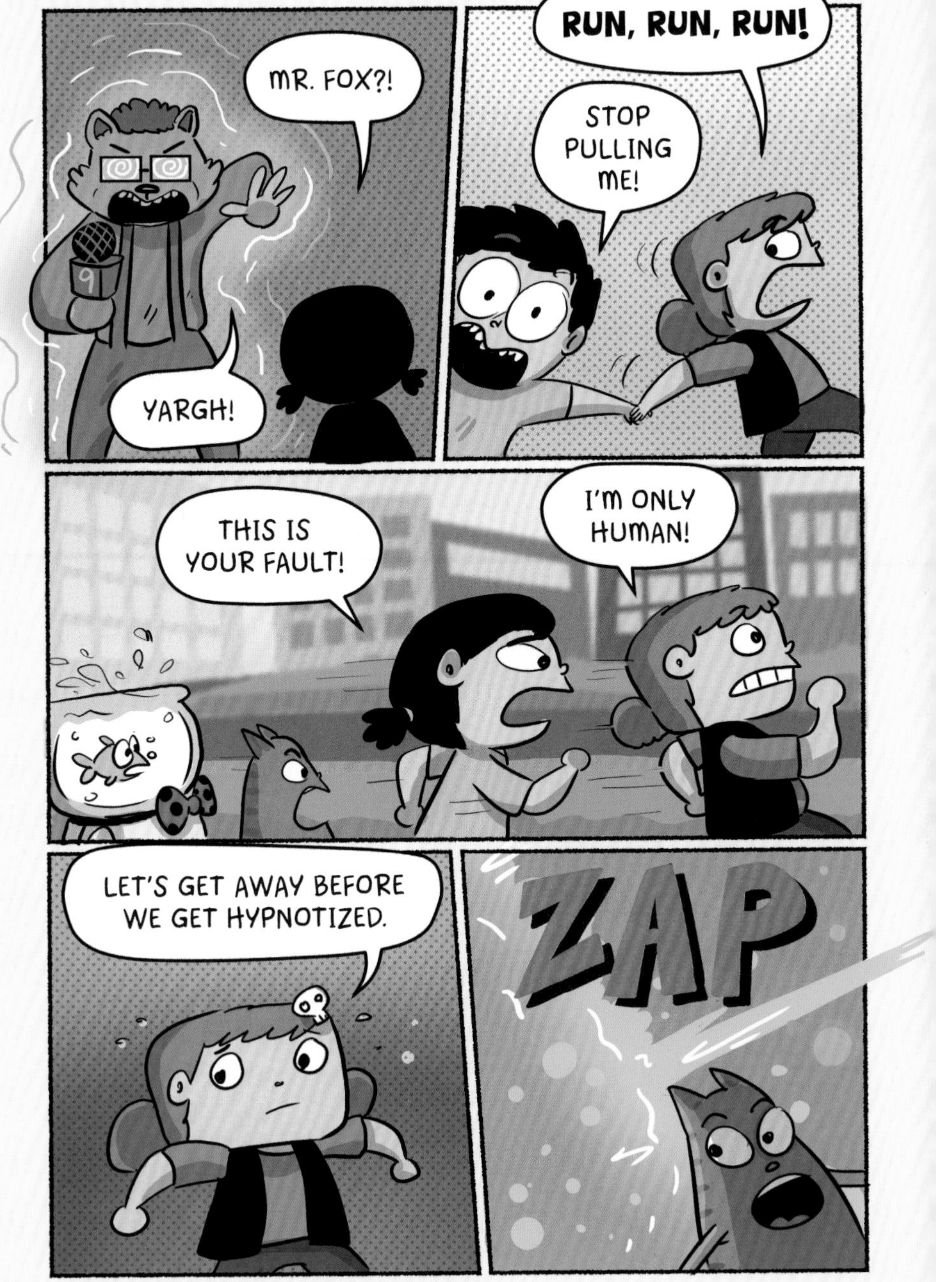
MR. FOX?!
YARGH!
RUN, RUN, RUN!
STOP PULLING ME!
THIS IS YOUR FAULT!
I'M ONLY HUMAN!
LET'S GET AWAY BEFORE WE GET HYPNOTIZED.
ZAP

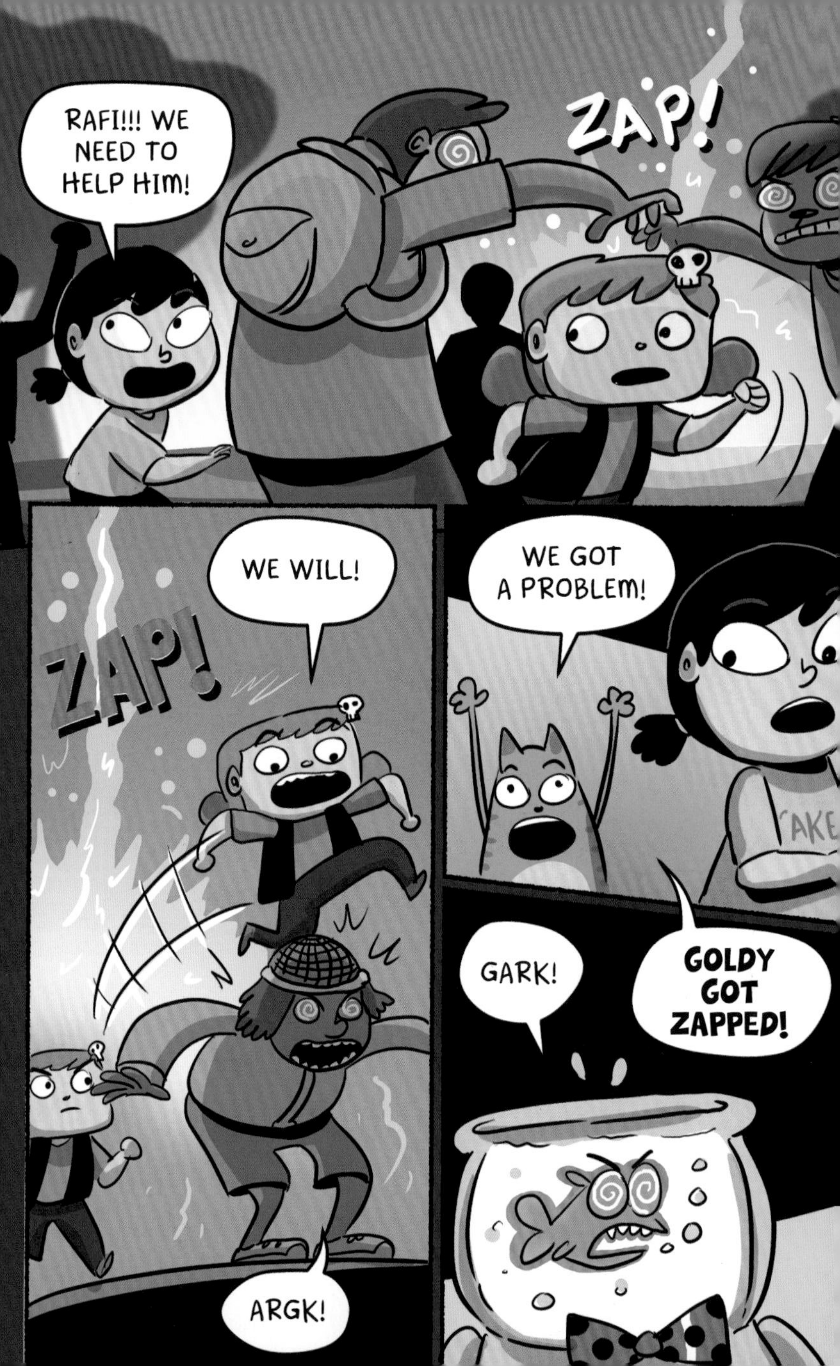
RAFI!!! WE NEED TO HELP HIM!
ZAP!
WE WILL!
ZAP!
ARGK!
WE GOT A PROBLEM!
GOLDY GOT ZAPPED!
GARK!

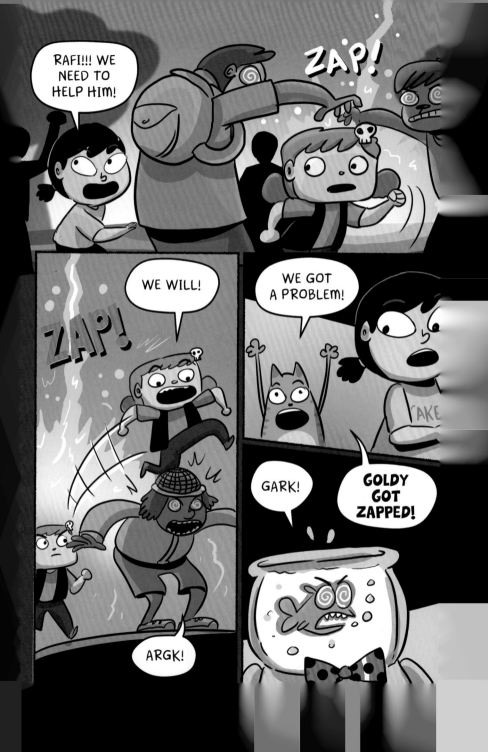

CHAPTER 9 NOWHERE TO RUN!

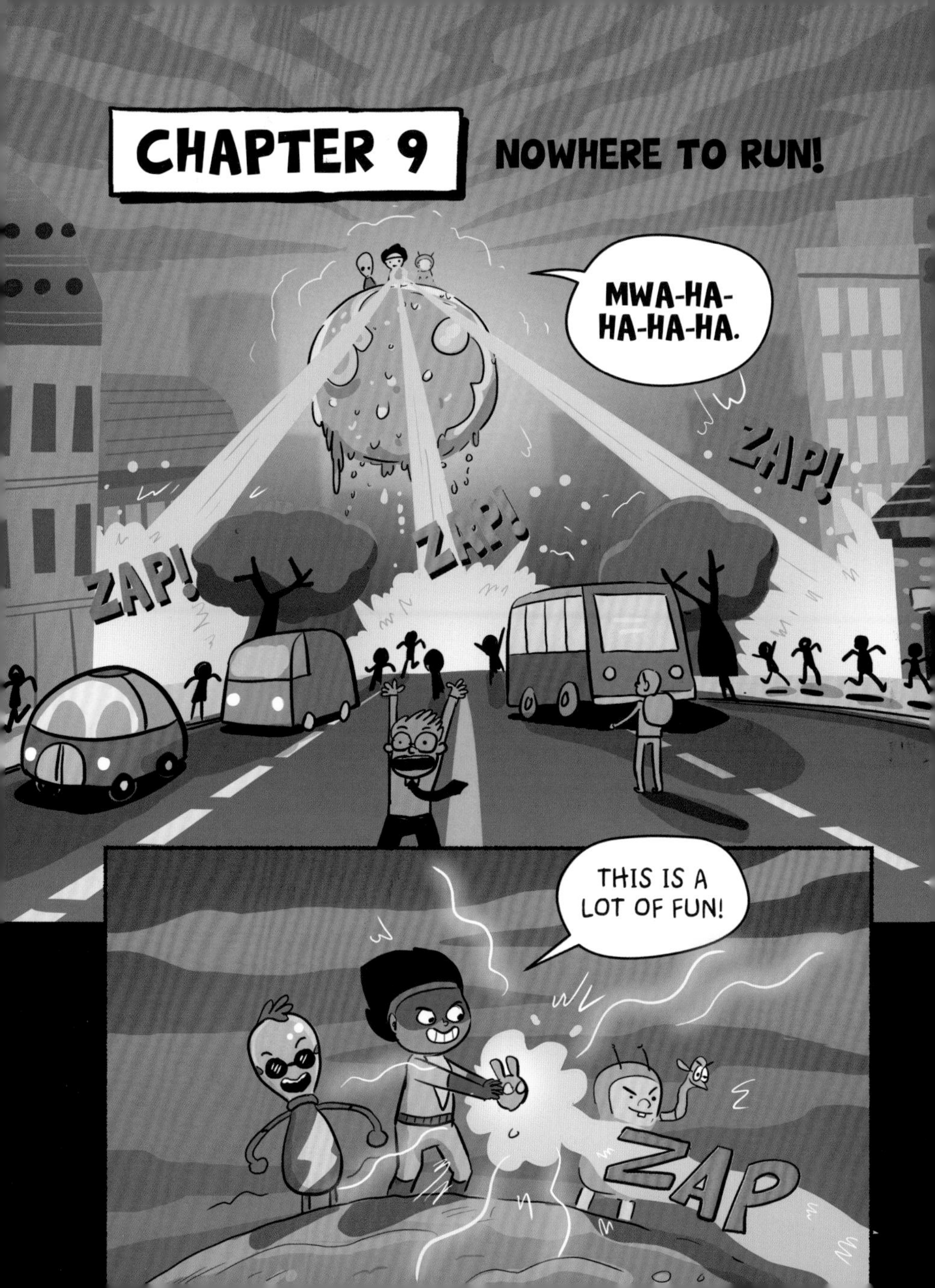
MWA-HA-HA-HA-HA.
ZAP!
ZAP!
ZAP!
THIS IS A LOT OF FUN!
ZAP

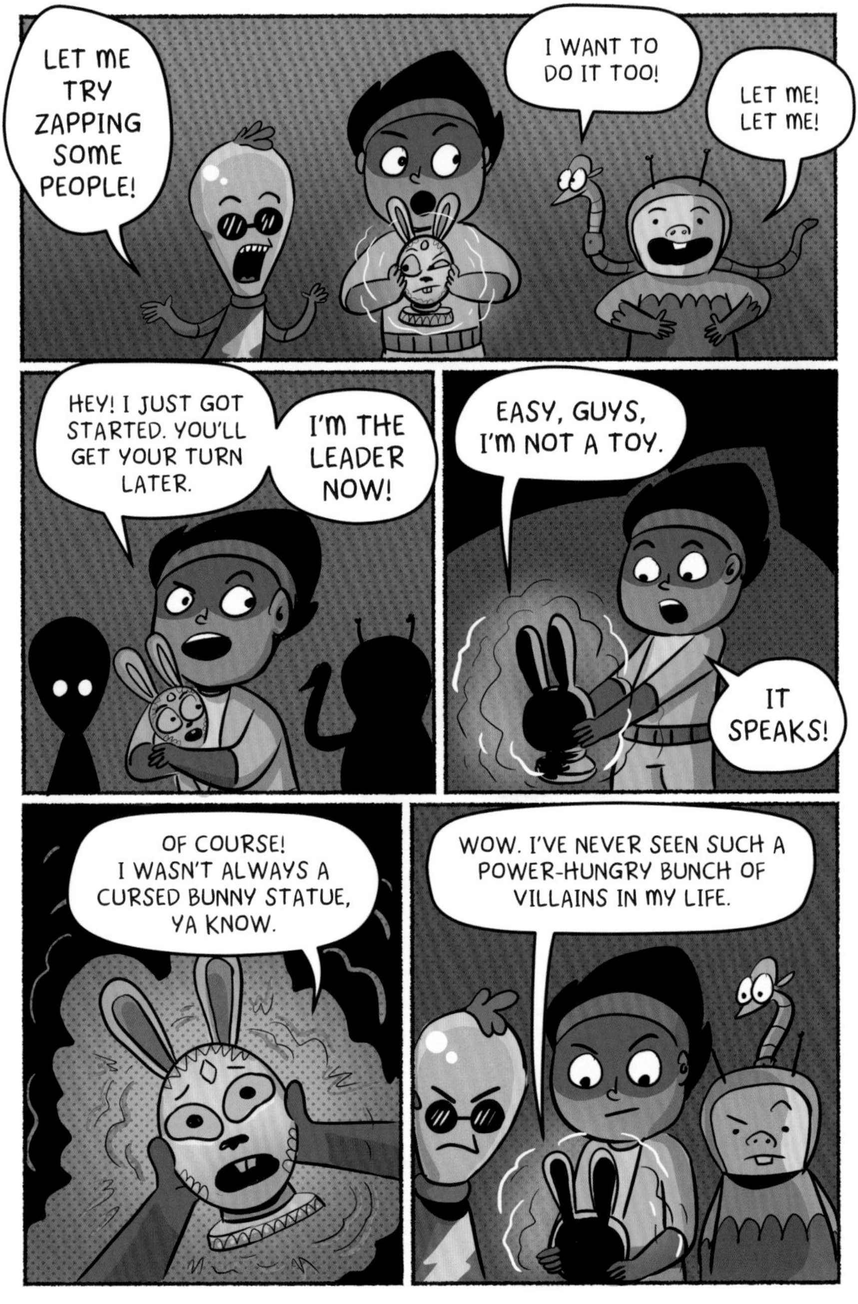

LET ME TRY ZAPPING SOME PEOPLE!
I WANT TO DO IT TOO!
LET ME! LET ME!
HEY! I JUST GOT STARTED. YOU'LL GET YOUR TURN LATER.
I'M THE LEADER NOW!
EASY, GUYS, I'M NOT A TOY.
IT SPEAKS!
OF COURSE! I WASN'T ALWAYS A CURSED BUNNY STATUE, YA KNOW.
WOW. I'VE NEVER SEEN SUCH A POWER-HUNGRY BUNCH OF VILLAINS IN MY LIFE.

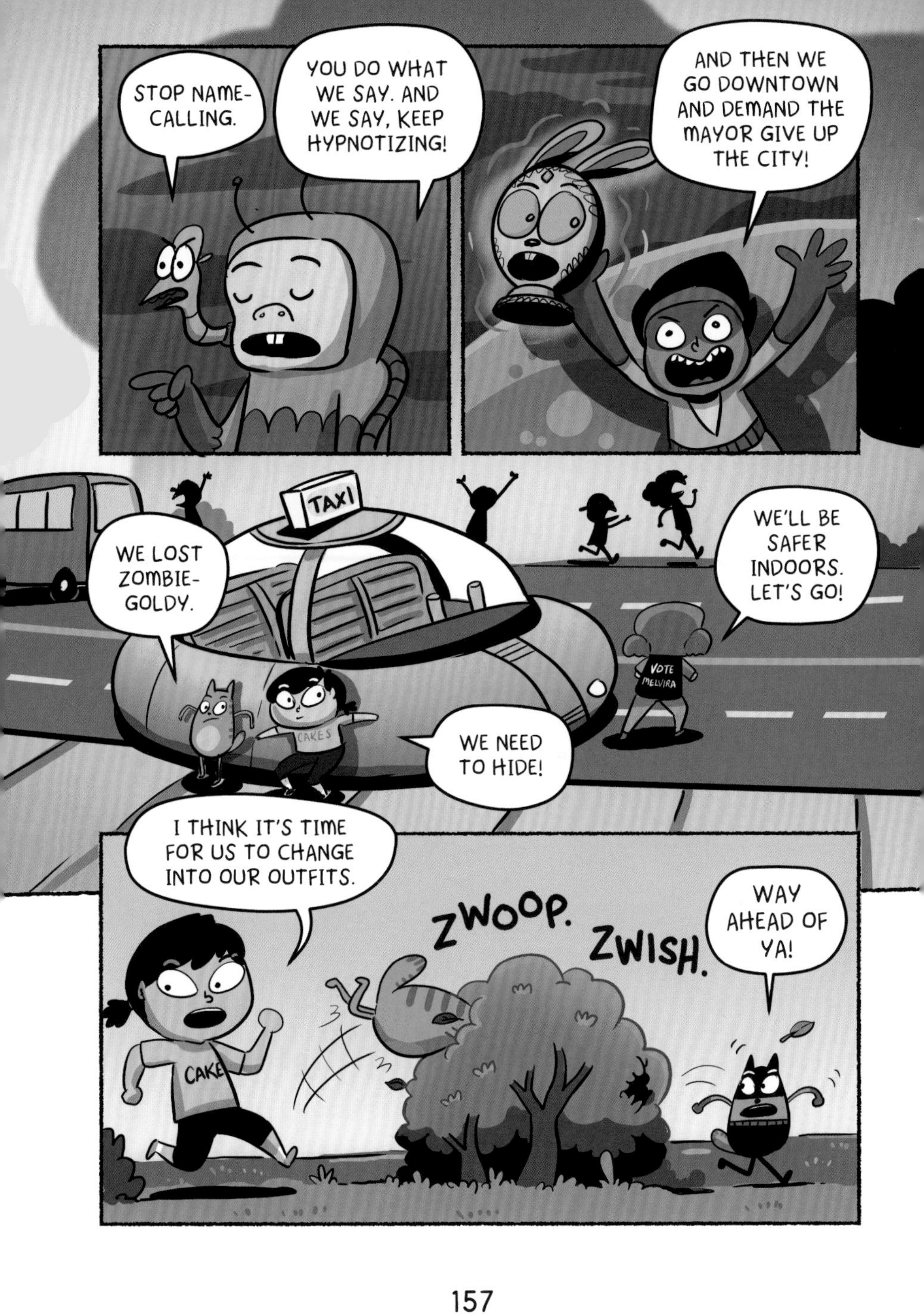
STOP NAME-CALLING.
YOU DO WHAT WE SAY. AND WE SAY, KEEP HYPNOTIZING!
AND THEN WE GO DOWNTOWN AND DEMAND THE MAYOR GIVE UP THE CITY!
TAXI
WE LOST ZOMBIE-GOLDY.
WE'LL BE SAFER INDOORS. LET'S GO!
VOTE MELVIRA
CAKES
WE NEED TO HIDE!
I THINK IT'S TIME FOR US TO CHANGE INTO OUR OUTFITS.
ZWOOP.
ZWISH.
WAY AHEAD OF YA!
CAKE

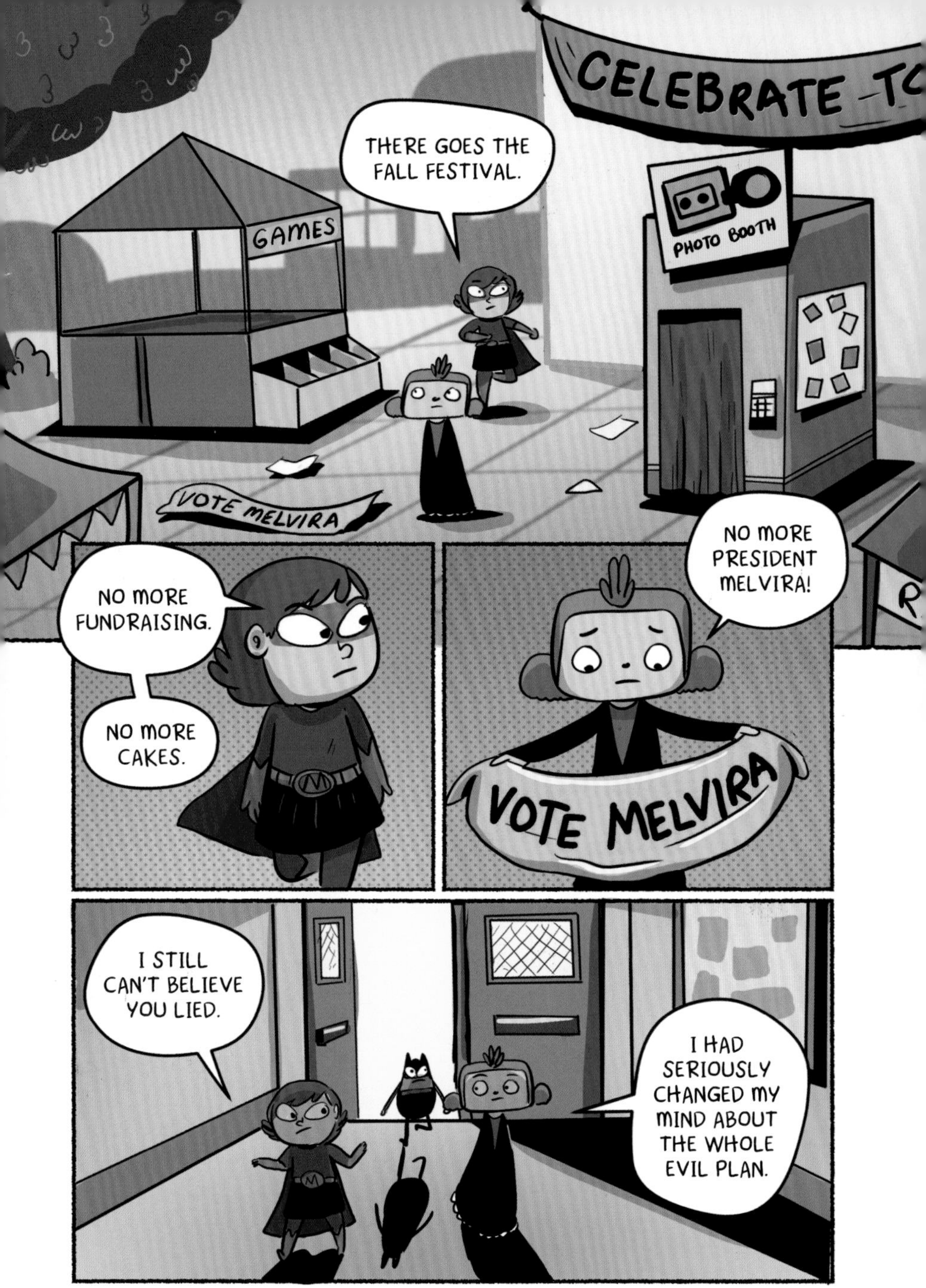
CELEBRATE TO
THERE GOES THE FALL FESTIVAL.
GAMES
PHOTO BOOTH
VOTE MELVIRA
NO MORE FUNDRAISING.
NO MORE CAKES.
NO MORE PRESIDENT MELVIRA!
VOTE MELVIRA
I STILL CAN'T BELIEVE YOU LIED.
I HAD SERIOUSLY CHANGED MY MIND ABOUT THE WHOLE EVIL PLAN.

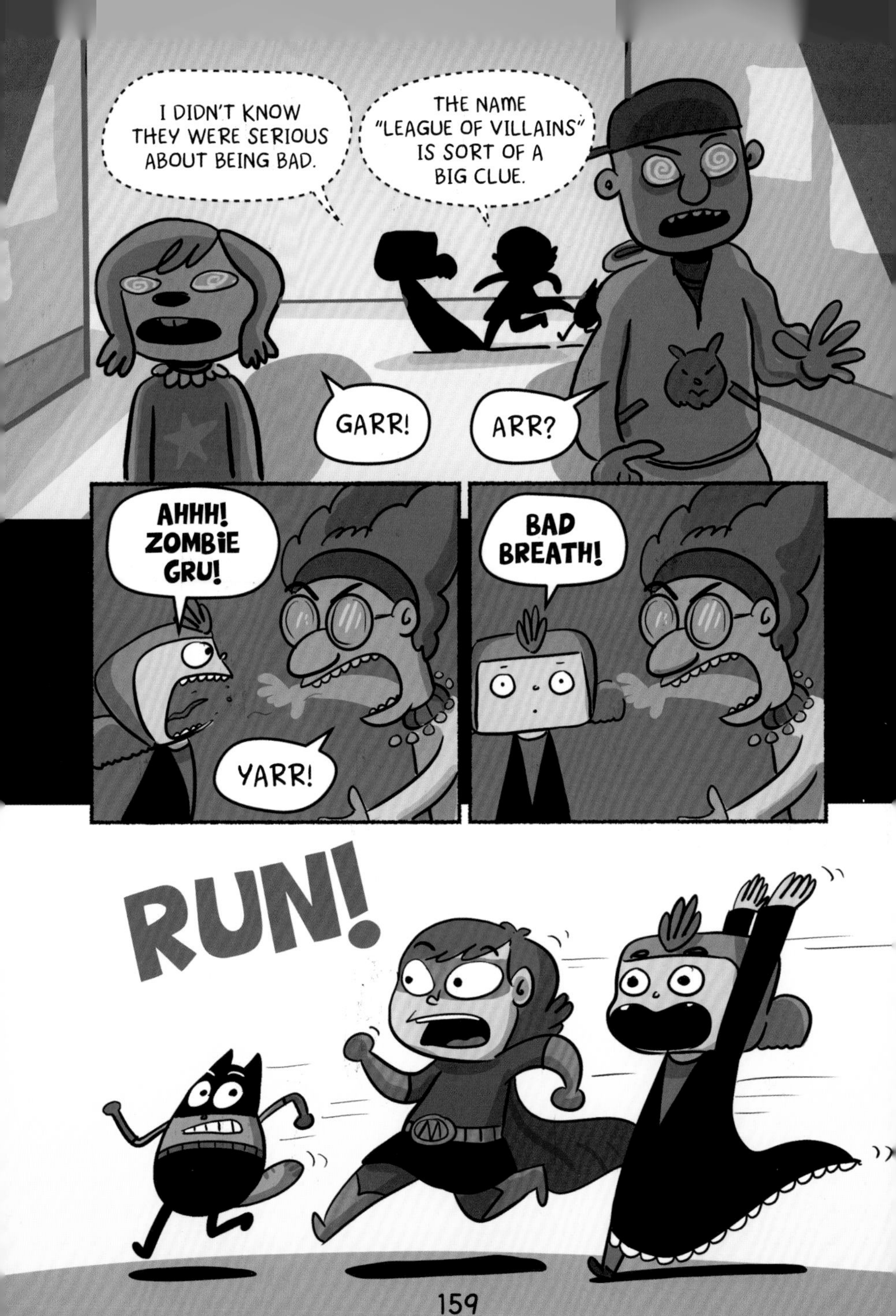
I DIDN'T KNOW THEY WERE SERIOUS ABOUT BEING BAD.
THE NAME "LEAGUE OF VILLAINS" IS SORT OF A BIG CLUE.
GARR!
ARR?
AHHH! ZOMBIE GRU!
YARR!
BAD BREATH!
RUN!

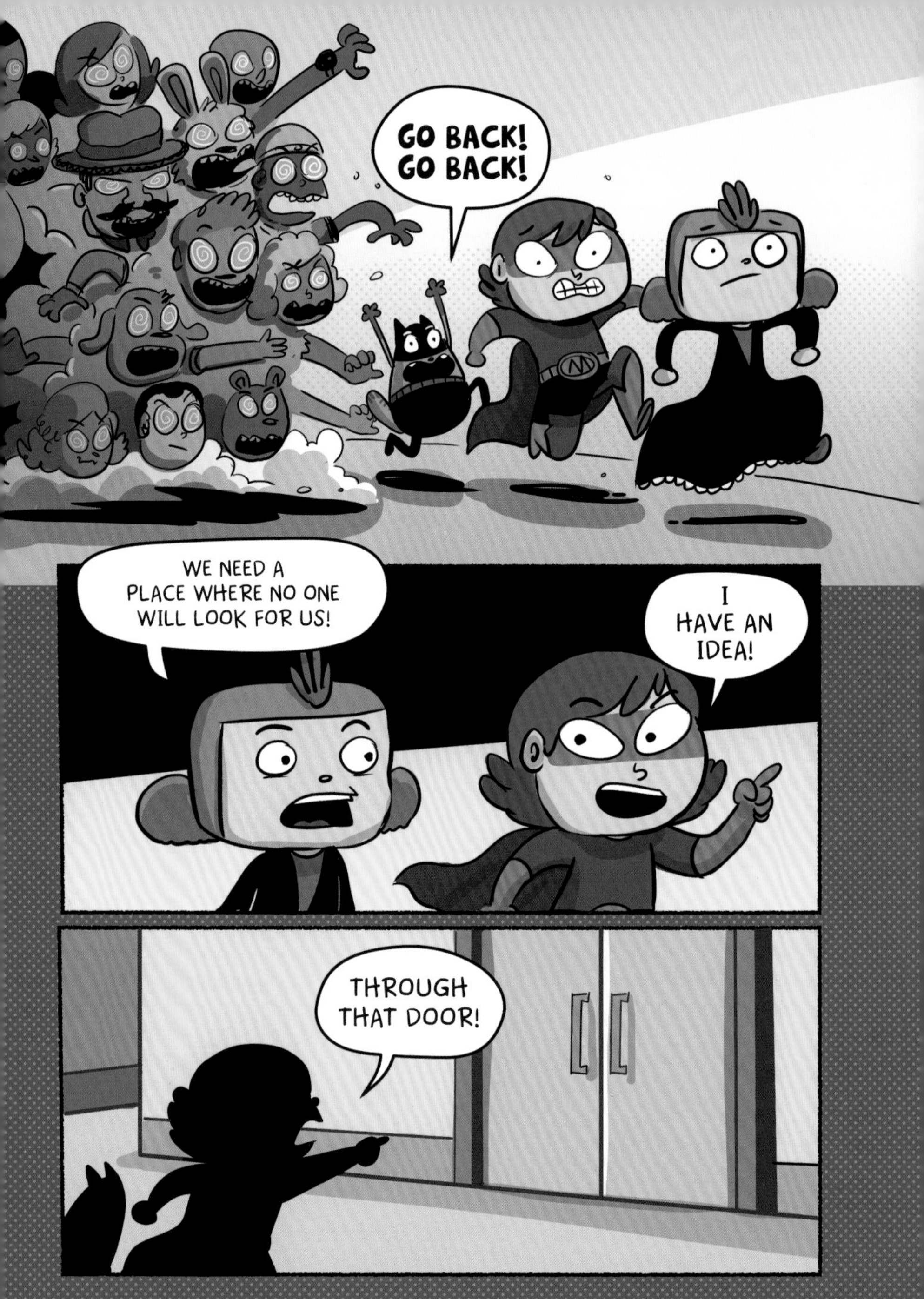
GO BACK! GO BACK!
WE NEED A PLACE WHERE NO ONE WILL LOOK FOR US!
I HAVE AN IDEA!
THROUGH THAT DOOR!

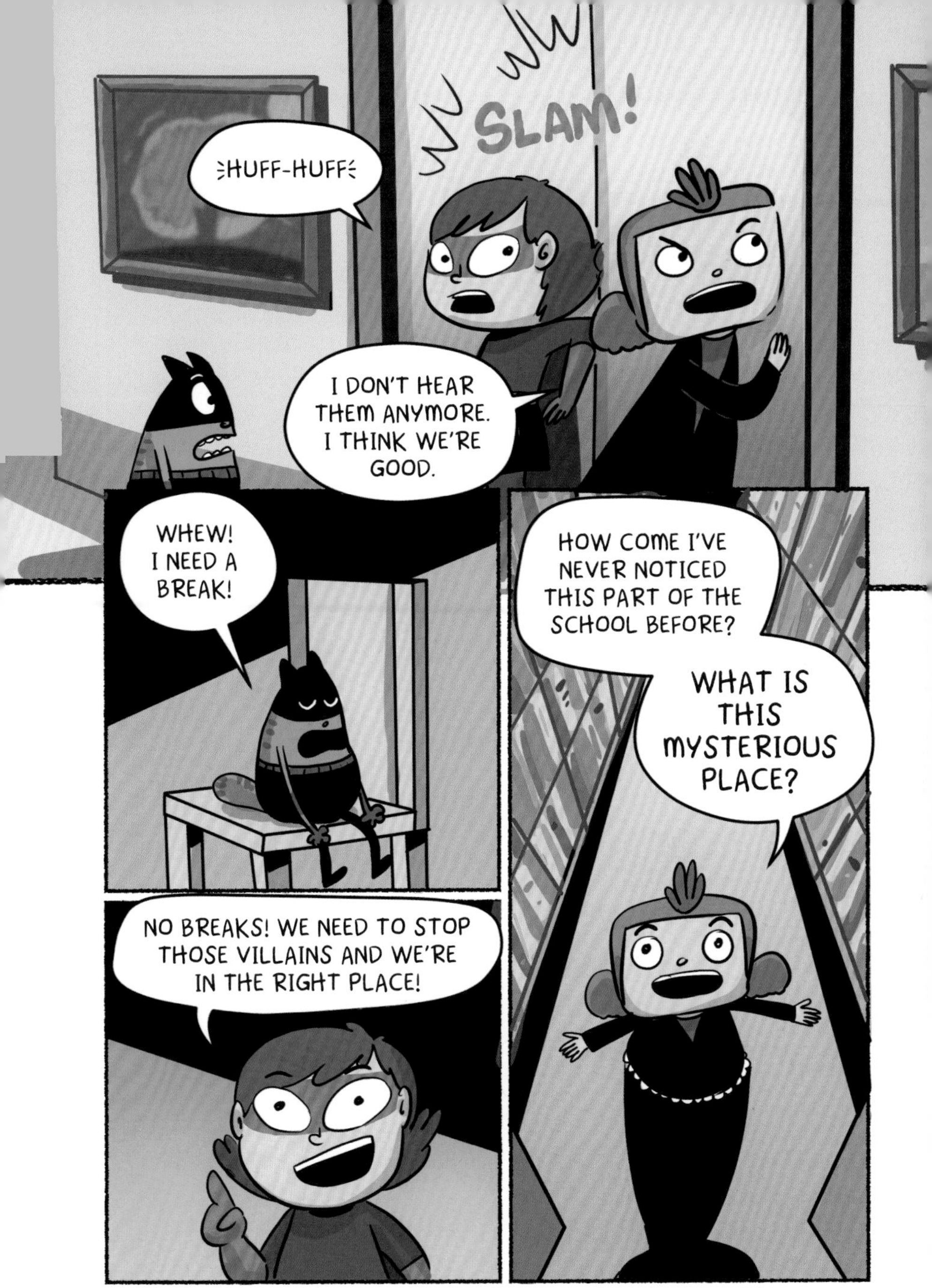
SLAM!
HUFF-HUFF
I DON'T HEAR THEM ANYMORE. I THINK WE'RE GOOD.
WHEW! I NEED A BREAK!
NO BREAKS! WE NEED TO STOP THOSE VILLAINS AND WE'RE IN THE RIGHT PLACE!
HOW COME I'VE NEVER NOTICED THIS PART OF THE SCHOOL BEFORE?
WHAT IS THIS MYSTERIOUS PLACE?

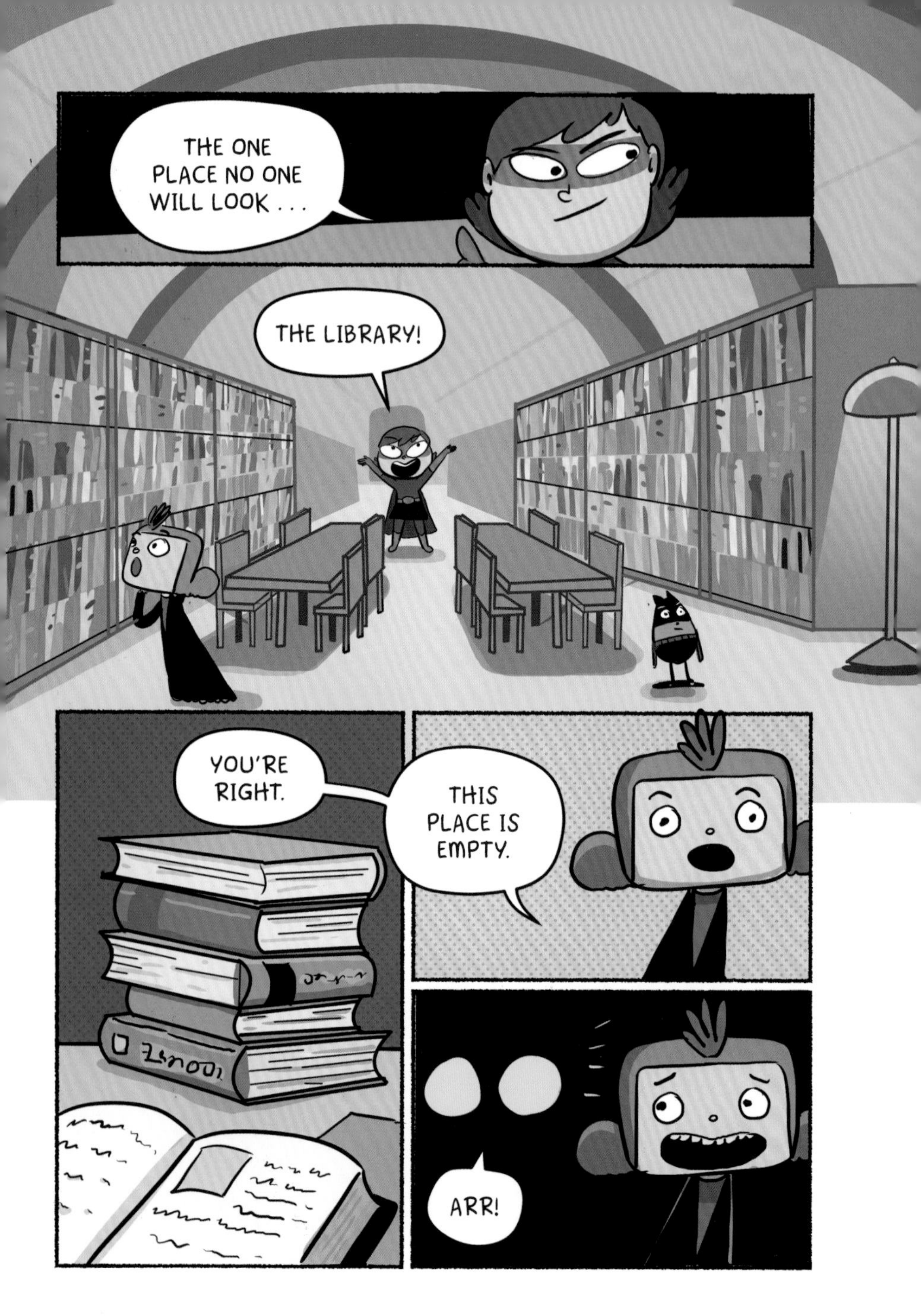
THE ONE PLACE NO ONE WILL LOOK . . .
THE LIBRARY!
YOU'RE RIGHT.
THIS PLACE IS EMPTY.
ARR!

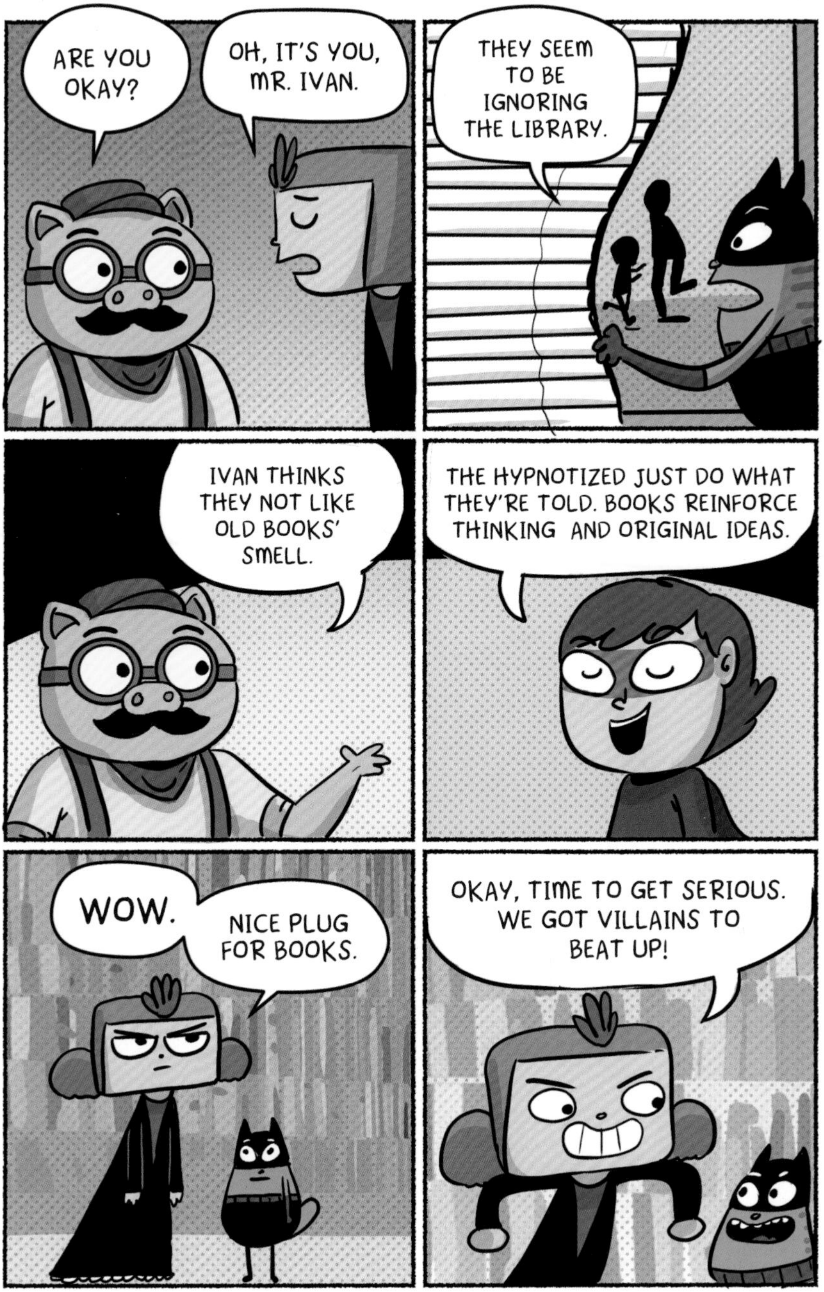
ARE YOU OKAY?
OH, IT'S YOU, MR. IVAN.
THEY SEEM TO BE IGNORING THE LIBRARY.
IVAN THINKS THEY NOT LIKE OLD BOOKS' SMELL.
THE HYPNOTIZED JUST DO WHAT THEY'RE TOLD. BOOKS REINFORCE THINKING AND ORIGINAL IDEAS.
WOW.
NICE PLUG FOR BOOKS.
OKAY, TIME TO GET SERIOUS. WE GOT VILLAINS TO BEAT UP!

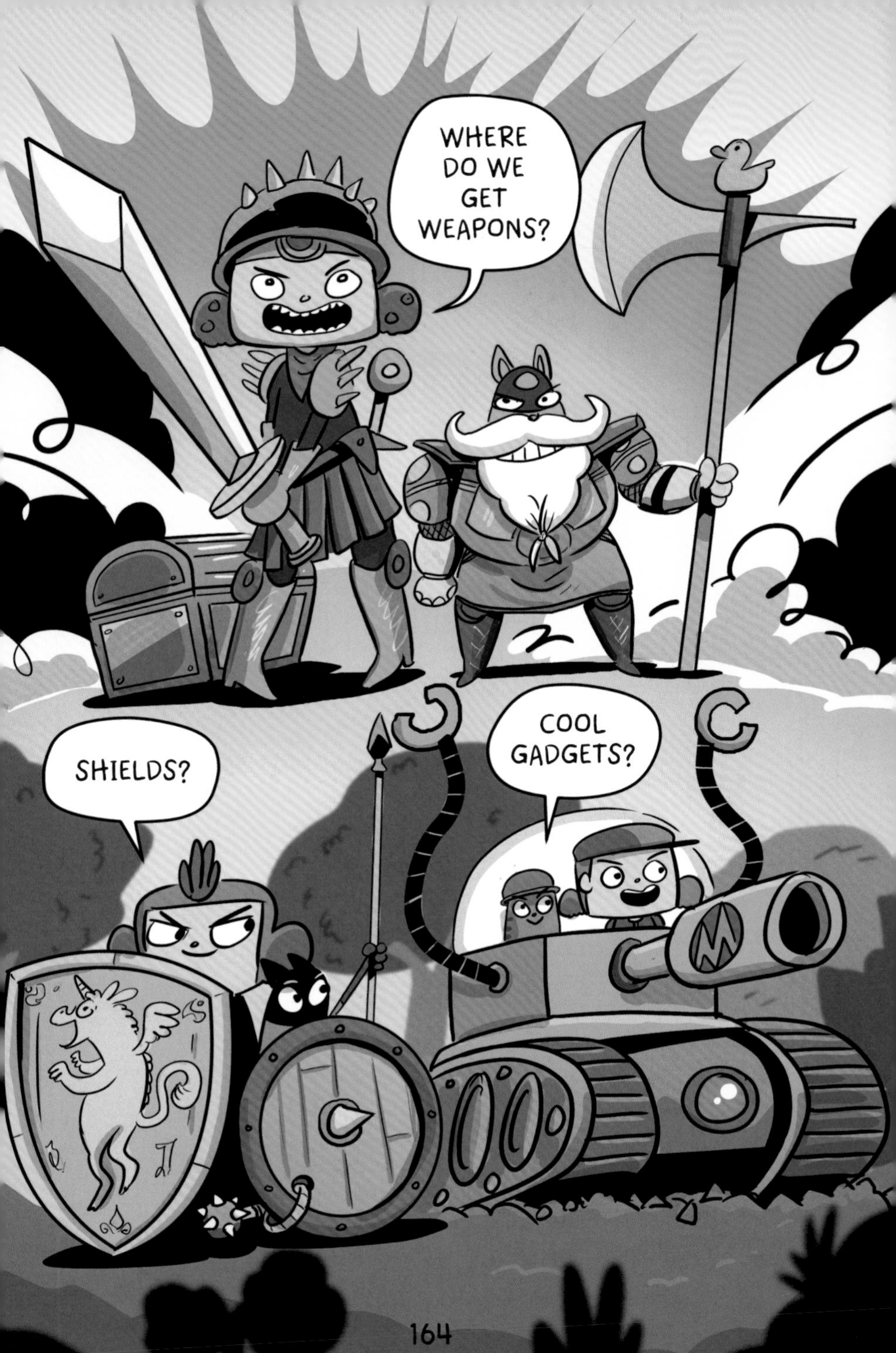
WHERE DO WE GET WEAPONS?
SHIELDS?
COOL GADGETS?

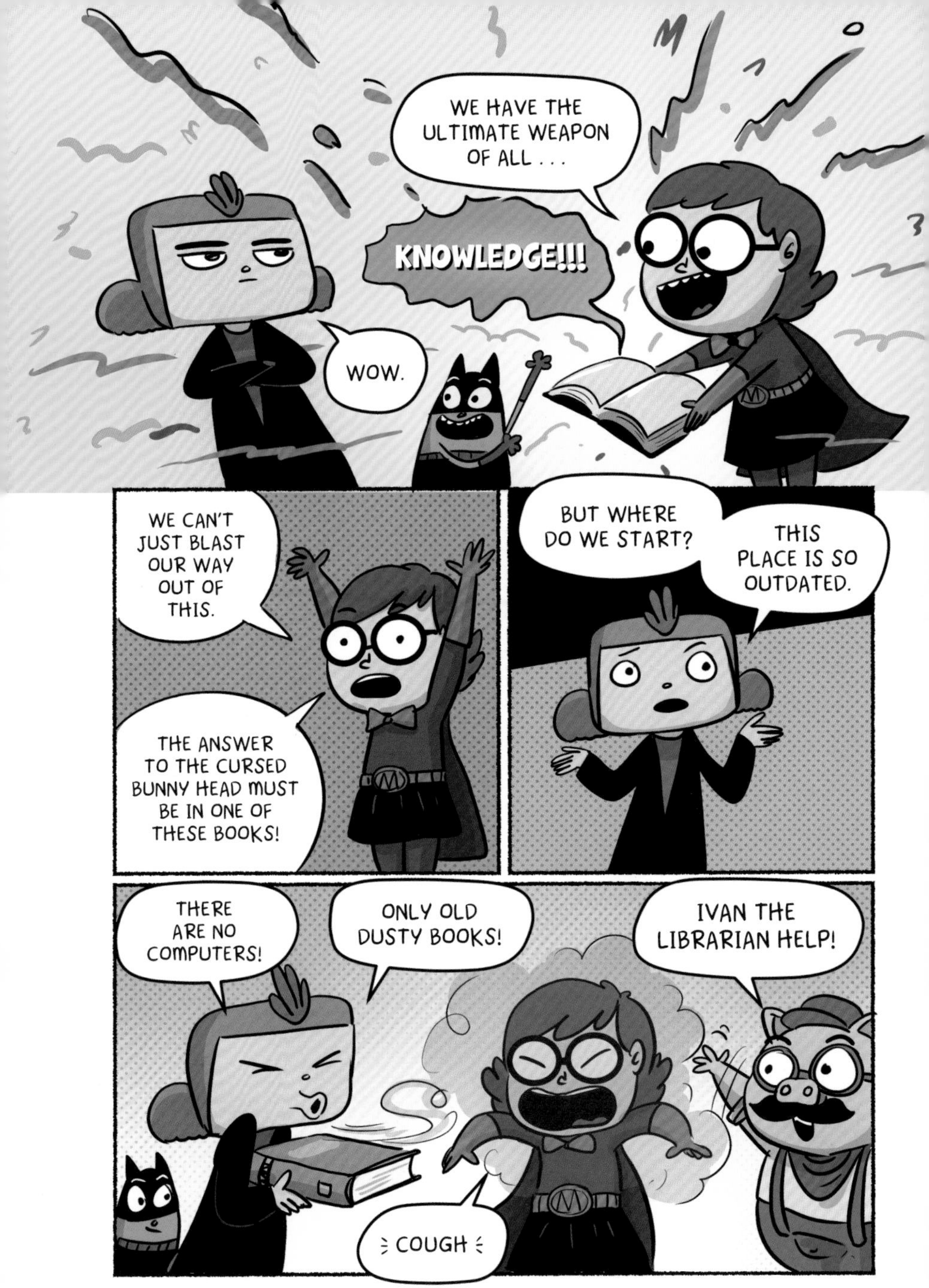
WE HAVE THE ULTIMATE WEAPON OF ALL . . .
KNOWLEDGE!!!
WOW.
WE CAN'T JUST BLAST OUR WAY OUT OF THIS.
THE ANSWER TO THE CURSED BUNNY HEAD MUST BE IN ONE OF THESE BOOKS!
BUT WHERE DO WE START?
THIS PLACE IS SO OUTDATED.
THERE ARE NO COMPUTERS!
ONLY OLD DUSTY BOOKS!
COUGH
IVAN THE LIBRARIAN HELP!

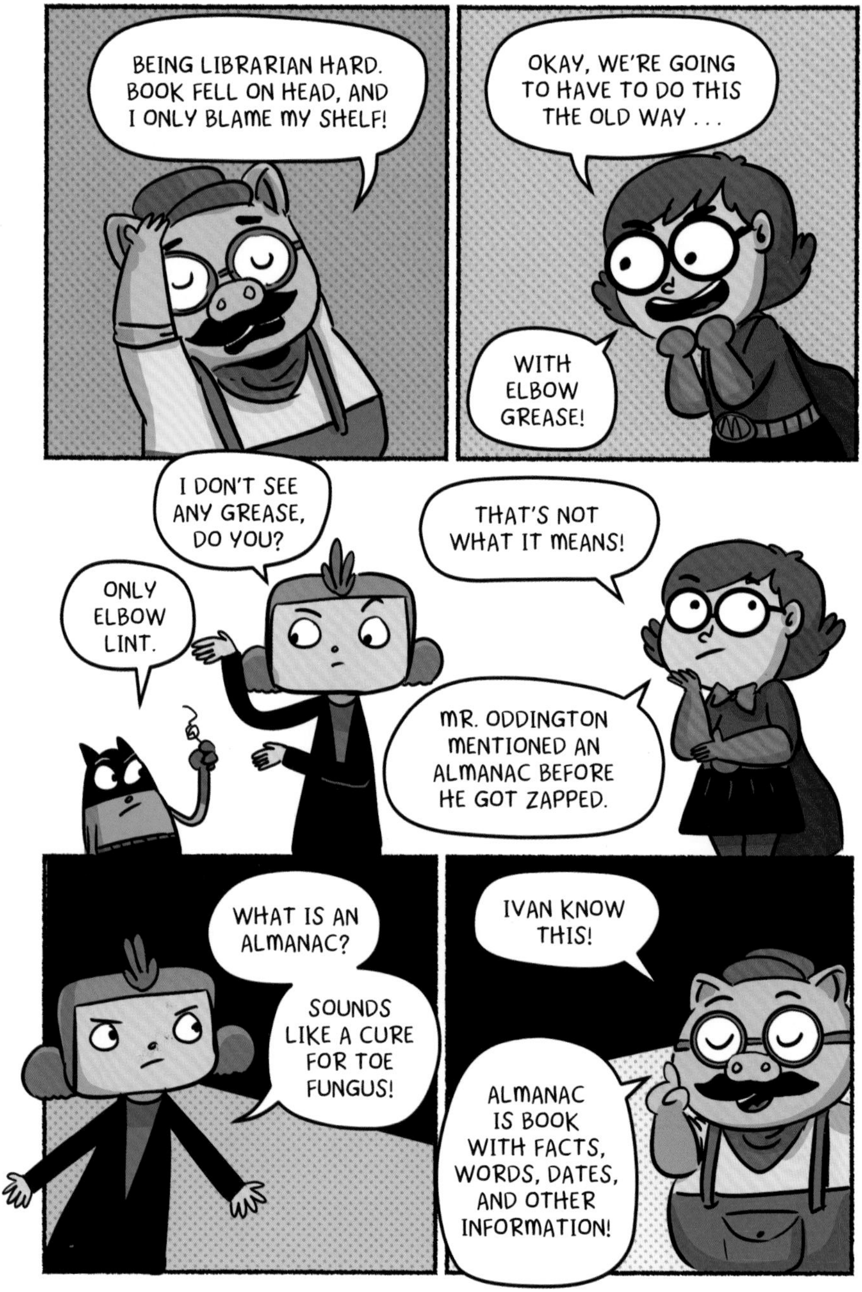
BEING LIBRARIAN HARD. BOOK FELL ON HEAD, AND I ONLY BLAME MY SHELF!
OKAY, WE'RE GOING TO HAVE TO DO THIS THE OLD WAY . . .
WITH ELBOW GREASE!
I DON'T SEE ANY GREASE, DO YOU?
ONLY ELBOW LINT.
THAT'S NOT WHAT IT MEANS!
MR. ODDINGTON MENTIONED AN ALMANAC BEFORE HE GOT ZAPPED.
WHAT IS AN ALMANAC?
SOUNDS LIKE A CURE FOR TOE FUNGUS!
IVAN KNOW THIS!
ALMANAC IS BOOK WITH FACTS, WORDS, DATES, AND OTHER INFORMATION!

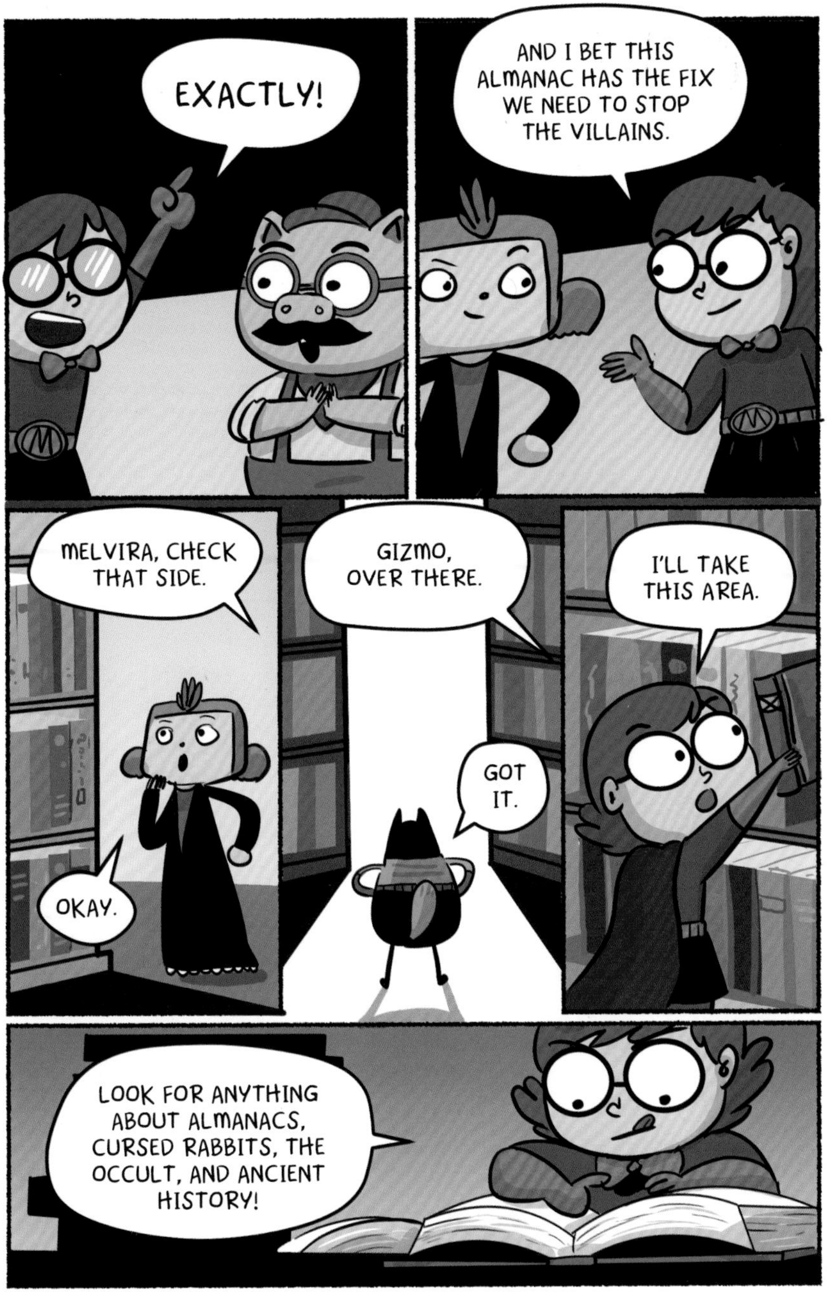
EXACTLY!
AND I BET THIS ALMANAC HAS THE FIX WE NEED TO STOP THE VILLAINS.
MELVIRA, CHECK THAT SIDE.
OKAY.
GIZMO, OVER THERE.
GOT IT.
I'LL TAKE THIS AREA.
LOOK FOR ANYTHING ABOUT ALMANACS, CURSED RABBITS, THE OCCULT, AND ANCIENT HISTORY!

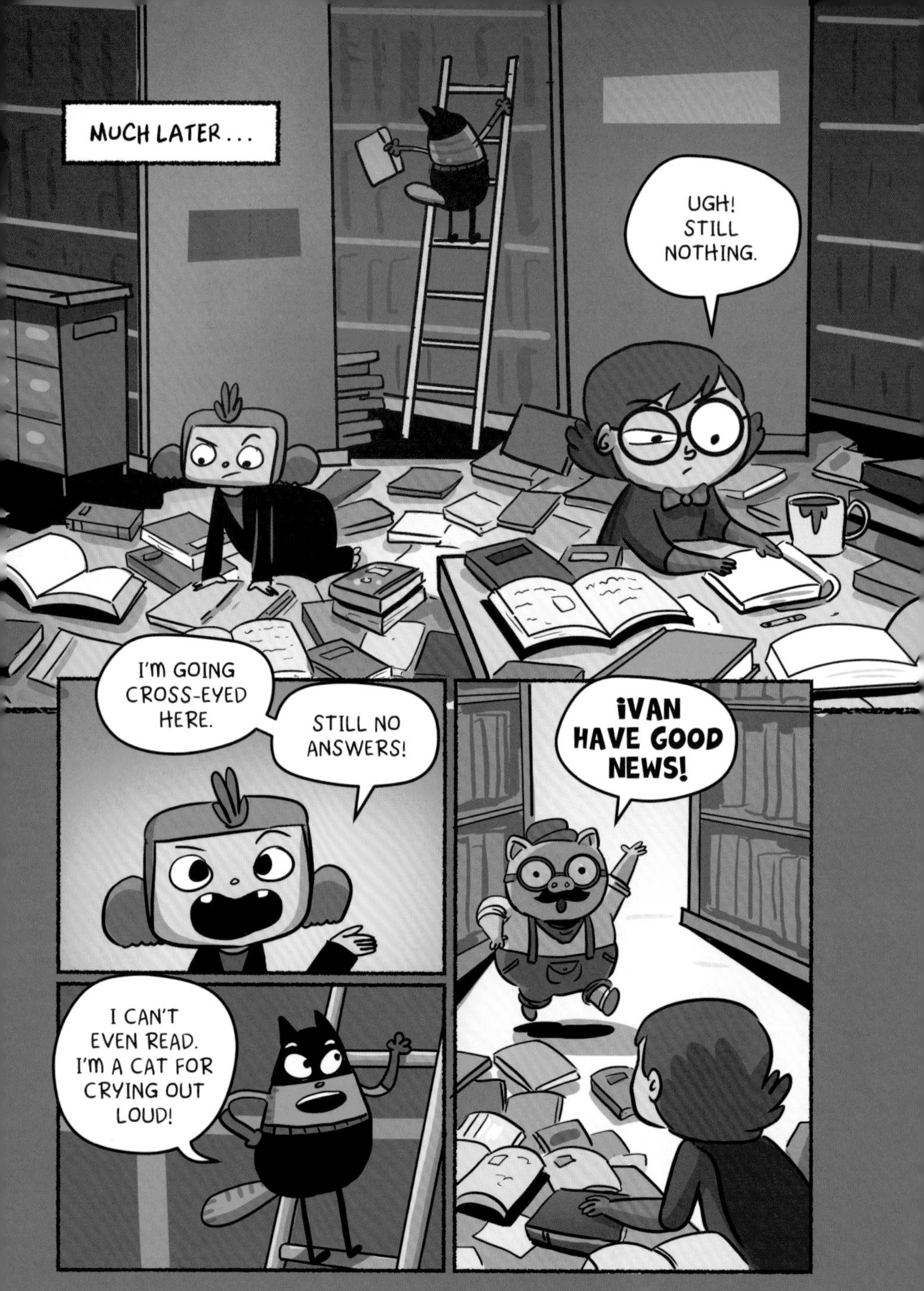
MUCH LATER . . .
UGH! STILL NOTHING.
I'M GOING CROSS-EYED HERE.
STILL NO ANSWERS!
IVAN HAVE GOOD NEWS!
I CAN'T EVEN READ. I'M A CAT FOR CRYING OUT LOUD!

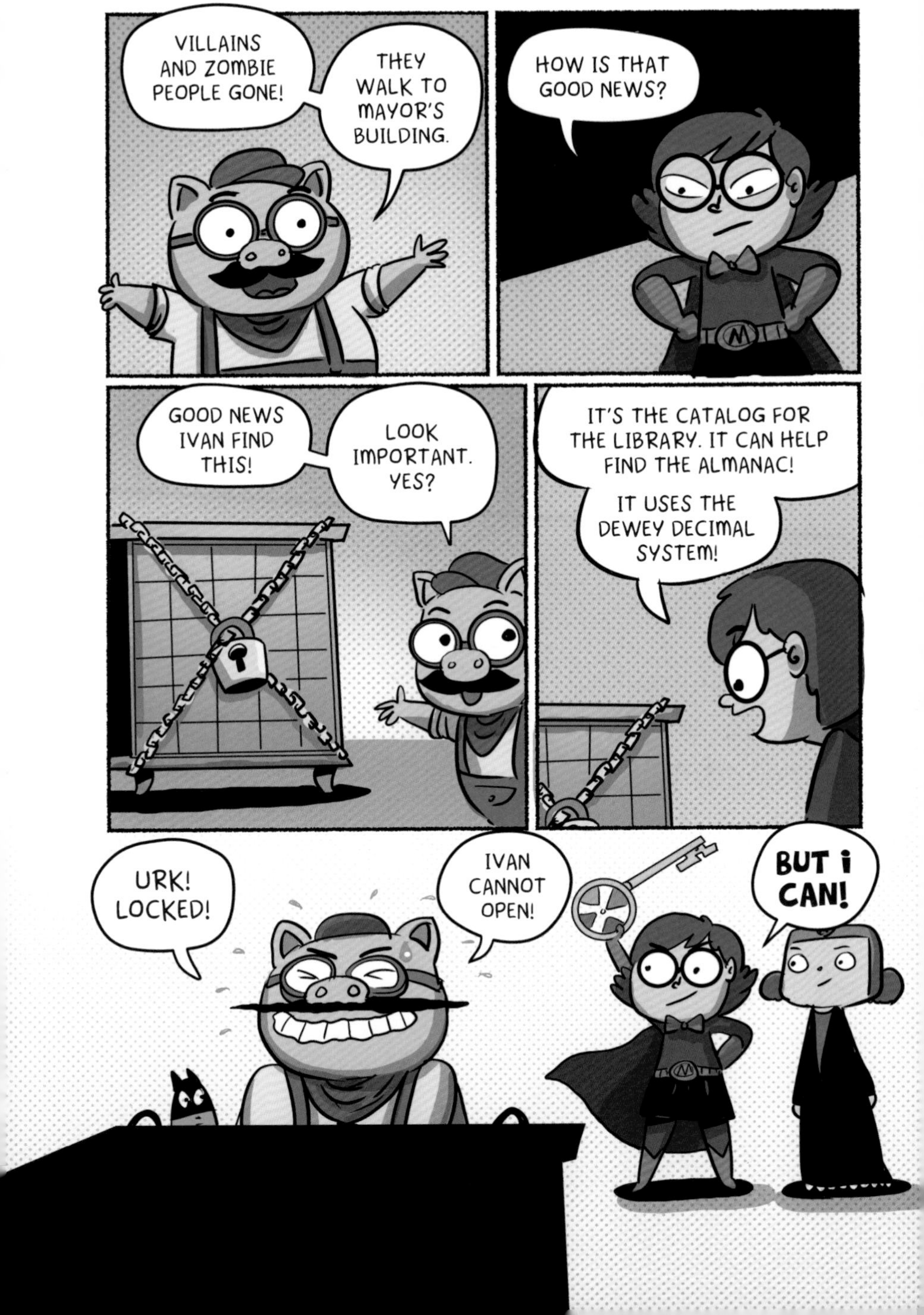
VILLAINS AND ZOMBIE PEOPLE GONE!
THEY WALK TO MAYOR'S BUILDING.
HOW IS THAT GOOD NEWS?
GOOD NEWS IVAN FIND THIS!
LOOK IMPORTANT. YES?
IT'S THE CATALOG FOR THE LIBRARY. IT CAN HELP FIND THE ALMANAC!
IT USES THE DEWEY DECIMAL SYSTEM!
URK! LOCKED!
IVAN CANNOT OPEN!
BUT I CAN!

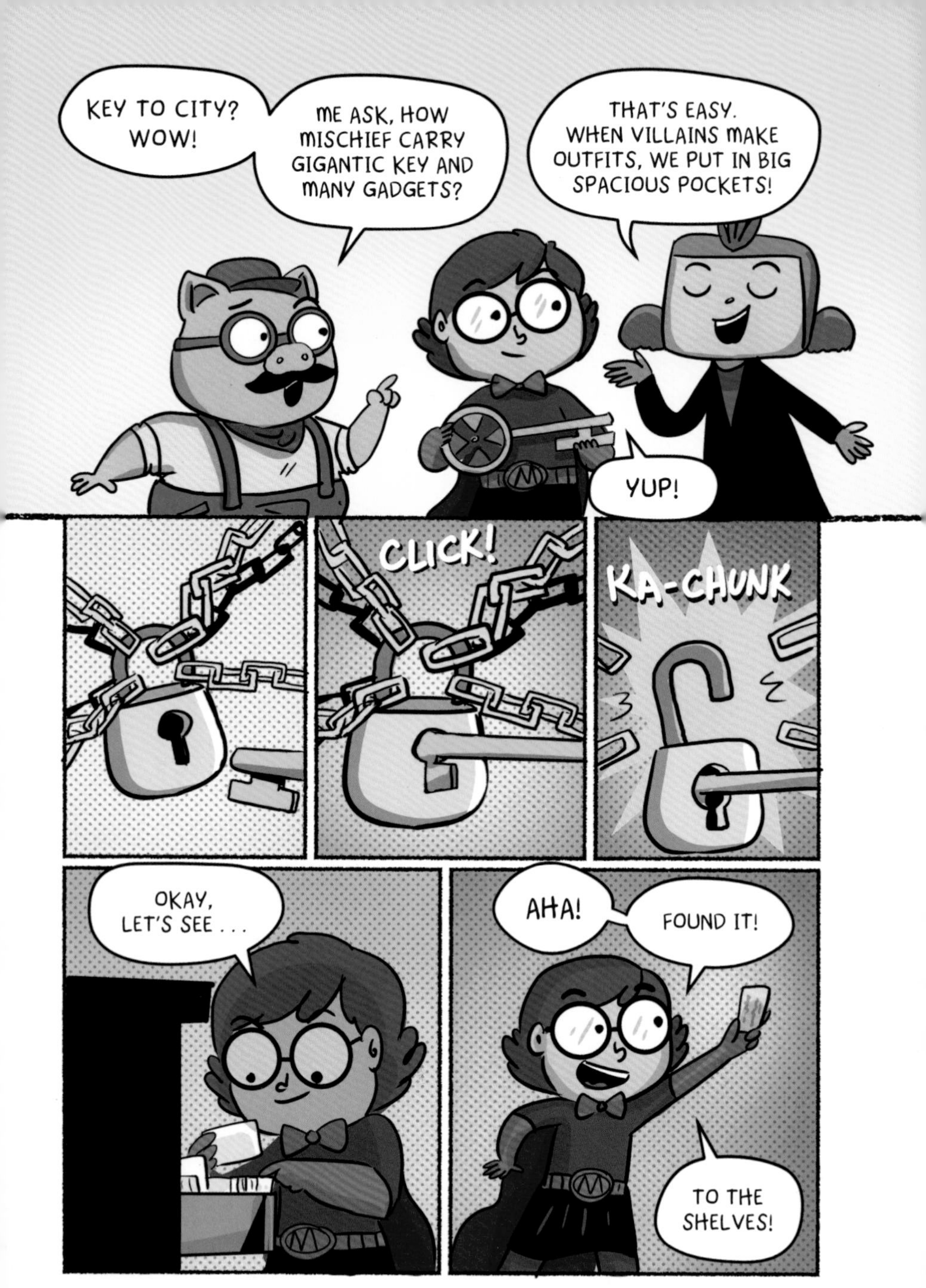
KEY TO CITY? WOW!
ME ASK, HOW MISCHIEF CARRY GIGANTIC KEY AND MANY GADGETS?
THAT'S EASY. WHEN VILLAINS MAKE OUTFITS, WE PUT IN BIG SPACIOUS POCKETS!
YUP!
CLICK!
KA-CHUNK
OKAY, LET'S SEE . . .
AHA!
FOUND IT!
TO THE SHELVES!

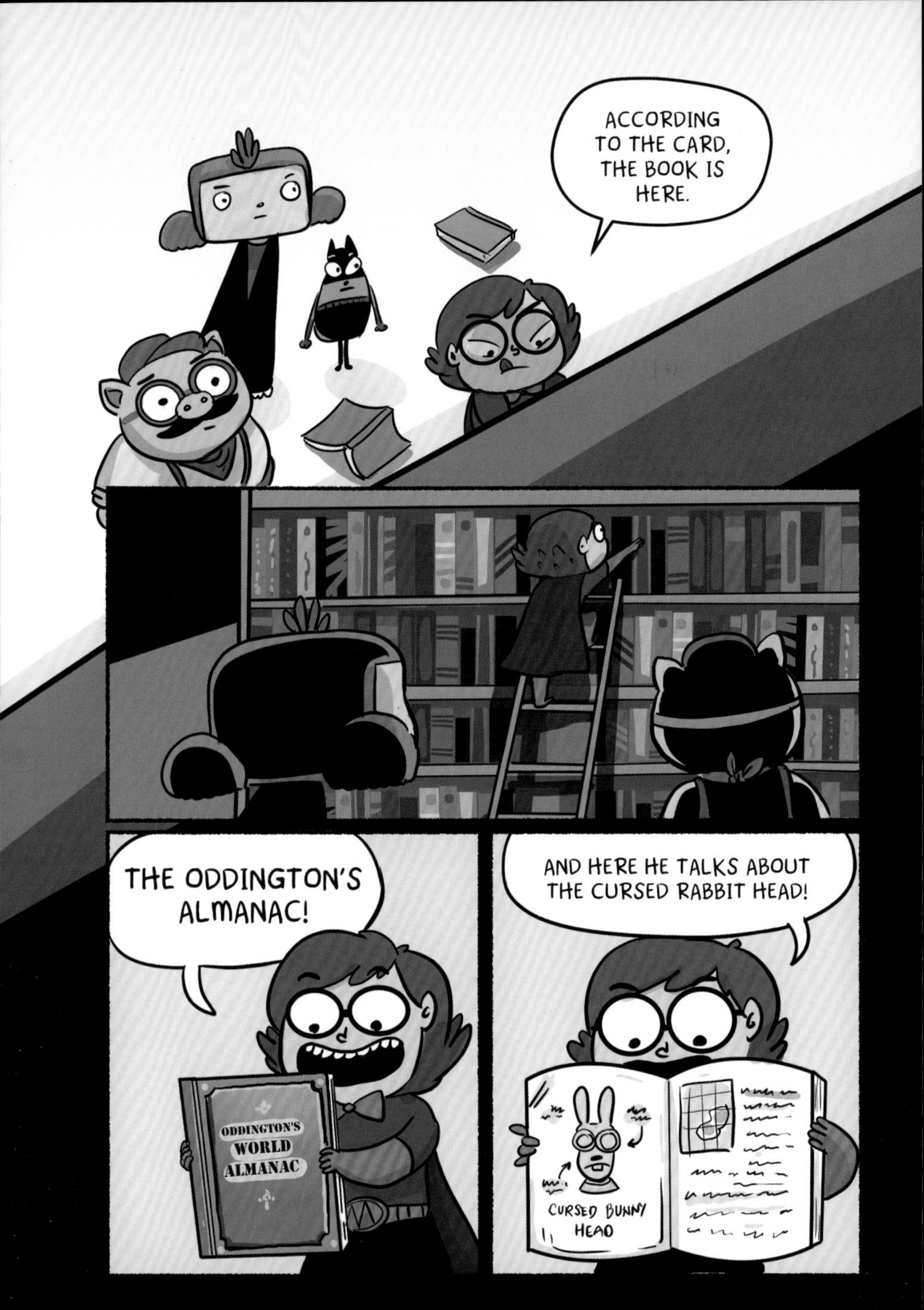
ACCORDING TO THE CARD, THE BOOK IS HERE.
THE ODDINGTON'S ALMANAC!
ODDINGTON'S WORLD ALMANAC
AND HERE HE TALKS ABOUT THE CURSED RABBIT HEAD!
CURSED BUNNY HEAD

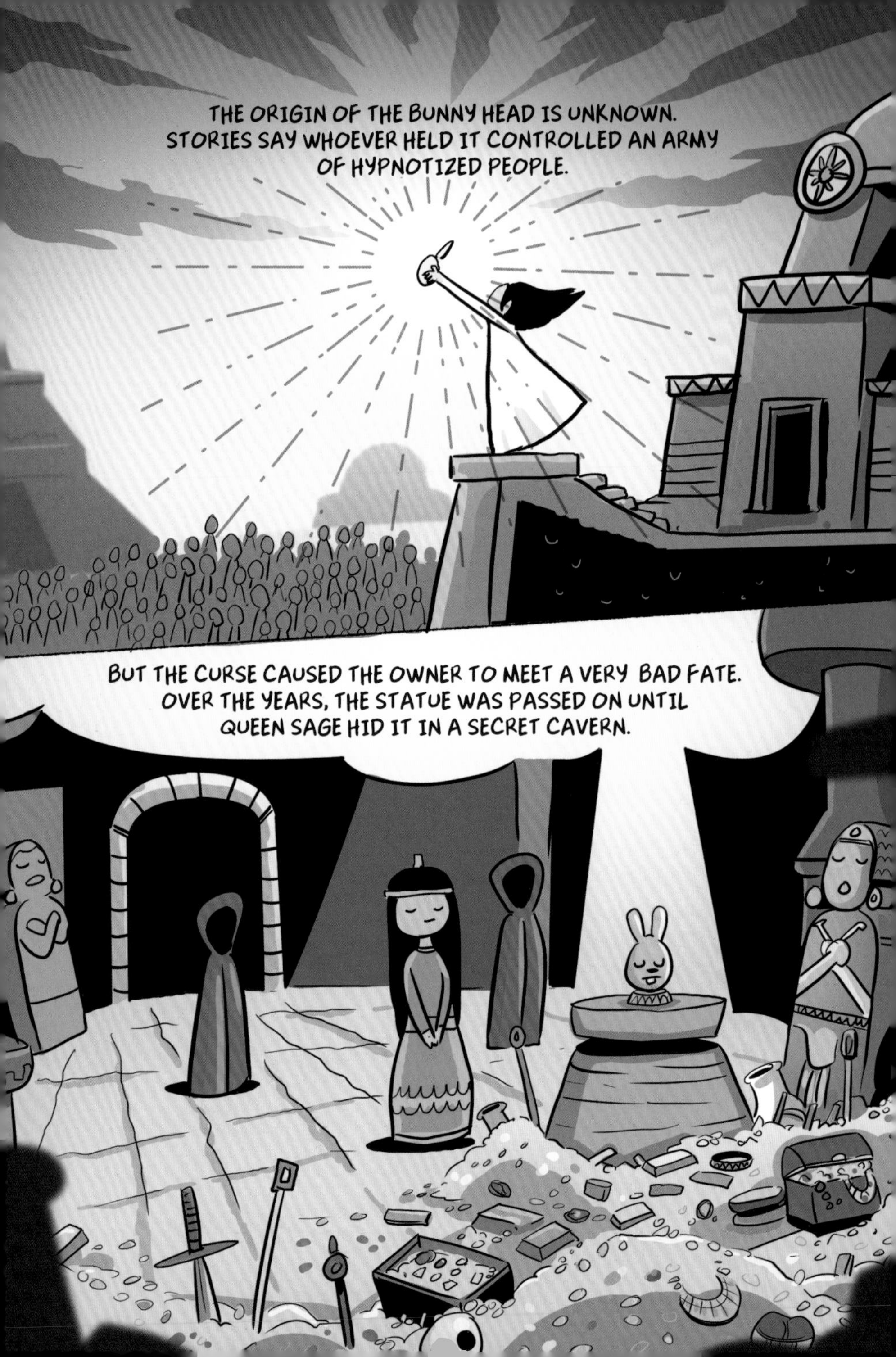
THE ORIGIN OF THE BUNNY HEAD IS UNKNOWN. STORIES SAY WHOEVER HELD IT CONTROLLED AN ARMY OF HYPNOTIZED PEOPLE.
BUT THE CURSE CAUSED THE OWNER TO MEET A VERY BAD FATE. OVER THE YEARS, THE STATUE WAS PASSED ON UNTIL QUEEN SAGE HID IT IN A SECRET CAVERN.

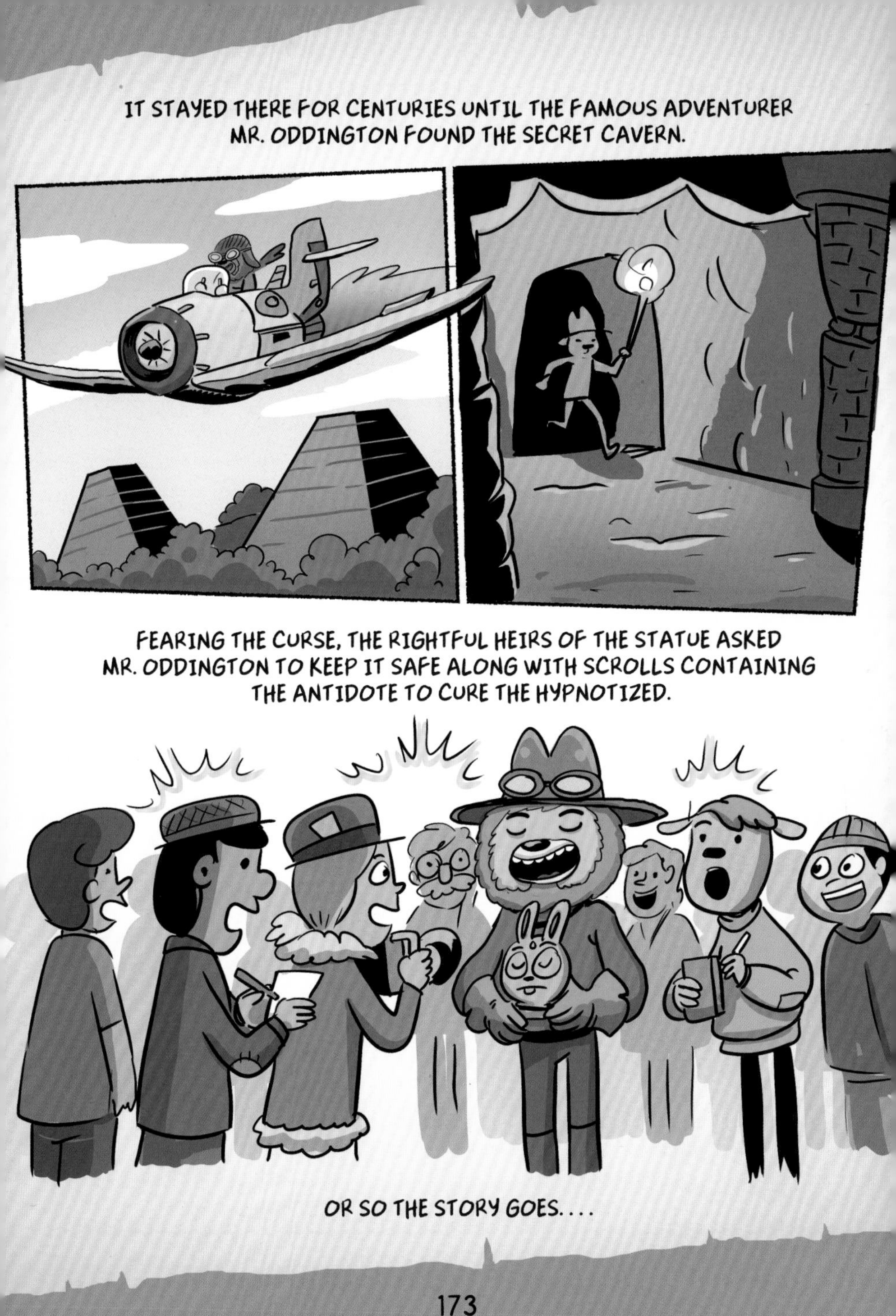
IT STAYED THERE FOR CENTURIES UNTIL THE FAMOUS ADVENTURER MR. ODDINGTON FOUND THE SECRET CAVERN.
FEARING THE CURSE, THE RIGHTFUL HEIRS OF THE STATUE ASKED MR. ODDINGTON TO KEEP IT SAFE ALONG WITH SCROLLS CONTAINING THE ANTIDOTE TO CURE THE HYPNOTIZED.
OR SO THE STORY GOES. . . .

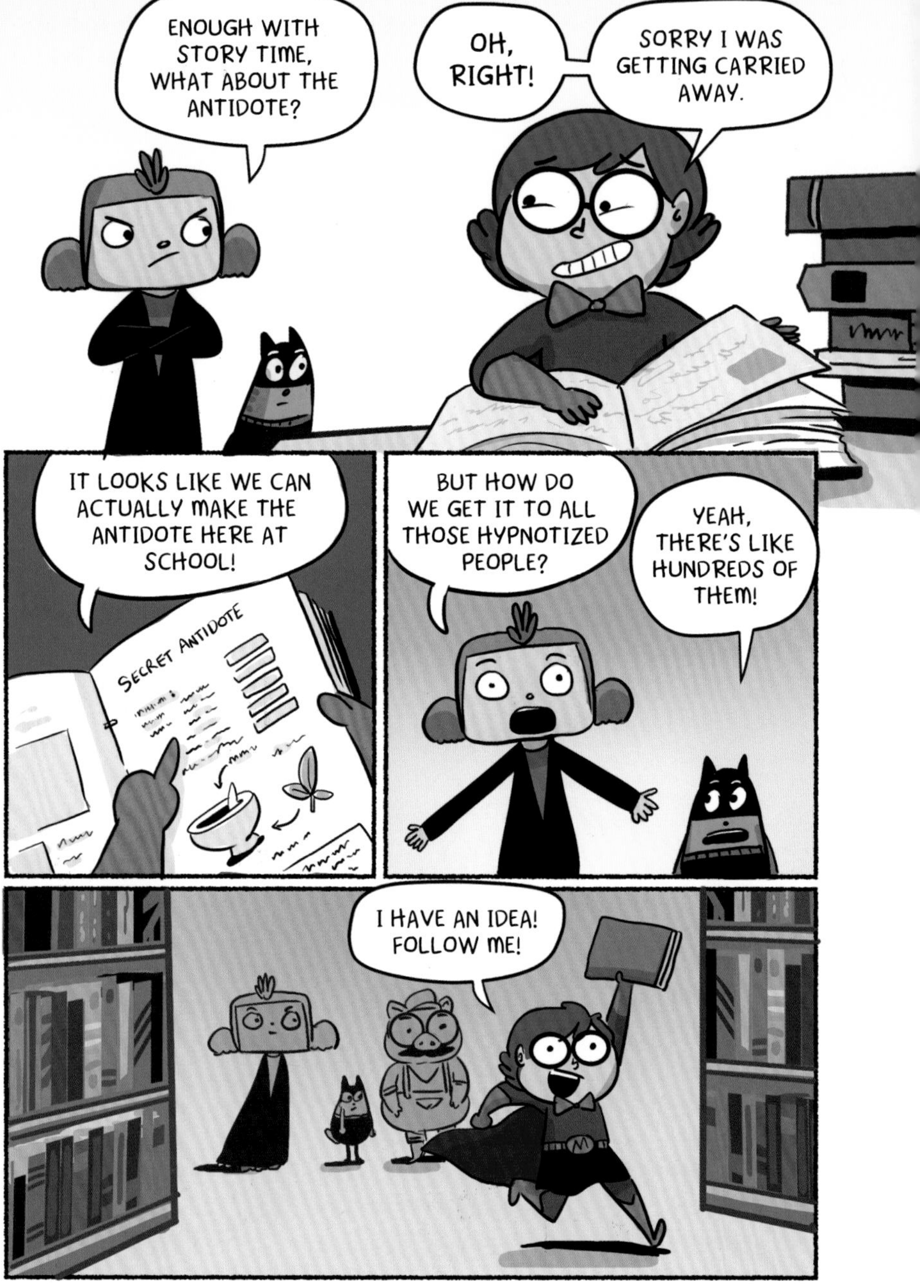
ENOUGH WITH STORY TIME, WHAT ABOUT THE ANTIDOTE?
OH, RIGHT!
SORRY I WAS GETTING CARRIED AWAY.
IT LOOKS LIKE WE CAN ACTUALLY MAKE THE ANTIDOTE HERE AT SCHOOL!
SECRET ANTIDOTE
BUT HOW DO WE GET IT TO ALL THOSE HYPNOTIZED PEOPLE?
YEAH, THERE'S LIKE HUNDREDS OF THEM!
I HAVE AN IDEA! FOLLOW ME!

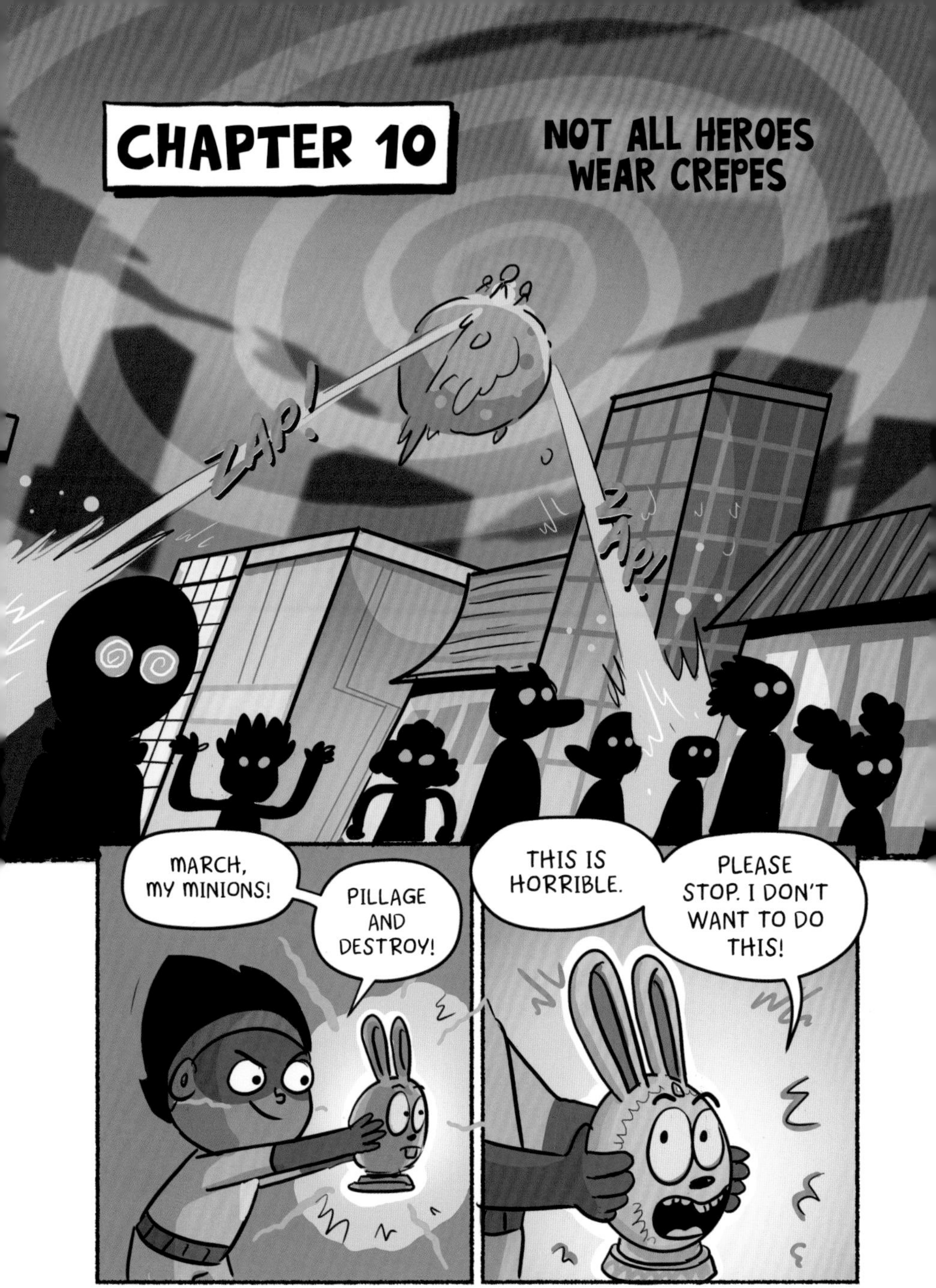
CHAPTER 10
NOT ALL HEROES WEAR CREPES
ZAP!
ZAP!
MARCH, MY MINIONS!
PILLAGE AND DESTROY!
THIS IS HORRIBLE.
PLEASE STOP. I DON'T WANT TO DO THIS!

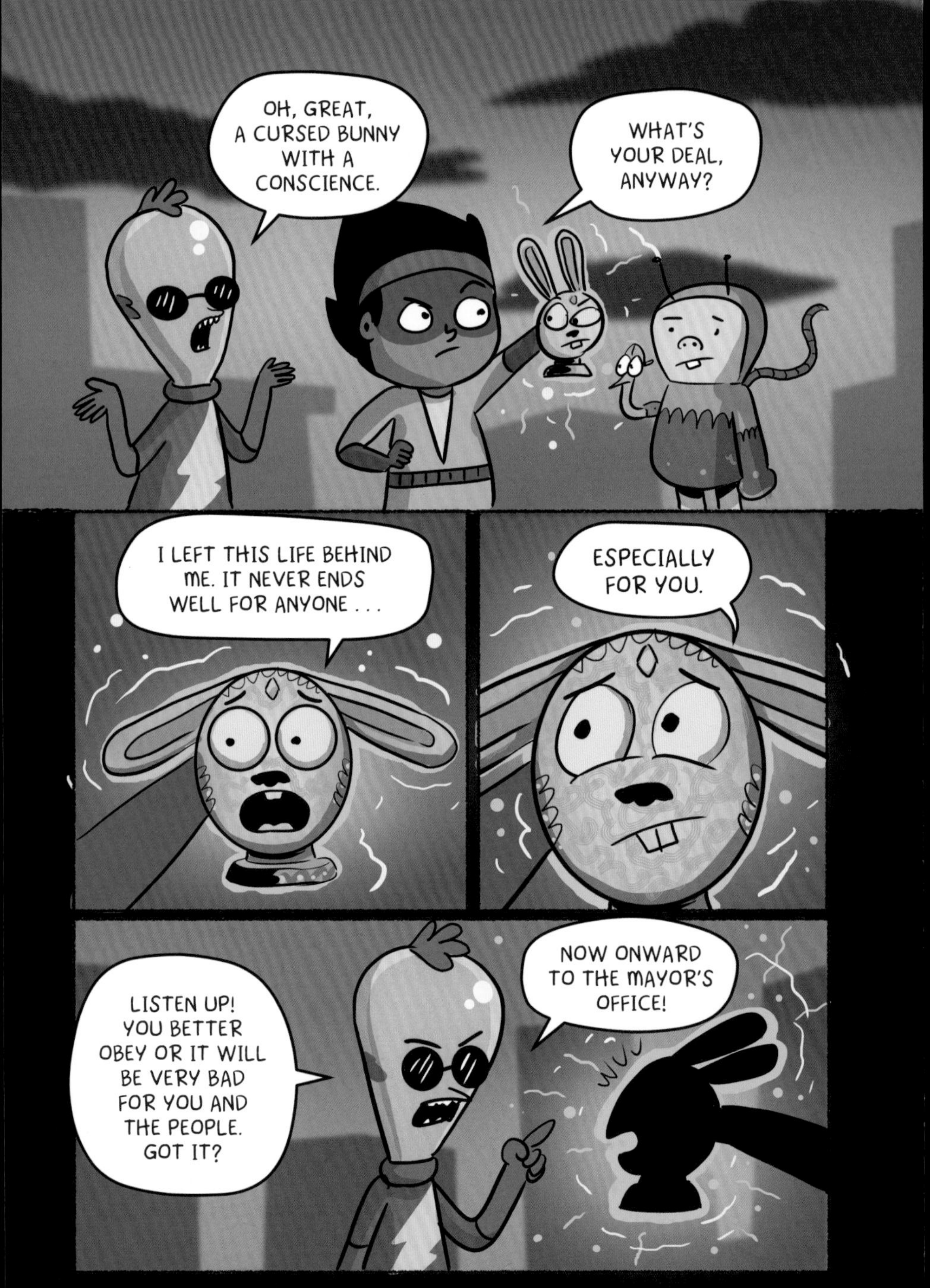
OH, GREAT, A CURSED BUNNY WITH A CONSCIENCE.
WHAT'S YOUR DEAL, ANYWAY?
I LEFT THIS LIFE BEHIND ME. IT NEVER ENDS WELL FOR ANYONE . . .
ESPECIALLY FOR YOU.
LISTEN UP! YOU BETTER OBEY OR IT WILL BE VERY BAD FOR YOU AND THE PEOPLE. GOT IT?
NOW ONWARD TO THE MAYOR'S OFFICE!

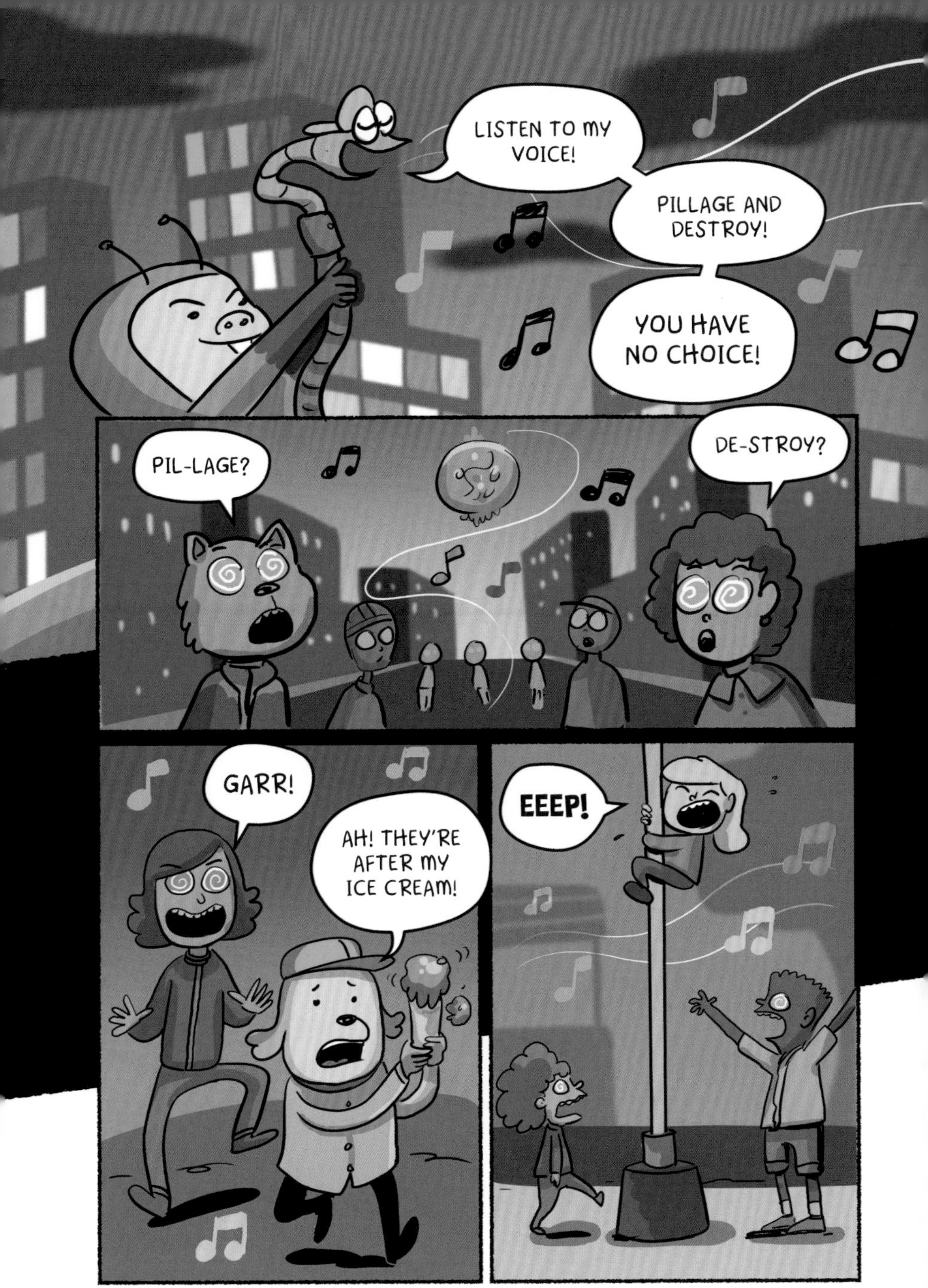
LISTEN TO MY VOICE!
PILLAGE AND DESTROY!
YOU HAVE NO CHOICE!
PIL-LAGE?
DE-STROY?
GARR!
AH! THEY'RE AFTER MY ICE CREAM!
EEEP!

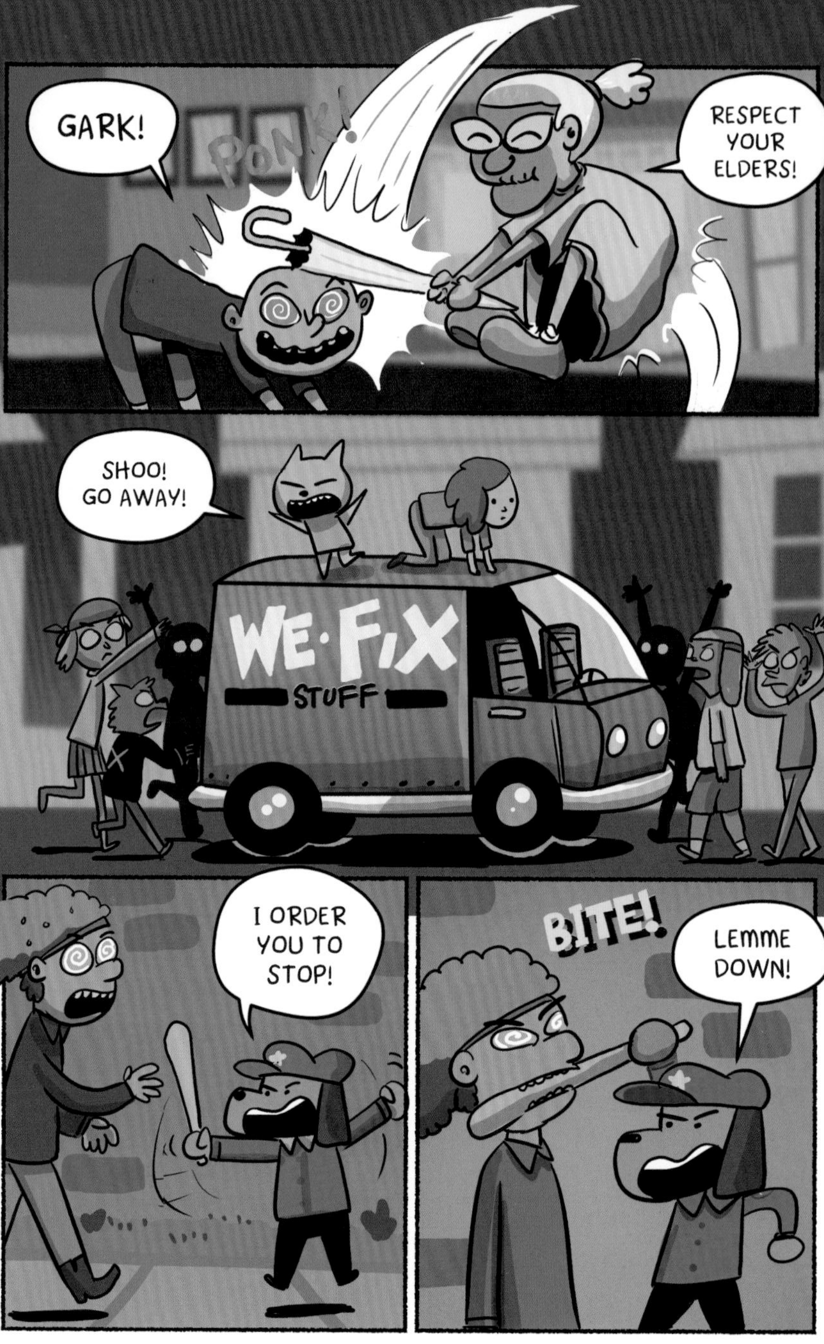
GARK!
PONK!
RESPECT YOUR ELDERS!
SHOO! GO AWAY!
WE·FIX STUFF
I ORDER YOU TO STOP!
BITE!
LEMME DOWN!

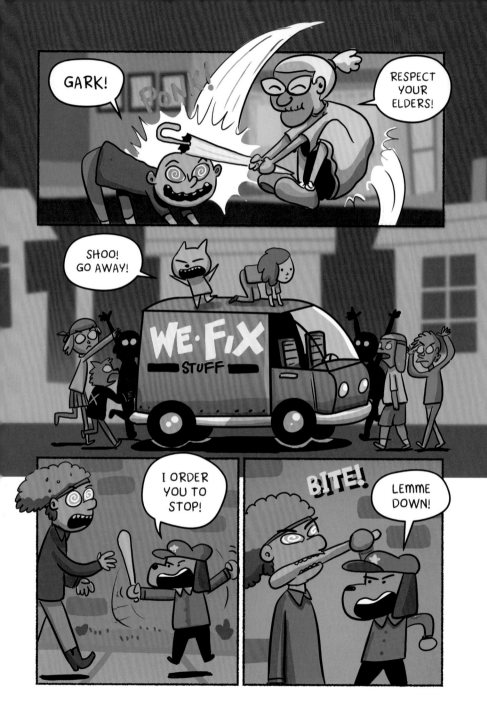

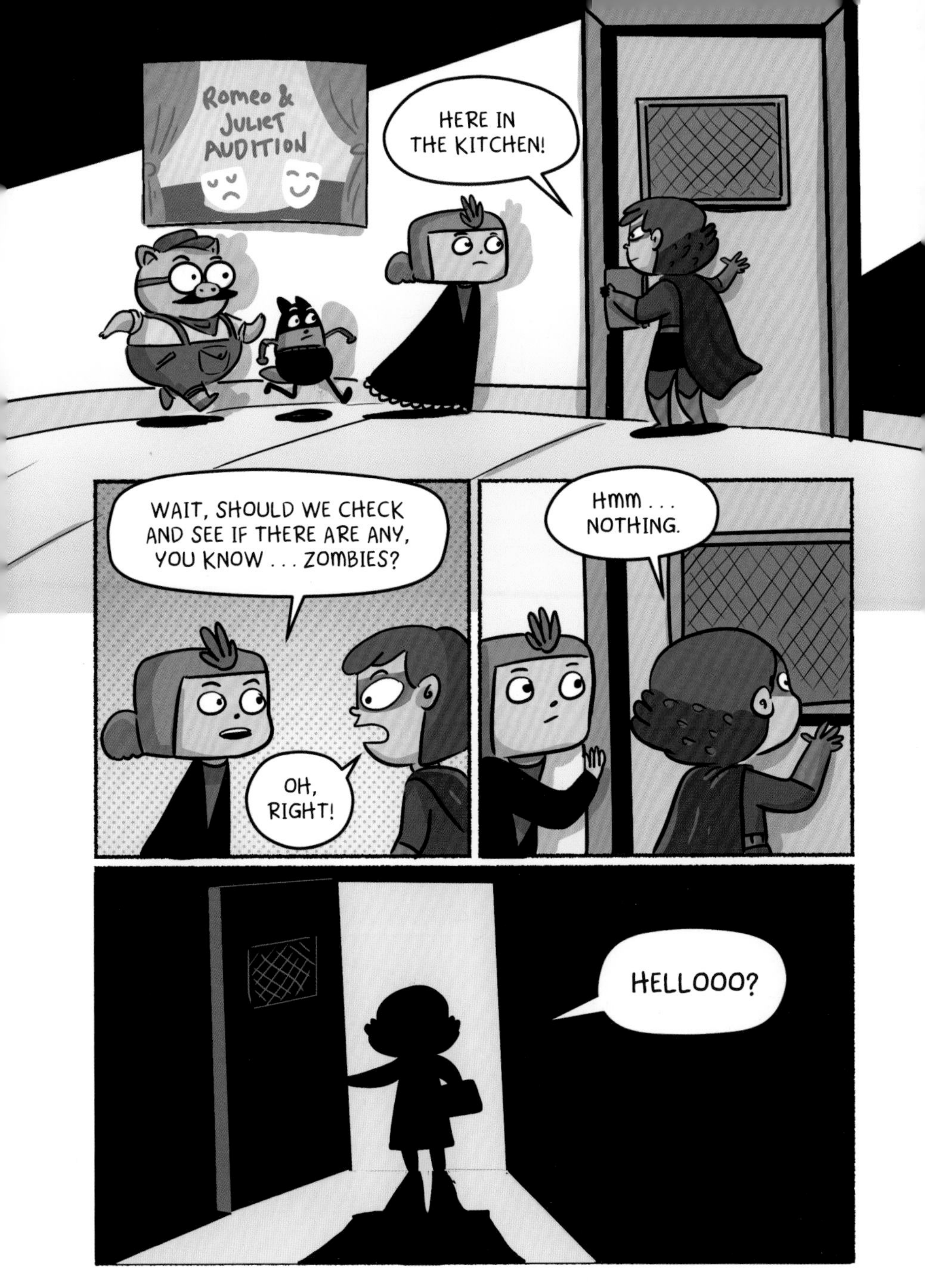
Romeo & Juliet AUDITION
HERE IN THE KITCHEN!
WAIT, SHOULD WE CHECK AND SEE IF THERE ARE ANY, YOU KNOW . . . ZOMBIES?
OH, RIGHT!
Hmm . . . NOTHING.
HELLOOO?

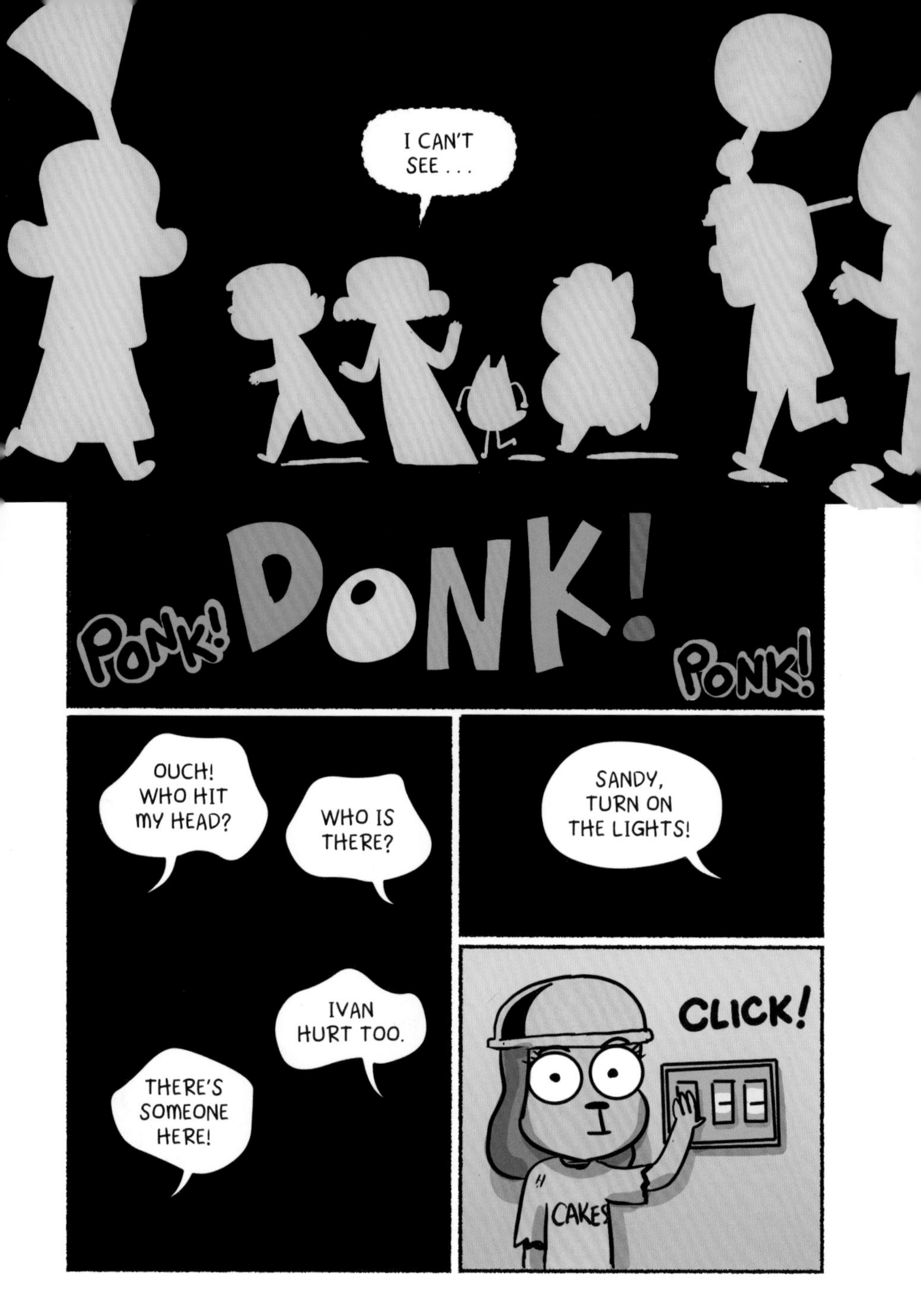
I CAN'T SEE . . .
PONK! DONK! PONK!
OUCH! WHO HIT MY HEAD?
WHO IS THERE?
SANDY, TURN ON THE LIGHTS!
IVAN HURT TOO.
THERE'S SOMEONE HERE!
CLICK!
CAKES

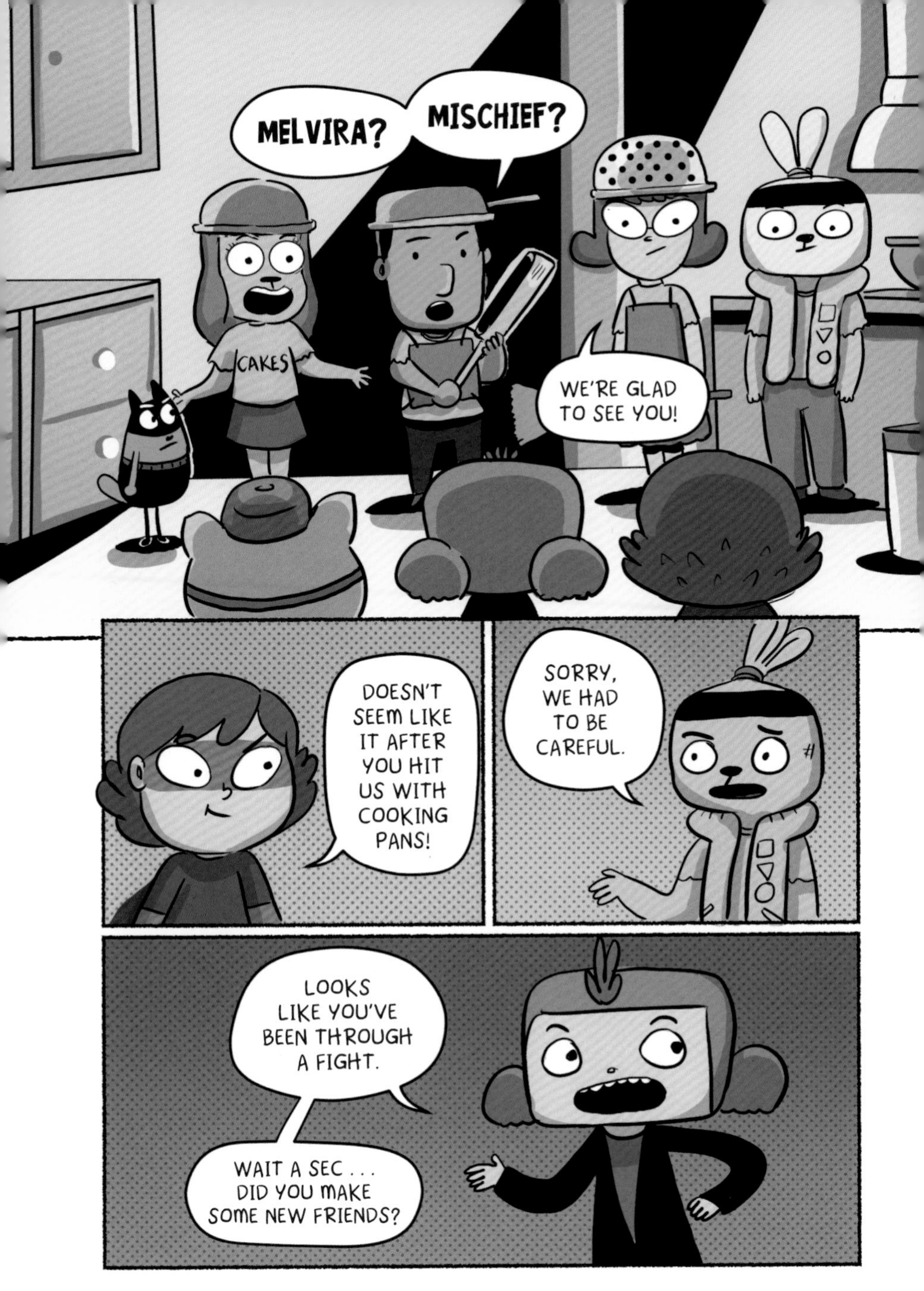

MELVIRA?
MISCHIEF?
CAKES
WE'RE GLAD TO SEE YOU!
DOESN'T SEEM LIKE IT AFTER YOU HIT US WITH COOKING PANS!
SORRY, WE HAD TO BE CAREFUL.
LOOKS LIKE YOU'VE BEEN THROUGH A FIGHT.
WAIT A SEC . . . DID YOU MAKE SOME NEW FRIENDS?

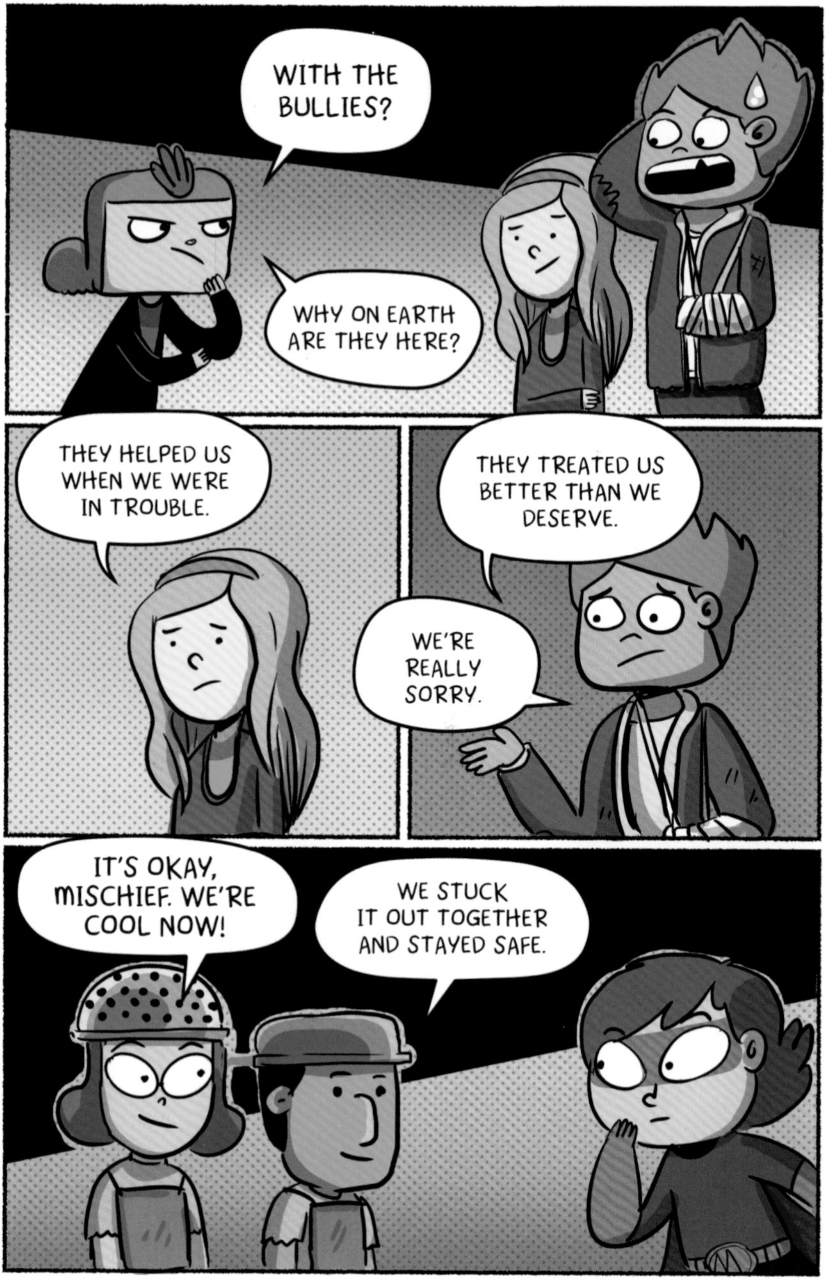
WITH THE BULLIES?
WHY ON EARTH ARE THEY HERE?
THEY HELPED US WHEN WE WERE IN TROUBLE.
THEY TREATED US BETTER THAN WE DESERVE.
WE'RE REALLY SORRY.
IT'S OKAY, MISCHIEF. WE'RE COOL NOW!
WE STUCK IT OUT TOGETHER AND STAYED SAFE.

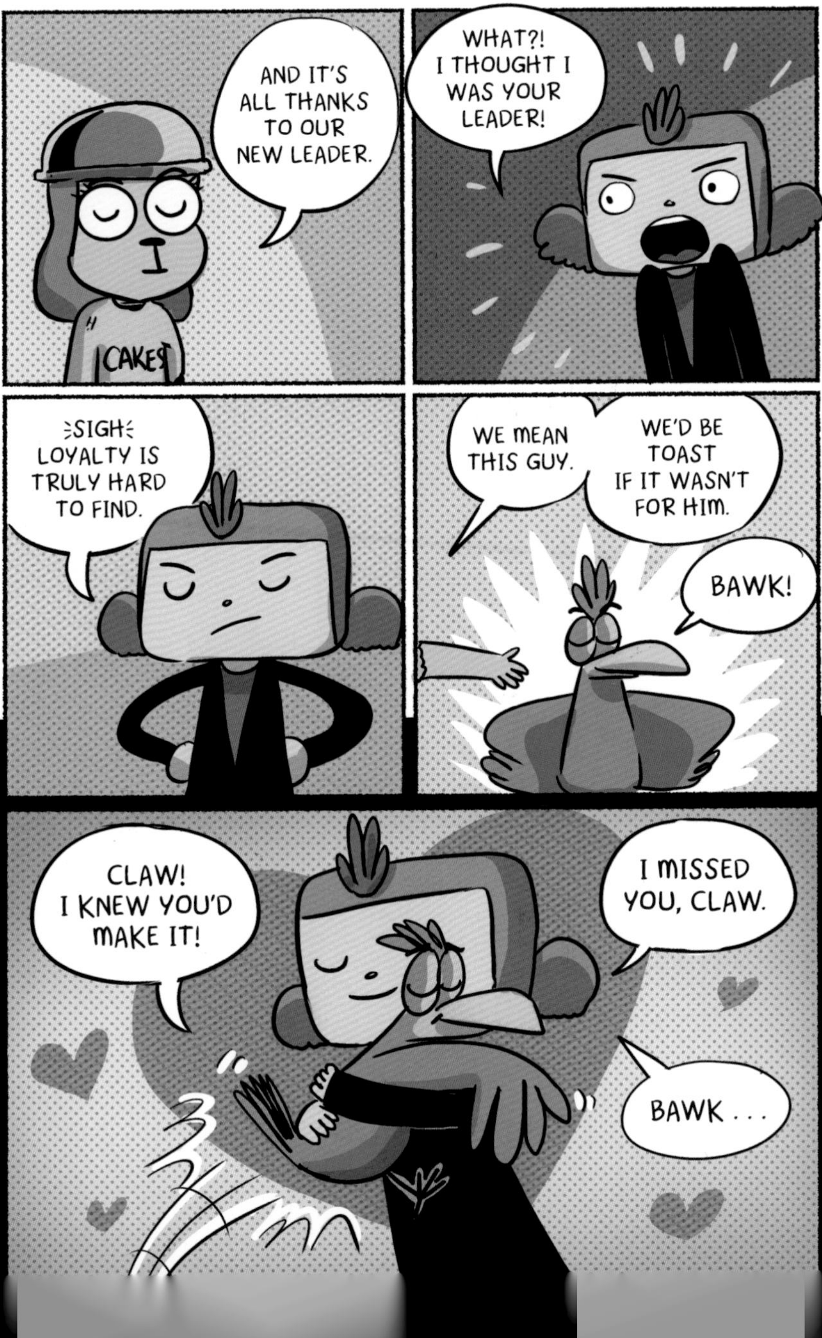
AND IT'S ALL THANKS TO OUR NEW LEADER.
WHAT?! I THOUGHT I WAS YOUR LEADER!
CAKES
SIGH LOYALTY IS TRULY HARD TO FIND.
WE MEAN THIS GUY.
WE'D BE TOAST IF IT WASN'T FOR HIM.
BAWK!
CLAW! I KNEW YOU'D MAKE IT!
I MISSED YOU, CLAW.
BAWK . . .

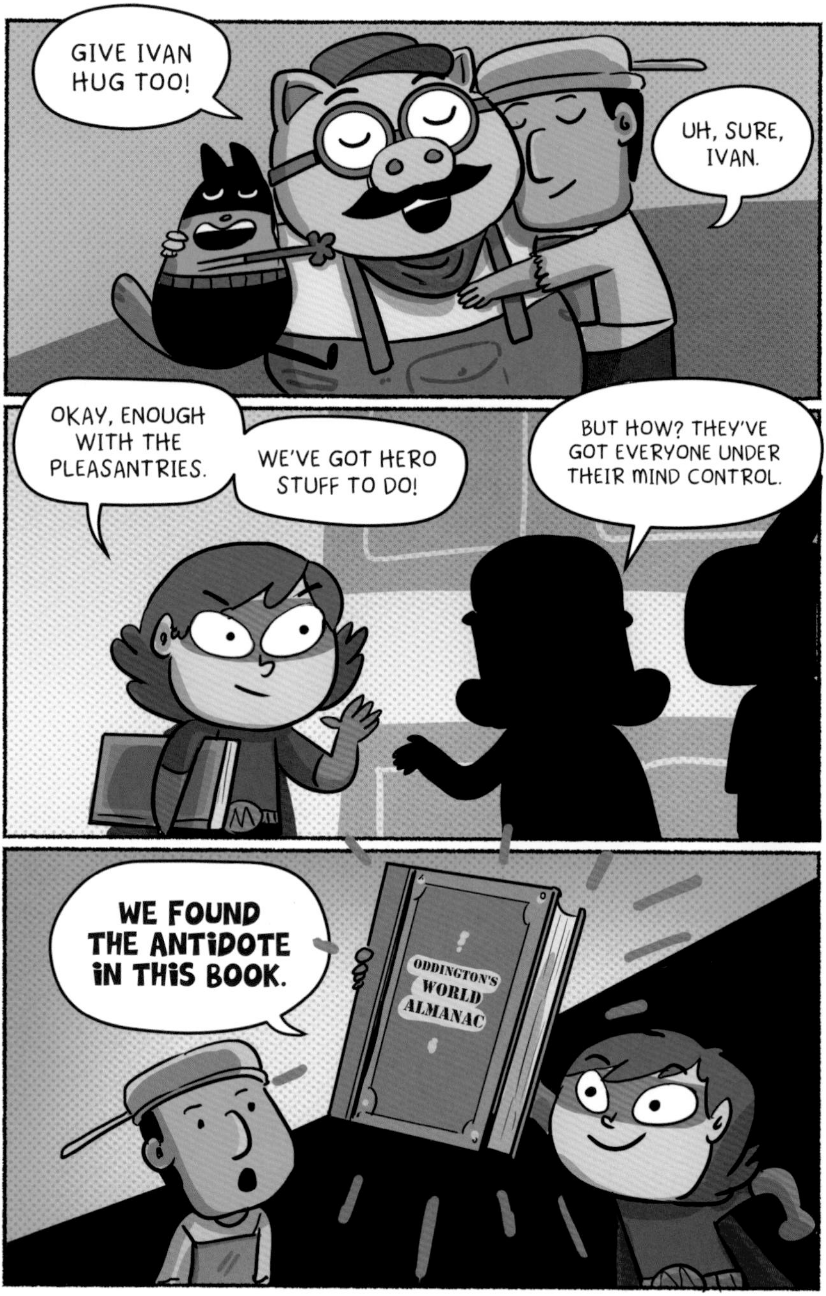
GIVE IVAN HUG TOO!
UH, SURE, IVAN.
OKAY, ENOUGH WITH THE PLEASANTRIES.
WE'VE GOT HERO STUFF TO DO!
BUT HOW? THEY'VE GOT EVERYONE UNDER THEIR MIND CONTROL.
WE FOUND THE ANTIDOTE IN THIS BOOK.
ODDINGTON'S WORLD ALMANAC

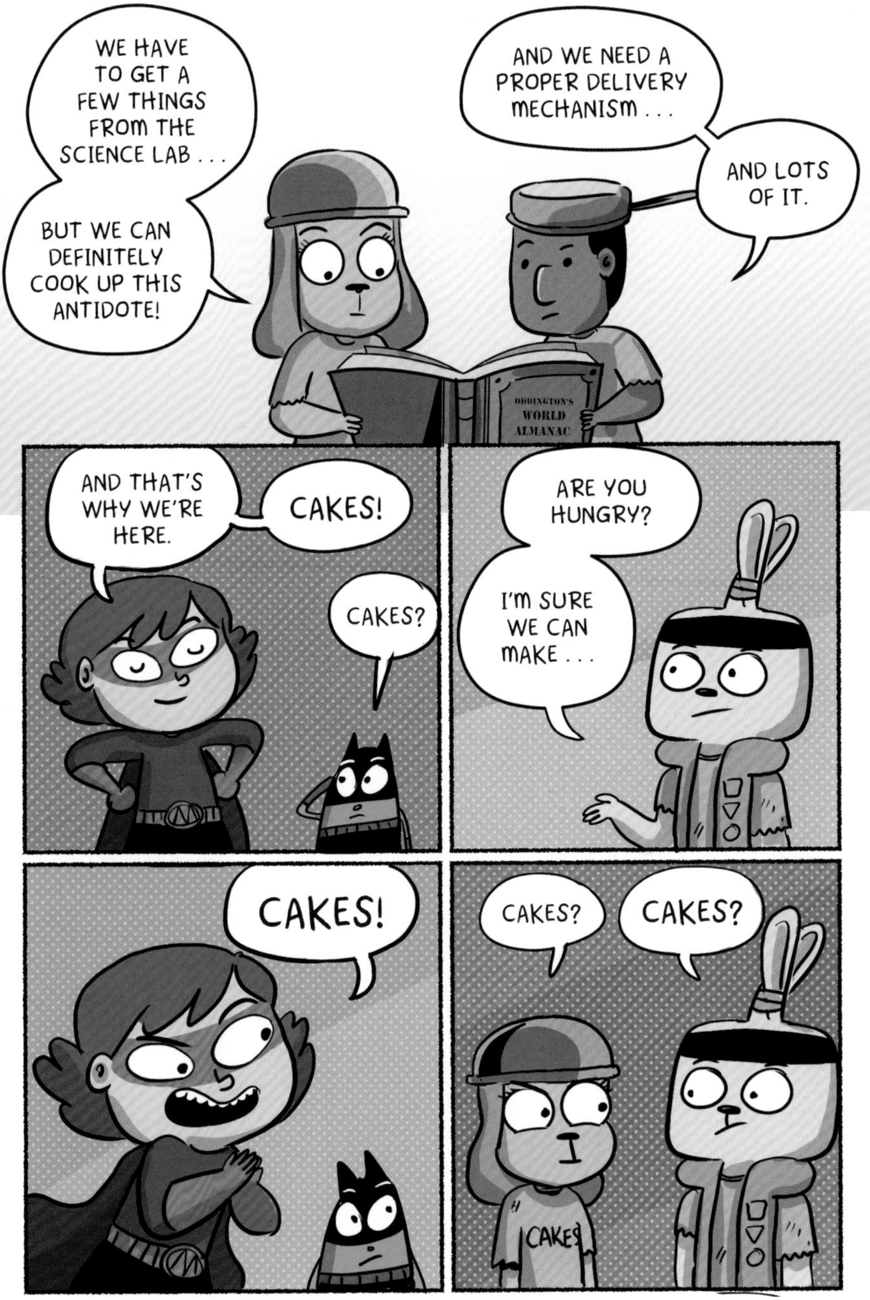
WE HAVE TO GET A FEW THINGS FROM THE SCIENCE LAB . . .
BUT WE CAN DEFINITELY COOK UP THIS ANTIDOTE!
AND WE NEED A PROPER DELIVERY MECHANISM . . .
AND LOTS OF IT.
ODDINGTON'S WORLD ALMANAC
AND THAT'S WHY WE'RE HERE.
CAKES!
CAKES?
ARE YOU HUNGRY?
I'M SURE WE CAN MAKE . . .
CAKES!
CAKES?
CAKES?
CAKES

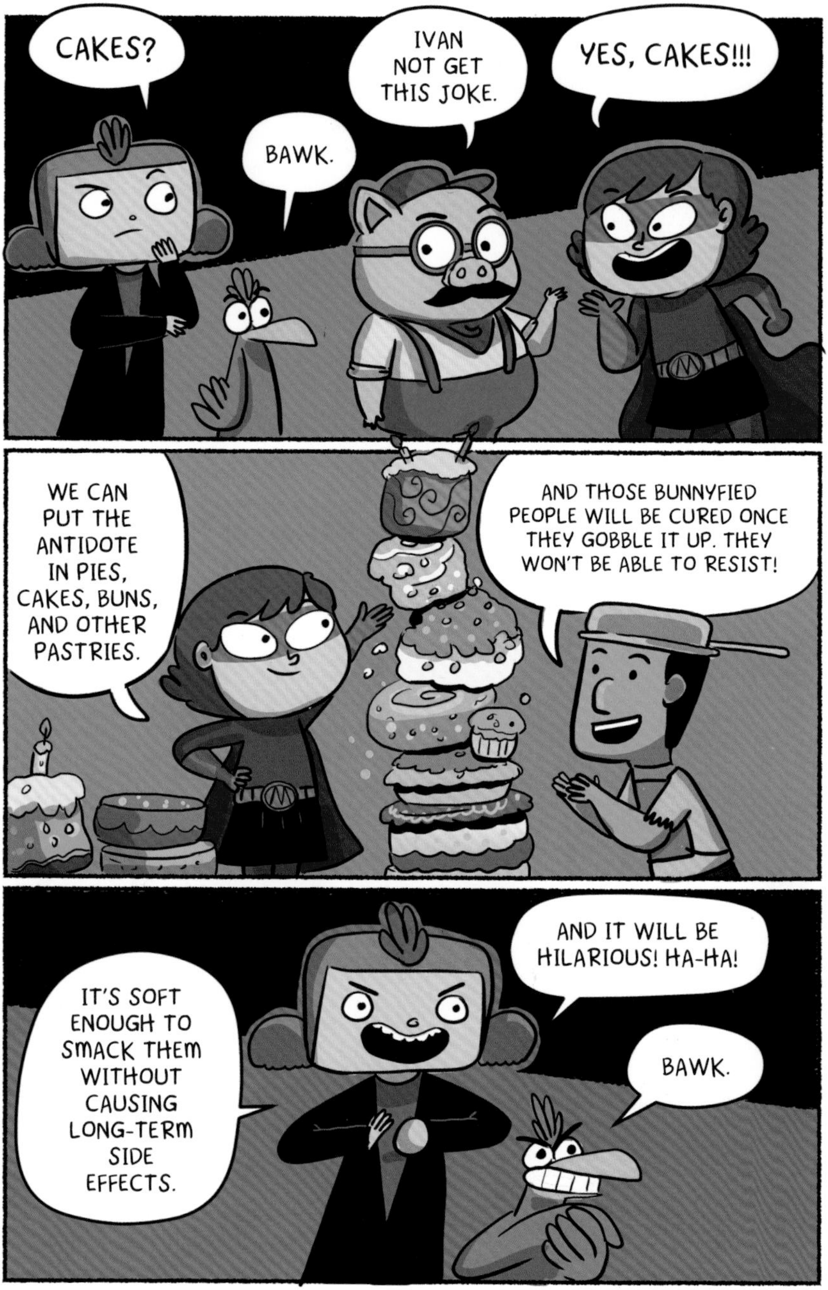
CAKES?
BAWK.
IVAN NOT GET THIS JOKE.
YES, CAKES!!!
WE CAN PUT THE ANTIDOTE IN PIES, CAKES, BUNS, AND OTHER PASTRIES.
AND THOSE BUNNYFIED PEOPLE WILL BE CURED ONCE THEY GOBBLE IT UP. THEY WON'T BE ABLE TO RESIST!
IT'S SOFT ENOUGH TO SMACK THEM WITHOUT CAUSING LONG-TERM SIDE EFFECTS.
AND IT WILL BE HILARIOUS! HA-HA!
BAWK.

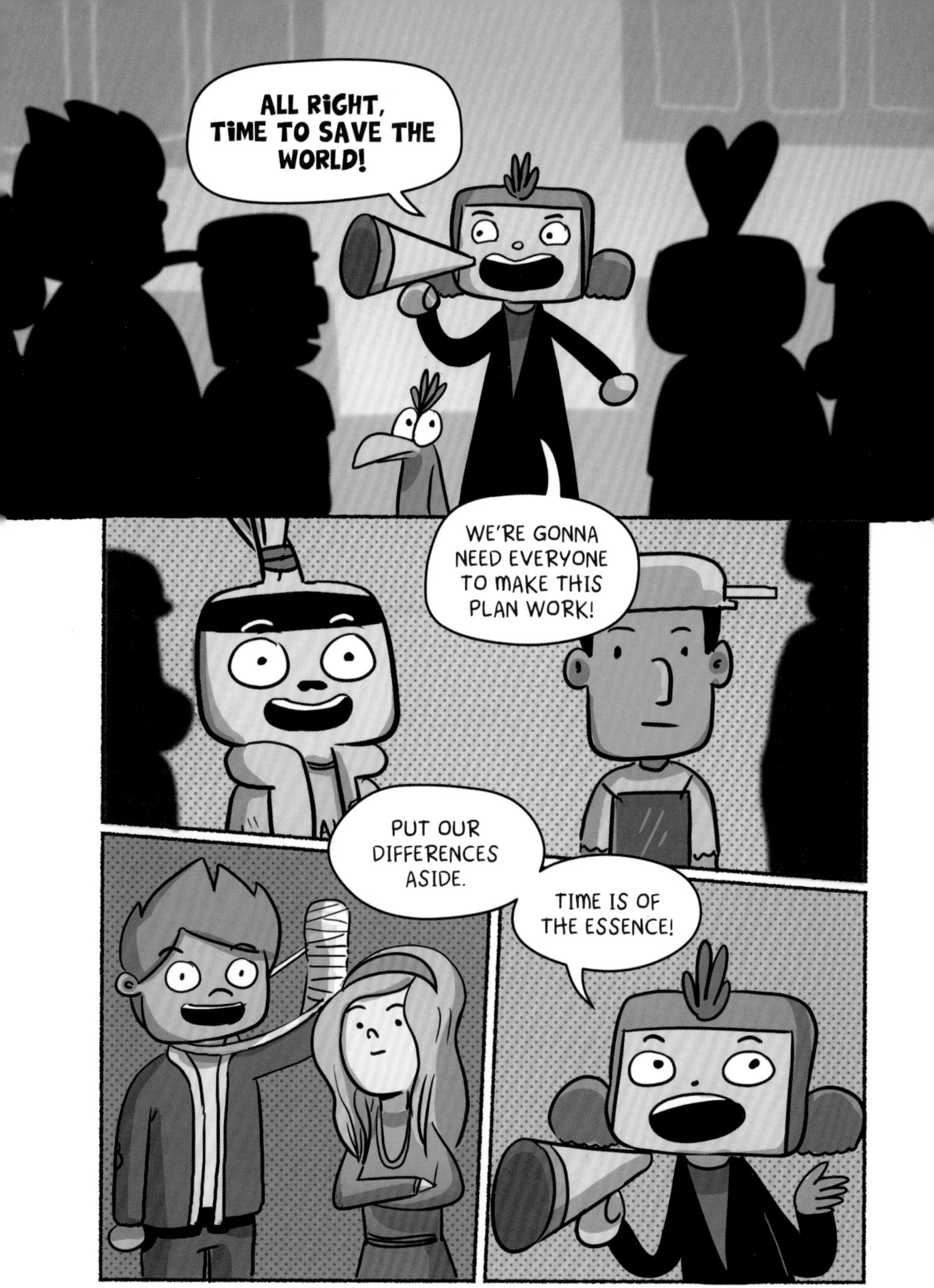
ALL RIGHT, TIME TO SAVE THE WORLD!
WE'RE GONNA NEED EVERYONE TO MAKE THIS PLAN WORK!
PUT OUR DIFFERENCES ASIDE.
TIME IS OF THE ESSENCE!

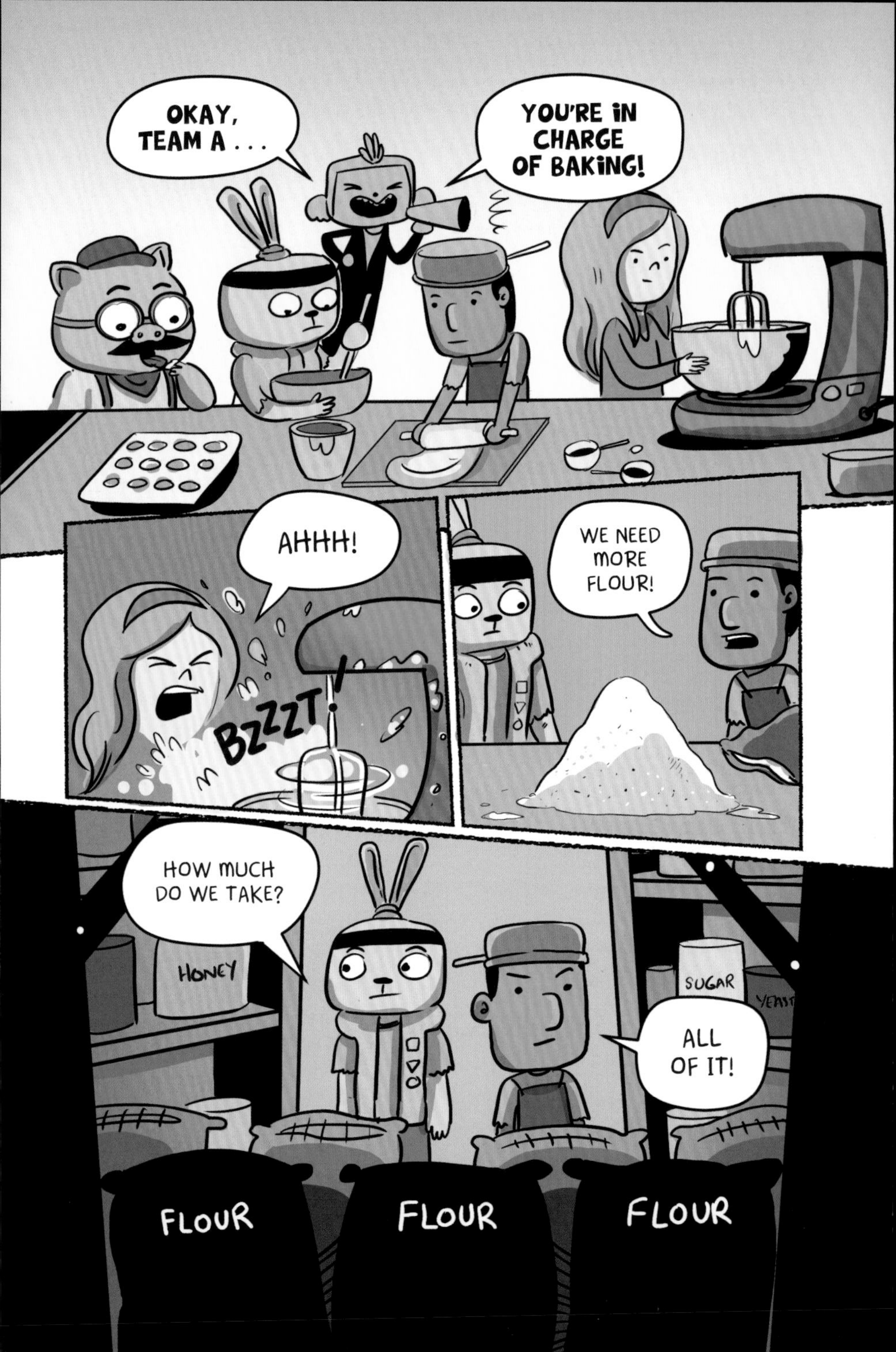
OKAY, TEAM A . . .
YOU'RE IN CHARGE OF BAKING!
AHHH!
BZZZT!
WE NEED MORE FLOUR!
HOW MUCH DO WE TAKE?
HONEY
SUGAR
ALL OF IT!
FLOUR
FLOUR
FLOUR

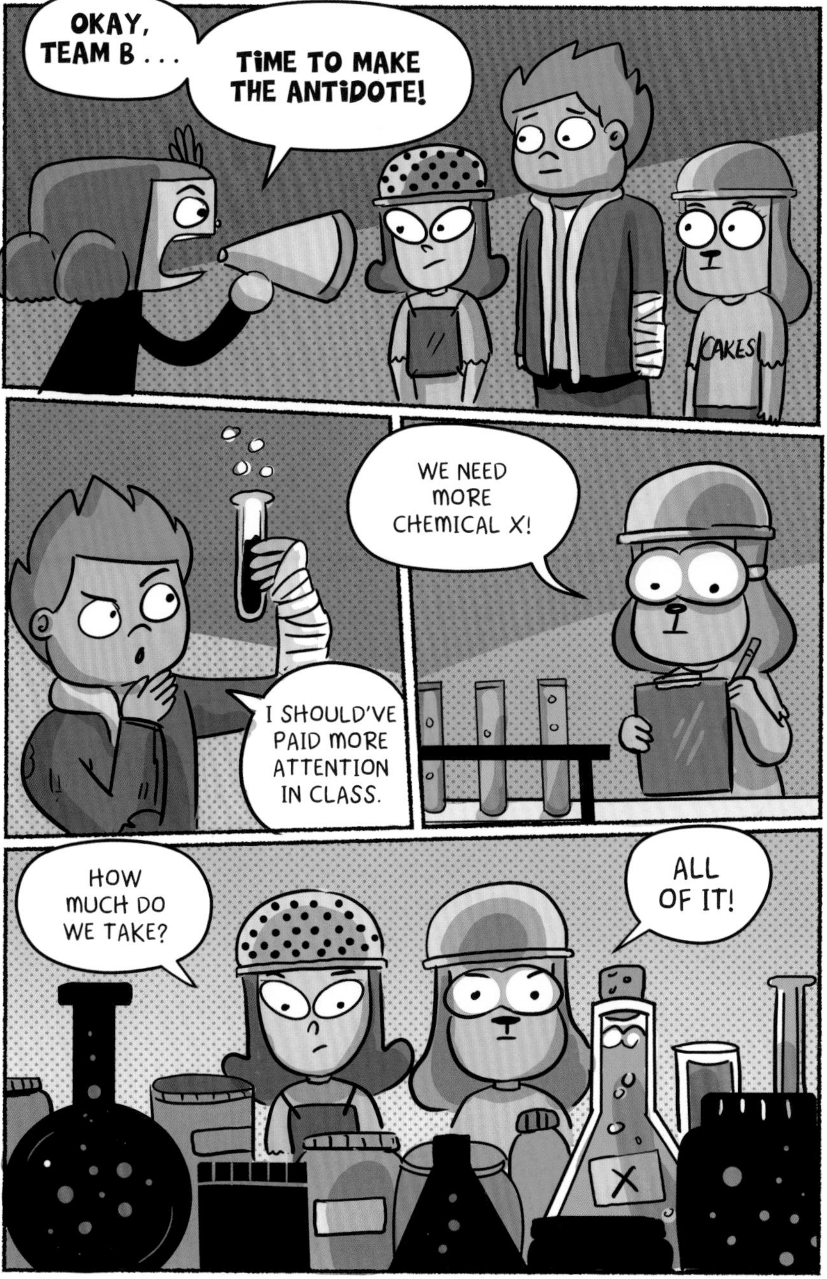
OKAY, TEAM B . . .
TIME TO MAKE THE ANTIDOTE!
CAKES
I SHOULD'VE PAID MORE ATTENTION IN CLASS.
WE NEED MORE CHEMICAL X!
HOW MUCH DO WE TAKE?
ALL OF IT!
X

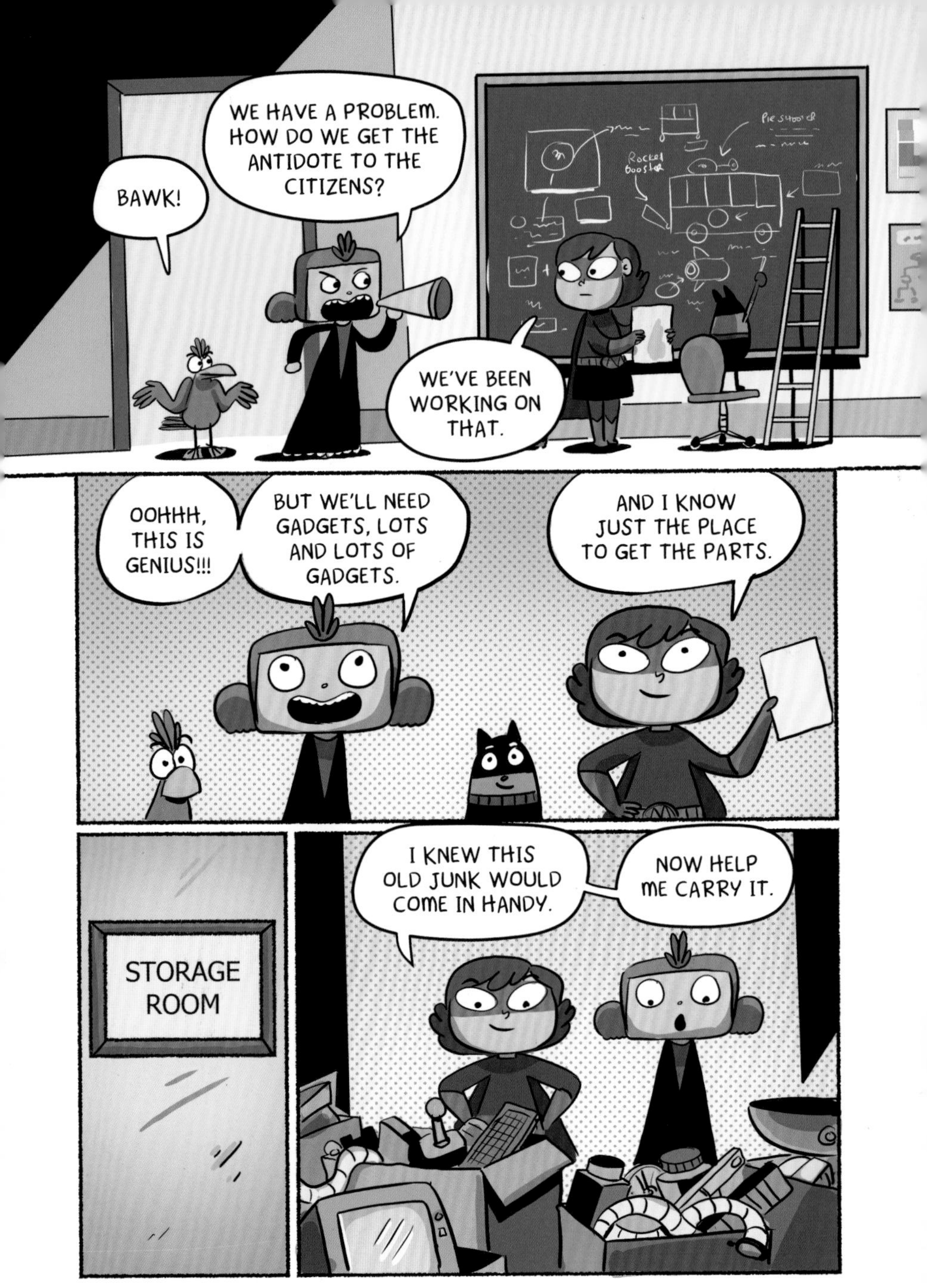
BAWK!
WE HAVE A PROBLEM. HOW DO WE GET THE ANTIDOTE TO THE CITIZENS?
WE'VE BEEN WORKING ON THAT.
OOHHH, THIS IS GENIUS!!!
BUT WE'LL NEED GADGETS, LOTS AND LOTS OF GADGETS.
AND I KNOW JUST THE PLACE TO GET THE PARTS.
STORAGE ROOM
I KNEW THIS OLD JUNK WOULD COME IN HANDY.
NOW HELP ME CARRY IT.

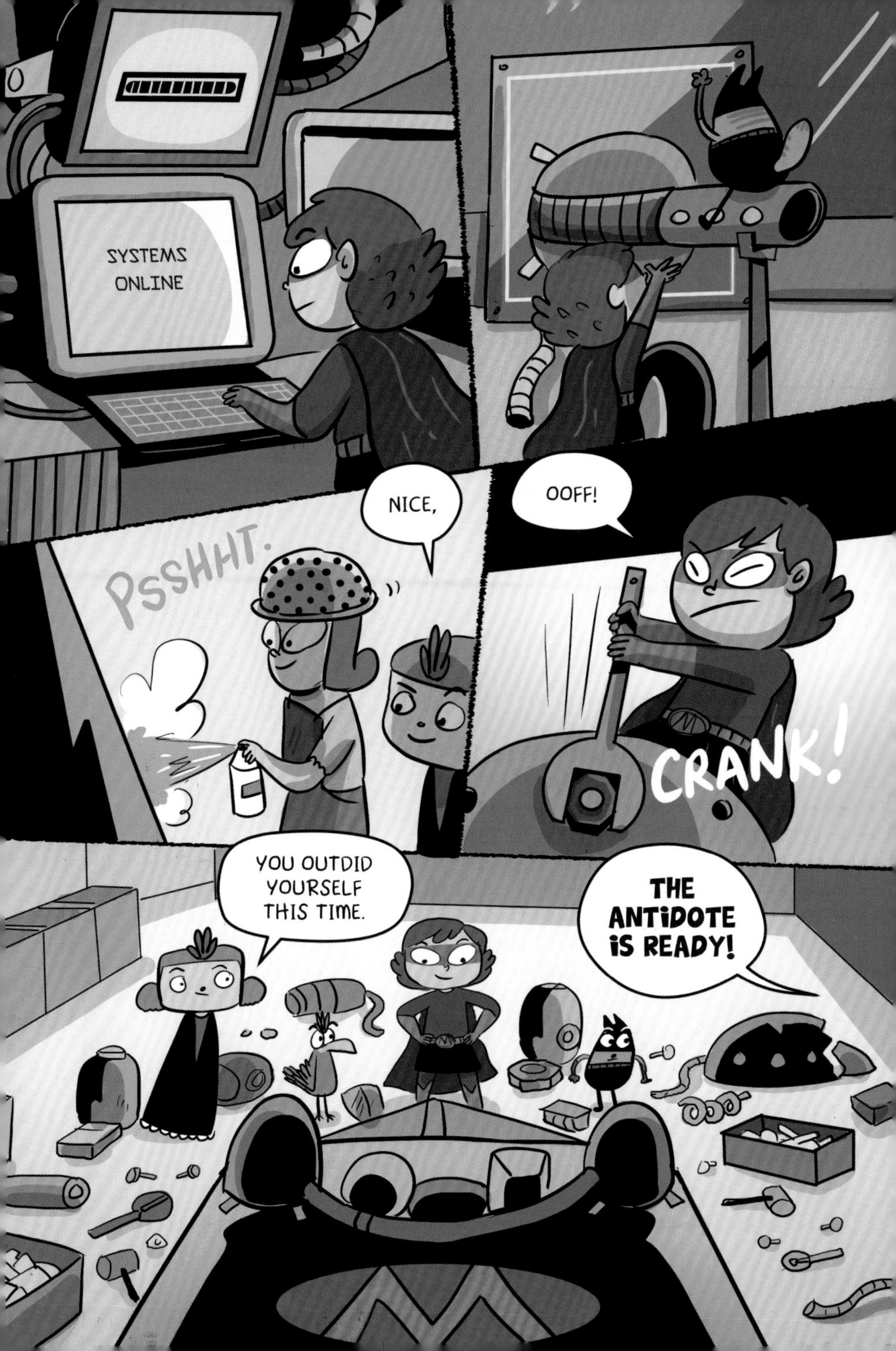
SYSTEMS
ONLINE
PSSHHT.
NICE,
OOFF!
CRANK!
YOU OUTDID YOURSELF THIS TIME.
THE ANTIDOTE IS READY!

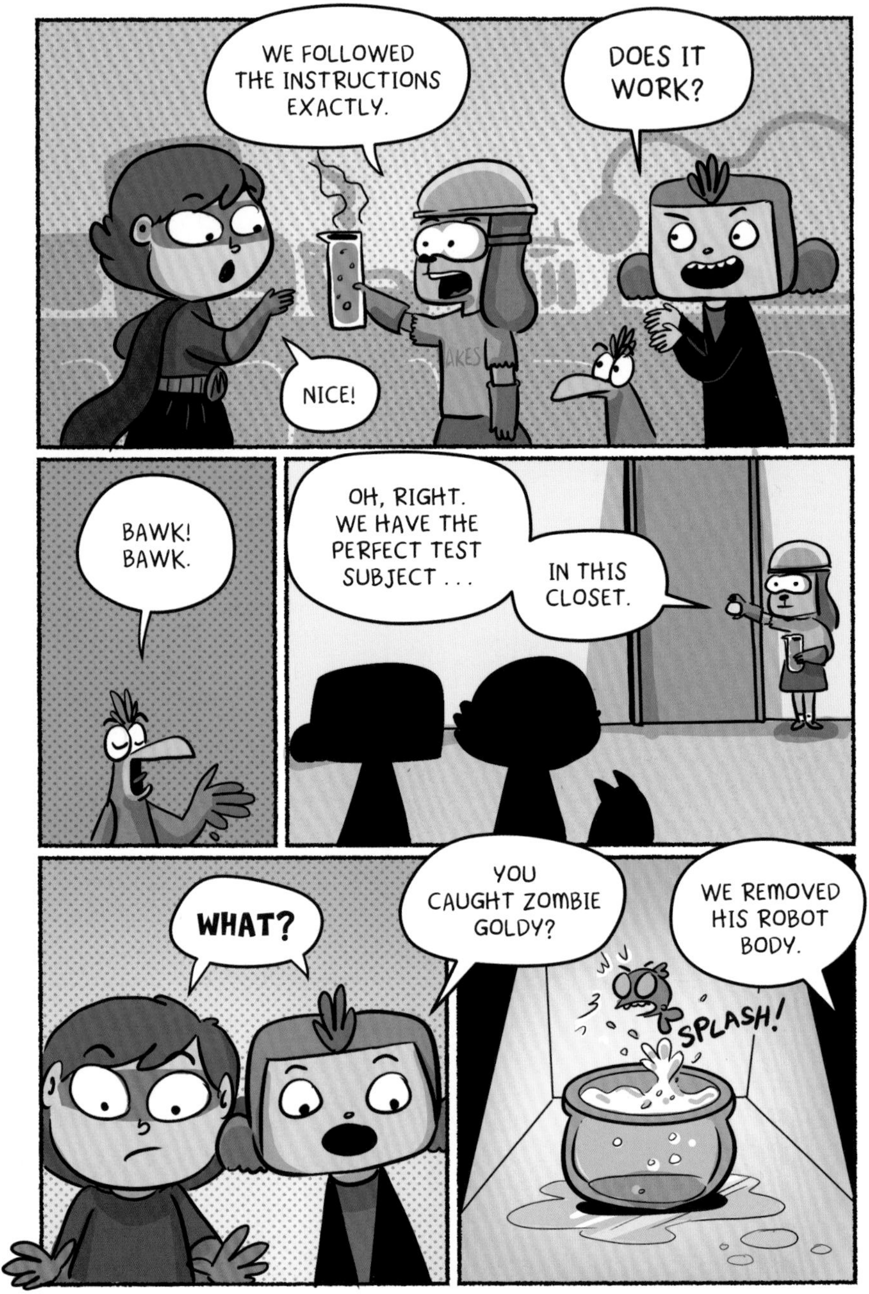
WE FOLLOWED THE INSTRUCTIONS EXACTLY.
NICE!
DOES IT WORK?
BAWK! BAWK.
OH, RIGHT. WE HAVE THE PERFECT TEST SUBJECT . . .
IN THIS CLOSET.
WHAT?
YOU CAUGHT ZOMBIE GOLDY?
WE REMOVED HIS ROBOT BODY.
SPLASH!

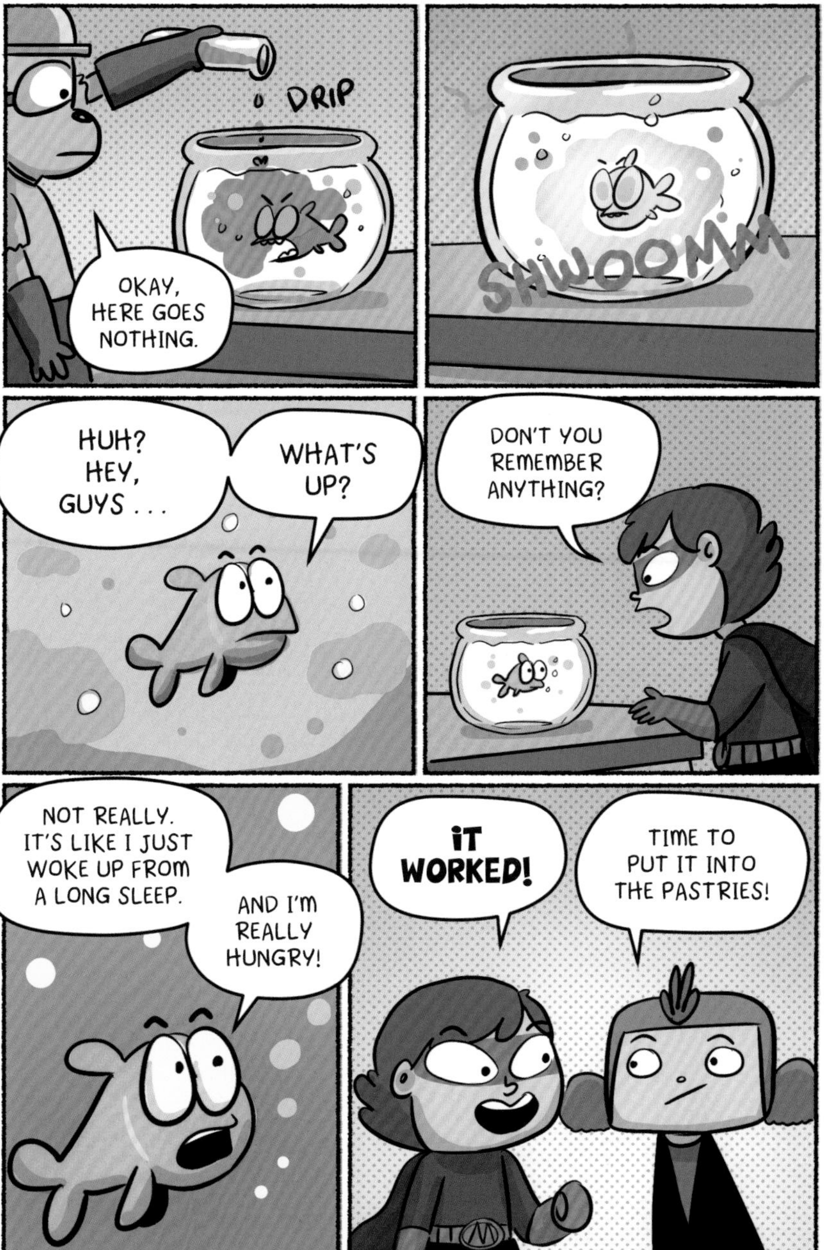
DRIP
OKAY, HERE GOES NOTHING.
SHWOOMM
HUH? HEY, GUYS . . .
WHAT'S UP?
DON'T YOU REMEMBER ANYTHING?
NOT REALLY. IT'S LIKE I JUST WOKE UP FROM A LONG SLEEP.
AND I'M REALLY HUNGRY!
IT WORKED!
TIME TO PUT IT INTO THE PASTRIES!

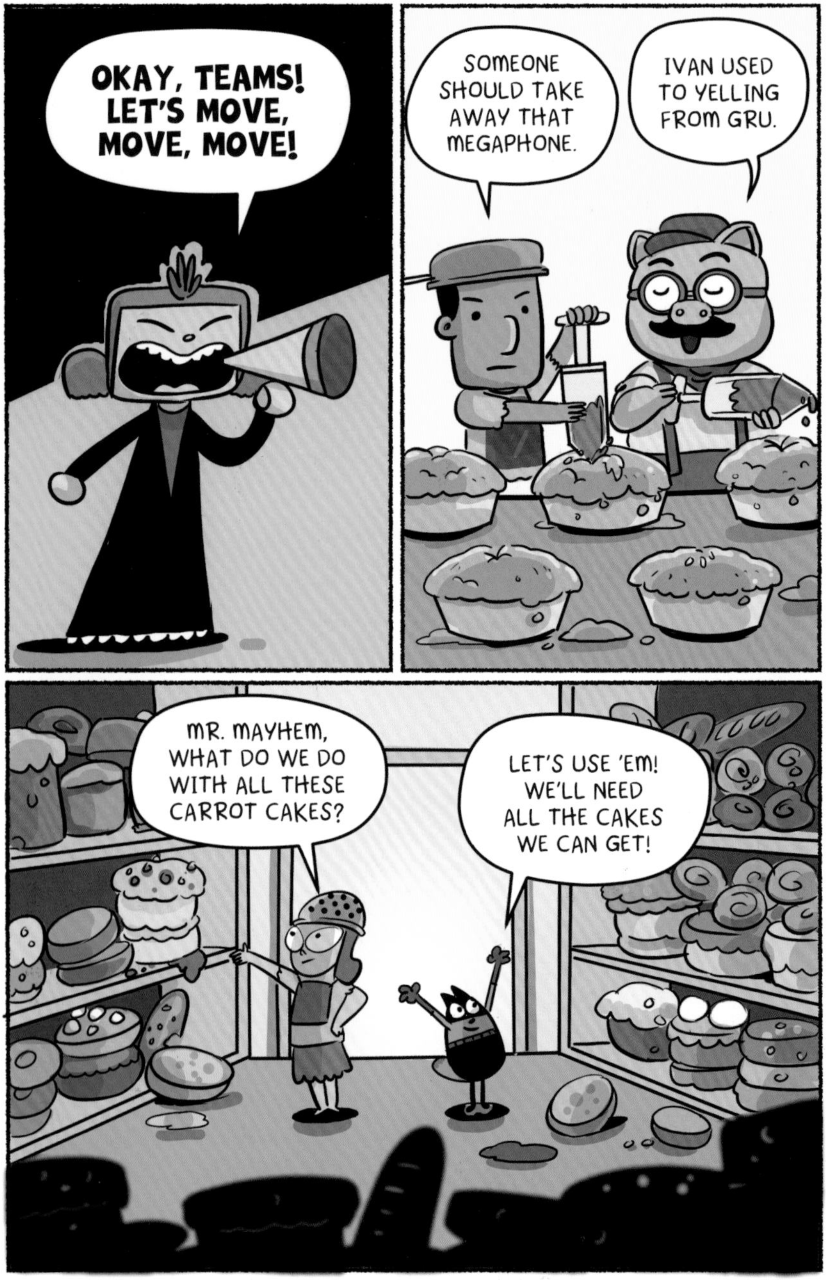
OKAY, TEAMS! LET'S MOVE, MOVE, MOVE!
SOMEONE SHOULD TAKE AWAY THAT MEGAPHONE.
IVAN USED TO YELLING FROM GRU.
MR. MAYHEM, WHAT DO WE DO WITH ALL THESE CARROT CAKES?
LET'S USE 'EM! WE'LL NEED ALL THE CAKES WE CAN GET!

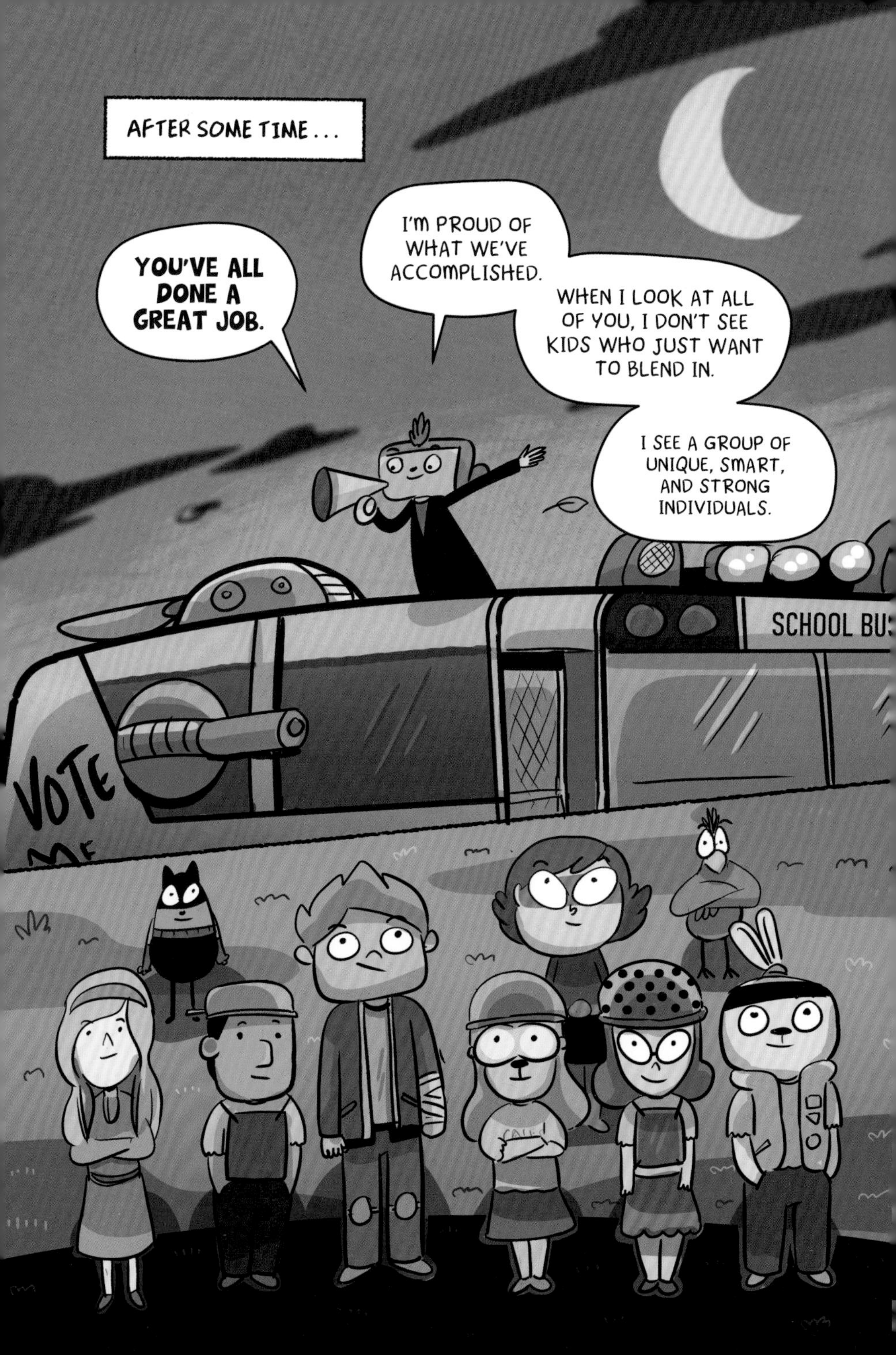

AFTER SOME TIME...
YOU'VE ALL DONE A GREAT JOB.
I'M PROUD OF WHAT WE'VE ACCOMPLISHED.
WHEN I LOOK AT ALL OF YOU, I DON'T SEE KIDS WHO JUST WANT TO BLEND IN.
I SEE A GROUP OF UNIQUE, SMART, AND STRONG INDIVIDUALS.
SCHOOL BU
VOTE

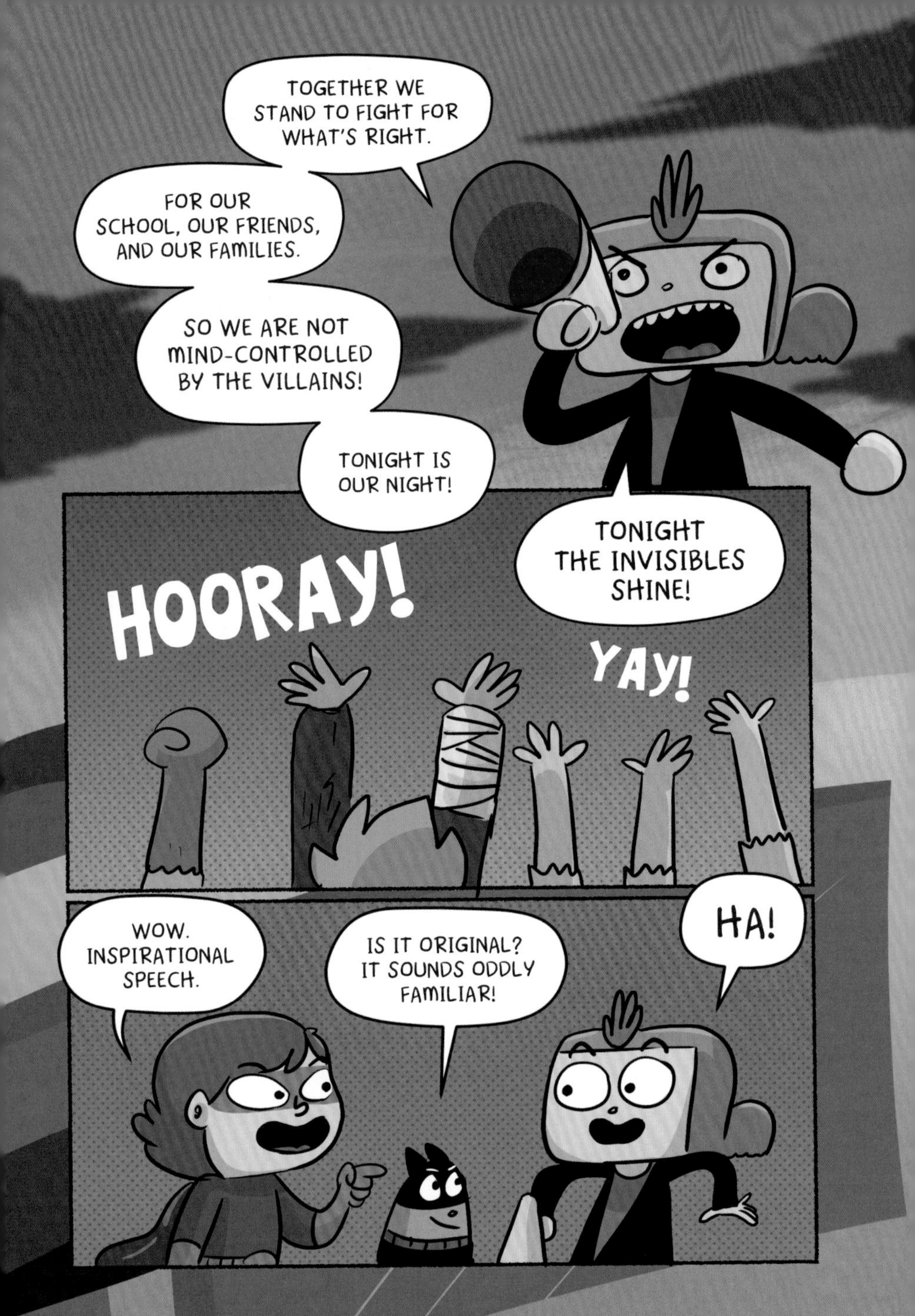
TOGETHER WE STAND TO FIGHT FOR WHAT'S RIGHT.
FOR OUR SCHOOL, OUR FRIENDS, AND OUR FAMILIES.
SO WE ARE NOT MIND-CONTROLLED BY THE VILLAINS!
TONIGHT IS OUR NIGHT!
TONIGHT THE INVISIBLES SHINE!
HOORAY!
YAY!
WOW. INSPIRATIONAL SPEECH.
IS IT ORIGINAL? IT SOUNDS ODDLY FAMILIAR!
HA!

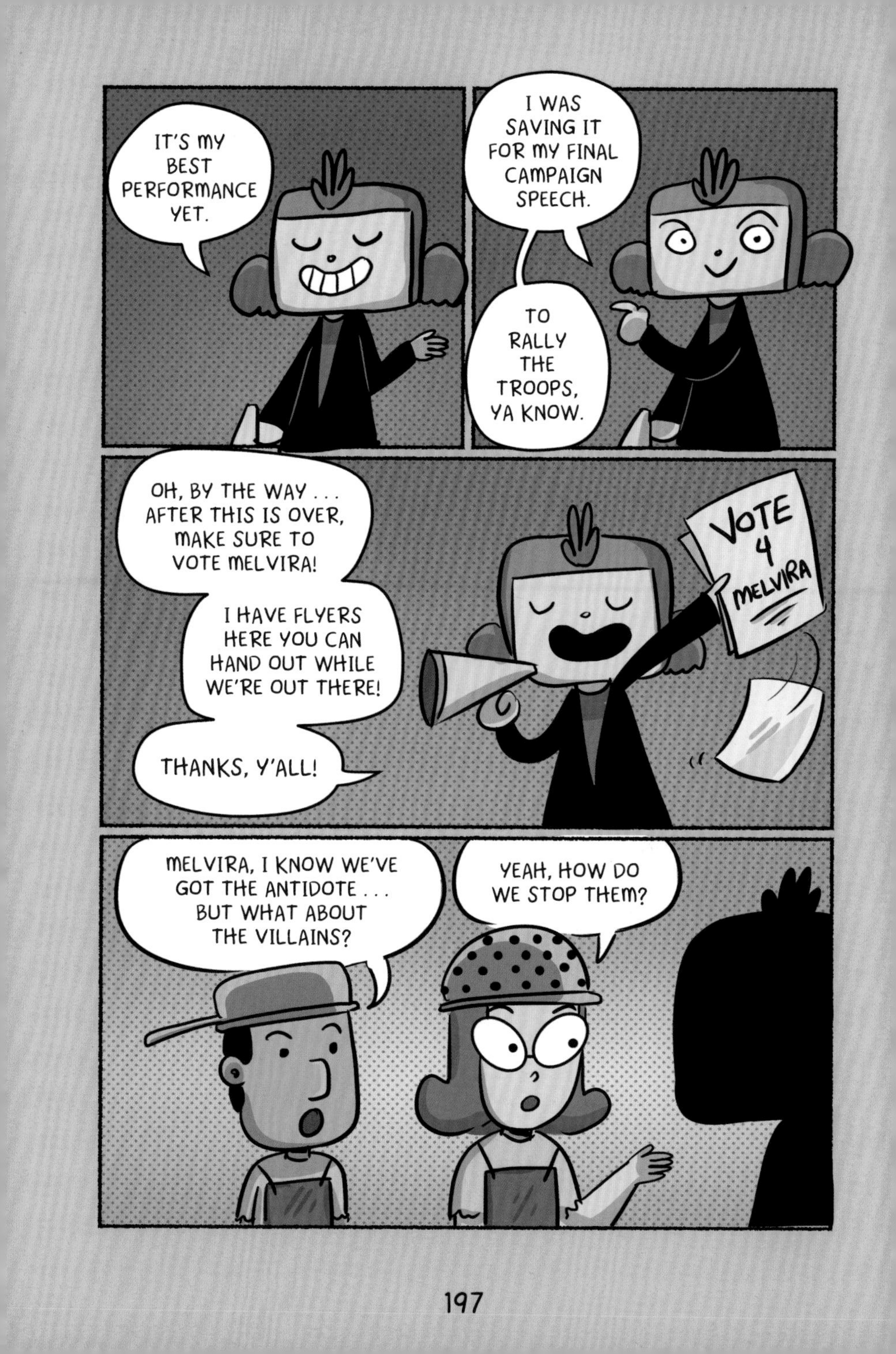
IT'S MY BEST PERFORMANCE YET.
I WAS SAVING IT FOR MY FINAL CAMPAIGN SPEECH.
TO RALLY THE TROOPS, YA KNOW.
OH, BY THE WAY . . . AFTER THIS IS OVER, MAKE SURE TO VOTE MELVIRA!
I HAVE FLYERS HERE YOU CAN HAND OUT WHILE WE'RE OUT THERE!
THANKS, Y'ALL!
VOTE 4 MELVIRA
MELVIRA, I KNOW WE'VE GOT THE ANTIDOTE . . . BUT WHAT ABOUT THE VILLAINS?
YEAH, HOW DO WE STOP THEM?

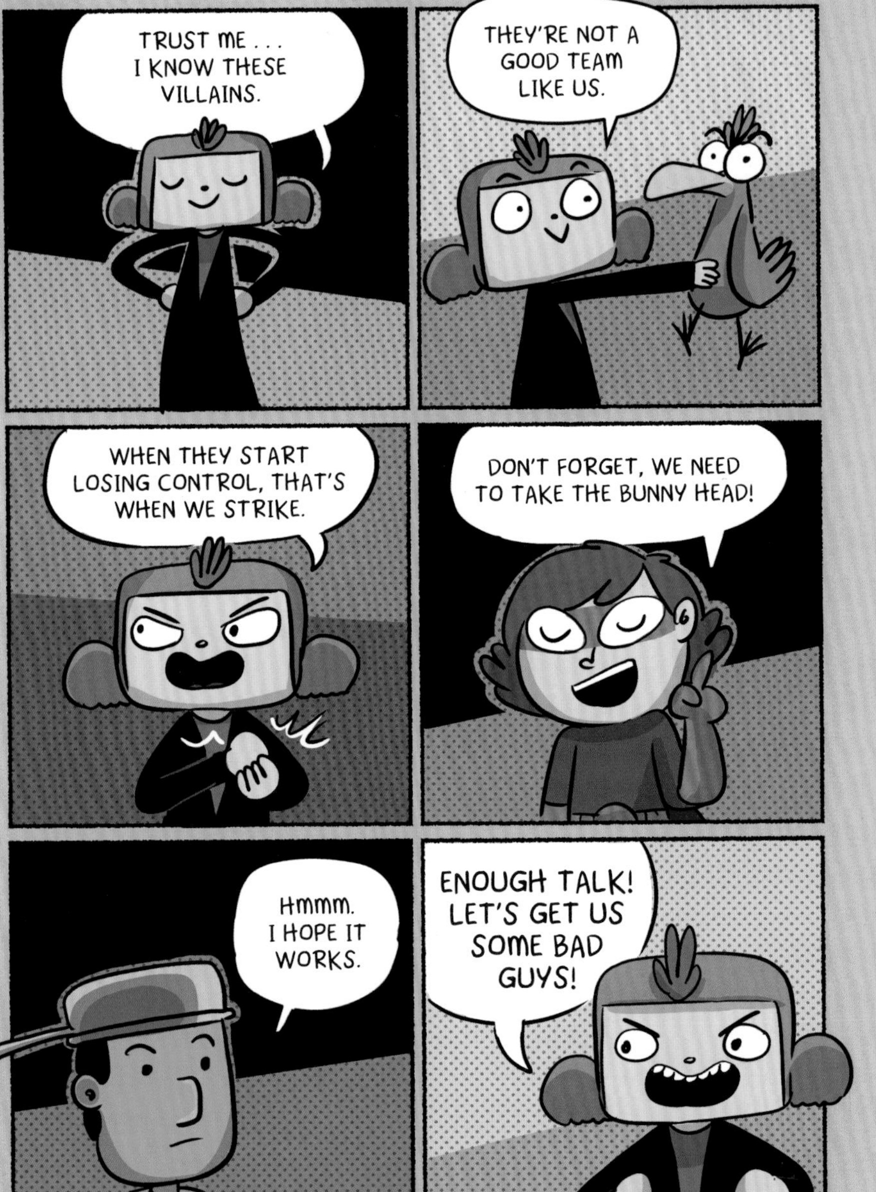
TRUST ME . . .
I KNOW THESE
VILLAINS.
THEY'RE NOT A
GOOD TEAM
LIKE US.
WHEN THEY START
LOSING CONTROL, THAT'S
WHEN WE STRIKE.
DON'T FORGET, WE NEED
TO TAKE THE BUNNY HEAD!
Hmmm.
I HOPE IT
WORKS.
ENOUGH TALK!
LET'S GET US
SOME BAD
GUYS!

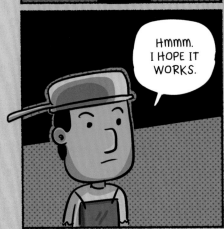

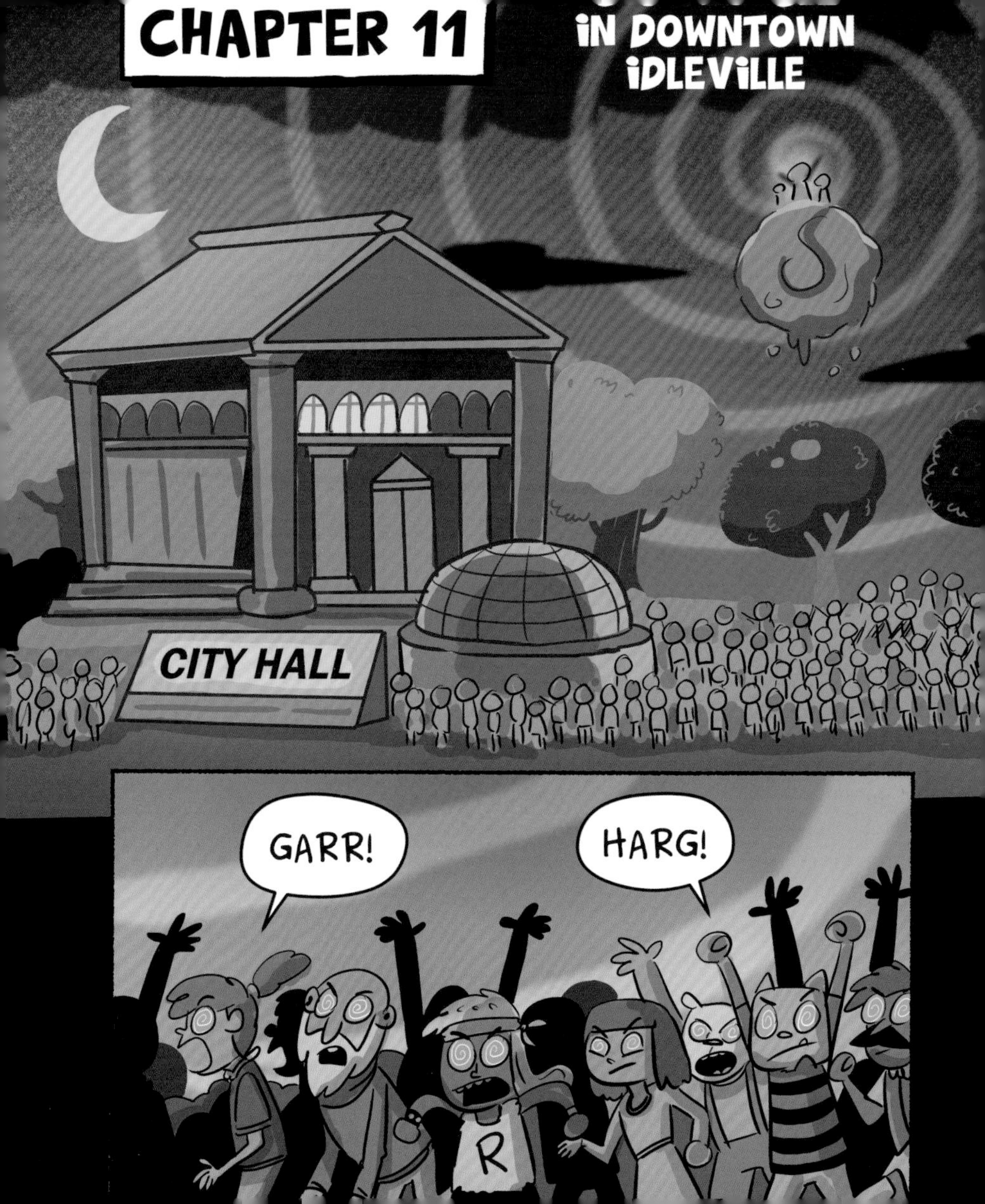
CHAPTER 11
IN DOWNTOWN IDLEVILLE
CITY HALL
GARR!
HARG!
R

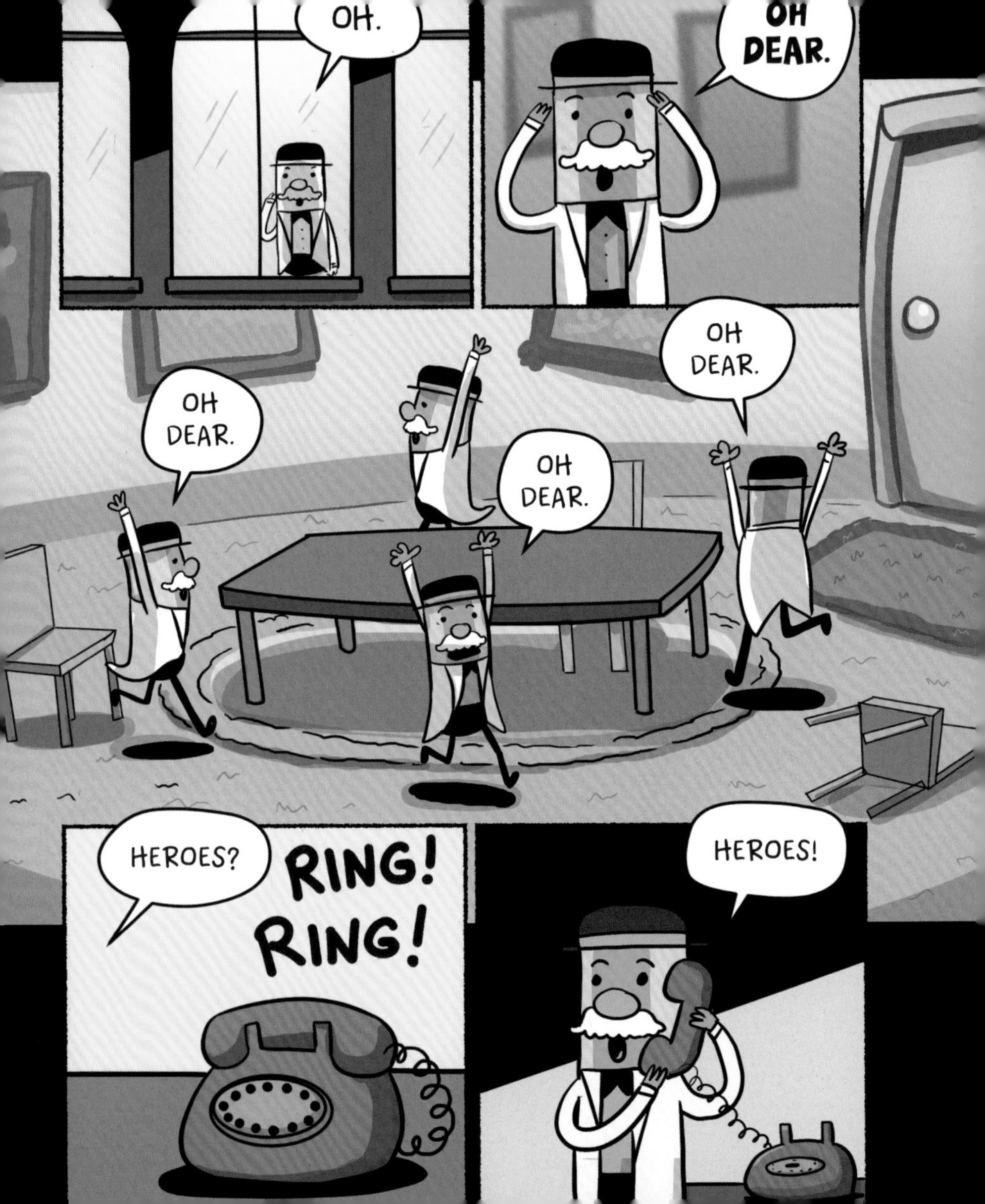
OH.
OH DEAR.
OH DEAR.
OH DEAR.
OH DEAR.
HEROES?
RING! RING!
HEROES!

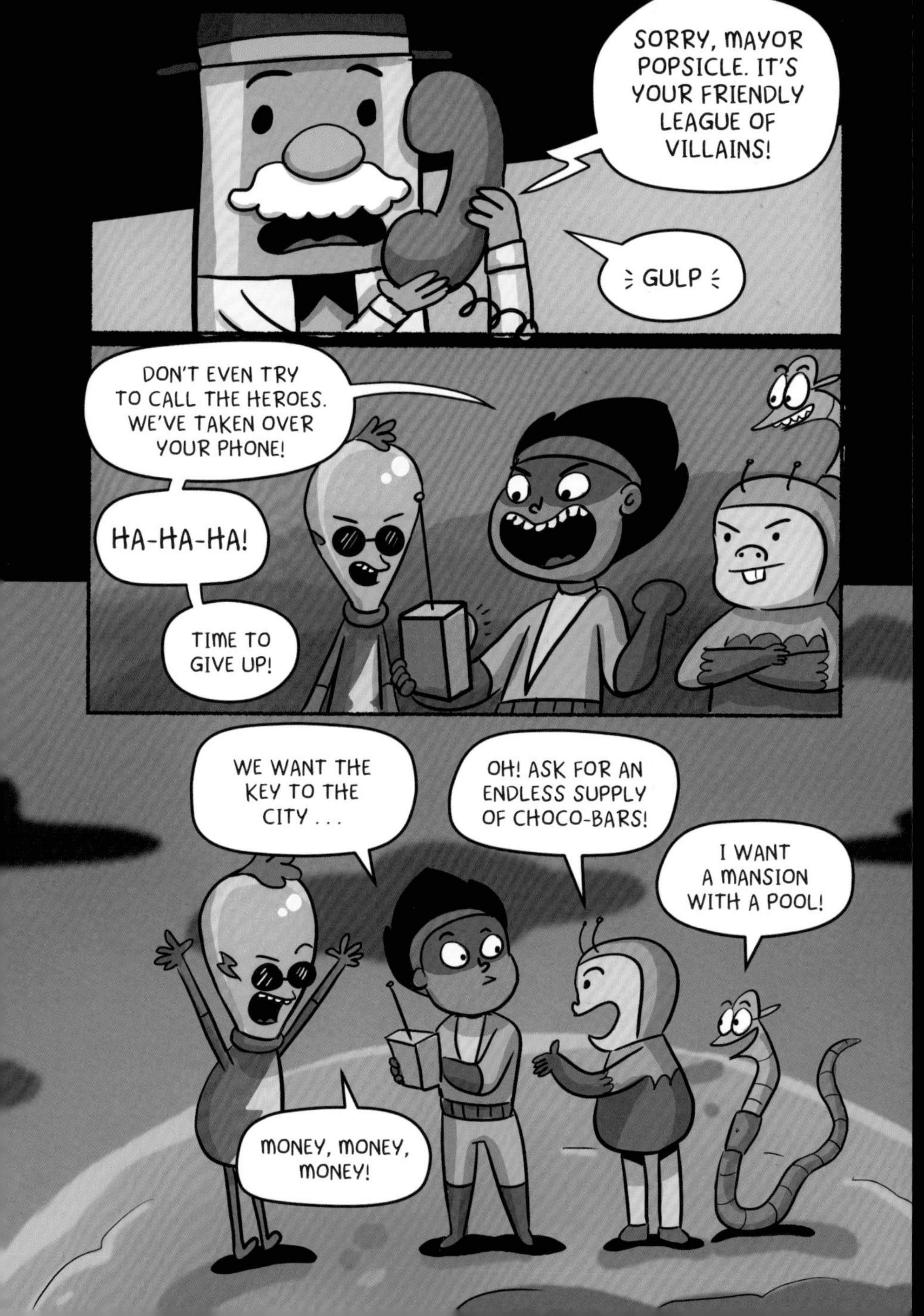
SORRY, MAYOR POPSICLE. IT'S YOUR FRIENDLY LEAGUE OF VILLAINS!
GULP
DON'T EVEN TRY TO CALL THE HEROES. WE'VE TAKEN OVER YOUR PHONE!
HA-HA-HA!
TIME TO GIVE UP!
WE WANT THE KEY TO THE CITY . . .
OH! ASK FOR AN ENDLESS SUPPLY OF CHOCO-BARS!
I WANT A MANSION WITH A POOL!
MONEY, MONEY, MONEY!

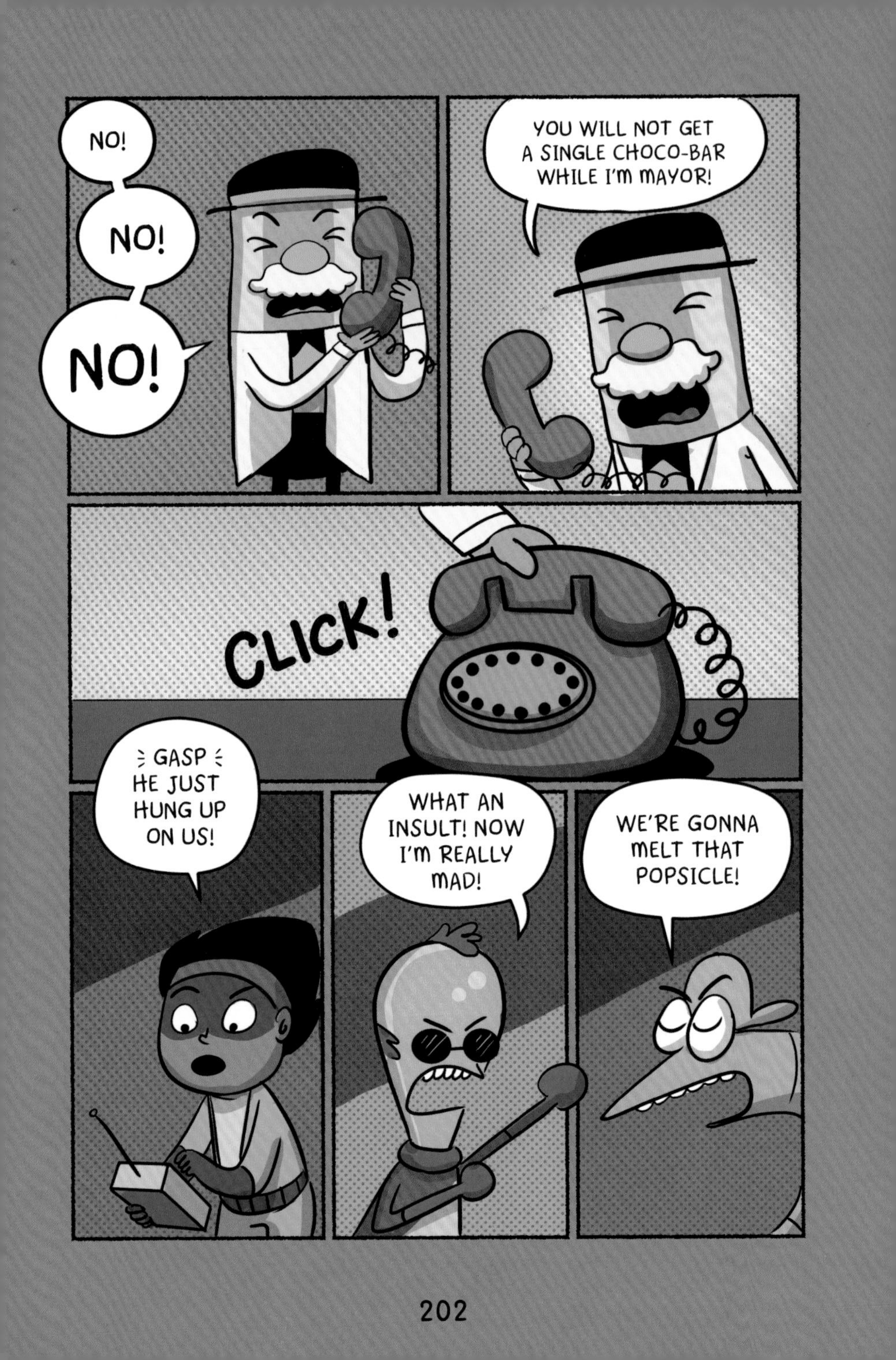
NO!
NO!
NO!
YOU WILL NOT GET A SINGLE CHOCO-BAR WHILE I'M MAYOR!
CLICK!
GASP
HE JUST HUNG UP ON US!
WHAT AN INSULT! NOW I'M REALLY MAD!
WE'RE GONNA MELT THAT POPSICLE!

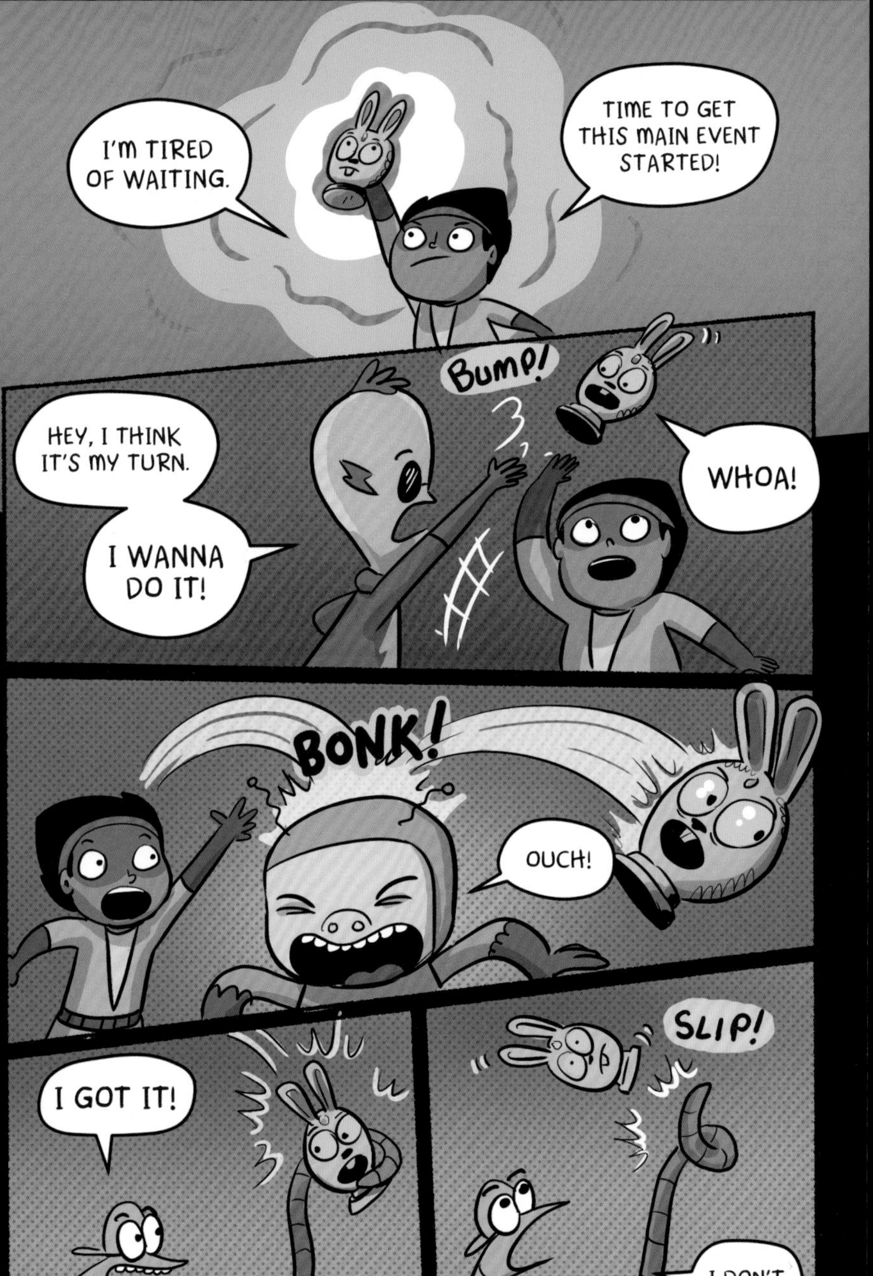
I'M TIRED OF WAITING.
TIME TO GET THIS MAIN EVENT STARTED!
BUMP!
HEY, I THINK IT'S MY TURN.
I WANNA DO IT!
WHOA!
BONK!
OUCH!
I GOT IT!
SLIP!
I DON'T GOT IT.

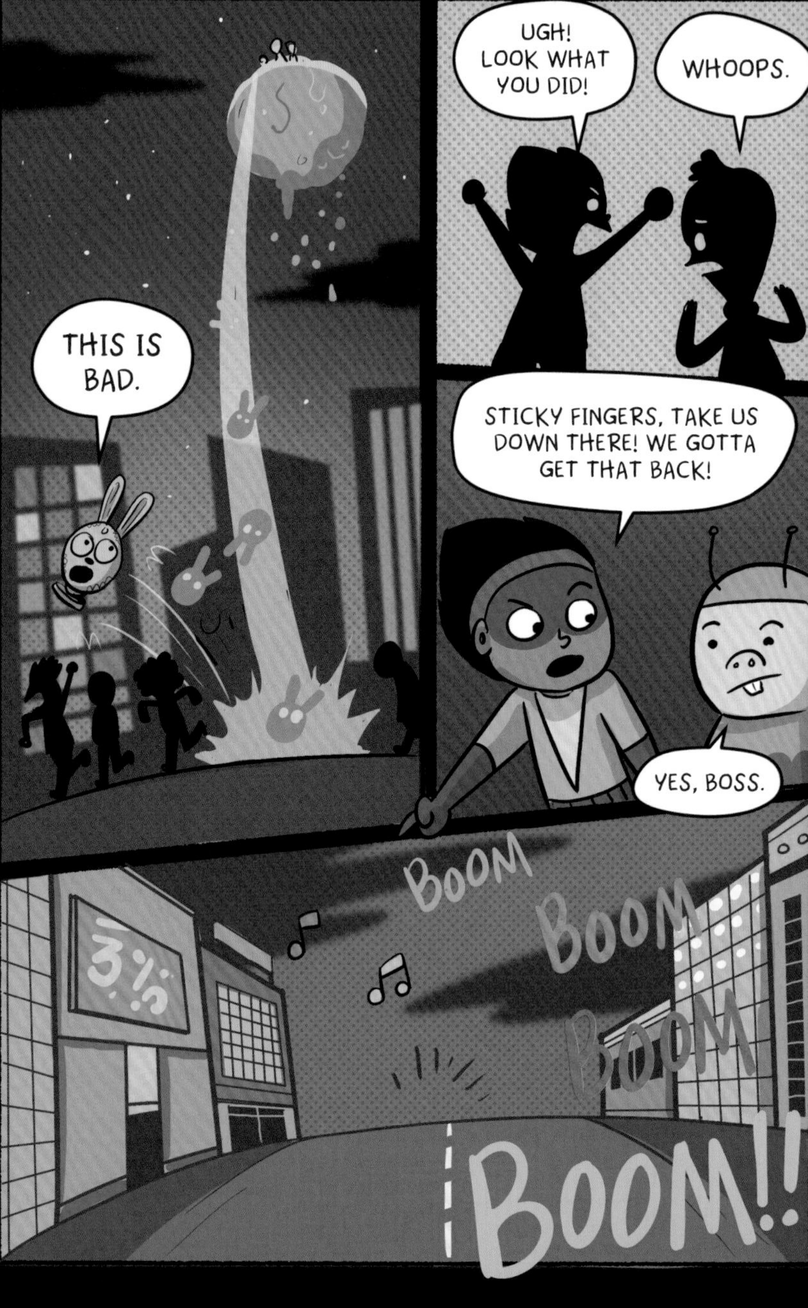
THIS IS BAD.
UGH! LOOK WHAT YOU DID!
WHOOPS.
STICKY FINGERS, TAKE US DOWN THERE! WE GOTTA GET THAT BACK!
YES, BOSS.
3%
BOOM
BOOM
BOOM
BOOM!!

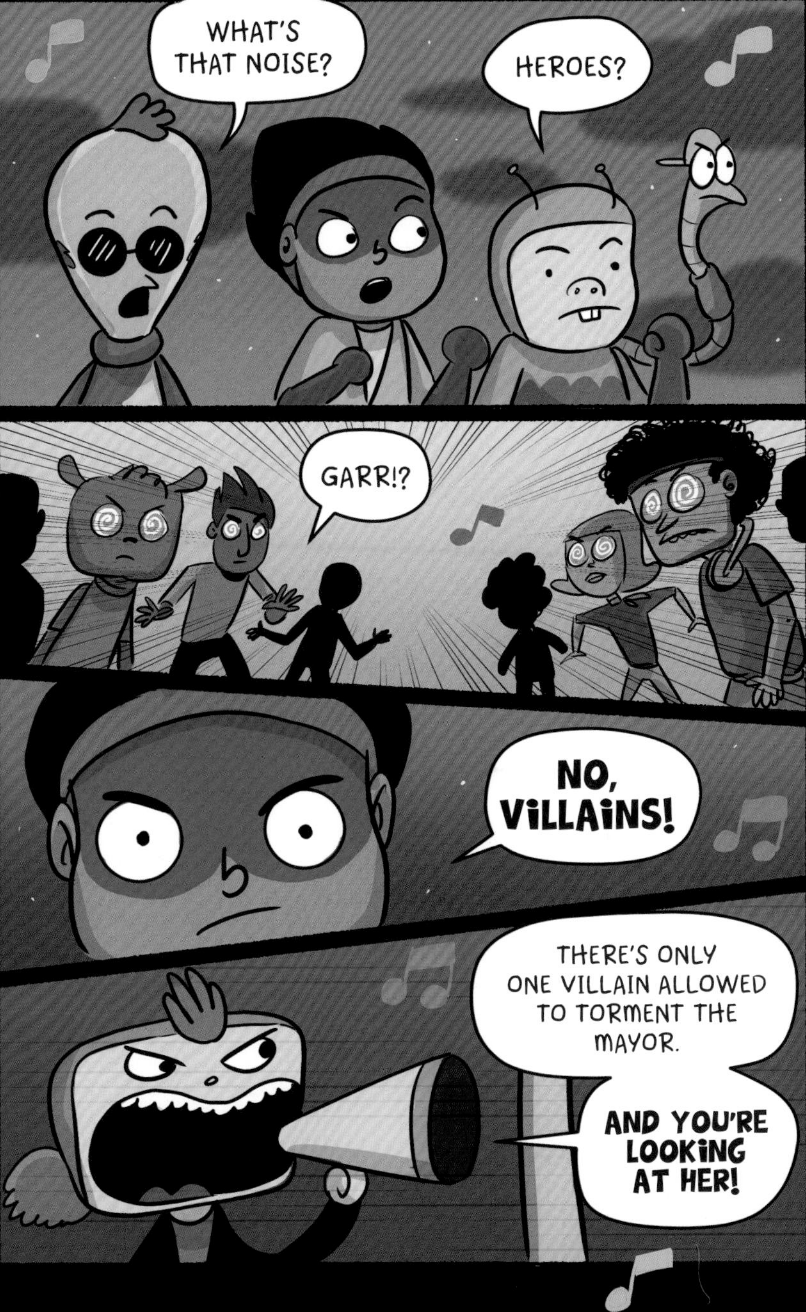
WHAT'S THAT NOISE?
HEROES?
GARR!?
NO, VILLAINS!
THERE'S ONLY ONE VILLAIN ALLOWED TO TORMENT THE MAYOR.
AND YOU'RE LOOKING AT HER!

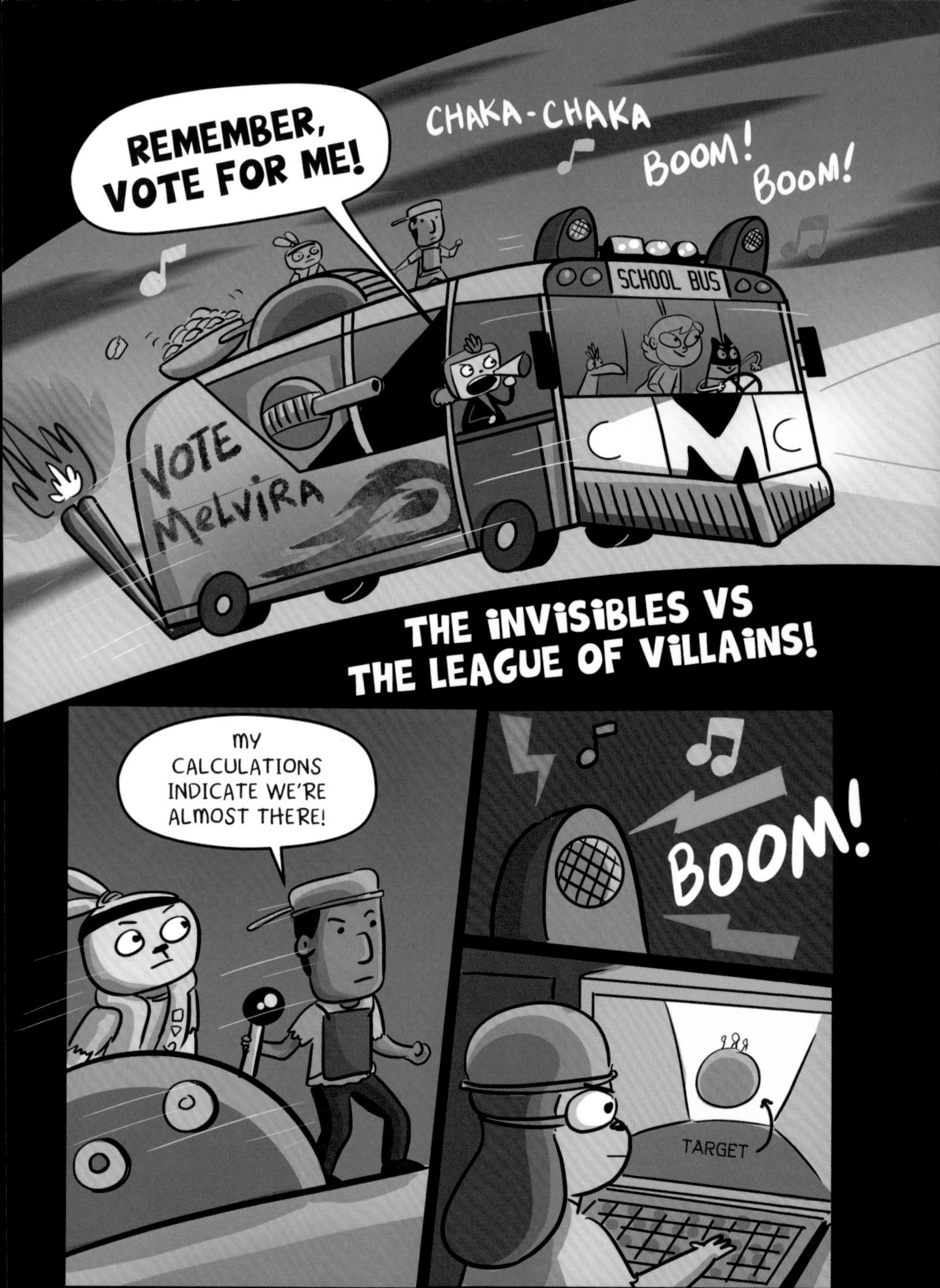
REMEMBER, VOTE FOR ME!
CHAKA-CHAKA
BOOM! BOOM!
SCHOOL BUS
VOTE Melvira
THE INVISIBLES VS THE LEAGUE OF VILLAINS!
MY CALCULATIONS INDICATE WE'RE ALMOST THERE!
BOOM!
TARGET

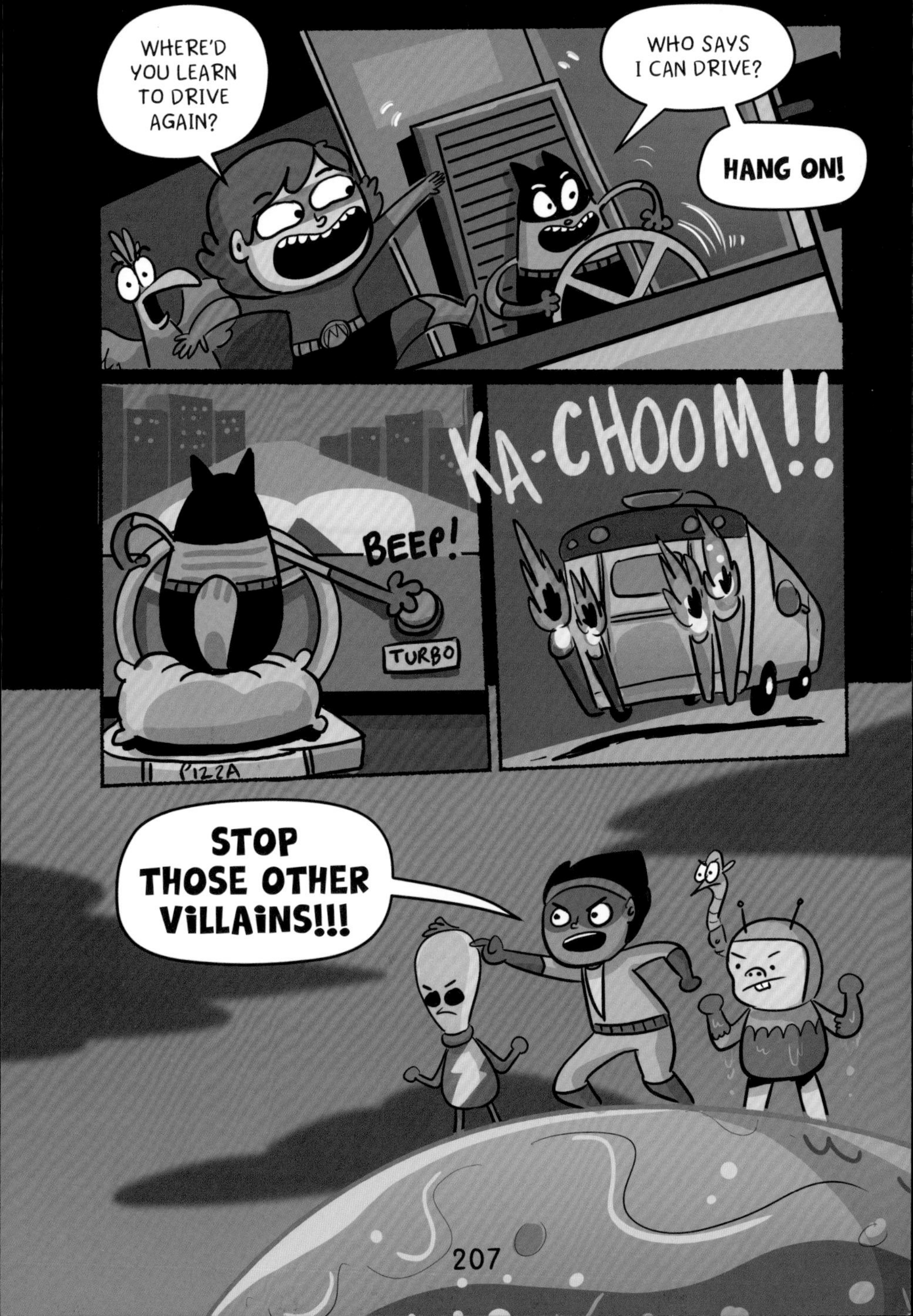
WHERE'D YOU LEARN TO DRIVE AGAIN?
WHO SAYS I CAN DRIVE?
HANG ON!
BEEP!
TURBO
PIZZA
KA-CHOOM!!
STOP THOSE OTHER VILLAINS!!!

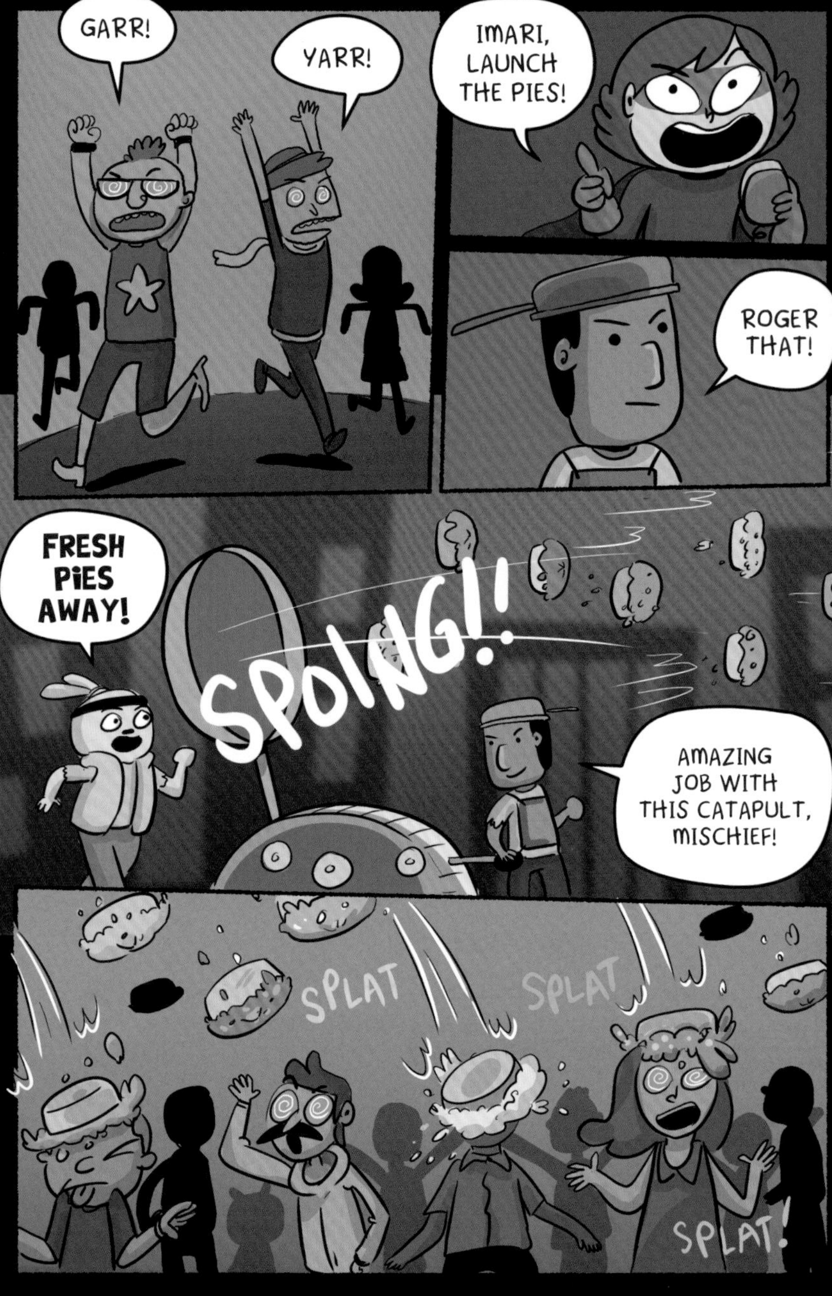
GARR!
YARR!
IMARI, LAUNCH THE PIES!
ROGER THAT!
FRESH PIES AWAY!
SPOING!!
AMAZING JOB WITH THIS CATAPULT, MISCHIEF!
SPLAT
SPLAT
SPLAT!

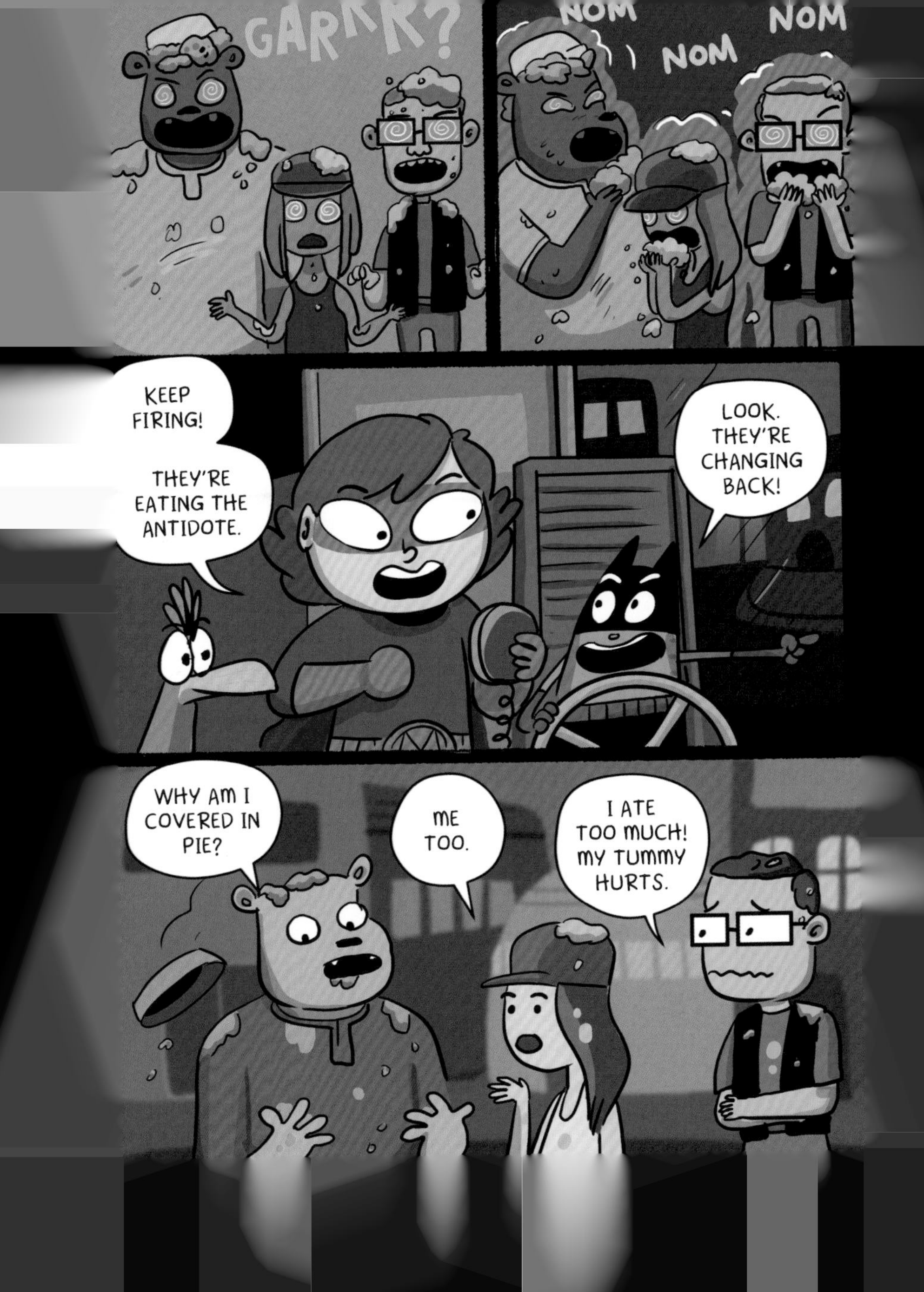
GARRR?
NOM
NOM
NOM
KEEP FIRING!
THEY'RE EATING THE ANTIDOTE.
LOOK. THEY'RE CHANGING BACK!
WHY AM I COVERED IN PIE?
ME TOO.
I ATE TOO MUCH! MY TUMMY HURTS.

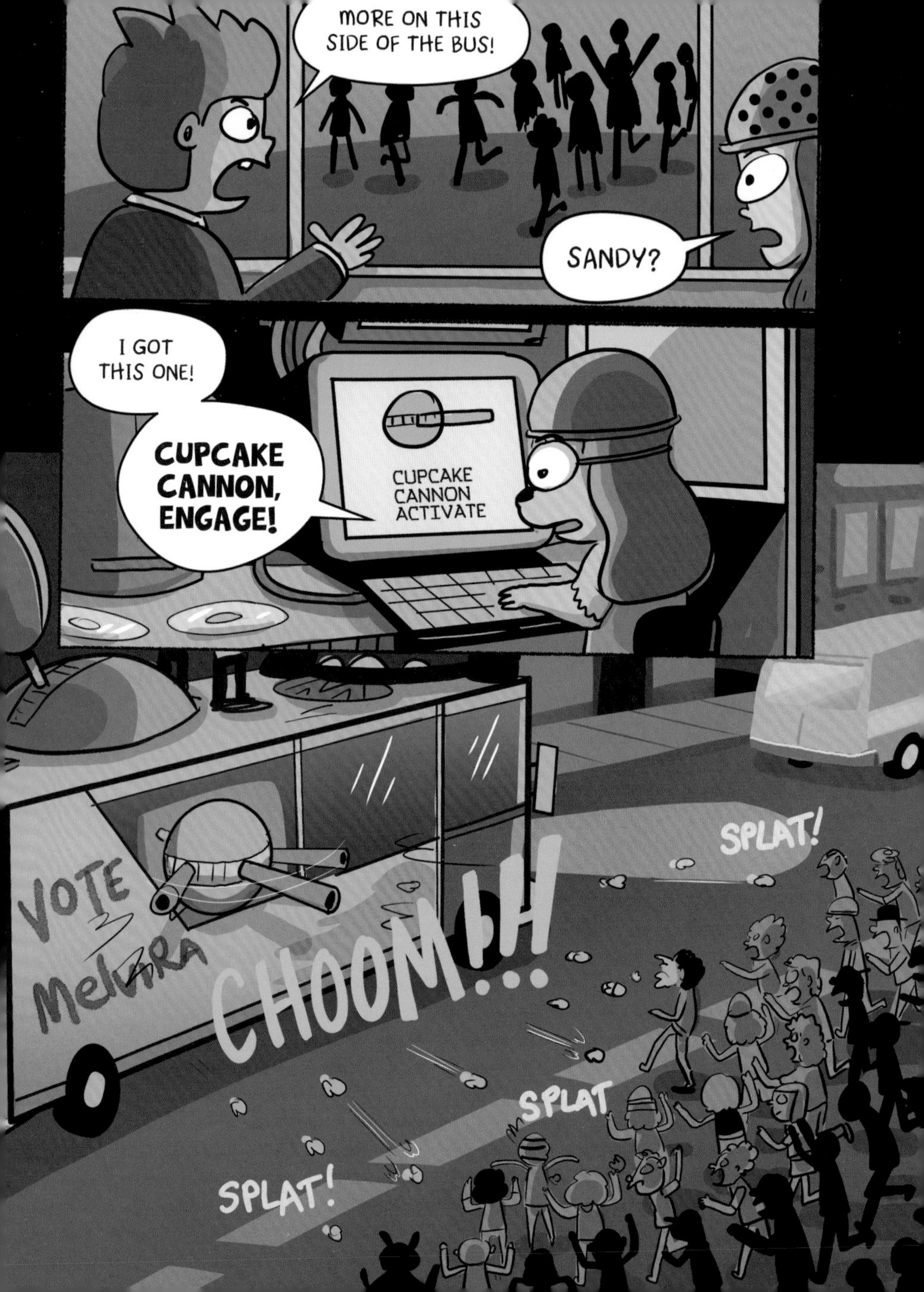
MORE ON THIS SIDE OF THE BUS!
SANDY?
I GOT THIS ONE!
CUPCAKE CANNON, ENGAGE!
CUPCAKE CANNON ACTIVATE
VOTE
CHOOM!!!
SPLAT!
SPLAT
SPLAT!

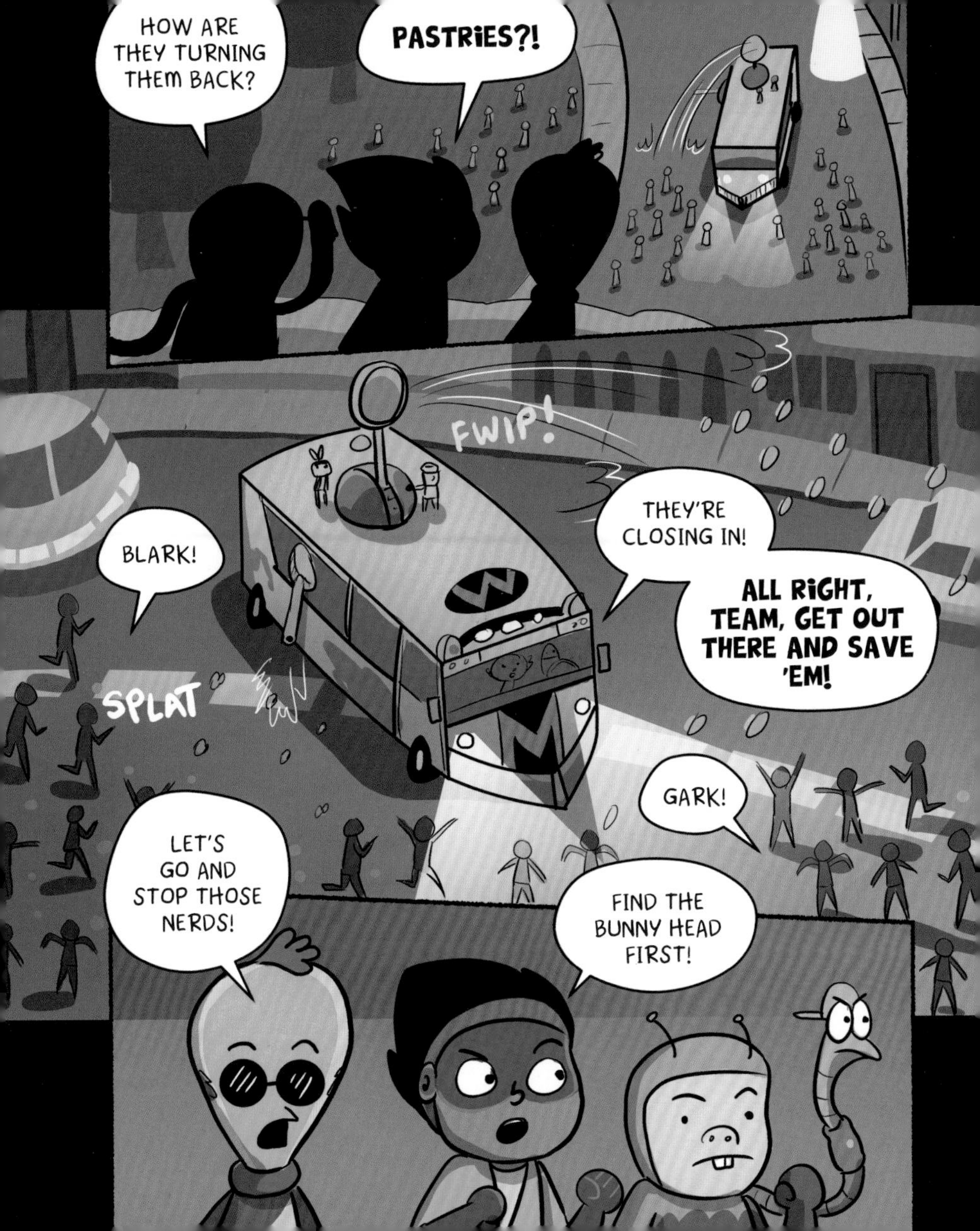
HOW ARE THEY TURNING THEM BACK?
PASTRIES?!
FWIP!
BLARK!
THEY'RE CLOSING IN!
ALL RIGHT, TEAM, GET OUT THERE AND SAVE 'EM!
SPLAT
GARK!
LET'S GO AND STOP THOSE NERDS!
FIND THE BUNNY HEAD FIRST!

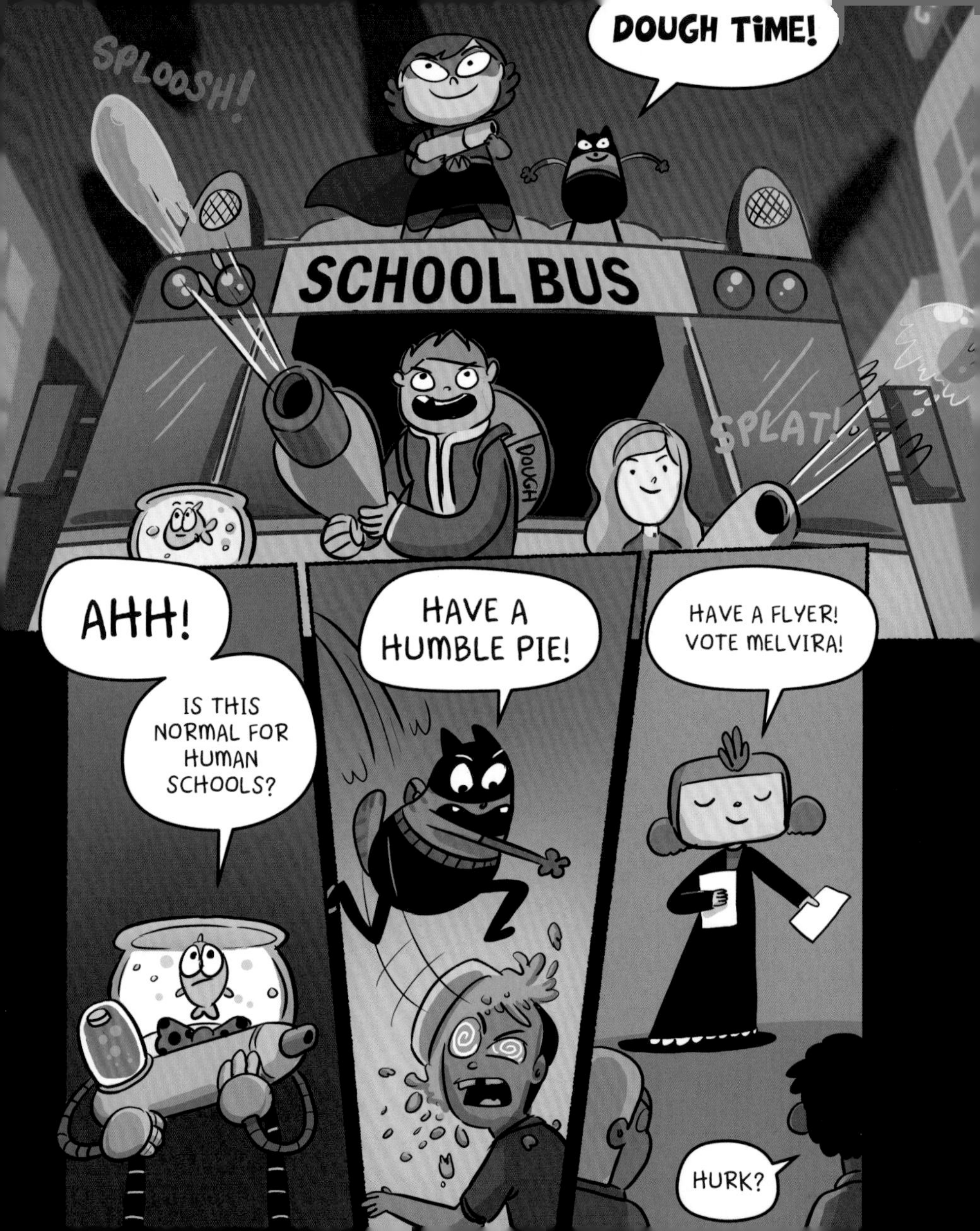
SPLOOSH!
DOUGH TIME!
SCHOOL BUS
DOUGH
SPLAT!
AHH!
IS THIS NORMAL FOR HUMAN SCHOOLS?
HAVE A HUMBLE PIE!
HAVE A FLYER! VOTE MELVIRA!
HURK?

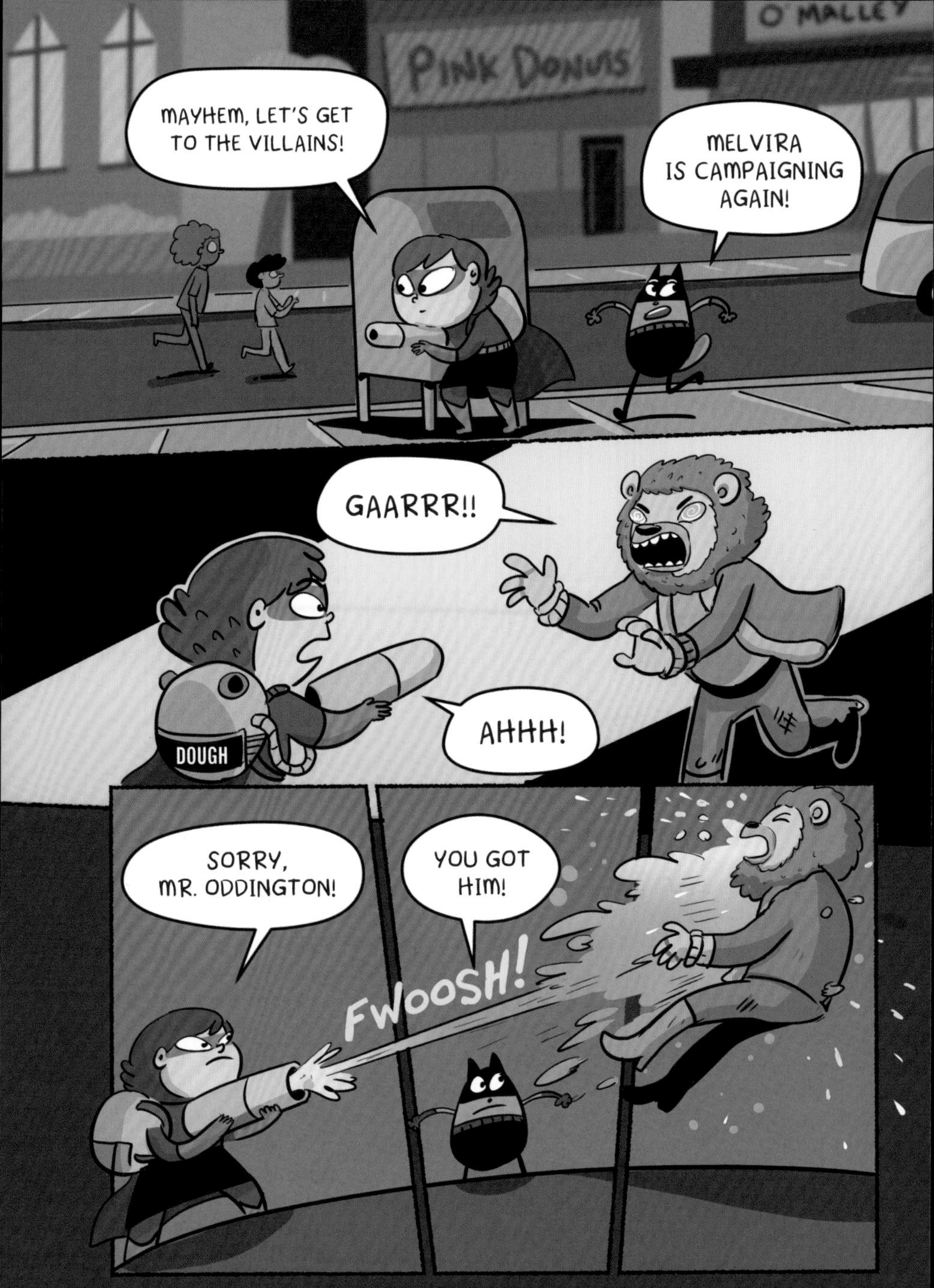
O'MALLEY
PINK DONUTS
MAYHEM, LET'S GET TO THE VILLAINS!
MELVIRA IS CAMPAIGNING AGAIN!
GAARRR!!
DOUGH
AHHH!
SORRY, MR. ODDINGTON!
YOU GOT HIM!
FWOOSH!

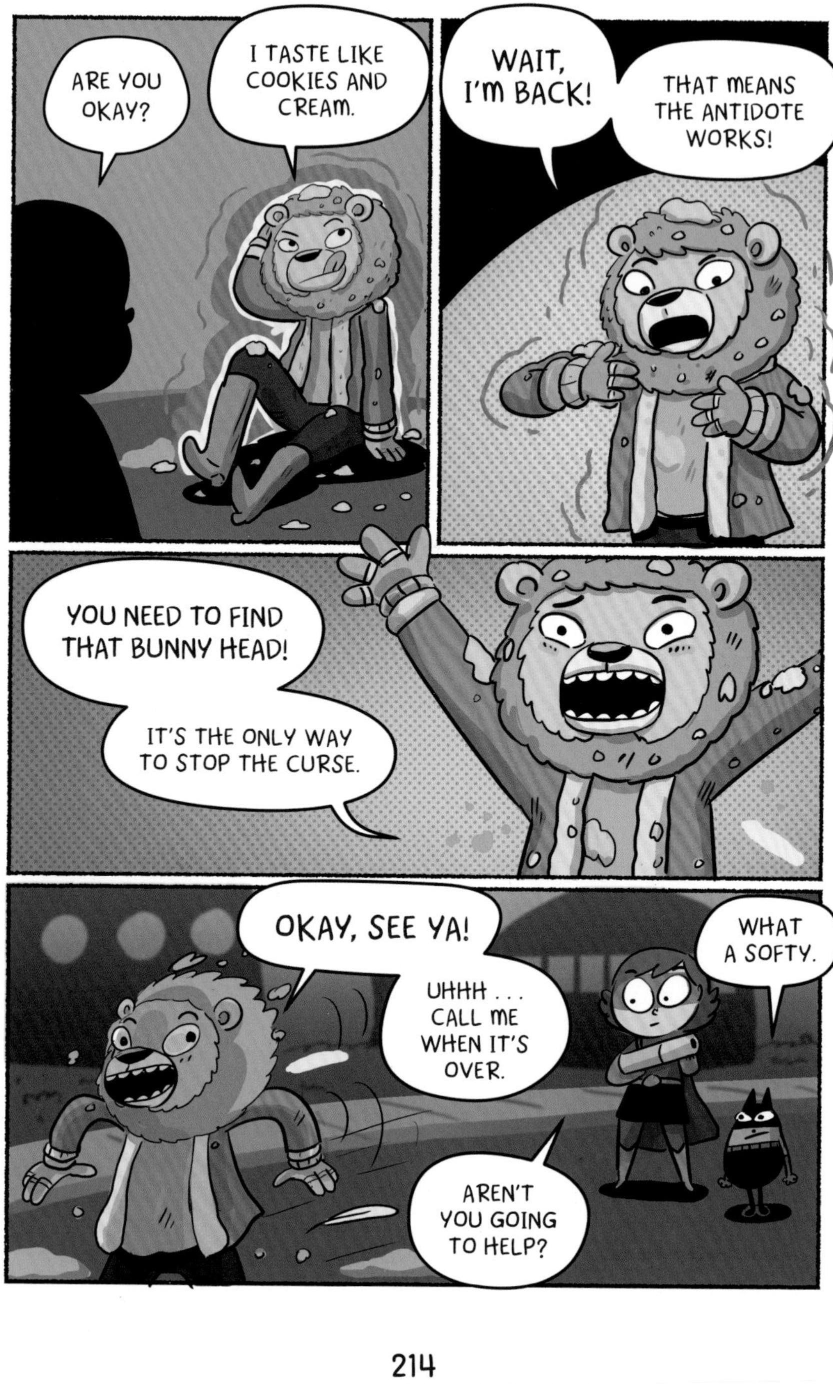
ARE YOU OKAY?
I TASTE LIKE COOKIES AND CREAM.
WAIT, I'M BACK!
THAT MEANS THE ANTIDOTE WORKS!
YOU NEED TO FIND THAT BUNNY HEAD!
IT'S THE ONLY WAY TO STOP THE CURSE.
OKAY, SEE YA!
UHHH . . . CALL ME WHEN IT'S OVER.
AREN'T YOU GOING TO HELP?
WHAT A SOFTY.

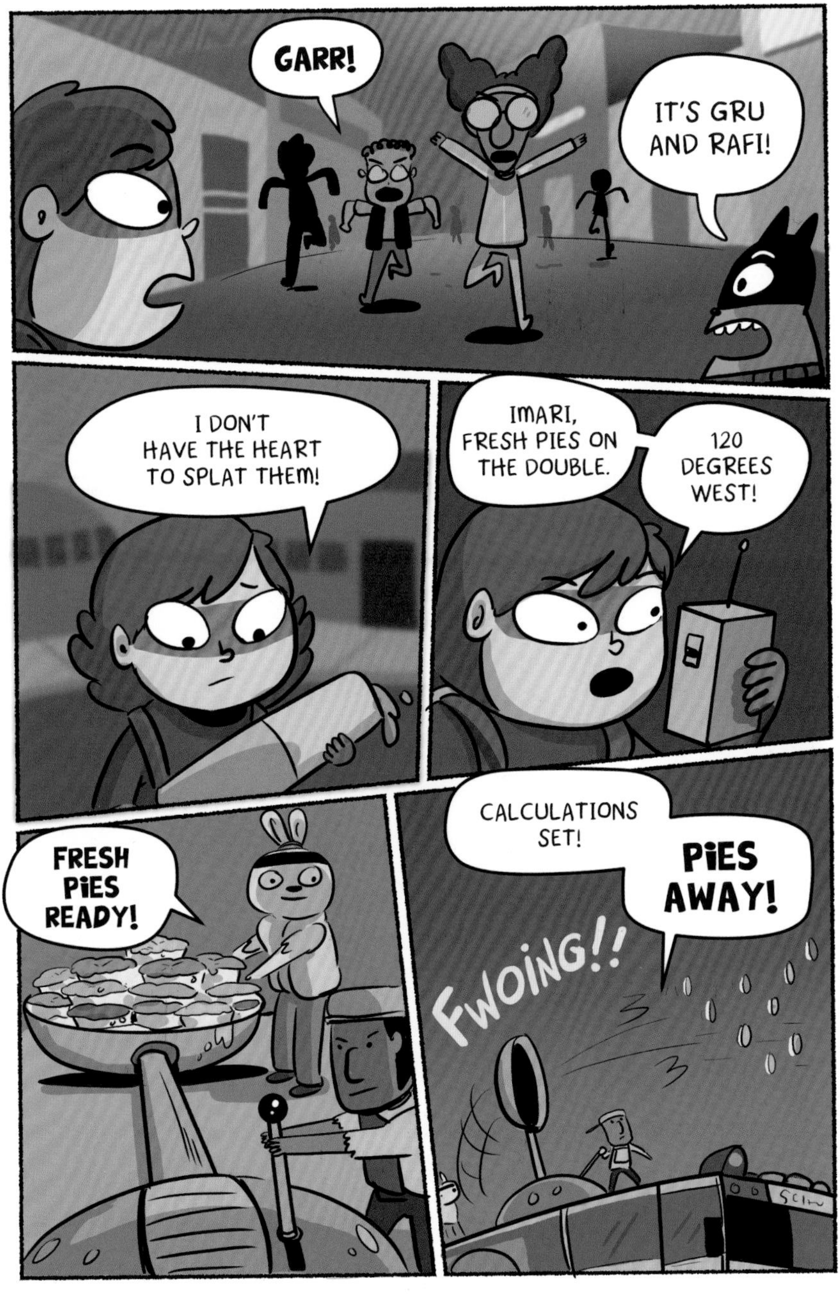
GARR!
IT'S GRU AND RAFI!
I DON'T HAVE THE HEART TO SPLAT THEM!
IMARI, FRESH PIES ON THE DOUBLE.
120 DEGREES WEST!
FRESH PIES READY!
CALCULATIONS SET!
PIES AWAY!
FWOING!!

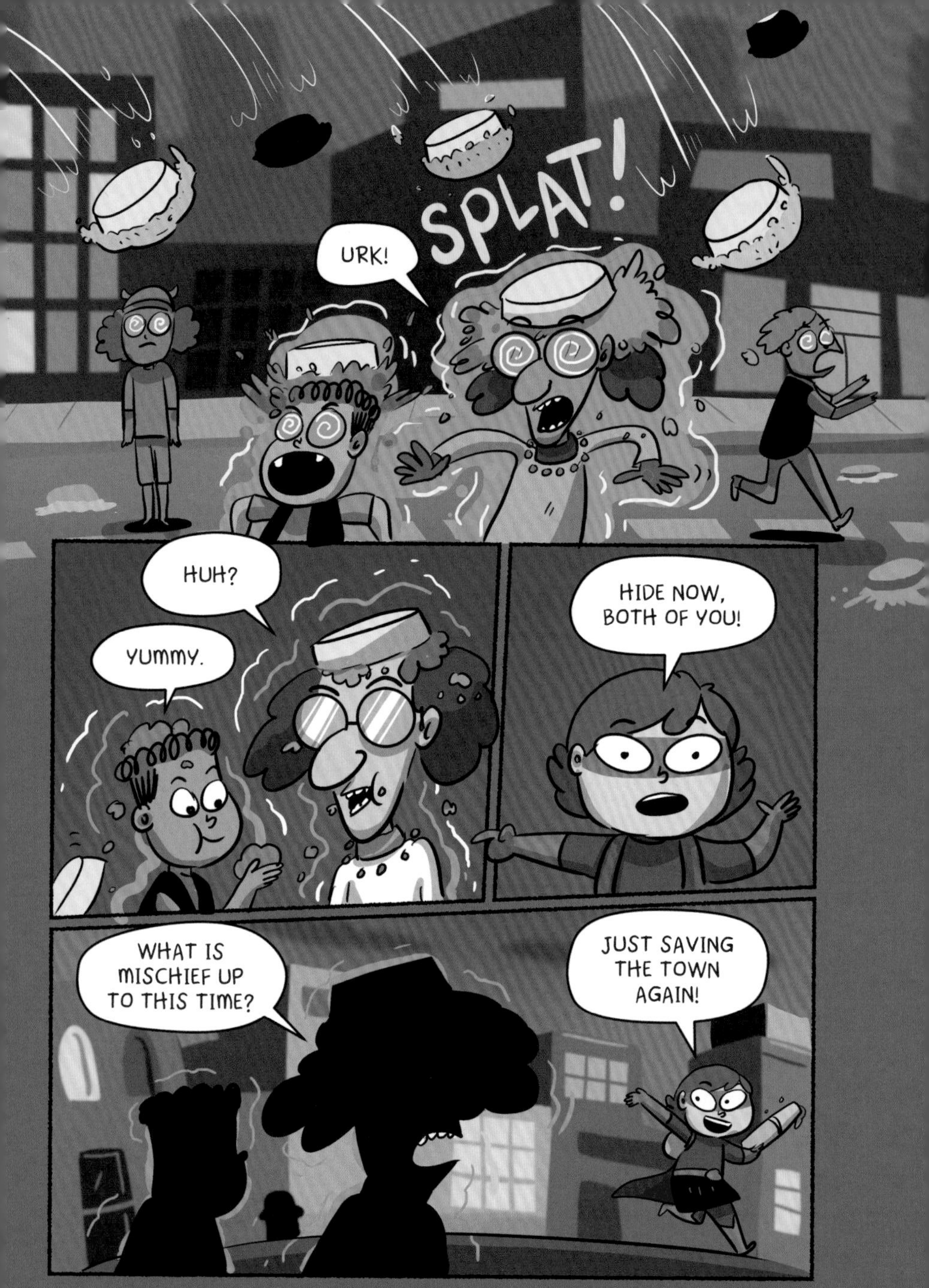

URK!
SPLAT!
HUH?
YUMMY.
HIDE NOW, BOTH OF YOU!
WHAT IS MISCHIEF UP TO THIS TIME?
JUST SAVING THE TOWN AGAIN!

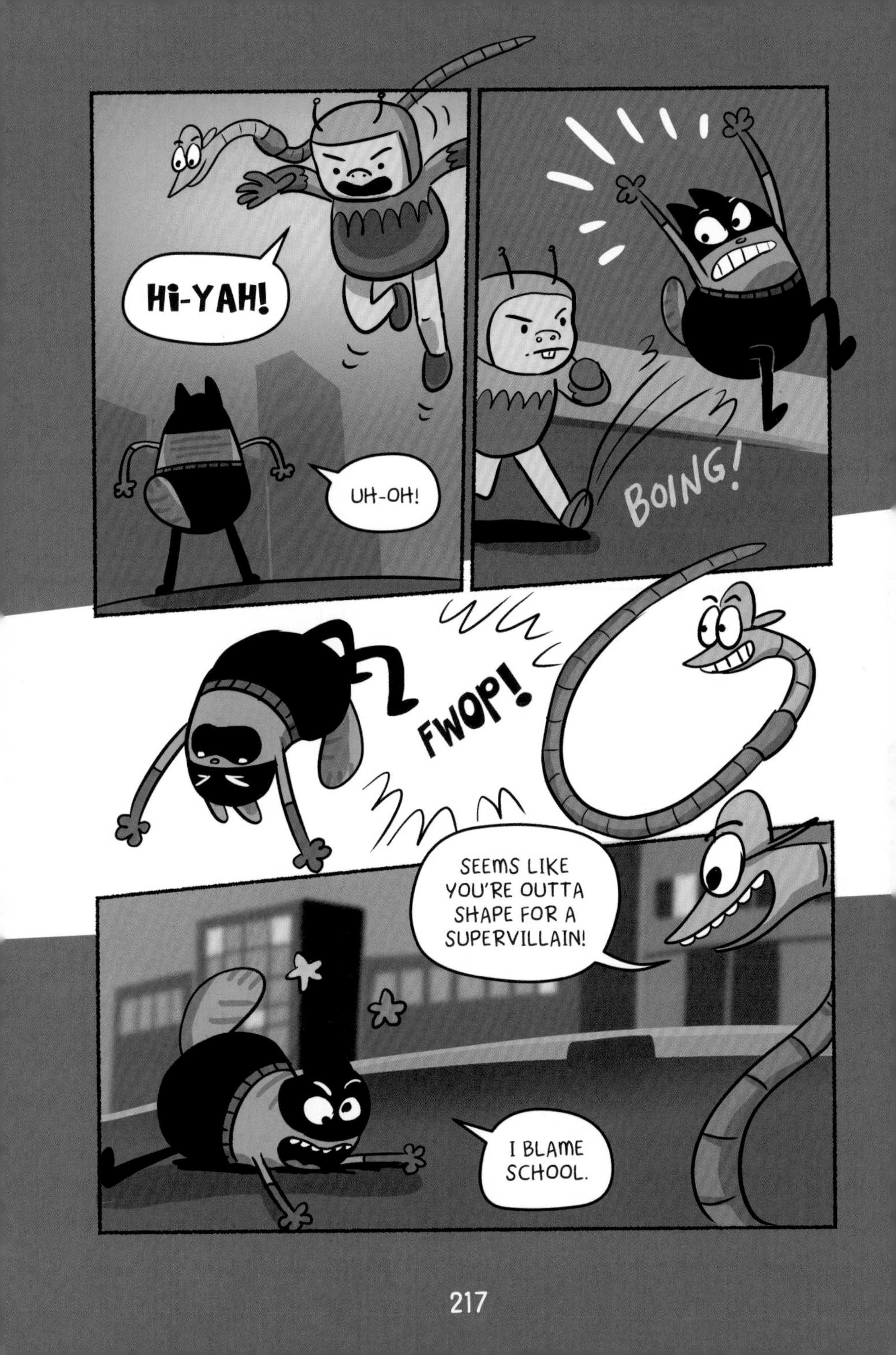
HI-YAH!
UH-OH!
BOING!
FWOP!
SEEMS LIKE YOU'RE OUTTA SHAPE FOR A SUPERVILLAIN!
I BLAME SCHOOL.

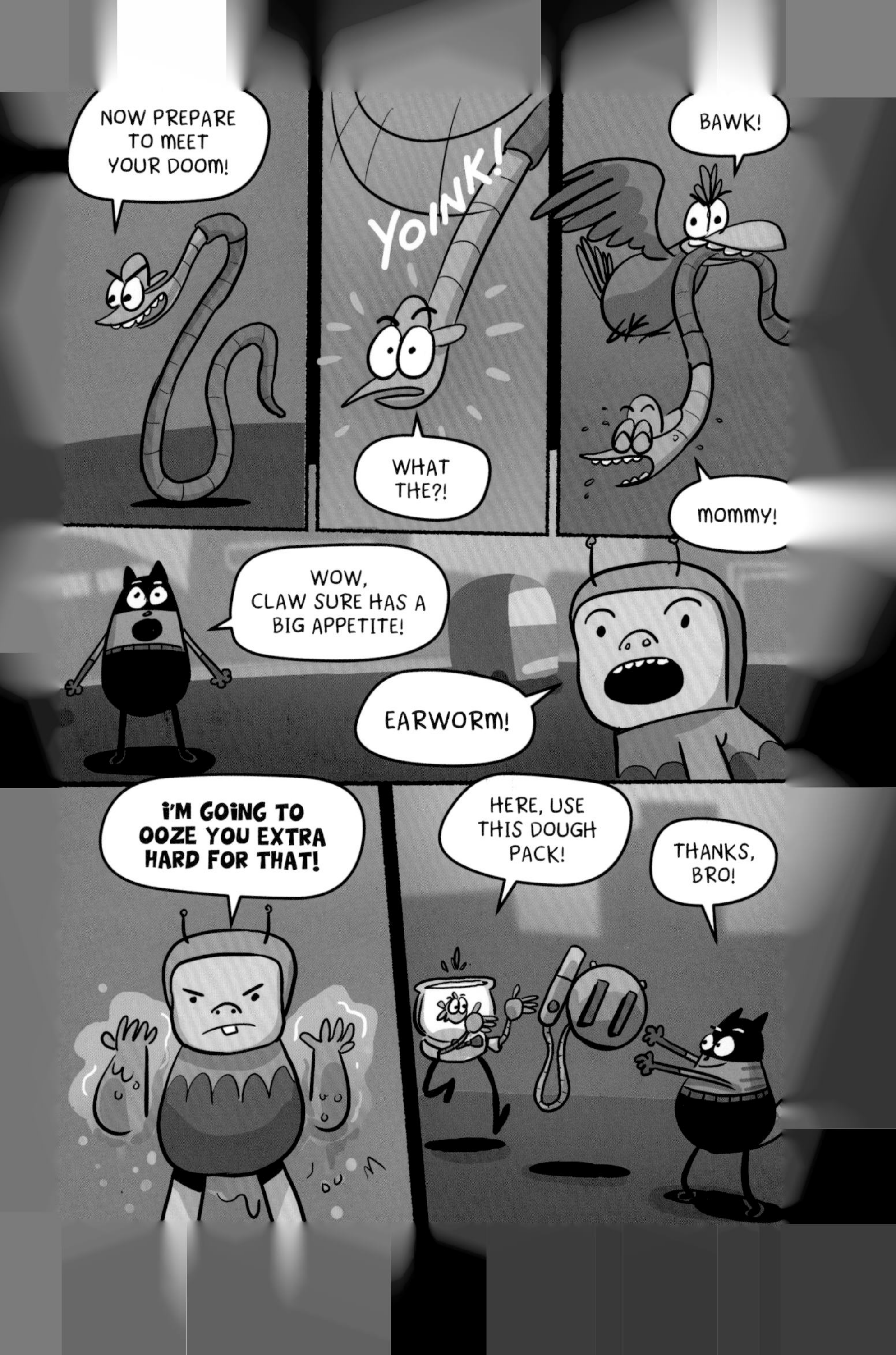
NOW PREPARE TO MEET YOUR DOOM!
YOINK!
WHAT THE?!
BAWK!
MOMMY!
WOW, CLAW SURE HAS A BIG APPETITE!
EARWORM!
I'M GOING TO OOZE YOU EXTRA HARD FOR THAT!
HERE, USE THIS DOUGH PACK!
THANKS, BRO!

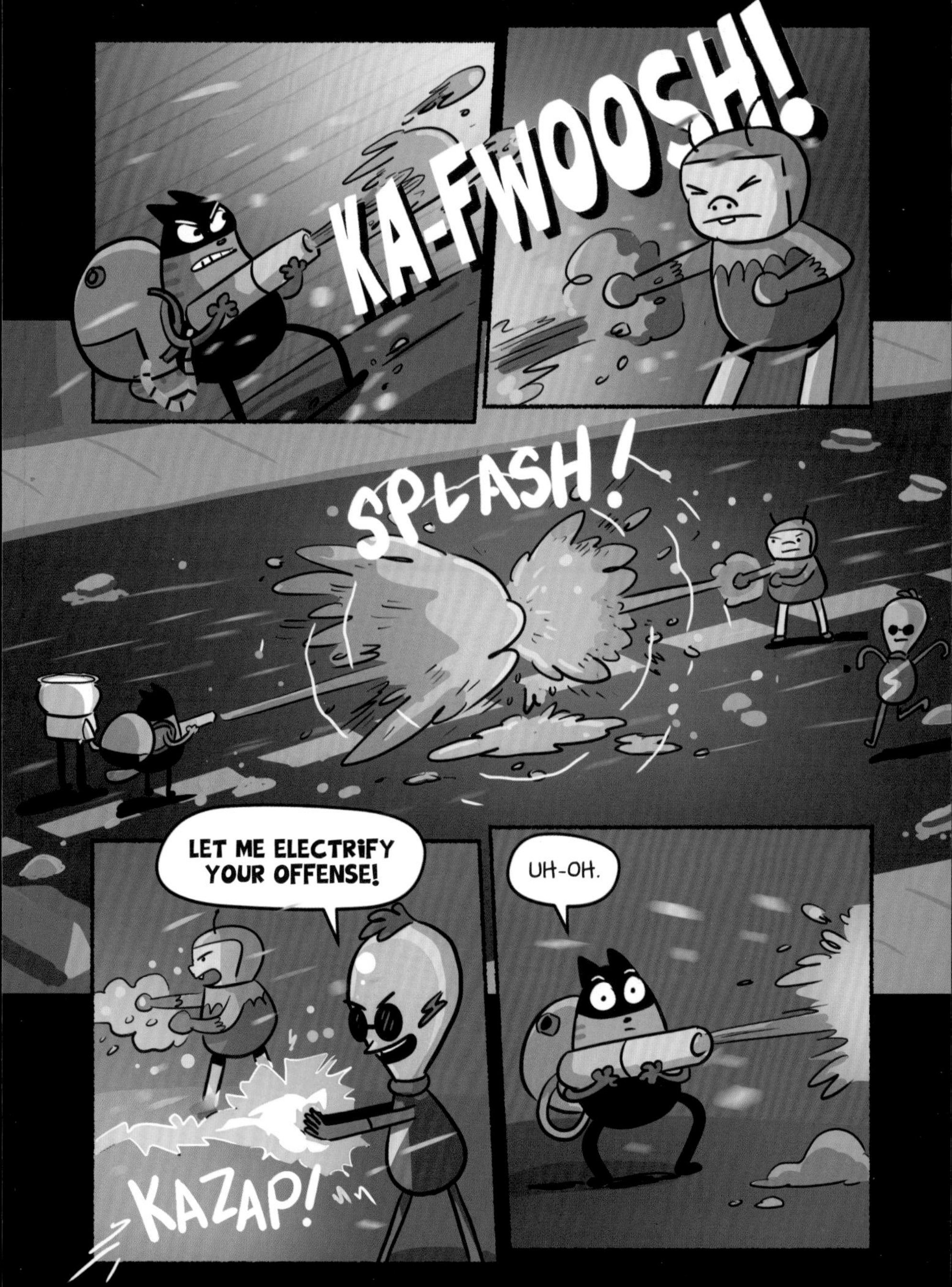
KA-FWOOSH!
SPLASH!
LET ME ELECTRIFY YOUR OFFENSE!
KAZAP!
UH-OH.

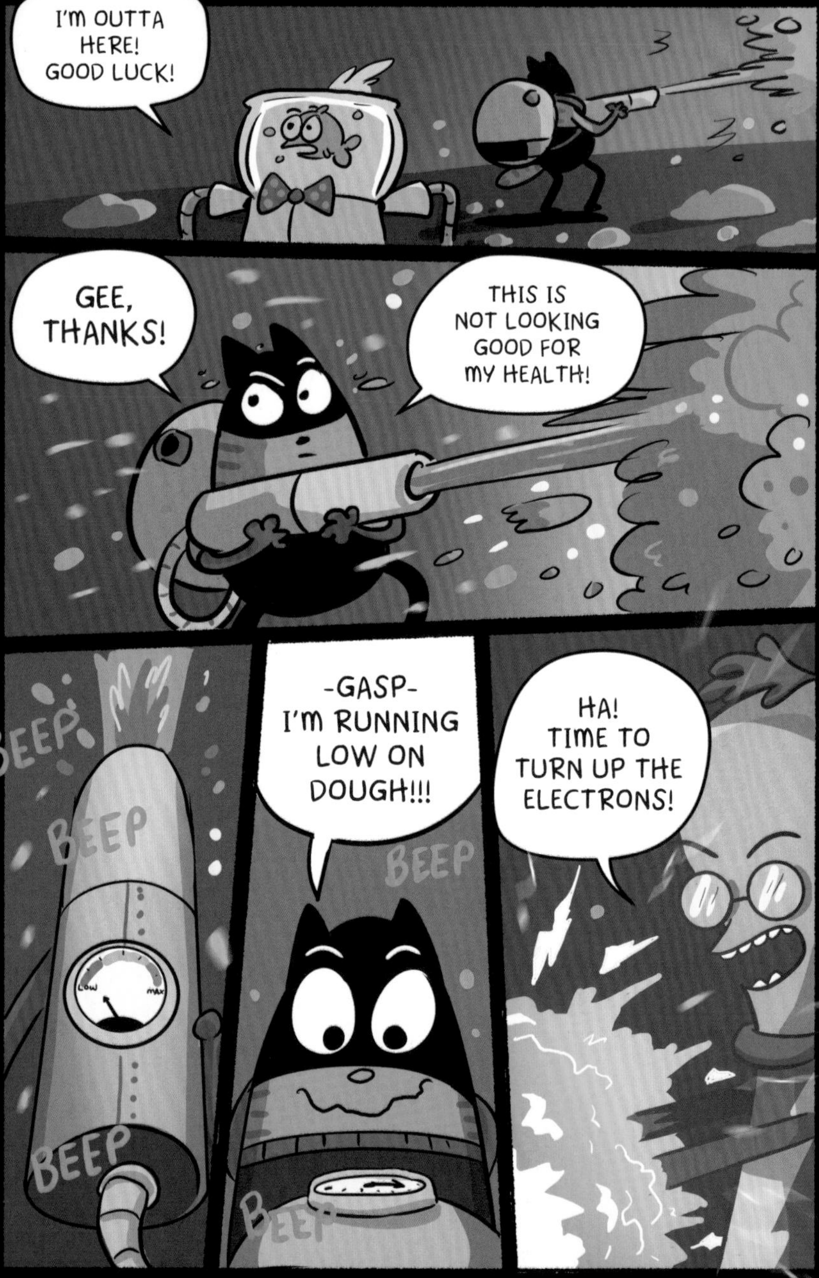
I'M OUTTA HERE! GOOD LUCK!
GEE, THANKS!
THIS IS NOT LOOKING GOOD FOR MY HEALTH!
BEEP
BEEP
BEEP
LOW
MAX
-GASP- I'M RUNNING LOW ON DOUGH!!!
BEEP
BEEP
HA! TIME TO TURN UP THE ELECTRONS!

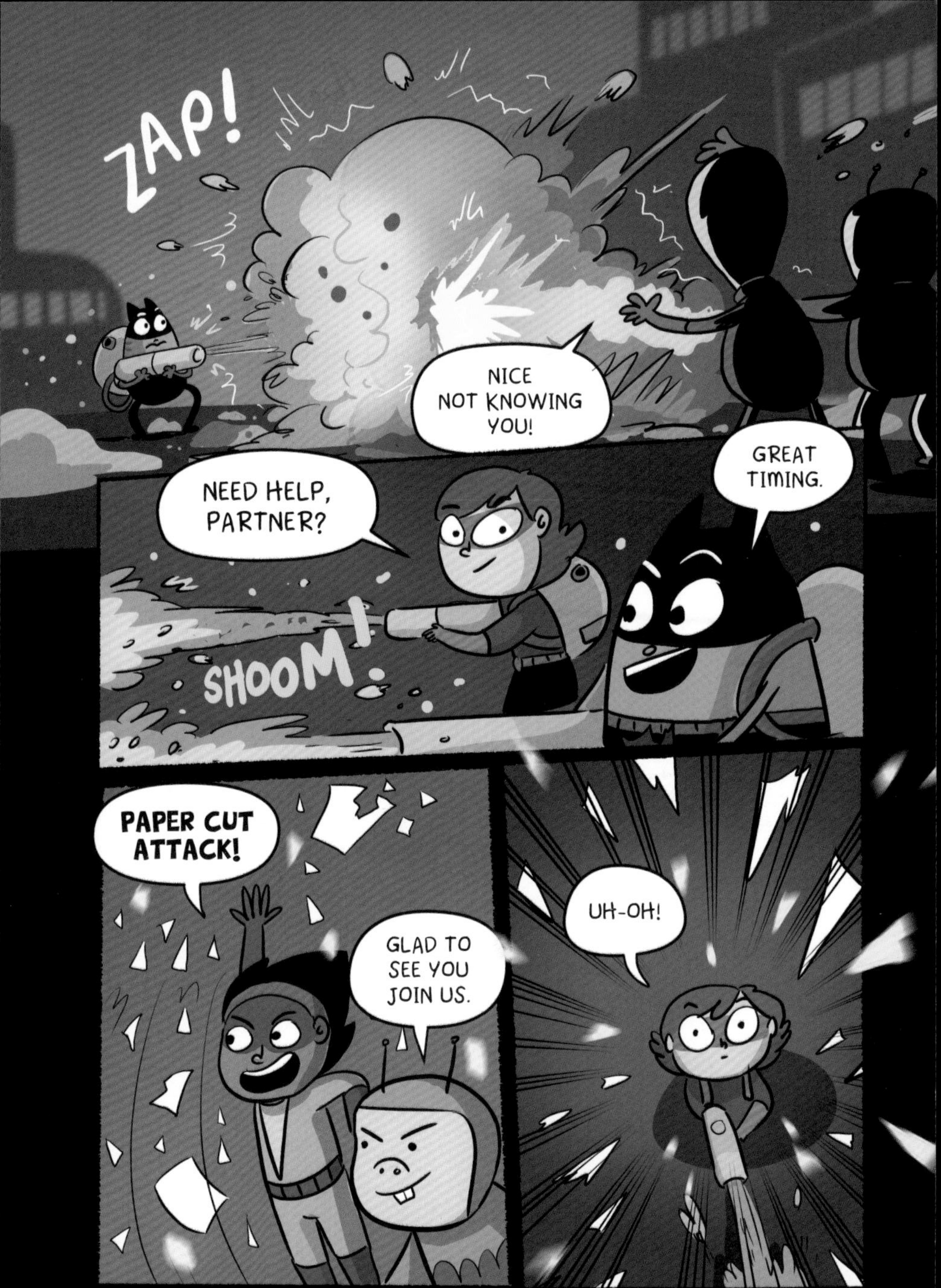
ZAP!
NICE NOT KNOWING YOU!
NEED HELP, PARTNER?
GREAT TIMING.
SHOOM!
PAPER CUT ATTACK!
GLAD TO SEE YOU JOIN US.
UH-OH!

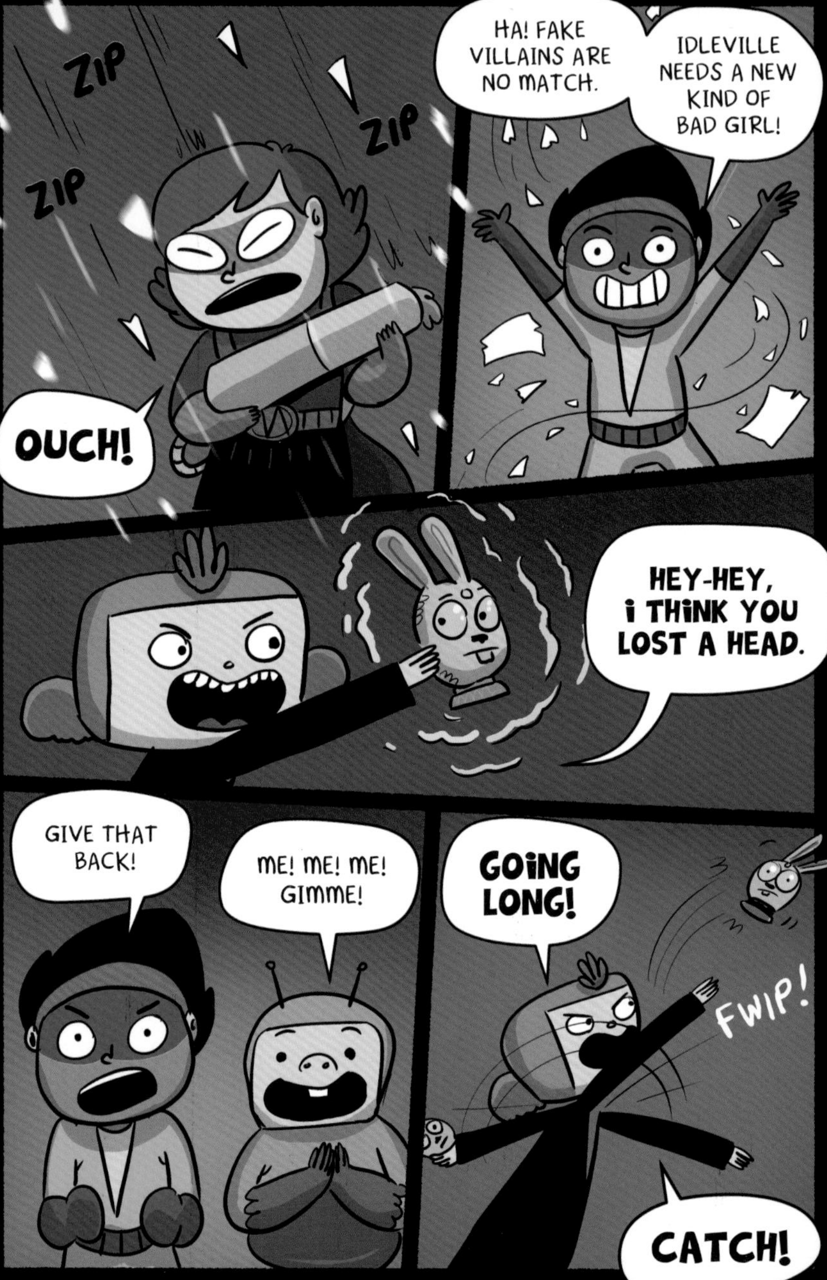
ZIP
ZIP
ZIP
OUCH!
HA! FAKE VILLAINS ARE NO MATCH.
IDLEVILLE NEEDS A NEW KIND OF BAD GIRL!
HEY-HEY, I THINK YOU LOST A HEAD.
GIVE THAT BACK!
ME! ME! ME! GIMME!
GOING LONG!
FWIP!
CATCH!

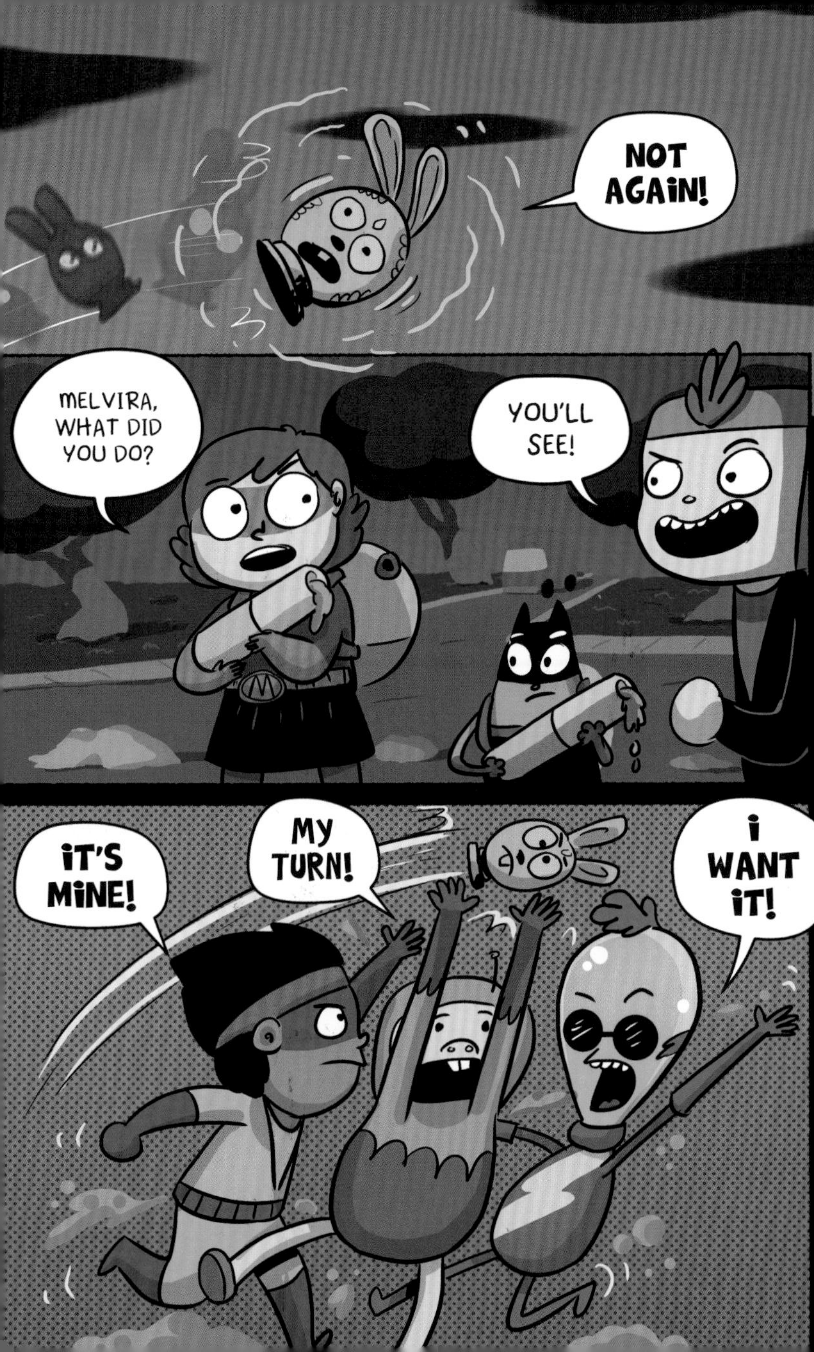
NOT AGAIN!
MELVIRA, WHAT DID YOU DO?
YOU'LL SEE!
IT'S MINE!
MY TURN!
I WANT IT!

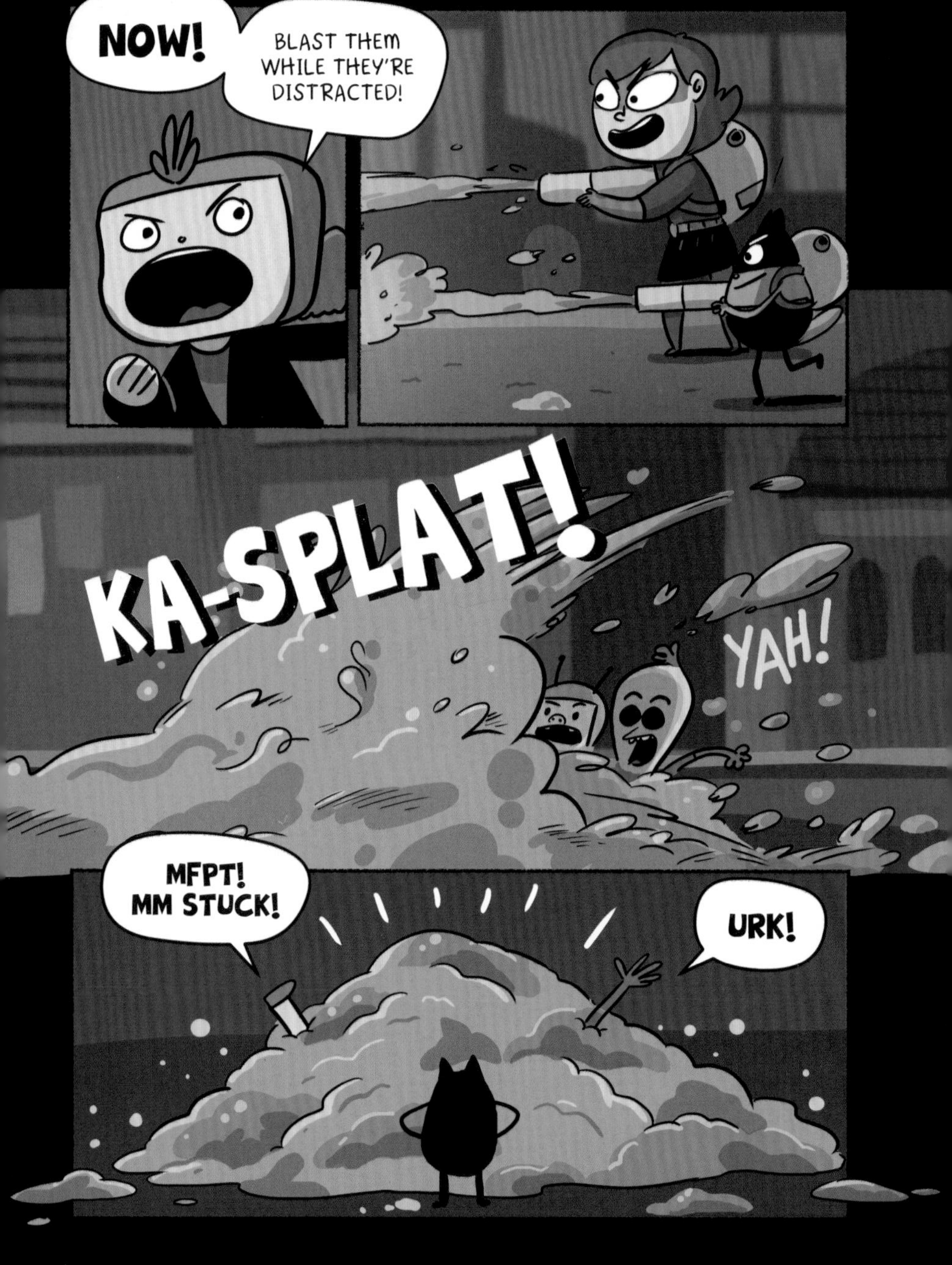
NOW!
BLAST THEM WHILE THEY'RE DISTRACTED!
KA-SPLAT!
YAH!
MFPT! MM STUCK!
URK!

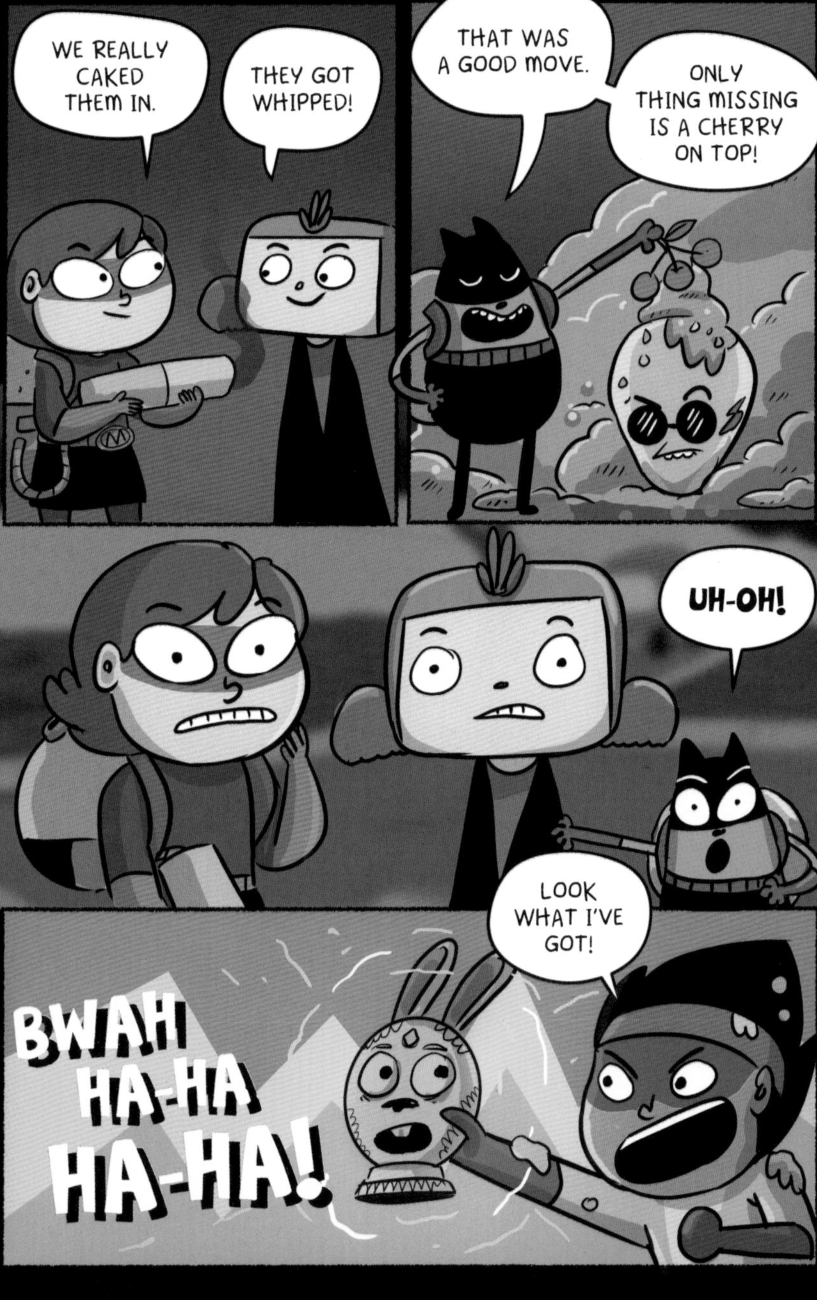
WE REALLY CAKED THEM IN.
THEY GOT WHIPPED!
THAT WAS A GOOD MOVE.
ONLY THING MISSING IS A CHERRY ON TOP!
UH-OH!
LOOK WHAT I'VE GOT!
BWAH HA-HA HA-HA!

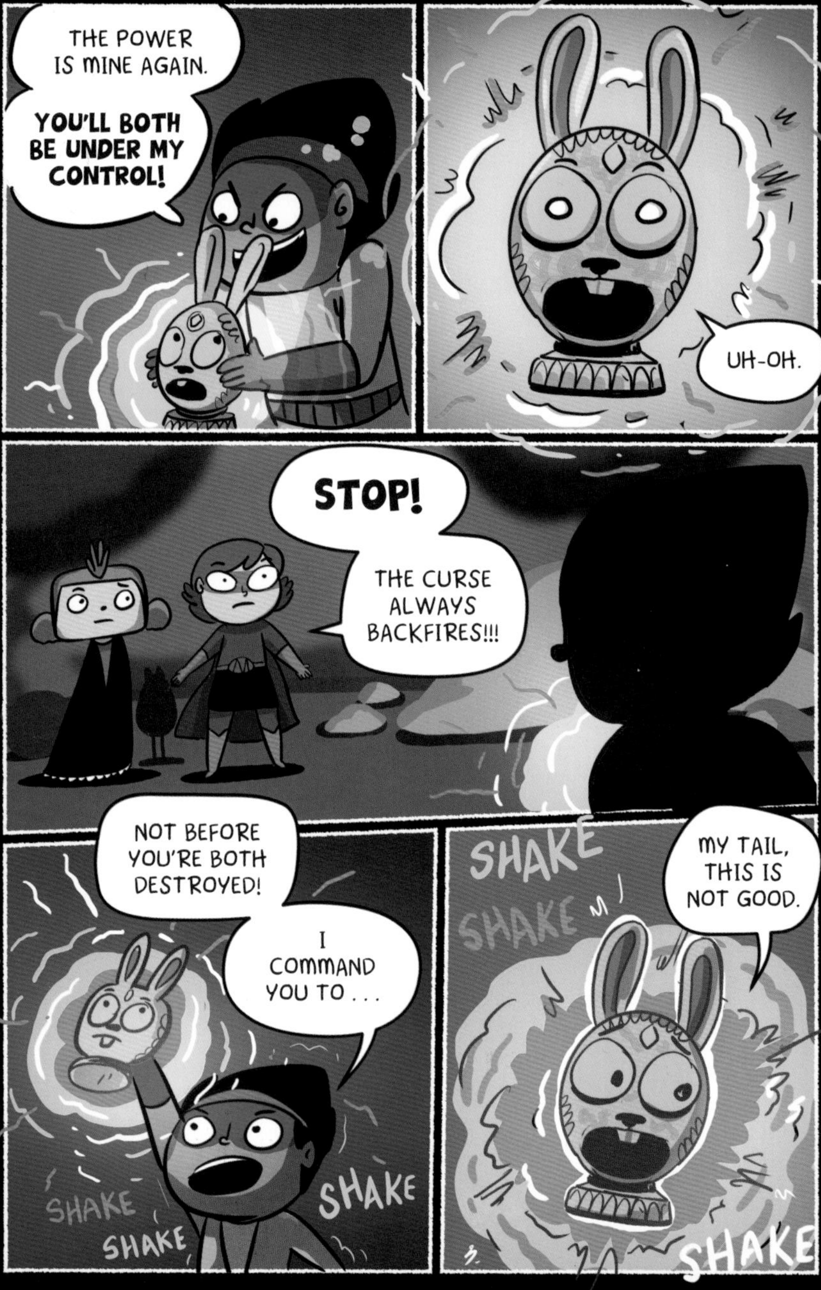
THE POWER IS MINE AGAIN.
YOU'LL BOTH BE UNDER MY CONTROL!
UH-OH.
STOP!
THE CURSE ALWAYS BACKFIRES!!!
NOT BEFORE YOU'RE BOTH DESTROYED!
I COMMAND YOU TO . . .
SHAKE
SHAKE
SHAKE
SHAKE
MY TAIL, THIS IS NOT GOOD.
SHAKE
SHAKE
SHAKE

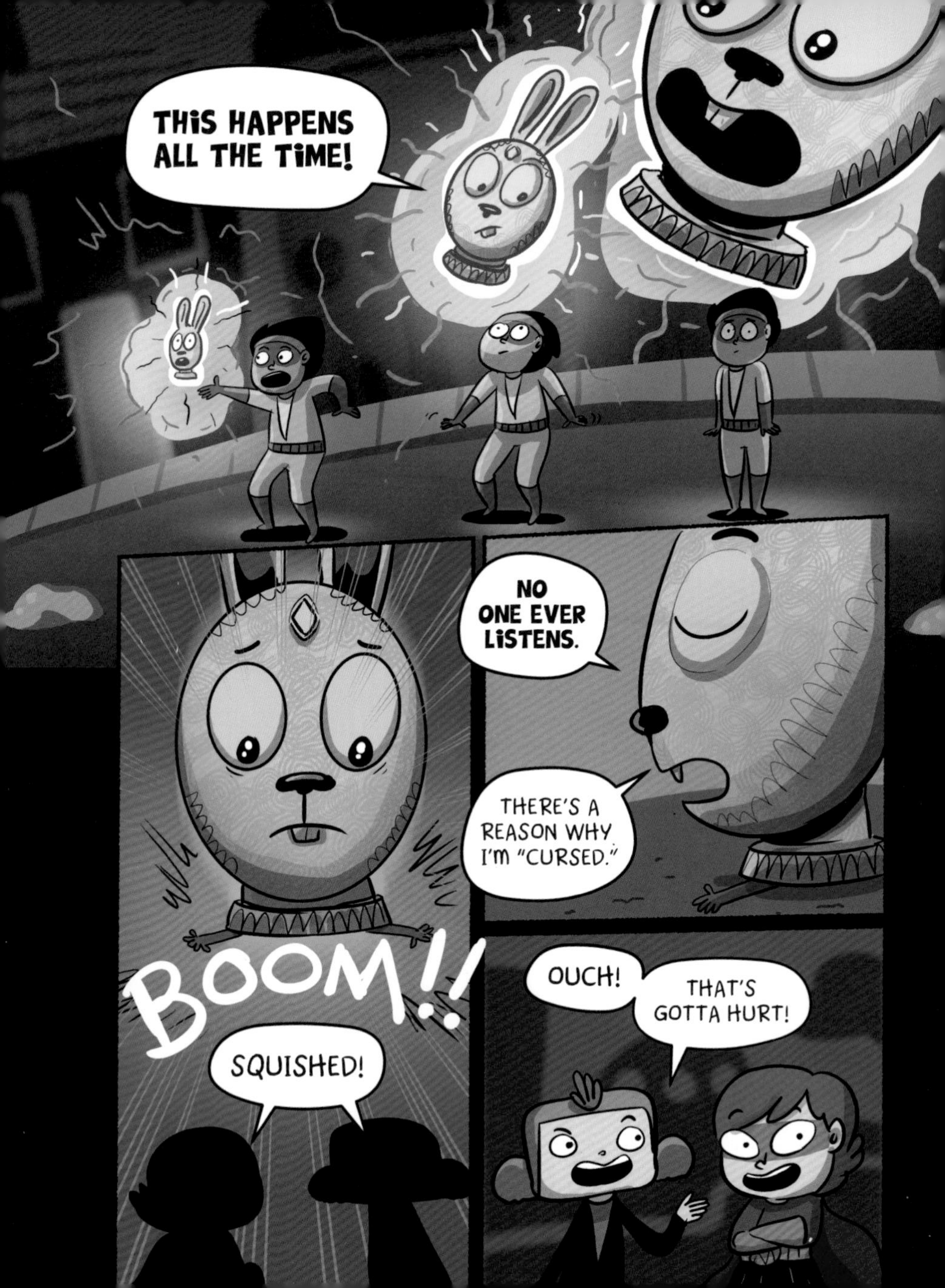
THIS HAPPENS ALL THE TIME!
NO ONE EVER LISTENS.
THERE'S A REASON WHY I'M "CURSED."
BOOM!!
SQUISHED!
OUCH!
THAT'S GOTTA HURT!

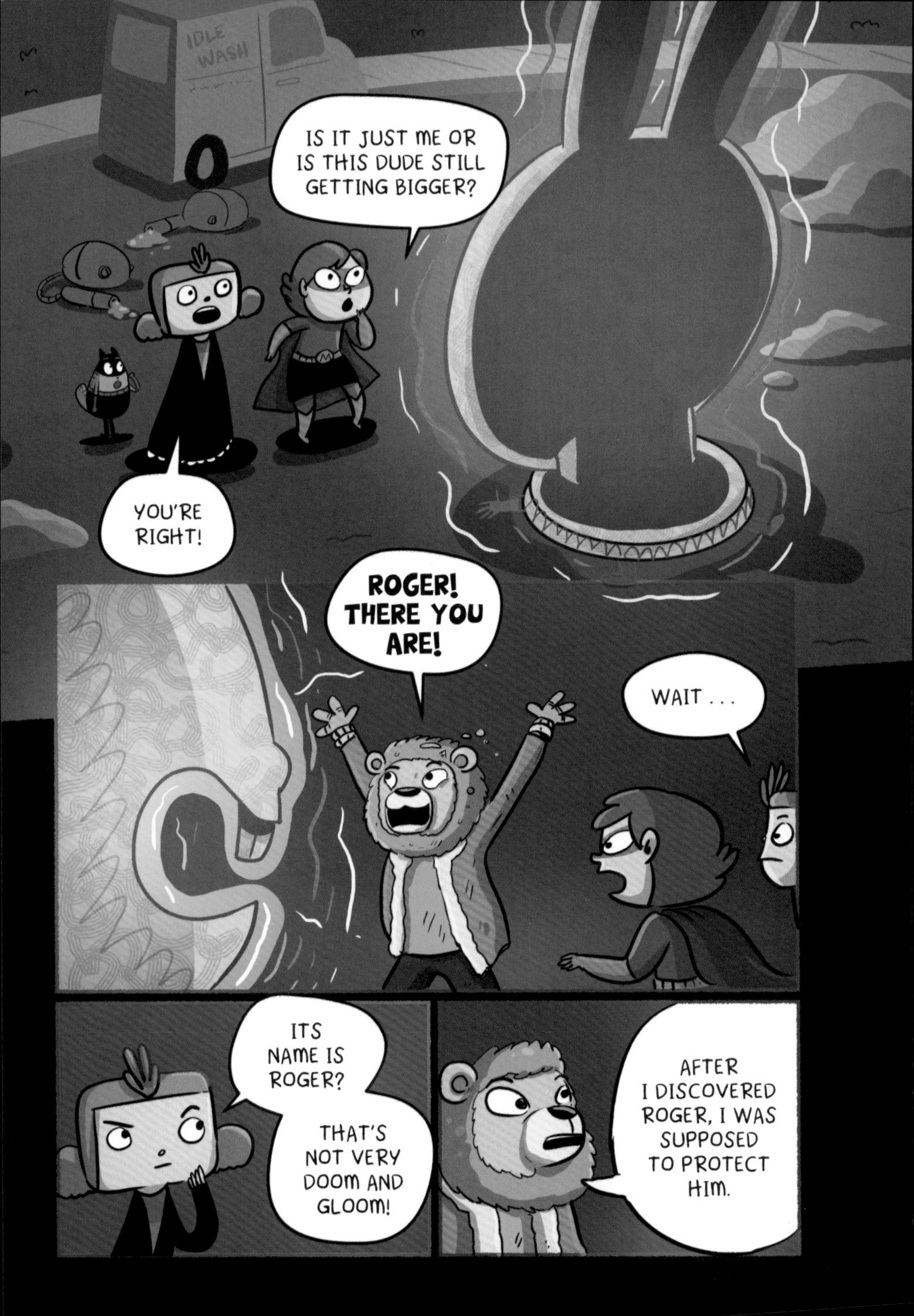
IDLE WASH
IS IT JUST ME OR IS THIS DUDE STILL GETTING BIGGER?
YOU'RE RIGHT!
ROGER! THERE YOU ARE!
WAIT . . .
ITS NAME IS ROGER?
THAT'S NOT VERY DOOM AND GLOOM!
AFTER I DISCOVERED ROGER, I WAS SUPPOSED TO PROTECT HIM.

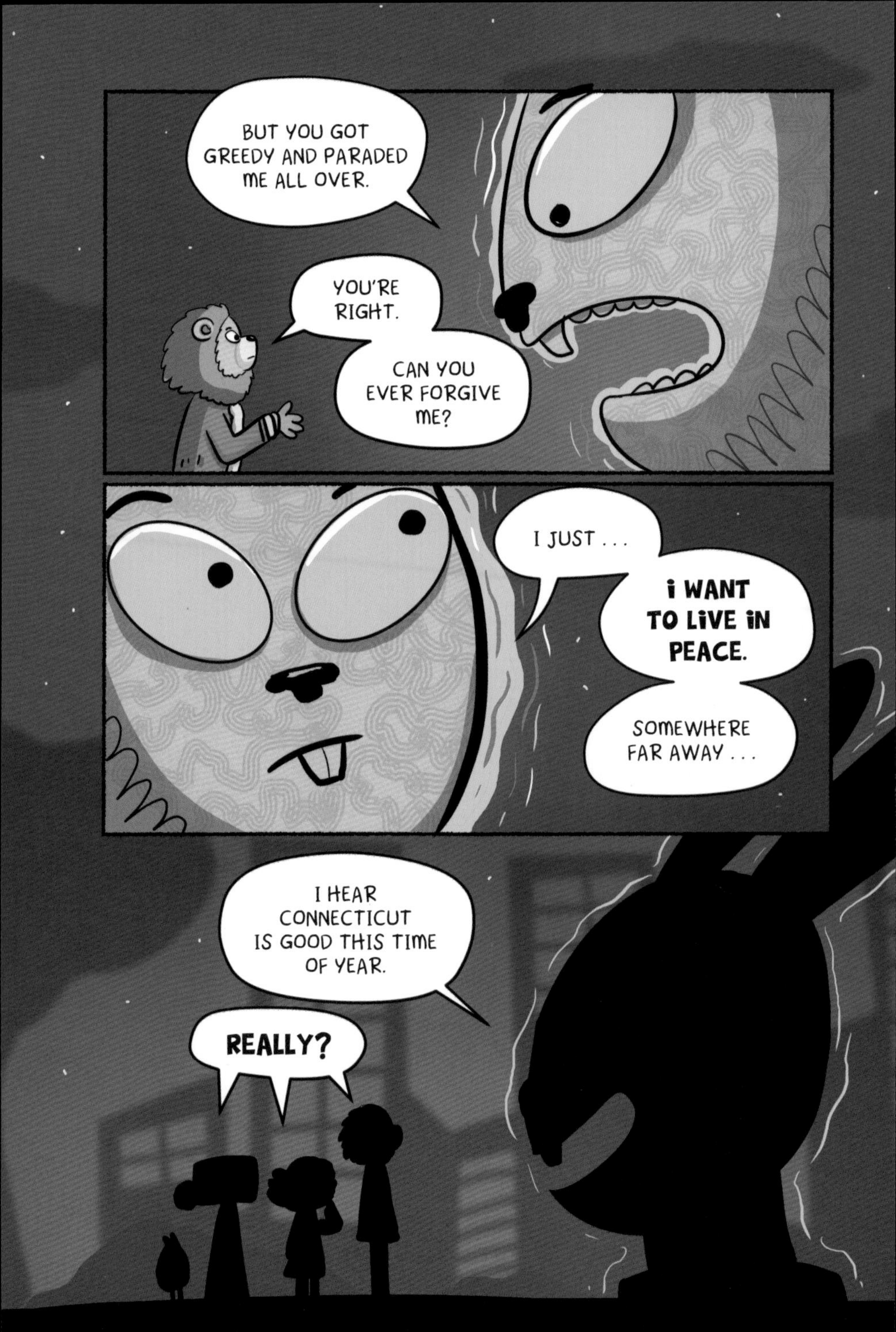
BUT YOU GOT GREEDY AND PARADED ME ALL OVER.
YOU'RE RIGHT.
CAN YOU EVER FORGIVE ME?
I JUST . . .
I WANT TO LIVE IN PEACE.
SOMEWHERE FAR AWAY . . .
I HEAR CONNECTICUT IS GOOD THIS TIME OF YEAR.
REALLY?

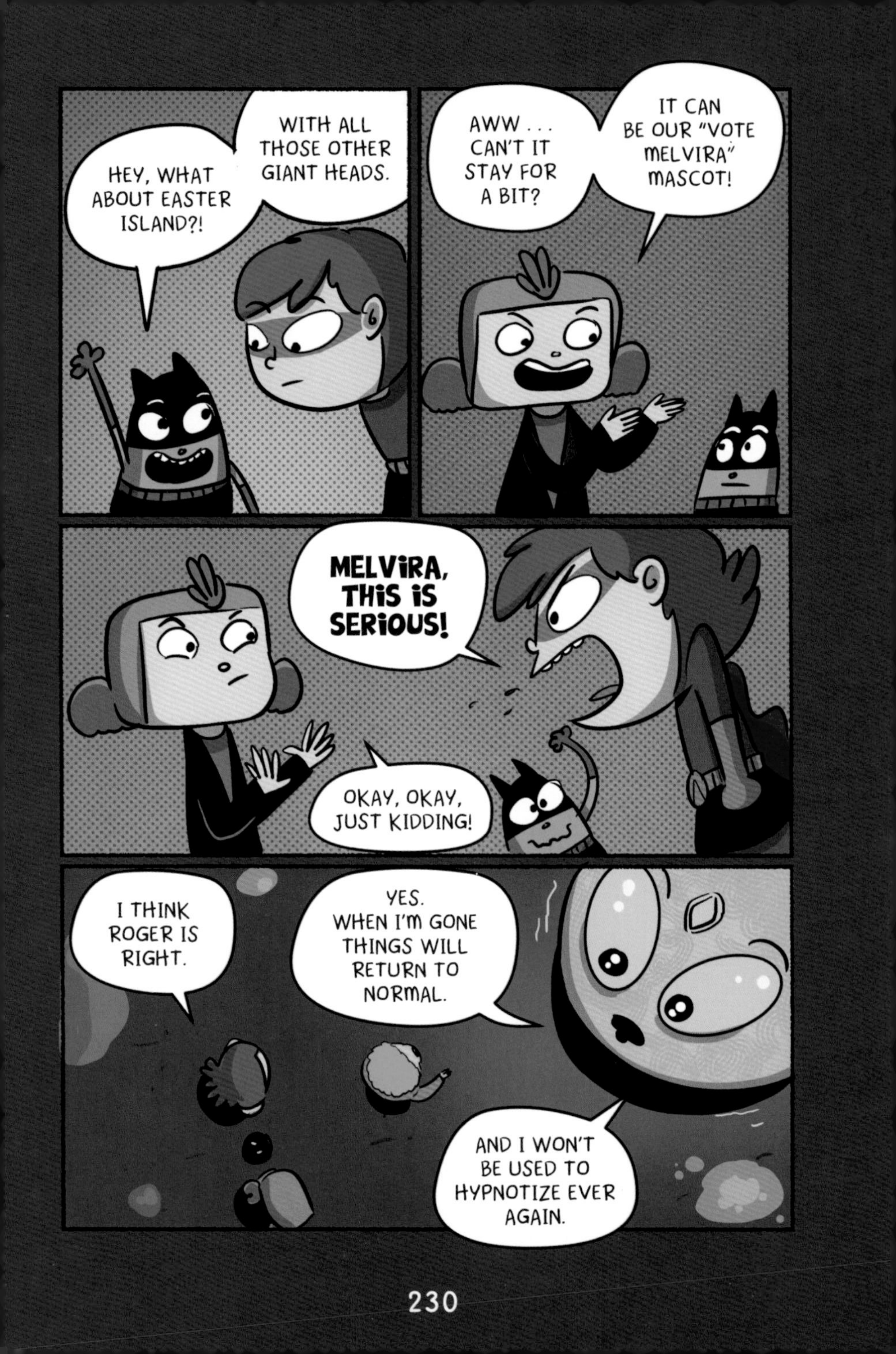
HEY, WHAT ABOUT EASTER ISLAND?!
WITH ALL THOSE OTHER GIANT HEADS.
AWW . . . CAN'T IT STAY FOR A BIT?
IT CAN BE OUR "VOTE MELVIRA" MASCOT!
MELVIRA, THIS IS SERIOUS!
OKAY, OKAY, JUST KIDDING!
I THINK ROGER IS RIGHT.
YES. WHEN I'M GONE THINGS WILL RETURN TO NORMAL.
AND I WON'T BE USED TO HYPNOTIZE EVER AGAIN.

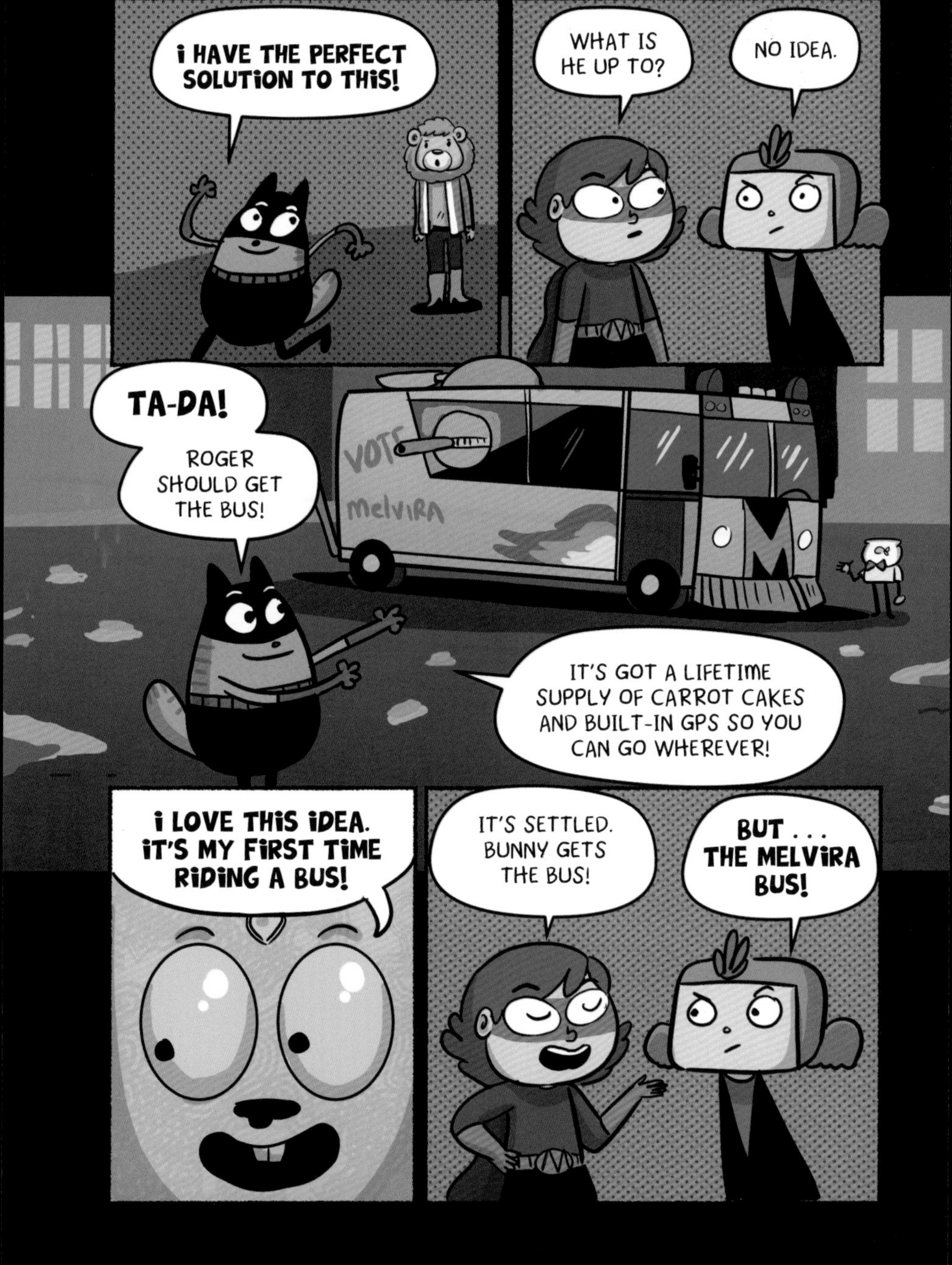
I HAVE THE PERFECT SOLUTION TO THIS!
WHAT IS HE UP TO?
NO IDEA.
TA-DA!
ROGER SHOULD GET THE BUS!
VOTE melvira
IT'S GOT A LIFETIME SUPPLY OF CARROT CAKES AND BUILT-IN GPS SO YOU CAN GO WHEREVER!
I LOVE THIS IDEA. IT'S MY FIRST TIME RIDING A BUS!
IT'S SETTLED. BUNNY GETS THE BUS!
BUT . . . THE MELVIRA BUS!

CHAPTER 12 BYE-BYE, BUNNY

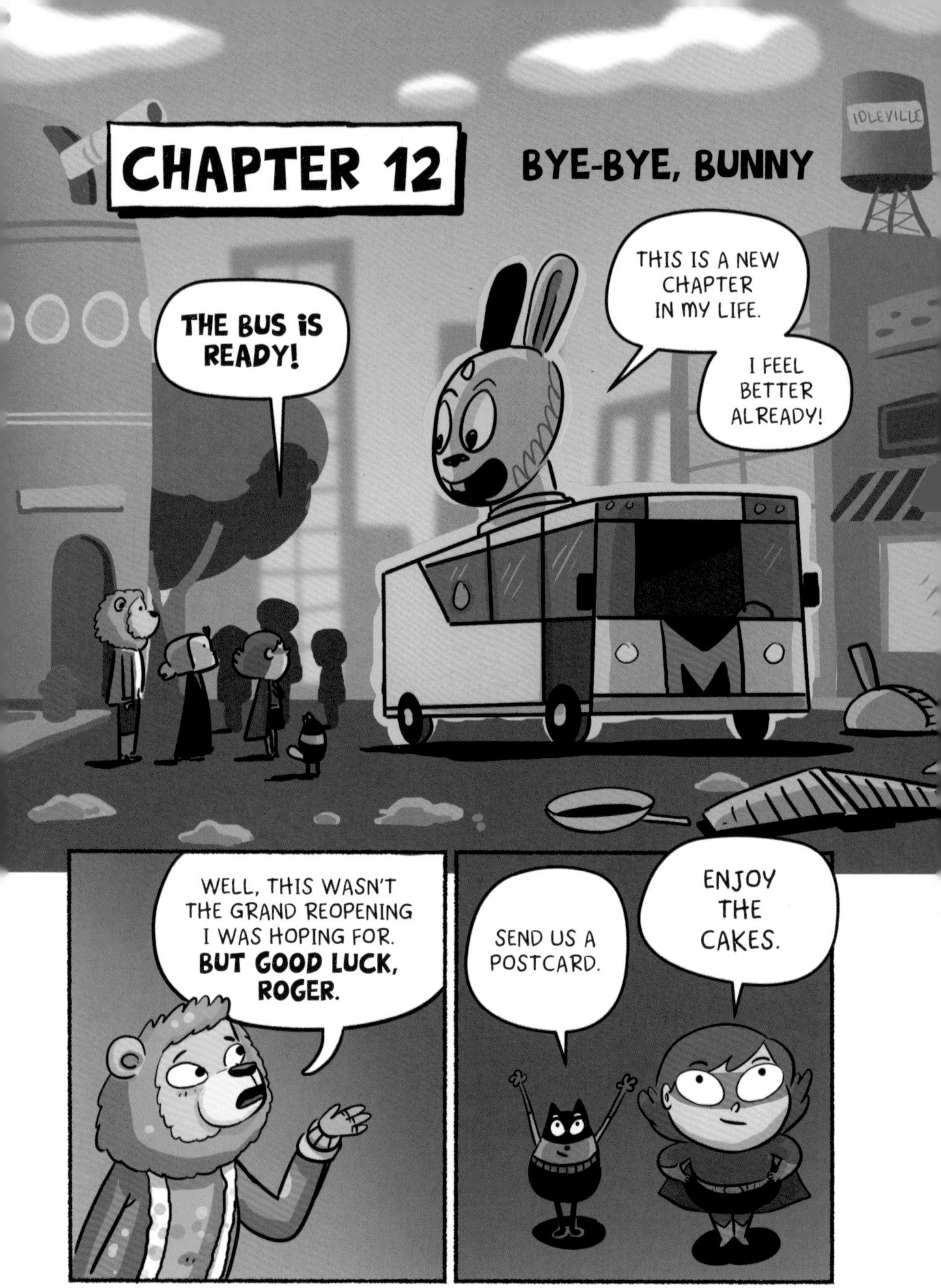
IDLEVILLE
THE BUS IS READY!
THIS IS A NEW CHAPTER IN MY LIFE.
I FEEL BETTER ALREADY!
WELL, THIS WASN'T THE GRAND REOPENING I WAS HOPING FOR. **BUT GOOD LUCK, ROGER.**
SEND US A POSTCARD.
ENJOY THE CAKES.

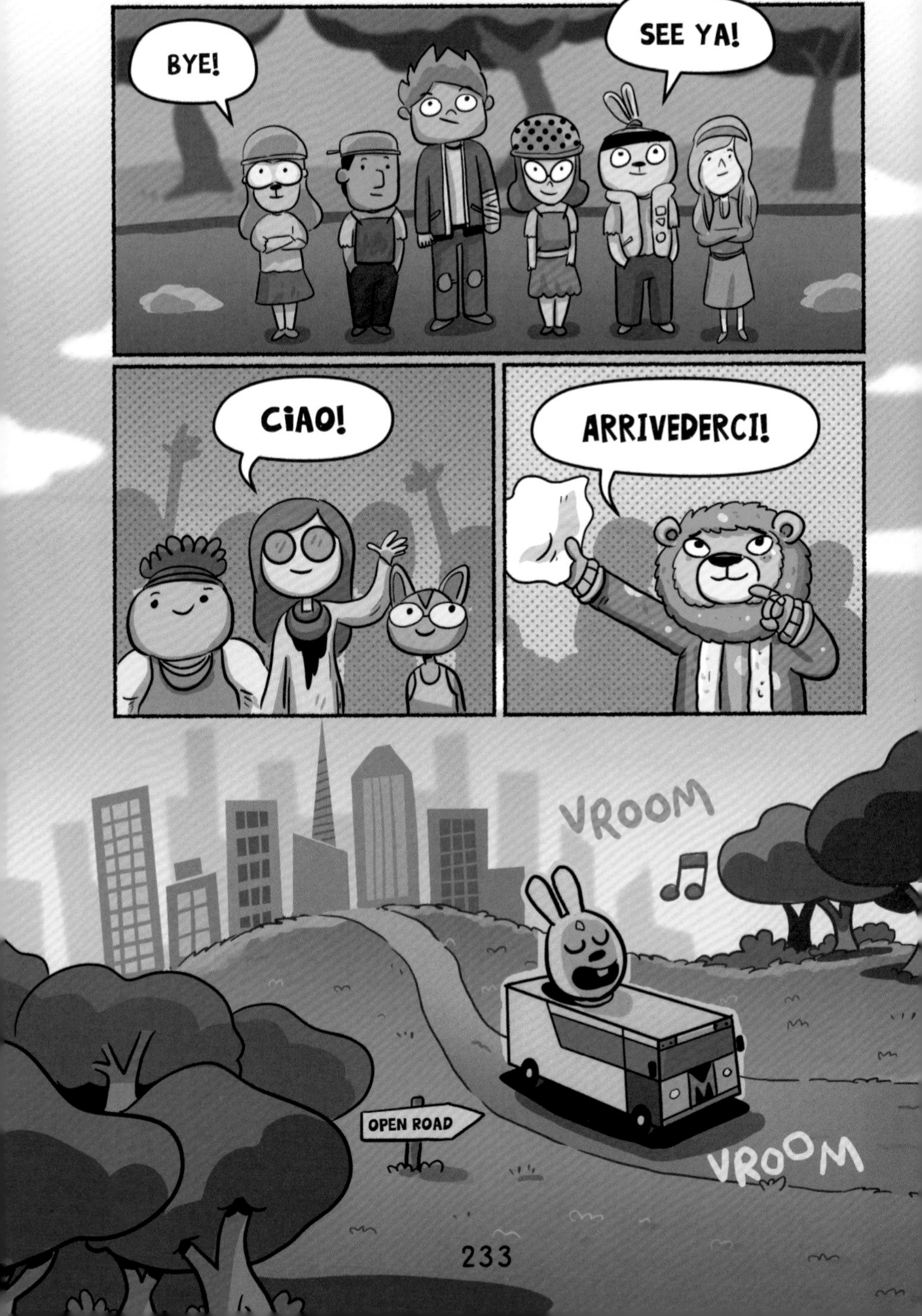
BYE!
SEE YA!
CiAO!
ARRIVEDERCI!
VROOM
OPEN ROAD
VROOM

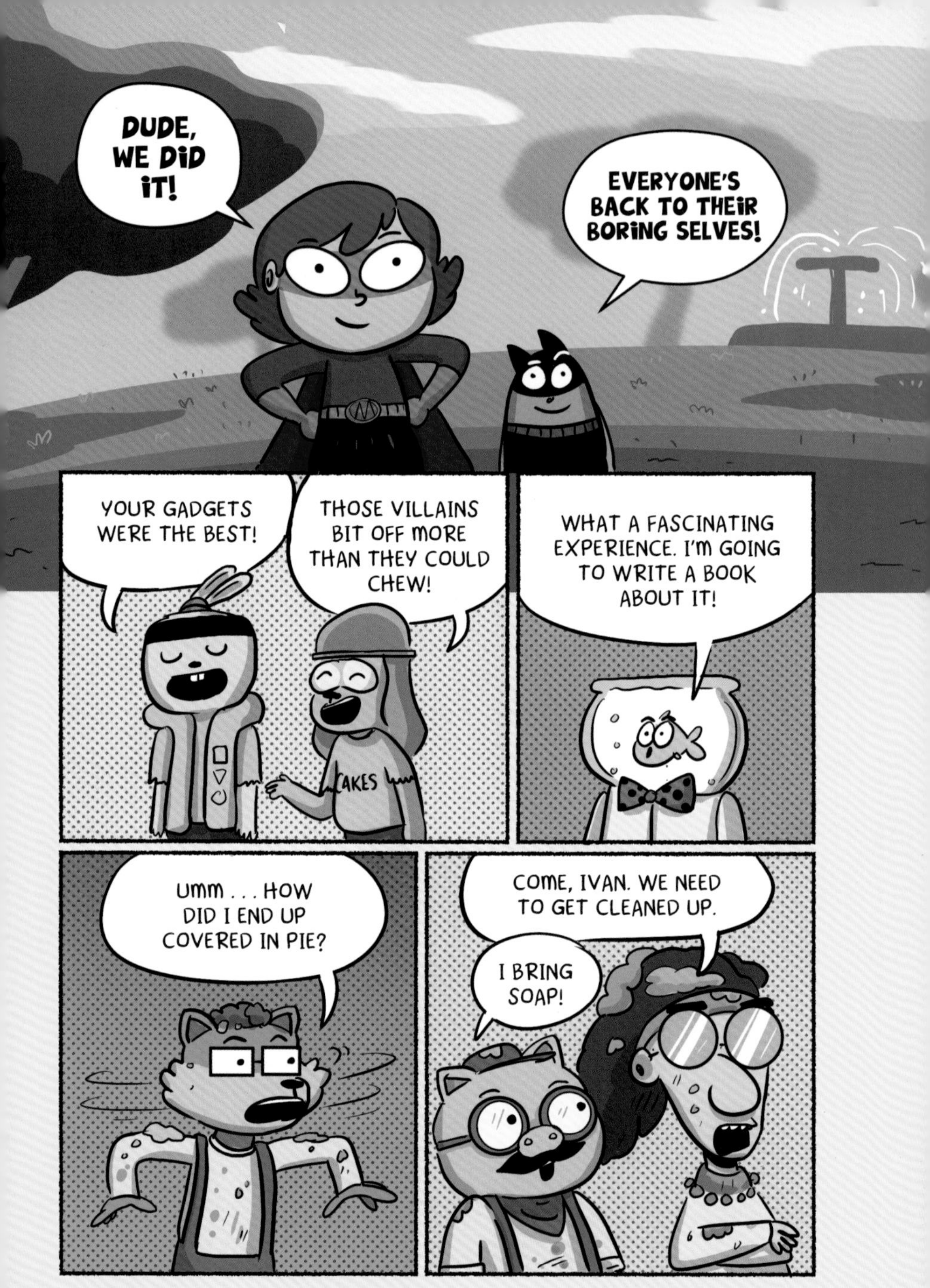
DUDE, WE DID IT!
EVERYONE'S BACK TO THEIR BORING SELVES!
YOUR GADGETS WERE THE BEST!
THOSE VILLAINS BIT OFF MORE THAN THEY COULD CHEW!
CAKES
WHAT A FASCINATING EXPERIENCE. I'M GOING TO WRITE A BOOK ABOUT IT!
UMM . . . HOW DID I END UP COVERED IN PIE?
COME, IVAN. WE NEED TO GET CLEANED UP.
I BRING SOAP!

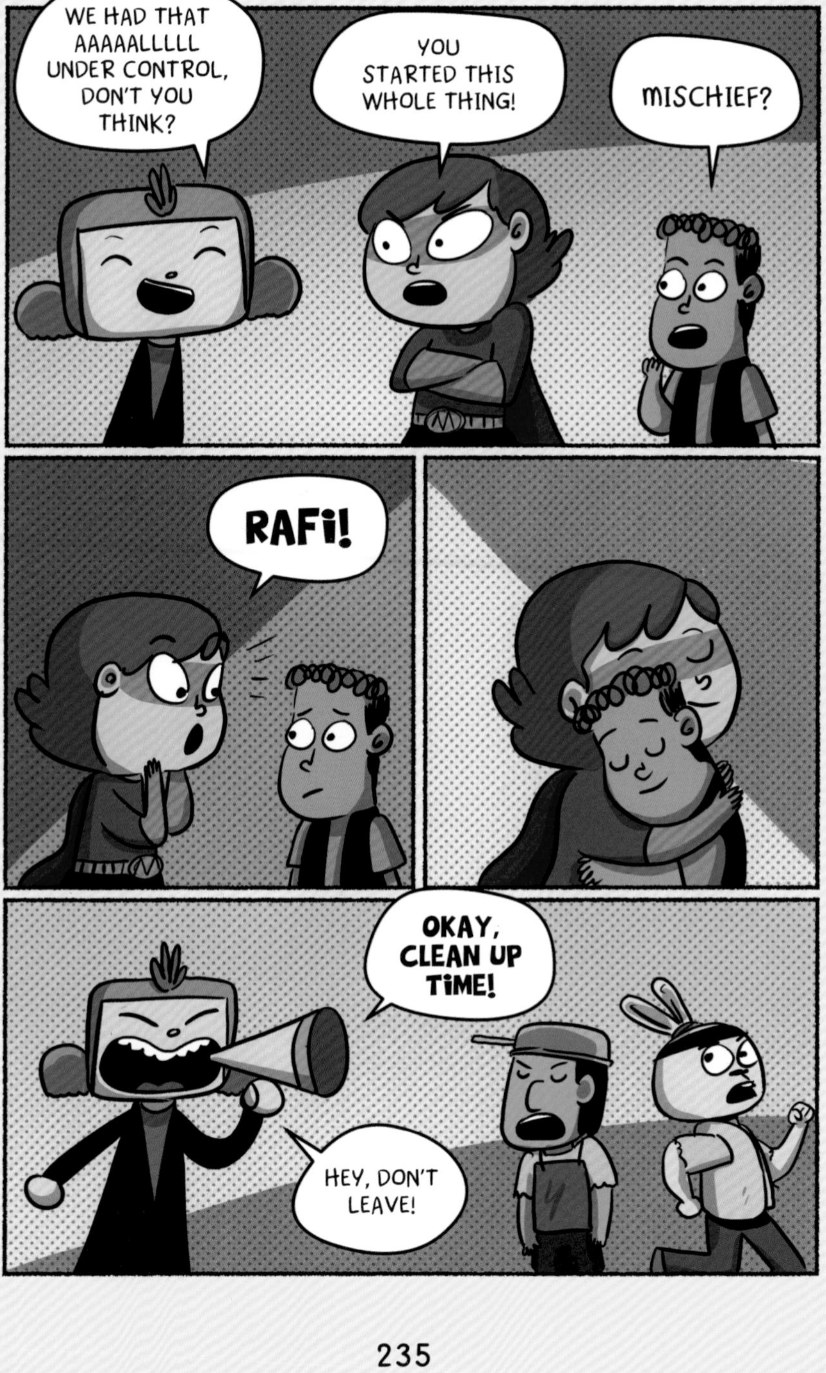
WE HAD THAT AAAAALLLLL UNDER CONTROL, DON'T YOU THINK?
YOU STARTED THIS WHOLE THING!
MISCHIEF?
RAFI!
OKAY, CLEAN UP TIME!
HEY, DON'T LEAVE!

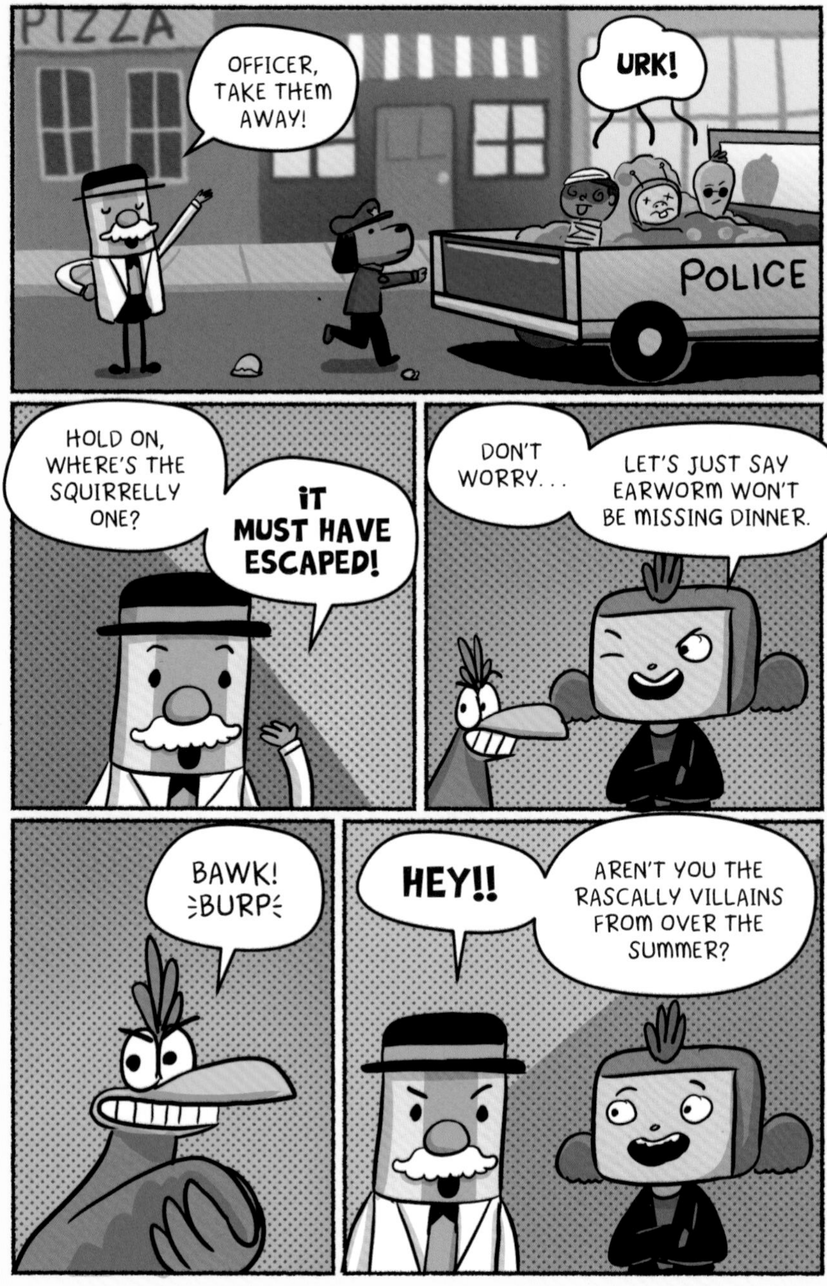
PIZZA
OFFICER, TAKE THEM AWAY!
URK!
POLICE
HOLD ON, WHERE'S THE SQUIRRELLY ONE?
IT MUST HAVE ESCAPED!
DON'T WORRY. . .
LET'S JUST SAY EARWORM WON'T BE MISSING DINNER.
BAWK! ⋛BURP⋚
HEY!!
AREN'T YOU THE RASCALLY VILLAINS FROM OVER THE SUMMER?

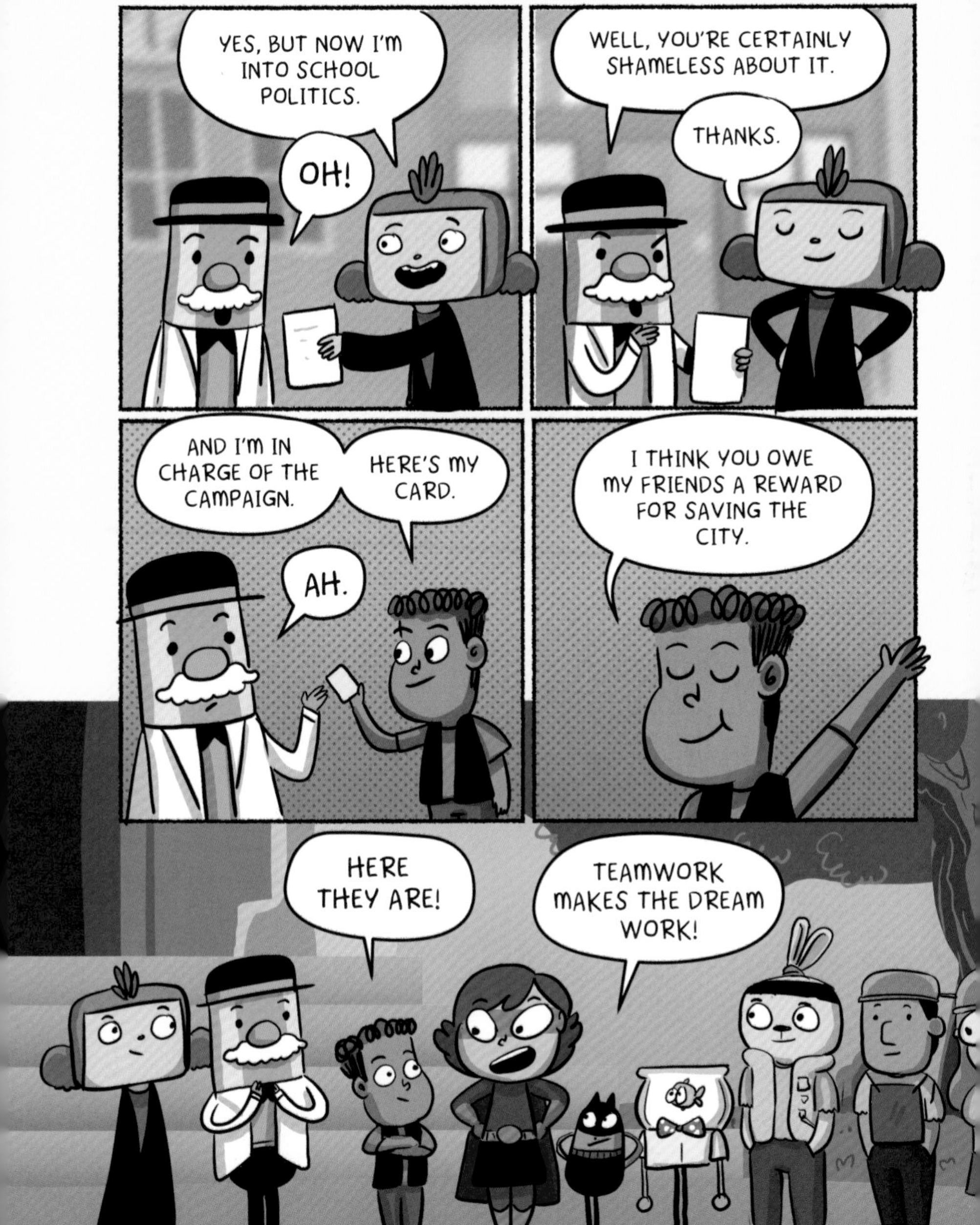
YES, BUT NOW I'M INTO SCHOOL POLITICS.
OH!
WELL, YOU'RE CERTAINLY SHAMELESS ABOUT IT.
THANKS.
AND I'M IN CHARGE OF THE CAMPAIGN.
HERE'S MY CARD.
AH.
I THINK YOU OWE MY FRIENDS A REWARD FOR SAVING THE CITY.
HERE THEY ARE!
TEAMWORK MAKES THE DREAM WORK!

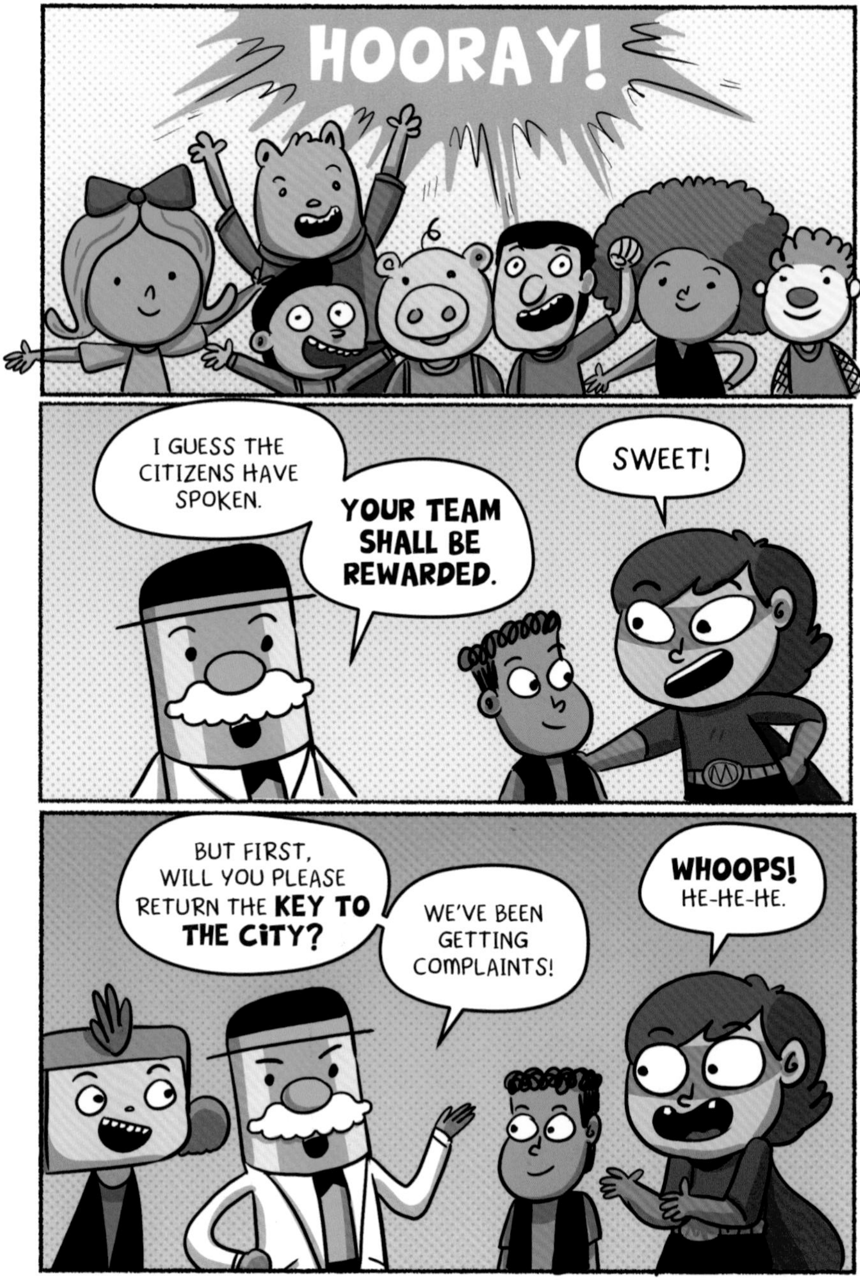
HOORAY!
I GUESS THE CITIZENS HAVE SPOKEN.
YOUR TEAM SHALL BE REWARDED.
SWEET!
BUT FIRST, WILL YOU PLEASE RETURN THE KEY TO THE CITY?
WE'VE BEEN GETTING COMPLAINTS!
WHOOPS! HE-HE-HE.

CHAPTER 13

A FESTIVAL, YET AGAIN!

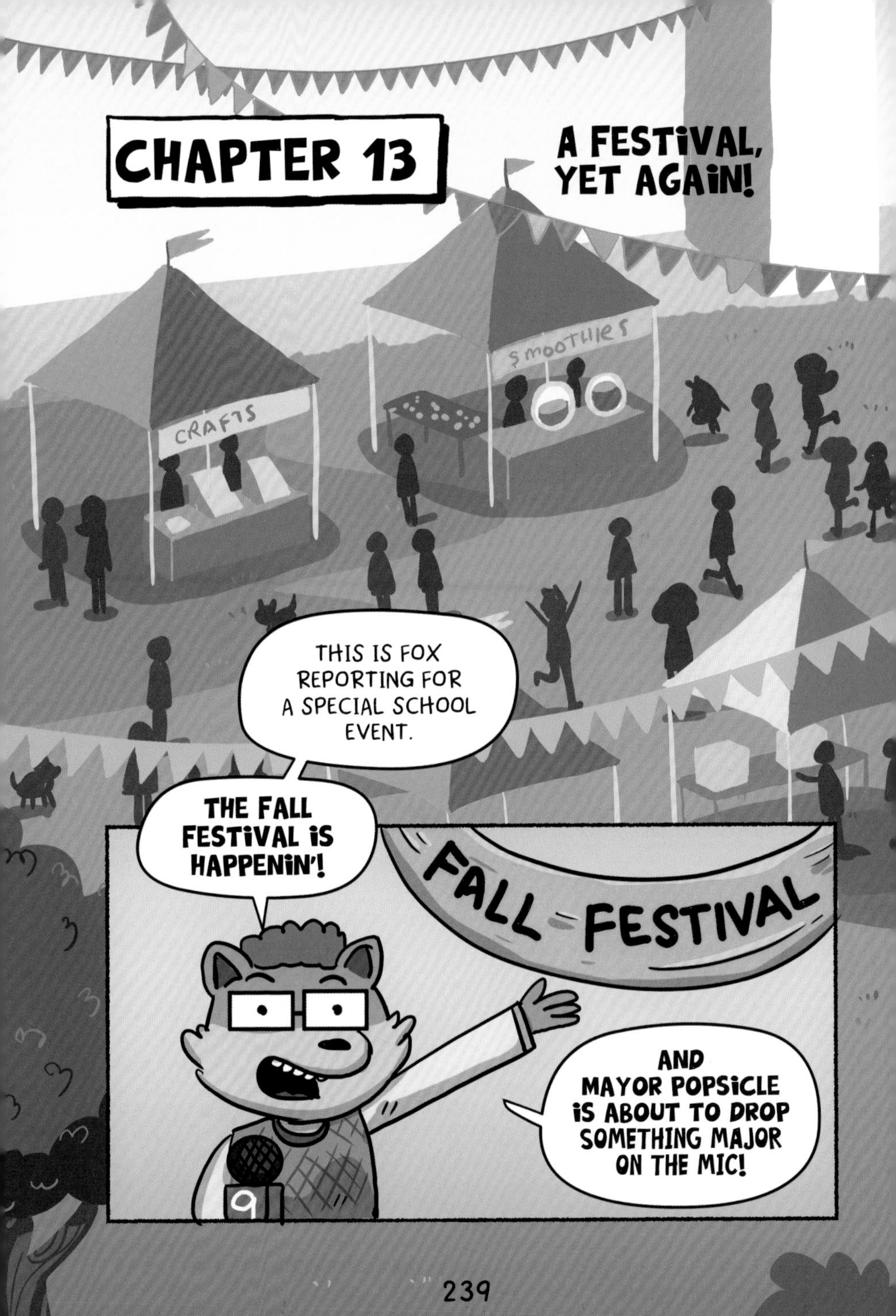
SMOOTHIES
CRAFTS
THIS IS FOX REPORTING FOR A SPECIAL SCHOOL EVENT.
THE FALL FESTIVAL IS HAPPENIN'!
FALL FESTIVAL
AND MAYOR POPSICLE IS ABOUT TO DROP SOMETHING MAJOR ON THE MIC!
9

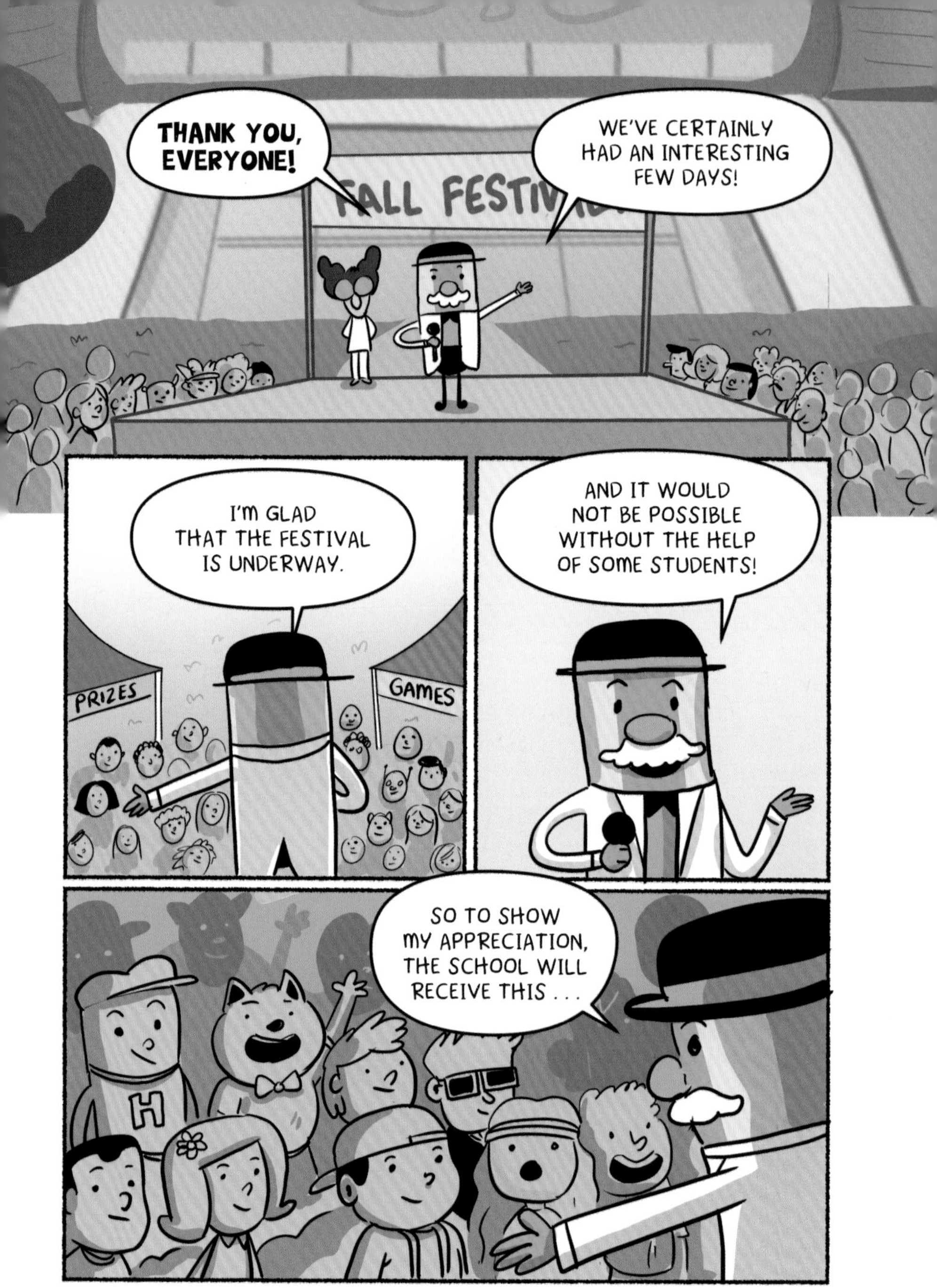
THANK YOU, EVERYONE!
WE'VE CERTAINLY HAD AN INTERESTING FEW DAYS!
FALL FESTIV
I'M GLAD THAT THE FESTIVAL IS UNDERWAY.
PRIZES
GAMES
AND IT WOULD NOT BE POSSIBLE WITHOUT THE HELP OF SOME STUDENTS!
SO TO SHOW MY APPRECIATION, THE SCHOOL WILL RECEIVE THIS . . .
H

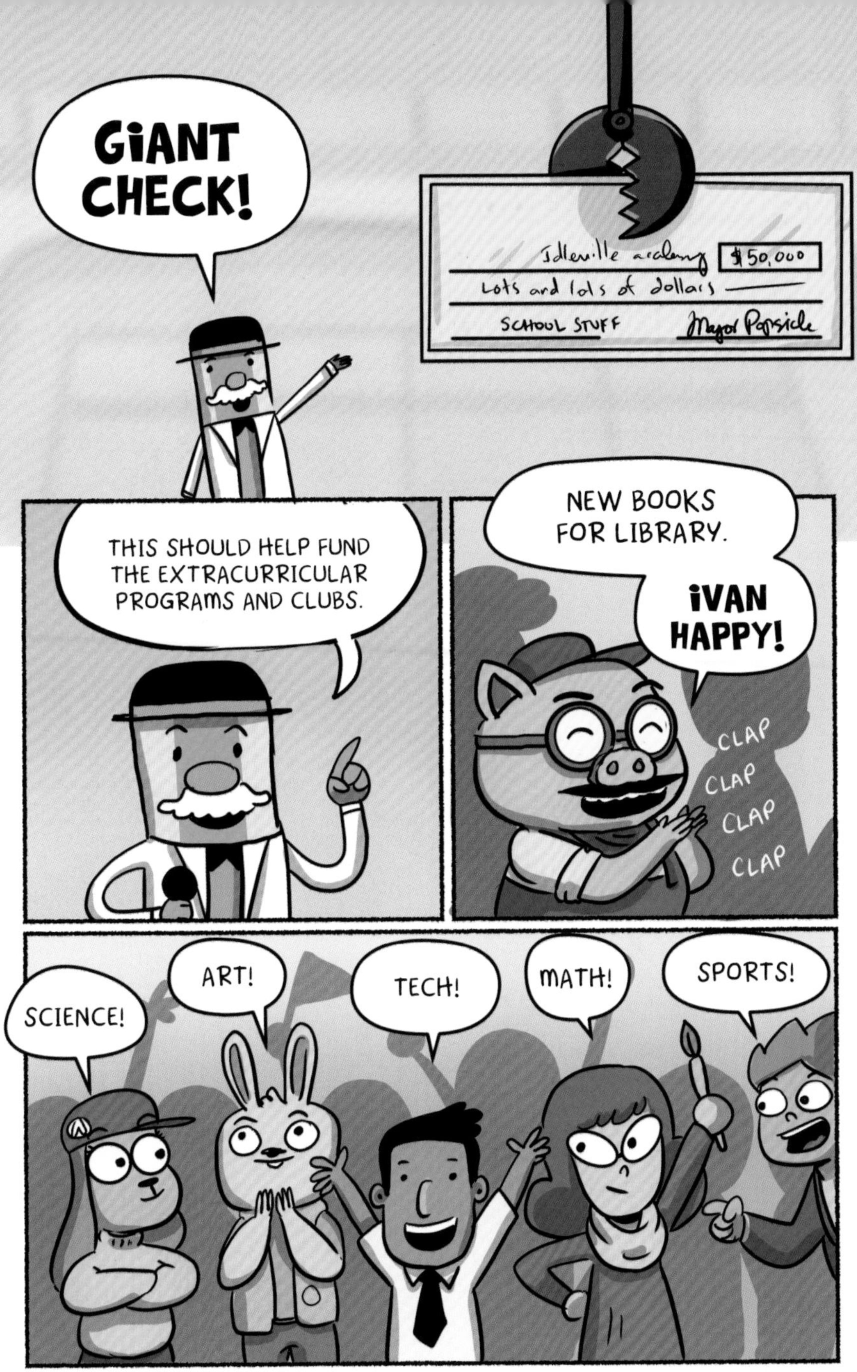
GIANT CHECK!
Idleville academy
$50,000
Lots and lots of dollars
SCHOOL STUFF
Mayor Popsicle
THIS SHOULD HELP FUND THE EXTRACURRICULAR PROGRAMS AND CLUBS.
NEW BOOKS FOR LIBRARY.
IVAN HAPPY!
CLAP
CLAP
CLAP
CLAP
SCIENCE!
ART!
TECH!
MATH!
SPORTS!

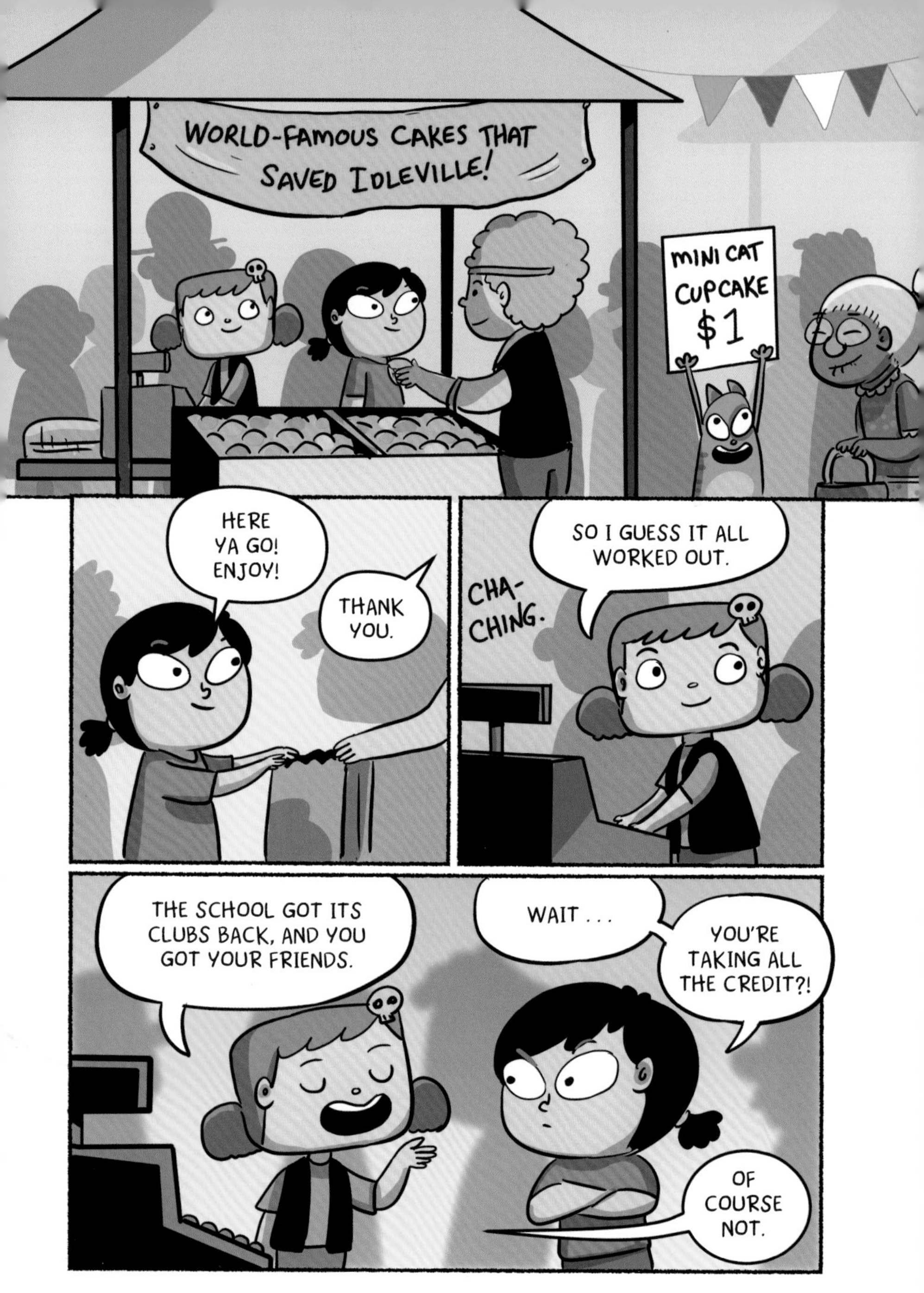

WORLD-FAMOUS CAKES THAT SAVED IDLEVILLE!
MINI CAT CUPCAKE $1
HERE YA GO! ENJOY!
THANK YOU.
CHA-CHING.
SO I GUESS IT ALL WORKED OUT.
THE SCHOOL GOT ITS CLUBS BACK, AND YOU GOT YOUR FRIENDS.
WAIT . . .
YOU'RE TAKING ALL THE CREDIT?!
OF COURSE NOT.

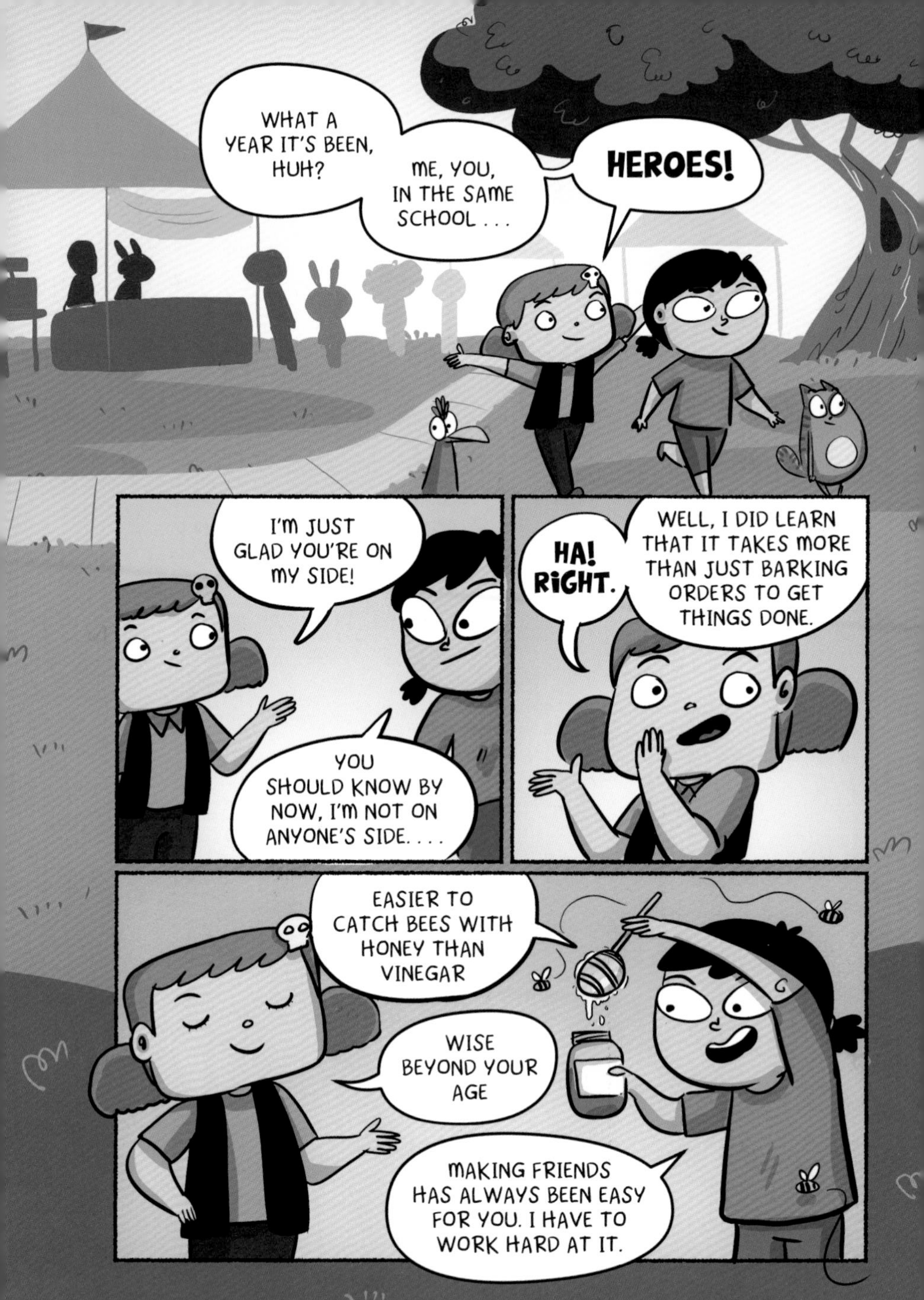
WHAT A YEAR IT'S BEEN, HUH?
ME, YOU, IN THE SAME SCHOOL . . .
HEROES!
I'M JUST GLAD YOU'RE ON MY SIDE!
YOU SHOULD KNOW BY NOW, I'M NOT ON ANYONE'S SIDE. . . .
HA! RIGHT.
WELL, I DID LEARN THAT IT TAKES MORE THAN JUST BARKING ORDERS TO GET THINGS DONE.
EASIER TO CATCH BEES WITH HONEY THAN VINEGAR
WISE BEYOND YOUR AGE
MAKING FRIENDS HAS ALWAYS BEEN EASY FOR YOU. I HAVE TO WORK HARD AT IT.

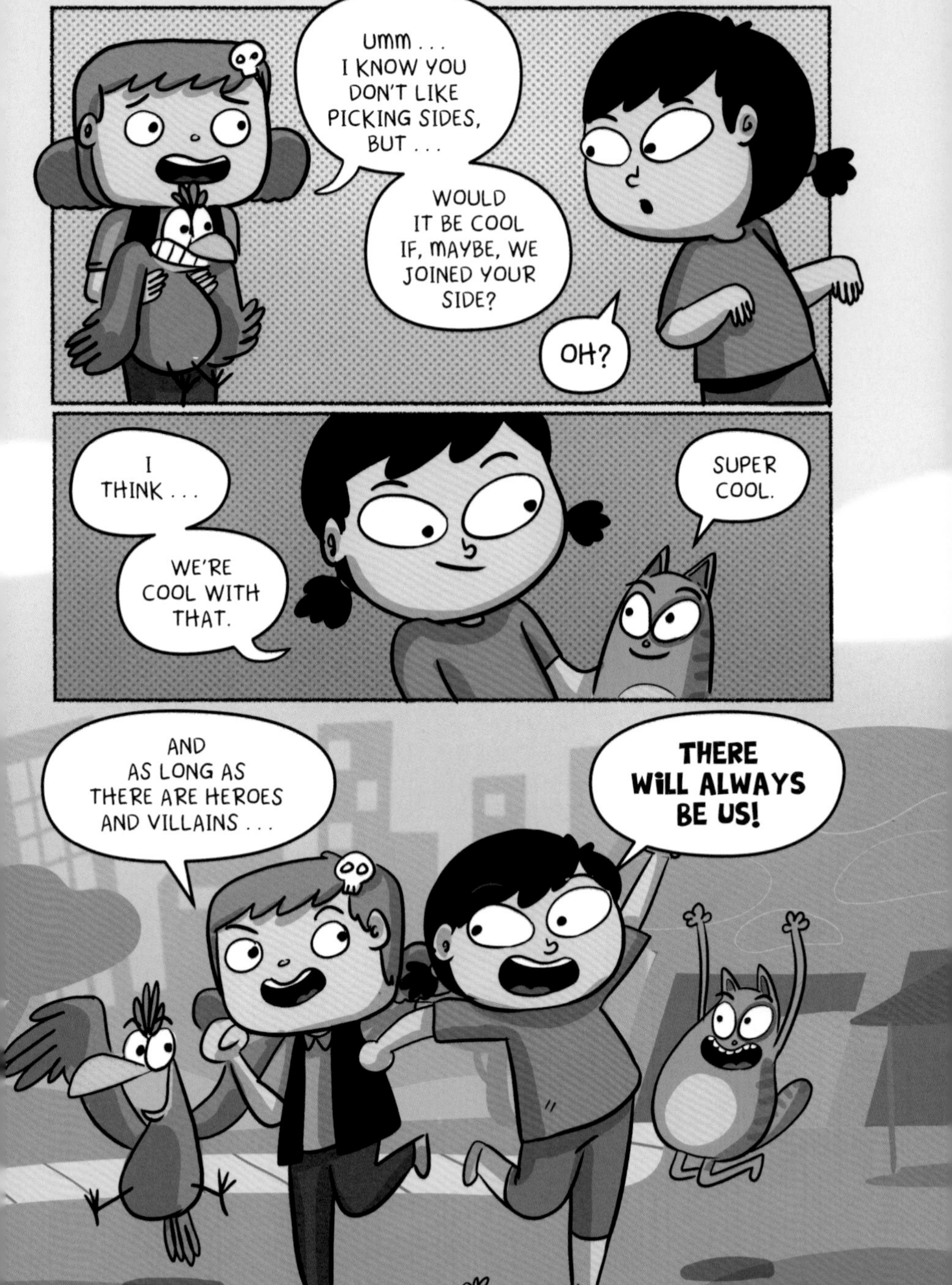
UMM . . . I KNOW YOU DON'T LIKE PICKING SIDES, BUT . . .
WOULD IT BE COOL IF, MAYBE, WE JOINED YOUR SIDE?
OH?
I THINK . . .
WE'RE COOL WITH THAT.
SUPER COOL.
AND AS LONG AS THERE ARE HEROES AND VILLAINS . . .
THERE WILL ALWAYS BE US!

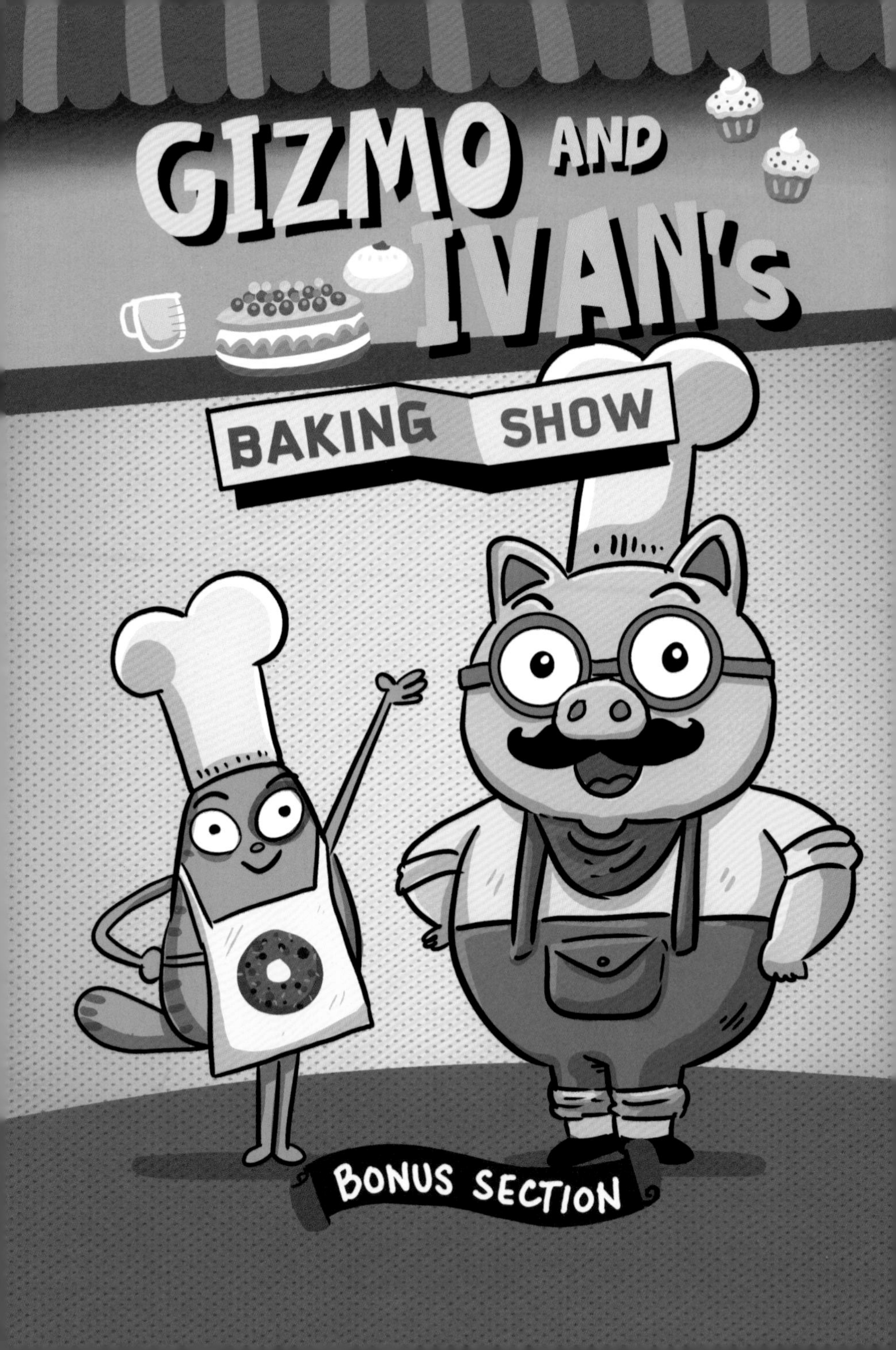
GIZMO AND IVAN'S
BAKING SHOW
BONUS SECTION

LET'S MAKE CARROT CAKE!

For today's show, we're making my favorite - Carrot cake!
Follow the recipe and don't forget to ask for help if you need it!

INGREDIENTS

- ☐ vegetable oil spray for greasing pan
- ☐ 1 1/4 cups all-purpose flour
- ☐ 1/2 teaspoon baking soda
- ☐ 1/2 teaspoon baking powder
- ☐ 1/4 teaspoon ground nutmeg
- ☐ 1/4 teaspoon ground cinnamon
- ☐ 1/4 teaspoon salt
- ☐ 2 large eggs
- ☐ 3/4 cup white sugar
- ☐ 1/4 cup light brown sugar
- ☐ 2/3 cup vegetable oil or melted and cooled butter
- ☐ 1 teaspoon vanilla extract
- ☐ 8 ounces carrots (3 medium-sized carrots)

Carrots must be grated in advance.

LET'S GET BAKING!

1.

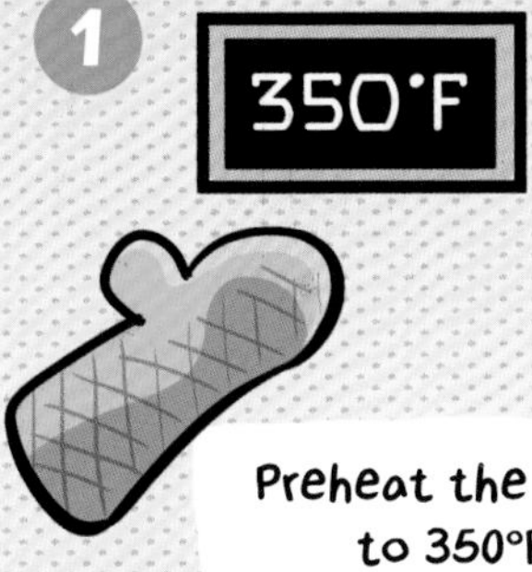
350°F

Preheat the oven to 350°F.

2.

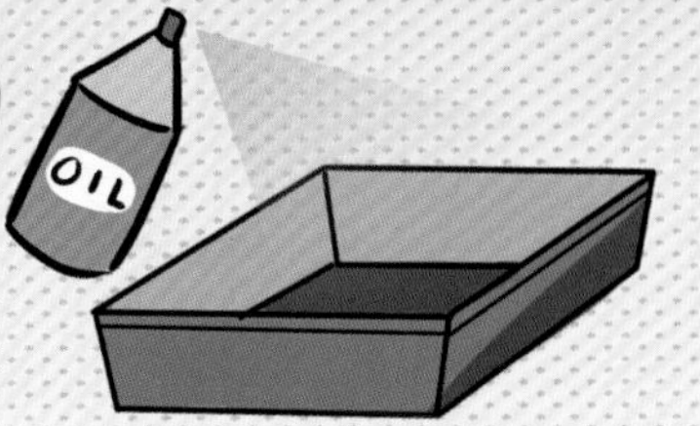
OIL

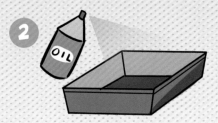

Get an 8-inch square baking pan and lightly grease the bottom and sides with vegetable oil spray.

3.

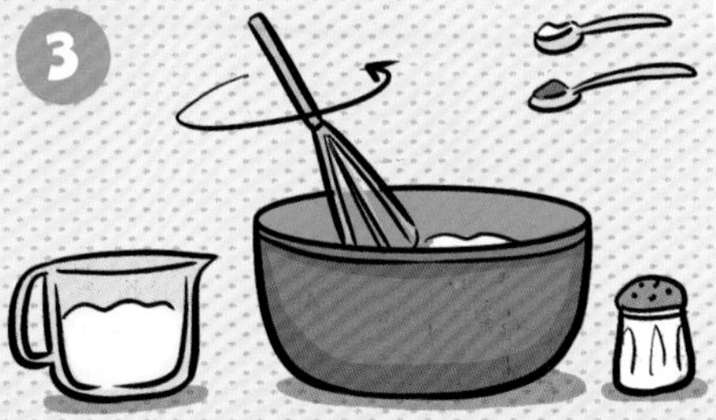

In a medium bowl, combine and whisk together the flour, baking soda, baking powder, cinnamon, nutmeg, and salt.

4.

In a large bowl, combine and whisk the eggs, white sugar, brown sugar, oil (or butter), and vanilla for several minutes.

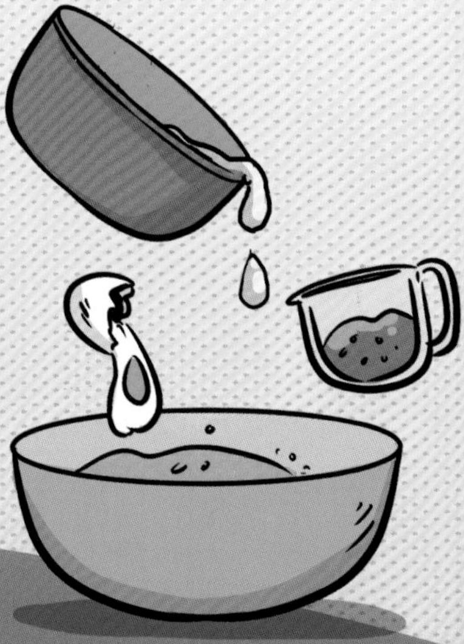

5.

Add the flour mixture from the medium bowl into the large bowl. Stir well using a spatula or wooden spoon.

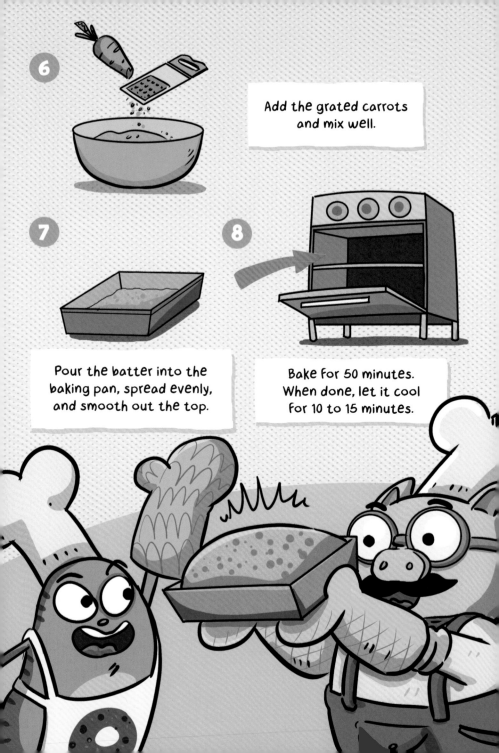

6

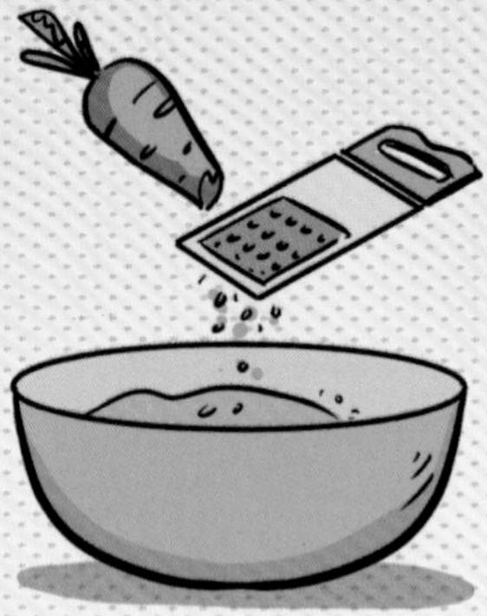

Add the grated carrots and mix well.

7

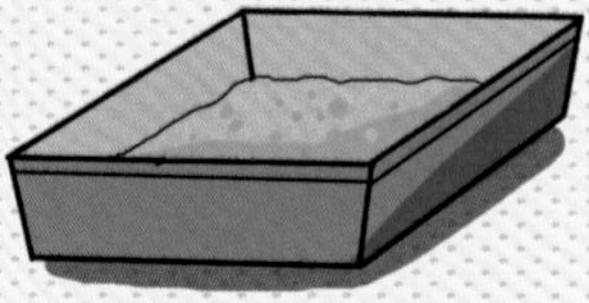

Pour the batter into the baking pan, spread evenly, and smooth out the top.

8

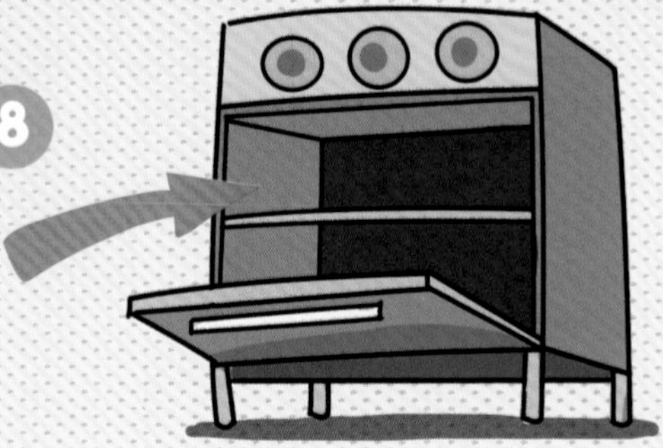

Bake for 50 minutes. When done, let it cool for 10 to 15 minutes.

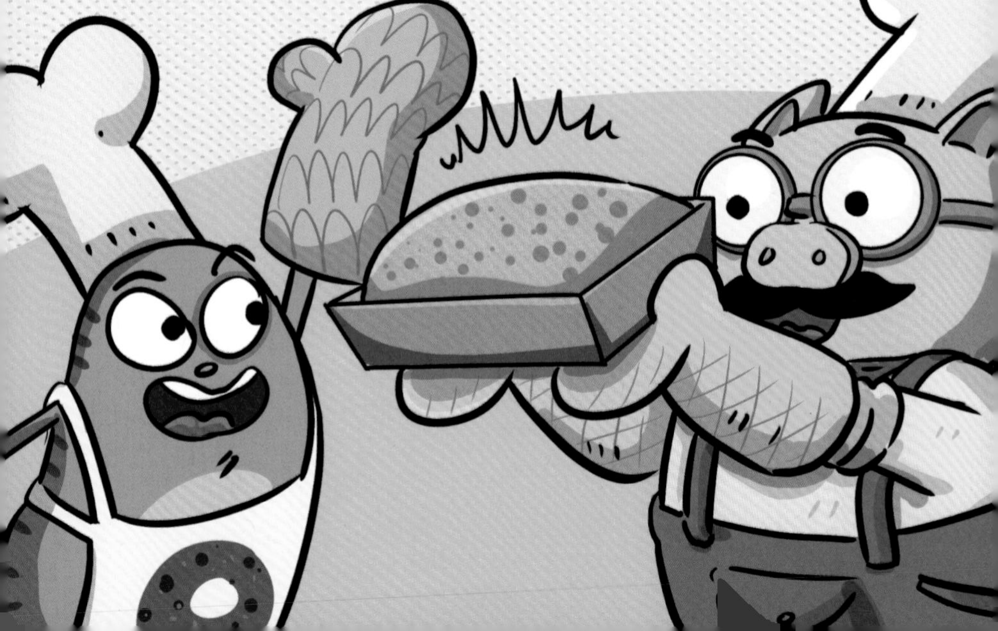

TOOTHPICK TEST!

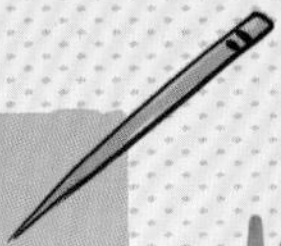

To check if your cake is baked, stick a toothpick in the center of the cake and pull it out. If the toothpick comes out clean, then your cake should be baked! If it comes out with batter sticking to it, then the cake needs more time to bake.

Yummy!!

CUT INTO SMALL SHAREABLE SLICES AND EAT!

MORE WAYS TO ENJOY:

Here are other ways to put together a carrot cake. Can you think of other ingredients you would add to make it yummier?

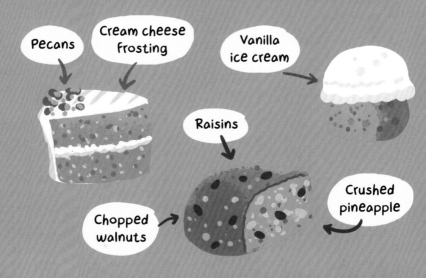

Pecans

Cream cheese frosting

Vanilla ice cream

Raisins

Chopped walnuts

Crushed pineapple

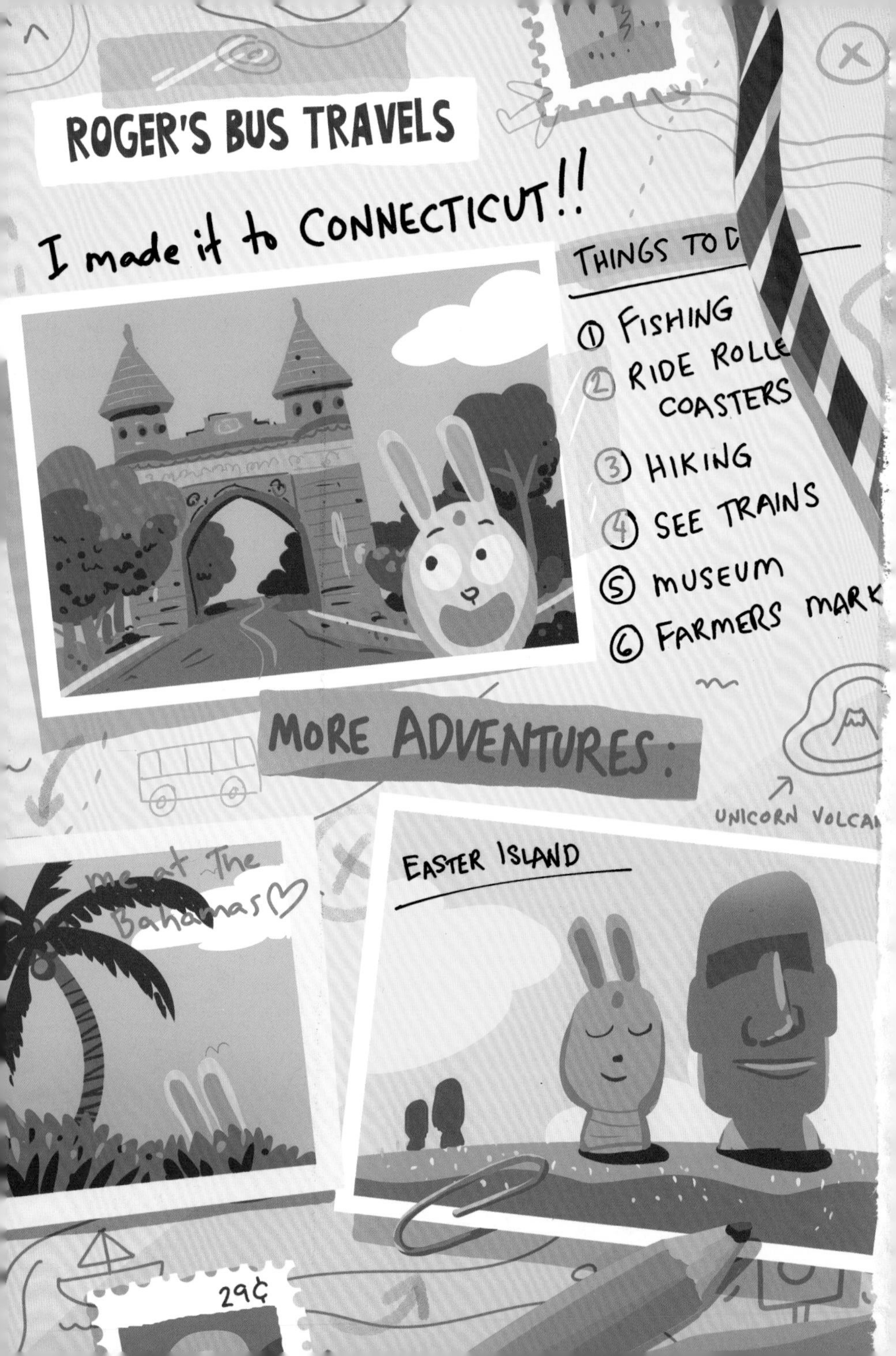
ROGER'S BUS TRAVELS
I made it to CONNECTICUT!!
THINGS TO D
① FISHING
② RIDE ROLLE COASTERS
③ HIKING
④ SEE TRAINS
⑤ MUSEUM
⑥ FARMERS MARK
MORE ADVENTURES:
UNICORN VOLCA
EASTER ISLAND
me at The Bahamas
29¢